I0772734

The Human Inside: Reditus

Book 2

Y.T. Cheng

For Annabelle.

If you're out there watching over us from among
the stars, then this one is for you.

Contents

Time can be one of your greatest allies... or it can be your greatest enemy. It witnesses the journey of life from the moment of birth, through growth, and eventually, when it ends. Death then joins in, and everything moves on. Just as nature intended. It can measure over vast distances. Take a moment to think about how long it's been since the last time you took a road trip. How many hours did it take to get from point A to point B, in whichever mode of transportation you took? Almost everything has a schedule. In the vision of a scientist, time created a special kind of ally for humanity.

Dr. John Kendrick, the owner of A.I. Industries, had always considered time to be something he had a love-hate relationship with. When he was a student, he was told that getting a doctorate would be about... this many years. He didn't like how long it was, so he simply answered he would do it in half the time. With his intellect and his skills, he was able to get two while acquiring his PHD. Somehow, in the middle of all of that, he fell in love with someone who wanted to have a family with him. To be accurate, he found a partner interested in sharing his vision of the family he wanted.

In school, it felt like it would take too much time to implement all the ideas that he had sitting in his great mind. That's why he motivated himself to do well academically. He wanted to use all the time he had to get away from the classroom and tackle the real world.

With his knowledge, everything he learned, and all that he wanted to do, time still found a way to take away many of the important things that he had in his life. After the death of his parents, Dr. Kendrick found himself inheriting a massive legacy. He thought that he and his wife would manage. Unfortunately, time had other plans, and he found himself alone. Just another reminder of life's harsh realities, where loss meets the inevitable and carries on.

It all changed when he decided to pick himself up off the ground. When he had taken the time to finish his mourning and recovered from his losses, he began working again. The physical and emotional strain slowly mended with time. From that, he found and created his family.

It started with a bunch of kids. His company took them in off the streets and raised them. These children were outcasts, orphans, and survivors. A.I. Industries searched and rescued as many as they could. Dr. Kendrick's idea of creating the first cybernetic human beings in history was moving forward.

Trying to change the world alone would be a near impossible task. With each child that he rescued and with each of them volunteering to go on this perilous journey with him, he hoped that their world would be changed forever.

Tragically, some would pass on while Dr. Kendrick grappled with the unforeseen challenges of being one of the first scientists to officially recognize how difficult it all was. The first amborgs who survived, however, would be the results of his dream.

On many occasions, Dr. Kendrick has admitted that if he'd known if his endeavors would result in unexpected tragedies, and if he had the capability to time travel, there would certainly be some events that he would try to go back to and change. This is a sentiment that many share. The current amborgs today also think about this subject a lot. However, if one was to go back and alter the past, then who knows what that would create today? Dr. Kendrick believes that it is better to accept that time will continuously flow as it pleases. He still maintains love for it but also hates it every now and then.

He has witnessed time treating his coworkers and classmates well. Some weren't as lucky, something he understood since he has also seen some of the bad moments that most humans suffer in their daily lives. There have been numerous instances that have left him stunned, or moments when the amborgs find ways to increase his stress levels.

Despite all the trials and the challenges of running A.I. Industries, and overseeing his family of amborgs as their father figure, there is one important note that he will always remember. He will always be glad to have his family. If time had treated them just a bit differently, then it is quite possible that things would have turned out... well, very differently. To get rid of the anxiety that time often gives him, he's forever grateful that the amborgs, his creation, will continue to protect the world and will constantly fight for it.

Even when the odds are stacked against them, they will be the ones to face the threat and defend those that are unable to fend for themselves. The amborgs, whether in the public eye or their own personal lives, will respond. Sometimes time will be on their side, or it could also be against them.

The circumstances can be unfair at times. Ain't that one of the most annoying things about the universe?

■ ■

Access granted: Welcome back to the A.I. Industries public database. Enjoy your session. Amborg Archives have been unlocked.

Caution! Possible editing in progress of the following files. Please be patient as the information is being updated for your viewing needs. Data for the Epsilon-Alpha conflict in the year 2137 is available. Please enjoy.

Alpha Universe
Deep Space: Sector 0068
ER-F4 Task Force
2213 July

"Captain, please report to the bridge."

Captain Chastain opened his eyes and jerked forward. Somehow, he had been dreaming of being home with his family, enjoying the comfort of his recliner. Now, he sighed as he took in the familiar sight of his room and the desk he was sitting at aboard his ship, the Alexandria. Papers covered every inch of the locked-down steel table, unfinished from the night before. He would have to finish his reports as soon as he possibly could, but they just kept piling up. Upon hearing the order from his executive officer over the intercom, he yawned, leaned back and stretched his arms to try waking up properly. Then, he pushed his seat back and stood up. He walked over and unlocked his door, and it slid open. He promptly exited his quarters.

If he had been vacationing aboard a luxury cruiser or passenger liner, he would have been able to witness a spectacular view of the stars. The windows would be sealed and constructed to illuminate the beauty of the passing void of space. However, his vessel had been remodeled entirely only two years earlier. It was now a combined exploratory science and military class ship. All that he was allowed to see was dull and worn-out gray metal plating. The rusty steel pipes had several buttons along the side of the walls that controlled the corridor barriers in the event of a hull breach.

Before he could take a step, he heard some light footsteps coming from his right. Chastain turned his head and stepped to the side to clear a path. A crewman was jogging towards him.

"Lieutenant Ja'kor. You ever think about slowing down when you're off-duty?"

The young officer smiled as he stopped his jog and immediately straightened up. He gave Chastain a quick salute, which he reciprocated. When the formalities were all taken care of, both men relaxed.

"You always taught me to stay alert sir," Ja'kor panted in reply with an eager grin. "Best way to survive in space is to not go too soft."

The Lieutenant fixed his eyes on his superior, looking down and back up, then leaned in close. Chastain raised an eyebrow when he realized he was being scrutinized.

"You uh... just wake up from a nap or something?" he teased with a cheeky grin.

"Watch it kid," Chastain scoffed, then nodded with a sigh. "Another jab like that and I'll have you sit in the brig to check that attitude."

"Understood sir."

"How's your wife?" Chastain changed the subject immediately as the two of them began to walk together.

"Our daughter is due any day now," Ja'kor replied as he followed alongside. "I can't wait for our next shore leave. You uh... don't happen to know...?"

"No," Chastain replied firmly. "No confirmation from command. We might be out here for another month. Maybe more."

"Yes sir."

Even though Ja'kor sounded professional, Chastain could hear the disappointment in his voice.

"You'll be home with your family again soon," Chastain said as the two of them stopped.

"Aye sir," Ja'kor nodded. His eyes lit up upon hearing his Captain's reassuring words. "Thanks."

"As you were."

The two men separated at a T-intersection. Ja'kor resumed his jog and ran forward while Chastain turned to take the left. As he walked the hollow hallways, listening to the sound of the Lieutenants retreating footsteps echoing off the walls, he recalled what it was like when he was merely a junior officer.

"Exercising again..." he muttered."I remember a time when I was that energetic once. Bridge, bridge, bridge. I hope there's good news."

He found himself at a junction, faced with three doors. He pressed a button and in an instant, the elevator doors in front of him opened. Despite the off-putting flickering lights, Chastain stepped inside, turned around, and pressed the panel.

"Bridge," he stated when the panel flashed red.

Nothing.

Chastain glanced downwards at the screen. He put his hand up to it and pressed it more firmly. Keeping his finger on it, he spoke loudly to the flashing panel.

"Bridge," he repeated.

The panel flashed green and then with a small jerk, the elevator began to move. The voice recognition was all shot up. He made a mental note to get someone on that as soon as possible. Engineering was probably already busy with how much work they had piling up. Elevator maintenance was likely very low on their list of priorities.

Suddenly, his communicator chimed, and a voice spoke up.

"Captain," his Executive officer's voice repeated. "Please report to the bridge. Urgent update."

Chastain reached towards his right wrist and activated his communicator. A brief chirping noise answered, indicating it was set to receive his message.

"This is the captain," he answered as the elevator continued to whir in the background. "I am already on my..."

He looked at the intercom and pushed the button again. The beep that usually signified it was ready for him to speak had suddenly fizzed out. The light was working but not receiving audio. Grumbling, he made another mental note to write a report for the engineering department. The intercoms were acting like the kind of cheap broken radios that kids played with.

"Intercoms are still half-broken," he muttered. Brainstorming quietly, he thought of the likeliest scenarios that could have caused this. If they couldn't communicate effectively in the event of an emergency, they were dead. "Ship-wide communications are faulty and now everyone on the bridge thinks I'm late. Excellent."

It took a few more seconds but the whirring of the elevator began to wind down as the Captain felt the speed begin to drop.

As the elevator arrived at the bridge level, the doors chimed and hissed open. He stepped off and looked around. Bridge members were passing to and fro in this section. They all straightened up when Captain Chastain exited the elevator. Many of them were saluting quickly. Silently, he saluted them back, which allowed them to return to their tasks.

The Captain approached the end of the hall and stepped through an open archway. He saw a glowing round table, the ship's map display, in the center, but he began to walk around it. There were a few crew members gathered around it, and Chastain glanced at the officers near the consoles. They were all on headsets and engrossed in their tasks, so they didn't notice him. Instead of interrupting them, he merely pressed on. The people around the map table looked in his direction as he approached. They immediately straightened up and saluted him. He continued to walk by, but quietly saluted again, prompting them to return to their posts.

He exited the map room, and the doors in front of him quickly slid open. As the doors parted to the sides, he made his way onto the bridge, heading straight for his seat in the center. Below him, through the transparent floor, he could see crew members at their stations, glued to their monitors. Just like in the map room, they were all wearing headsets and monitoring their systems closely. Up by the captain's chair, there were fewer screens, but a good number of people were bustling around.

Once his presence was noticed, he braced himself for what came next.

"Captain on deck," a female crewman announced as he approached his chair.

Everyone immediately abandoned their work and stood at attention. In a swift and fluid motion, they turned to face him, raising their arms in a salute. It was almost like someone had asked them all to freeze and smile for the camera. For the third time since stepping off the elevator, Chastain acknowledged them with a quick salute and dismissed them. Without missing a beat, they went back to work. He walked over to his chair and sat down.

"Everything alright, sir?"

Captain Chastain looked up to see his first officer, Lieutenant-Commander Riley, standing in front of him with an inviting cup of coffee. Riley had been assigned to the Alexandria for about six months and was just getting the hang of how he liked things. The caffeine called to him. Taking the steaming cup, Chastain smiled and took a sip. Cream without sugar, exactly how he preferred it.

"Not too good," he muttered as his throat warmed up. The coffee was only partially effective as he let out a sigh. "Send a report to Engineering that repairs to the intercoms in various parts of the ship still need attention. It's supposed to have been fixed by now."

He glanced down at his wrist band and activated it. It turned green, but after a few seconds, it fizzled, and the color faded as it powered down.

"Connection is... really faulty," he reported.

"Understood," Riley replied with a quick nod. She stood rigidly by his side with her hands behind her back. "But Engineering's report this morning might explain why. They've been focusing on the shields for maximum yield for the pending mission. It will probably be some time before they properly fix ship-wide communications. The chief wanted to make sure we weren't caught with our defenses down if anything went wrong."

Chastain looked at Riley sternly. She turned away in embarrassment when she realized she had just given extra unnecessary details in her response. The Captain let out another sigh and nodded his head. Riley and the Chief Engineer did have a point. It was probably safe to prioritize their defense first. That was how the saying went. It was the best offense.

"Just get it done," he stated firmly. He still sounded nervous when he thought about the bigger picture for the safety of his ship. "But without communications in all parts of the ship, we'll be crippled when the Tandeeri decide to pay us another visit. So have engineering rotate two shifts to accommodate. Tell the Chief to work on five active shift rotations. I know they hate overtime but make it a top priority. I'll contact command about getting them the money."

"Yes sir."

That's how it should be done, he thought. Everything on the ship should continue to operate every small detail with maximum effort. But in Riley's case, there was a lot of inexperience under her uniform. Even though she'd been there a considerable amount of time, she devoted more effort to her adjusting to life aboard the Alexandria instead of actually caring for the ship itself. As first officer, this was not the performance that Chastain wanted to see, even if Riley was doing her best to achieve expectations. Why did his previous XO have to be sent home due to a case of severe psoriasis?

Unfortunately, under the circumstances, there was no way to bring back his more experienced XO. He had to make do with what he had in young Riley. Chastain focused on their mission at hand, though he did need to speak to her privately later. Hopefully, he could motivate her and the other newer officers to take more initiative around here.

"I take it our trip to our destination went well?" he asked as he sipped from his cup again and turned on the console in his armrest. "Give me a sit-rep?"

"Yes sir," Riley replied informatively. The screen on his armrest displayed their fleet formation. "Our fleet has reached the isolated area and preparations have begun for the next phase. They've maneuvered into the formation you laid out yesterday."

"And how are the preparations going? Did we charge up in time?"

"Main power cells are finishing the charge as we speak and will be ready to fire within thirty minutes," Riley reported without hesitation. "There were no issues during the night shifts."

"Well, you know what that means then?"

Chastain turned to Riley, giving her an inquisitive look. His eyes widened as he smiled gently, hoping she would know the answer. Unfortunately, she just blinked and didn't respond. She broke eye contact, trying to think, but then tilted her head back toward him. Her silence made him look down at his display, chuckling softly to himself.

"It means," he said as he read more of the report, "that the ship should be ready for whatever happens. You can relax a little, Riley."

"Yes, sir," Riley cleared her throat. "I'm just... It's still taking me some time getting used to how easy-going it is under your command."

"We're not the Marines," Chastain snickered. "Don't tell them I said that. Now, fleet update? Any problems with our formation?"

Captain Chastain's display then showed their ships under his command. Expeditionary Reconnaissance Fleet Four was highlighted in blue. The radar was a standard x, y, and z axis image of a Cartesian Coordinate system with a sphere outline indicating the "bubble" that surrounded the Alexandria, since it was at the center. The other ships in the fleet were also the center of their own spheres on the map, but they appeared as other triangles in a specific formation.

"The S.C.E. New Welkin is off our port bow on the left flank, position two-seven-zero mark three-two," Riley highlighted the triangle next to theirs. Theirs had the initials "**S.C.E. TF1**" in bold and the New Welkin's triangle was "**S.C.E. TF4**." Riley began to highlight the others. There were seven in total, including Alexandria. "We have the Sola in reserve directly behind us and the Ramstein on our starboard position."

As Riley continued describing the fleet status, he pondered the final preparations of his mission. Seven ships. That was all that they could spare for this mission. It wasn't enough, but at least they had a sizable force. The next part of their objective was now the hardest. Well, to Chastain, it was always what made him very uneasy.

"Then I guess we wait," Captain Chastain nodded once the fleet report became clear and concise. "Well done, Riley."

Chastain then looked up and issued orders to one officer sitting nearby.

"Signal the Ramstein to speed up and run a parallel course with us off our starboard bow. I want them to adjust course to assist the Ying Lee. I think the Wenfra Santiago can handle the rear guard with the Soko-Kang. Now I don't want anyone to fall behind. So, send word to the New Welkin and Ramstein. Tell them to launch an extra fighter patrol."

"Aye sir," a communications specialist replied off to the side. "Contacting the fleet."

Another thought crossed his mind as their mission began.

"Also, send the word out on our encrypted channels," he said. "Request for backup. Anyone out there who can get to us if there's trouble would be really useful. If things go wrong, we need help."

Another specialist acknowledged the order and began to transmit the message.

"Our current numbers are quite adequate," Riley informed the captain quietly from the side. "Is there something bothering you?"

"Our task force is pretty decent," Chastain replied, "but one can't be too sure."

"Sir?"

Chastain glanced over at Riley, who was leaning forward to make sure the rest of the bridge officers nearby couldn't hear what they were saying.

"I understand that we don't know each other that well," she declared. "I know that I'm still considered to be a new and inexperienced officer. However, I have recognized that same look that you have right now in the past months."

"Yes," Chastain admitted with a curt nod of his head. The two of them kept their conversation quiet as the rest of the bridge bustled with activity. "I'm getting that sense of caution. It's much more intense than the last mission we were on. Would you care to give the order to deploy escort squadrons?"

He turned to his first mate, who looked taken aback. She had never actually given the order before, which was what he wanted to change. *Time to put some more experience into her pocket*, he thought as she stepped forward and nodded. Chastain watched as she looked around and began to make good on the opportunity. It was probably good that he had refocused their efforts back on the task at hand.

"All stations standby to lower shields. Divert power to the launch bays," she ordered. "All escort fighters, standby for launch. Gun emplacements maintain a field of view for cover. Commencing patrol mission in two minutes."

"Very good," Chastain nodded. It wasn't how he would have done it, but it was a perfect textbook way of carrying it out. He activated the ship intercom on his armrest. Maybe this would have a better connection. He cleared his throat, "Engineering?"

"Yes sir," a voice replied from his chair speaker. "Chief here."

"We are launching fighters," Chastain informed them. "I know your people are stretched thin but if you can keep the ship together for the next half hour, you're all going to be our saviors. If necessary, sacrifice power from the engines to speed up the process. I'd rather be done sooner than be sitting ducks a little while longer."

"You got it sir. I'm ready to tap into the engine cores now. Oh, and thanks for acknowledging my department. It's nice being reminded we keep the ship together."

The line was closed as Chastain smirked. Staying in one place for too long always sent chills up his spine. The waiting game sometimes would put pressure on his mood. It was always the calm before the storm. His combat experience and instincts were telling him that it wasn't alright, that there would be trouble coming around the corner, and that corner was coming up fast.

After a couple more seconds, he pulled up a screen that showed the fleet's current status. There were several loud and distant booms in the background. Outside the windows of the bridge, they could see many lights flying away from the port and starboard sides of the ship as the first fighters began to deploy into space.

Chastain noticed a bunch of smaller triangles appearing on his map display. Riley informed him of another report from the hangar bays, saying they were getting the reserve squadrons prepped as well. It would be another minute or two before they were ready. As the deployment continued, Chastain kept an eye on the radar. Sensors and the taskforce's scouts were reporting an all-clear on the perimeter.

"Riley," he said as he looked over the readiness levels. Feeling satisfied, he glanced at the ship's energy readings. The power was rising on another screen that he was putting on the display in front of him. "I want you to..."

A loud alarm instantly began to sound off from one of the radar stations. The red alert switched the ambient lighting to dark crimson instantly. Seconds after the first alarm, Chastain looked out of the corner of his eye straight down at the crew members just below his seat. He saw that each of the monitors beneath the see-through glass began flashing red. He prepared for the incoming radar report.

"Contact! Several signatures detected!" he heard the radar officer report. "On intercept approach!"

"Where?" the captain demanded as he handed his coffee mug to Riley, who quickly took it somewhere else. He could see his officer was hesitating. "Can you identify? Your training son! Bearing and range?!"

The crewman at the radar station was listening and checking his screen.

"Less than a light year ahead and approaching from three-one-two mark thirty-eight! Closing in fast! Bogey signatures... Identified! Tandeeri fleet inbound!"

"Battle stations! Scramble the rest of our fighters and get them out there immediately!" Chastain commanded once he got a clear direction of where they were coming from. "This isn't a drill! General quarters! Fleet wide alert! We are engaging the enemy!"

The captain yelled out his orders as clearly as possible, but was nervous all the same. The Tandeeri were deadly and extremely dangerous. Every encounter the S.C.E. had with this particular species always ended in defeat.

The klaxon alarm rang overhead, broadcasting across the ship.

"Action stations! Action stations! Set condition one throughout the ship. This is not a drill. Repeat. Action stations! Action stations! Set condition one throughout the ship. This is not a drill."

Hopefully, the rest of the fleet was doing the same and readying their crews for battle. Chastain heard the announcement from his communications officer as he mentally prepared to focus on the coming battle.

"Status?" he demanded.

"All stations checked in. Condition one set throughout the ship. Ready."

"Tactical!" Chastain turned to the next officer sitting nearby.

"Sir!" she replied.

"Charge the R-batteries, standard battle levels. Seventy percent at eight second salvos! Deploy missile emplacements! Load all volleys. All external mounts standby. Prepare secure channel to fleet. Transmit new coordinates on my mark. We are changing the defensive perimeter. Auxiliary power to the shields!"

"Yes sir!"

Chastain then turned back to the officer before her.

"And comms!"

The communications officer immediately turned around and looked to the captain for his next set of orders. He clenched his fist tightly and took a deep breath to fight the tension building on his nerves.

"Contact and send a distress call to anyone in range," Chastain said quickly. "We're accelerating our mission parameters, and we need help now. Tell them our fleet has been discovered and we have engaged. Riley!"

Riley instantly returned to the Captain's side. There were several coffee stains on her wrists and the lower waist of her uniform. Although she was burned, she maintained a steady composure.

"Get the asset into her transport," Chastain said, ignoring her pained expression. He hoped that she was doing the same and powering through it. "Tell her we're sending her over now! I don't care if we're not ready. We'll drain power from the thrusters if necessary. We're making a wormhole now! Apertus modem procedures. You take charge and oversee the transports!"

"Captain! As your XO, I can't abandon you on the bridge!"

"There's no time to explain," Chastain replied sternly. "You oversee the asset and complete our mission! You're the best person I know who can do this!"

"Regulations state...!"

Chastain immediately slammed his fist on the chair, cutting her off. He had already made it clear that they were low on time. How much clearer did he have to be?

"Enough with regulations!" he snapped. She flinched at the sudden raise of his voice. "Well, now I'm making this a direct order, Lieutenant! Get down there. Protect the asset. Make sure she boards her ship. And get her the hell out of here!"

Riley gulped as she stood there in shock. Chastain knew that she wouldn't dare disobey a command. She nodded and ran off towards the elevators without another word.

"Sir? Distress signal is being transmitted," the comms officer suddenly declared. "Scanning for incoming responses."

"Tactical! Have alert squadrons proceed to Bravo rallying points and standby for the go-ahead to alpha! Scramble the last of our fighters."

The tactical officer acknowledged this and began to send a transmission to the Alexandria's pilots. Chastain used that opportunity to coordinate his fleet. He enlarged the map display on his chair as he began typing a message to the tactical console.

"New coordinates," he said as he finished entering them in. "Transmit! Order the fleet to prepare the modified defensive perimeter!"

"All ships, Alexandria" the tactical officer stated calmly into her headset. "Modified coordinates being transmitted."

Another voice broadcasted on the bridge.

"Alexandria, Stinger. We are outbound and have arrived at point Bravo. Standing by."

It was the wing commander of Alexandria's fighter squadrons. Stinger was one of Chastain's most experienced pilots. With his fighters out of Alexandria's airspace, he could begin to maneuver his ship and ready his weapons.

The rallying points were preset destinations for their fighters to fly to. Each ship in the fleet coordinated and shared this information to avoid accidentally crossing into each other's "bubble". Chastain picked Bravo point, which moved his fighters out of the way of Alexandria's heavy guns. On his signal, he would send his pilots to Alpha point in order to intercept the enemy fleet.

"Alright!" Chastain commanded as he looked at the map display again. "Send transmission to the Ramstein and the Hazel Ying Lee. Break formation. I repeat. Break formation and assume defensive pattern Lima."

"Aye sir. Ying Lee, Alexandria," the tactical officer transmitted. "Defensive pattern Lima. Repeat. Assume pattern Lima."

The reply was broadcast from her console, but Chastain was able to hear it.

"Alexandria, Ying Lee actual. Lima confirmed. See you on the other side."

The Ying Lee's Commander remained calm and level-headed, which made Chastain smile a little. Hopefully, Commander Hodges would be alright as he took his destroyer and began to break away.

On the map display, Chastain watched the triangle labeled "**S.C.E. TF6**" change course. He had ordered Hodge to take the Ying Lee up on the Y-Axis and begin turning to starboard. The destroyer fired its ventral maneuvering thrusters and was moving away. There was no up or down in space but on his map display, he watched the "**TF6**" triangle begin to move upwards and turn to heading zero seven eight. This allowed the Ying Lee to have a clear and full view to port. Her weapons would have a clear line of sight.

The tactical officer was also issuing the same order to the Ramstein.

"Ramstein, Alexandria," she declared. "Defensive pattern Lima. Repeat. Defensive pattern Lima."

"Alexandria, Ramstein actual," the transmission came in. "Chastain, this is Rocker, Lima acknowledged. Moving to cover the Ying Lee."

The cruiser directly next to them began to surge ahead. **"S.C.E. TF2"** was on the move. Instead of turning the ship to starboard, Captain Rocker of the Ramstein turned its rear thrusters to move diagonally. Her bow was still facing forward, since it had been moving to run parallel with the Alexandria. Chastain wanted the Lima formation to give their ships plenty of distance. Once their defensive perimeters were set, the Ramstein could cover their flank.

"Ramstein's fighters are clear and proceeding to rendezvous with Stinger's formation."

Rocker and Captain Belara of the New Welkin did the same thing once the order to scramble their fighters had been given. When the task force was assembled, they had set up their deployment strategy ahead of time. They would send one squadron each to fly with the Alexandria's fighters, leaving them with one remaining squadron.

Chastain could see tiny shapes on the map that represented the fighter groups. They were also triangles, but with circles enveloped around them and diagonal lines to symbolize a fighter squadron. Stinger's fighter squadron was surrounded by five more. His symbol had a star, indicating that his squadron had the flight leader commanding them. There were six symbols in total for the six fighter squadrons that the Alexandria could carry. She was a modified heavy cruiser with larger hangars in comparison the New Welkin, Ramstein, and Soko-Kang, which only had a standard hangar complement of two squadrons total. Alexandria was perfect for taking in smaller vessels or damaged craft for repairs and ideal for providing overwhelming numbers if the situation called for it. However, being a modified heavy cruiser meant they were the bigger target. If they went down, who knows how long the rest of their fleet would last?

The Ramstein dispatched one out of two of their own squadrons to join the main fighter group. The other stayed close to provide cover for their base ship.

"R1" or Ramstein First Squadron, was the symbol on the map moving to meet with the Alexandria's "A" squadrons one through six.

"Tactical," Chastain commanded, "movement order to the Soko-Kang. I want them to take over the Ramstein's former position!"

Leaving one destroyer to watch the rear was risky. If the formation moved forward, then they could be hit from behind if the Tandeeri snuck their forces all the way around.

"Have Soko-Kang send both its squadrons to assist the Santiago and spot for anyone trying to flank us," he said insistently.

"Aye sir. Soko-Kang, Alexandria. Occupy Ramstein's former position and divert fighter groups to assist Wenfra Santiago. Acknowledged."

"Alexandria, Soko-Kang. We won't last long if we get flanked."

"Understood. Hold your position at all costs," Chastain replied firmly.

They were right. However, he believed that the Soko-Kang and the Ying Lee could manage on their own. One destroyer as the rear-guard would be at the most risk if the Tandeeri looped around.

"I want the Madison Marsh to fire port thrusters and climb," Chastain glanced at the map and typed in the coordinates. "Position marked. Tell them to get clear of our firing solution."

"Alexandria, Madison Marsh," the tactical officer relayed the order. "New position marked. Clear our line of fire. Repeat. Clear the line of fire."

"Madison Marsh, Alexandria, copy that. Coordinates locked. Initiating."

Their last destroyer, that was also at the head of the fleet, switched course. Just as he was about to give orders to the last ship awaiting instructions, a ping sounded from the radar station.

"Captain!" the radar officer reported. "Enemy ships are deploying! Closing fast! Tandeeri fighter squadrons inbound!"

"Contact the New Welkin!" Chastain's stress levels shot up as he watched the red dots on the map growing closer to his fleet. "Hard aport! Prepare starboard defenses! Ready our portside weapons. Standby enemy suppression barrage."

As his tactical officer relayed the commands to the two remaining ships in their fleet, Chastain watched the map and glanced out the bridge viewports on his left hand side. He saw the New Welkin begin turning; their starboard thrusters were burning brightly as the bow was being pushed away and their main engines were coming into view. Captain Chastain turned to look ahead and saw the Destroyer Madison Marsh perform a Y-Axis climb as it moved out of the Alexandria's way.

Like a curtain rising on a stage, the enemy fleet came into view, heading directly towards them.

The Tandeeri ships were massive, even in the distance. Once they closed the gap and reached their position, they would probably barrel through them like an avalanche. The Alexandria was the largest ship in Chastain's task force. Based on their previous encounters, intelligence had described the Tandeeri capital ships to be about three times their size. Although he personally had never gotten to see one up close, he knew that the Tandeeri fleet was comprised of only this type of vessel with massive fighter squadrons. They had the size, strength, and the advantage in numbers. It was like they were the pins with a horde of flying bowling balls hurtling toward them. These bowling balls also contained massive amounts of power. It had to be equal to about a hundred suns. This was an exaggeration, of course, but Chastain still didn't feel like getting hit by one of their energy blasts.

"Come on," he gritted his teeth as he watched the map. "Get clear, Desmond."

Captain Desmond of the Madison Marsh was still maneuvering his ship out of the line of fire. By now, the New Welkin had finished executing a ninety degree turn to port and its starboard R-batteries were charging on deck. Their red lights were glowing brightly. Chastain could also see the turrets, missile launchers, and guns taking aim.

"Stinger, Alexandria," a message came in from the fighter group. "Sir, the enemy is closing. Enemy fighters are approaching. Are we clear to proceed to engage at Alpha?"

"Negative," Chastain replied. "Stinger, the fleet will provide covering fire. Hold your position."

Stinger acknowledged the order as Chastain suddenly got a communications ping on his display.

"Captain!" his tactical officer spoke up. "Message from the New Welkin! It's Captain Mo'lahk."

Did he spot something that I missed? Captain Chastain didn't have time to think. Waste too much time and they would all be killed.

"Patch him through," he nodded and listened to the transmission.

"Welkin actual, Alexandria," Captain Mo'lahk's voice spoke through Chastain's speaker on his chair. "Chastain, I believe the Marsh and Ying Lee are exposed without fighter support. Permission to pull my squadrons to assist?"

Chastain did a quick check of the map. A few more seconds, and the Alexandria would have a firing solution along with the New Welkin once the Madison Marsh moved out of the way.

"Negative," he answered Mo'lahk. "We need them out there... Our destroyers can manage on their own."

His tactical officer suddenly spoke up.

"Sir!" she reported urgently as her eyes remained glued to her console. "The Madison Marsh is clear! Zone clear."

"Weapons free!" Captain Chastain ordered without hesitation. "Defensive fire! Enemy suppression barrage, all weapons with clear sightlines, initiate!"

Moments later, there was a massive rumbling from below deck. He could feel the vibrations through the floor as he saw multiple streams of rounds from the point-defense guns flying out towards the enemy fleet. A few of the gun batteries joined in, and he heard muffled booms from the deck. As they hurled ordnance at the Tandeeri, bolts of bright red light fired from the R-batteries. The New Welkin's entire starboard side was lighting up almost all of her weapons in comparison. Once their combined barrage began, Captain Chastain immediately gave the next order.

"All fighters," he declared firmly. "Attack point Alpha."

"Alexandria, Stinger," the tactical officer relayed the order. "Alpha point is green. Alpha point confirmed. You are clear to engage."

"I copy Alexandria," Stinger replied on the comms. "All fighters, weapons free. Engage Tandeeri at point Alpha and stay clear of the fleet's barrage!"

Chastain glanced at the map again. The fighter group began to move fast. He saw Stinger leading the main fighter group to a position that was a little outside the range of the task force, but it was a direct shot to several red dots. They would not only try to intercept any Tandeeri ships, but try to be a distraction. The Ying Lee and the Madison Marsh would not have fighter cover, but for the plan to work, they had to try to separate in order to make the Tandeeri choose their targets.

He had to count on the other captains in his fleet to hold the line as long as possible. Captain Chastain tried to contact Riley.

"Chastain to Riley. Come in Riley."

There was a moment of silence, but then a communications ping responded.

"Yes sir," she reported.

"What's your status?" he asked, keeping a close eye on the map for any surprise moves.

"The ships are fueled and ready to go!" she answered promptly. "I'm programming the decoys as we speak. The asset is ready for transport."

"Great news! Standby to have them launch when we give the signal."

"Aye sir."

Captain Chastain ended the conversation and tried to hail engineering. The next phase of the mission was going to involve a lot of power.

"Bridge, engineering!" Chastain said into the channel. "Chief Kolst!"

It didn't take long for a response.

"Chief here," the Captain heard the gruff voice of his department head answer loudly. "Go ahead sir!"

"I need all the power we have!" Chastain looked over the ship's energy readings and examined the map. "How long does the main cannon need to charge for a wormhole?"

"My main generators are holding on but if the Tandeeri hit us, we're history!" Kolst responded hastily. "Maybe if they hadn't paid us a house call, we could handle it alone!"

"Well, that's why we came with a fleet. We're not the only ship out here," Chastain answered. "What do you need? How much time?"

"Is another one of the frigates available?!"

"Yeah but... what did you have in mind for...?"

Before Captain Chastain could finish, more bright lights appeared from the deck. The R-batteries had just fired another salvo at the Tandeeri fleet. Unfortunately, this caused another problem. A sudden small explosion crackled over the comms channel, causing the Captain's eyes to widen in alarm as he anxiously focused on the device in front of him. He heard a startled yelp from Kolst, followed by a series of loud pops that echoed through the line. The voices of the engineers on the other end were frantic and filled with urgency. It sounded like pandemonium down there.

"Oh gods, there goes the auxiliary..." Kolst yelled angrily. Chastain could tell he had turned his head away from the microphone to assess the apparent damage that he himself couldn't see. "That's not good at all!"

Captain Chastain heard Chief Kolst's voice fade a little in the background, but it was still audible.

"Damn it!" he yelled at someone nearby. "Tell weapons station delta to lower their power charge! The R-batteries on the port bow just burnt out the backups! Captain!"

Suddenly, the Chief's voice was directed loud and clear back to Chastain.

"Kolst! What just happened?"

"A big shit-show!" Kolst replied furiously. He certainly sounded frustrated even though he was trying to maintain professional decorum. "Captain, we are not going to be able to divert power from the mains to weapons and the main cannon at the same time! The ship will be dead in the water! We're probably not even going to need to get hit by a Tandeeri energy blast!"

"Alright then, here's what we'll do! Kolst! Let's patch you in with Luthor!" Chastain said, thinking quickly. He looked over to his tactical officer. "Contact the Ramstein! We need to converge both of our main cannons and cross the beams to generate the wormhole!"

The Captain glanced back down at the comms channel on his armrest. Sweat poured down his head as he improvised a new plan.

"Will that be enough, Chief?" he asked.

"We're going to have to time this really accurately," Kolst answered promptly. "If we miss, this mission will end a lot faster than we like."

"Then let's make sure we don't miss," Chastain nodded, then realized the Chief couldn't see him over a comms channel. He looked up, shook his head to focus, and put his head back in the game. "Tactical! Coordinate with the Ramstein immediately. I need a firing solution for both of our ships. Charge the main cannon and divert all non-essential power! Signal the fleet to tighten our defenses and keep us safe for a few minutes!"

Waiting for their main cannon, as well as the Ramstein's cannon, was going to feel like an eternity. Engineering from both ships had to focus on monitoring the energy charge while the helmsman and tactical officers would need to calculate where they had to point the ship and shoot so it would hit at the same time. The Alexandria and the Ramstein would have to fire at a fixed point and cross the beams successfully in order to generate the artificial wormhole. Kolst was right. If either ship missed, then the mission was over and all they would have was an expensive fireworks show.

"Captain Chastain to Riley," he issued his next command to the hangar. "How soon until you're ready to launch?"

"One more minute!"

Another transmission came in. The bridge heard Stinger's voice as he broadcasted a sitrep.

"Alexandria, Stinger here! We're taking a beating! Tandeeri fighters are about to overrun us!"

Damn it. Captain Chastain clenched his fist as he looked at the map. On the display screen, his main fighter group was surrounded by more and more red dots. Where were they all coming from? Just once, he wanted to try and get close enough to hit one of their capital ships. It looked like it wasn't going to be possible at this rate.

"Stinger, Alexandria actual," Chastain huffed as he pinged the fighters with a new order. "Emergency recall. Initiate! Get your pilots out of there and fall back to the fleet. Have the Welkin's and Ramstein's squadrons return to their own commands. I need you back here now."

"I copy that Captain," Stinger replied. "Disengaging! Rear guard, give us cover!"

"Tactical," Chastain looked at the map and highlighted the destroyers. "Signal Madison Marsh and the Ying Lee. Provide cover for the retreating fighters."

"Alexandria, Ramstein actual," Chastain heard Commander Rocker on the comms channel. "We've detected Tandeeri fighters off our starboard bow. We're going to need cover while we help you create the wormhole!"

"Understood Ramstein... standby!"

This wasn't good at all. The battle was causing their own power supply to dwindle with every passing moment. If the Ramstein was suddenly attacked, then they would lose the opportunity to generate the energy needed for mission success. The New Welkin was turned to port, their main gun pointed away from where they needed to create the wormhole. If he ordered the Welkin to turn and bring its main cannon around, they would lose the suppression barrage in that direction, and they would be flanked again. He had an idea and hoped it would work.

"Ramstein!" Chastain ordered. "Hold present position and prepare your main gun! The Soko-Kang is moving to cover your flank!"

His tactical officer contacted the Soko-Kang, which was already enroute to the Ramstein's original position in the fleet formation. Chastain then issued a move order for the last destroyer he had in reserve.

"I want the Wenfra Santiago to support the New Welkin! All batteries, pick your targets carefully! Have all R-batteries reduce energy levels!"

"Captain sir! If the rear guard moves away, won't we be exposed at the stern?"

His navigator brought up an excellent point, but if the Tandeeri fleet was closing in, what choice did they have?

"The main fighter group will circle around once they reach us! We will be covered until it's time to send the asset through!"

Chastain looked down at his display again. They needed twenty more seconds before they could fire, but they also had to coordinate with the Ramstein. His tactical officer suddenly spoke up again.

"Incoming message from the Ying Lee and the Madison Marsh! Both are being targeted by enemy capital ships!"

"Onscreen! Divert all our guns! All stations! Get ready to provide cover!"

The main Tandeeri capital ships were in range and coming in towards the point guard. A display screen ahead at the front revealed the enemy ships, and it wasn't a pretty sight. Glowing bright lights had appeared at the bows of the ones at the head of their formation. These were massive, charged energy attacks. When launched, the Tandeeri asteroid-sized balls of energy would inflict heavy damage to anyone or thing caught in its path. They weren't extremely fast, but if they couldn't avoid or shoot them down, they were screwed.

"Five capital ships have fired their main weapons!"

Chastain highlighted the map display. He quickly marked the closest energy ball, which was on a direct path to the Madison Marsh. He pinged the New Welkin, who happened to be in perfect position to help. The Alexandria would also do the same since Chastain wasn't worried about the Ying Lee, which was furthest away from the Tandeeri attack.

"Cover the Madison Marsh! Make your shots count!"

Immediately, the Welkin, Alexandria, and the Madison Marsh jumped into action to counter the enemy blasts. Three capital ships launched a single energy ball at her, which meant they had to take out all three. Chastain watched as the three of their ships successfully hit the first one, which glowed brightly and dissipated. As the attack began to fade, they shifted their fire to the second one. It was really close.

The Welkin's reserve fighters intercepted the second blast and neutralized it. Chastain's eyes went wide when he saw the third blast still coming for their destroyer.

The Madison Marsh attempted to turn on its own axis and steer the bridge away from the Tandeeri energy blast, but it ended up taking the hit directly. The ship emitted a massive crackling sound as it lit up like a giant Christmas tree. Chastain turned to the sensor station, and they all looked on in horror.

"Deploy the search and rescue craft!" he ordered. "Sit-rep!"

"She's drifting," his lookout reported. "Unresponsive!"

"Alexandria actual, Madison Marsh," he said as he tried to transmit a message. "Come in! Can anyone hear us? Desmond! Can you hear me?!"

"Captain," the sensor officer added, "heavy damage detected. All systems overloaded! Scanning for survivors! No response to emergency hails."

The decision to turn the ship on its starboard axis was probably what saved the ship from being completely destroyed. There was more armor on the ventral side, and it was a strong defense to protect the crew. However, getting hit by the energy blast had rendered them unable to fight. One ship down meant that the rest would follow if they didn't hurry.

"Come on," Chastain said as he looked at the Madison Marsh. "Riley! Come in!"

"Captain Chastain," Riley answered. "The transports have launched! The asset is up and away!"

"Then we better be ready too," Chastain let out a brief sigh of relief. He spoke back into the channel to Engineering. "Are we ready to fire?"

"I need forty seconds!" Chief Kolst answered urgently.

"Forty it is! I'm sending the transports now!"

Chastain watched as another symbol suddenly appeared next to the Alexandria on the map. It was a square instead of a triangle. The asset they needed to protect was attached to a small squadron of transports. Most of them were empty and piloted remotely from operators in the hangar. They flew alongside as decoys in order to draw enemy fire. The asset was in one of five escape pods that would try to make for the wormhole, but he didn't know which one.

"Attention transport operators," he announced. "Hold your formation and begin maneuvering to the designated coordinates. Fighters will escort you for as long as possible. Remember what we practiced!"

As the ship continued to charge the main gun, Chastain directed his attention over the next few seconds to the rest of the fleet. The Wenfra Santiago had taken a position alongside the New Welkin and had the flank secure. Captain Belara had also dispatched SAR craft to assist the Madison Marsh, which was still unresponsive. However, Chastain wasn't worried, since his sensor station reported that there were still people alive onboard. The Tandeeri fleet had redirected their efforts elsewhere instead of finishing her off. The Ramstein was also coordinating with Chief Kolst, and they were almost ready to fire. The Soko-Kang was descending on the Y-axis to cover the fleet if the Tandeeri weren't going to waste the time to attack their rear. Each ship did have enough armament on the ventral side, but having someone covering that side was extremely helpful.

"Alexandria, Stinger," Chastain broadcasted to his fighter group. "The asset is on the way. Provide cover at all costs and don't let the Tandeeri shoot her down."

"Copy that," Stinger answered. "All fighters, on me. Sparkler formation."

"Captain!" Kolst declared. "Ready when you are!"

"Contact Ramstein," Chastain said as he looked straight ahead. "On my mark. Five second count. Prepare to fire main cannon!"

"Alexandria, Ramstein," the tactical officer relayed the command. "Standby to fire main cannon. Five second count on our go-ahead."

The battle raged on in the background as they awaited confirmation. Then, the tactical officer reported to Captain Chastain.

"The Ramstein is ready, Captain," she turned her head and nodded. "On your count."

"Alexandria to the fleet," Chastain opened the channel and broadcasted. "Standby. Ramstein. Begin count and fire main cannon in... Five... Four... Three... Two... One... Mark."

A low rumble emanated from the ship ahead. A piercing, high-pitched whine followed as the bow started to glow more intensely. Once it maxed out, a massive explosion rocked the floor, sending vibrations through the ship. The bright red energy clashed with the light green of the Tandeeri lasers as the Alexandria's main gun fired off a colossal laser dead ahead. Meanwhile, they spotted another huge red beam coming from the Ramstein, ready to intercept.

As the battle continued, the energy pulses from the two S.C.E. ships collided together, and the result was enormous. The timing was perfect. Both beams struck at the same point. With a flash of light, a massive explosion occurred and, within moments, the process began to take shape. The fabric of space was instantly torn apart, and a miniature wormhole began to form at the center. A mix of colors danced and swirled with each other.

A rift appeared and took the place of where the beams had been. Like a flashlight appearing in a dark tunnel, a clockwise-swirling vortex of a beautiful crimson color formed, gradually growing larger. It was too small for their capital ships, but just large enough for the asset's transport pod. Chastain kept an eye on the transport as it headed straight for it.

From the bridge, the lookout officer watched as the transports and their fighter squadrons rushed by the starboard side and began to make a beeline for the wormhole.

"All ships," Chastain ordered. "Defend the asset. Engage the enemy!"

"Sir," the tactical officer reported. "Signal from the Ramstein. They are low on power!"

Glancing out the forward viewport, he noticed that the energy weapons were firing at a much slower rate than they had been before. The power used from the main gun had sapped so much energy that both the Alexandria and the Ramstein's defenses were working at a slower capacity. Unfortunately, they had to put everything they had to the mission first.

"Cover the asset!" Chastain shouted as he saw Tandeeri ships changing course. "We're still in this fight! We can't turn back!"

The Alexandria took aim and began firing at the newly determined targets. Thanks to the energy drain, the rate of fire was slower. The Tandeeri capital ships were turning towards their wormhole and the enemy fighters were on an intercept course. It wouldn't be long before Stinger and the decoy transports would come under attack.

"Captain, Tandeeri capital ships are approaching our wormhole! Five of them have changed course!"

Just as he'd anticipated, the Tandeeri had switched targets. He figured they would manage to work out which target to prioritize. If that was the case, it meant that the Madison Marsh was safe now that the enemy had redirected their attention. Chastain looked at the map. Even at full speed, the asset along with the four other decoy pods and fighter escort were only a couple of minutes away. He needed time.

"Course correction to the Santiago," he commanded. "I want her to assist the Ying Lee and defend us from enemy fighters! The New Welkin must maintain their suppression barrage. All SAR units make for the Madison Marsh! Have the Soko-Kang advance and take point! All remaining ships will defend the asset!"

His crew transmitted the orders to the rest of the fleet. He hoped this would buy them some time to check on themselves. Once more, Chastain opened a direct line to Engineering.

"Kolst! Come in," he said as clearly as possible. "Chief! Can you hear me? Status?"

There was a brief moment of static, then he got a response.

"Captain," Kolst coughed back. "The blast from the main gun took almost every last shred of power we had. I can't believe we still have a functioning engineering department!"

"What's the damage?"

"Let's just say I don't want to be here if the Tandeeri actually hit us," Chief Kolst replied grimly. "We were already struggling to keep the ship patched up before this mission began. All of it is useless now. We are losing power. All auxiliary generators are non-functional. Half the mains are out and the rest are barely holding us together! We're going to lose shields, life support, and weapons in minutes!"

Captain Chastain pulled up a small screen highlighting the Alexandria. Chief Kolst was right. The main cannon had used up so much energy in one go, that now the ship's map diagram was turning a heavy shade of red. Just before the main cannon fired, it had been almost entirely green. It was as though someone had yanked off a bandage before the wound had time to heal.

"Our ship is bleeding to death," he muttered before speaking up again to Chief Kolst on the channel. "Kolst, I'm shutting down non-essentials. If we do that, will that buy some time to fix any of the auxiliary systems?"

"You give me as much time as you can, I'll make sure that we don't get spaced."

"Done!"

Captain Chastain immediately looked up and called out his next command.

"Attention all hands. Emergency status! Code 31! All personnel evacuate non-essential areas immediately."

"Aye sir," his tactical officer sounded the alarm. "Broadcasting code 31 across the ship!"

"Switch to minimal life support and transfer remaining power from all available primary and secondary subsystems to engineering!" Chastain commanded as the alarm blared. "All energy batteries. Reduce charges again to twenty percent at twelve second salvos. All weapons stations, pick your targets. We need to stay in this fight as long as possible. I am counting on every single one of you. Good luck!"

A sudden transmission was broadcast across the bridge.

"Alexandria!" Chastain heard Stinger's voice. "I just lost my wingman! A few bogeys have broken through us! The pods are under attack! I'm going after them! We need reinforcements!"

They could all hear the fear in his voice, but Stinger continued to fight against the overwhelming odds, regardless. If they failed here, then all the casualties that led to this moment would have been for naught. But they had nothing left. Even with both of the fleet's remaining destroyers moving up to the front of the formation to take on the enemy fighters, they were still outnumbered.

If he needed Belara, the New Welkin would require time to properly turn about, which wasn't possible, considering it was the only cruiser in their ranks that was continuing the suppression barrage. If she stopped firing, the Tandeeri had a direct shot at them with the defense perimeter down. She would also be exposed while attempting to change course.

The Madison Marsh was still powerless and drifting. There was no word from Commander Desmond. All remaining S.C.E. fighters covering her were dealing with their own problems. The entire fleet was stretched thin.

"Stinger, Alexandria actual," Chastain bit his lip and clenched his fist in anger. He didn't want to say this, but he had to. "All fighters are currently occupied. There aren't any more reinforcements!"

"Understood Alexandria!" Stinger panted in response. "Then let's give them hell with all that we have left!"

"Captain! Enemy forces are attacking the wormhole!

The comm officer's updates were very much correct. Captain Chastain looked at the area surrounding the wormhole and realized there were enemy fighters diverting to shoot at the wormhole. Their attacks did minimal damage and the wormhole remained stable, but the Tandeeri cruisers were closing in. Bright lights in front of their bows indicated they were planning to fire more energy blasts just like the ones that had crippled the Madison Marsh. Chastain found himself unable to think of what to do next. His ship was low on power, and he had played every card he had. He just needed a few more seconds so the transport could make it through, but they were overwhelmed.

"Captain! I have an incoming signal! A response to our beacon!"

Chastain's eyes widened as he looked over at his tactical officer.

"Oh thank the gods."

"I have IFF beacons from nine allied vessels! We are being hailed."

A deep and commanding tone was broadcast for everyone to hear.

"Attention fleet four of the Expeditionary Reconnaissance task force. This is the S.C.E. Firestar. Inbound with reinforcements."

"The Firestar?" Chastain's sensor officer shot him a surprised look. "No way."

They all heard another voice transmit a message. This time it was a woman's voice.

"Alexandria, Firestar actual," her voice spoke professionally, but there was a bit of disappointment detected in her tone. "We are engaging the Tandeeri fleet. Entering your defensive perimeter."

Within moments, everyone aboard the bridge of the Alexandria noticed the Tandeeri ships veer away from their wormhole. As they were drawn off, Chastain focused on one pod that broke away from the decoys and soared through the portal. Before he could send one of the accompanying transports to follow it, enemy fighters converged on the wormhole. They fired multiple blasts and struck right on the rims. Flashing brightly, the wormhole began to close as it destabilized and it began to collapse upon itself. The rift disappeared and the spot where it had been turned back to normal.

"Mop up those fighters! Have our reinforcements send the capital ships packing."

The pride of the fleet, one their most advanced starships, the Firestar had arrived. Once it entered the combat zone, everyone on the bridge looked out the viewport just in time to see it immediately begin firing all weapons at the enemy. In comparison to their current state, the Firestar and her own fleet was at full strength. The Tandeeri ships were scrambling to get away while they faced a massive arsenal of firepower. The battle was over within minutes as the enemy fleet retreated.

A wave of relief washed over the entire room. Cheers erupted, and several of the bridge crew began clapping. They had managed to make it through another terrible ordeal.

"Hail the CAG please," Chastain sighed, taking deep breaths to calm the adrenaline coursing through his veins.

His tactical officer nodded and opened a channel on her console.

"Stinger, Alexandria actual. Captain Chastain wants to speak to you. Are you clear?"

"Roger Alexandria," Stinger answered. "Go ahead."

Captain Chastain pulled a communicator out of a cabinet sitting next to the tactical officer. The light turned green as he held it up to his ear.

"Stinger, have the songs of Aurora Delias reached you?" he asked calmly.

"Negative sir," Stinger sighed in relief over the line. He let out a chuckle as he happily responded. "I still got some fight left in me. I'd like to make an informal observation."

"Alright."

"Our reinforcements are kicking ass and it's a pretty fantastic view, sir."

"Noted," Chastain smiled as he also glanced out the viewport. "I want you to pick a squadron and rally volunteers. Nine of your best. I need you for a patrol. Send everyone who's left back home. Let's start fixing everyone up."

"Yes sir," Stinger acknowledged over the line. "I'll get volunteers. Everyone else is RTB."

Captain Chastain switched the communicator off. As it turned red, he stored it back in the cabinet.

"We still have work to do," he said. "Get me a casualty list."

"Understood sir," his tactical officer answered.

To his radar officer, he pointed at the console.

"Keep an eye out in case the enemy reappears," he instructed. "Begin coordinating with search and rescue."

The officer nodded, acknowledging the order, and turned his attention to his console. He kept a close eye on it as Chastain made his way back to his seat.

"This is the captain. All hands, we have achieved mission success. All emergency crews, please proceed with repairs," he said as he began the announcement to the entire ship. His instructions were clear, and he managed a firm and calm tone to help everyone else onboard relax. "Hangars, emergency protocol. Prepare for incoming. All weapons crews, stay alert. Thanks to all of your courage and dedication, we will fly another day. Check in with your department heads immediately and let's figure out our next move."

As he ended the announcement, Chastain looked up to see Riley returning to the bridge. Her uniform was slightly disheveled, but she maintained a cool composure.

"So," Chastain grinned cheekily. "We sent the right pod through... right?"

"Yes sir," Riley answered promptly, his joke flying over her head. "There were quite a few of us that were there to witness the asset select the one she needed. I watched it the whole entire time and..."

Riley stopped when she got a proper look at him, noticing his mischievous grin. When she realized that she had fallen victim to his antics, she grew mildly annoyed.

"Permission to speak freely?" she shook her head as her eyes narrowed. "That's not funny sir."

"It was a little bit," Chastain held up his hand and stifled his laughter. He ignored the fact that she hadn't actually received permission from him to speak openly. "Alright, we made a bit of a mess here. Let's make sure our reinforcements aren't the only ones picking up after ourselves."

Riley nodded and proceeded to an officer nearby to oversee operations. As she began to help, Captain Chastain attempted to contact Chief Kolst.

"Bridge, Engineering," he said. "Status?"

"I can happily report that we have not been obliterated," Chief Kolst replied. "You think I'll get enough time to properly fix the ship?"

"How long do you need?" Chastain asked curiously.

"One month," Kolst answered firmly.

"Yeeaah no," Chastain mumbled thoughtfully, hunching over. "We're never going to have that much time. You have one week at the most."

"Hooray."

Chief Kolst's sarcasm was the last thing he heard as the transmission ended. As Chastain leaned back in his chair and let out another sigh of relief, his communications officer spoke up.

"Captain! Incoming hail from the Firestar actual."

He perked up upon hearing this. He'd heard the news that she would be in command of the newest flagship of the S.C.E. It had been a few years since they last spoke. Chastain straightened up and softly cleared his throat.

"Put her through," he stated.

A display screen appeared in front of him. No one else had the same screen, which meant that he was the only one being contacted. As the image focused and revealed the person calling, he nodded politely.

"Admiral Ra'aiah," he smiled warmly. "It's good to see you again."

"Agreed. However, you have a lot of explaining to do."

Here we go… Chastain's smile faded, turning into a fearful frown. If there was one thing he didn't enjoy, it was the post-action report. The survivors of the battle were about to face one of their biggest fears. It was essentially a huge audit. Who knows if the council was going to be lenient with them.

"It looks like I have to start at the beginning," he sighed.

Chapter 1: Apertus Modem:
Blast from the Past

Earth Orbit: 250 miles
Apogee Station
2138 July

The door to the main control room hissed open and Jacob stepped inside for the start of his shift. He was followed by 17 others to start their next eight hours. Another team of 18 would relieve them later through those same exact doors, and so on. There were always 18 people keeping a lookout, twenty-four hours a day. The same boring routine. To Jacob, this schedule was starting to get irritating and only added to his depression as he slowly lost his motivation with every passing moment. Not even his coffee was helping like it did before.

Security teams, custodial staff, sentry drones and maintenance bots were going about their jobs in the room while his seventeen coworkers received their pass downs from the last shift and took their positions. As a few of them logged in and began to work diligently at their computer terminals, Jacob sighed as he walked to the eighteenth chair and greeted the man who was logging himself out. He stood and faced Jacob.

"Nothing much to report," he said as the two of them lifted their palms and turned them over. Both men did a visual inspection as Jacob listened carefully. "You have scheduled maintenance on the eighth antennae at section six. Two teams of engineers have been out there for the last three hours. We power cycled a few systems and they're all up and running. All quiet."

"Thanks, I have the station," Jacob stifled a yawn.

"All yours."

The other tech grabbed his jacket off the back of the chair and walked away. Jacob removed his own jacket as the previous shift began to leave. He placed it on the backrest of the chair and sat down. Yup, the same old boring routine. A couple of months ago, they were all focused on their work, taking it seriously. Now, they were beginning to feel trapped. It didn't help that they were also literally closed off from Earth for at least three more weeks.

"At least the pay is good," he muttered as he shut his eyes. The best way for him to maintain his sanity for the duration of his contract was to preserve a lot of self-motivation. "Just keep telling yourself that. Just keep saying that."

He sighed again as he leaned back and stared longingly up at the shiny ceiling. His chair let out a squeak as he stretched. Once he straightened himself up, he turned to face his screen again. After a brief facial recognition scan, his computer automatically logged him in and displayed his data sheets.

"Alright. Let's see what we got."

The previous technician's pass down was accurate. The antennae maintenance was already written and scheduled in the logbook. The engineers had been assigned to the task and were set to begin repairs soon, with a backup team already allocated. They would take over before the first team would lose oxygen. It was also nice of the last shift to power cycle his terminal. It was performing much faster than it was yesterday. Jacob noticed this as he sifted through the different tabs.

Another pretty awesome thing, aside from his paycheck, were the amborgs living onboard Apogee. Since the completion of the facility, the amborgs had been staging more and more training missions off-planet which provided additional forms of entertainment for the staff. All things c onsidered, what the station lacked in ideal job prospects, it made up for in luxury, quality, and high salaries. After all, every one of these things was crucial since Dr. Kendrick owned it all.

Jacob stared through the sealed reinforced glass bulkhead in front of him, keeping an eye on his readings while taking in the view of his home. It looked like another day on Earth. Aside from the fact that a typhoon was blowing off the Madagascar coast and some heavy storm clouds were raining down on Western Europe, the view from the space station seemed to be quite normal. This put a thought into Jacob's head as he brought up a few pictures from his files.

"I really should send mother a video message later," he reminded himself, writing an entry into the security logs. As he scrolled through them, a photo popped up depicting himself and a kind grey-haired lady wearing glasses. "She'll want to hear from me."

"Jacob," one of the other technicians spoke up, pulling him back into the present, "would you mind fine-tuning the wide-range radar? I'm picking up something strange just past Saturn."

"Sure thing," Jacob replied as he shifted his attention back to his keyboard and typed in the commands. "But it could just be a meteor shower, Bill."

"I don't think so," Bill said with uncertainty. "I've never seen meteors scramble up our readings before. Not like this. This is Dr. Kendrick's best equipment after all."

"Alright alright. Let me look. I'll get on the horn with NASA, too. See if they can patch in."

Jacob began to troubleshoot the problem. First, he had to boost power to the radar system that Bill was monitoring. He watched a progress bar appear as he performed the transfer. After he did that, he relayed a message to NASA.

"Houston, this is Apogee Station, over?"

A response came through after a brief crackle through the radio.

"Roger, Apogee, how are things up there?"

Jacob looked at his screens and the progress of the power transfer to the radar sensors. Everything seemed to be fine, but something caught his attention.

"Houston," he said, frowning at the readings. "We have detected an occurrence just outside Saturn's orbit. It is scrambling our wide-range sensor readings and power transfers are not clearing the imaging. Can you confirm?"

Jacob paused as he waited for their answer. After a brief silence, the same person spoke again.

"Copy that Apogee, we see the occurrence too," the communications specialist answered in a deep voice. "Our equipment also seems to be going fuzzy. We're trying to divert power now. Transfer initiated. Is it clearing up on your end?"

"No, it isn't Houston," Jacob said, double-checking. He glanced at Bill who was shaking his head. Extra power didn't seem to fix anything. "We've triple checked already and it's not getting any better. Request permission to divert one of the Jupiter probes to home in on the unknown phenomenon?"

"Roger that Apogee," NASA replied. "Permission to realign... Jupiter X45B probe to the unknown is a go."

"Thank you, Houston."

Jacob pointed at another technician, who nodded in response. Silently, she entered the calculations into the computer. As she diverted the probe, the remaining techs gave Jacob their full attention as he turned to face them.

"Ok guys, we got something on radar," he said, taking charge. "It might be nothing but let's do this by the book. Split it into three groups of six and keep track of this phenomenon. I'll take the lead on this. Bill, you take two. Is whatever this is still scrambling us?"

From where he sat, Bill gave a thumbs-up and nodded.

"Yeah, Jacob, I don't think this is a meteor shower."

"You might be right."

"Oh wow, did you just agree with me?"

Jacob rolled his eyes when he noticed Bill staring at him incredulously. He snapped his finger and pointed downward. Bill chuckled and went back to looking at his own screen.

"Yeah, it could be Santa Claus," Jacob replied, shaking his head. "We know it isn't a meteor shower so let's hurry up and find out. I don't like it when someone tries blinding us. Let's get an amborg up here to help. Tell them we need an immediate consultation. They should be finished with their zero-G training."

Bill nodded again and pressed a button near his computer, which generated a loud ping that rang across the control room. As the signal for an amborg was transmitted, Jacob turned at the sound of another technician calling out to him.

"Jacob, the probe has been aligned and is centered on the unknown. We should have an image in a few seconds."

"Thank you," Jacob said as he rechecked the trajectories and then put the probe's transmission onto a view screen. "Let's see what we got... Oh crap..."

Everyone quietly fixated on the screen, waiting for the static to clear and the image to focus. The entire control room began to fill with murmurs, and disappointed groans could be heard when nothing happened. A tense atmosphere fell over the control room as everyone gave each other nervous glances. Jacob was starting to feel worried. This was not what they expected.

"Are you kidding?"

Disgruntled, Jacob tried to reconfigure the settings once again.

"This unknown is screwing with our monitors too," he sighed in frustration. "Can't see anything... Uh Houston do you copy? Can you get eyes on what Jupiter X45B is seeing? I think there's a problem."

It didn't take too long for them to send a reply. What they had to say didn't fix the problem.

"Sorry Apogee, the feed is distorted here as well. We see what you see and right now it's no use. Our monitors are unable to identify. We have definitely never encountered this phenomenon before."

"You may not have, but that may not be entirely accurate."

Jacob turned at the sound of heavy footsteps approaching from the entrance to the control room. Heads turned as everyone glanced at the man who had arrived. He wore the trademark amborg uniform jacket with a glowing "2" in bright neon green on his back and a smaller one on his chest pocket. His shoulder pauldrons featured the A.I. Industries logo, with the number one positioned below, signifying his rank as a First Group amborg. This was Amborg 2, the second person in history to successfully become an amborg.

"Houston, this is Ziggy, reporting from Apogee station control," he announced as he took position next to Jacob. He politely dipped his head to everyone in greeting and spoke to NASA. "May I be of service?"

"Amborg 2, it's a pleasure. We could use your help clearing this up and also your input about this phenomenon."

"Then we shall have answers once I have attempted to provide assistance."

Jacob watched as the First Group amborg extended his hand and placed it on the console. A loud humming emanated from the monitor as Ziggy connected to it.

"What are you doing?" Bill asked curiously.

"I am drawing power from my energy reserves and channeling into the radar system's components," 2 replied calmly as he concentrated. "This will clear the image for a few moments."

"Only a few moments?" Jacob asked.

2 looked up and gave him a cold stare. Jacob gulped. He probably just insulted him. Jacob braced himself and readied an apology, but 2 spoke back to him civilly.

"I don't have enough power to run this equipment for too long," he responded curtly. "Also, I can only hope it'll clear it up. This will theoretically work. I'm afraid that I don't know if this will work entirely."

The monitor began to flash and whine louder from 2's power, attracting everyone's attention to the main view screen. Jacob watched in awe as the monitor completely filtered out the static and the image became clear as day. What they witnessed, however, left everyone in disbelief. On the screen, the Jupiter probe's camera was focusing on a rip in space itself. But it wasn't possible, was it? Jacob immediately reached for his keyboard and started running scans.

"Uhh, Houston, are you seeing this?" he asked, his eyes shifting between his monitor and the main viewscreen.

"Apogee... we have no idea," NASA responded. The reply sounded stunned. "We have checked and rechecked but... The only thing we can possibly ask to explain this is... have you accelerated the procedures? Ahead of schedule."

Jacob, knowing full well what they were talking about, promptly sent a reply.

"Houston, this is Apogee and we're not doing anything," he said rather quickly. "Could someone call Dr. Kendrick? He's gonna want to take this call."

"I've already been trying his hotline," Bill called out to him. "He must be busy with something."

"Keep trying," 2 encouraged him. "He has a 95% chance of responding within 40 seconds."

"Uh... Ziggy?" Jacob's eyes widened as he pointed at the main viewscreen. "The big tear in space is expanding."

"Well that's an image," someone said in awe.

"Literally or mentally?" 2 asked, tilting his head and looking around.

There was no response as they continued to look on.

On the monitor, the tear in space opened wider. It turned bright red as it began to rotate in a circle. In a matter of seconds, the diameter expanded so much that 2 had to adjust the probe camera to zoom out, at which point, everyone fell silent. Several people gasped. It had only ever been discussed in textbooks, research papers, and by the most famous physicists on Earth. Yet here it was, right before their very eyes.

It was a wormhole. The first that Jacob had ever seen. As the technicians continued to take readings, the monitor abruptly blurred out. Jacob looked over to Bill's station to see that 2 had removed his hand from the console. He suddenly appeared weak, barely able to stay upright.

"Pardon me," he said shakily as his breathing became ragged.

Each word was illuminated by lights emanating from his wrist. 2 had switched to his bracelet to continue talking to them. It must have taken everything he had to hold out that long. He took deep breaths to try and stabilize himself.

"That required way more power than I originally calculated," his robotic voice echoed from his gold bracelet. "It took quite a bit of energy out of me to maintain a complete picture. Apologies. It truly was an amazing sight, but I must return to my charging chamber after this."

"It's alright 2, you did your best," Jacob said, smiling as he looked back at the screen. "That was a fantastic image."

A small warning light began flashing on his panel, followed by a loud beeping noise. *Strange,* he thought, *that indicator means a meteorite is heading towards earth.*

"Check the radar!" he commanded. "We got something heading for Earth!"

"Jacob," one technician answered. "I am detecting another object from the vicinity near the anomaly. Radar seems to be clearing up, but I can confirm this meteorite… originated from the wormhole."

"What? How? Houston, are you getting this?"

Checking his console, Jacob could see that they were quite right. His screen was no longer fuzzy, which was immediately confirmed by the people at NASA. The wormhole anomaly had vanished. That was probably why the radar was clear. The image from the probe on the monitor showed nothing. Since their systems were cleared up and back to normal, they could concentrate on the incoming object that had been detected.

The entire room focused on their monitors and together, they successfully identified an object, thanks to their probe, and saw that it was moving away from the coordinates of the anomaly. 2 even managed to grab the keyboard next to Jacob's and began typing. Based on its trajectory, the unknown object was speeding towards Earth.

"Hey Jacob, that object. It's kinda moving in fast. Very fast. I can't get an exact lock on its trajectory. It's like it's evading our scans whenever we manage to get our cameras on it."

Bill's agitated tone caught Jacob's attention. An idea popped into his head. Thankfully, the only enhanced human being in the room had gotten to it first.

"May I?" 2 asked politely. "I can track the object."

Without a word, Jacob nodded. He and his team watched as the amborg began to work his magic. 2's fingers were nothing but a blur as he typed at what must have been 3000 words per minute. He was amazed that the keyboard didn't begin to smoke or catch fire. Within seconds, he put a dot on the radar screen.

"This object may be fast, but not quick enough," he announced triumphantly. "It is on a direct course with the planet and will enter the atmosphere in thirteen minutes."

Jacob was impressed. Since amborgs generally kept to themselves, this was his first time actually seeing one at work. He had only ever seen old mission footage of them in action. Occasionally, they would help, but they were usually busy with their own schedules aboard Apogee station. Though at times when they did feel like offering their support, the workload became much lighter due to their high efficiency. Still, after watching that, Jacob knew that Dr. Kendrick's teenage-looking cyborgs were pros at handling serious business.

"I wish I could do that. The stories about you guys being hyperactive machines certainly are true."

"Yes, they are," 2 said with a smile. "I even had time to check my power levels, write a poem, and thought about my next spacewalk. Have we managed to reach Dr. Kendrick?"

"Not yet," someone called. "It's definitely gone past 40 seconds."

"Keep trying," 2 said. "We may have to figure out his current schedule."

"Wait," Jacob said suddenly. "You mean you don't know what he's up to? I thought amborgs kept track of everything."

"Yes," 2 said bluntly. "But privacy is something we greatly respect above all in human relations."

"Oh. I see."

"Also, it is possible we may have to alert the space jumpers... I can see the object now."

Jacob turned to face 2, who was gazing blankly out the window. He cast a glance, unsure if it would work, but decided to give it a shot anyway. As he narrowed his eyes, all he could make out were stars. He figured that 2, with his enhanced vision thanks to his advanced eye implants, was perceiving something far beyond his own sight.

"Ok, I don't have spidey-vision," Jacob announced, realizing that he must have looked ridiculous. "And I'm pretty sure the rest of us don't either."

Jacob looked back at 2, who was still peering out the window. He wasn't sure why he had accidentally tried to mimic the amborg's actions, but it gave him a clever idea.

"Legolas!" he said casually. "What do your elf eyes see?"

"How humorous... I am seeing... the object now," 2 said with a concerned look. "Recording images and transmitting to all consoles. It appears to be... or resembles a transportation pod of some kind... I estimate it is large enough to house one individual."

A few others chuckled discreetly at Jacob and 2's banter. However, the room fell silent after 2 reported what he was seeing. Nobody moved at all. They were all anticipating more news as 2 continued to stare out the window.

"Jacob," he said suddenly. "Inform the space jumpers that... we have a potential first contact. And... We need containment. Now. Until the world is prepared to know, initiate threat con delta. On my authorization."

Without saying a word, Jacob picked up a phone and immediately sent a call straight to the Station's security forces.

"Attention all hands," he said, his hands beginning to tremble. "Threat con delta authorized by amborg 2! Threat con delta! Action stations! Space jumpers...!"

Jacob glanced at 2 and hesitated. The amborg met his gaze and nodded firmly.

"...M-mobilize!" Jacob stammered as he concentrated on finishing the announcement. "Space jumpers! I repeat! M-mobilize!"

My whole entire world just turned upside down in less than a few minutes. He started to sweat as he dropped the phone back onto the charging station. *This is going to be an extremely long day.*

Jacob took a few moments to write down his reminder to call his mom. He didn't want to miss any opportunity or else, worst-case scenario, he might never have another chance.

■ ■

Somewhere over the Great Plains of Africa
Half an hour later

"We're in the pipe. Five by five. Ha! Now that never gets old!"

Captain Sheila Hicks held the controls as the cockpit managed to stop shaking violently. Her copilot, Lieutenant Benji Frye, listened in and waited for communications from Apogee to reestablish. Both were strapped into their seats tightly as their dropship faced the full brunt of atmospheric reentry. The silence of space was replaced with a massive rumbling that reminded Frye of each time they rocketed back up to the station after a mission. The sounds from the outside of the ship resembled that of a popcorn machine on steroids. Gravity was starting to act on them, and the turbulence was hitting them hard. Suddenly, they received a transmission from the other dropship that had descended down to Earth alongside them.

"Foe Hammer, this is Night Song."

"We copy you," Frye replied as he glanced at Hicks. "Go ahead."

The man over the radio was Captain Sam Planck, the pilot of another dropship that had deployed from Apogee Station.

"Communications reestablished," Planck reported over the radio. "No problems on our end, we are forming up behind you."

"Roger that," Frye answered. He turned to Hicks. "We're all set Cap! Both ships made it planet-side!"

"Acknowledged!" Hicks said with a grin. "Apogee Station, come in! Apogee Station, do you read?"

The radio crackled as they heard their dispatcher's voice answer them.

"Go ahead, Echo flight. We see you on our scopes."

"Attention Apogee Station," Hicks reported. "This is Echo Two-Oh-Nine. Atmospheric reentry completed safely. On approach to crash site. Echo Two-Three-Two has our six."

"Roger Echo flight, proceed to heading two-two-zero for one minute. The skies are clear. Begin your descent."

"Copy," Hicks answered. "Apogee Station, what exactly are we heading towards?"

The emergency alert had only given them a short amount of time to rush to the hangar, begin an emergency pre-flight start, and load the squads of Space Jumpers aboard their dropships. Normally, each time they launched and headed planet-side; they would have an emergency briefing outlining the details of their mission. This time, they had received nothing. Just the coordinates of where they needed to go, which was concerning.

"Standby Foe Hammer."

That was all that Hicks heard. She and Frye exchanged glances as the ship continued to fly through the rough winds. Both read each other's expressions as they spoke off comms.

"That doesn't sound reassuring..." Frye said, looking at the heading and checking their engine readings.

"I agree," Hicks replied. "Something must have shaken them up. This is big."

An answer abruptly came over the radio.

"Echo flight, this is what we have for you. Apogee Control and NASA informed us that some portal tore through the dimensions of space. Shortly after, we had an unidentified bogey that entered the atmosphere. Now you're in Africa because we have visitors. Do you have a visual of the craft?"

"Yes sir, we are closing in and scanning now. No disruption to our equipment. We can confirm it is not of Earth origins, right? Do we know what it is?"

"I'm going to be honest with you, we have absolutely no idea."

"Can I say it?" Frye asked on their private channel.

"No," Hicks answered promptly before switching back to the Apogee dispatcher. "Apogee, approaching the DZ, deploying Space Jumpers."

Hicks steadied the ship and began to cruise at a slower speed. She turned her head and switched on the intercom.

"Chief! Wakey wakey! 30 seconds to drop! Let's get boots on the ground! I'm opening the para-doors!"

The troops inside felt a sudden lurch as the thrusters outside the ship roared. Two doors towards the rear opened, letting in the sound of rushing wind. The Crew Chief, Staff Sergeant Dean Hammond, stood in the center and held up both of his hands so that everyone could see his instructions.

"Scouts! Get ready!"

Four marines towards the back leaned forward. Even though all of them weren't jumping, they all fixed their eyes on him intently.

"Stand... UP!" he yelled, motioning both hands upwards like he was lifting a window.

The four marines towards the doors stood on command.

"Equipment check!" Hammond tapped both of his shoulders a few times.

The four standing marines began to inspect the equipment they wore. They checked their bags for loose objects and made sure that all their straps were clasped tightly. Within a matter of seconds, they confirmed everything was secure and faced Hammond.

"Sound off for equipment check!" he yelled once he saw the safety check was done.

Each of them called out to him in sequential order.

"Four ok!" the marine closest to him yelled back as he tapped the shoulder of the next person in line.

"Three ok!" the next one nodded and repeated the process.

"Two ok!"

Hammond watched the last marine, who would be the first to jump out, give him a thumbs up.

"One ok!"

Hammond brought his hand up to his helmet's radio and contacted the cockpit.

"Lead scouts ready!" he called into the radio. "Give them the boot?!"

"Let's kick them off!" Hicks answered.

Seconds later, the green light beside both open doors at the back of the ship flickered on. Both Hicks and Frye had given them the go-ahead.

"Go, go, go!" Hammond shouted.

The first four marines immediately stepped through the doors, two on each side. After they left, Hammond spoke into the radio.

"Jumpers clear!"

An alarm buzzed loudly as the para-doors closed tightly, abruptly shutting out the roaring of the wind. Those remaining onboard began receiving instructions. This was the emergency briefing.

"All troopers, be advised," the Apogee station dispatcher reported. "Initial scans of the ship were captured before atmospheric interference made us lose sight of it. Possible miniature craft with one potential passenger inside. This ship is not from Earth. Repeat, this ship is not from Earth. Steel yourselves. This is the real deal."

Everyone pivoted and stared up front in unison. Several of them began glancing around, wide-eyed in disbelief, almost as if they had just heard an inappropriately timed joke. Hammond swallowed but held his composure. He shifted his gaze toward Captain Lee Harrelson, the squad leader, who was scanning the rest of his team.

"At ease," he commanded, prompting everyone to make subtle adjustments in an attempt to relax. "Steady there, troopers. Apogee station, we copy on your last, what is our response command?"

"Potential first contact scenario," Apogee station replied. "Order your soldiers to buck up. Keep them in line and make sure that they don't get trigger-happy. Avoid a firefight at all costs. Engage only as a last resort. The top brass want you to take extreme care."

"Copy that."

The soldiers checked their weapons, a few started panting nervously. Harrelson surveyed each of them again, his brow furrowed. He cast a quick glance at Hammond who gave him a shrug. He scoffed, turned back to the team, and raised his voice as loud as possible.

"Alright jumpers, you heard that order! Fire only on my command and ONLY when I give that order. Understood?!"

They all shouted in unison.

"YES SIR!"

"In the event that something happens to me," the trooper continued, "You do not fire unless my X.O. orders it. GOT IT?!"

"YES SIR!"

"BE HAPPY TROOPS! WE'RE ABOUT TO WITNESS AN HISTORICAL MOMENT! FIRST CONTACT WITH AN ALIEN SPECIES! AND YOU ARE ALL ALIVE TO WITNESS IT!"

"YES SIR!"

"BUT IF THEY ARE HOSTILE, THEN DON'T BE HAPPY! WE WILL FIGHT THEM BACK AND SHOW THEM THEY CAN'T COME TO OUR PLANET AND MESS AROUND WITH US! DO YOU GET ME?!"

"YES SIR!"

"LET'S GIVE THEM A GREETING FROM THE EARTHLINGS!"

The lights inside the ship turned a deep shade of red as Hick's voice over the intercom rang out.

"Touching down marines," she said as they felt the dropship slow its descent. "Exit in five seconds. Good luck troopers. Let's meet whoever was crazy enough to land on our home planet."

The back hissed as they watched the ramp lower. The hydraulics whirred loudly as the massive frame opened to lay down their exit. The dropship hit the ground with a sudden lurch. Hammond and Harrelson ordered the troops to stand and move out.

"Go! Go! Go!" Hammond bellowed as the ramp lowered completely and sunlight quickly streamed in.

Everyone sprinted out as they cleared the ship.

"Disembark! Now! Move out now!"

It didn't take them long to secure the area. Everyone fanned out cautiously, scattering to put space between each other. As they secured their position, they saw Captain Planck's dropship touch down a short distance away. Once the troops aboard that ship disembarked, the Night Song's thrusters fired again. Planck's ship emitted a deafening screech as it took off. Hicks kept her dropship's engines idling, keeping it in place. Echo Flight had their tasks. Planck would cover them and provide aerial surveillance while Hicks would standby on the ground.

After it was clear, Harrelson gave the signal, and his marines took point and advanced towards the crash site. The Night Song's marines fanned out to establish and hold the perimeter. No one fired a shot, which was expected since they were under strict orders, but they clung tightly to their weapons, anticipating a possible ambush. The lead troopers moved forward and took their position at a safe distance from the unknown vessel, which was currently sitting in the middle of a field. It was still sizzling from entering the atmosphere. Small fires and smoke surrounded the area. They gathered closer to the vessel, moving tentatively.

"Apogee station," Harrelson reported. "Are you getting this?"

"Roger," the operator replied. "We see what you see. An emergency session of the United Nations was just convened, and your video is live for A.I. Industries. Please proceed carefully."

"Roger that. Approaching the ship now," he replied. "For record keeping, this is Captain Harrelson, 1st platoon, Bravo company, 205th Marine Regiment. Reporting live for A.I. Industries. Second platoon is securing the perimeter. My squads are approaching the unidentified spacecraft."

Nobody spoke as they all took slow and deliberate footsteps through the grass. They kept their weapons trained on the target, holding their fire as they stopped a few meters away. Evidently, none of them knew what to do. Was the craft going to respond or should they make the next move? Harrelson knew that the longer they waited, the quicker the tension and anxiety would build, and that would be the end to a peaceful solution. If there actually was a possibility for one. After a few seconds to contemplate, he made up his mind and advanced ahead of his troops.

"Come on boys, we got to see if there's anything we can find out. This job ain't going to do itself," he said bravely while simultaneously concerned. "Cover me."

Interesting that the amborgs on Apogee couldn't spare time to jump with us, he thought, feeling all eyes on him. *What are we? Cannon fodder?*

"Sir, it might not be safe!" someone yelled.

Despite how obvious that was, what other choice did they have?

"Only one way to find out," Harrelson replied confidently, raising his voice so they could all hear him.

Without hesitating, he lifted his hand from his rifle and pressed his hand up to the shiny plating of the hull. He wasn't sure if it was going to be hot or cold when his glove made contact. Fortunately, it felt cool to the touch, and he eyed the craft suspiciously, waiting for something to happen.

They remained silent and motionless. It was like trying to avoid waking a hibernating bear. Harrelson stood with his rifle in his left hand and his right glued to the plating. Seconds passed by, but nothing happened. Just another awkward silence.

"Craft not responding to physical contact," he stated out loud for the record as he continued making observations. "It certainly feels real. Apogee station? Got any other ideas? Should we try to prep it to be brought in?"

"Hold on that suggestion," the radio crackled as the operator quickly replied. "Your bio-readings show nothing different. All normal. No change from the ship either."

"Copy that Apogee. I'm happy to report I'm still normal. I think. Do the amborgs or Dr. Kendrick have any ideas? We could probably..."

Harrelson was interrupted when the ship hissed and released a puff of steam. A little jet of steam shot up but missed him entirely. Harrelson retracted his hand and backed away. Then, a hatch sprang open.

Every marine close to the vessel trained their weapons on the hatch's opening, but Harrelson quickly held up his hand, silently ordering them to stand down. Personally, he was glad they hadn't opened fire. That had certainly got his heart going and he had thought for a split second that he was dead the instant his hand touched the alien ship. After a moment to steady himself, he stepped forward warily and glanced inside. At first, the steam blocked his vision, but once it cleared, he had an unobstructed view of the inhabitant inside and froze. Everyone began to move forward, lowering their weapons as they all curiously drew closer.

Captain Harrelson stared in absolute shock. This wasn't possible. A.I. Industries had made it clear years ago. Being a veteran from the Dominoe Incident, he remembered every person he had fought alongside with. The face of the person seated inside the vessel brought back memories. The news of her death had spread world-wide but now, his mind was unable to comprehend what he was looking at.

"Sir... Apogee. Are you seeing this?" he said into the radio.

"Harrelson. That's affirmative. We see it... but, we can't make sense of this."

"What do we do sir?" Harrelson's gaze was fixed intently on the pod's sleeping occupant.

"We're calling Kendrick. He's going to want to see this."

"I am seeing this."

The voice over the radio sounded familiar. He had heard it before and even met the man it belonged to on quite a few occasions. One of the brightest scientists on the planet. Hearing it helped him to simmer down and stop trembling.

"Dr. Kendrick," Harrelson let out a sigh of relief. "Please advise. How should we proceed?"

Every marine lowered their weapons as Harrelson waited to hear Dr. Kendrick's response. Maintaining his composure, Harrelson spoke into the radio and double checked that his body camera was fixed on the alien craft.

"Just keep your camera sighted on the occupant," Dr. Kendrick replied calmly. "Continue documenting."

■■■

A.I. Industries
Dr. Kendrick's Main Office

"George? Please signal for Serina."

Dr. Kendrick stroked his chin, removed his glasses, and wiped them just to make sure he wasn't hallucinating. A part of him hoped that his eyes weren't mistaken. He was fixated on the live stream from Harrelson's camera and tried his best to avoid letting the marines hear the growing fear building within him. Beside him, George Ramirez, one of his closest colleagues, was frozen in place, staring at the feed in disbelief.

The camera was aimed at the occupant's clothing inside the pod. This provided them with an ideal close up of what initially shocked them both. It was an A.I. Industries jacket. One that was made for the amborgs. The design looked slightly flashier, but it certainly looked like one of theirs despite it coming from outer space.

"We're sure this is not from... here?" George managed to ask his first question.

"George, unless someone managed to sneak to that alien craft in the last 25 seconds..." Dr. Kendrick turned and let out a faint chuckle, "Cloaked themselves invisible, stole one of our Amborg jackets and dressed an unconscious person, I am pretty sure that what was in the pod when it opened is definitely... Not. From. Here."

Noting what was printed on the jacket, he was right. Over the left chest pocket was a glowing neon double-digit number. A number that didn't belong to any active or any current amborgs. No one in their ranks had been designated or given that in years. In fact, it was one of the only numbers that was officially retired. Yet there it was in broad daylight.

"Captain," Dr. Kendrick cleared his throat, "Have your troops stash their weapons and put them away. Secure the area. I don't like the idea of this but... please take the occupant inside into custody. We need to begin containment and prepare a formal statement."

"Yes doctor," Captain Harrelson replied.

"Apogee Station," Dr. Kendrick switched the radio channel and contacted his staff members. "Ready a transport. All amborgs in space are to return to Earth immediately. Remain on alert."

"Well, that about wraps it up! I love system updates! Well... when we don't stumble across any deadly viruses."

A light flashed from the light strip on the wall. A familiar female A.I. sprung up in holographic form with a blue outline. This was Serina, one of the top artificial intelligence programs living at A.I. Industries. When she appeared, she bounced up onto Dr. Kendrick's desk, no bigger than a Barbie doll. She looked up at the two men with a cheerful smile and a quick salute.

"Ok, I got your call! So, what was so important that all the A.I.s were locked out of this meeting? Sounds serious."

"It is," Dr. Kendrick replied immediately. He quickly looked down at her. Not giving her a second to think, he spoke sharply, "Now, listen to me. Serina, turn away from the screen."

"Uhh sure... Are you ordering me not to watch? Because even if I turn away, I hate to break it to you, but I can still 'see' it. You know? I can just access the TV without looking if my Wi-Fi connection is still on."

The look that Dr. Kendrick gave her was enough to make her smile fade. She had, in fact, turned away from the screen when he first told her to, but when he didn't respond the way she expected, she knew she had accidentally buried herself in a hole thanks to her calculated level of humor. Immediately sensing the tension in the room, she stopped talking and listened carefully.

"Sorry," she cleared her throat, flashing brightly and straightening her posture. "What is it?"

"Serina," Dr. Kendrick said sternly as he glanced away from her and turned back to the screen. "The only known human being that defied the impossible and became an artificial intelligence."

"Yes?" Serina asked skeptically, wondering why he was stating the obvious.

"You are that A.I. standing right here in my office. And somehow, you are also... right there."

Dr. Kendrick bit his lip. He clicked his teeth and then sighed. He lifted a hand and motioned for her to turn around. She followed his movement and slowly turned to face the screen. As she began to watch the live video feed, Dr. Kendrick saw her turn a bright blue to a pale ghostly white.

"What?" Her eyes widened in shock, her breathing becoming rapid. "What. The. Hell??"

"Uh," George glanced at her nervously. "Is she hyperventilating?"

"They don't breathe George," Dr. Kendrick reminded him. He spoke calmly to Serina, who seemed to be fading through different shades of color. "Serina, listen to me."

"What the hell is that?" Serina demanded.

"I believe the better question is, how?" Dr. Kendrick replied as he gazed at the screen.

"Uh... Serina?"

Dr. Kendrick shifted his attention to George again, worry etched on his face as he watched Serina. Following his gaze, both men stared as she began to flash and turn fuzzy on the spot. They stepped back. She almost looked like someone had spilled water on her hardware.

"Has she ever done that before?" Mr. Ramirez raised his voice.

"Serina!" Dr. Kendrick exclaimed.

With a jump, Serina let out a squeak and snapped out of it. Her holographic image stabilized and the color to her silhouette began to return. She began to look more stable, but her eyes darted around in confusion. George appeared alarmed while Dr. Kendrick sternly held his composure.

"Yes?" she blinked as she turned to look up at them.

"Are you alright?"

Serina looked away from Dr. Kendrick's gaze, flashing red but switching back to blue in an instant. Once she began to look more normal, she nodded to them.

"Diagnostic check," she reported. "Completed. I am fine."

"Are you sure?" Dr. Kendrick asked suspiciously. "We've never seen any A.I. glitch like that before."

"Like you said..."

Serina gazed up at them with a serious expression. All traces of her light personality disappeared as she put on her game face. She was ready for action. A small wave of nostalgia washed over Dr. Kendrick. He hadn't seen that face since her days as an amborg.

"I'm not an ordinary A.I." Serina declared. "This is the real deal. It just surprised me... that's all. It's not a nightmare or a dream. I just... needed to make sure that I was awake."

After a moment of silence, Dr. Kendrick thought about his next decision. Whatever was going on, he knew this wasn't going to be simple. He needed help. The only people he could rely on were those he trusted unequivocally. Glancing at George and Serina one last time, he decided to go with the option that felt right.

"Very well," Dr. Kendrick nodded decisively. He gave his next command without hesitation. "Emergency Recall. All amborgs, Serina. I want all staff, personnel, outposts, and every single person notified and ready for action. Now."

There was no going back. Serina heard the order and firmly nodded.

"Right away."

Serina pivoted and took a step towards the wall. With a quick leap and a bright flash of light, she disappeared. They watched her move along the wall and then up into the ceiling. When she was out of sight, the two men glanced at each other.

"What did she mean when she said she needed to make sure she was awake?" George asked quietly. "She... can dream?"

"She told me it was an experiment she attempted last year," Dr. Kendrick answered in the same soft tone. "I don't know the full details. She won't say what happened. All I know is... that was the only other time I've seen her so shaken up."

"Doctor?"

Serina's voice spoke over the P.A.

"Emergency recall in effect," she reported. "However, some amborgs aren't immediately responding. I don't think everyone heard me."

Dr. Kendrick turned to George. Unconcerned, he nodded his head and spoke up.

"That's not what's going on but thank you, Serina. In fact, I anticipated this possibility. Now, it's time we send for them."

"Sending people to notify the amborgs or bringing our employees back... It will take time to recall everyone," George replied in a cautious tone. "Even the amborgs who are in deep cover or working incognito can't just drop everything on the spot. It will take a week. Minimum! If it works out perfectly! And if the world finds out, it will turn into a..."

"Chaotic logistical nightmare," Dr. Kendrick finished the statement.

"If that's your way of saying a real shitshow, yes."

Dr. Kendrick glanced at George and shrugged.

"I don't like to cuss."

He was right. The amborgs would have no problem returning to A.I. Industries in a short amount of time. Would it be enough? Mobilizing everyone else would quickly turn into a mess if mishandled. Everyone already on site would have to begin kicking into overdrive. If the world began to catch wind of what had just landed on their planet, then there would be instant panic. Still, every second they wasted wasn't helping.

"Serina?" Dr. Kendrick called out to her. "We have three days. Continue expediting recall. Bring them home."

Chapter 2: Lions, Vigilantes, Bread? Oh My

Hell's Gate, Kenya
Emergency Recall minus 32 minutes
6:56 PM Eastern Africa Time

"Luten base, calling Raven. Over? Raven, check in."

An hour had passed since the radio had sparked to life. Right on schedule as always. It was the standard hourly check-in call. Thanks to his earpiece, the sound hit his ears only, otherwise he would have given away his position. Fortunately, anyone who happened to be in the vicinity would have merely heard the wind and the surrounding environment. Technology once again proved superior. Even someone passing by wouldn't have noticed a gloved hand rise and hit the speaker button.

"Raven reporting," a quiet voice responded. "With all due respect sir, I wasn't expecting you to call me. Do you always feel the need to supervise every single one of us?"

"Well son," a kind and sincere voice chuckled over the radio. "I wouldn't be much of a leader if I didn't take the time to hear from you. Status?"

"Sorry Colonel," Raven replied softly. "Nothing to report this time. No movement or activity. Baker team must have succeeded... otherwise... I would be punching in on my timecard. Unless the insurgents are disguised as zebras, then all clear, sir."

"Copy that Raven, stand by for further instructions. We might just pull you back earlier. Also... you cut it out with the sass."

Carter 297 of the Second Group took his eye off his scope. He laid prone on his stomach and overlooked a vast grassy plain. He lowered his sniper rifle to listen to the transmission.

"Colonel," he replied. "I sent an update back to base a few minutes ago. Is there anyone investigating why my radar's acting up?"

"Stand by Raven," the Colonel answered. "We've just received a transmission from Dr. Kendrick's space station. They're trying to tell us something but it's buggy. Something is going on... and we'll update you once we hear more. We're trying to boost the connection."

297 peered up at the sky with curiosity. It had been a while since he'd last heard about Dr. Kendrick's recent endeavors. A big announcement regarding some sort of long range survey mission into outer space was the most recent bit of news. Whatever that was about, it was taking place far above his position.

The space station? He wondered. *Did the Apogee station encounter something?*

It was probably a meteor shower or something. Plenty of objects that traveled through reentry from space throughout history were usually the cause of communications issues.

He slowly raised his head a little more and checked his surroundings. Once he was certain that it was clear, he picked up his rifle and stood. If anyone else had been watching him, it would probably have gotten him killed. Nevertheless, he accepted the risks. He looked to the skies, his gaze trailing the clouds floating above. He didn't expect to see anything aside from that but still, he had a gut feeling that something was... up. Literally and metaphorically. Something didn't feel right.

A few moments passed, nothing happened. Shrugging the feeling away, 297 sighed and prepared to return to his previous position. He was about to crouch forward and lie back down in the tall grass when something caught his eye. He stopped himself and remained crouched on one knee. He lifted his rifle scope to his eye and scanned the area. The zebra herd had disappeared.

Concerned, 297 immediately switched to his peripheral vision camera and rewound his memory banks. This was a feature that only amborgs, robotic drones, or those that had purchased eye implants had. He took a deep breath, focused, and began searching through the footage in the last few minutes.

The zebra herd he'd seen moments before reappeared in his vision. He rewinded the footage back about 40 seconds and then ran the playback. Based on the footage, the herd had detected something strange. Like him, they had also sensed something wrong. Their animal instincts acted as a warning system, alerting them to potential danger. One of the zebras, possibly the leader of the pack, suddenly perked its head up. Noticing the signal, the rest of the herd stopped grazing. They all raised their heads, and in seconds, they bolted, almost as if they'd felt the presence of hunters. When the video ended, Carter shut off the recording and brought his thoughts back to the present. He scanned the area carefully. How was it possible he had failed to notice the herd fleeing? Once he had some free time, he'd set a reminder to run a diagnostic check on himself.

"I've gone soft…" he said, feeling at a disadvantage as he clenched his rifle. "They disappeared without my noticing."

All he could hear now was the wind. The sounds of the wildlife had died down entirely. The zebras were long gone, and the birds were no longer singing. Everything had fallen eerily silent. 297's eyes narrowed as he disengaged the safety and raised his rifle. He picked his feet up slowly, stepped forward, and kept an eye out for hostile activities.

"Now why would you be running away?" he whispered, listening for any movement. "What did you see? What sent a chill up your spines? Hunters? Poachers?"

His answer came in an instant.

As if on cue, a sudden boom echoed across the plains. 297 stopped and whirled around. That had come from above. He quickly activated his cybernetic scanner and looked up to identify the source of the unexpected noise.

"What?" he said aloud. "That was not a bomb or explosive. It came from the atmosphere."

That was definitely a sonic boom generated by something traveling faster than the speed of sound. Shortly after hearing it, 297 looked up and saw something streak across the sky and crash off in the distance. The ground rumbled as he felt the impact reverberate across the land. The ground shook, but he managed to remain upright. Based on how fast it had fallen and hit the ground, he knew one thing. That wasn't a meteor.

"Command, this is Raven," 297 tried to contact Luten base. "Come in, over. I got something that just flew overhead on my current position."

"Khhzzt…Say again, Carter kkzz… Repeat?"

"Command? Colonel? Can anyone hear me?"

He glanced at his radio and noticed that the interference was worse than before. His radar was still fuzzy and knocked out. Now his communications were cut off. It was atmospheric interference.

Excellent, he thought, *No backup or support.*

If anyone was trying to kill him, then this would be an ideal opportunity for an ambush. He was alone, by his choice, in the middle of nowhere. He recalled all the distractions and traps the amborgs had fallen for in the past. Most of their enemies were clever, coming up with all sorts of tactics to cut them off, isolate each other, and take them down. Even with everything they had survived, there were still plenty of criminals that held serious grudges. He could only hope that no one had managed to discover his true identity.

Cautiously, he glanced around and decided to head towards the place where the object crash-landed. It wasn't too far away, based on what he could see. Even though it meant he would deviate from his current task, he felt that he couldn't ignore it. 57 had always said that probable cause was a great start to either an adventure or trouble.

Changing course and beginning his hike towards the crash site, he followed a smoke trail originating from a spot only a few clicks away. Technically, he was supposed to be trying to reestablish contact with his base, but since he was originally told to keep an eye out for suspicious activity, this still fit his mission requirements. Being alone in the field wasn't necessarily a terrible thing. The majority of the time, his commanders disliked it whenever he separated from his squad. Together, in groups, his friends were deadly and capable of handling any threat. Going solo also yielded the same results, but he couldn't showcase his true strength due to the fact that not everyone knew he was an amborg.

If anything bad were to happen to him, they would be facing a highly trained and skilled U.S. Green Beret Special Forces soldier who also happened to be an amborg, one of the strongest humans on Earth.

As he slowly marched towards the crash site, the sound of two more sonic booms pierced the sky, causing him to stop and look up again. A loud whooshing filled the air, followed by the distinct sound of engines roaring in the distance. Something big was coming this way.

"Rapid response," he said.

From what he was able to pick up, it was the sound of advanced Grumman boosters firing. He'd heard the sounds of these thrusters before. They were commonly installed on modern spacecraft.

"Those can't be..."

He continued to move carefully, keeping his eyes locked on what was approaching the crash site. He spotted two modified dropships descending from the sky on a landing approach. He recognized the markings and the insignias on the fuselages. He knew who it was.

"Those are the space jumpers," 297 said as he felt energy building up in his chest. "From space!"

My amborg side is kicking in, he thought, *I forgot how exciting my life was.*

This had to be the real deal. He never expected to be witnessing an actual deployment from space.

297 increased his speed and took up a position overlooking the crash site. What lay before him was breath-taking. A massive crater had formed with

something large sitting in the center, surrounded by flames and small pillars of smoke all over in a large radius. The space jumper ships initiated their landing procedures and moved into position.

He watched the dropships hover in midair, their engines rotating to face the ground below. Both ships remained in place and the side doors opened. Moments later, the jetpack troopers deployed. 297 saw one squad of four troopers from each ship jump out and descend. Eight scouts in total flew overhead and circled over the target like vultures. From his concealed position, 297 crouched low, his eyes fixed on the troopers who touched down to secure the area. Fortunately, no one had spotted him.

As the dropships picked a landing site and deployed their landing gear, the powerful booster engines kicked up debris, scattering dust, mud, and grass in all directions. The ships executed a soft landing and the rear cargo ramps opened, allowing the rest of the troops aboard to rush out. 297 saw them exit the ships and clear the area. One of the dropships took off while the other one remained in place. He watched the main group begin to move towards the center of the crater in a standard encirclement formation.

Doesn't look like an ordinary meteor to me, he thought.

Relying solely on his own eyes rather than his rifle scope, 297 silently observed from his position. If it had been an ordinary falling object from space, it would have caused a lot more damage. No, what the troopers were circling was a ship of some kind. It had slowed down and hit the ground at a lower velocity.

Over the next few minutes, he observed the leader of the marines engage in a series of interactions with the object. 297's suspicions were confirmed when he saw steam shoot out of the vessel and a part of it sprang open. He quickly looked up the amborg "First Contact" protocol in his database.

He knew that this ship was definitely not something he had seen before, which only seemed to spark his curiosity. Life from outer space had touched down and he was one of the witnesses.

As he compiled his own results from the data he was acquiring visually, a sudden alert sounded at the back of his mind. It wasn't an ordinary one. This was a beacon built into his implants when he was first cybernetically enhanced. He had only seen it used a few times in the last decade. Amborg Industries had activated the emergency recall.

"Well, this just gets better and better," 297 smirked as he sent his reply.

━━━━━━━━━━━━━━━━━━━━━━━━━━━━━━━━

Beloyarsk Power Plant
Sverdlovsk Oblast, Russia
Emergency Recall minus 19 minutes
9:09 PM YEKT Time

It was cold. Not cold enough for snow but definitely frigid enough to where most would want to stay indoors. Far away from 297's position in Africa, the temperature was significantly colder in Russia. A few individuals that were dressed for the weather were going about their business as usual. In the middle of a park overlooking a pond, a woman sat on a bench and waited patiently.

"Lovely lady! I don't think I've seen you before."

The woman's green eyes turned left to see who had the nerve to bother her. Someone was trying to throw her a line in Russian. Unconcerned, she saw a man strutting up to her confidently. After a second, a smug smile formed on her lips as she recognized the familiar voice.

"Well, I see that you finally decided to show," Katrina 4 spoke softly. "If you were anyone else, you'd probably be dead for approaching me with that stupid pickup line."

"Well, I was practicing my Russian."

Amborg Stuart 8 dipped his head politely. 4 tilted her head toward the edge of the park bench, allowing him to sit beside her. The two of them sat there acting nonchalant. As they initiated a quick connection and shared intel, 8 presented her with a progress report.

"Where is she?" 4 looked around curiously. "Did 9 fall behind? I've been waiting."

"Hiding the bodies of the security guards who were tailing you a while back," 8 answered. "I'm surprised that someone of your skills and stature would allow yourself to be followed so easily."

"Well, I had to," 4 said with a half smile. "I had to catch their attention, but I didn't want to shake them off. It's too important that they don't discover that the amborgs are here."

"Now that you mention it," 8 looked around cautiously. "Why are we here? You were quite secretive, as usual."

4 pulled her hand out of her pocket and rested her arm on the backrest of the bench in response. This didn't seem reassuring at all. 8 stared at her nervously as she flashed a mischievous smile. She was plotting something again.

"If it goes well," she spoke in an upbeat tone, "you'll see. Anyway, how's it going 35?"

"Wonderful Katrina, just abso-freaking-lutely wonderful..."

4 continued smiling as 8 realized that she'd just transmitted a message. She was on a radio channel that he wasn't aware of. She linked him in, and he was added to the group chat. 8 realized that she had been monitoring someone else this entire time.

"Is that you, Ryan 35?" 8 asked.

"Greetings my old friend." Ryan 35 of the Second Group responded in a begrudging tone.

8 was happy to hear from another amborg, especially one he hadn't had a chance to speak to for a few weeks.

"Last I checked, I thought you were working as a psychologist for your human cover," he said while 4 smirked and casually rested both her elbows on the park bench. "What are you doing out here?"

"I was working as a psychologist. That piece of information is accurate," 35 replied grimly. "Until Ms. Kat 4 decided to show up while I was vacationing here with a mission that required an amborg. She threw rank in my face, being a senior First Group member, and now I'm stuck infiltrating a Russian power plant. Apparently, it is under the influence of a corrupt owner which could lead to a disaster of nuclear proportions."

This sounded more and more like a heavily planned mission than an interrupted leave of absence. Knowing what 4 was like in the field, it wasn't actually that surprising. Before, the First Group usually had very fast and direct methods of carrying out their tasks. 4 was an accomplished tactician among the amborgs. She prioritized long-term planning, focused meticulously on details, and emphasized coordination in her missions.

"I'm amazed 35 happened to be here at the same time we were," 8 said, nodding with approval. "You didn't call him here like me, did you?"

"Well let's just say," 4 said innocently. "I still have access to his location, schedule, and skills. You could say it was almost... coincidence that I came here on assignment and that he also happened to be living across the street from my hotel room."

There was a brief pause, almost as if time had frozen. 8's smile faltered as he nervously spoke up, breaking the silence.

"You're scary, you know that?"

4 didn't reply. She merely smiled and continued to lean back and relax on the bench while 35 continued to grumble on in the conversation.

While the two First Group amborgs sat comfortably incognito, it was a different story for the volunteered amborg who got roped into this mission. Meanwhile, several miles away, a covert infiltration operation was underway.

At the Beloyarsk power plant, 35 had successfully managed to sneak inside. He carefully glanced around the corner, listening to the group communications channel. Once he determined that the coast was clear, he advanced further, maintaining a 360-degree awareness of his surroundings. He headed towards the entrance.

"Be quiet!" he transmitted to the others as he nonchalantly walked over and crouched next to a pillar. "I'm trying to infiltrate a compound here! I still don't understand why I had to do this. Couldn't you have called your buddies from the Fourth Group? They're new right? Make them do this."

"First of all," 4's voice replied assertively in the radio channel at the back of his mind. "Just because someone is new doesn't entitle everyone to pull the 'make the new guys do it,' tactic. Besides, the fourth group has been operating since just after the Domino Incident, which tells me you need to rework your definition of new, 35. Now get a move on... since you're already there."

"Because you ordered me here!"

35 sighed and lifted his left arm to examine his bracelet. He quickly activated a button, and a holo-emitter instantly surrounded his entire body. Within seconds, he was wearing a lab coat with a bunch of other accessories to go with his newly established disguise. Quickly converting his hand into a mirror, he checked to make sure that his face was now completely altered. Satisfied, he stood up and walked out of hiding. He headed towards the entrance and casually stepped inside.

The security guards looked up from their desk as 35 walked forward and held up a fabricated badge. The one closer to him took a brief look and nodded, indicating that 35 had secured his way in. His credentials checked out and looked convincing enough for them.

He proceeded past the checkpoint and through another pair of doors that opened to reveal a long hallway. 35 began walking past glass windows on both sides of the walls. In his peripheral vision, he could see labs filled with what appeared to be workers in chains. His eyes widened a fraction, but he maintained a normal composure and double-checked that he was transmitting live footage to 4.

"Yikes," 35 shuddered as he spoke to them privately. "Are you both seeing this? This isn't good. Didn't we ban this practice a few centuries ago?"

"The video is streaming perfectly," 4 replied. "This is exactly what we needed. I knew something was odd about this place."

"That's a lot of workers..." 8 observed.

"There is," 35 silently replied in his head as he reached the end of the hall. "Civilians probably. All in chains. I think those rumors were true. A nuclear power plant on the outside, but inside, a converted heavy weapons lab utilizing manual slave labor. Looks like this section is making guns. Enough for a battalion of troops."

35 entered the next hallway and looked down the corridor. There weren't any windows in this one, but he found an elevator. He walked over and pushed the button to call it down. He had to find a computer terminal in one of the administrative offices to acquire more information.

"Is someone planning to start another war?" he asked, looking around to make sure there was no one else approaching.

"I doubt it," 4 said quietly. "Based on what I'm seeing of your video feed 35, this is most likely a main supplier to the black market. I never would have suspected that they camped themselves and set up an entire operation in a nuclear power plant. Very clever. The risk is quite dangerous. If we went in guns blazing, one bad explosion and then we reenact Chernobyl. Nuclear meltdown. Fortunately, we have the resources and technology to quickly reverse the damage, but we can't fix the loss of life if something goes wrong. We're going to have to disable these weapons or find a way to recover them to make sure they don't get into the wrong hands. And do all of that without destroying the place."

"Yeah," 35 said as the elevator doors opened. "I'm going up a few floors. I'm going to try to hack into a computer to see if I can copy the database and pinpoint the exact location of where the rest of the weapons are being stored. Maybe I can sabotage their operations covertly while I'm here."

"Copy that 35. Proceed carefully. I am authorizing you to use any means at your discretion. Uh, just don't nuke us by mistake."

"I'm not going to be that careless..."

35 entered the elevator. A computer database in this place would most likely be in one of the main offices. He waited quietly and patiently as the elevator moved up towards the top floor. Thinking about his next move for infiltrating the higher levels, a sudden ding interrupted his thoughts as the elevator came to an abrupt stop and the doors slid open.

A couple of scientists walked in. 35 casually greeted them in Russian as they pressed the button for the floor they wanted. They continued their conversation and excluded him, which allowed him to relax a bit. He had to avoid as much contact as he could with the other employees. The possibility of anyone realizing that he didn't actually work here would increase if he so much as said the wrong thing. 35 waited silently as the elevator continued its ascent, but a couple of floors later, it stopped again with a ding, and more passengers got on. A couple more people in suits followed by another trio of scientists in white lab coats joined them.

This was starting to concern him.

A crowded elevator in the middle of a power plant? What were the odds of that? 35 looked down but kept his eyes on the new arrivals. This much traffic in this kind of place was very odd. Wonderful.

He was right to be suspicious. All the passengers were pressing in on him and shifting him to the middle of the elevator. This definitely reminded him of a scene from a movie he'd seen before. Then, it dawned on him what was happening. As the elevator slowly ascended, 35 began to speak in fluent Russian, causing everyone to become silent. Might as well get this over with.

"Hello everyone," he said calmly. "This is going to end painfully for all of you. Do not worry, I am not here to kill anyone. All occupants will be knocked unconscious in a fair manner. However, for the record, I must ask one question. Would anyone like to get out?"

"You're really polite despite the fact that they're about to gang up on you..." 4's voice spoke in the back of his head in a rather questioning tone.

"Not now 4," 35 replied to her in his head as he waited.

He quickly exited the amborg group chat. The instant he finished speaking with his real voice, chaos erupted. A massive scuffling broke out as the occupants began attacking 35. The people closest to him tried to subdue him by tackling and shoving him towards the wall. It was evident from their movements and combined strength that they were all expert martial artists. Capturing him alive was their sole objective. It made sense. They probably wanted to interrogate and beat some information out of him.

"Hey 35."

"What is it?" 35 asked mentally when 4 reconnected him to the group chat. "I'm kinda busy right now you guys... Oh how cute, they think those will work on me."

35 eyed the ones moving in front of him while he was pinned tightly against the wall. Several of them had drawn stun sticks. They could either use these to beat the crap out of someone or switched to electrocute them. In 35's eyes, this didn't seem to be an effective strategy.

It was clear they hadn't recognized he was an amborg. If they tried beating him, he was capable of withstanding the pain. Amborgs had a high threshold for it. Electrocuting him was most likely just going to tickle him. Still, continuing to pretend that he was a helpless human being was probably ideal for him for this infiltration. Once he was isolated in whatever torture chamber they had, he could break out and switch the plan up.

"I'm receiving an incoming alert 35," 4 explained in the transmission. "Stand by for further instructions."

"I'm not going anywhere," 35 replied defiantly, continuing to struggle against the multiple people trying to restrain him. "I guess I can pretend to be helpless a moment longer."

35 watched apprehensively as they began to activate their stun sticks. The sound of electricity filled the elevator as they all slowly moved closer to him. The sticks crackled and glowed with electricity. To an ordinary person, those would probably hurt. Maybe he could at least pretend they were stinging him if they decided to poke him with them.

"We have new orders 35," 4 stated as someone in the elevator ordered 35 to surrender. "Priority one message from home. It's an emergency recall from Dr. Kendrick. I guess this mission will have to wait."

35 ignored the passenger's repeated commands to stand down as he listened to 4's messages. Did he hear that correctly? An emergency recall?

"You mean...?"

Her response was immediate.

"Time to go home."

35 paused for a moment. That was that. His mind raced as he quickly strategized his extraction route and started to consider what the emergency recall could be about. Those orders by Dr. Kendrick were no joke. Once he had a plan in place, he redirected his focus back to the task at hand. It was time to deliver a world of pain.

"I'll call you back," 35 sent his next message quickly as he saw someone's fist swinging towards his face. "I need a minute."

The amborg quickly shook off the people clinging to his right arm. With it freed, he grabbed the man's fist before it could hit his face and redirected it towards someone on his left side. He lifted his right leg and kicked the first person in front of him, sending them straight into the closed elevator doors. With lightning speed, he curled his right fingers into a fist and landed a punch on the person to his left. Bringing his arm back, he delivered a powerful elbow strike to the person behind his right shoulder. One by one, 35 punched, grabbed and threw all the attackers around the elevator. Despite their attempts to fight back, it was not effective. The stun sticks weren't doing their job, but before any of them had the chance to contemplate this, 35 powered through each blow and eliminated them. When he was down to the last man, 35 punched him with so much force that the man flew straight into the window, shattering it on impact. With one quick step, before he could fall, 35 grabbed the legs of the unconscious businessman and pulled him back in.

"I made a vow. No deaths today," 35 declared as he placed the unconscious man on the floor. "This is and has always been one of our main directives. If you'll excuse me, we'll have to do this again another time."

The door to the elevator opened as it reached the top floor. Face to face with a group of heavily armed guards, 35 was ordered to surrender and identify himself. He couldn't help but find it pretty funny.

"You guys haven't identified an amborg before?" 35 muttered. "Interesting."

"Aren't you finished yet 35?" 4 asked impatiently over the coms. "We got to go now."

"You guys should probably go on ahead," 35 said as he lifted his hands slowly in surrender. "I got this."

"Well, you got to send a reply to the priority one," 4 said half-heartedly.

"I know, just give me a sec," 35 replied as the guards ordered him to step off the elevator. "Tell me, how did they know I was an imposter? Pretty impressive response time and security measures."

"From what 8 and 9 can see in the building schematics… That is, the recent ones we just downloaded off the back alleys of the internet," 4 explained. "There's a new facial recognition software update in the cameras which identified that you weren't part of the actual staff, and it alerted them. Cutting edge and really expensive…"

"Ah technology," 8's voice joined 35's messaging system. "So primitive but getting better and better. Humans seem to have evolved over the last few years."

"Better indeed," 4 agreed. "But not advanced enough. 35 are you done yet?"

"Just finishing up. You'd think that they would have learned not to mess with me after seeing an elevator full of their friends that I took down all by myself."

35 turned to look back at all the guards he'd left behind him. In that brief conversation, he had started just outside of the elevator and proceeded to run right through the hall of guards. The wider space in the hall gave him plenty of maneuverability to utilize his maximum speed while the others continued their conversation. By doing so, he had most likely exposed himself as an amborg, but with Dr. Kendrick sending out the emergency recall, their priorities had changed.

"I am withdrawing from the area," he reported as he ran around the corner. "Please give me an extraction point to rendezvous at."

"Show off," 4 and 8 replied in unison.

He smirked and made his way to the stairs up to the roof. He would have to ask for an A.I. to help him scrub the security footage of the events that took place here at the plant. The amborgs would have to return another time to finish this mission.

"Family reunion time," 35 said as he opened the door to the roof.

■ ■

Portland, Oregon
Tillia's Bakery
Emergency Recall minus 11 minutes
9:17 AM Pacific Time

"How many times have I told you? I'm not that old... I can still do this."

"Grandma, no. You are old."

Across the world, in North America, amborg 999 was shifting three large boxes into the corner of a small-town bakery. She was spending time away from duty, unaware of what was going on overseas. The old lady that owned the place watched peacefully from behind the counter.

"I'm only one hundred and sixteen," she replied with a chuckle.

Angel ignored her. She properly placed the boxes where she had been instructed and opened one. She checked the invoice and examined the contents. Both matched, so 999 checked the next box, and then the next. Meanwhile, Grandma Tillia wiped down the counter top with a rag.

Grandma Tillia had owned the bakery for quite a long time. She gained custody of it many decades ago when she returned from a life of pain, loss, and chaos. Apparently, the bakery was one of the few possessions that her family had passed onto her, and it was the peace that she discovered that she needed. Or that was how she had described it.

She was well-known for her high-quality baking skills and for her tough attitude, despite being only five feet tall. She and her husband had run the place together until his death several years ago. According to her stories, she was a fifth-generation descendant of a family of cooks. Before the Third World War, her ancestors owned a large chain of at least thirty family-style restaurants, but the business dwindled over the years. Over time, after all the closures, property sales, and real-estate conflicts, it was possible that this bakery was probably the last one still standing that remained a part of their legacy.

Grandma Tillia continued to take care of the place as best as she could on her own despite the struggles in the community. With her own children all grown up and working elsewhere, she cured her empty nest syndrome by taking care of hungry folks and children who passed by.

Now, why was amborg 999 of all people helping out around a place like this, while wearing civilian clothes to hide her true identity? The answer was simple. Grandma Tillia was one of the individuals who originally rescued her off the streets and helped raise her during many years of her childhood. Very few people knew this particular story about Angel, the cold-hearted lone wolf of A.I. Industries.

"I may be old, but I also notice things," Grandma Tillia called over to 999.

"Oh?"

999 walked over to the entrance of the store and grabbed another stack of three big boxes. She casually lifted them and carried them inside like they weighed nothing. Grandma Tillia glanced outside to make sure no one could see her utilizing her superhuman strength. It would catch a lot of unwanted attention if any fans of the amborgs spotted 999.

"You seem to be visiting a lot nowadays," Grandma Tillia said, confirming that the coast was clear. "Is there anything wrong? Something you not telling me?"

"What's so wrong about seeing my favorite grandma?" 999 replied with a neutral expression as she continued towards where she was arranging the other boxes. "I just like coming home to you."

"Well, it used to be a visit every few weeks," Grandma Tillia paused her cleaning to walk around the counter slowly. "Now it seems like it's every few days. And every time, you're always working. So hard, too. We hardly have a chance to talk anymore. Don't you ever just... sit down and have a nice conversation?"

"Only if I have something to say."

"So, say it," Grandma Tillia placed a hand on the counter to steady herself. "Why don't you talk about it?"

"You know why," 999 sighed, turning her head to the side as she tried to see where to place her boxes.

Suddenly, a faint trilling noise caught their attention and they turned to listen. It was a tiny alarm beeping from the door. Both froze in place, and the old lady peered outside.

"Oh! The porch sensor!" Grandma Tillia said sharply. "Someone's coming!"

In a flash, 999 flinched and instinctively jerked her arms upward. She launched the top two boxes in the air, and they landed in the corner with the rest. Regaining her composure, she tightly gripped the remaining box in her hands and proceeded. Now, she was pretending the box was heavy and slowing her down.

If anyone saw her in her casual clothes carrying weights beyond what she physically looked capable of lifting, then her cover was blown. Quickly, both made sure to play it cool and maintain a façade of normalcy. 999 needed to act casual and avoid raising suspicions.

A woman carrying a baby walked in through the door. She was followed by three kids, who were obediently sticking close. They were also joined by another adult. 999 noticed a military uniform on this one, but the hat masked the soldier's face.

Grandma Tillia smiled at the family and welcomed them in.

"Hello Brena," she said with a warm smile and raised her arms. "How nice of you to drop by! Who's the soldier with you? Or should I say... there seems to be a mysterious draft following you."

The soldier chuckled, understanding the joke, and looked down at her camo-patterned uniform. People always cracked camouflage jokes whenever they spotted someone in uniform.

"That's very funny actually," the soldier said with a laugh.

"What?" Grandma Tillia teased, looking past the entrance. "Brena, there seems to be a disembodied voice coming from right behind you!"

Brena and the soldier giggled. She adjusted her grip on her baby and gave Grandma Tillia a hug as the kids scrambled over to the glass case and peered at the pastries inside. After they let go, she placed her bag on the nearest table and let out a huge sigh of relief once the weight was off her.

"She's new to the area," Brena panted as she caught her breath. With her baby in her arms, she sat down in the chair. "She heard about your bakery and wanted to try it out!"

The soldier removed her cap politely.

"Oh! Look!" Grandma Tillia exclaimed playfully. "It's a floating head!"

999 set down her box and, out of the corner of her eye, noticed that the soldier was an officer. There was also something familiar about her. Had she seen this woman before?

"Everyone at the base says this is a place you have to visit. Thanks for showing me where it is. I almost thought my GPS was lying to me."

It suddenly dawned on her. 999 immediately recognized the soldier's voice, and there was no mistaking that face. She had met this particular person 10 years ago. It was back at The Academy during the Domino Incident. The amborgs had rescued her and fought with her.

"Deliza," 999 said as she wiped her hands on her shirt and took a few steps forward. "It would appear you have been promoted. A Lieutenant now."

Deliza turned and got a good look at 999. She eyed her civilian clothing with a hint of recognition in her eyes. She gave a subtle nod and smirked. The two of them silently acknowledged their shared history.

"Alice," she winked. "Good to see you. I think you're the last person I expected to see here."

"We're friends," 999 explained to Grandma Tillia, who was looking at the two of them with curiosity. "She's trustworthy. We saved each other's lives."

Deliza's eyes widened. Did 999 say that just to keep her cover intact? It almost sounded like she had just given out a compliment. Whether it was genuine or not, she never thought she'd see the day that 999 would actually acknowledge another person for their past efforts.

"She does seem quite capable. I think I figured that one out for myself," Grandma Tillia answered with a slight chuckle. She turned to shake Deliza's hand. "I'm glad to hear that my bakery's reputation hasn't sunk into the mud. You're welcome here anytime."

"Wait a minute… Alice?"

Before Deliza could utter a word of thanks, Brena suddenly rose from her seat. She stared at 999, squinting her eyes. She felt uneasy being scrutinized and attempted to look away.

"It can't be? Alice? Is it really...?"

It was no good. Her attempt to try and hide failed as Brena approached with her baby, drawing everyone's gaze. She stared intently at 999, concentrating as if there was a time limit. She used one free hand to rummage into her jacket pocket and flipped out a pair of glasses. As she placed them over her eyes, she leaned in close to 999, who leaned away slightly.

"Alice!" she exclaimed. Her eyes sparkled as her enthusiasm leaped out. "It is you! I thought you seemed familiar but... I couldn't tell! Until the Lieutenant said your name that is. I am so sorry it took me a while."

999 returned her fascinated gaze awkwardly and tried to search through her memory banks. Unfortunately, all of her childhood memories prior to becoming an amborg weren't exactly ingrained in her head. It wasn't a part of her life that she enjoyed remembering so she had forgotten most of it. Still, she couldn't deny there was something about Brena that seemed vaguely familiar.

"I'm sorry," 999 dipped her head apologetically. "But I don't remember you. We knew each other?"

"I'd be surprised if you did remember," Brena chuckled. "But we met when we were kids! Remember? I was always bumping into things and falling all over the place. You and the other kids pitched in and got me my first pair of glasses? Remember? It really helped make things a lot better."

"It sounds familiar..." 999 shrugged. That was a lie. Memories were starting to resurface prior to her cybernetic enhancement, but she tried to block them out. "I'm sorry. My childhood was difficult."

"I totally get that," Brena said. "But I'm glad to see you all grown up! I never thought I'd see you again! Especially when I heard about what happened to this place after I moved away."

"Wait. What happened?" Deliza asked curiously.

Brena turned to Deliza and paused as she gathered her thoughts. Without hesitation, she started to relay the story. 999 and Grandma Tillia both exchanged a look, but Brena had begun to speak.

"Alice here was a very shy but tough girl," she said, putting a finger on her cheek. "She was always with this boy. Almost all the time, you know? A boy with a prosthetic arm. I wonder if he's still ok? I think he was hurt very badly. Anyway, when they were older, I heard stories about the mob..."

"Brena!"

Grandma Tillia stepped forward and forcefully tapped her cane on the floor. The impact echoed across the room. The kids stopped playing and turned to stare at her inquisitively. Startled, Brena and Deliza halted their conversation and turned to the old lady, who gestured towards 999. They saw that 999 had gone completely silent and appeared uneasy. She was clearly uncomfortable as her breathing became ragged and her fingers started to tremble.

"Oh," Brena said, placing a hand over her mouth. "I'm so sorry. I let my mouth run again..."

Deliza remained quiet, looking between Brena and 999. Obviously, this was a very sensitive subject. 999 cleared her throat calmly.

"I'll... step outside for a minute."

999 walked past them gently, patting the head of one of the kids who gazed up at her before she walked out the door. They only heard her footsteps as she went out onto the front porch. The door slowly started to close after 999 exited.

As it shut, Brena bit her lip and looked down nervously.

"Should I say something?" she asked Grandma Tillia with a worried expression. "I really should apologize."

"Give her some space," the old lady sighed as she watched 999's silhouette. "I'm afraid Alice still has a hard time forgetting the past. It cost her everything."

"But you seem to have greatly helped her right?" Deliza pointed out with a soft smile. "I don't think I've ever seen her be so open around other people before. She's in casual clothes and showing emotion. More than usual. I never would have pegged her as the baking type."

"It's because she chooses who she trusts carefully," Tillia dipped her head down. "This place is... important to her and also a place that she feels very guilt-ridden over."

"I don't follow."

Deliza glanced at the two of them skeptically. Brena held onto her baby, gently cradling her back and forth as she explained.

"Grandma Tillia helped a lot of us to survive," she said. Deliza noticed that Brena appeared to be holding the baby much closer to her heart. "Her shop here was like a beacon of hope to the community. But after it burned down..."

Brena turned and tipped her head to motion towards the front door.

"Things changed," she lowered her voice softly.

Deliza turned to glance at 999, who was still standing outside. She looked at Grandma Tillia and pointed towards the entrance.

"She... burned down your bakery?" Deliza asked slowly.

Grandma Tillia's expression darkened. Her gaze caused Deliza to clear her throat and clamp her mouth shut. Deliza rarely encountered anyone that could deliver such a cold and terrifying look, especially a little old lady that didn't even seem capable of hurting a fly. She almost felt a sense of familiarity from Tillia. The look that emanated from her eyes was that of a protective mother. She imagined that Brena also had that strength hidden away somewhere inside of her if she ever needed to defend her kids.

"I'm sorry," Deliza swallowed a little. "That was insensitive."

Grandma Tillia glanced over her shoulder. 999 remained outside on the porch. She turned to face Deliza again.

"No, she didn't burn down the place," she replied sternly. Deliza saw her clench the handle of her cane tightly. "She believes she was responsible though. This community, a long time ago, tried to defy the mob to protect her. They came for her. They wanted... to take her away and put her to work in those terrible underground brothels. When we refused and tried to protect her, they burned everything. Just because they didn't like that we had chosen to fight back. But it was at that moment that we all stood together right in their greedy faces to protect our children. That's how important she was to us. We wanted to protect her future."

"The place looks really great though," Deliza glanced around, looking closely at the interior. "It's hard to believe that it once burned down."

"You can rebuild some things over and over again," Grandma Tillia smiled. "But some things may be lost for good. Just like him."

Deliza reached into her pocket and whipped out her phone. She entered Grandma Tillia's bakery into the search bar and decided to browse the internet for significant events and anything of note.

"Ok, let me look this up," she muttered. "I feel like this is something I need to know more about. Who is... uh, him? You don't mean...?"

In the years that she knew 999, there was only one man she'd seen that spent a lot of time at her side. However, before anyone could say another word, they heard footsteps outside. The front door burst open, and the bells rang as they saw that 999 rush inside.

"I have to go," she said quickly. "You should turn on the TV."

Following her instructions, Grandma Tillia swiftly looked at the monitor sitting above the counter and blinked. The Bluetooth remote in her ear activated the television. They saw an urgent news bulletin appear on the screen.

"... A strange disturbance occurred moments ago over the plains of Africa. Witnesses claim that they saw an asteroid of some kind flying across the sky heading towards the ground. Many in the area reported multiple loud disturbances. The area has already been sealed off and no one is commenting. A leak from NASA has revealed that this strange set of events may be linked to experiments aboard the Apogee Station..."

"Not good," 999 muttered.

Deliza's phone suddenly began to ring. She quickly pulled it out of her pocket, held it in her palm, and answered it. As the call went through, a holographic screen appeared in front of her.

"Hello?" she asked, keeping a side-eye on Brena and Grandma Tillia. They had their eyes fixated on the TV, but she saw 999 sneaking a glance back at her. "Deliza here."

"Are you secure?" the voice on the phone demanded.

Deliza quickly switched her settings. The display turned off and disappeared. She brought her phone up to her ear. Now that the call was encrypted, she could speak freely over the line.

"Yes sir," she answered immediately. "Go ahead."

"Lieutenant, urgent recall," the person on the phone stated. Deliza could hear his voice waver for a moment, but listened carefully. "All passes for military leave are canceled, effective immediately. Report to base. Speak to no one."

"Understood," Deliza replied. "May I ask what's going on?"

"Speak to no one. Report to base. End transmission soldier. Move out."

The call was cut off after the man repeated the order. Although he had sounded serious and very straight-forward, the fact that she had heard his emotions slip just from the tone of his voice told her two pieces of information: something had spooked him and whatever it was that had canceled their leave was big. Really big.

"Damn," Deliza lowered the phone from her ear. "I thought I could get 'em that time. The people working the phones sometimes let some extra details slip."

"I am being recalled, too. Dr. Kendrick initiated an emergency recall."

Deliza turned to look at 999, who had a very serious expression in her eyes.

"Well, if you're being called in, now we know for sure. This is big," Deliza muttered. She analyzed 999's behavior and guessed that she was doing the same to her. "Military mobilization and the amborgs, too?"

"Perhaps this will bring us together again," 999 mumbled.

They both glanced at Brena and Grandma Tillia, who were completely immersed in the news bulletin and clearly hadn't heard their conversation. Deliza hurriedly made her way over to them but tried to avoid appearing hasty. 999 followed.

"I'm so sorry," she apologized as she pocketed her phone and pulled her hat out. "But I gotta go. Something just came up."

Grandma Tillia nodded at Deliza before turning her attention back to the TV. Brena quietly gave an encouraging smile, then went to go control her kids. Deliza gave 999 a quick salute.

"See you out there, maybe," she said as she prepared to put her hat on.

"Good luck," 999 answered courteously.

"Brena," Grandma Tillia spoke softly as Deliza exited the bakery. The door closed behind her as Tillia gently tapped Brena's shoulder. "Would you mind giving Alice and I a moment alone?"

"Oh, of course," Brena nodded.

Brena, while holding her baby, was trying to watch the TV while attempting to round up her kids, who had started chasing each other around the tables. Grandma Tillia took the opportunity to walk 999 to the front door.

"They're calling you?"

"Yes Grandma," 999 answered with a firm nod.

"Stay safe my child," Grandma Tillia lifted her hand and stroked 999's cheek. "Protect and watch over him at all costs."

"I will always do so," 999 said with a determined look in her eyes.

"I know I have already asked you thousands of times," Grandma Tillia smiled gently. "But if you two make it through this, will you bring him back to see me?"

"He'll come home soon," 999 nodded. "I promise, when it's right, it will happen."

"I'll be here, waiting as always, for you and your best friend, 917."

Grandma Tillia watched with a smile as 999 left the bakery. Letting out a deep sigh, she turned and walked towards Brena. Together, they listened to the news report and waited in anticipation to find out what would unfold.

Kendrick, Grandma Tillia gripped her cane tightly and quietly prayed, *Please keep your word and keep them safe. All of them. These kids are our future.*

▪ ▪

Port Hope
San Pedro, California
Emergency Recall minus 18 minutes
9:10 AM Pacific Time

The potent salty scent of the ocean permeated the air, carried by a steady breeze that wafted and meandered along the California coastline. Right as 35 prepared to enter an abandoned nuclear power plant, right before Angel 999 had to say goodbye to her grandmother, and right before 297 would witness one of the Earth's most notable historical events in the making, one other amborg operation was in progress.

Port Hope was in San Pedro, which was the area in between Long Beach and the Port of Los Angeles. Over 90% of all commercial shipping came through here in order to enter or exit the United States. If sending by air proved too costly, then importing from the ground or the sea was the next best option. Unfortunately, the remaining 10% usually came with dark deeds.

This was exactly what a certain group of vigilantes were planning to stop. Staged on a four-story building with a clear view of the docks, a few hooded individuals sat still, keeping a lookout. Some of them were unpacking sniper rifles, setting up their operation. One man with a grey beard inserted a Bluetooth device into his ear and held up a small radar dish. He pulled the trigger and it switched on. His listening device, capable of detecting audio from up to a mile away, helped him eavesdrop on his enemies so he could glean any useful information from their conversations.

"Alright, the boss wants the next shipment out within 30 minutes!"

"Did you hear that? Looks like we still got a window."

The old man observed all the activity going on at the harbor. He lifted a hand and waved it down twice. Some footsteps shuffled behind him, and the group was joined by about four more hooded individuals.

"We have plenty of time," he grinned as he used his eye implants to mark targets for his snipers. "Besides, my grandson was kind enough to send us one of his siblings as backup. It'll help us finish this."

A robotic voice spoke through the channel.

"A relative of David 117's is a friend to the amborgs."

Mark felt his spirits rise. He wanted to share his excitement but unfortunately, their mission involved them being quiet and stealthy for as long as possible. If the bad guys knew that they were here, then it would turn into a firefight. Still, it felt like a morale boost every time he heard another of the amborgs praise their alliance. 117 had certainly bridged a trustworthy relationship between their two groups.

Before, if they didn't have the support of one amborg, then Mark would have had to plan for some extra contingencies. Prior to introducing himself to his grandson, David 117, all those years ago, some days, it felt like an uphill battle for his band of vigilantes. Now, things felt so much easier whenever they were the ones backing up an amborg. As his crew had started to say, "One amborg guaranteed success. Two was overkill."

Amborg 777 was in the field reporting back to him as they prepared for a raid on the docks. These criminals had set up camp on the wrong port. They weren't going to get away with this mystery shipment.

"Alright everyone," Mark spoke into the channel. "Looks like they mean to make a run for it. If they hit international waters, we won't be able to catch them. Let's make sure we stop them here."

"Excuse me, Mark?"

"Copy 777," Mark answered. "Go ahead."

"Attempting to infiltrate the main gate," 777 replied. "There are four guards in total. Two above, and two at the gate. I can eliminate one if you get the other three."

"Stand by," Mark responded as he zoomed in with his enhanced vision.

There was a tower next to the gate and he could see two armed guards standing at the top looking down upon the area. There were two more placed at both sides of the gate, which they needed to get through.

"I am proceeding to the guard on the south side."

From their position, Mark's gaze tracked 777's figure, who was strolling up to the guard on his right.

"I see them," he said. "Snipers, pick off the two guards in the tower and the one on the left. Standby for 777's command."

In his personal HUD, he saw the green dot on 777's back indicating he was a friendly. The four guards in his field of vision were marked with red circles. He watched the mark for the guard on the left side suddenly display an orange dot in the center of its red circle. The two tower guards also were marked by the additional orange dots. Three of his snipers were locked on and had the targets in their sights. The guard on the right, as 777 sauntered right up to them, had a green dot appear in the center of the red, which meant that 777 was signaling that he would take this one out.

"We have targets acquired," Mark reported over the radio. "We have a northern wind, three miles an hour, but it shouldn't affect us. Ready for your signal."

After a brief pause, Mark watched 777 continue to interact with the guard. He saw the guard slowly lift his rifle when he heard the command.

"Now!" 777's voice rang out over the radio.

Not taking his eyes off the gate, Mark answered.

"Fire!"

At the signal, three silenced shots simultaneously went off as the snipers opened fire. At the same time, 777 rushed the guard in front of him and discreetly knocked them unconscious. Mark watched the other three guards get hit by his vigilantes. Three precise headshots hit their targets, and puffs of red mist burst out, killing them instantly before they even hit the ground. As the front gate was cleared, they watched 777 move the guard he had taken out aside and placed him on the pavement.

"Setting a charge on the gate," 777 reported to them. Mark saw him look in their direction and gave them a hand signal. "I am proceeding inside. Set up for the raid."

Mark nodded and looked to his people.

"Understood," he said as he started waving at everyone hiding on the other rooftops. "Snipers, you're on overwatch. Cover us as we move in. Everyone else, move to breech. Make it snappy."

A moment later, Mark stepped onto the ledge and attached a grappling hook to the building. He quickly leaped forward and lowered himself down to the first floor, followed by several others. When everyone was safely on the ground, they unhooked their lines and proceeded to 777's previous location at the gate. Mark's group moved swiftly through an alleyway. Just before they crossed to the front gate, he received an alert.

"Whoa! Hang on! Movement! Sir, I got a truck heading towards the gate!"

Mark stopped and held up a closed fist. Following his lead, everyone behind him took up a holding position and crouched down, ready for any potential threat ahead. The team stood in line cautiously, listening intently to the sentry's report.

I got an inbound," the sentry explained. "One freight truck. Looks like a late arrival."

"How long do we have?" Mark asked.

This was not on the itinerary. This truck had to be a stray that might've been delayed or something. The gang seemed anxious to leave as soon as possible before the authorities could arrive. Actually, this could possibly buy them a few more minutes.

"74 seconds until it reaches the gate. Should we take them out?"

"No," Mark answered thoughtfully. "I've got a plan. 777, if you can hear me, we're going to follow you in on this shipment. Do not blow the gates yet."

"Copy that," 777 answered. "Please proceed carefully."

"I'm an old man with aging cybernetic implants," Mark let out a sigh. "I'm always careful."

He quickly glanced back and gestured for everyone to follow him. At his signal, they sprinted across the street, carefully checking their surroundings. Once at the gate, Mark had them huddle together to assess the situation.

"Alright, let's not hang around too long," he said. He pointed at the man behind him. "Wade, conceal this explosive charge on the gate and then cover us."

Mark pointed to the next two vigilantes as Wade nodded and ran to the gate.

"Alejandra and Krazinsky, get up on the tower and clean up. Hold position."

He pointed at the next person in the group while Alejandra and Krazinsky readied another pair of grappling hooks.

"Chuck," he instructed quickly as they heard the pistons of the grappling hooks fire. "You and I will stand-in as the guards in front of the gates. We will distract that truck and take it over quietly. The rest of you, hide. I want Cortez, Cooper, Fisher, and Bob on the truck once we make the move. Everyone I left out stays outside the gate until we blow it open."

Alejandra and Krazinsky both ascended the tower. It was like watching Batman and Batgirl in white color schemes fly up and out of sight.

Everyone else deployed and began to tidy up the area. They had less than a minute to get ready. Mark and Chuck were removing their hoods and quickly taking off their jackets. They had to switch their outfits with the actual guards fast. Meanwhile, Wade set up a small portable holo-projector to camouflage the explosive charge on the gate, rendering it invisible unless someone approached closely enough to notice the faint distortion. Up above, Mark trusted that Alejandra and Krazinsky were also executing a quick wardrobe change while ensuring the tower appeared inconspicuous.

"Sir, I have a question before the truck gets here."

Mark slipped on the guard's jacket as he listened to the radio.

"Is this important Bob?" Mark replied as he and Chuck straightened each other's outfits.

"Kinda?" Bob answered quickly. "How come with everyone else, you use their last names? You only use my first name when it's with me."

"No offense Bob," Mark replied with an annoyed sigh. Chuck was grinning and holding back a laugh. "But this can wait. So, get ready."

"Yes sir."

He heard one of the other vigilantes chuckle over the radio channel.

"You're still hung up about that? Come on Bob..."

Ignoring whatever conversations they were having, Mark and Chuck exchanged a firm nod and made sure they looked both presentable and intimidating. Mark picked up the enemy's rifle from the ground as they prepared for their next move. As they set the stage, Mark listened as his sentry spoke once more over the radio.

"The truck is 10 seconds out."

They all heard the engine of an old industrial truck approaching, the sound of its chugging growing louder as it drew nearer. Though it was definitely outdated, it was perfect for criminal activity. As it got closer, they saw it slow down, the brakes squeaking as it prepared to turn into the front gate entrance.

"Alright," Mark muttered into the channel. "Act natural and let me do the talking. Get ready for the trap."

The truck stopped in front of the gate, and Mark raised his hand to wave it down. He went to the driver's side, which was Chuck's current position. He stood behind Mark as he greeted the driver, who rolled down his window.

"You're right on time," Mark said in a gruff and serious voice. "Any later and we would have left you behind."

"Tell me about it," the driver snarled, turning to look down at Mark. "The boss is such an ass. Gave us a shitty truck and they expect us to get here on time? If they're so rich, why don't they try doing the work themselves?"

"That's a mood," Mark scoffed.

"Hey, you're not the usual guy," the driver stared inquisitively, a note of suspicion in his voice. "I don't know you at all. You new?"

"Obviously," Mark shrugged. "Doesn't matter how old I get... I still got to make a living."

"Hmm... You sure don't look like one of us. Oh well, I ain't judging. Where's Bob? He didn't show up or something?"

Mark paused for a moment, then understanding crept over him. He nodded and let the driver see him smile.

"Ah. Bob, great guy. Yeah, where is he? That's a good question. Well, it's a very funny story!" Mark's eyes widened, nearly letting out a laugh. What a coincidence. Apparently, there was another Bob. "He's hijacking you right about now."

"What?"

The door on the passenger side was flung open, and the other thug riding along was dragged out. Vigilante Bob swiftly knocked him out, while Mark leaped up to the door and socked the driver in the face, knocking him out cold. The old man climbed back down, opening the door with a triumphant smile.

"What a coincidence..." Chuck said as he dragged the driver out of the truck, while Fisher climbed into the driver's seat with Cooper on the other side.

"Yeah," Mark answered as he shook his head.

"Sir?" Wade said to Mark over the channel. "I'm going through the other guards' stuff. The gate guard's name is actually Bob."

"Aww, we knocked out Bob," Alejandra joked from up above.

"He seemed like a good guy," Krazinsky added.

"Shut up guys," Bob from the vigilante group grumbled.

"For the record Bob," Mark said over the channel as they got ready to open the gates. "Bob is easier and more fun to say. You try going into battle saying Papilopidilo repeatedly and ten times fast in a sentence."

"Hey," Bob sounded happy as he prepared to hide on the truck, "you said it right that time."

"You're welcome," Mark replied, respectfully dipping his head towards Bob.

"But still, why not shorten my last name or give me a nickname?" Bob asked curiously.

"Bob is better," Mark answered. "Now shut up and let's get the gate open and get in there."

"This is 777 to grandpa, I need you in here now."

777's words caused Mark's smile to fade, and he whirled around to look towards the gate. Just what he needed, David 117's siblings also called him grandpa. He would have to make a rule about this before another amborg got too comfortable with the nickname.

"Ok, my call sign is not 'grandpa,'" Mark stated firmly over the radio. He took a moment to regain his composure. He cleared his throat and spoke normally. "We're just now coming in with a truck of whatever these guys are smuggling. Hang in there."

Mark and Chuck opened the gate, allowing Fisher to drive the truck straight through. As he and Cooper drove the truck inside, Mark saw Bob and Cortez hanging from the undercarriage, out of view. He gestured up at the tower to Alejandra and Krazinsky, signaling them to act normal and cover them. Once it was time, Wade and the rest of the vigilantes would wait for their signal to blow the gate and come in after them with reinforcements.

Mark and Chuck followed the truck into the docks before the gate shut. Once the truck began to move towards their destination, they quickly ran to the side and ducked into the shadows.

"Alright 777," Mark said as they hurried past a warehouse, staying low. "I have four of my teammates in a truck belonging to this gang heading your way. Chuck and I will back you up at your signal. We're ready to breach the gate."

"Excellent thinking," 777 replied. "We should consider making a move in a minute. I know what the cargo is, and we have to stop them."

"Well, if it's that important, then we're standing by for the signal," Mark answered as he did a quick check of his equipment while Chuck kept a lookout.

Suddenly, 777's voice spoke over the channel.

"Oh no."

Alarmed, Mark and Chuck both glanced at each other. That didn't sound good.

"Uh... what's going on?"

"I am transmitting an emergency message to your vigilantes in the truck," 777 quickly replied. "The gang members are directing the truck to park somewhere I really don't want them to be..."

Mark took a deep breath as fear began to creep in. He hoped that 777 was not about to say what he thought he was going to say. Still, he had to ask for confirmation.

"And where is that?" he asked in a worried tone.

"Right next to where my explosives are hidden," 777's voice responded with dread.

"Are the explosions necessary?" Mark asked.

"The other trucks over there are empty and off-loaded, but I wanted to set off that explosion as a distraction to draw everyone away while I apprehend the leader," 777 explained. "Your people are in the blast radius. I am transmitting instructions. Please confirm with them that they need to back off immediately!"

"Fisher!" Mark said into the radio. "Did you copy that?"

"Yeah boss," Fisher replied. "Gun it in reverse so we don't die. Easy."

"Uh... might want to speed things up or help us out. Like right about now..."

It was Cooper's voice that joined Fisher's. Mark could hear the nervousness in his tone.

"Shit," Fisher said softly. "Sir, they're coming up to the truck. We're about to get made..."

If Mark had to guess, some gang members were probably wondering why Fisher and Cooper hadn't exited from the truck. It also probably looked even more suspicious that they hadn't shut off the engine. Sitting here idling for too long definitely made them stick out like sore thumbs. Had the plan to hijack the truck compromised the plan?

There was no time to think about the consequences. Mark heard 777's voice over the radio.

"Detonating the charges," he warned them immediately. "Three seconds!"

Mark clenched his fist. They had seconds.

"Fisher! GUN IT! Wade! Open the gate!"

Right after his warning, Mark heard two explosions. One went off around the corner where Fisher had driven the truck. Several shouts and screams suddenly filled the air, signaling the start of the battle. From behind, they heard another loud boom and the crashing sound of the gate as it was forcibly blown inwards. No turning back now. Mark could only hope that Fisher managed to get his team out of danger.

"Charge!" he commanded into the radio. "Don't let them escape! Decoy truck! If you can hear me, get to safety! All teams! Converge on 777's position and take the docks!"

Mark's vigilantes went in guns blazing as he plowed ahead with Chuck at his side. He didn't allow age to physically slow him down. In fact, every mission always made him feel young again, thanks to his implants.

"Keep it tight!" he ordered as he and Chuck took down three gang members in a coordinated attack.

"This is 777," they heard over the radio. "Approaching the main lounge. I have subdued the captain of the ship."

"Copy that," Mark answered as he punched an enemy drone, sending it crashing to the ground. The face plate shattered as he ripped its neck apart. "Chuck!"

Chuck turned to listen to his next set of orders.

"I'll cover you," he instructed as he pointed in the direction of where Fisher had driven the truck. "Go check on the others! They're not responding and we need to see if they got out of that blast radius."

"I'm on it!" Chuck replied, running ahead.

"The rest of you," Mark held his hand up to his earpiece. "Secure the docks! Make it quick and don't let anyone escape!"

Mark caught up with Chuck. As they ran out into the open, they were immediately detected, and a barrage of bullets began raining down in their direction. Reacting quickly, Mark and Chuck split up. Chuck deftly navigated between various cover points, while Mark remained exposed to divert enemy fire. His implants proved invaluable in tracking incoming fire, enabling him to dodge and successfully evade the enemy's attacks. The two of them eventually reached a corner and entered the space where the gang members were positioning the shipping containers from the trucks. As soon as they arrived, they were able to assess the situation and see what had unfolded.

The explosion had destroyed three parked trucks, and a fire was now spreading. Amidst the chaos, a few emergency drones were diligently working to contain and extinguish the flames, seemingly oblivious to the ongoing battle. Mark noticed a trail of bad guys laying prone and scattered around, which was likely 777's handiwork. Some gang members were still disoriented and confused as they tried to get back on their feet. Chuck and Mark redirected their attention to their hijacked truck, which was located several feet from the blast site, but there were no signs of activity coming from it.

"They got hit!"

Chuck was right. Mark took a quick glance and noticed that the windows of the truck were shattered. Both occupants inside were unconscious.

"Bob? Cortez? Where are you two?!"

As Chuck attempted to extract Fisher and Cooper from the truck, Mark looked around for the others. He didn't see their bodies, which was a good sign.

"I need help here," Mark said over the channel. "Do we have eyes on the decoy team? Locate Bob and Cooper!"

"Sir," he heard a voice respond, "I got their tracker. Both are active, but unresponsive. Looks like they're moving northeast, behind that building."

Mark replied with a quick thank you and turned to face that direction. With his HUD, he noticed a marker highlighted by one of the snipers leading to another section of the docks. In his line of sight, an administrative office obstructed the path to the marker, which was on the other side.

"Chuck," he said as he took off towards the door. "Secure the area! I'll be back!"

Mark ran up to the door of the building and scanned it. No traps detected. He kicked the door open and proceeded inside. The vigilante that had reported Bob and Cooper's movements had sent him the tracking data. On the map display of his wrist bracer, he kept track of the distance between him and his two friends. He just needed to find a door at the opposite end of this office and exit to the other side.

He arrived at the center of a cross-section and found himself facing three hallways: one on his left, right, and straight ahead. He stopped and listened quietly. From his right, he heard what sounded like four sets of footsteps rushing towards him. Thinking fast, he pulled a flash bang from his belt, pulled the pin, and positioned himself behind a corner. With just the right timing, he hurled it around the corner.

"What the?!" he heard someone exclaim as the grenade plunked onto the floor.

With a bright flash of light, a deafening bang reverberated through the space. Mark put on a pair of goggles to shield his eyes from the light while his headset blocked out the noise. Among the chaos, he could hear cries of pain erupting from his enemies affected by the grenade. Mark dashed around the corner and attacked.

There were four of them, just as he had anticipated. Mark swiftly incapacitated the first gang member, wrapping his arm around their head and deftly flipped them to the ground, rendering them motionless upon impact. Without pause, Mark pivoted to the next target, executing a similar takedown maneuver before delivering a decisive punch to the stomach for added measure. Rising to face the remaining two, Mark saw that they had one hand on their weapons and another covering their ears from the flash bang. If he didn't do this carefully, they could impulsively pull their triggers and fire blindly. Stepping between them, he disarmed the pair, quickly incapacitating one with a punch and following up with a powerful backspin kick that brought down the final enemy.

With the immediate threat neutralized, the only thing Mark could hear was a bunch of pained groans as he scanned for any additional enemies. Satisfied that the area was secure, he took the opportunity to kneel down and restrain the four gang members by binding their arms and legs to prevent any potential escape attempts. With the captives immobilized, Mark continued down the hall and proceeded towards the exit. There was no time to linger.

When he reached the door, he looked out the window and scanned the surroundings. He hadn't detected any traps at this entrance, but he decided to play it safe and check anyway in case of a possible ambush. Once he confirmed it was safe, he cautiously opened the door and stepped out onto the top steps, turning to look in the direction of the beacons, and spotted them immediately.

Bob and Cooper were being forcibly dragged across the ground by a few gang members. They were probably going to take them somewhere to torture them, or worse. Considering that they were obviously pissed that they'd been raided, they were likely not going to show any mercy. Mark had to act fast, or his friends were going to get seriously more hurt than they already were.

Thinking fast, he readied a small explosive charge, stuck it to the railing of the steps, and bolted to a nearby shipping container. Hidden from view, he climbed up and sought out the high ground. He watched the enemy drag his two vigilantes away as he snuck from one container to the next, preparing to ambush them. Mark pulled out a flash bang grenade and prepped to detonate the explosive he'd set up on the railing. He scanned the area where he was going to drop in to initiate the rescue.

"Alright," Mark took a deep breath. He was ready. "Time to get my friends back."

He used his wrist communicator to activate the explosive. When the light turned green, he pressed it and heard a tiny beep. A split second later, an earsplitting boom echoed through the chaos, smoke and fire bursting up from his previous position. The sound added to the cacophony of gunfire and the battle raging across the docks, but it worked perfectly. The group dragging Bob and Cooper stopped and turned sharply. Now that their attention had been redirected, Mark tossed the flash bang at them. Just before he saw it make contact with the ground, he leaped from his position and aimed his landing right for the center.

The group focused on the explosion and formed a defensive perimeter, keeping their eyes on their surroundings in every direction, except one – directly above. That was the opening Mark was going for.

I am getting way too old for this, Mark thought as he did a somersault in midair and prepared to hit the ground.

With the help of his external leg implants, he hit the ground, executing a perfect superhero landing from a height of about twenty feet. It was a little rough on his knees, but fortunately, he was able to absorb the impact of the drop. The force of his landing shook the ground, briefly knocking anyone nearby off balance.

Without hesitation, Mark drew a knife and sliced the weak spot of a drone directly behind him. He jumped up and brought the knife down on the back of its neck, disabling its power supply, and kicked it to the ground. He shifted his gaze to the left and saw another drone preparing to shoot him. Mark hurled his knife at the drone's faceplate, knocking its head back, and watched it crash to the ground.

Without wasting another second, Mark pivoted and slid left, sweeping a human gang member off their feet. As they hit their head on the ground, Mark grabbed their gun, took aim, and fired at four gang members out of his reach. Two of them, a drone and a human, were still dragging his colleagues, but Mark killed them with two well-aimed headshots. He continued to fire, emptying the rest of the magazine and hitting the next two gang members with every last bullet. The last drone barely had time to turn around and fired its rifle at him, but Mark rolled forward to dodge the incoming rounds. Thankfully, the drone's weapon jammed, rendering it unable to pull the trigger. Mark straightened up and quickly raised his arm, empty gun in hand, and threw it as hard as he could. It struck the drone in the face, causing it to stumble back. Mark crouched down and sprinted to the drone at full speed. As he closed the distance, he spun on his heel and delivered a huge kick to the drone's chest. He heard a loud snap as his foot connected with its chest plate, shattering it. He landed on his feet and watched as his enemy went flying into a nearby shipping container, creating a loud clang as it left a massive imprint in the metal. Sparks flew as the drone crashed to the ground. It didn't get back up. With the area now clear, Mark hurried to check on Bob and Cooper.

"Alright," Mark transmitted to his group. "I saved Bob and Cooper, they're ok but they need to be extracted. I'm heading back to help with the clean-up."

"Uh boss? I think you might need to see this."

Mark paused for a moment, then responded.

"Copy that, what did you find?"

"Amborg 777 is pretty pissed," Chuck reported.

A few of his vigilantes arrived and checked on Bob and Cooper. After confirming they were safe, Mark headed towards the cargo vessel that the criminals had intended to use for their escape.

"I'm on my way."

Once he returned to the assembly area, he saw his vigilantes rounding up the gang members and tying them up. The fire from their explosives had been put out, and it appeared that the area was now under control. He didn't see any sign of 777, which was odd.

"Alright," Mark said, and shrugged. "What's the problem? I don't see a pissed amborg anywhere. Are you sure?"

"We're pretty sure." Chuck confirmed unsteadily.

Mark's eyes followed the direction he was pointing. He turned, glanced up, and suddenly lurched slightly. From the side of the ship, he noticed a few bodies hanging by chains.

"Oh, that's a new one," his eyes widened.

"We think that's the ringleader, next to him is the captain and the first mate of this ship. We saw 777 throw them over the side. All chained up and everything."

Upon closer inspection, Mark could see why his vigilantes were anxious. The three men hanging from the side of the ship were visibly battered, with chains tightly wound around their chests and wrists. They'd been left alive, but it was still a disturbing sight. An amborg had done this?

"Ok," Mark gulped while they all stared. "Police the area and hold until the authorities get here. I need two teams to follow me. We're boarding the ship. 777, come in. Can you hear me?"

"Affirmative," 777 replied softly, but his tone sounded cold. "You need to see this."

"We're on our way," Mark answered calmly.

He turned to see some of the vigilantes gathering behind him. Many of them looked concerned.

"Alright, search the ship and stay in contact with each other once you're below deck," he instructed. "Just be careful and don't piss off 777 when you see him. I'll handle this."

"You mean handle this as in, talk to him?" Chuck took out his earpiece and covered his microphone. He carefully made sure he wasn't broadcasting on a live channel. "Or handle him as in... take him down?"

Mark glanced at Chuck. He didn't have a response. All he did was make sure that Chuck could see his expression. Mark shook his head, feeling uncertain. He took a few steps towards the ship, maintaining his composure.

"Watch the perimeter," he stated firmly.

"You know I have your back, right? What do we do if the worst happens?"

Mark stopped and turned to look back at his colleague. Chuck's eyes were unwavering, but Mark could hear how concerned he was. Chuck's earpiece remained detached, and his microphone was still covered, ensuring their conversation remained private. 777 hadn't heard them, and they wanted to keep it that way. Mark curled his fingers and decided to respond. He had to keep them focused on the current matter at hand.

"I'm still quite capable," Mark declared, covering his microphone. "The worst has yet to come. Secure the area while I secure the ship."

Mark didn't wait for confirmation from his friend. He turned away and climbed up the stairs to get aboard. When he made it to the top deck, he looked down and saw Chuck directing everyone on the docks. He was pleased that his crew was continuing to focus on their tasks, allowing him to trust in their capabilities and giving him less to worry about. A few of his vigilantes had already gathered on the deck, readying themselves to board and search the ship.

"What are you all doing?" Mark lifted both of his arms questioningly. "Go inside already!"

"We're afraid to go in there," one of them answered.

Mark leaned over to get a look at the vigilante who'd replied. It was a woman wearing a hooded sweater.

"You're new right?" he asked. "Your name's... Brandy?"

"Breann," the vigilante corrected, lifting her head and revealing a pair of green eyes.

"Sorry, Breann. You claustrophobic, Breann?" Mark asked.

"Sorry?" Breann asked.

"Are you claustrophobic, yes or no?" Mark impatiently repeated the question.

"No sir," Breann answered.

"Well good," Mark said as he walked up to the hatch and peered inside. "Because if any of you are afraid to follow me or give me some back up, you're in charge of cleaning our barracks for a month. Now let's get a move on and finish the job."

Mark took another look at the hatch and noticed that the door had been ripped off entirely and cast aside on the floor nearby. The ship doors alone were made of pure steel. Only an amborg or someone else equally strong was capable of pulling off a feat like this. He could understand 777 pulling it out and setting it down gently during the battle, but it had been thrown violently away, as if in a fit of rage. Something had pissed him off. An angry amborg was deadly to have on-site. Mark couldn't let his vigilantes see how unnerving this was to him.

Without another word, Mark stepped through the hatch and began to make his way through the corridors. Behind him, he heard the sound of his vigilantes stepping over the threshold.

"777," he reported. "We are making our way inside. We're following your beacon."

"I hear you," 777 replied on the channel. He sounded solemn. "Please come to the main cargo bay. I apologize for what you're about to see."

Mark pulled up the map and scanned the interior schematics of the ship. He located the main cargo bay and saw 777's beacon sitting in the same spot. Once he confirmed his destination, he mapped the fastest way there.

He turned back and waved for his team to follow. After taking a few steps, Mark made a turn and found the stairs that headed below. The lights were flickering, but he was able to make out the next level. Slowly, Mark descended and looked down the hall. His eyes widened as he stopped.

"Everything ok sir? Oh shit..."

Mark looked down the hall and heard Breann gasp from behind him. She descended the stairs and positioned herself right behind his shoulder, peering ahead to get a clear view of the scene before them.

The hall was littered with bodies. Men, women, and children. A few criminals, their destroyed weapons and bullet casings strewn about, had also been taken down in this hallway of death. Mark proceeded cautiously, initiating a scan as he went.

"I need some more help on the ship," he radioed to everyone outside. "We got bodies in here. Someone contact LAPD and get them here. Now."

"D-did... the amborg do this?" someone behind Mark stammered.

"No," Mark said as he walked over a nearby body and inspected it. "I'm pretty sure that Luis 777 of A.I. Industries and brother to my grandson... did not murder civilians, strip them of their valuables, and found the time to lay them on the ground along these walls. But these gang members, I'm pretty sure he took care of them."

Mark and the vigilantes continued down the hall. The criminals looked like they'd been physically beaten to death. His eyes swept over the deceased civilians laying on the ground, taking note of how each of them had died: some had gunshot wounds, others showed signs of physical trauma with bruises and welts covering their bodies. Many of the bodies were still radiating minor traces of heat, indicating that the attack happened recently.

"Check for survivors," Mark stated. "If any of these criminals are alive, you take them prisoner. Any civilians that you find, save them. These assholes have a lot to answer for."

"Sir?" Breann asked in a trembling voice. "What were they trying to do here?"

"Let's find out," Mark replied.

The trail of bodies that lined the hallway was incredibly traumatizing. Fortunately, having seen his fair share of death throughout his life, he was able to handle it well. The younger vigilantes, however, were probably shocked beyond reason. Since Breann was a new addition to his crew, "one hell of a first day" would be a serious understatement. These poor kids did not deserve to witness such a massacre.

Once they reached the main cargo bay, Mark was taken aback by yet another crazy sight. At first glance, its height could have easily topped the hallway they'd just walked through. Situated a few feet away from the hatch was what appeared to be an enormous cage.

"Is this a cargo ship? Or a deportation facility?" Mark felt his anger boiling up in his throat.

"It's worse."

The door to the cage had been torn off, and the vigilantes discovered 777 kneeling within the enclosure. He was surrounded by children. There were probably several dozen, all alive, chained and tied up together. 777 was gently trying to free each child. Mark looked in a corner outside the cage and noticed some of them huddling together. Each child that was freed from their bonds immediately left the cage to join the others.

"Advise the LAPD we stumbled across... a trafficking operation," Mark transmitted. "We need some people in here to police a ton of civilian bodies and get some kids out of here. We need triage set up on the docks. All hostiles have been taken down. We are all clear."

Mark turned to his team.

"Everyone check all the hallways, see if there are any more bodies," he instructed. "Search the ship. Let's find a quick way out of here so these kids don't have to see all of... that."

The vigilantes dispersed, but Mark grabbed Breann by the shoulder.

"If you or anyone else wants to step off," he let out a gentle sigh. "I'll understand."

"We'll be ok sir," Breann lifted her hands up to her hood and clenched the sides tightly. "I signed up for this."

"No," Mark sympathetically patted her on the back. "Not for this. Do me a favor and call Dr. Lira Rodriguez. Tell her we need all the help we can get. We stumbled into something way bigger than we expected."

"My second mission," Breann muttered, "And I need therapy... A lot of therapy."

"You did go from protecting a family of refugees to... this."

Mark gestured around the room. When he realized that his joke didn't make her laugh, he put his arms down and switched back to work-mode.

"Sorry, my grandson doesn't get my humor at times too," he admitted with a sigh.

"No, it was a little funny," Breann nodded.

"Call the doctor when you get a second," Mark said, dipping his head. "Let's get this done."

"Yes sir."

On Breann's first day, she had gotten exposed to something absolutely unthinkable. Dr. Rodriguez, who was their main counselor, was probably going to be working overtime. The incident they witnessed today was definitely going to be a topic of discussion for everyone later. None of them were going to be sleeping well for a while after this.

"So let me get this straight," Mark turned and walked towards 777. "We caught a gang trying to hightail it out of the country and stumbled onto a make-shift prison ship?"

"Yes," 777 cut another set of chains off a little girl with frizzled hair and gloomy eyes.

Mark knelt down and activated a gadget on his wrist bracer. A bolt cutter popped out and he kindly gestured to the first kid he saw. The little boy ran up to him, his blue eyes lighting up as he realized that the old man in the hood was friendly and preparing to free him.

"I was expecting weapons, drugs, or their money, but who are these kids?" he asked as he broke the chains off the boy with bright blue eyes. "Alright, go wait outside the cage with your friends, ok?"

"Thank you," the boy uttered. Following his instructions, he walked out of the cage and waited with the other freed children.

"Orphans?" Mark asked as he moved onto another child. "This is a large-scale trafficking ring. I'm guessing an underground slave organization."

"Tragically, the answer is yes," 777 replied. "But we need to identify these kids... and the bodies all over the ship. I think many of them lost... Correction. I think they were all separated from their parents. Recently."

"All of the..."

Mark stopped himself. He focused his attention on the little girl in front of him, smiled warmly, and cut her chains. He'd almost said "bodies" in front of the group. He didn't want to cause any alarm or reveal that there were a ton of dead bodies disturbingly close, less than 15 feet away.

Mark shared his findings from his scan of the hallway they'd recently passed through, "... the uh... people we passed by here are still warm, it was all... executed recently. Rigor mortis hasn't even begun to set on many of them."

"I concur," 777 answered calmly. "My scans show that they were... taken care of... by the gang members within the last two hours."

"If we had acted sooner," Mark put on a brave face as he freed two more kids. "We could have stopped this."

"I also regret to say that I agree," 777 replied.

"Once my team clears the halls and polices the bodies," Mark cast a quick look at 777, checking on him, "we'll get these kids the help they need. Then we figure out who did this."

"Thank you."

There were very few organizations that had the resources to head something like this. The leader that 777 captured and flung over the side had managed to stay under the radar from the authorities. An impressive feat, but also terrifying. The questions raced in his mind as he worked with 777 to cut more and more chains. Who were all these kids and why were all these bodies disrespectfully laid out along the halls of this ship? If Mark's growing theories were correct, there was something sinister going on that would soon attract a lot of attention, ultimately demanding answers.

Despite how gruesome this scene looked, Mark did remember a key detail about the unconscious gang members that they had walked past to get to the cargo bay. Personally, he felt relieved knowing that 777 hadn't gone too aggressively overboard.

"You know, you showed a lot of restraint," he said as they freed another four kids that were clinging onto some worn-out stuffed plush toys. "You didn't kill any of the gang members in here. It looked pretty bad but... they're all ok."

"I wanted to hurt them," 777 spoke softly. "They've hurt everyone here."

"I'm pretty sure you made that clear with that..." Mark paused as he looked up thoughtfully. "...display that we witnessed outside. I don't entirely support that decision but, well done."

"I appreciate it," 777 replied.

"But," Mark cleared his throat as another chain was cut, "if it was the right thing to do, you'd be feeling better. Do you, uh, feel better?"

"I will once we get all these kids out of here."

It wasn't a direct answer to his question, but Mark knew that 777 was still dealing with a lot of issues. He wanted to make sure that the amborg next to him was still able to focus on the task at hand. If things got too emotional, then they would lose control and that would affect their judgment. Over the last ten years, Mark had seen the amborgs show incredible resilience in stressful situations, but that was the problem. They didn't talk about it and at times would bottle it up inside. Sometimes for too long.

The sound of footsteps caught Mark's attention. Breann had returned with some reinforcements.

"Luis," Mark watched some of his crew disperse to console the kids. "What do you say we get some air? Let's go top side and talk."

"But there are still kids here."

"I know," Mark replied as he stood up and allowed another person to take over freeing the kids. "But you don't have to do this by yourself. Come on. I'll get you a drink."

Mark turned and led 777 out of the cage. The rest of his vigilantes switched with them and got to work.

Eventually, the two of them found themselves overlooking the cleanup operation. Mark had contacted a friend with the LAPD and she had promised to personally oversee the police operation. The authorities had arrived and were coordinating with Mark's vigilantes. Emergency medical teams had set up a triage area to care for all the children and surviving civilians that had been pulled out of the ship. Teams of people were rounding up all the prisoners, clearing the bodies, and beginning to examine official records to identify the deceased.

"You know, I got to be honest...I'm glad that you're here with this discovery."

Mark and 777 turned to see their friend approach. It was Commander Bradley, recently appointed head of LAPD's Metro SWAT division.

"Back up," Mark gazed at her with a glint in his eye and smirked. "Did you just compliment me?"

"Yes, she did," 777 responded.

"Shut up," Bradley crossed her arms. "It's already a nightmare explaining to the Chief about your sudden appearance. A.I. Industries openly asking the vigilantes and not us looks bad."

"I'm afraid that time wasn't on our side," 777 replied. "Once I received intelligence about what was happening, we called for a much faster response."

"Yeah, yeah, I know the drill," Bradley nodded. "As a commander, I can't really agree with your methods but off the record, I know you kids are quite capable. Mark, thanks for your help."

"Sure. But uh, they're not going to cast this aside, right?" Mark asked.

"You boys stumbled across something horrifying," Bradley began to walk away. "It's gotten a lot of attention. Watch your backs."

With that, Commander Bradley turned and headed towards a gathering of a few other officers. Mark and 777 were left alone and continued to observe.

"I saw a mother lying on the ground."

Mark turned to 777. Anything the amborgs saw was recorded. It was highly unlikely that this experience would ever fade from his mind. He silently listened to 777 vent about what he'd witnessed.

"The mother had a baby in her arms," he described the scene to Mark. "It looked like before they both died, she was trying to protect her child. There was a little stuffed bear next to them. It was soaked in blood."

"I'm sorry you saw all of that," Mark consoled him in a gentle but mournful tone.

"We should have gotten here sooner," 777 stated.

"We can't save everyone," Mark said. "We didn't know what was going on here."

"It isn't fair…"

"I'm afraid that life and death are always going to be that way. It's tough being the one who survives, but you can't let that guilt weigh on you."

777 turned and gazed at Mark. This mission had hit him very hard, and he could see how upset he was.

"How do you…?"

777 suddenly stopped talking. He turned his head, breaking eye contact as he redirected his attention. Alarmed, Mark tried to follow his line of sight, curious to see what he'd spotted. Was there trouble on the horizon?

"It's an emergency recall," 777 announced.

Right now? The timing couldn't have been worse. Mark remembered exactly what this meant. He'd been involved in helping David 117 and numerous others in its planning and had personally witnessed Dr. Kendrick utilize it twice over the last decade.

"Dr. Kendrick is calling?"

"No," 777 replied. "It's just a recall. I must return to A.I. Industries."

777 abruptly looked down at his bracelet, which had begun to flash brightly.

"Never mind," 777 lifted his wrist. "Now, he's calling."

The call connected, and Dr. Kendrick's face appeared on a small video screen displayed from his bracelet.

"Luis," Dr. Kendrick greeted him. "And I see Mark is here as well."

"It's really good to see you John," Mark nodded politely with a smile. "You're a sight for sore eyes."

"I can imagine," Dr. Kendrick responded. "I just saw the updates you sent me, 777. My apologies that it was after I initiated the emergency recall. How are you feeling?"

"I shall be honest," 777 answered, "It has been quite terrible."

"Well, I'm afraid that we need you back home," Dr. Kendrick let out a sigh. "Serina is sending you details, but I need you."

"Cut him a break, will you?" Mark interrupted as 777 received the files on his bracelet. "We literally discovered a pit of dead civilians that this gang was trying to smuggle into International Waters. There are hundreds of bodies here."

"And if 777 doesn't return immediately, there may be plenty more of them," Dr. Kendrick declared sternly.

"Whoa," 777's eyes widened. Mark glanced over and noticed that he was looking at the data privately.

"This better be good," Mark grumbled as he crossed his arms.

"777, please make preparations to return immediately," Dr. Kendrick instructed. "Before you leave, please transfer my call to Mark."

777 nodded.

"May I also send the data Serina just sent me to him as well?"

"Well, he's going to find out about it eventually," Dr. Kendrick sighed. "Do as you wish."

"Dr. Kendrick, your orders in the emergency recall require us all to report in by the end of the week," 777 said, "May I continue with my current mission?"

"For what purpose?"

"All these kids here," 777 looked down at the docks. "I can't just leave yet. Please, let me make sure they're taken care of, and I'll come home."

"Very well," Dr. Kendrick replied, "Please return before the end of the week."

"Thank you," 777 nodded, "Transferring your call."

As 777 made a quick swiping motion from his bracelet, Mark's earpiece emitted a ringing noise. He saw Dr. Kendrick's call on the display of his bracer, prompting him to accept or deny the call. For a brief moment, Mark toyed with the idea of disconnecting the call and refusing to answer as a joke. Before he had the chance, though, 777 asked a question.

"How do you handle seeing all that death? How are you able to remain positive in the face of such traumatic incidents?"

"Luis," Mark replied as Dr. Kendrick's call continued ringing. "You've seen my war record. I've lost a lot of friends over the years. People that I wish I could message and hear from again. But they're gone. I've already accepted that. I still had to deal with the pain."

"But," 777 glanced at Mark, looking at him from head to toe, "you appear to be fine."

"I lost my son, my daughter-in-law, and the best guys and girls I knew. All of them didn't deserve to die so young. Part of what gets me through the day is David 117, you, and my current friends and family. I don't know if this will also help you, but I find that talking about it with a professional helps, too. Taking care of yourself mentally is a long road for a lot of us. I've just been on this particular road for years."

777 silently nodded and turned. As he walked away, Mark received a data transfer from him. When he started perusing the files, he finally answered Dr. Kendrick's call.

"Was it necessary to keep me waiting?" he spoke in irritation, which made Mark grin.

He glanced down at his bracer and Dr. Kendrick's face appeared on the mini-projector. He looked impatient and annoyed.

"Luis asked me a serious question," Mark replied, "I think you should cut him some slack after he gets back to A.I. Industries."

"We may not have the luxury of that."

Mark focused on Dr. Kendrick's face on the video screen a little more closely. Before asking the burning question weighing on his mind, he instead opened the files transmitted by 777. He browsed the files while Dr. Kendrick waited patiently, allowing him to look at the details uninterrupted.

"Whoa," he uttered, turning his head to look at the video screen. "This just happened?"

"I'm trusting you with this information because despite our differences before, you're still a relative of someone I value as one of my own. Can you tell me where David 117 is?"

Mark raised an eyebrow.

"You're the head of A.I. Industries and the smartest man on the planet... and you don't know where my grandson is?"

"All the amborgs and I have a mutual agreement," Dr. Kendrick explained in a grim voice. "We are a family and family... does not stick their noses all the way in each other's business."

"Why do you even need me to tell you?"

"Because he's ignored the emergency recall and none of us can reach him," Dr. Kendrick sighed. "I know he spoke to you before he left on holiday. Will you tell me?"

"Sure," Mark looked up thoughtfully. A smile broke out on his face.

"Alright," Dr. Kendrick interrupted impatiently and conceded. "What do you want?"

"Well, some of my gear is getting a little outdated," Mark grinned, showing his teeth. "Some of my vigilantes could use some new pieces, here and there."

"Done. Anything else?"

Mark continued to grin. He enjoyed watching Dr. Kendrick's expression go from annoyed to fearful in a matter of seconds.

"I'll send you the full list," he pressed a few buttons, which made Dr. Kendrick groan.

"Wonderful," he muttered, rolling his eyes. "Wait, you're joking. I can't just authorize..."

Mark laughed as he ended the phone call. It was such a shame. Sometimes cell reception wasn't too reliable at times.

Chapter 3: A Vacation Interrupted

Lake Red Rock, Iowa
Emergency Recall plus 39 minutes
12:07 PM Central Time

A sudden shrill cry pierced the air, cutting through the serene stillness of the morning. Outside of a beautiful cabin, a man was making his way back from an early hike on a nearby trail, his heavy winter boots quietly crunching in the frozen dirt. David 117 of the Second Group paused on the cabin's porch and glanced up. Against the backdrop of a bright, cloudless sky, a hawk circled overhead, its outstretched wings casting a shadow over the frosty ground below.

117 inhaled deeply, letting the crisp scent of the pine trees surrounding the cabin fill his lungs as his sensors took readings. A gentle breeze brushed against his skin as he admired the sunlight filtering through the branches. He stayed there for a few moments, taking it all in. As much as he wanted to linger outside, a small inner voice reminded him that he had more pressing matters to attend to. 117 looked to the sky once more and watched the hawk fly out of sight. He reached for the door handle, turned it gently, and stepped inside.

During his hike, 117 had been mulling over something special he had planned for that morning. He removed his jacket and boots at the door and made his way into the kitchen. It had been modeled to emulate a 19th century American West style that his grandfather had always considered a classic. Since neither of them had lived during that era, 117 had to rely on historical photos at museums, which offered glimpses into a world long past. No matter how many times he'd been told to embrace the nostalgia, 117 just treated it like an ordinary cabin. To those around him, he may have appeared to be falling short of their expectations as a homeowner.

He opened the fridge and retrieved a carton of eggs, bread, and an assortment of fruits. Setting them on the counter, he began to wash some oranges, apples, and grapes, preparing them to be arranged in a simple, small ceramic fruit bowl. After letting the fruit sit on a clean towel, 117 grabbed some bread and brought it over to an antique toaster oven he'd salvaged from a junkyard. After scouring the internet for schematics and a few hours of work during his downtime, he managed to restore the old toaster to its original condition. He inserted the bread, closed the door, and pushed the "on" button. A timer began ticking as the toast started to heat up. While the toaster oven worked its magic, 117 went to fry some eggs.

He grabbed a cast iron frying pan from its hanging spot and placed it carefully on the burner, turning on the heat. As the flames heated up the pan, he gathered the rest of his ingredients on the counter nearby. He picked up three eggs and prepared to crack them open over a clean bowl. Unlike most chefs who typically cracked eggs over a skillet, he preferred this method to avoid accidentally crushing or exploding them with the amount of force he used. Eggs are delicate things, cracking them open properly demanded a controlled touch to prevent making a mess, especially since he possessed superhuman strength. He was guilty of many egg-splosions dating all the way back to the first time Mandy encouraged him to take that cooking class.

117 gently leaned forward, held one egg in his hand, and concentrated. He remembered what 3 had once suggested to him and tried to hang on to her exact words: *"You have to carry an egg carefully like you would an open paint can; don't swing or drop the can or the paint will get everywhere. But, when cracking the egg, break it like you would a wooden plank; aim with precision and focus to achieve a clean break."*

"She makes it seem so easy," 117 gave himself a countdown and slowly tapped the egg against the rim of the bowl.

He heard a faint crack, just as he was anticipating. He maneuvered his thumb to the crack and carefully separated the shell. Without any sudden movements, he pulled the two halves apart and allowed the inside of the egg to drop. The yellow egg yolk fell into the bowl cleanly. It didn't crumble to pieces like he was expecting it to.

"Success," 117 let out a sigh of relief. "Two to go."

It probably took him an additional two minutes, one per egg to get the last two into the bowl. The level of stress he felt to get this right was just like the time he had to disarm a bomb that someone had snuck into a shopping center several months ago. Relieved, he grabbed a spatula and gently mixed the yolk, stirring slowly and not rapidly to avoid splattering it all over the place. When he was ready, he transferred it to the pan, which had finished heating up while he took his time cracking the eggs.

The eggs sizzled loudly as soon as they hit the frying pan. 117 adjusted the heat and began to scramble them. Hopefully, they'd turn out exactly how his grandfather had taught him.

Straightening up, David 117 turned and walked over to the nearby cabinet. He pulled out some plates and grabbed a tray to begin his setup. As if on cue, the toaster bell dinged, signaling that the toast was done. 117 stepped over and pulled down the door. He grabbed the toast, ignoring how hot they were, and delicately swung around to place them on one of the plates.

117 glanced at the eggs and suddenly remembered that there was one more step to his grandpa's instructions. He walked over to the pantry and retrieved some dill weed. He sprinkled it over the cooking eggs and stirred them as they solidified, making sure they were just slightly browned.

With only a few more seconds left for the eggs to cook, 117 hurried over to the sink and grabbed a small, clear vase. He quickly filled it with water and then went over to the windowsill where a beautiful wild flower colored in swirls of pastel pink and purple was basking in the sunlight. He carefully placed it in the vase and turned around to set it next to the toast, adding a touch of elegance to his breakfast.

Once that was all set, he returned to the frying pan. 117 shut off the heat and did a visual scan. They were done. He gently lifted the pan, carried it over to the tray and scooped the eggs onto the main plate. As he let them sit, 117 brought the pan and spatula to the sink. His hands became blurs as he washed and dried them in a matter of seconds.

After setting them aside, he grabbed all the fruit that he had washed and, just like the dishes, used his superhuman speed to prepare them. Somehow, he managed to peel the oranges into slices, pluck the stems from the grapes and slice the apples into even slices. Why was it always the fruit that he had no issues with? Shrugging that thought aside, 117 organized a fruit bowl and added that as the finishing touch to the breakfast tray. He grabbed some silverware and placed them with a napkin on the side.

Even though he knew that he had shut off everything correctly, he followed basic safety protocol and did a quick scan of the kitchen. He made sure the kitchen faucet was off, the flame burners were not accidentally left on, the toaster oven was empty and switched off, and the fridge was securely closed. Once the safety check was done, 117 nodded with satisfaction. Breakfast could now be served.

117 picked up the tray and left the kitchen. He gingerly walked up the staircase and balanced the tray in his hands. According to the others, his track record was spotless when it came to carrying things up or down flights of stairs. Without any distractions, he successfully made it up to the second floor and walked down the hall to the room at the end.

117 shifted the breakfast tray to his left hand and slowly opened the door with his right.

"Oh, now that smells nice."

Audrey was still in bed, lying on her stomach and half-asleep, a book sitting on the mattress off to the side. Despite her drowsiness, her sense of smell was as sharp as ever. 117 walked over to her side of the mattress, prompting her to shift into a sitting position.

"I believe you have slept past your alarm," he gazed down at her in amusement. "Did you sleep well?"

"Every night for the last ten days," Audrey mumbled as she set her book aside on the bedside table. "Can we stay on vacation forever?"

"I am afraid that is impossible. I cooked breakfast for you."

Audrey eagerly watched as 117 placed the breakfast tray in front of her. When it was all set, she stared in awe at the delicious meal before her.

"Wow, this looks so amazing too!" she clapped her hands together and smiled at him.

"Thank you," 117 sat next to her as she picked up a fork and dug into the eggs.

"I'm really glad you're here David."

"The feeling is mutual Audrey."

"Do you have to talk like that??"

"Like what?" 117 asked with a puzzled expression.

"Very technical. You sound just like you did when we first met 10 years ago," she stared inquisitively at him. "Are you pretending to sound like that, or did you actually forget?"

"I have not forgotten anything ever since I became an amborg. I thought it was a nice idea to reminisce about when we started dating," 117 admitted. "It actually did sound a little painful to my ears since you brought it up. Saying something so formal does get old fast."

"Well, it is a nice idea," Audrey grinned as she leaned in and kissed him on the cheek. "And it was one of my favorite things about meeting you back then. You swooped in and saved me."

117 smiled warmly as he relaxed and let her enjoy her breakfast.

"My handsome husband," Audrey smiled as she kept chewing. Then she pointed down at her tray with her fork. "Did you want some of this?"

"It's all for you," 117 answered with a smile. "I don't need a lot of food."

"Did you eat something when you went out for your morning run?"

"A protein bar," he answered with a nod.

"Uh... honey?" Audrey's smile faded when she bit down on some more egg. "I think you goofed. I just bit an eggshell."

117 perked up. His smile faltered as he quickly glanced at the tray.

"That can't be," his voice wavered a little. He then looked up at Audrey. "I was sure..."

117 stopped when he noticed that she was grinning mischievously at him. He sighed and let out a chuckle.

"You... got me," he replied.

"It's too easy," she laughed.

"You, Mandy and so many other people are so good at that," 117 sighed, "I still have problems figuring out the jokes."

"How is Mandy? Did you manage to call or text her last night?"

117 nodded.

Mandy was 117's old technician and his second pair of eyes and ears when he deployed into the field. Just after he became an amborg, she was one of the first human friends that he made. His selection process and being paired up with her led them from one mission to the next.

"She's also enjoying her own vacation," he replied. "I didn't get too much time though; it was late when I managed to contact her."

"Oh right," Audrey blinked. "There's a time difference."

"Which of the two of us is the forgetful one?"

Audrey smacked 117's shoulder and it was his turn to grin. She definitely loved this side of him more. Years ago, he was so meek and shy. Wait, how did the others describe him? Helpless? Well, either way, it didn't matter so much now. According to what she and everyone else saw of David 117 today, it was clear that he was becoming more expressive and emotionally connected with each passing day. He was continuing to evolve and surpass the complex technology that had brought him back to life.

She decided to change the subject.

"So how are things at home?"

117 paused, seeming to hesitate.

"If you are asking about Carter..." he suddenly looked at Audrey, annoyance in his expression. "He's fine."

A few years after the Dominoe Incident and during their budding relation-ship, Audrey's artificial intelligence program, Carter, had reached a crucial junction in his life. Most A.I. had a lifespan of about 20-30 years. Every five and ten years, there would be a special maintenance review to assess each program's feasibility. This was done so that any of the research institutions or corporations could determine whether an A.I. needed to be retired or replaced by a completely new one. An A.I. reaching the end of their life wasn't exactly performing at their max potential in comparison to a newly developed program that was fresh off the assembly line.

In Carter's case, he had reached 15 years of service and was due for a check-up shortly after 117 and Audrey got together. Unfortunately, his service model was rather rare and outdated because her father had been very attached to keeping him in the family. Unfortunately, there weren't a lot of companies that could take him in due to heavy A.I. growth and modernization. The ones that could examine Carter were extremely expensive. Many stated that his particular model was obsolete. To help ease the stress that was weighing on Audrey's shoulders at the time, Dr. Kendrick personally took Carter in and gave her a *"friends & family"* discount. She had just graduated from the Academy and was extensively searching for a job, so Carter being taken out of her hands by A.I. Industries had helped a lot.

Not only did Carter have a successful checkup, but the R&D specialists had also surprised Audrey with a complimentary upgrade. They'd given him a proper holographic form, which meant that he was no longer an A.I. that was just the squiggly line that she had grown up with. His program had a physical appearance, and he was also performing better than ever.

Now, he spent half his time staying at A.I. Industries and occasionally reporting to Audrey. She did miss having him around at times, but she knew that he had accomplished one of his dreams of working with the other A.I. at Dr. Kendrick's company. Audrey was overjoyed and supportive of his decision to stay there. What she worried about constantly, though, was all the trouble he always seemed to be involved in.

"Are you sure?" She raised an eyebrow at 117. "It's not exactly normal whenever I seem to call and check in with him."

"I admit that there have been some issues from before," 117 said slowly.

"Some??"

Audrey began to count on her fingers, interrupting him.

"There was the time that he and Serina caused a global blackout," she listed off the top of her head, "The time that he caused a lockdown of A.I. Industries... twice. You told me a story about how he got another A.I. trapped in a printer for hours. And what about the time that a computer virus got downloaded which caused all the Amborgs to break out into song and dance...?"

"That brings back unpleasant memories," 117 looked away embarrassingly.

"Oh yeah, those recordings were spectacular," Audrey snickered a little. She placed a hand on his shoulder reassuringly. "I never would have imagined you participating in a musical number."

"That's probably one of the only times you'll ever hear me sing," 117 replied casually. "Besides, we went through so many genres, styles, and popular songs that the virus was bound to hit me too."

"Actually, I wasn't checking on Carter. I swore not to ask while we were on our trip together, but it's been on my mind for a while."

Audrey set the breakfast tray aside so that she could sit up straight and look 117 in the eye.

"Things have been so nice lately that I've been forgetting about work, and it's been wonderful."

"Is there something wrong with our vacation?" 117 asked. "Because I am a little confused."

"I'm just trying to tell you that things have been so nice ever since we both took time off that I feel bad for forgetting to bring this up with you."

"Oh."

117 still wasn't sure if he fully understood. He decided to let Audrey keep talking.

"You know," she said, "he's also quite a good singer too."

117 glanced at Audrey. She canted her head and grinned. He immediately knew who she was referring to. He tilted his head back and forth slowly.

"Oh. Him," he said as his smile faded. "Right."

"I don't think he's been the same since..."

"I know," 117 interjected. "It affected him deeply."

Audrey leaned away from him. He turned and noticed that she looked slightly hurt.

"Ok, why do you do that?"

Audrey rose from the bed and walked around it so that she faced him. He looked up at her with a slight tilt of his head.

"What do you mean?" 117 asked innocently.

"Is it such a sensitive subject that you and the others feel it's necessary to interrupt me when I want to check in on him? For God's sake David 117, he was the best man at our wedding, and you won't even let me in enough to care about my own brother-in-law. Well... one of them at least."

Audrey could see the pain in 117's expression. Even though he wasn't expressing it out loud, she could see the facial tics that were giving it away. When he didn't respond, she sighed.

"Can you at least tell me where he is?" she asked.

"917 is the only one who can disclose this information to you," 117 replied firmly. "The truth is, if Dr. Kendrick won't tell the rest of us, then I'm afraid there is not much left to say about it."

"I'm just worried," Audrey began to pace. "There have been rumors about him."

"I'm not surprised considering you work with a ton of highly ranked military officials."

"Listen please," Audrey let out a frustrated sigh at being interrupted again. "It's been a long time since we've seen 917 on a deployment. The rumors aren't good. They're saying that he got excommunicated. I never knew that could even happen to an amborg."

"He is definitely not excommunicated," 117 replied quickly. His defensive response snagged her attention. "All I know is this. You're right, before... he was much more optimistic. He is also still a good friend. He's just taking time alone now. And before you ask again, I don't know where he's gone. I can only assume that it was serious enough to the point where Dr. Kendrick ordered him to leave."

"That sounds a little extreme..." Audrey's eyes widened.

"Indeed," 117 nodded. "He left and apparently, didn't say anything to Angel."

"But aren't they best friends? He just up and left her this whole time?"

"The answer to both questions are yes," 117 sighed. "Unfortunately, she's also in a similar situation and it's worrying the rest of us as well."

Everyone at A.I. Industries knew that Alice "Angel" 999 was 917's closest friend. Both had been inseparable ever since the two of them joined the Second Group. They weren't physically joined at the hip like the twins, 92 and 93 or the Third Group triplets, but their friendship was one of most iconic ones. Most employees and staff at A.I. Industries had always been intrigued by the contrasting dynamics in their personalities. 999 had always been a strong fighter but was extremely introverted with severe trust issues. 917 was the complete opposite. He had so much enthusiasm, optimism, and was so outgoing that you would sometimes forget that 999 was right there backing him up at times. A quiet amborg paired with one of the most upbeat ones was certainly a unique relationship. Serina had often said that if Angel opened up a bit more, her and 917 would have a relationship similar to the one Serina had with 117 in the past. Well, before she passed on and became an A.I.

"Does she talk to anyone besides 917?" Audrey asked.

"Dr. Kendrick maybe," 117 answered with a shrug.

It wasn't a wrong answer to her question. 117 genuinely didn't know. Audrey could hear how uncertain he was.

"If I'm being honest," he added, "since he's been gone, she's been hurting more. I'm not sure if it's getting any better. I don't know what to do."

"You are the leader of the Second Group," Audrey said as she knelt in front of him and clasped his hands. "If anyone needs a friend, you're the right person to extend a hand."

"You're not just saying that because... if you reach out to Angel, you face some unfavorable odds?"

"Well, the last time I spoke to her, I thought she was going to crawl through my screen and kill me like that girl from that horror movie we watched! At least the amborgs could stand a chance!"

117 and Audrey laughed. He held her hand gently.

"Aside from 917," he said, "the only other amborg capable of handling Angel 999 is Serina 43."

"And she's kinda dead," Audrey held a finger up to her lips and winked. "I know."

Out of nowhere, a red light flashed from 117's bracelet, followed by a warning beep. Audrey looked down nervously as 117 activated his bracelet and checked the notification.

"Perimeter alert," 117 murmured in surprise, suddenly perking up.

"What?"

Both of them jumped to their feet.

"Someone walked past one of my motion detectors," 117 stated while Audrey ran to the closet.

"You installed motion detectors? Here?" she asked as she slid the doors open and brushed some clothes aside.

"It was a precaution in case our enemies figured out my travel itinerary."

Audrey reached inside and placed a thumb on an electronic pad. It lit up green and revealed a small screen displaying a set of numbers. She entered the security code and after a quick chime, the back of the closet slid open, unveiling a small gun cage.

"Maybe it's Dr. Kendrick?" she asked as she grabbed a rifle and handed it to him.

"Dr. Kendrick wouldn't jump over the fence, honey," he said as he inspected it, then took the ammo magazine that Audrey passed to him. "He usually just hacks the front gate and strolls right in. He values our privacy and hasn't looked at our itineraries for the past four years. All he does is just sign the approval form once it reaches his desk."

"I wish my boss would do that..." Audrey sighed, pulling a sniper rifle out of the cage.

"It took four weeks just to point out that I had put my PTO request on his stack of folders in the inbox."

"Cover me from the cabin?"

"On your signal," Audrey loaded her rifle and nodded her head.

The two of them exited the bedroom. He turned left to head downstairs, and she turned right to go up into the attic where the sniper's perch was located. Once he reached the first floor, he immediately made his way to the front door and opened it gently.

He stepped outside and plotted an intercept course. He had only seen one bogey hop the fence and trigger the alarm. Hopefully, this could be easily taken care of. If a cybernetically enhanced assassin had tracked him down, they would probably be in for a deadly fight. Making sure that Audrey was safe inside the cabin was his highest priority.

"Initiate lock down," he instructed into a small monitor next to the door handle.

There was a loud click as the light turned red.

117 walked away from the cabin and headed to the nearest tree. He was just about to fall silent and listen for the oncoming target when something on his radar caught his attention. Whoever it was didn't appear to be approaching the cabin in an attack pattern, but rather strolling towards it nonchalantly at a normal pace. They weren't even trying to hide themselves. If someone were targeting him or Audrey, they would be more discrete in their approach. As they drew closer, 117 understood why.

An amborg beacon appeared on his radar, easing his tension. 117 could hear the crunching of leaves and the snapping of twigs as the footsteps drew closer.

"Is this how you greet a friend?"

Remaining in his hiding spot, 117 transmitted his response through his bracelet, broadcasting it publicly.

"Well, you did jump the fence," he answered. "Most people would have called from the gate."

"True. Unfortunately, I didn't have the gate combination. Paging you from there would have been boring. So, I decided to give you a little scare."

117 emerged from his hiding spot and was greeted by a familiar face. Standing before him was a woman who's youthful appearance, just like every amborg, also resembled that of a teenager. She was bundled up in warm clothing suitable for the cold weather. 117 switched the safety on his weapon and smiled warmly.

Katie 57, another Second Group amborg, took off her gloves and pocketed them in her windbreaker. A small brown bag was wrapped around her shoulder, and 117 noticed a rifle slung on her back. He decided to throw her a curveball to see how she'd react.

"And if I decided to attack first?" he asked cautiously as he swung his own rifle around his shoulder. "Before you activated your beacon? How would you feel about that?"

"I'd say that you had a perfectly normal response. Well within amborg-established protocol."

117 and 57 cautiously matched each other's footsteps, smiling pleasantly as they approached each other.

"I think that your form is a little off," she stated. "You still have that small twinge in your step from when that building collapsed on us eight months ago."

117 let out a satisfied sigh as he extended his hand towards 57. She shook it, and the two of them burst into laughter.

"117, I highly doubt that someone would have disguised themselves as me, forged an amborg beacon, and gotten this far."

"Rules are rules," 117 replied as they both let go. "Until you arrived, I was the only amborg out here with one civilian under my care. I must keep her safe."

"Fair. Nice place you have out here," 57 gestured towards the cabin while admiring the surrounding scenery. "It's good to see you 117. This place seems like a nice getaway."

"Likewise. Hang on one moment," 117 politely dipped his head and turned towards the cabin. He sent a message directly to Audrey. "It's ok honey. It's Katie 57. All clear."

"Oh? It's Katie? Great!" Audrey answered happily. "I'll be right down. The lack of shooting was making me nervous."

"What's the occasion?" 117 turned to face 57 again.

There was only one person who knew exactly where he and Audrey were. The only way that 57 would know about his vacation spot was if Dr. Kendrick had told her. If he had told her, then that meant it was important enough to come here personally.

"Emergency recall," she replied bluntly. "You and a few others didn't respond."

"For all of us?" 117 raised an eyebrow. "I didn't see anything on the news about any upcoming disasters or notable events."

"This...isn't public," 57 stated, choosing her words carefully. She glanced at her watch on her right wrist. "If it was, I imagine your wife would be the one informing you of this."

"Informing what?"

117 and 57 turned to acknowledge Audrey, who was approaching them with excitement. She cheerfully hugged 57, and the two of them greeted each other warmly.

"You didn't fly in your drop-pod today?" she asked curiously.

"It would have looked strange if an amborg in full uniform deployed out in the middle of Iowa," 57 explained. "I hitched a ride instead."

"You took an Uzoomly?" 117 asked. "From A.I. Industries?"

"Of course not, a driver wouldn't want to go all the way from home to here," 57 shook her head. "I was dropped off at the nearest town, and Craig and Dexter took me here."

"You had two drivers?" Audrey looked confused.

"No," 57 clarified and explained. "Craig was the driver, and he had his dog Dexter with him while he was working. They were so nice. I tipped them extra for their trouble."

"Did he have anything to say about the fact that you were armed?"

117 gestured at her rifle. She glanced at it and smirked.

"Hunting trip," 57 answered smugly. "Didn't really ask anything else after that."

"It's surprising that he bought that story," 117 gave her a look of concern.

"Well, he did get a lot of money for the trip. Pay enough and they don't pry."

Even if she was in a civilian disguise, it probably raised a lot of questions to anyone that had the chance to speak directly to 57. It was the fact that she was carrying almost nothing but a rifle without any extra ammunition or supplies and casually declaring that she was on a "hunting trip" that appeared a bit suspicious to anyone who cared to notice. Any actual expert or hunter that lived off the wilder-ness probably would have reported her for looking like such a terrible amateur.

"Anyway," 117 sighed. "You were saying? The emergency recall?"

"Recall?" Audrey suddenly looked alarmed. "You're leaving?"

"I apologize for cutting your vacation short," 57 said with a look of reassurance. "But I'm afraid it's all hands on deck."

"I understand that and I look forward to a family reunion," 117 said as he glanced at Audrey, "but I'm afraid you haven't explained what the emergency is."

"I'll explain while the both of you pack?"

57 motioned towards the cabin door and waited for their response. Audrey and 117 both knew what had to happen. They understood that it was necessary to expect the unexpected.

"Deal," Audrey sighed.

The two of them walked alongside 57 and let her head inside first. Audrey hesitated, turning to look at her husband with a nervous expression. He quickly raised his hand and stroked her cheek reassuringly. After sharing a brief loving moment, they proceeded into the cabin together.

"Dr. Kendrick wants us to rally all of the other amborgs that haven't responded to the recall order," 57 said as she took the lead, ascending the stairs with the other two in tow.

"How many didn't respond?" 117 asked.

"At least 16 of us," 57 answered as they entered the bedroom.

57 walked to the corner and pulled out the chair that was sitting in front of the table. She motioned to Audrey to sit down.

"Here," she said politely, "117 and I will pack. Make yourself comfortable."

Audrey smiled and thanked her, then made her way over to the chair.

57 and 117 propped their rifles against the wall while Audrey's sniper rifle was carefully put into the gun safe in the back of the closet.

From her comfy position in the corner, Audrey watched the two of them get to work. 57 started by securing the gun safe, then rapidly began to pull clothes out of the closet and tossed them to 117, who meticulously folded and organized them on the bed.

The two cybernetically enhanced humans pulled out their suitcases and efficiently packed everything away. Their special abilities made everything they did seamless and convenient. Audrey listened intently to the details 57 was describing as they continued to work in rapid motion.

"Less than an hour ago, Apogee Space Station detected an anomaly," she said as she folded two shirts and handed them to 117. "A wormhole was detected."

"The A.S.S. detected a hole in space?"

117 and 57 stopped to look at Audrey, who quickly averted her eyes in embarrassment.

"Sorry," she muttered sheepishly. "I couldn't help it."

"Dr. Kendrick's space station did come with an unfortunate acronym," 117 shrugged.

"Yeah, that was funny," 57 replied with an amused grin.

The two of them resumed packing.

"Anyway, this wormhole appeared and the next thing we knew, an object from it landed in Africa."

117 paused and suddenly pivoted towards 57, who was zipping up one of their bags. Audrey's smile vanished, all humor replaced with shock.

"Excuse me?" she gasped, eyes wide.

"You don't mean..." 117 pondered curiously and looked at 57 in awe, "an extraterrestrial?"

"Yes and no."

57's short response only confused the two of them.

"How could it be yes or no?" 117 asked as he and Audrey both glanced at each other. "Did something come from outer space or not??"

"What landed in Africa is definitely from space," 57 explained as she took the last jacket out of the closet and folded it. "It was what we found inside that concerned us. 117, do you remember when we had those long discussions about the possibilities of life beyond our solar system?"

117 nodded.

"When we opened this pod or transport," 57 stated, placing the jacket in another open bag and zipped it up. "We found an occupant inside. Emergency protocol 16B-2-A4-01."

"Whoa..."

117 looked stunned. Audrey stared blankly at the two amborgs. This definitely seemed like some sort of code that only they knew about. She bashfully raised her hand.

"Um... can I ask what that means?"

57 and 117 turned to look at her.

"Yes, but if you didn't have clearance, our responses are limited due to this being restricted information," 57 stated.

"But my wife actually is authorized," 117 smiled proudly. "She was promoted three months ago, which significantly granted her higher access with her new rank."

"Ah, congratulations," 57 replied, dipping her head courteously. "I am afraid that information never reached me. Your promotion is a wonderful thing to celebrate."

"Thanks Katie," Audrey replied, "but could one of you tell me what you're talking about?"

"A code 16 for the amborgs is an incident involving outer space or has taken place in space," 117 explained. "The 'B' means that it's an invasion from space or an object crashing on Earth. Since the entire world isn't at war, we are at condition 2 which means that this visitor from space is not hostile. A4 is the code for alternate dimension or multiverse incident."

"Whoa..." Audrey gulped. "Having clearance is scary... What's the zero-one at the end?"

"This would be our first incident ever recorded," 57 added.

"And honey, I know you understand what classified means," 117 coughed. "But we are obligated to remind you that..."

"Of course," she replied before he could finish, nodding her head slowly. She raised her hand as if she were taking a vow, "Don't tell anyone what you just told me. I know."

If she had a different career entirely, it was possible that the secrets hiding in her husband's brain would never be revealed to her. The amborgs were very meticulous when it came to protecting certain bits of information. So much so that they would take it to their graves, and it would die with them.

"Did you really spend all this time coming up with all these different kinds of protocol?"

"We have a lot of time on our hands," 57 shrugged, answering Audrey's question.

"Which might change due to recent events," 117 said. "How did you know that this incident was related to the multiverse?"

117 had picked up two bags and slung them over his shoulders. He was about to head out and have Audrey follow him when 57 grabbed his arm and stopped

him. He hadn't noticed that she'd hesitated to answer the question. This concerned the two of them, especially when they saw how serious 57's expression was.

"What is it?"

"Dr. Kendrick wanted you to see this," she answered softly. "There's no way to sugarcoat this 117. I was told to tell you directly."

57 turned and signaled to Audrey to join her and activated the projector from her bracelet. Footage from the Apogess Station Space Jumpers began to play, showing the events leading up to the crash and the opening of the pod that had arrived from space. As the camera focused on the figure inside the pod, 117 flinched and Audrey let out an audible gasp.

"Yup, Dr. Kendrick reacted that way too," 57 said as she shut off the footage. "So did a lot of us. Are you ok?"

"I... don't know..."

117 felt a wide range of emotions beginning to flood his mind as he struggled to process everything. It was like seeing a ghost from his past, so surreal and thought to be lost forever. Now he could really see why this recall was put into effect. It was unbelievable how something that seemed impossible had somehow become a reality.

"Here's what Dr. Kendrick has ordered us to do," 57 said to keep them on track, recognizing their apparent shock. "We will send Audrey to safety or drop her off back in D.C. For the amborgs that were unable to respond to the recall, we will have to go and get them. Discreetly."

57 picked up her rifle, slung it around her shoulder, and grabbed 117's weapon.

The three of them went downstairs and headed outside to where 117's car was parked. As he unlocked the vehicle and opened the trunk, 57 shifted 117's rifle to her right hand and brought up her left wrist, activating a display showcasing a list of names.

"117 has been notified and we are proceeding to pick up the next amborg," she reported.

On the display, 117's name was crossed off and grayed out. The next name below was highlighted. However, 57 frowned when a strange detail snagged her attention. A crucial piece of information was missing.

"Huh. That's strange..." she said, doubled-checking to make sure she didn't miss anything. "I don't have a location to go to."

"For who?" Audrey asked as she opened the door and climbed into the back seat.

117 glanced at the list as he loaded a bag into the trunk while 57 removed his rifle and emptied it before safely storing it on a custom-built storage rack.

"Jack 917," he stated.

"Ooh, how interesting," Audrey said, intrigued, as she watched them organize the trunk.

"Why would his location be hidden?" 57 asked, her confusion deepening as she swung her rifle around and unloaded it. "Let me call Dr. Kendrick."

"Why indeed?" 117 glanced at Audrey, and they both shrugged.

The back of 117's trunk had another accessible gun rack, which 57 put her rifle in. When it was secure, 117 loaded the last of the luggage and closed the trunk. As it shut, he and 57 made their way to the front of the car.

57's bracelet started ringing as she initiated an outgoing call. She called dibs on driving, and 117 casually agreed, climbing into the front passenger seat. Audrey faced forward and buckled up. Everyone sat quietly for a moment as 57's phone call connected to the car's Bluetooth. With an audible click, Dr. Kendrick's face appeared on the dashboard monitor.

"Hello Katie," he greeted them with a smile. "Have you met up with David?"

"I did," 57 answered with a nod. "However, both of us are confused about picking up the next amborg on the list you gave me."

"Oh? Oh wait... Right. Oh."

Dr. Kendrick appeared slightly bothered when 57's words sunk in.

"Hello Dr. Kendrick," 117 said politely. "We were just wondering why 917's location was blacklisted?"

There was a pause as Dr. Kendrick curled his lip and nodded.

"Right, ah..." he let out a strained mumble. "Jack..."

57 and 117 exchanged glances.

"Is now the appropriate time to ask what happened to him a few years ago?" she asked innocently. "Can you tell us? It seems like you are reluctant for us to go get him considering you recalled every amborg back to A.I. Industries."

"Yes and no," Dr. Kendrick stated firmly. "You may ask, but I will not give you a full answer."

"That seems to be a repetitive answer lately," 117 grumbled.

"As stated, when I sent Katie to meet you David," Dr. Kendrick sighed as he rubbed his forehead. "This emergency recall means, 'all hands-on deck.' Regardless of personal or past issues, every amborg is to report in as soon as they're able. There are several reasons as to why I have not disclosed any information regarding Jack's current whereabouts. So, with that being said, I will tell you where to find him if you promise me that you won't pester either of us for answers. The world may be facing a crisis and I need all amborgs and every person I can reach to prepare."

"It just sounds so strange that he's off the grid," 117 voiced his concern.

"I'm waiting to hear you promise me."

Dr. Kendrick crossed his arms and became silent. 117 and 57 both turned to look at each other again and decided to compromise. It was probably the only way they were going to get anywhere with this, especially considering that they were in a hurry. 117 suddenly realized one other thing.

"Oh right," he said, and he looked behind him. "Audrey, I think Dr. Kendrick wants you to promise too."

"Your wife is in the car too?!"

Dr. Kendrick's eyes widened, but he paused before nodding.

"Oh wait," he said, "I remember now, you requested time off to spend time with her. I signed off on that a while ago."

"Hi Dr. Kendrick," Audrey said from the backseat with a smile. "I promise too! If that means anything!"

"Yes, I promise," 57 stated in agreement.

"I promise," 117 added.

"Thank you," Dr. Kendrick sighed. After a moment of silence, he adjusted his glasses and spoke again. "Jack 917 is located here."

A map on the dashboard appeared. A red dot indicating the place they were going to synchronized and was uploaded to 117 and 57's bracelets. As the coordinates were uploaded and the location began to reveal itself, Dr. Kendrick continued, "Your destination is Fulton Federal Penitentiary."

"WHAT??!"

Audrey clamped a hand over her mouth, concealing her sudden outburst as if she'd accidentally revealed an embarrassing secret. 117 and 57 stared, equally shocked, at the map on the screen. There seemed to be a lot of unexpected news today. Each of them exchanged glances to make sure they heard correctly.

57 cleared her throat as she checked the destination again.

"Prison? He is in a maximum-security prison?" she asked slowly in a nervous tone.

"The place that the First Group deemed to be inescapable?" 117 added. "The prison that we personally tested to see if it was escape-proof? Where none of the amborgs were successful?"

Audrey was the last one to finish their questions.

"Where they sentenced and executed the Assassin?"

Audrey's breathing became ragged for a moment. 117 turned around and held out his hand, which she grabbed and clung to as tight as she could. Not feeling any pain, 117 listened to Dr. Kendrick's response.

"Yes, to all of that," he replied. "I apologize Audrey. I had forgotten that you were there as a witness."

Shortly after the Dominoe Incident, one of the world's most terrifying and deadliest blitz conflicts, the man that orchestrated the entire attack had been put behind bars for good by the amborgs. The government sentenced him to death for killing countless people, including Audrey's older brother, Thomas, when the incident had found its way to the Academy. She had been invited to the prison along with hundreds of others to witness the entire thing. She hadn't been allowed in the direct observation room, so she remembered that they had gathered in one of the courtyards and watched it unfold from a television screen. Even though she was just a visitor, the conditions there were something else. It had left quite a disturbing impression on her, and she had hoped she would never set foot in a place like that again.

"Oh, I'm fine but..." Audrey steadied herself as she used both hands to cling to 117. "But I really need to ask..."

"How exactly is 917 in prison?" 57 interjected.

"Yeah, that," Audrey nodded.

"Well," Dr. Kendrick replied bluntly, "I already told you that I cannot fully disclose that information. If you were to remember certain... coinciding events from around the time he left, then you should start piecing that puzzle together."

"You allowed him to be put in prison? One of the world's most secure ones? Why?"

57's face was full of concern, but her tone had gotten quite serious. She was outraged at this particular turn of events. 117 could feel her anger rising.

"I can't tell you that," Dr. Kendrick replied, glancing down. 117 sensed a hint of sadness in his eyes.

"So, you just let them lock him up? You didn't fight for him all this time?"

"Katie 57," Dr. Kendrick said sternly, glaring up at them. "Do you think I would really abandon one of you like that?"

A tense silence filled the air as 117 and Audrey glanced at 57 nervously. Dr. Kendrick using her full name was never a good sign. 57 merely looked down and exhaled as she tried to calm herself.

"No sir."

57 took control of the wheel and started the car. The conversation could continue while on the road. Shifting the car into gear, she pressed her foot on the gas and steered away from the cabin. 117 let go of Audrey's hand and continued to listen to Dr. Kendrick.

"I can't say anything beyond that," he repeated. "Jack is the only one who can decide what to share with you."

"But what are we supposed to do?" 117 asked calmly. "During an emergency recall, everyone will be on their way back to A.I. Industries. Will we receive any support?"

"No," Dr. Kendrick replied, "That will not be necessary."

A thought crossed 117's mind. He didn't exactly like where this train of thought was going.

"Dr. Kendrick..." he gulped. "You aren't. Surely, not even you would consider doing this. Are you ordering us to break him out of prison?"

"I don't recall giving such an order," he answered promptly.

"Uh, if I'm allowed to be the normal human in this conversation," Audrey raised her hand politely. She nervously let out an exaggerated chuckle. "But as an officer of the U.S. Military, perhaps I should return to Washington before you start talking about committing potential off-the-books felonies?"

"That is appreciated, but unnecessary," Dr. Kendrick said as he lifted a hand up to point at 57 and 117, "I am saying that you should use your imaginations. You don't need to break him out of prison. I suggest you ask them."

"Ask?" 117 raised an eyebrow.

"You'd be surprised at how certain situations resolve themselves... as long as you ask nicely."

"I have way too many questions surfacing..." 57 said as she concentrated on driving.

"I know that these are rather mysterious circumstances," Dr. Kendrick said. He leaned forward and dipped his head apologetically. "But please bring him home. The emergency recall applies to everyone, and I need every amborg.”

“We’ll get him,” 117 acknowledged the message and responded obediently.

“I have other matters to attend to now, but call me and report in later.”

“Yes Dr. Kendrick,” 57 replied softly.

Dr. Kendrick turned his gaze to 57. He opened his mouth again, but nothing came out. The video call ended and the image on the dashboard disappeared. As the preference settings on the dash went back to normal, 57 plotted a quick route to the penitentiary.

“Audrey,” 117 said as he glanced in the back. “I believe it would be best to get you on the next train back to Washington right away.”

“Before we reach the train station, I believe that we should do as Dr. Kendrick says and discuss what happened chronologically over the last few years.”

117 glanced at 57.

“Are we disclosing more classified information?” Audrey asked curiously. “Is my clearance level good for this?”

“Actually yes,” 57 replied. “Amborg records and matters restricted to Earth are probably less secretive than outer space incidents.”

“Well, with that being said,” 117 said as he gazed forward. “It probably began after Brazil.”

“No 117,” 57 interrupted as she stopped at an intersection and waited for the light to turn green. “Everyone knows what happened in Brazil and the events after that. I’m trying to think about what 917 would have done that was so severe that he got put in prison.”

Audrey actually did know about the big amborg deployment in Brazil back then. She hadn’t realized that following that event, 917 must have been dealing with something serious enough for him to not be forthcoming about it.

“It’s something worse than Brazil?” she asked curiously.

57 saw the light turn green and drove straight.

“There were rumors,” 117 pondered, crossing his arms. “Dr. Kendrick did give him and Angel time off to recuperate but... after that... 917 went off on his own without her.”

“You never told me this...” Audrey struggled to think. “Unless... are you talking about the time that he and 466 rescued 501 from that group of maniacs?”

“That was before Brazil,” 117 answered.

"When was the incident where you had to take down some cultists in the middle of the woods?"

"Also before Brazil," it was 57 who answered. "It was very unfortunate for them. They didn't realize until it was too late that the amborgs had marked them for capture. That was a good time."

"I remember that he came back from traveling to Mexico. That was after Brazil."

"You are correct," 117 replied. "After Brazil, most of South America was redeveloping and needed our help. However, I don't believe there was any isolated incident involving 917."

"Didn't he encounter amborg-killers? With 18?"

"Yes, but hold on," 57 interrupted. She turned and stared at 117. "You told Audrey about the amborg-killers?"

"Actually, that one was Carter," Audrey chuckled nervously. "He told me about how A.I. Industries were encountering people engineered to target the amborgs. So, I got worried about 117 when I heard that there were some incidents."

"I love and respect you Audrey," 57 sighed as she continued to drive the car. "But you need to be careful where you stick your nose in our classified archives."

"But if it's relevant to 917," 117 suggested, "then it helps when I get my wife's perspective. She also happens to have a great deal of insight as a normal human."

Audrey sighed and turned to look out her window at the passing scenery. As the car passed through a small town, they turned a corner and headed towards the train station.

"There were unconfirmed rumors," 117 said, glancing at the people on the sidewalk. "I didn't want to talk poorly about 917, but I had a theory."

They stopped at a red light and watched a crowd of people cross the street.

"A lot of us were saying that he had gone rogue and used his enhanced abilities, which was against our code of conduct. I don't think that's the full story, so I only ever had that theory."

"But that's the problem. No one ever denied anything when 917 left," 57 said as they approached the train station. "The way that Dr. Kendrick was acting so secretively. Audrey? 117? It would take a very serious crime or offense for an amborg to be locked away in maximum security. A prison that we tested and made sure was escape-proof. He had to have done something that the rest of us wouldn't have dared to follow through on."

"Do you think he went rogue, and Dr. Kendrick punished him?"

"Well, I heard the rumors that he went out on an unsanctioned mission. Dr. Kendrick sealed all files on it, even reprogrammed the security drones to not talk about it, but I witnessed him leaving and coming back that day. Before he left for good. I heard that it was 917 who destroyed the Cypress criminal syndicate single-handedly purely for personal reasons without authorization."

"I heard about that story," Audrey remembered vague details about it from a news report she'd seen. "But there were never any confirmed details that an amborg was responsible."

"No one confirmed anything. At least, not A.I. Industries," 57 shook her head with a shudder. "The timing of when 917 was gone matches with that incident. But... everything that I'm thinking of doesn't make sense based on Dr. Kendrick and 917's personalities. It doesn't match their behavior in the past. Dr. Kendrick loves all of us as his family. So... how could he just abandon 917?"

"What's she saying??" Audrey looked at 117 nervously.

"Dr. Kendrick implied, and this is only a guess," 117 said slowly, thinking about his next words carefully. "When 57 got upset at him earlier, his response made it sound like he did try to prevent them from locking 917 behind bars. Dr. Kendrick still seems reluctant to bring him back even with a worldwide emergency recall."

"Exactly! Why not just say that?" 57 suddenly asked. She still sounded slightly irritated. "Why is he acting like, 'Oh, I did try to stop one of the amborgs from going to jail.' But then he also acts like 917 deserved to be in this situation. Isn't he supposed to be our dad? The man who raised us? It's like he didn't care and that scares me."

"I think he still does," 117 replied.

"117," 57 sighed. "Do you remember that 917 was the first and only amborg to be enhanced out of a coma?"

"Yes," 117 replied with a nod. He looked in the back and saw Audrey nodding, too. "This is common knowledge. 917 was first found in a hospital and Dr. Kendrick saved his life."

"Have you ever wondered why Dr. Kendrick tried to save his life? Why out of all the thousands of people out there that he was looking for... he picked him? A kid, in a coma, and who couldn't even consent to the whole thing?"

"I don't think that has anything to do with this."

"What if it does?"

The light turned green, and she drove forward.

"Over time, when we started gaining our emotions back, we all learned how to express ourselves properly," 57 explained as she looked left and right. "917's enhancement was different. If you ever tried asking him about it, the answer was always the same."

"Right," Audrey suddenly exclaimed. "He doesn't remember!"

"Every other amborg in existence right now was taken in and raised," 57 explained. "You had a family connection, 117. That was a personal connection. For you and Serina 43. For the rest of us, like me, we were nobodies. Then you have 917 who wakes up from a coma, has no memory of anything before that, and suddenly has superpowers. I'm worried about the fact that... maybe 917 tried to fight his way free from Dr. Kendrick and wanted to find out who he is... and he had to do something illegal to get answers."

"Well, let's go and talk to him," 117 said a few moments after absorbing the details of her explanation. "We know where he is, and we'll welcome him with open arms."

"You think this is a good idea? Trusting 917 or Dr. Kendrick's word?"

"It might be the best shot we have," Audrey suggested. "917 has always been a friend. He probably just didn't want us to see how much he's been hurting or the weight of the burden he's been carrying. Lots of people are trying to be the strong and silent type. Maybe you can get through to him. Even after being sent away, he probably needs you there to hear him out."

"And if he doesn't talk about it?" 117 asked.

"Like Dr. Kendrick said to us," Audrey replied, "it's 917's decision. It's his business, and if he keeps it to himself, then so be it. Respect that. All that matters is that he answers the recall."

The car made it to Osceola, and 57 turned into the train station's parking lot. 57 found a parking space and claimed it as Audrey unbuckled her seatbelt.

"Whatever happened," she said as she leaned forward, "917 is still your brother and an amborg. You need him back. I'm always going to be nosy but... it sounds like it might be time to listen to him and not push him into a corner. He'll only close himself off or fight back if that happens. You all have been through so much. The people that are probably the best ones to talk to him are the ones who've gone through similar experiences, right?"

117 and 57 remained silent, unable to form a response. Audrey got out of the car and 57 popped the trunk open. 117 stepped out to go around back. As they unloaded her bag from the back, Audrey hugged him.

"I am not ready," he said as he pressed the button to close the trunk.

"I know," she said playfully.

As the trunk closed, 117 turned and wrapped his arms around her.

"I love you," she said, tilting her head back for a kiss.

"My feelings for you remain unchanged," he replied as he leaned in, and their lips met.

"Really?"

57 had rolled down her window, watching them say their goodbyes.

"If Mandy was here," she shook her head, "she'd be making you say it."

"I was trying to be classy," 117 shrugged as Audrey giggled.

The two of them separated and Audrey grabbed her bag. She walked past the driver's side and waved to 57.

"Please be safe," she said. "Help keep an eye on him?"

"I'll do my best," 57 nodded.

Audrey turned and blew a kiss to 117.

"I do love you," he said, which made her smile.

"I know."

With her bag in her hand, she walked away from the car and headed towards the station. 117 got back in the car and buckled up. They watched Audrey disappear into the crowd before 57 shifted gears and prepared to leave.

"It never gets any easier, does it?" 117 sighed. "Saying goodbye?"

"All the more reason to motivate you to fight harder," 57 pointed at the station. "That. That right there is what you protect. Let's make sure that you both see each other again."

"You don't think we're actually going to have to fight our way into the prison? Will we?"

"Two amborgs with no backup and no support with a window of a few hours?" 57 did some quick thinking as they navigated through the parked cars. "It's possible but I think it should only be considered a worst-case scenario."

"Have you figured the success-fail rate?" 117 asked, doing his own calculations.

"If we fight to break him out," 57 replied. "I calculate less than 11%. Dr. Kendrick's suggestion of asking them is probably the peaceful way through this."

"Agreed," 117 nodded. "Let's go to prison."

Chapter 4: Nothing but the Truth

S.C.E. Firestar
Main Conference Chamber
Post-Battle Report Debriefing

"With the submission of your final testimony, you understand that failure to provide complete details from this moment on, you could be subjected to a disciplinary investigation if facts are omitted, altered, or changed?"

Captain Chastain inhaled, let it out through his nose, and nodded firmly.

"To keep to standard protocol," he replied, "I understand. As always."

He stood in front of a podium that was directly across from a long-curved table. Sitting there were 11 individuals all wearing formal uniforms. They weren't battle-dress uniforms like the one he wore. They were much cleaner and more formal. Their uniforms were a mix of grey, dark blue and silver. The only difference being that they were decorated as higher-ranking officials. Significantly higher ranks. This was the Admiralty board for the S.C.E. fleet. They would be responsible for reporting their findings of this debriefing to the S.C.E. council.

The spotlight shone brightly on the third person on his left. The logo of their organization and this admiral's name plate were on the left side of his chest. The bright light showed the two-tone colors of his jacket; the main fabric sections were dark gray while the accent areas were black. Like Chastain's uniform, the rank was displayed on the neck and along the shoulders. Maybe it was just him, but he preferred the olive-green color of his own uniform that the starship captains and commanders wore.

"Captain," this admiral said in a soft voice as he glanced down at a holo-pad. Without looking at him, he asked his question. "Although the mission was technically successful, your fleet was in quite a predicament. You could have lost two of your vessels."

"Objection."

To his right, Chastain heard the S.C.E. appointed military attorney speak up, cutting off the admiral.

"Admirals, that is a hypothetical assessment by Admiral Avalon," he declared in a strict and cold tone. "Captain Chastain's fleet did not lose the

S.C.E. Madison Marsh or a second unspecified vessel. No other vessel came close to being considered a loss."

"Sustained," a loud voice not at the curved table boomed across the entire room. "Admiral Avalon, rephrase your question."

Chastain turned to glance at his attorney, Davies, whose visor glowed red. He was partially blind in his left eye and had to wear a medical headset that allowed him to see clearly. If the light on the visor was shut off, Chastain would have thought that he was just wearing sunglasses indoors. Both quietly faced the admirals and awaited their word.

"Yes sir," Avalon cleared his throat. He set the data pad down, looked at Chastain properly and spoke again, "Even though your fleet did not sustain the loss of any of your ships, there were still casualties among the crew and personnel. It is the opinion of this board that you could have spent more time preparing for this operation. Do you think you could have prevented the number of casualties if you had allowed yourself more time to wait for reinforcements?"

"Objection!" Davies spoke again, causing Chastain to sigh.

He didn't like being interrupted, but when it came down to legal matters, who was he to argue with an educated lawyer? The legal advisors and officers trained in these matters weren't joking around.

"Hypothetical scenario. It has already been established by the council to avoid theories preventing the outcomes of past events."

"Sustained again," the loud voice spoke out again, this time more sternly, rattling the whole table. "Admiral Avalon, get to your point or we shall move on."

"Yes sir," Avalon dipped his head respectfully. "Captain Chastain, why did you proceed with the mission without amassing reinforcements with your fleet? Did you believe that the mission would be successful with what you had?"

"Yes, I did," Chastain replied, giving his answer calmly. "My own ship was already understaffed, undergoing repairs during our deployment, and as you can see from the testimonies of the other commanding officers within my fleet, we were all facing difficulties. I contest that if we had delayed any longer for our fleet readiness to be at a hundred percent, then the mission would have ended in failure. Besides, if we had delayed, wouldn't that have meant that we would have failed to carry out the operation in the time frame that we were given by the board of admirals? I'm pretty sure I stated in the record many weeks ago about my concerns. Did that by any chance come to light before this debriefing began or should we just start my court-martial?"

"Captain..." Davies muttered from the side under his breath, "don't give them any ideas."

The board of Admirals did look slightly uncomfortable and embarrassed at Chastain's response. Even though Davies was probably ready to pull his own hair out, Chastain confidently stood his ground. His wit was one of the reasons he still had his command.

He quickly glanced to the side to get a look at the other captains and commanders of his fleet who were attending this meeting. Everyone from his fleet were there, quietly observing the debriefing, except for Captain Desmond, who was still recovering from the battle. He and the Madison Marsh had survived, but it was that ship that carried the most casualties in the aftermath. He also saw Admiral Ra'aiah at the end glaring at him with crossed arms. Chastain merely smirked and faced the board again.

"I withdraw my question," Avalon responded quietly, and the spotlight on him shut off.

As he plunged into the shadows, the spotlight clicked on again on the next person.

"Actually," the admiral sitting next to him raised a finger, and she was illuminated, "I am curious. Captain Chastain, what was your motive for carrying out the mission despite your fleet's smaller-than-usual composition and complement of crew? Were you under any personal pressure or trying to rush things in order to carry out this mission?"

"Objection," Davies cut in, causing Chastain to keep his mouth shut. "Relevance to the mission?"

The admiral dipped her head and answered promptly.

"State of mind," she stated. "A commanding officer in charge of a vessel must always be putting the mission first. Otherwise, they must safeguard their ships, the lives of their crew, or lastly, themselves. I want to know what Captain Chastain was thinking before and during the encounter with the Tandeeri fleet."

"I allow the question," the voice thundered across the chamber again. "Captain Chastain, please answer."

"My state of mind..."

Chastain replied in a respectful tone. He glanced upwards.

"Judge," he said and then he lowered his gaze to face the admirals. "Admirals."

He made sure to choose his words carefully. He needed to be fast before Davies could chime in with another objection.

"I was not under any pressure to rush this mission," he stated. "I knew what was at stake and appearance-wise, it looked like something that a newly graduated cadet put together to present in their final exam back at the fleet academy. I carried things out the way I did with what I had available. That is the simple answer. I teach every single officer, cadet, and person aboard my vessel to understand that when we get underway, they could lose their lives in space. They risk themselves on every mission. Every operation assigned to us by high command is not an easy task. If it were easy, then we'd all be sitting safely in the confines of our homes without a care in the universe."

Chastain cleared his throat as the board listened intently.

"Most of the crew were inexperienced when we were assigned this mission," he continued. "My first officer, Riley, did an exemplary job when faced with her first taste of battle. Even understaffed, my department heads came together, and we needed that pressure to help motivate us to fight for our survival as well as the success of the mission. I firmly believe that if I had waited to staff my ship completely, or waited for more ships to join us, then we would have had more casualties or more hands to hold. Davies, don't object, I know you're going to say it's a hypothetical statement."

Chastain had lifted his hand to Davies, who had opened his mouth. At his signal, he stayed quiet as Chastain turned to face the board again.

"At some point, every person aboard a starship needs to learn that if they don't do their job or carry out their tasks, they will die," he stated. "My ship was struggling to stay together physically but because we had such high stakes, my crew performed admirably. We made sure to motivate ourselves in the circumstances we had to get the job done. For those that weren't lost and the lives that we saved, they definitely earned their wings and stripes."

"Any other questions? Admiral Gina?"

Admiral Gina looked up when the loud voice addressed her. She had maintained a neutral expression during Chastain's explanation, but now her lip curled slightly. She nodded with a hint of satisfaction as she answered the voice of the judge presiding over them.

"No sir," she answered as she placed her right hand over her chest.

Just before the spotlight shut off, Chastain grinned. Not only had she made that subtle hand gesture to signal that she was done with her line of questioning, he noticed that it was also a silent declaration of respect to him. She couldn't say it out loud, as it would reveal her personal opinion. The board always needed to remain unbiased. Admiral Gina, at least, was telling

Chastain discreetly that she respected his decisions. Her silhouette was all that remained when the light shut off. A few seats away, the light came on again and everyone listened to the next admiral.

"Since you brought it up, this was going to be my next question anyway," she announced. "You stated in your report that you violated S.C.E. protocol and ordered Lieutenant-Commander Riley off the bridge. Why did you disobey regulation?"

Chastain paused for a moment. No objection from Davies. Wonderful! He was allowed to talk.

"It was in the interest of carrying out the mission," Chastain replied with a firm nod. "Riley is a close friend of the asset Serina 43. I believed that before we sent her over into an alternate universe alone, a friendly face would be a pleasant sight to see just in case we didn't make it."

"That sounds like a particularly grim perspective. Unnecessary as well."

"A familiar face, whether it be a friend or a loved one," Chastain answered with a twitch of his eye. "They are a reminder as to why we fight. Who or what we fight for matters. If I'm about to die, I think about my wife. I see her expression and her smile whenever my ship is about to fall under attack. It certainly makes me want to fight harder than thinking about a Kalorian Pigma."

Before the admiral could protest, the one sitting next to him cleared his throat and the spotlight moved to him.

"To steer the matter back on track," he said, an amused expression on his face. It appeared that Chastain's little slice of humor hit appropriately. "I think what Admiral Lisa is hinting at is... why would you praise Commander Riley's actions as 'exemplary' when she wasn't even aboard the bridge and assisting your command in the battle? The reason why you went against standard protocol is, in my opinion, acceptable. But it's just interesting how someone would earn your praise when they actually had nothing to do with the overall conflict."

"I disagree, Admiral Bokasc," Captain Chastain spoke up. "Riley was the most important part of the battle. She was aboard my ship and with our fleet in the middle of a high-stakes mission. Her actions led to a mission success. I'm sure that the board will find that fact to be the reason why we are here celebrating instead of feeling demoralized."

"To send your first officer off the bridge is still risky, even if you were attempting to favor sentiment."

Chastain stared at Lisa and sighed.

"I've known you ever since you first commanded a starship, Lisa. Same with almost everyone in this room. I still firmly believe I chose the option that would give us the best outcome for the mission. Riley oversaw the delivery of the asset personally, and Serina 43 got to say goodbye to a friend and gain a reminder as to why we're fighting this war."

Admiral Lisa glanced at the admiral who had interrupted. He merely put his hands on the table and lowered his head. The spotlight on him shut off and Lisa glanced at Chastain.

"No more questions," she stated.

"So, Riley's actions are to be commended?" Chastain asked for clarification.

"That may be true but…"

Oh great. Chastain exhaled once more. *What else were they going to criticize him for now?* He turned to look at the next person sitting in the center as the spotlight turned back on.

"…there is the matter of you failing to send Serina 43 without any assistance."

"Pardon me Admiral Joola."

Another admiral interrupted by raising his hand, signaling for Davies to remain quiet. The admiral's face was illuminated in the dimly lit room, commanding everyone's attention.

"I think we can all agree that the decision to send 43 to the Epsilon universe was successful, yes?"

The rest of the admirals on the board began to murmur, but from what Chastain was able to hear as they all deliberated among themselves, it sounded pretty good. Admiral Joola, who was the only other person who had the floor, nodded in agreement.

Admiral Hamman smiled when he saw that the rest of them agreed.

"After reviewing the footage, data, and the testimonies of the Expeditionary Fleet's fighter pilots and the squadron leaders," he explained, "it appears that tactically, having every ship flying to divert enemy fire away from Serina 43 led to her escaping the battle unharmed."

"I can agree that the mission was a success," Admiral Joola's large blue eyes blinked as he crossed all four of his arms. His orange skin seemed to turn bright red, likely from embarrassment. "What I am concerned with is how the inhabitants of Epsilon will react."

Admiral Joola leaned forward and pointed his finger at the table.

"Captain Chastain separated the shuttles carrying Serina 43's escort away from her to prevent the enemy from shooting her down," he said, doing a small recap to stay on topic. "This accomplished the objective. But was it a wise decision to send her into an entirely different universe without extra supplies or protection? When she reveals herself to them or if they discover her, what are the chances that the Epsilon universe will decide to keep her alive long enough to deliver our message? What's to prevent them from hurting or killing her?"

"Admiral Joola," the echoing voice of the judge spoke across the room. "From a certain point of view, your questions center towards hypothetical scenarios. Rephrase your questions."

"Judge? If I may?"

The spotlight revealed Admiral Lisa again. Chastain looked at Hamman, Joola, and her now steering the discussion away from him.

"Serina 43 is highly trained and skilled," Admiral Lisa pointed out. "She is an amborg. She will appear to them as human, and we must put our faith in her. For many years, she was taught how to survive on her own without an escort or extra supplies. Now that she has crossed the threshold of our very universes, we should focus on our efforts here more than ever while she carries out the next part of the mission."

"Surely," Hamman stated to Admiral Joola, "an amborg can carry out this mission. Wouldn't you agree, Admiral Joola?"

Joola didn't answer. Chastain glanced at the table and turned an eye towards Davies. Was the awkward silence good or bad? The person sitting next to Admiral Joola cleared her throat. A fourth light switched on and illuminated the woman sitting there.

"If there are no further questions," she stated, "then I believe we can conclude this debriefing."

The entire admiralty board was suddenly bathed in bright light, making everything completely visible. Captain Chastain noticed 11 admirals now looking right at him, and stood up straighter.

"For the record, this is First Admiral Leahy of the S.C.E. Admiralty Board. This debriefing and review of the Fourth Expeditionary Reconnaissance Fleet's actions on July 7th of the recent battle of Sector 0068 is officially declared as a success. While initial findings did raise a few valid concerns..."

Right, valid. Captain Chastain almost wanted to cut them off, but knew that would be the wrong thing to do. Davies would blow a gasket if he opened his mouth.

"...Captain Chastain, commanding officer of the S.C.E. Alexandria, lead ship of this operation, has demonstrated quick-thinking under pressure and this led to a satisfactory victory with minimal casualties. It will be noted that despite repeated acts of eccentric behavior, Chastain brings forth methods of improvisations and off-the-book tactics that prevented any further loss of life. After the final vote, the board of Admirals would like to send out commendations and citations to those that performed admirably in the line of duty. All rise."

Someone yelled across the room.

"Attention!"

Chastain stood at attention, his posture becoming rigid. Beside him, he heard Davies snap his feet together, mirroring Chastain's stance. From the left, the captains of his fleet and Admiral Ra'aiah followed suit, rising from their seats and joining in the show of respect. In perfect synchronization, they all saluted the admirals, who returned the gesture with equal formality.

"Captain Chastain, arrangements for your fleet have been sent to your executive officers," the booming voice spoke over them again. "Please enjoy some well-earned time off. Your entire crew is given one week's leave. Bring your ships into port for your commendation ceremony. We shall begin repairs straight away as you begin your break."

"Yes, your honor," Chastain answered. "Thank you judge."

Everyone lowered their arms.

"Dismissed!"

The image in front of Chastain dissolved as a projector shut down. The admirals and the table before them vanished from sight. The conference room lights flickered on, illuminating the space once more, and everyone began to readjust to the normal lighting. *Why did all the debriefings have to be done with a dark background? Something about that has always felt ominous.* Chastain blinked a few times, allowing his eyes to adapt to the new brightness. The few admirals that stayed on the line waved to him.

"Captain Chastain," Admiral Avalon cleared his throat. "A word please?"

He politely stepped around his podium and up to the holographic images of those that were still in the conference call.

"Well, that never gets old," he snickered. "It's always fun when they hang up the call. Something about your images dissolving into nothing is so satisfying."

"Remind me again," Admiral Gina looked at the others. "Why did we vote in his favor?"

"Because let's face it," Chastain chuckled. "You kids actually care about me. And thank you Gina for looking out for my state of mind. It's more than..."

Chastain snuck a glance over his shoulder. Admiral Ra'aiah was talking to Captain Mo'lahk.

"...a certain someone else who recently got promoted to admiral is doing," he finished as he faced the others.

"We just want you to know that it wasn't supposed to sound that harsh," Admiral Lisa explained. "Even though we did question or bring up concerns... we didn't want to make it seem like we were humiliating you."

"To be fair," Chastain answered as he smiled warmly at Lisa. "I embarrassed and humiliated you when I taught you how to fly starships. Now that you all outrank me, I totally understand your need to kiss asses and keep climbing the ladder."

"If you just stuck to protocol," Avalon sighed. "You would be on the board of admirals. Let us recommend you again to join us here."

"I belong on the bridge of my ship," Chastain replied. "What was the one piece of advice I taught your classroom when you graduated from command class?"

"Don't let them promote you," Gina stated. "Don't let them plant you at a desk."

"Don't let them retire you," Avalon muttered as he added the next segment. "Don't let them transfer you."

"Don't let them do anything that takes you off the bridge of your ship," Lisa finished.

"Look at that," Chastain shook his head and let out a laugh. "You and half of this table ignored me spectacularly. Why? What were you all thinking when you left your ships and basically sentenced them to die without you there to protect them?"

"Sometimes, an admiral has more privileges than a captain."

Chastain turned and grinned when he saw a familiar face. Admiral Ra'aiah appeared next to him, joining the conversation.

"Is it alright if I talk to him, in private?" Admiral Ra'aiah glanced at the other three.

All of them nodded.

"Good luck sir," Avalon said, and his image faded from view.

"We'll call again," Lisa said as she waved goodbye. "Have a good shore leave."

"I'll be sure to prioritize your fleet repairs," Gina dipped her head politely. "It's the least I can do for you, sir."

As the three admirals disappeared from view, the sound of footsteps could be heard approaching as someone else joined in.

"Sir, with all due respect," Davies groaned, "I don't think many of them appreciate your acerbic wit."

Chastain smirked.

"How else am I going to stand out from all those textbook desk-jockeys?"

"I unfortunately agree with your attorney," Admiral Ra'aiah didn't look amused. "You're dismissed Lieutenant Davies. If there's any paperwork to sign or whatever... send it to me and I'll annotate it."

"Yes admiral," he answered quickly and walked away.

"Whatever happened to saluting a superior officer?"

Admiral Ra'aiah crossed her arms as she looked up at him. He merely snickered as he kept his hands at his side in clear defiance of the rules.

"Oh, I'm sorry," Chastain smiled. "I'm afraid my shoulder seems to have cramped up from being a kiss ass."

"And if you took things more seriously, those three would be right and you would be an admiral by now," she replied angrily. "You could be on the board and making more of a difference if you stopped playing around! Why can't you use those skills of yours and build a bigger influence?"

"Now now," Chastain couldn't help but chuckle a little, which seemed to aggravate her even more. "Don't be so angry. It's not good for your complexion."

Before he could hear her response, he began to leave the conference room without asking for permission to be dismissed, knowing that this would most likely rile her up.

"As you were," he heard her say to the others still mingling. A moment later, he heard her footsteps growing louder as she chased after him. "Don't you walk away old man! We're not done here!"

"Well of course not," Chastain said nonchalantly as he continued walking. He headed towards the nearest hall with windows that would give him a view out into space. "That's why I'm leading you away from the crowd so that we can have a nice family chat."

"I outrank you captain!"

"And you're doing such a wonderful job," he said sarcastically. "Thanks for the reminder but really, is this any way to treat your godfather?"

"When we're on duty, we have to keep things professional."

Chastain finally turned around as she continued to grumble. Things like rank didn't concern him. Even if they weren't blood-related, every time he looked at Ra'aiah, he felt happy to be in the presence of family. Now she was all grown up and he still wasn't sure if he approved of that technicality.

"I really doubt it's that big of a secret," Chastain said as a few crewmembers walked by. "Considering that everyone knows who your parents are. What's wrong with being open about our family ties?"

"You may be one of my father's closest friends," she said, pointing a finger at his chin. "But we are not here for a family reunion, Uncle! There are a lot of things at stake here!"

"You've turned into quite a stick in the mud ever since you got promoted," he sighed with a sad look in his eyes. "They give you the flagship of the fleet and suddenly, you're no fun anymore. I mean, in comparison to the other admirals at command, I'm glad you're still in charge of a starship. But why such a big one? You compensating for something that I don't know about?"

"Stop that," Ra'aiah snapped at him. She almost looked like she was pouting. "I still have fun and I am not compensating."

There we go. Chastain was laughing internally. That little annoyed child-like tone was what he was listening for.

"Oh yeah? What happened to your boyfriend?"

"Ex-boyfriend," Admiral Ra'aiah furiously muttered through gritted teeth as her fists clenched. "He was 52 and still living with his mother."

"Well, he's Keellavokian," Chastain replied casually. "Their parents are quite attached to their young. I'm surprised you even started dating one. Quite a bold decision if you want my opinion about it. Oh wait, that's right, I did give you my opinion back then and what was that you said? Right, you said you were fine."

"It was an unhealthy and disturbing attachment. He took me out three times and apparently that was how we got engaged," she let out an aggravated sigh. He could hear how stressed out she was. "We broke it off when his father tried kidnapping me. That's the last time I take my parent's advice and post on a dating app."

"Your mom and dad just want to see you doing well in many aspects of your life," Chastain patted her on the shoulder.

"I have told them and you repeatedly that I'm fine," she shrugged his hand away. "It's not like either of them were tripping over themselves to try and rescue me at the time."

"Maybe it's because you keep saying you're fine but you're actually not?"

Chastain held up his hands in surrender when she glared at him again. He laughed as he backed away.

"Oh, come on, that was funny."

"I just don't understand why you can't be serious enough at your job to want to move on… away from starship duty," she said as she shook her head. "What if I'm not there to help you the next time? This is war. You and your crew need all the help you can get. I don't understand why you didn't wait for us to reinforce you before you ran off to carry out the mission. We were supposed to be in this together."

"Because if you always follow the rules exactly as they tell you or if you wait too long, then your shot will be gone."

He looked out the window and saw the S.C.E. Alexandria flying alongside them. There were several small ships and crew out on the deck in spacesuits patching up the outer hull before they would begin the trip to the nearest port.

"I do understand what's at stake here," he explained, "and it makes me afraid. But I have my sense of humor and spirit to make sure that if it's my time, then I'll happily accept it. Especially if it means that people who can't fight can live to see the universe just a little longer. What good am I sitting at a desk if the war goes badly for us? Hmm?"

Admiral Ra'aiah was about to say something again, but everything flew out of her head as she stood next to him. The two of them watched the Alexandria as the fleet maintained its course.

"The stars are quite pretty, aren't they?"

"Uncle," she said, "They always look like that…"

Chastain turned and smiled at Ra'aiah again.

"You can't get this kind of view if they promote you and put you at a desk," he said cheekily. "Now you want some real advice? You are in command of one hell of a ship. It's modern and new, just like you. If sitting on a seat on the bridge is what makes you happy, then don't leave. You make more of a difference commanding thousands out here... than from a dull office on a planet with gravity."

Admiral Ra'aiah gazed out at the stars to try and see if she could also spot what it was that caught Chastain's eye. Space was unpredictable, and if you underestimated that, it was lethal. Yet, he seemed right at home out here in space.

"Uncle, I heard a rumor," she said softly.

"Oh? What is it?"

"High command wants to merge your fleet with mine," Admiral Ra'aiah explained. "They'll prioritize your fleet's repairs but once they're ready, you'll be under my command for the next phase of the mission. I know they'll send you the orders... but I wanted to let you know that's what I heard."

So the Fourth Expeditionary Reconnaissance Fleet would be reassigned? That sounded exciting.

"Well," Chastain nodded his head. "If I'm relinquishing my fleet command, I'm glad that it's to you. At least I trained you and everyone else well. They could have saddled me with some greenhorn fresh from the Academy and we'd all be screwed."

"You would have been screwed if I hadn't gotten to you in time," Admiral Ra'aiah stated.

"I'm glad you did," Captain Chastain smiled in relief. "I'm just happy you still care about me."

Admiral Ra'aiah sighed as she continued to stare at the stars.

"Even with your shore leave coming up," she said, "home is still a long way out. We might not be back for a while again."

"Ha, everything I need is right here," Chastain beamed happily.

"I have supplies or materials that I could send you if the Alexandria needs assistance."

"Not what I meant but... close enough."

Chapter 5: Extreme Amborg Solitude

Fulton Federal Penitentiary
Madisonburg, Pennsylvania
Emergency Recall plus 3 hours 16 minutes
5:23 PM Eastern Time

"Attention inmate, you are being summoned. Please stand up on the marker."

The pleasant sound of the prison A.I.'s voice grabbed 917's attention. He had been looking through the small quadruple reinforced two by two window out into the courtyard when the announcement echoed in his cell. He turned around and saw the light shining on the center of the floor glow and begin to pulse.

917 moved away from the window and walked towards the middle of the room. Once he stepped onto the circular light, the pulsing stopped, and the color turned green.

"Please stand still. Beginning confirmation scan."

"You know... I haven't left this cell in three months. I'm pretty sure I can save you the trouble and just tell you that it's still me..."

There was a whirring noise as the floor sensor switched on.

"Scanning. Error. Scanning. Inmate confirmed. Please remain in the circle. The doors will open momentarily. Do not step off the sensor or you will be disciplined."

917 crossed his arms. The A.I. spoke again.

"Please uncross your arms and stand still. Otherwise, you will be treated as hostile for failure to comply."

"I can see that new upgrade in your system is working," 917 chuckled softly as he let his arms drop to his side. "As long as you don't say what my weight is out loud, I will comply."

917 fixed his eyes on the cell door and within moments, there was a loud pounding from the other side. The noise was deafening. 917 could feel the vibrations reverberating all throughout the walls, which probably would have scared a deaf person awake. He stared coldly at the door as he heard the locks

opening. There were several loud clicks and he heard hydraulic pistons firing in a sequential order. After another minute of this, it became quiet, until there was another loud bang. He heard the machinery in the walls begin to come to life and the cell door started to swing open. The five-ton weighted steel door opened at a snail's pace as he waited to see who would be greeting him.

Standing in the entrance was an enormously muscular guard. In his hands, he wielded a nine-millimeter standard issue and a steel rod. 917 focused on the guard, and a smile suddenly broke out across his face. The prison A.I. spoke again.

"Please follow the guard. You may now step out of the circle. You have been cleared to leave your holding cell."

The light in the circle switched off and 917 stepped forward. The guard moved to the side and let 917 come out.

"Keep your hands up where we can see you," he instructed.

"Opening my cell with your weapons ready is dangerous," 917 spoke aloud as he walked out of the cell. "Everyone might get the wrong idea, Dawson."

"Sorry sir," Dawson replied as he holstered his gun. "Procedure. You are a maximum level prisoner."

Once he was outside of the cell, he noticed four lasers trained on his chest. With a casual glance, 917 spotted two sentry guns on the walls, poised to fire at him. There were a couple of security drones aiming their weapons at him as well. Dawson waved at them, and the lasers deactivated, and the automated weapons switched off.

917 walked down the hallway with Dawson trailing him closely. The sound of clanking metal footsteps echoed from behind, signaling the drones following them. Looking ahead, 917 saw two other heavily armored guards stationed at the end of the hall, flanked by another pair of security drones.

"You guys are doing a good job," 917 stated as they began walking at a slow pace. "So, what's going on? Who's here to see me now?"

"Warden said to get you out as soon as possible," Dawson answered. "Someone's here to get you."

"Get me?" 917 asked as they stopped before the checkpoint.

The guards and the drones scanned 917 and Dawson. After a quick check, they were allowed to step through the door into another passageway. The door hissed open, and they both stepped through. The drones didn't follow, remaining in the maximum-security wing.

"Do you know who it is?" 917 asked as they followed the signs lining the upper parts of the walls.

"Must be someone important," Dawson muttered in a soft register. "All I can say is, whatever's going on, the warden seems on edge about something."

"How interesting," 917 replied, also lowering his voice.

917 had the entire layout of the prison memorized. He knew what path they were heading down, even with Dawson escorting him. Normally, prisoners had to be handled by the guards, using force to control them in a certain way. In this case, 917 cooperated and Dawson respectfully kept his hands to himself.

After they passed through a few more winding corridors, they made it to a small rail system. It was the exit to this building. Functioning like a miniature subway, Dawson and 917 waited as they saw a roofless cart making its way to the station. Once it came to a complete stop, the doors slid open and the two of them climbed aboard. As they got situated, the doors closed. Once secured, the motor revved up and the cart departed the station. The tracks took them through a tunnel, and they started coasting at a moderate pace.

"Are you sure I'm getting out?" 917 asked. "You sure this isn't some sort of prank?"

"No sir," Dawson replied. "I think this is the real deal."

917 turned to glance back at Dawson, who appeared to be serious, but sensed an underlying uncertainty. Looking closely, he noticed that Dawson was sweating a bit. There was definitely something that had him acting more nervous than usual.

"The warden?" 917 asked for confirmation.

"The warden," Dawson nodded firmly.

"Well then Dawson," 917 faced forward. "If I am getting out... for real, then I guess I won't be back for a while."

A meeting by the warden himself was a big deal. It was rare for him to have personal meetings with prisoners.

The cart slowed down and exited the tunnel. Along the walls, 917 could see a large number one appearing. Their ride had entered building one, which was outboarding and processing, and where the warden's main office was located. The main visitor's area was stationed on the lower floors.

Once the cart came to a stop and opened its doors, 917 and Dawson stepped off and began to leave the station. 917 made to turn left, but Dawson cleared his throat.

"Uh, this way sir,"

"Outboarding is this way Dawson," 917 gestured towards the elevators.

"Sorry sir," Dawson said, gently placing a hand on 917's shoulder. "Two VIPs want to meet before you see the warden."

917 raised an eyebrow. Dawson appeared quite insistent, so he let out a sigh and turned around to walk in the other direction. This didn't seem right. The warden and Dawson were the only two individuals in the prison that knew who he really was. If Dr. Kendrick was trying to signal the emergency recall from A.I. Industries, shouldn't they be expediting his release instead? Who was it that had decided to pay him a visit? Unless...

This isn't just a visit. 917 rolled his eyes. *It better not be who I think it is.*

917 and Dawson reached a door and stood in front of it. It was a casual interrogation room. It was referred to as "casual" because these kinds of rooms were often used by the parole boards or criminal investigators for final rulings.

"Oh, come on," 917 turned to look at Dawson. "You got me out of my cell, and I have to do this??"

"Sir," Dawson stated, "you have to follow the exact procedures."

"I can't sit through hours of deliberation by some investigators," 917 replied, clearly agitated. "Don't make me go in there!"

"Believe me," Dawson said, looking desperate. "The sooner you go in there and talk this out, the sooner you can leave."

Dawson casually glanced over his shoulder. He opened the door so that he could push 917 inside.

"What do I do if it all goes downhill here?" he asked quietly.

917 looked at Dawson and sighed.

"There hasn't been an incident in about three years," 917 stated. "So just ride it out here, keep your head down, and count the days until you get transferred."

"I doubt the warden will approve it," Dawson muttered as he backed away from the door.

917 turned to face Dawson politely. Even though this particular action didn't sit well with him, 917 still wanted to express his gratitude to his friend. Both men dipped their heads respectfully to each other as they said their goodbyes.

"He will," 917 nodded. "I'll make sure of it. So, in the meantime, just for appearances, I'm sorry for all the times I punched you."

"Wait... you're not serious," Dawson cowered a little as he gazed fearfully at 917. "Are you going to break my nose again?"

"Actually, I was saying that you should punch me," 917 cleared his throat. "Just make it look good."

"I've never been comfortable fighting you sir," Dawson sighed, his eyes darting around anxiously.

"It's just a show," 917 said with a disappointed expression. He started to shake his head and began criticizing. "And also, if you're trying to transfer to the Pennsylvania police department, you got to take some initiative. You want to be here babysitting the rest of your life? Or do you want to get the guts to be tougher? You got to fight to get ahead to where you want to... Gah!!"

917 suddenly felt Dawson's fist connect with his face, interrupting him mid sentence. He pivoted to the right as his left cheek took a massive blow from the guard. It didn't actually cause any kind of pain or injury, thanks to the protection of his cybernetics. While he couldn't help but feel a sense of pride for Dawson's surprise attack, 917 also felt a bit annoyed at being interrupted while in the middle of talking. Still, his punch had successfully caught him off guard, and that rarely happened.

"Are you ok?" Dawson asked, clenching both fists.

"Was that even a punch?" 917 asked, straightening up. "That felt like 15% of your strength..."

Based on the amount of force that he knew that Dawson was capable of, it definitely didn't feel like he had put all of his power into it. The amborgs had excellent accuracy when measuring out someone's strength.

"I'm sorry sir," Dawson shrugged. "I see you as a friend more than an enemy. I can't motivate myself to really punch you."

"Ok, well do it right this time," 917 groaned. He motioned and pointed at his core. "Hit me in the stomach twice. Use both fists and give me a combo."

"If I do that," Dawson nodded at his instructions and raised his arms again. "There's something I've always wanted to know. Ever since I was assigned to look after your cellblock. How is someone as nice as you in maximum security?"

It was a question that unfortunately, 917 wasn't allowed to directly answer. Dawson couldn't know.

"You know? I get that a lot," 917 replied casually. "It's above your pay grade but... let's just stick with the short version. I broke some rules, and I got in trouble for it. You get the full version if you make it as a police officer for Pennsylvania. I'll be in touch."

Dawson still seemed perplexed at this response. It didn't fully satisfy his curiosity, but what else were they going to do? He quickly lunged forward and with his right fist, delivered a huge punch into 917's stomach and followed with another blow from his left.

Unhurt, 917 keeled forward and measured the force from the punches. There was much more power put into each one, and he was pleased with the results in comparison to when he was hit in the face.

"Ok," 917 reported calmly as he slowly stood straight again. "Much better. I'll see you around Dawson. Tell your family I said hi."

"Thank you, sir," Dawson replied, leaning over and pressing the door control. "Good luck."

As it hissed closed, 917 nodded and gave him a smile.

"Take the day off tomorrow," he instructed. "I think it would be best to call out."

"Uh. If you say so?"

That was all that Dawson was able to say before the door slammed shut. 917 turned around and examined the room he was in.

In the middle of the room stood a long steel table, firmly bolted to the floor. There was a single chair on his end and two on the opposite side. The idea was for the prisoner to take the lone chair while a lawyer or prosecutor would sit on the far end. Over in the corner on the left was a security booth for prison guards to keep an eye on things. A long, dark-tinted window stretched along one wall, hinting that someone might be watching him from the other side. To the right, there was a large booth protected by bullet-proof glass, featuring nine seats. The whole place felt eerily empty, leaving 917 puzzled.

"So how are we doing this?" he asked out loud, directing his attention to the dark window. "What is this?"

A door on the other side of the room opened, revealing a man dressed in a sharp business suit. As he entered, the door closed behind him, and he gave a quick greeting. 917 recognized him immediately the moment he walked in. It was the warden.

"You can speak freely now," he said. "This room is free of guards, and no one is on the other side of that window."

The warden gestured at all the empty seats. 917 glanced at the cameras in each corner of the room and noticed that the red lights on each one of them were switched off. He saw himself and the warden in the reflection of the lenses. Adjusting his vision, he enhanced the scanner and glanced at the other side of the room at the tinted window. There was no one in there. When he was confident that they weren't being watched, 917 nodded and walked forward.

"So, what's going on outside?" he asked. "I assume Dr. Kendrick called?"

The warden nodded. He pointed at the table.

"Yeah, he did," he stated. "Emergency recall. He's initiated a priority one message to all amborgs. If you would, please take a seat, Jack."

"Sit down? Why? I received an emergency recall which I couldn't answer because I was in prison and in the public eye, it's illegal to break out," 917 shook his head. He remained in the same spot, refusing to budge. "Now under the agreement that you, Dr. Kendrick, and I established four years ago, this directive overrules and expedites a discreet and immediate release. My status should now be reactivated. Therefore, I must leave. Is he here?"

"Dr. Kendrick?" the warden replied as he crossed his arms. "No. He seemed a little busy, with how fast he called and hung up on me before I could even say, 'how's it going?' All he told me was that he needs you back."

"That's all?" 917 raised an eyebrow. "Are you sure, Kenny? Well then what are we waiting for?"

"As much as I do want to obey Dr. Kendrick's orders, I can't do anything just yet," Kenny scratched his eyebrow. "He did send for you but... they... how do I put this? They want to talk to you first."

"And... who exactly is here to speak with me?"

917 looked at Kenny suspiciously. Who had convinced him, the man overseeing this prison, to comply with their demands over Dr. Kendrick's orders? He was already beginning to feel like he knew who it was.

"Look," Kenny held up his hands. "I'll go get them right now. I don't want any trouble. They said before I let you go, they wanted to catch up first. Under no circumstances am I to allow you to go back to your cell. And they also didn't want me to let you leave until they talked to you."

"I guess it seems like I have very few options when you put it that way."

917 let out a sigh and stepped towards the chair.

"Looks like freedom will have to wait," he said as he grabbed the chair.

Kenny watched as 917 gave in and took a seat at the table. An automated voice spoke through the speaker system. A sign descended from the ceiling, displaying the words in multiple languages for them to read.

"Please keep your hands in sight and on the table at all times," the announcement said.

Once he was perfectly still, 917 raised his arms up for the warden to see. He then gently placed them on the table and relaxed. When he saw that he was ready, Kenny nodded and turned to leave.

"Oh, I have one thing to say, if you are leaving this prison."

917 glanced at Kenny, who was halfway out the door. He hesitated, one hand on the doorknob, and looked back.

"Only if you agree to transfer Dawson out," 917 spoke quickly.

"Will you please stop encouraging my guards to leave this job?"

A look of annoyance crossed Kenny's face, while 917 grinned.

"Dawson doesn't want to do this for the rest of his life," he declared. "You let him go to Pennsylvania PD and he will be much happier. He's not built for this place."

"I'll... get on that," Kenny lowered his head in defeat. "Look, just be careful out there alright? Whatever's going on doesn't seem good."

"If it involves us," 917 said, "Then it's definitely not your area of expertise."

"Just watch your back," Kenny said. "You had mine when you got here. Once you get out there, I can't do that anymore. So, this is goodbye."

917 nodded. Kenny gave him one last solemn look before he stepped out and shut the door. Both men silently waved each other off without another word. 917 sat in silence, deep in thought as he waited to see who would come to speak with him next. Hopefully, this would be quick.

Moments later, the door opened again, catching 917's attention. He perked up slightly at the two familiar faces entering the room. Now it made sense.

"David 117 and Katie 57," he let out a small laugh. "I guess the secret's out."

117 and 57 walked up to the table and took a seat. 117 smiled gently.

"You know, it feels really strange to see you on the other side of the table."

"Likewise," 917 shrugged. "I wasn't expecting the two of you to be interrogating me."

57 and 117's eyes widened. They quickly snuck a glance at each other and held up their hands defensively.

"This is not an interrogation," 117 clarified. He paused, bit his lower lip, and then fully turned his head to 57. "Right?"

"That is what we agreed on," she nodded reassuringly. "An actual interrogation would not be a pleasant sight."

917 stared at his friends. *Could this conversation get any more awkward?*

"Ok then," he said, holding up his hands, then let them hit the table. "Why are we still sitting here then? When we need to get back? If we're in a hurry, shouldn't we speed this up?"

"Interesting," 117 observed carefully. "So, you are curious about the recall."

"Well 117, I wasn't exactly in a position where I could just walk out of my cell," 917 replied. "If Dr. Kendrick wanted me out of here, then it must be bad out there."

"Look," 57 said as she pulled a folder out of a bag that she had carried in. "Dr. Kendrick ordered us to bring you back and to ask for your release from prison. Although we are trying to do this in a timely manner, it doesn't mean that we can't have some time to catch up. He did technically give us a certain number of days to get you home."

917 pointed a finger straight up at the ceiling.

"Catch up? Just like that? So casual? And you thought that prison would be the best place to do this?"

917 raised an eyebrow as 117 and 57 exchanged glances. They faced him again and nodded simultaneously.

"We just wanted to ask you a few questions," 57 stated as she placed the folder on the table, leaving it closed.

"Can I ask why you're carrying around a paper folder?" 917 eyed it suspiciously. "Pretty old-fashioned if you ask me."

57 had had the folder hidden inside her travel bag ever since she left A.I. Industries. It was small enough and was easy to keep safe. The fact that it was printed on an actual physical sheet of paper was what got 917's attention. It also added more of an explanation to how serious this was. Paper documents being hand delivered to certain recipients meant that someone was trying to avoid it spreading on the internet. Whatever was in the folder was not meant for the public eye.

"I already know what's in it," 117 eagerly raised his hand with a casual grin. "She's kept it sealed the entire trip here for you."

"I'm honored..." 917 sighed. "And I assume that until you get answers, you're not going to tell me what's in it?"

"Well, you've been gone for almost four years," 117 said. "And it turns out, you've been here that entire time. Do you want to talk about it?"

"It's complicated," 917 replied.

117 looked at 57. She didn't take her eyes off 917 and stated her question.

"Do you think that you deserve to be in here?" she asked.

"Yes, I do," 917 answered with a firm nod.

117 and 57 didn't seem convinced. It didn't sound right at all.

"We've seen the records that they cooked up for you in this place," 117 said as he pulled up the prison database on his wrist bracelet and scrolled through the information. "The warden has you labeled as a dangerous inmate, but you don't exactly exhibit the behavior of one."

"I'm in maximum security because those are the only cells in this prison designed to hold people like us," 917 explained. "Otherwise, anyone with an enhanced prosthetic could easily break out. I know you're going to keep asking why I'm here so let me save you the trouble. You've heard the rumors, right?"

"Well," 57 said, turning her eyes up to think. "There's a lot of them."

"You should know that Dr. Kendrick never exiled or banished me," 917 stated as he let out a sigh. "But I had to be punished for taking matters into my own hands. Angel and I weren't doing too well emotionally after Brazil. So, everyone encouraged us to go on less missions and spend some time recovering. That's when I went to a town called Silhed."

This sounded familiar to the both of them. 117 remembered seeing the name of this place on the news.

"Silhed?" 117 asked in confirmation. "You convinced Dr. Kendrick to approve Project Silhed a month before you left. A.I. Industries sponsored reconstruction and renovation projects there."

"It never came to light because that town was destroyed," 57 recalled what the news footage had claimed. "You were there?"

"I was," 917 nodded as he looked down at the table. "Silhed was just outside of Athens, Ohio. It was a nice community. Everyone knew each other there. It was the kind of place to go if you wanted time off or a place to hide away from your problems temporarily. That was before it got taken out."

917 didn't look at either of them, choosing to stare at his palms instead. 57 and 117 saw that he was twiddling his thumbs and shifting uncomfortably in his seat.

"The Cypress syndicate came in and tried to take it over. Silhed refused to relinquish control. I wasn't there when it happened. By the time that I made it, everything was destroyed. Everyone was killed. There were kids, babies, and teenagers that hadn't even gotten a chance to live a full life. There were retired grandparents and senior citizens. Families. Parents. Cypress killed every one of them. All these gangs that can't take no for an answer pissed me off."

"Did you report this?" 117 asked.

"Of course I did," 917 said softly. "But no one was going to do anything about it. When I got a distress beacon, I responded but it was too late. Cypress covered their tracks well, but I figured out that they were responsible. I never got approval for the mission. Dr. Kendrick told me he wouldn't sign off on it. Something about the Cypress syndicate having the Ohio state government by their throats. No one could intervene."

"And then you decided to proceed anyway," 57 nodded in understanding.

"Are you comfortable with sharing what happened after?" 117 asked gently.

"I went after them," 917 declared, looking remorseful. "I went to their base, and I took them down myself. I did exactly what they did to Silhed and I destroyed them. If I hadn't, they would have hit another innocent community. I went back and accepted punishment. Dr. Kendrick was not exactly in the best mood."

117 and 57 remained silent, processing 917's words. 57 remembered they were still on a time crunch, so she cleared her throat and asked in a soft tone, "Why didn't you come to us? Any of us?"

"Because if I had," 917 replied. "You would have all followed orders and tried to stop me."

"We probably would have," 117 said, but even as he said it, he didn't feel entirely certain about his own words.

917's retaliation hit him deep in his own feelings. He recognized that same rage and thirst for destruction. It had happened to him before. When Serina 43 was fatally injured many years ago, he experienced a flood of intense negative emotions. Fortunately, everyone had been there to support him and stop him from pursuing revenge. 917's circumstances were different. Everyone knew that he had already been hurting for a long time but when he lost the town of Silhed, something that was supposed to help him heal, it probably caused him to snap, and no one had been there to help.

"Dr. Kendrick declared it an unsanctioned mission and I willingly came here," 917 finished the story. "After he pulled some huge favors and managed to keep my name out of the media, he said that it would be best to self-reflect somewhere safe and where I couldn't lash out the way I did."

"In prison?" 57 looked around. "I mean, it sort of makes sense... but I don't see why it had to be covered up and he just put you in here. Couldn't he have just suspended you from duty for going over our heads?"

"Well, how do you think it would have looked?" 917 shrugged. "The first amborg that woke up from a coma, destroyed a crime gang single-handedly and didn't spare any of them. That would have damaged the reputation of A.I. Industries and Dr. Kendrick would have been put under the spotlight. The government has already spent plenty of years trying to prove why we aren't necessary anymore. This would have given them one big excuse to shut us down."

"It was all to save face," 117 surmised.

"I admit I didn't choose the best outcome..."

917 trailed off when he noticed 57's expression turning grim.

"So why?" she demanded. "Why didn't you come to us?"

"Like I already said, it would have been a waste of time," 917 replied in a calm tone. "It was unnecessary for them to kill the entire town of Silhed. I was angry... and when I was done crying, I lost control. You want to know why? Charlie, Olivia, Emma, Billy, Lysander, Tancred, Fabio, June, Michael, Alex, Tori, Diana, Bruce, Peter, Johnathan..."

917 stopped to lean forward and put his hand on the sealed folder.

"Those are just the kids I buried that day," he said as his lips trembled. "Want me to name everyone else I knew in Silhed? I remember them all and they are never coming back."

117 and 57 both wanted to say that it was not necessary to go on. Neither of them could utter a word. Not after hearing him list the names of those that were gone.

"I'm sorry," 57 said, "For sounding like I doubted or didn't trust you."

"Would you still trust me?" 917 asked as he held up the paper folder and waved it in the air. "Especially for this?"

"I do. So does Dr. Kendrick," 117 replied. "That's why we came. We just wanted to know, but we shouldn't have pushed you for answers."

"You've lived here since?" 57 muttered.

"It wasn't all bad," 917 said, preparing to open the folder. "Maximum security has quite a reputation. Most of the others kept away from me."

917 pulled the tab at the end of the folder and unsealed the document. He reached inside and pulled out some papers.

"Jack 917," he recited as he glanced at the top page. "For your eyes only. Really?"

"I didn't print it," 57 replied.

917 let out a sigh and set the top page aside. A quick snap of his fingers and the paper suddenly caught fire. Unfazed, 917 let it burn away on the table. It was printed on flash paper. One spark and it would ignite and vanish without a trace. The amborgs ignored this and 917 looked at the only other sheet that was included in the folder. His eyes widened as he looked at it carefully.

"What the hell is this?" he exclaimed, not taking his eyes off the photo.

"Now you know why we're all being recalled."

917 managed to save the image in his mind as the photo also began to catch fire. He carefully set it on the table, and he watched it burn out. Once it had been completely destroyed, leaving no trace, he turned to look at 117 and 57. He looked spooked.

"No offense 117," 917 stated, pointing at the spot where the papers were just incinerated. "Last I checked, before I got put in jail, wasn't Serina 43 dead?"

"Apparently not," 117 answered.

"And you're positive that none of you tried practicing necromancy?"

"I'm pretty sure the signs of that would be obvious if we decided to pursue dark magic," 57 said with a concerned look.

"Well, I think we should wrap this up and tell the warden I'm ready to be released."

917 stood up, the other two following suit. 117 walked over to the door and knocked on it. It opened and the warden poke his head in.

"All set?" Kenny asked.

"We're set," 917 stated. He paused and looked at the other two amborgs. "Right?"

117 looked at 57, who nodded.

"Yes, let's get out of here."

Kenny motioned for 117 and 57 to exit.

"Follow the signs and wait outside the entrance," he instructed. "Quickly. I'll take Jack the other way and have him get his things."

117 and 57 nodded and proceeded left while Kenny led 917 to the right.

"Just like last time alright?" he whispered. "I can't be seen escorting you out. The drone around this corner has been programmed to reactivate when it sees you and will take you downstairs. The guards have only been instructed to take you to get your personal effects."

"I know," 917 replied. "I was there the last time?"

"Very funny," Kenny replied sarcastically. "Come on, I don't have a photographic memory like you. I must repeat these instructions because sneaking you out of prison isn't exactly a common practice here. If the public were to find out, it'd raise a lot of questions. Be serious, will you?"

917 stopped in his tracks, causing Kenny to stop as well. He looked at the amborg in the orange prison suit questionably. 917 gave him a hard and serious stare. It didn't last long because seconds later, a smile broke out on his face. Kenny scoffed and placed his hands on hips.

"Alright, I'm sorry," 917 snickered. "You said be serious, then I'll act serious now. Ok? I just enjoy messing with you a little."

"Look, it's just really difficult pretending to treat you like a serious criminal when you and I both know that's not true. I told Dr. Kendrick that there would be no problems with you in here. So far, you've had my back plenty of times... and I can't tell anyone about it. You know what that's like?"

"Actually, yeah I do," 917 nodded. "But that's what makes our friendship one-of-a-kind. We just have a bond!"

"I swear to God," Kenny looked like he was about to burst. "Sometimes I wish you won't come back."

917 felt amused at seeing Kenny act so flustered. It was hard to believe that he was the warden of this prison at times. Some had questioned whether he had the proper discipline for this place.

The two of them resumed walking and rounded the corner.

"Will that be all, warden?" 917 said.

"Yes," Kenny nodded. "Good luck."

917 walked around the corner and noticed a deactivated drone standing alone in the middle of the hall. Once he approached it, the red eye on its faceplate lit up. Its head straightened as it turned to face him.

"Prisoner," it stated. "Follow me."

One elevator ride later, 917 stepped onto the ground floor of the outboarding center of the prison. Chain link fencing running from the ceiling down to the floor lined every walkway. A security drone escorted 917 through several aisles, and when he passed through an entrance, he was joined by a few human guards who guided him to a security booth. The woman behind the counter activated a scanner that projected a beam of light across 917's face. Once his identity was confirmed in the system, she handed him a key.

The guards then directed him through another open archway. Once he was through, he approached a man sitting behind a desk. He activated a scanner and 917 held up the key for him to see.

"Your belongings are in this box number," he stated, handing 917 a yellow paper when the scanner confirmed the key he was holding. "You may get dressed and collect everything within 10 minutes. Congratulations on your release."

917 thanked the man politely and proceeded to the door, which was now flashing green. A loud buzzer sounded as the door unlocked and slid open. The guards remained outside as he stepped through the threshold. The door closed behind him as he approached a table. A robotic arm descended from the ceiling.

"Six-one-three-eight-two-four-zero," 917 stated the number written on the yellow paper.

A little upbeat chime sounded as the robotic arm disappeared around some shelves. After a moment, it returned with a big steel storage container in its claws. It set it down on the table for him and retracted. Once it disappeared out of sight, 917 saw a TV screen drop from the ceiling. A ten-minute timer began to count down.

917 inserted the key into the box and turned it, hearing a click as it unlocked. He lifted the lid and found all his belongings neatly arranged inside. His clothes were folded nicely, and smaller items were placed in manila envelopes for safe-keeping. Each envelope was labeled with its contents. He read the full inventory list printed on the inside of the lid.

917 first changed out of his orange prison pants and into a pair of black slacks, securing them with a leather belt from his storage box. After that, he took out a black T-shirt and set it aside. Removing the prison shirt, he folded it neatly before donning the black shirt. Finally, he grabbed a cotton zip-up hoodie and slid his arms through it.

Once all the clothes were unpacked, he moved on to the personal effects. He picked up the small envelopes and emptied them out. He grabbed three items: a wallet made from black leather, a necklace with a small silver rose pendant, and a gold bracelet.

He quickly pocketed the wallet, slung the necklace over his head, and picked up the gold bracelet. Instead of immediately putting it on, he held it in his hands for a moment, studying it.

The bracelet suddenly beeped and a green light over a white LED strip switched on. 917 put it on his left wrist and allowed it to calibrate. It had been about four years since it was stashed away. As it became fully synchronized to his implants, 917 transmitted a message from his mind to the bracelet.

"Identity authenticated," his voice broadcasted from the bracelet. It pulsated with every word. "Amborg Jack 917, Second Group, A.I. Industries."

Switching to his actual voice, he spoke his next sentence out loud.

"Emergency Recall received," he said. "Will return asap."

917 pulled his sleeve down over the bracelet and put the prison clothes into the box. He closed the lid, set it on the edge of the table, and turned to head for the door. As soon as he stepped out, the guards showed him to the exit.

They didn't follow him as he entered the main lobby. They watched him as he passed through a security gate and continued towards the final set of doors that led outside. 917 approached the doors, and they slid open.

As he exited the prison, 917 paused and took in a breath, tasting the outside air. His nose sensors immediately flagged something he couldn't stand. Pollen. Slightly annoyed, 917 quickly switched on his filters and braced for the attack on his allergies. Millions of dollars invested in the designing and upgrades on his body, and modern science still hadn't figured out how to cure allergies.

The way of the future my ass, 917 thought as he let out a sigh.

He resumed walking and spotted his friends patiently waiting outside the entrance to the parking lot. David 117 and Katie 57 were engaged in conversation, but turned their attention towards him as he approached.

"You have a very interesting file here in this prison," 117 said. "Maximum security prisoners don't have a shot at early parole. Yet, after you were transferred out, some kind of glitch changed your prisoner ID. This particular ID allowed you to leave the prison. Another kind arrangement with the warden?"

"If I showed my other prisoner ID number to guys on the first floor," 917 glanced back and pointed with his thumb over his shoulder, "they would think I was trying to escape."

"You actually have two prisoner files in here?" 57 asked, incredulous. "One for maximum security and one for hanging out with the folks with misdemeanors?"

"Really smart you two," 917 rolled his eyes. He spoke sarcastically as he walked past them into the parking lot. "Why don't you talk louder? I don't think they heard you."

"That'd probably be the shortest prison release in history," 57 shrugged to 117.

"Well, if we were to catch him now and toss him back in there, it might be a new world record," 117 replied.

"I'm right here," 917 said without turning back. "I actually miss the days when we would keep certain comments to ourselves. If only we had some sort of private channels in our brains to do that. Oh wait."

57 and 117 exchanged a cheeky grin with each other. 917 paused and glanced back at them irritably. Sensing his annoyance, they quickly composed themselves and tried to look nonchalant as they also stopped.

"Better yet," he said, slowly turning his head and looking around the lot. "Maybe the amborg who just came out of prison shouldn't be the one walking in front. I have no idea which car is yours."

"Right, sorry. It's that one."

57 led them to their car parked near the entrance. 117 unlocked it and she went for the driver's seat.

"New model?" 917 asked as he opened the back passenger door.

"Last year, actually," 117 replied.

The three of them climbed in and 57 started the engine. She shifted it into gear, and they left the prison parking lot.

"You think we're going to have time to stop on the way back home?" 917 asked. "I want to visit an old friend of ours."

"Well, it does depend on where you want to go," 57 stated. "We do need to get back after I pick up the last person on my list."

"Great," 917 sighed. "Who is it?"

"3 has also failed to answer the emergency recall," 117 said.

"Oh. New York?" 917 perked up. "Well that's great then, we can stop in Brooklyn."

117 and 57 glanced at each other. 117 looked in the rearview mirror and noticed that 917 was smiling, looking rather pleased. The sudden uplifting change in his mood was certainly an improvement from when they were back inside the prison.

"Well, if we're making a short detour into Brooklyn," 57 said as she entered the stop into the GPS, "I can manage that since we're still ahead of schedule. But may I ask why we're visiting there?"

"It's an emergency recall," 917 replied. "Before we report in, I need to deliver a message. I promised to deliver it in person."

117 looked confused for a second as he turned around to look at 917.

"But if you were in jail... how did you...?"

"You'll see when we get there."

917 crossed his arms and leaned back, closing his eyes.

"Anyway, since we're on the subject of friends," 917 yawned as he got comfortable, "How's 501 and 466? Are they doing ok?"

"Good," 117 answered. He wasn't happy about 917 changing the subject again, but it looked like he had properly finished stating his request. "Both are fine."

"Glad to hear that," 917 spoke softly as he drifted off. "They're good kids."

"Actually," 57 said cheerfully, "you both would be happy to know that for this gathering of amborgs, they were actually sent out to retrieve another unresponsive family member."

"Good for them," 917 muttered. "Who were they going to drag back home?"

There was no answer. 117 turned his head and gazed at 57. From the backseat, 917 opened one eye and peered at the back of 57's head.

"Who did they get assigned to bring home? Katie??" 117 asked. "Where were they sent?"

"Italy," 57 replied calmly.

117 and 917 both responded simultaneously.

"Oh no."

"You did tell them explicitly to be discreet, right?" 117 asked nervously. "Did you leave them with those instructions?"

57 chuckled nervously but remained silent, causing 117 to bury his face in his hand. From the backseat, 917 let out a soft laugh and closed his eyes again.

"You know?" 57 replied. "I knew something had slipped my mind."

"Oh, this is going to be fun," 917 concentrated on falling asleep. "Wake me when we get there, or when the Italian mob puts out a contract on 501. Always wanted to see a wanted sign with Donut's name on it."

117 could hope that this wouldn't be the case. The last thing that A.I. Industries needed was to accidentally anger the mafia.

Chapter 6: International Mishaps & Priorities

Livorno, Italy
V.N. Mafia Headquarters
Emergency Recall plus 1 hour 35 minutes
8:03 PM Central European Summer Time

"Attenzione. Attenzione! This is local surveillance! We have sighted two unidentified figures approaching the headquarters of the Italian mob boss, Alberto Biagino!"

There was a loud crackling noise as someone answered. The radio line opened again and another man spoke angrily.

"Che Cavolo! What do you mean? No one has been allowed to move in. Stop them! We are only supposed to watch the building!"

"It isn't us! No one has left their post! We have confirmed! It's an unscheduled visit!"

"Who could be dumb enough to oppose the Italian mafia on their own???"

Dominic 501 twitched his head. He looked up at the empty balcony of a nearby house. Disappointed, he turned and walked across the courtyard calmly. Now he was starting to wish he hadn't heard what was being discussed over the police communications line.

"Dumb? That's a really bad thing to judge about someone," he huffed with a very annoyed expression and shut off the police channel. He felt a bit better when he didn't have to listen to them anymore. "I sure would like to teach those officers a lesson... How rude."

At his side, his friend and partner, Carolina 466, kept pace with him. She chuckled softly as she also shut off the channel. The two Third Group amborgs were supposed to remain incognito. Blowing their cover would complicate things.

"Now now," she said calmly, "We are not here for that, remember? We're just monitoring their com lines to make sure they aren't planning anything stupid. As long as we just remain casual, then it will all be fine."

"Who knew that Kiden 18 would be working for Alberto Biagino," 501 looked up at the entrance to the hideout. "She said that she had connections here but... I never imagined."

"The older amborgs always keep really cool secrets like this," 466 smiled as she admired the architecture. "It's just... so interesting every time you learn something new about them."

466 continued to marvel at the buildings. In Italy, the architecture was rich with culture in comparison to where they were from. From what she had found out, she was born in New York, where all the tall and imposing skyscrapers made of steel felt so overpowering. Here, the stone buildings were much softer by comparison. Their round rooflines and delicate colors were warm and inviting. Vines of all sorts grew everywhere, crawling up the sides of the buildings, adding vibrancy and scents. It was comforting.

501 and 466 both agreed that it was beautiful, even as the evening sky made the lighting too dark to appreciate it in its entirety.

Remembering what their current task was, 466 snapped out of her daze and turned to the door. She rapped on it a few times with her fist. When there was no answer, she turned to look at 501, who shrugged in response. 466 lifted her hand gently and knocked a second time. In an instant, a slot on the door opened and both amborgs heard a man's voice speak from inside.

"Password?" he declared in Italian.

"We don't have one," 466 replied nonchalantly as she flipped through her Italian dictionary. "Uh. Buona sera come stai? Lei parla inglese?"

Unfortunately, this made the guard close the slot. Had she spoken incorrectly? They had already expected this kind of response, so it was obvious that they needed to make another attempt. 501 and 466 exchanged knowing glances and nodded. 466 knocked on the door again, this time with more confidence to convey their intention. The slot opened once more.

"Ok I was kidding about the password," the man said, chuckling silently. He responded in English to them in a heavy Italian accent. The next words to come from behind the door were in a more serious tone. "But you should know who lives here. Now leave. Otherwise, you will be in trouble for more than trespassing."

"Boy," 501 spoke into the slot. "You know, you seem to be pretty nice for a doorman of the mafia."

"I know who I work for, my boy." the man said grudgingly. "Also, being nice has its advantages. You get treated better by these people if you don't give them bad attitudes. Once again, please leave. The longer this conversation goes, the more likely someone might decide to kill you out of boredom. Both of you look too young and handsome to be dealing with my boss."

501 and 466 grinned at each other. It was very flattering to hear that, despite only being visible through a small square hole.

"But we can't leave. Not yet," 466 protested, "We are here to see someone."

"An appointment, eh?" the old man asked carefully. "I doubt it. Kids like you? What business could you possibly have here? Oh dear, I'm going to regret asking that, aren't I?"

"Yes, we do have an appointment... Sort of," 501 stated. He was starting to feel a little surprised that the local Italian police weren't doing any more to interrupt their progress. But then he remembered it was probably because police interference was the last thing the Mafia needed on their doorstep. "Although we may be young in appearance, we do have an important matter on our hands. Our sister works here and it's really urgent that we speak to her."

There was a brief pause, then the old man spoke again.

"Sister? Yeah right," he said sternly, "and I'm the pope's long lost brother."

"You may know her," 466 said as sweetly as she could. She ignored the doorman's sass and continued to reason with him. "Her name is Kiden? Does that help?"

"I... er... Never heard of her," the man replied rather hastily. "No one by that name works here!"

501 and 466 gave each other a look. It was the man's flustered voice that gave it away.

"That is incorrect," 501 smiled as he spoke into the door slot. "We have built-in lie detectors, so we know you are giving false information."

"Now we know Kiden really is here," 466 said cheerfully.

"Ok look."

The slot closed. Both stood there awkwardly for a second. Had the man run off and left them on the front porch?

"Did you actually upgrade your lie detector?" 466 asked.

"The new patch didn't work out so well for the triplets," 501 replied softly. "It's got a few bugs, so I skipped it."

Another moment passed, and they heard several clicks from inside. 466 leaned forward and listened. Internal locks and clamps. This door was much more secure than they'd realized. The door knob turned, and the door opened a fraction. The two amborgs peered through and caught a glimpse of an old man's shadow from within.

"Fine I lied," the doorman spoke in a much more frightened tone. "I did it because you kids just named one of our top freelancers! Anyone who has business with her winds up in very bad shape. Now please leave before you end up the same way!"

The door instantly slammed shut. Unfazed, 466 and 501 knocked on the door again.

"Would you be willing to let us in for a fee? We are in a hurry. You seem like a nice man, unlocking the front door like that for us!" 466 called as she pulled a roll of money out of her back pocket. She turned and spoke privately to 501. "Wow, 18 has quite a reputation..."

501 nodded in agreement as the slot opened again. They heard the sound of clicking again as the doorman frantically locked the door back up.

"No little girl," the man said nervously, "I remember the last time I took a bribe. Introduced the mafia to a whole new benefactor... Business has never been so wonderful."

"But that's a good thing," 501 said observantly. "Isn't it?"

A loud laugh came from the door slot.

"In my experience, my boy, I'm more used to the boss in a bad mood. It's seeing him so happy from all the good things that have been going on... that's what's so scary to me. All it will take is one wrong thing to happen and it's all undone!"

501 and 466 stared at each other. Confusion began spreading all the way to their central processors.

"Something tells me we may have misinterpreted those mafia movies..." 501 whispered to 466. "The real-life methods of interaction we are implementing are not yielding expected results as portrayed on film. I believe this clarifies why the others say that we shouldn't assume everything on film is real."

"Yeah," 466 nodded. "I remember the lecture about not always believing internet rumors."

"How many times do I have to ask you to leave? You are just as stubborn as Kiden..."

Ignoring the doorman's protests, 501 and 466 both turned away from the door and leaned their heads towards each other.

"Perhaps we should change tactics?" 466 asked. "This is not getting us anywhere and we are running late. There can be no delays."

501 put his hand to his chin and tried to imitate 117 whenever he needed to brainstorm an idea.

"Possibly," he pondered, "Maybe we can... Mmm... No, that won't work. How about we try... 466?"

Without waiting for him to even offer confirmation, 466 turned her attention back to the door and stamped her foot on the pavement. Her foot hit the stone hard, causing a loud hollow echo that rang throughout the entire courtyard.

"Ok you leave us no choice," she said as cheerfully and as loudly as she could. "We have tried to be as reasonable as we could by your standards. But if you don't grant us passage, we'll have to force our way in."

"You wouldn't..." the man replied through the door.

"Oh dear," 501 said nervously as 466 curled her fingers into a fist. "Sir. I'd take her seriously. All of us are equal in strength but it gets worse when she's angry. Please step away from the door and a little to the side. Oh! Like-maybe-right-now!"

There was a loud shuffling noise as 466 surged forward. She planted her non-dominant foot on the porch and brought her fist upward. The force of her punch broke the door off its hinges and sent it flying inside with a loud crash. 501 stared in shock, his eyes practically bulging out. 466, her fist still raised in midair, was also caught dumbstruck by the destruction she had just caused. The doorman nervously leaned into sight, his eyes wildly flicking back and forth between the broken door and the two equally shocked amborgs on his doorstep. If the police were still watching, 501 could definitely sense the weight of all eyes on them now, mouths gaping in the midst of the current scene. They hadn't felt this much attention in years. The others had specifically ordered them not to go overboard.

"466... I think that was too much force," 501 said anxiously.

466 retracted her fist and looked at her own hand. She looked at the broken door and got rid of her fighting stance.

"I didn't realize... that the door was so weak," she stammered as she did a scan. "I only charged to about 40%."

Any higher than that and the entire front of the building probably would have collapsed.

They heard some shuffling as the doorman appeared from behind the entryway. He walked out past the two amborgs without looking at them and got down on his hands and knees. Kneeling onto the cobblestone a few steps behind them, he took a deep breath and sighed very deeply. It almost sounded like he was about to cry. They then realized that he was on all fours, possibly praying. 501 and 466 translated his Italian and realized he was expressing thanks for somehow managing to stay alive. After he was done quietly muttering his gratitude, the two of them watched as he sat on the pavement with an utterly blank expression on his face.

"I have failed..." he sighed dejectedly, throwing up his hands. No one had asked him to surrender, but he looked defeated. "We need someone new to be the doorman. This job is too difficult on the mind."

466 felt a little terrible for driving the poor man to the verge of tears. He waved his arm to them, signaling that he didn't care anymore. 501 and 466 acknowledged this by thanking the man briefly and took their chance to enter. The two of them scanned the hall as they clambered through the open passage.

"I wasn't trying to punch so hard," 466 chuckled nervously, "You'd think that a door belonging to the mafia would be... built much stronger. Not just an ordinary door."

"I guess movies really can be inaccurate about certain things."

They immediately entered another passage. Expecting some alarms, 501 and 466 proceeded with caution. When they realized that there weren't any at all, they walked down the hall a little quicker and entered the main living room.

They immediately put their hands up.

There had to be at least 25 armed individuals all aiming weapons at them. They had literally walked into a massive kill box. The only question now was, who was going to make the next move? If this went sideways, then there would be casualties.

"I don't suppose we could reimburse you for the door?" 466 asked.

"You, the one who punched my door down. There were other ways to resolve this. But now I'm only going to ask you once."

501 and 466 watched a tall heavy-set man stalk forward. He was the one who had spoken first. The two amborgs recognized him from his photos in their databanks. He had prominent, leonine features and a close-cropped beard and mustache, with short brown hair and blue eyes. He wore dark pants and an expensive dinner jacket over a silk maroon buttoned shirt. It was

loose-fit and comfortable, since they could see the top two buttons of the shirt were undone. A simple voice analysis officially confirmed it.

Alberto Biagino, the current head of the Vincenzo 'Ndrangheta Mafia. He was considered to be one of the most powerful human beings in the world, according to Interpol. Both amborgs stood very still as he sized them up.

Although he approached them unarmed, he did have a super intimidating aura about him that put them on edge. Regardless, they began thinking about what to do next if he gave the order to have them shot.

"Surrender yourselves immediately," he demanded. "Otherwise, we will shoot you."

"Even if you did," 466 stated, "it wouldn't work."

"And why not, little girl?"

"We just want to get our friend, our sister, and leave," 501 stated.

"Well, you didn't have to destroy my door," Alberto fumed. He pointed at the two of them and then at himself. "I didn't break it down, traumatize my doorman, and just waltz in here like it was an open invitation!"

"That was an accident," 501 stated. "Can we please see Kiden? We'll fix the damages."

"You're certainly right about that!"

They watched someone else step out from behind the group. They all shifted as a woman came into view. 501 and 466 looked relieved when they saw a familiar face.

"What were you two thinking?!"

466 cringed suddenly at the outburst. 501 flinched, but waved nervously.

"Hi big sis," he said meekly.

First Group amborg, Kiden 18, frowned at the two of them. Not just any normal frown, she looked at 501 and 466 as if they had just triggered the ultimate trap of their lives. The two of them began to tremble with fear. They felt they were about to spontaneously combust if the First Group amborg continued her stare of death at them.

18 was slightly shorter than most of the people in the room. Despite cybernetic augmentation increasing every amborg's height, she was just under six feet. She didn't let her height of 5'11 stop her from commanding a huge presence. 501 and 466 watched with impressed looks in their eyes when several mafia members started to lower their weapons as 18 stepped forward, partially shielding the two of them from a potential attack. Her faith

was remarkably strong, if confidently standing with her back to several drawn guns was anything to go by.

Kiden wore an impressive suit herself. They avoided her angry gaze and admired the design. Italian-style jacket and tapered trousers, covering up her powerfully built form underneath. She was dressed elegantly, but also ready for a fight, according to their analysis. With her dark, smooth features, she looked cool, even though she didn't look pleased at all.

"Don't you 'hi' me like it's alright," she said angrily. "Two amborgs in plain sight walking right up to the entrance?! Demolishing it?! You may have disguises on but you've terrified a lot of people! Do you want to scare the local populace into thinking something is wrong?! We have to be subtle especially now that we are out in the real world! What were you idiots thinking?! You literally have just created an international catastrophe! Do you realize whose door you broke down?! Who it belongs to?! Alberto Giabino is the head of the most powerful Italian Mafia syndicates in the history of the planet! And you just blasted in like there'd be no consequences."

"Does that mean we get to talk now?" 466 asked softly as the two of them bowed their heads. They kept their hands up.

18 turned to look at Alberto. He didn't appear to be as angry as her, but he lifted his hand and waved his fingers down. Every person in the room lowered their guns, but kept them out menacingly.

"Speak now while I still allow it," 18 scoffed as she put her hands on her hips and faced them.

"Well, you had a stubborn doorman," 501 said.

"Oh, this explanation already sounds fantastic," Alberto said to 18.

"Also, the door was way too weak," 466 admitted. "I just wanted to express a show of force given our time constraints. We decided to just go for it."

501 and 466 waited for a response.

"You don't always get the best results if you rush in headfirst," 18 said. "You improvise to make sure you get the best possible outcome for everyone you're affecting. I am going to have to report this to 117 and Dr. Kendrick when we get back."

"Oh no!" 501 whined. "That's the last thing we need."

"You two did succeed in expressing how badly you needed me to return," 18 said. "But it could have been handled better in a much more diplomatic way. Obviously, you failed. Therefore, your supervising amborg will be notified of your reckless behavior."

"Reckless?" 466 gulped. "But…"

"You forced your way in," 18 said, shaking her head. "Do you realize how bad this is? We're extremely lucky the police don't have any cameras in here."

501 and 466 snuck a glance at each other and apologized quickly.

"We're sorry."

18 held up her hand. With a silent and stern look, she made sure that the two Third Group amborgs stood still and remained quiet. She turned around to speak to Alberto.

"You know we're covering the cost of the door," she said.

"I appreciate it but what do we do about these two?" Alberto asked softly. "They came up to my home in full view of everyone and did this."

"What do you think?"

"A.I. Industries certainly responded quickly," Alberto pondered. "Africa has Dr. Kendrick agitated. We both knew they would send for you."

"Wait," 501 called out to them. 18 and Alberto turned to see 501's look of surprise. "You know about Africa?"

"Yes, we already knew about Africa," 18 explained. "The boss almost wanted me to go snatch a piece of it back for him as a souvenir! Even if they are trying to keep it hushed up, there are a lot of people already figuring it out! Now shush!"

"Not every detail," 501 said quickly. "It's about…"

"Shush! And will you two please put your hands down? You look ridiculous."

501 fell silent. He and 466 lowered their arms and stood there calmly. Alberto leaned in to speak to 18 privately, even though they could still hear the conversation.

"You could have responded immediately," he said.

"Now it's my fault? Is that it? I happened to be in the middle of business when the huge blaring emergency alert appeared on my display screen," 18 replied angrily. She tapped the side of her head as a reminder. "The one that's built in my head?"

Alberto glanced at 18 and let out a sigh. This seemed like a good sign. He appeared to be calming down. 466 felt uneasy when she noticed Alberto glance at her, and a mischievous grin appeared on his face. She didn't like the look of that, especially when 18 noticed, too. Instead of addressing it, she also turned to stare in their direction.

"You know, there is one thing that might satisfy me," he stated as he shifted his gaze to 501. "Your friends do need to face punishment."

"I don't know if I like where this is going," 501 piped up anxiously.

"Fight them."

501 and 466 stared. They both turned to look at each other and then at 18. Alberto nodded. They had heard him correctly.

"I've never seen amborgs spar before," he said, walking over to a bar in the corner.

"That's what you want?" 18 asked, raising an eyebrow.

"I can't just let these two walk off my property unfazed," he nodded as he poured a drink for himself. "They came in here and started a fight. The way I see it, you fight them. We will properly give them a punishment while also having you leave here, escorting them out without sharing with the entire world that you are one of them. As you Americans say, 'two birds with one stone.'"

18 pondered this for a moment.

"I did need to find a way to discreetly go home," she nodded.

18 stepped forward as Alberto's crew backed away, creating a clear space for them. She slowly took off her jacket and handed it to someone walking past, who swiftly took it away.

"Whoa! Whoa!" 501 stated. "Hang on, we didn't come here to fight, 18! Our orders were to bring you back!"

"What were the exact orders for this Emergency Recall?" 18 asked as she pulled her sleeves back. "Recite the words for me."

"Dr. Kendrick told us to bring you back..." 466 began to speak. Then her eyes widened. Realization spread as she finished, "By any means necessary."

"Under condition nine, paragraph two," 18 nodded her head. "All amborgs required to report in for an Emergency Recall are authorized to use any or all methods available to ensure and maintain their human covers, civilian identities, or status to avoid jeopardizing potential operations, missions, or standard lifestyles that have been previously established."

"But 18, why is it that...?" 501 pointed at everyone shuffling around. "Everyone here seems to know that you're an amborg."

"It was easier to explain to them," 18 cracked her knuckles. "Telling the Italian government or the authorities? Not exactly something I'd like to see happen."

"Do we actually have to do this?" 466 asked.

The room was opening up fast as the discussion continued, and within moments, there was plenty of space for the three of them in the center of the living room. The answer was obviously yes.

501 and 466 both looked at each other again.

A.I. Industries didn't want to start a conflict with the Italian Mafia. This was established a long time ago. Unfortunately, 18 was right. The two of them had created an international incident and it would get worse if it went public. It was good that they had switched to civilian disguises, but everyone wouldn't feel so happy if they discovered an amborg like 18 working for Alberto Biagino.

"Come on," she said. "I'm going to train you."

18 raised her hands and got into a combat stance.

"Will this by any chance involve actual injuries?" 501 asked timidly.

"Fight me with everything you've got."

That was 18's only command as she waited for the two of them to make their move. 501 looked at 466.

"Are we actually doing this?" he asked.

"I don't think we have any other option," 466 replied.

The two of them decided to raise their arms, curled their fists, and stepped away from each other. It was a two on one fight. Both amborgs would have to try and concentrate on one target. One of the toughest targets that they ever had to face.

18 was notorious for her fighting style and her skills. They knew from her records that she favored Brazilian Jiujitsu, but she seemed to be in a Muay Thai stance. Her right foot was in front facing twelve o'clock and her left foot was back and to the side at shoulder width. She had brought up both her hands, lowered her chin, and kept her eyes fixed on them. Her hands weren't fully closed, but she kept her fingers curled like she was holding a pair of binoculars.

Her feet were supposed to be bouncing around. They assumed that she would prepare to throw a lot of kicks at them, since Muay Thai utilized a lot of fast and powerful legwork. She was standing still, planted like a tree. Until they moved to attack, she was probably not going to reveal what method she wanted to counter with.

501 switched to a private channel for the next part.

"Now!" he told 466.

Both amborgs moved in for an attack. 501 tried to swing his right arm to attack, but 18 suddenly side-stepped towards 466. Dodging his attack, she ducked as 466 adjusted to try and swing at her head.

When 466 missed, 18 used the opportunity to straighten up and swung her right arm. 466 brought up her arm to block the attack. She narrowly avoided getting punched in the face, but was still knocked off-balance. 18 then quickly turned to face 501 who was gearing up for another move.

He charged at 18, extending his arms in an attempt to tackle her. 18 knelt and ducked, which forced 501 to leap and somersault forward. As 18 stood back up, 466 suddenly appeared on her left side, jumping high in the air, and delivered a side-split kick. Bringing up her elbows, 18 blocked it and got knocked back. Her feet skidded as she maintained a standing position.

In one split-second move, 18 drew a short dagger from her belt and threw it towards 466 before she could recover from the jump attack. 466 reacted by performing a front cartwheel, calculating the timing. Her foot struck the dagger, deflecting it towards the floor. 18 was curious as to why she didn't simply dodge the knife, since there was no one directly behind her to be hit if the dagger had continued flying in that direction.

She watched 466 kneel after performing her stunt, and was preparing to stand back up when 501 surged forward. He'd given her time to recover before quickly grabbing the knife off the floor and launching himself towards 18. 466 had been intentionally trying to arm him with a bit of unnecessary, but stylish, flair.

501 swung the knife, holding it in a forward position in his right hand, wrapping his thumb around the grip. He brought it down in a diagonal slash, which 18 stepped back to avoid. Not giving her a moment, 501 pivoted and switched his knife to a chambered reverse-grip position and tried to stab her again. This left his shoulder exposed as 18 brought up a foot and kicked him, which gave them a bit of distance. However, she couldn't follow up since 466 was coming in for another attack, forcing her to prioritize her defense. The two of them had a very excellent strategy, from what she could tell. They had definitely kept up with their training. Unfortunately, the longer that they failed to take her down, the quicker she could analyze their weaknesses and exploit them.

The more that they moved, the more time it gave 18 to calculate her counterattack. 466 executed a sweeping kick, aiming to trip or knock her over, while 501 attacked from above with slashing strikes. Their coordinated strategy was designed to prevent 18 from focusing solely on one opponent, keeping her on her toes and unable to predict their movements. By constantly changing up their tactics, they aimed to keep 18 off balance and unable to get too comfortable with any one technique.

Their strategy appeared to have worked, because the last thing 18 expected was 501 to perform an impressive 520 Taekwondo kick. With 466's failed attempt to hit her legs, 18 was vulnerable to 501's powerful strike. She was struck in the chest with enough force to knock her off her feet and send her skidding across the floor. Their coordinated efforts and ability to keep 18 distracted allowed 501 time to alter his style and catch her off-guard, ultimately leading to a successful attack that left her reeling from the impact.

Impressive, she thought as she picked her head up. *117 and 43, you were excellent mentors. But I know their styles. Just as well as I know every single amborgs' styles.*

18 quickly stood up and surged forward. Increasing her power levels, she leapt at 466 and brought her fist forward. 466 blocked it, but it was no good. She was sent flying into a wall while 18 switched to 501, who made the mistake of turning his head in shock, leaving himself wide open. He turned his eyes back, but it was too late. 18 had already moved into his personal bubble.

501 took the knife in his hand and thrust it forward. 18 blocked it with her left hand, brushing it aside, and used her right to land a blow to 501's head. 18 spun around, pivoting on her left foot, and swung her left arm. 501 brought up his own left hand to block it, but 18 delivered a high kick with her right leg. She finished him with a left-right-left combo with her fists and then kicked his exposed leg while he was trying to block the punches.

"David and Serina taught you well," 18 socked 501 in the stomach, causing him to double over. "But remember this."

With her other arm, 18 punched upwards, lifting 501 up into the air. 18 immediately followed up with another powerful punch before 501 could hit the ground. The impact caused him to cry out in pain as he was flung across the room, colliding with the wall. Some paintings and pictures shattered as he crumpled to the ground.

"I trained David and Serina," 18 declared, "Just like I trained every other amborg."

This left 466, since 501 had been incapacitated. She was still recovering from the last attack when 18 closed in and launched a roundhouse kick. Anticipating her move, 466 quickly performed a back handspring to create some distance. Not willing to let 18 close the gap again, 466 executed a side-flip, using her right heel to counter 18's next strike. The second she landed, 466 immediately knelt down, readying herself for another attack. She sprang back up and attempted another kick, but 18 was prepared for it. Her hand met 466's foot, both of them parrying each other's attack.

18 advanced with a back-spin kick, but 466 managed to dodge it. Both then attempted right flying kicks simultaneously, but blocked the attacks. 466 followed up with a roundhouse kick and a left-spin hook, but 18 skillfully weaved out of the way, evading both strikes. Undeterred, 466 tried to bring up her leg again to unleash a flurry of kicks. *What was she trying to do? Be like Chun-Li from Street Fighter?*

18 whirled around and expertly dodged the next kick, then elbowed 466, causing her to lose her momentum. It was over for her. In a fluid motion, 18 seized 466's right arm, maneuvered under it, and spun her around, almost as if they were on a dance floor. Crouching slightly, 18 bent her knees, preparing the finishing blow. She dragged 466 by the arm in a circle, disorienting her. With a quick release of her arm, 18 spun around and launched herself into a flying roundhouse kick, her leg connecting solidly with 466's face.

The sound of the blow echoed through the room as 466 was back flipped and landed hard on her stomach. 18 remained standing, observing the two prone amborgs on the floor. Everyone watching the fight were completely awestruck. They had seen 18 fight before, but have never witnessed her effortlessly demolish two other amborgs. She was terrifying.

"You didn't actually kill them, did you?" Alberto glanced over nervously.

"The only people in the world I usually use that much power for are other cybernetic individuals," 18 wiped her face as she held out her hand. "They're going to be fine. If they had been normal humans, they would be dead."

The person that had taken her jacket ran forward and put it in her hand. She thanked them with a polite smile, put her jacket back on and, voila. She suddenly looked normal, as if the fight that she was just in hadn't even happened.

"For a minute there," Alberto pointed at 466, "I almost thought you lost when they managed to land a couple of hits on you."

"They've been training and working hard," 18 replied with a smile. "I'm impressed with both of them."

"You are going to tell them when they wake up?"

"Maybe," 18 shrugged.

Some of Alberto's men had gone over and tried to pick up 501 and 466's bodies. Unfortunately, that wasn't working out too well, so 18 stepped in.

"It takes teams of people to lift up one amborg," she explained as she knelt next to 466 and swatted someone's hand away from her chest. "Each of us weigh a lot more than you think."

"How many people?"

18 looked at the man who asked the question. She waved her hand at him, telling him to step back.

"Teams," she enunciated as she repeated her answer.

18 lifted 466's head and scanned her vitals. As she did so, she pulled some smelling salt packets out of her jacket pocket. Quickly, she put them under her nose and waited a few moments.

466's nose twitched, and she jerked awake. She coughed as the salt burned her nostrils. The alarms in her head flared and she clutched her head.

"Easy!" 18 said as she rubbed 466's shoulder.

"Ow," 466 groaned. "My head."

"Yeah," 18 chuckled. "You took a big hit from my foot. Just take a minute to reorient yourself. I think the bruise will be very convincing when we get out of here."

466 blinked as she tried to focus.

"Now let me ask you one thing," 18 said.

"What is it?" 466 turned to look at her.

"Were you both trying?" 18 asked with a smirk. "For real?"

"Yes, we were," 466 nodded. "Our strategy. It would have worked."

"Keep dreaming," 18 chuckled. "Alright, I need to wake up 501."

"Wait," 466 started, but swayed a little. "Let me do it! Whoa, dizzy..."

"It's ok 466," 18 said reassuringly. "I can handle this."

466 was struggling to get to her feet when 18 walked over to 501. He was lying in a pile of plaster and stone that had broken off the wall he had flown into. 18 casually leaned down to roll him onto his side and woke him up the same way she did for 466.

"No! Don't touch me!!"

18 dodged 501's swinging arm as he regained consciousness, quickly backing off to create distance between them. 501, completely disoriented, kicked his feet on the floor in an attempt to slide away, only to back up into the wall. More plaster fell as he turned his head frantically.

"You can't wake him up from that close!" 466 quickly stumbled over to 18's side. "He's still not feeling better from that one time!"

"What?" 18 asked. "One time? Oh! *That* time?"

501 tried to focus, but continued to look around wildly. He waved his hands in front of his face, as if trying to push something away. 18 could see specks of plaster in his eyes. 501's actions were clearly defensive, bordering on a panic attack.

"501!" 18 said gently to him. "It's ok! You're safe! You blacked out because I hit you, remember? You weren't kidnapped!"

501's movements came to a stop, and he became still. Unsure if he had heard her, 18 signaled everyone behind her to stay in place. They watched as he carefully lifted his fingers up to his eyes and tried to clean off the plaster.

"Oh right," he coughed. "This is Alberto Biagino's home, right? 466 and I came here. Kiden 18!"

"Yeah, that's it," 18 let out a sigh of relief. "Glad you're back with us."

After things had calmed down, 501 was back on his feet. He and 466 were now seated on bar stools, joined by Alberto and 18.

"A drink?" Alberto offered as he poured himself a glass.

"No thank you," 466 said politely.

"May I ask what that was all about?" Alberto took a sip and dipped his glass towards 501.

"There was an incident about five years ago," 18 said. "We had to save 501 from some... really disturbing criminals."

"In 2132," 466 said as she held his hand gently. "We were both out on a normal day. We got separated and he was kidnapped."

"I didn't think anyone was capable of kidnapping any of you," Alberto's eyes widened as he looked at 501, who remained quiet.

"The other amborgs that were available at the time came after him," 466 said with a smile. "I didn't know where to start searching, but they came when I called for backup. For a while, 501 couldn't sleep properly."

"What did they kidnap you for?"

Alberto politely glanced at 501, who looked up and made eye contact. 501 turned his head down and shook it.

"I don't feel comfortable sharing," he mumbled. "Can we change the subject? The important thing that we need to resolve is, can we go home and take 18 with us?"

Alberto looked at 18 questionably. Without directly saying it out loud, the expression on his face practically asked if they were ready to go.

"I've been brainstorming some discreet exit plans," 18 answered as she nodded to Alberto. She pointed at 501 and 466. "As far as the Italian authorities are concerned, they witnessed these two breaking into your home. If I were to escort them out, we could inconspicuously leave and go home. It would look like Biagino's forces were able to win against you and he ordered his men to escort you someplace off-site."

"Well, it looks like she's got it all taken care of," Alberto put out another glass.

"Uh, begging your pardon sir," 501 pointed as the glass was put on the bar counter. "We didn't want to drink."

"Oh, this isn't for you," Alberto said as he poured the second glass and filled it up. He gestured to 18. "This is for Kiden."

501 and 466 watched as 18 picked up the glass, clinking it softly with Alberto's as they silently toasted each other. 18 took a sip before returning the glass to Alberto, who then placed it carefully on a shelf. Looking closely, 501 and 466 noticed that the shelf served as a memorial, adorned with photos and other glasses filled with alcohol.

"A drink for the road," Alberto declared. "It will remain here until 18 returns. A tradition of ours. For those that are about to embark on a long journey. When she makes it back, she finishes the drink with me."

"What about those other glasses?" 466 glanced at the shelf and counted several others that looked like they had been sitting there for a while.

"Still waiting for some of them to make it home," Alberto gave them an encouraging smile, but they could see the sorrow in his eyes. "No one is ever really gone. They're just not home right now. Isn't that right, Kiden?"

"I'm coming home," 18 nodded respectfully. "We'll make it back."

501 and 466 stared in awe. The head of the Italian Mafia and one of their own had such a strong friendship that he was willing to give her this high honor. It was truly remarkable. He was wishing her a safe journey and hoping she would come back alive. They never thought they'd see this happen.

"Alright you two," 18 said. "Go get yourselves tied up. They're going to bring a car around for us. Once you get in, we'll be out of here."

"Ok."

501 and 466 both stood and followed a few of the men into another room. Before she left, 18 turned to Alberto. There was one more favor she wanted.

"You mind pouring them both a glass?" she asked.

"Of course," Alberto smiled as he pulled out two more crystal glass cups. "They earned it, in my opinion. You have an incredible family. Take care of each other."

"Ci vediamo presto," 18 bowed her head before turning to walk away.

There was a reason why she turned away before he could even bid her a proper farewell. 18 never liked being too emotionally sentimental. So, Alberto said his goodbye quickly. He also didn't want her to see how sad he was about her leaving.

"Addio Kiden 18," was all she heard him say as she disappeared around the corner.

18 found herself leading 501 and 466 to a line of three dark vehicles idling in the main courtyard of the estate. A few of Biagino's men stood guard as the vehicles' engines purred.

"Not every detail," 18 said as a man opened the back door of one of the cars for her companion.

501 and 466 both turned to look at 18.

"That's what you said when you realized that Alberto knew about Africa," 18 clarified as 501 and 466 were escorted into the car.

18 walked up to the driver's side and opened the door. She thanked the man who stood guard and closed the door. Once she was behind the wheel, she followed the lead vehicle, and they departed the courtyard.

"What was the detail that we didn't know about?" 18 asked when the three amborgs were alone. "I assume you could only tell me when we were alone. Amborg to amborg?"

"Yes," 501 nodded.

"You can talk freely now," 18 gave them a small smile as she gazed at them in the rearview mirror. "I'm not putting up a fancy façade for the mob now."

"We really are sorry," 466 said apologetically.

18 nodded. She knew that 501 and 466 felt remorse for their actions. It was really sweet of them to do so. So, she decided to help them move on.

"I know. Details, transmit." 18 ordered in a soft and gentle tone. "Now."

Within seconds, 501 transmitted all the relevant information that was kept top-secret from human eyes. 18's eyes widened as she looked over the data.

"What on earth?"

"Actually," 501 interjected. "It's from off this earth, to be exact."

"Really? Captain obvious?" 18 sassed him.

"I-I mean, you know?" he stammered. "I was clarifying with a joke. Heh… Ok never mind, it didn't work. Sorry."

"I think we should just shut up now," 466 chuckled anxiously.

"Uh, no," 18 released a deep breath of annoyance as she turned down the road. "You need to provide more details than that."

501 and 466 turned their heads to look behind them and saw that the other vehicles in their convoy hadn't turned with them. 18 had driven off down a side path that seemed to lead away from the main road. The other vehicles were a diversion so that they could sneak away.

As 18 navigated to keep them all under the radar, 501 and 466 both relayed all the current information that they were authorized to share. 18 stayed silent as they both talked about 57 being chosen to go after the other amborgs who hadn't responded to the call. They even shared how Dr. Kendrick had sent them to get her. Apparently, he had some concerns sending the two of them since 501 and 466 both had tendencies to draw unexpected attention to themselves. He was probably not going to be surprised when 18 showed him the cost of repairs that Alberto would be billing to A.I. Industries.

"Can I ask a question?"

18 nodded when she heard 501 speak up.

"What is it?"

"The mafia," 501 said. "They knew you were an amborg. You told them?"

"Well, I told him I was an amborg a couple years after I started freelancing for him," 18 admitted grudgingly. "He's a friend, despite the colorful track record that he and his family have. But I managed to gain complete trust with Alberto. He and Dr. Kendrick have an undisclosed agreement, and I volunteered to maintain that connection."

"So, you've done contract killings for the mob?" 466 asked.

"Not all of my jobs with them were that extreme," 18 replied. "Alberto has access to a lot of intel in Italy and their connections across the world have helped with our international operations. I was more or less just a glorified mercenary that was working away from home and helping the other First Group amborgs with logistics. After the Dominoe Incident, I convinced A.I. Industries to start moving their reach outside North America. We needed to help oversee more projects and you can't help the world without including more of the world."

"So that's why you haven't been home," 501 guessed.

"International projects and worldwide problems sometimes demand that we are gone for a while," 18 sighed. "Still, it does feel good sometimes."

"What does?" 466 asked.

18 smiled as she temporarily set aside the problems that they would have to face once they returned to A.I. Industries. It was easier to just concentrate on driving instead of all the information that the others had just dumped her.

She didn't want to think about what they would have to do about Serina 43's mysterious double that appeared from space. Someone was going to have to interrogate her, and that was probably going to be difficult for whoever decided to volunteer or was chosen for that task. They also had a huge problem with the fact that their space division was miniscule in comparison to the possible threat from the vastness of outer space. The entire planet was in danger and there was no way that they were prepared for something of this scale.

There was one thing that still gave her some semblance of hope lingering in her mind as she maintained a confident smile for the two young Third Group amborgs sitting in the back.

"Going home," 18 said. "We got a flight to catch, so why don't you two break out of your restraints and relax? I'll wake you when we make it to the rendezvous."

501 and 466 suddenly remembered the physical pain that they'd endured earlier. As they freed their wrists, 501 massaged his stomach as 466 put a hand on her head. 18 laughed a little as they both struggled to get comfortable. This would probably be one of the last moments they would get to properly rest. The moment they all reported back to A.I. Industries, it would be nonstop work once they were called to action.

Chapter 7: The Check, please?

It was the peak of the dinner rush that night in Manhattan. Every table was seated, orders were constantly coming in, and every plate was being circulated in and out of the kitchen, the dish pit, and the expo line. Every staff member all over this grand restaurant contributed to giving the best customer service and fine dining experience possible. They had to, especially since the owner was one of the best there was. Although they weren't aware of her true identity, she constantly maintained a watchful eye on the system that she established over the last decade.

"Bill, tuck in your shirttail, you'll look more professional that way. I didn't train you to be a slob."

One of the servers walking by halted in place, looked down, inspected his uniform, then bowed to the woman standing in front of an office.

"Yes, Ms. Carson."

Once he was out of the way, Missy 3, a.k.a. Melissa Carson, noticed another detail that added to her mild displeasure. She made sure that the next person could see her look of disapproval. She stopped another server, a girl, from exiting the kitchen.

"Eliza," 3 said sternly. "I don't deny that you have got a great physique, but button up your shirt. You're serving some of the most important people in this city, so show some decorum or I'll cut your cash tips for the shift. Sell the food, not yourself, you hear me?"

"Sorry chef!" Eliza blushed, quickly setting her tray down and frantically fumbling with her shirt. "Won't happen again!"

"This isn't Hooters," 3 reminded Eliza loudly. "Just be glad I'm not your manager from where I found you."

Forcing the men and women to dress so skimpily in that place is a terrible dress code, 3 thought, shuddering. *You'd better break that habit fast Eliza, especially in my restaurant.*

Clearing her throat, 3 grabbed a small microphone along the wall and made an announcement across the entire kitchen.

"We may have made that food critic last week very happy," she declared, "but we need to keep running this place as if another one is coming through our doors! Everyone that dines with us leaves here satisfied or I will be unhappy! That's the only way this whole restaurant runs!"

Not everyone had stopped to listen to the announcement, but she knew they'd heard her while they worked nonstop. A loud chorus responded as she returned the microphone to its holder and stepped away to observe the kitchen again.

"Yes chef!!"

3 stood with her arms crossed as she surveyed the entire kitchen. Although her stance signaled that she was still on the prowl for any mistakes, she allowed her crew to see a proud smile spread across her face to indicate her satisfaction. Still, small mistakes from her staff hadn't gone unnoticed as she glanced at the plates of food exiting out the doors to her customers. It was pretty much another normal day for the restaurant. 3 turned away and decided to approach another chef with a wrinkled complexion and a mustache. He was fanning himself with a clipboard to keep cool.

"Hanging in there George?" she asked politely.

They greeted each other with an elbow bump—a kitchen "handshake."

"Of course, Ms. Carson," he chuckled. "I may be old, but I can keep up."

"Now how many times do I have to tell you? You call me Melissa," she said.

"To me, Melissa, you'll still be the little girl bartering for a job all those years ago." George smiled fondly as he reminisced. "That day during your job interview, it was as if the end of the Domino Incident delivered a miracle chef to me."

"It's hard to believe it's been exactly nine years," 3 replied in wonder.

Suddenly, she turned sharply. She had once again spotted another mistake.

"That prime rib better not set foot outside this kitchen Donny!" she bellowed, making everyone near her tremble. "Remake and rush it! You have seven minutes."

George laughed as the young server stumbled, balanced the plate carefully, whipped around, and sped back in the opposite direction with a quick "yes chef!" Like hell she would allow an incorrect steak order to head out to someone who wanted their meal perfect.

"It looked good enough to me," George muttered as 3 glared after the retreating server.

"Oh, come on George," she scoffed. "You and I both know that was overcooked."

The old chef merely laughed again.

"I never thought I'd see the day when you'd be running this place, Melissa," he admitted.

"Flattery does not help you get another break. Just think of it as my way of saying thank you when I first started," 3 said reassuringly. "You helped me start out as a chef. You taught me everything there is to know here. The success of this place is because you…"

"You are the success," George cut in. "You just absorbed my teachings and made it better."

Before the two of them could continue their conversation, they were interrupted by one of the servers.

"Miss Carson?"

George and 3 turned to look at the man approaching them. He had come in through the double doors that led to the dining room. It was Elias, one of her lead servers. 3's smile faded when she saw his expression. Something was wrong.

"What is it, Elias?" 3 asked courteously. "The kitchen is pretty busy."

"I have a rather strange order," Elias replied promptly.

"How strange?" 3 asked.

"It's very… ludicrous." Elias waved his hands back and forth.

3 focused her gaze on him, crossed her arms, and raised an eyebrow. She didn't like where this was going. She hoped that she wouldn't have to call the police or something along those lines.

"Is it the health inspector?" she asked. "We're not expecting them for another two months."

Elias shook his head.

"Did someone grope one of the servers inappropriately? Do we need to cut them off from any more alcohol and get their faces photographed for our files?"

Photographing troublesome customers or guests was for the staff's safety to avoid future incidents if they decided to return to the establishment. 3 was not going to let anyone get hurt under her watchful eye. Elias shook his head again.

"No."

"Alright Elias." 3 placed a hand on her forehead. "I don't have time to play 20 questions. What is going on that you had to tell me directly?"

Elias glanced nervously towards the doors to the dining room. He bit his lip as 3 and George waited. He seemed interested, whereas she was starting to get annoyed. Finally, Elias opened his mouth.

"There's a party here uh, well, that is... They k-kind of ordered everything off the menu," he stammered. "And pardon me chef but... I don't know what to tell them."

3's eyes widened. She looked at George, who mirrored her expression with a look of surprise on his face. It couldn't be, could it?

"There's no way." 3 shook her head calmly. "They're pranking you. Just ask them to choose what they want or have them leave if they're just going to keep messing with you."

"Begging your pardon ma'am," Elias spoke softly as he twiddled his thumbs. "They insisted. They wanted everything."

3 continued to frown.

"How many people in this party?" she asked.

"Three. Two men and one woman."

In 3's mind, she activated her scanner and was already looking at the camera footage of the restaurant's dining room. She located the tables that Elias oversaw and searched for this three-person party. When she found the right table, her eyes twitched slightly. No wonder she had detected multiple amborg signatures earlier. During the dinner rush, she had gotten busy, so she had ignored them.

3 turned her head and grabbed the microphone off the side of the wall. There was only one thing to do in this situation.

"Stop!" she commanded.

The entire kitchen instantly paused, the only sounds that could be heard were the sizzling of the stoves and the air vents circulating cold air across the room. 3, trying to keep a straight face, immediately informed them of what was about to happen.

"Attention everyone," she announced. "We have some special guests tonight. They want everything. Get started and serve Elias' table 1. They're not leaving here unsatisfied. Let's cook!"

She put the microphone back into the wall and looked at Elias.

"You tell your party of three that we'll be bringing out the appetizers first. Refill their drinks and let them know that we'd be happy to serve them. Got it?"

"Yes chef," Elias nodded. As he turned to leave, he looked back and checked for clarification. "But... your menu, all of it at full price will be..."

"Elias, take care of them," 3 replied. "We will deal with that later. Let's give them a dinner they'll never forget."

Elias bowed his head and turned to exit the kitchen. 3 glanced at George and gave him a stern look. Without hesitation, George cleared his throat and yelled at the line of chefs.

"Everyone needs to get on that ticket when it comes in! Let's get started!"

A tense moment passed as everyone exchanged nervous glances. Were they actually about to serve everything on the menu to one table? The idea was completely unprecedented, and they all knew it. It had never been done in the entire history of the restaurant. 3 didn't appreciate the precious seconds they were wasting converting oxygen to carbon dioxide.

"Well?" she tilted her head down and gazed ferociously at them, raising her voice. "What are you waiting for?! You heard him!"

The atmosphere seemed to crackle with electricity as if someone had just shocked the floor beneath them. Instantly, everyone sprang back into action, their energy levels seemingly amplified. George rolled up his sleeves even tighter in preparation, flashing 3 a thumbs-up and a confident smile. She caught his eye and took it as her cue to start moving. Nodding her thanks to him for taking charge, she began walking around the kitchen calmly and conducted an inspection.

"I want one chef from each station to report directly to me before food goes to that specific table," she ordered. "We will check and recheck so we can do this successfully!"

The appetizers started to roll off the expo line as the food runners resumed their work. It was simple: they would grab whatever plates the kitchen put under the heated countertops, move to a screen that scanned the food, and be directed where to go. Each runner had to verbally confirm into a speaker near the screen which table number they were going to, otherwise they would risk accidentally dropping off food at the wrong place. From the moment they stepped into the dining room, it was all down to them remembering on their own. Fortunately, half the food runners were robotic drones and they had a near-perfect record. However, the same couldn't be said for the human food runners.

The servers would occasionally grab plates as well. Elias would come and help deliver food to various sections of the restaurant. Whenever a plate was going to his section, he made sure that it was done right. 3 was glad that he was a lead server. He was very efficient at his job, and she had made it clear that his table 1 were VIPs.

The appetizers all made it out, and after several minutes, the bussers started bringing the plates back. Elias came in with a few of them and was getting ready to run back out, but 3 stopped him.

"Well?" she eyed the empty plates. "What do they think?"

"I think if they have entrees the way they finished the appetizers," Elias wiped the sweat off his brows, "they're going to be sick."

This made 3 smirk slightly. She was already aware of who was out there enjoying her food. Confirming it with her camera footage from the dining room surveillance also made it easier. However, to someone like Elias, her remote connection to the restaurant systems from her neural implants was not publicly known to the rest of the staff.

"I think they can handle it." She merely nodded and waved at him politely. "Take it slow."

Without question, Elias uttered a quick "yes, chef," and straightened up. For a split second, a weird look crossed his face, as if something in her behavior had aroused suspicion. Instead of pursuing the matter further, he adjusted his tie and proceeded through the doors.

Every time he came back in to report on what was happening, 3 made mental notes of his responses and any changes to his behavior. According to Elias, the party of three had strong ravenous appetites that were starting to draw a lot of attention from the other diners. Every plate brought to their table disappeared, as if sucked in like a black hole. They were devouring everything in an orderly fashion. Elias felt it was safe to say that they weren't critics, in his humble opinion, but very hungry. It seemed almost inhuman. Despite their rapid eating speed, and the sheer volume of food that was being consumed, they were apparently being extremely polite, courteous, and quite respectful to the surrounding tables. This behavior only made 3 smile, and she took it as a challenge.

"I don't like that look," George grinned. "It means you're about to light a fire."

"It's the only one I've got," 3 said as she took off her jacket.

She walked over to the door of her office, stepped inside to grab her apron off the hanger, and stepped out. Allowing the door to close, everyone near her watched as she put it on and tied it.

"Chef," one of the servers said, bewildered and with wide eyes. "You're stepping onto the line? But they're not even critics."

"Let's just say they're like family." 3 tied up her hair and patted the server on the shoulder. "Back to work Daniel. Clear a spot!"

Daniel looked quite honored as he backed away and bowed his head respectfully. He was feeling starstruck at the fact that 3 had patted his shoulder. This let everyone know that she was in a particularly good mood. The chefs on the line cleared out of the way so that 3 could join them.

"Alright team," she commanded. "Give me three salmon, add secret sauce, three filet mignon, two medium rare, one with extra garlic and the third is medium, throw on an onion ring. Caesar salad with dressing on the side. California cobb salad, no eggs please. Toast a baked potato. I've got this table myself. Josiah, serve the soup. Miranda, fresh pasta please. Understood?"

"Yes chef!" the entire line responded as they got to work.

In about 28 minutes, 3 was done making the primary meals for the VIPs. The rest of the kitchen began to ferry out other dishes one at a time at a slow pace. There was only so much space for their table. Putting every entrée on the menu in front of them would cause quite a problem. There'd be no elbow room at all.

"Where are they packing all of this food?" Josiah exclaimed as they watched the bussers bring back the empty steak and salad plates. "They're eating like they've been starving for weeks!"

"Chef," Miranda asked 3 when they stepped off the line to take a breather. "Can they afford this?"

"Oh yeah," 3 nodded. "Keep it going once they finish the pasta."

Elias suddenly came through the doors, frantically straightening his hair. They watched as he went to the sink and washed his hands.

"Ma'am," he reported, panting like he just finished a marathon. "They would also like dessert."

"That's fine. Our dessert menu isn't humongous," 3 smiled. "They can have it all."

The entire kitchen staff took note of Elias' peculiar response. He began to tremble anxiously. Finally, after a few moments of contemplation, he walked up and took a deep breath.

"Begging your pardon Ms. Carson. They want to buy dessert for every guest in the restaurant," Elias clarified his earlier statement.

A huge wave of silence washed over the entire staff. Everyone stared in shock at Elias. 3's smile faded. Out of the corner of her eye, she could see George frozen in place.

"Are they nuts?!" Josiah exclaimed.

"Shh!" Miranda nudged him.

3 shut her eyes. In one evening, her restaurant had probably faced the biggest night they had ever seen. Now this was the finisher. An order was still an order, and she was not about to refuse it.

"Alright then," she cleared her throat. "Let's get everyone's dessert orders for the night."

"Uh, Melissa?" George spoke up. "Are we going to be able to do this??"

3 faced the entire kitchen.

"This is the busiest night of this restaurant," she spoke firmly so everyone could hear. "I'm not going to force any of you to help me but I'm going to make sure we close tonight after making sure everyone is taken care of."

She gestured to everyone in the kitchen.

"Especially you," she smiled. "So, here's what we do. Servers, get out there to your sections and let them know a generous benefactor is buying dessert for everyone! I want two volunteers and one of the bakers to double check our current inventory! Let's see what everyone wants and get a complete count of what is left. If we're out of something that they order, we will suggest alternatives."

3 pointed to some of the chefs.

"If anyone finishes their tickets early, get in there and help the bakery!" she commanded. "Let's get started and plate some desserts for any tables that are finishing their entrees! Servers take the orders, and we will fulfill them! Understood?!"

A huge chorus of "Yes Chef" rang through the entire place.

"Food runners!" 3 looked at the staff members standing at the expo line. "We're not done yet. Get ready to back up the front of house staff."

Everyone immediately got started. She was extremely pleased with how resilient each person was. Their dedication was to be commended. There was no time, however, for 3 to reflect on her admiration for the staff. She quickly tightened her apron and went with George to the bakery to begin supervising the dessert tickets that would be coming their way.

As expected, they came flooding in on the screens and the bakers were instantly flustered. The customers were obviously ecstatic for complimentary desserts, and they wanted in on that action. This was going to be a long night for everyone.

Two hours later, they had finished and managed to plate the last desserts for the remaining tables. The chefs in the kitchen all began to wind down and begin their closing duties. 3 instructed the front of the house to close a half an hour earlier than usual. They no longer accepted walk-ins for the evening. 3 did a rough estimate in her head. They would have to restock half their inventory, thanks to how much food had been served. It was a very profitable evening, but they had to shut down. Otherwise, it would be too much. Everything that had to be done while the last customers were getting up and leaving was going to keep the cleaning crews here twice as long as normal.

"Ma'am." Elias approached 3 as the expo line began to shut down. "Here's the total bill for my table."

3 looked at the check that Elias had brought on a small electronic booklet, the display screen brightly lit as she checked the total amount at the bottom.

"Your table one, after ordering everything off our menu," she double checked to make sure it had been entered correctly. "Also, one dessert per person at every single other table in the entire restaurant brings us to a total of... Yup. That looks about right."

"Thank you for double-checking ma'am." Elias bowed his head. "I have never seen a total like that before. $17,324.50 from one table alone is impressive."

"I wonder what your tip is going to be," 3 shook her head, smiling at the bill.

"Too much for myself," Elias admitted. "It's good money but I would like to divide it fairly for everyone."

"That is greatly appreciated." 3 handed the book back to him. "First, get their payment. If they refuse or try to dine and dash, then come get me and I'll deal with them."

3 looked at her staff, noticing that many of them were exhausted and about to collapse.

"Take a break everyone!" she commanded. "Fifteen minutes! You all earned a respite. Well done! Let's clean up shortly and start sending you all home."

3 grabbed a stool and handed it to George.

"Take a seat, old-timer," she said. "You should rehydrate before you fall over."

"You think I could join you when you meet that party?" George chuckled as he took a sip from his water bottle. A few of the bakers were passing ice cream to each other. "I want to know who was insane enough to spend that much."

"First, take a break," 3 said firmly.

"Ma'am?"

3 turned to see that Elias had returned. She dipped her head politely to George and the rest of the bakery before walking away.

"I'll handle this," she said. "Just get ready to shut it down and go home for the night."

3 walked up to Elias and he handed the checkbook to her. She opened it a second time and looked down. The party had used a card to pay for everything and there was a 15% tip. There was also a small, bulging envelope that caught her attention.

"Isn't there some law that says tipping this much is illegal?"

"Not really." 3 opened the envelope and saw several thousand-dollar bills. "If it's left for you, legally, it's yours to do with how you like. They must have really liked you."

"The food service was what kept them happy," Elias spoke modestly.

"As your boss," 3 smiled, "I say, excellent job tonight. You earned this."

"They also asked me to come get you," Elias smiled.

"I assumed this was coming." 3 straightened up and she and Elias walked out to the dining room.

There was another corner where the servers could prepare drinks, ready water pitchers, and chill beverages with the ice machine in between their trips to and from the kitchen. Computers were set up on the counters for submitting ticket orders and accepting payment from the guests. 3 went to a nearby sink that hid just behind the water spigot and checked herself in the mirror. Her "Melissa Carson" identity had to still be spic and span if she was going to the front of the house to make any sort of appearance.

The customers she walked past noticed her, and all the nearby tables applauded. A few children were watching her eagerly, eyes wide with excitement. Keeping a casual demeanor and a warm smile on her face, she approached Elias' section to his table with her hands clasped firmly behind her back.

"May I join you?" she asked when she made eye contact with the three familiar guests.

"We would love it!"

David 117, Jack 917, and Katie 57 smiled at 3. They watched as she grabbed a chair from a nearby table and placed it at the edge of their half-circular booth.

"It's good to see you." 117 took a sip from his water.

"Funny," 3 replied with a grin. "I can't say the same about you."

57 glanced at the other two, baffled. Confusion spread among them.

"Pardon?" she asked.

"What were you three idiots thinking?"

3's tone was calm, and she kept her voice soft so that no one else would hear. She kept her composure professional, but they could see that she was not happy. 3 got a good look at the three amborgs in their civilian clothes sitting comfortably in the booth.

"I thought that the amborgs agreed that discretion was key," 3 explained. "I thought that we all discussed how important it was to maintain a low profile whenever we didn't want to be seen in public. So why did you all come strolling into my place and put us through the wringer?"

"With all due respect," 117 gulped, "we didn't think you'd come out to see us if we had asked."

"I might have," 3 shook her head, showing them her disappointed expression. "Now you've given us all extra work for closing duties."

117 and 57 glanced at each other and sighed. 917 reached forward and grabbed something from the center of the table. As he sat back and held it up in his hands, 3 realized that there had been a small pile of cash.

"What's that?" 3 raised an eyebrow as she watched 917 counting the bills slowly.

"Oh, we had a bet going," 917 explained. "After we came in and decided we were hungry, we knew that ordering everything would draw attention. I said that in less than a minute after seeing you face-to-face, you would get mad."

3 looked at 117. He held up his hands.

"90 seconds," he admitted.

"Two and a half," 57 awkwardly lifted her hand.

"Moving on," 3 interrupted. "If this is about the emergency recall, then I responded and sent a message to Dr. Kendrick saying I would return when I was able to. I can't just leave my restaurant out of the blue."

"Dr. Kendrick didn't say anything about your response." 57 tilted her head. She glanced upwards and tried to remember. "We were told to relay important information. Can we pass it on to you?"

57 had pulled out a small manila envelope and placed it in front of 3. It was like the one 917 had been given when he'd been allowed out of prison.

"Don't think that this brightens my mood," 3 said as she picked up the envelope.

"We thought you'd be pleased about us paying for our meal," 917 said. "It was delicious, and a lot of people are leaving here happy. Not only was this a nice marketing tactic, but it also proves that everyone's reviews online tell the truth. This place is amazing."

"As far as I'm concerned," 3 replied as she glanced at the table, "you three Second Group amborgs almost revealed my identity. How many recalls have been enacted over the last ten years?"

"Three," 117 answered.

With the folder in her left hand, 3 lifted her right hand and held up three fingers.

"Three," she repeated. "I have rules that were established after the first one. I confirmed it with Dr. Kendrick after the second one. Then on the third one..."

3 glanced at 917.

"I responded when I could," she said. "So, with that being said, it is good to see you. But I'm afraid you made this trip for nothing. I will join you all back home when I can at the set amount of time that has been established."

"And when exactly are we supposed to expect you?" 117 asked curiously. "You can't ignore this."

"Just because I didn't respond as efficiently as you doesn't mean I'm ignoring it," 3 said as she looked at the envelope. "I have an agreement to respond to Dr. Kendrick after 12 hours."

"Not good," 57 shook her head. She pointed at the envelope. "It has to be now."

3 lowered her gaze and glared at 57, but faltered when she noticed all three of their expressions. They were serious about something.

"Is this classified?" 3 asked.

"Yes," 117 answered.

"Then let me take this back into my office," 3 stood up from her seat. "For privacy. Whatever is in this envelope better not waste my time."

"I bet you 50 dollars that it will supersede your standardized 12-hour response timeframe," 917 said.

"I'm not taking that bet," 3 said in a low voice. "Please enjoy your desserts."

She straightened up and scanned the room. All eyes on her seemed to have been averted. The other tables nearby had gone back to their own business, and some were getting up to leave.

The others sympathized with 3's feelings on the matter. It was difficult to think about leaving her restaurant so suddenly. As the owner, it was unthinkable. Her duties as an amborg were calling to her again. Her family, her friends, were sitting here supporting the life she had always yearned for. If Dr. Kendrick was asking all of them to come back, then it meant she would have to say yes. Still, she did want to be sure of what she was doing.

The three amborgs watched as 3 turned back to them, as if she still had something to say. Instead, she merely walked back towards the kitchen.

"Do I detect some hostility?" 57 asked as they switched to a private channel.

"Oh no," 917 replied, a hint of sarcasm in his tone as he shrugged his shoulders. 117 and 57 gazed at him as they mentally chatted. "It's probably her 'Melissa' persona."

"It might be an act," 117 replied, turning his gaze to look towards the kitchen. "She's always been talented at socializing with people."

"Yeah but... if you were the owner of a place like this," 917 looked up at the ceiling. "Would you be mad at someone who just dropped in with the intention of overly supporting the restaurant?"

"We probably overdid it," 57 muttered.

They waited patiently for about five minutes. The restaurant had closed early thanks to such a profitable evening. As the last guests departed, many walked by their booth and thanked them for their generosity.

Eventually, the three of them debated whether they should also get up to leave. 117 suggested that they thank Elias for a lovely evening and that they should probably wait by the car.

Right as they slid out of the booth and stood, they heard footsteps approaching. 3 had returned, wearing a different jacket, and was carrying a bag.

"You three look ridiculous," 3 shook her head. She added herself to the private channel and her voice rang out in the back of their minds. "The conversations you have in your head are private but... if someone were to look closely, they'll know you're amborgs."

3 walked with them and they all proceeded to the front door.

"So, you opened the envelope?" 57 asked.

"Let's wait until we get to the car."

Those were the last instructions that 3 gave in their heads. After they stepped out the doors and the cold air hit their faces, she spoke in her actual voice.

"I'm having George oversee the closing duties for the night," she said with a smile. "Want to hang out? Let's go get some drinks or something."

"Uh," 117 replied with a confused look. "Are you allowed to just leave like that?"

"She owns the place," 917 pointed out. "I think she can do whatever she likes."

"Perks of the job," 3 let out a sigh. "Now who's driving? Where are we parked?"

57 led the way as they made their way down the sidewalk.

"We're not actually going for drinks, are we?" 117 asked.

"Of course not," 3 replied, pointing her thumb over her shoulder back at the restaurant. "That was just for the hosts at the entrance. We can talk freely now."

"I'm glad you're back with us," 57 replied.

"Let me be clear about something, Katie, David, and Jack. I'm not entirely happy."

3 walked alongside 57. Even though all three of them were slightly taller than her, they were all feeling anxious. Her anger was quite apparent, and they felt like they were about to face a scolding.

"Thanks to you three, I had to help the dish pit organize all those plates of everything you ate... Now we've missed the last train for the night. The next one won't be ready till morning. You can explain to Dr. Kendrick why we're late heading home."

The others followed 3 to the car. When they reached it, 117 unlocked it and was about to open the front passenger door when 57 stopped him.

"I'm too full to drive tonight," she muttered, shaking her head.

117 was happy to oblige and allowed her to climb into the passenger seat. She probably wanted to take a break since she had been driving for several hours. From Iowa to Pennsylvania and New York within one day was quite a feat of strength and endurance. If you kept an amborg behind the wheel for long enough, even they would eventually exhibit signs of physical exhaustion that most drivers faced. 117 walked around the hood to get in the driver's seat. 917 and 3 hopped into the back.

"Question," 917 felt confused, raising his hand. "You've seen the envelope, right?"

3 let out a soft grunt, indicating yes.

"So, you're coming home with us?"

"No, we're going back to my apartment," 3 replied. "I have some work to do, and it must be taken care of before it all goes to hell. There aren't any trains and calling for an airship to pick us up will draw a lot of attention. I highly doubt we are all interested in driving the entire night all the way back to A.I. Industries. Come back to my place and relax."

"But, if you saw the picture in the envelope," 117 said as he started the ignition, "we need to go home now."

"This whole issue with Serina 43," 917 said. "Does that not matter to you?"

3 turned and glared at each of them. She landed her stern gaze on 917, making him cower slightly.

"Of course it matters. But guess what, cloud-for-brains," she snapped, "I had to calculate exactly how much money that needed to be split for cashing out the tips. Thanks to your extra generous one, it reduced some of my employees to tears of joy when they saw how much we made in one night."

"And that's a bad thing?" 117 asked, glancing in the mirrors and switching his blinker on.

"Not finished," 3 snarled, which caused 117 to face front and shut up.

"Shutting up," he replied meekly. He took the opportunity to turn and merge out into traffic.

"George was kind enough to finish overseeing the closing duties with another one of my managers. He insisted that I leave early to hang out with you three since it was pretty obvious to everyone in the place that you all seemed to know me," 3 continued in a soft dulcet tone. 917 could see that she was hiding her annoyance, but it threatened to spill out again at any moment. "Your enormous appetites, the massive bill, and the really awkward private and silent conversation before I came out to get you. Tell me, were you trying to make a scene? Or did you just want to piss me off?"

"Well," 57 started, but 3 whirled to her.

"Shut! Up!" she roared.

57 shrank in her seat.

"I had to skip my own restaurant's closing duties," 3 barked out to them. It felt like they were being scolded by a parent. "I needed to calculate all of the financial payouts for every one of my employees, had to leave the kitchen in charge of cleanup duty which might be more work for the next morning thanks to all of what you put us through, and now we have to go back to my place so

I can take care of a lot of other things. I am a general manager and owner of a restaurant in the middle of New York, and I almost got my cover blown by you three. So yeah, excuse me if I need to go back home to unwind for a few minutes and get some of my affairs in order before reporting in."

So, she hadn't ignored the emergency recall. 3 just needed some time to plan for that. They had been too hasty in their approach. No wonder she was extremely annoyed.

"Don't you have other managers or people on staff that can handle all of what you do?" 917 politely asked.

"One's on maternity leave, another is on vacation and the last one, I gave the day off because she keeps getting cheated on and it's understandably frustrating at times. It's hard to concentrate on the job when you're upset, so I sent her home."

There was an awkward pause as 117 reached for the dashboard and pushed a button.

"That's rough buddy," a familiar voice played from the car radio. They all turned to stare.

57 held back her laughter. 117 timidly continued facing forward and didn't say anything else. 917 buried his face into one of his hands, trying not to laugh. 3 looked livid.

"Why did you play a meme?" she asked angrily.

"I wasn't sure if I was allowed to talk," 117 mumbled. "I felt bad for your manager. The one that got cheated on. I thought a classic internet meme would be appropriate."

"Excellent 117," 917 said sarcastically. "Just dig our graves right here on this very spot."

"Dr. Kendrick's orders are absolute," 3 sighed. "But you need to realize that like this numbskull who lived in prison", she jabbed a thumb at 917, "I need some prep time if I'm going to just up and leave my job."

"Wait," 917 turned his head sharply. "How did you know? Who told you?"

117 pulled over, parked the car safely, and turned off the engine. There was a pause as everyone stared at him, bewildered.

"Why did you do that?" 3 immediately rounded on him again when the car became silent. "We need to get moving."

"Sorry," 117 said nervously, scratching his head. "I don't know where you live, 3. I turned the car off because if we idle more than 12 minutes, we'll get fined."

"Oh," 3 blinked and realized the mistake. After a brief pause, she put her hand on the shoulder rest of his seat and looked at the dashboard. "I just texted it to your car. You can head there now."

117 looked at the address, nodded, and started the car up again. He shifted it into gear, glanced over his shoulder, checked for oncoming traffic, turned outwards, switched on his blinker, and inched out into the street a second time. 3 had decided to stop lecturing them and had calmed down while she rested in the back seat.

"Did they starve you? 917?"

917 had been looking out the window when she said his name. He turned and looked at 3.

"Pardon?"

"I knew you were in prison because I could smell it when I sat down across from you."

917's eyes widened. He lifted his sleeve and sniffed it.

"S-smell?" he stammered. "You can smell that I was in prison??"

"Aside from you confirming it just now," 3 nodded, "I've been trained to sniff and taste flavors from all sorts of food and drinks from around the world. Those prison uniforms have a unique scent. I've catered and cooked for prisoners before. Did they starve you?"

"I was well-fed," 917 replied.

"You ate the most food when you came in for dinner," 3 stated, crossing her arms. She didn't believe him at all. "Between 117 and 57, it was almost as if you had been starving for months and then you finally got a taste of genuine food. Did they starve you in prison?"

""No," 917 answered. "I swear, the quality of their food was good but not as good as yours. I missed your cooking."

"Thanks. It's understandable. After all it is a prison," 3 scoffed. "Glad to see that they're keeping food safety at average levels."

"Your food is always the best," 57 said from the front seat. "I just left an anonymous review online about my dining experience. It was great!"

"I agree," 117 nodded as he changed lanes. "I would submit a review as well, but I cannot be distracted right now."

"You haven't changed a bit since the last time I saw either of you," 3 sighed. "Still a bunch of young morons."

They made their way off the island of Manhattan and traveled across the bridge leading out of the city. It was hard to believe that the area they were driving in had been an urban battlefield over ten years ago, one they had all been involved in. All the brand-new structures and buildings stood tall and proud. The signs of the devastating conflict before seemed to have been wiped away completely.

"We have a few minutes," 3 suddenly said. "917, why did you go to prison?"

From the front seats, 117 and 57 quickly spoke up.

"Not it!" both said instantly, but 117 had been the fastest and 57 let out a groan.

"What are you doing?" 917 asked.

"Oh, we just figured that more people were going to ask so 57 and I were trying to see who could opt out of sharing," 117 replied casually.

"Fine," 57 sighed. "We just figured that you would be tired of having to explain the whole story again and again, 917."

117 went back to focusing on the road as 57 shared the details. 917 jumped in whenever it seemed like the story was straying off-topic, but they managed to give the whole story by the time they reached 3's apartment building.

"Wow," 3 said once 57 and 917 finished the recap. "I never realized that Dr. Kendrick would actually send one of us away like that. I almost wish I had replied sooner when the emergency recall was activated."

"I think it's fine," 117 said. "Under the circumstances, he probably understands why you couldn't answer. You also did have a personal rule set in place."

"That's the problem I've always had with the emergency recall," 3 sighed. "Not all of us can just be immediately summoned like that. We were all free to do with our lives as we pleased ten years ago. Coming back to handle large scale events is fine with me but if I'm being honest, I dislike being pulled away so suddenly from where I was. It's so inconvenient."

"It does sound like you're unhappy. Are you saying you don't want the responsibility of what we do?"

117 asked his question in a polite and calm manner, but his face showed concern at what 3 was saying. 3 locked eyes with him in the rearview mirror.

"Don't go putting words in my mouth David 117," 3 said sternly. "I will always come back whenever A.I. Industries needs me. If there's something that requires all amborgs available, then yes, I will be there. Sometimes, all I want before I switch lives is time. I understand that I made a mistake by not showing up for my actual job or even giving Dr. Kendrick a proper response...

but if we are all supposed to be this one big family, capable of almost anything, then he needs to trust us more."

117 drove until he found an empty space. As he slowly parallel parked, he listened to 3's words closely. 917 and 57 also listened intently.

"You don't have to depend on Dr. Kendrick all the time and he doesn't have to as well," 3 said when 117 came to a stop. "You all have your own personal lives to lead and there are people in your lives that you have to take care of. So, before I put on my uniform again, I want to make sure that the people I care about get their paychecks. I can handle all of that if I just get a few hours of personal time. I was mad because you three showed up unexpectedly and put me on the spot. The world, in my humble opinion, doesn't need Missy 3, an old crumbling veteran of the First Group, to be at the very front of whatever is coming. Being an amborg makes us necessary workers but it doesn't mean we should just submit ourselves to that lifestyle permanently. Until such time as the world comes to an end, then it's our job to make sure that we act as if it intends to keep spinning. If we prevent the end from happening, I want to go back to my restaurant and just live my life peacefully, the way it's supposed to be."

117 wondered if this was how the other First Group amborgs felt. 3 was definitely coming from a place that had taught her a lot. She had probably met hundreds of influential people that dined at her restaurant who'd shared life lessons with her. His entire life, after becoming cybernetically enhanced, he felt that he would always be doing what he did best, which was remaining at A.I. Industries. Her experience was a new and unique perspective that she had probably spent a long time thinking about.

"I mean, 57," 3 gestured to the front passenger seat and 57 turned her head towards them. "You like being a police officer, right?"

"It's a different perspective," 57 answered with a nod. "The fact that no one notices that there's an amborg hiding among their ranks often gives me a lot of insight into how we're perceived."

"Forget about that," 3 shook her hand. "Do you like doing what you do? Choosing to be a police officer was a decision you made back then because it's what you wanted, right?"

"Right. I wanted to keep protecting people but also not be seen as an amborg at times."

3 turned to 117.

"And you. You got married to Audrey. The leader of the Second Group with a normal human," she said tapping on his shoulder. "Why did you marry her?"

"I love her," 117 stated.

"Yes! Super important," 3 nodded encouragingly. "You wanted to marry her because you wanted to be happy, right?"

"Yes," 117 replied. "Right."

"Did you kiss her goodbye before you left her?"

"Uh, why is that important?" 117 asked, bemused.

"Did you do it?" 3 asked insistently. "Because those small moments in your marriage are things you should hold onto. It's what you fight for, right? More of those moments. Don't always be so quick to rush back into the line of duty. I wouldn't be surprised if Audrey wishes that you had stayed with her a bit longer before this whole entire incident."

3 turned to 917.

"And you," she declared. "Did it make you feel better? When you avenged Silhed?"

917 hesitated as he thought about his answer.

"Not entirely," his tone darkened. "But if I had waited until someone gave me permission, they would have gotten away."

3 held a somber look and got ready to open the door.

"The three of you," 3 looked at everyone in the car. "You all have these abilities because you wanted them, just like I did. It doesn't mean you should forget who you are."

She stepped out of the car and headed over to the apartment entrance. Following her lead, the Second Group trio gave each other quick glances, then exited the car. As they entered the lobby of the apartment complex, they couldn't help but wonder, was 3 right about them?

"Nice place," 57 commented as they looked around.

They followed 3 through the lobby. The business office was closed since it was after hours, and they noticed three booths in full view in the corner. A humanoid drone caretaker was seated in one of them, inactivated. 3 strolled up to it and pressed the button in front of it. A loud bell rang, and the caretaker sparked to life. A bright gold LED light shined in its eyes as it glanced at the person in front of it.

"Ah, welcome home!" They watched it wave its hand politely to them. "I am this residence's 24/7 caretaker. How may I help you today?"

"Apartment 902," 3 stated. "I have some guests staying with me for the night."

"Splendid," the drone said in a very upbeat manner. "Melissa Carson of residence 902. How many guests are staying with you for a... one night stay?"

"Three of them," 3 held up three fingers.

"I need their full names, if they wouldn't mind stepping up to the glass."

3 turned and stepped to the side. She gestured for one of them to come forward. 117 realized he was closest and walked up to the window.

"Greetings," he blurted out. "I mean, hi."

"State your full name," the caretaker requested in a kind tone.

"David... Uh... Walker!" 117 realized that he hadn't actually prepared a response and thought of the first last name to pop in his mind.

"Excellent," the caretaker nodded as it entered the name into the computer. "Next please."

The caretaker immediately turned and fixed its gaze on 57. The bright light from its eye had her mesmerized for a second and she nearly fumbled her words.

"Katie! Uh, Walker," 57 stated.

917 looked at the others, slightly amused. 3 gave him a don't-even-think-about-it look, but it was too late. The caretaker entered 57's name into the computer and then looked up at 917.

"Jack Walker," he grinned at the caretaker when he walked up to the booth.

"Oh my god," 3 muttered in annoyance. "This isn't what I meant when I said that, oh never mind."

"Welcome David, Katie and Jack Walker," the caretaker finished typing into the keyboard and submitted the information. "What a nice group of visitors! Please obey all rules of this building and enjoy your stay."

"Missed opportunity," 917 whispered as 3 grudgingly led them to the elevator.

"For what?" 57 asked.

"I should have said my name was Jay," 917 snickered.

"A missed opportunity indeed," 117 grinned.

"Children," 3 sighed, pressing the button to summon the elevator. "I work with children trapped in adult bodies."

They heard the ding and the elevator doors slid open. They slowly walked inside.

After arriving on the ninth floor, 3 stepped off the elevator first and veered to the right.

"What a cozy building," 57 looked at the (what color? "opaque" just means "not see-through") walls and the (ornate, stylish, fancy, abstract?) paintings hung up. "And you live on the top floor. The restaurant must be doing really well for you."

"Thanks," 3 answered. "Hold on."

They rounded a corner and spotted some unusual activity. As the four of them made their way towards apartment 902, they noticed a man and a woman standing outside another door. From the way they were dressed, it looked like they were coming back from a date. 3's neighbor, they guessed was the girl, because she was trying to enter her apartment. Casually, they all did a scan. She didn't have her keys out and her date appeared to be looming over her, creating an uncomfortable vibe. As they got closer, they listened in on the conversation to gather more information.

"Come on," the man smiled as he backed the woman against the door and tried to lean his arm high above her head. "The least you could do is let me in. I won't stay long."

"Uh oh..." 117 privately messaged the rest of them.

"I had a good night," the woman was trying to say, visibly uncomfortable. "But it's late and I need to turn in. Look, I'm trying to be nice here."

"Let me in and we'll have a good one," the man smiled, which caused the woman to glance downwards and to the side. "Come on, if you were nice, you'd invite me in."

Collectively, they had all heard enough. 3 moved ahead and made herself known.

"Hey!" she called out to them.

The man and the woman turned and noticed the four amborgs walking towards them. In their civilian clothes, they were still properly disguised, so it just looked like a small group of friends.

"Do you mind?" 3 asked sternly.

"Uh, Missy," 57 tapped 3 on her shoulder and stepped forward. "Maybe I should handle this one. Excuse me miss, sorry to interrupt, is everything ok here?"

Before the woman had a chance to answer, she got cut off by her date.

"We're all fine here," the man immediately replied, waving them off. "Don't worry about it. Thanks."

"We weren't asking you," 917 loudly cleared his throat. "She was talking to her."

The woman looked relieved when she saw that she had other people backing her up. She nervously glanced up at the man, then looked at them and shook her head frantically.

"That's that," 57 declared. "Please show yourself out, sir."

This didn't appease him at all. The man changed his whole demeanor in a matter of seconds. Complete red flag. His face was contorted with rage as he straightened up and walked menacingly towards them. If only he knew.

"What's your problem? Get lost! Who the hell do you think you...?!"

He didn't get a chance to finish the question. As he rushed forward, he reached out to grab 57's shoulder. She was just a couple of inches shorter than him, but his plan to assert some dominance backfired. Before he knew it, she had him in an arm lock, pinning him against the wall. He yelped in pain as 57 whipped out her LAPD badge from her pocket and flashed it at him.

"Listen," she declared firmly. "No means no and she has spoken. Now walk out of here before I book you for assaulting a cop! Your choices are either go home or go to jail!"

57 then let go of him and he stepped away from them. He massaged his shoulder and quickly departed without another word. 917 let out a laugh.

"You know, if he had looked more carefully," he pointed a thumb over his shoulder in the direction of where the man left and smiled, "he would have noticed that you're not a New York police officer. Your badge says, 'City of Los Angeles.'"

"Well, it does scare them off quite well," 57 smirked.

"Are you ok?" 3 turned her attention to her neighbor, who was nodding.

"Yes," she sighed. "My internet date went full... internet date."

"Well, we're glad to have been here," 117 stated.

"And you wanted to rush us," 3 rolled her eyes.

3's neighbor, thankfully, didn't hear her comment. She smiled brightly as she shook their hands, filled with gratitude. She looked much better than she had a few minutes earlier. Her smile could probably melt through ice.

"Thank you for helping me. I'm Lina!" she said.

"David," 117 introduced himself.

"Katie," 57 waved as she pocketed her badge while Lina shook her right hand.

"Jack," 917 nodded politely.

"Melissa," 3 said. "But you can call me Missy."

"Wait," Lina looked at 3 more closely. "As in Melissa Carson? You own Crystalline! I knew you were a chef, but I didn't realize you were a famous one!"

"Wait, how did you know?" 3 asked curiously.

"Sometimes I walk past your door, and it smells fantastic," Lina admitted. "Also, you're really loud in the kitchen sometimes. You blast music while you're cooking, right?"

"Right," 3 nodded. Suddenly, realization dawned on her. "Sorry. Wait, you didn't file a noise complaint, did you?"

"Oh no," Lina shook her head. "Your music isn't that loud. I can just hear you through the walls sometimes."

"What do you do in your kitchen?? Do you host concerts or something?" 57 asked.

"Loud music helps me cook," 3 replied, blushing slightly. "If I can tune out my music while I work, then I can properly work in my kitchen with all the other background noise out of the way."

"Well, I really appreciate you so much!" Lina nodded to all of them, her long black hair flowing as she did so. "It must be nice to have friends over after a long day. Are you really from L.A.?"

57 nodded.

"Yeah," she said awkwardly. "Long day is quite an understatement."

"I just moved here a month ago," Lina said as she looked at 3. "My apologies for not introducing myself sooner. I guess I should meet my neighbors first before going on dates with total strangers online."

Lina turned and gazed at 917. She looked him up and down quite curiously.

"Hou hoi sum gin dou lei!"

Everyone's translators instantly went to work in their brains. Lina was speaking Cantonese. 917 looked fascinated as he responded.

"Oh," he lit up and grinned. "Nei hou mei nu."

Lina blushed as she looked away and tucked her hair behind her ear. The other three amborgs knew exactly what he had said. Unfortunately, they had to keep their reactions hidden because Lina was a civilian and had no idea that they had built-in translation software.

"Hey," 3 cleared her throat. "No disrespect or anything but I don't speak Cantonese."

"I'm sorry," 917 dipped his head to the others. He turned and continued smiling at Lina. "It's just so rare to hear someone speak it in this part of the world."

"Well, I'm glad I met all of you," Lina smiled again. It looked like the incident from moments earlier had already passed completely. "I hope to see you again soon. I think I've kept you from your plans long enough. Goodnight."

Everyone said their farewells as Lina unlocked her door and stepped inside. As a precaution, they waited until they heard the lock click before proceeding to 3's door. 3 unlocked it and pushed it inwards.

"We are sure that guy from earlier is out of the building, right?" 57 whispered.

"Yup, I checked the security footage, he's gone. If he comes back, I texted the caretaker and reported it downstairs. Also, we're alone now," 3 grumbled as they all clambered inside. "You can transmit this conversation on a private chat. Why are you whispering?"

"Just looking the part," 57 shrugged as everyone passed through, and the door closed.

"Well, she was nice," 117 remarked as he looked towards the entrance.

"Here's hoping she gets a better date next time," 917 said as 3 turned on the lights.

"She was totally looking at you," 57 nudged him in the shoulder. "Smooth talking her with the Cantonese? Wonder what she'd think if she found out that she had been saved by four amborgs."

"Technically," 117 lifted a finger and pointed at 57, "you actually saved her."

"Well yeah," 57 shrugged. "But it was clear she liked tall 'shuai ge' prison boy right here."

"You get points for saying that correctly," 917 acknowledged 57's attempt at a Cantonese phrase. "Sounded more like the Mandarin pronunciation though."

"Anyway, I've got snacks in the fridge if anyone was actually still hungry," 3 pointed inside the kitchen as she walked to the living room. "I doubt it, but you can help yourself if you want."

3's apartment was beautifully furnished. The lights in her hallway had switched on when she hit the button. Once they stepped past the kitchen and into the living room, the sensors detected their presence, and the place was completely illuminated. In the center of the room, there were two steps that descended into a lovely pit that was lined with lush red carpet. A sofa, flanked by two armchairs on each side, encircled a coffee table in the center facing a huge TV. Above, an ornate glass chandelier glimmered. Just behind the TV were floor-to-ceiling windows, and other buildings could be seen through the tinted glass. Off to the (right/left?) were a flight of stairs leading up to some rooms right on the second-floor landing.

"Feel free to put on the TV if you want to amuse yourselves," 3 called to them as she ascended the stairs. "I need to do some work in my office. I'll let Dr. Kendrick know that we'll be back home in the morning. The bathroom is either this next door here or the one across from the kitchen. Third door up here is my room and the last two at the end are guest rooms if you need a break."

They watched as 3 walked up to the top of the stairs. She opened the first door and looked down at them before entering.

"Whatever you do," she said warningly, "don't trash the place or cause any issues. You think you can handle that?"

"Sure," 117 nodded, and the other two amborgs agreed.

3 then disappeared through the door upstairs, leaving the three of them alone. 117 stretched as they all went into the living room. No one was hungry, that was for sure. 57 took a seat on the couch and leaned back to rest. 917 decided to go to the bathroom for a minute while 117 walked up to the window.

It didn't have curtains, but instead, it was made of a new tempered glass with an impressive feature. It had the ability to change its tint color automatically depending on the circumstances.

When he approached the window, it began to clear up entirely, revealing the buildings across the street and offering a clearer view of the night sky.

"You know," 117 said as he looked at the building across from them, "3 might enjoy this place, but I probably couldn't. I prefer houses instead of apartments."

"On my salary as a police officer," 57 said as she let out a relaxing sigh, "I can only live on the third floor or below. Every apartment back in L.A. costs three times as much when you go up past the fourth or fifth floor. It's crazy. I was thinking of maybe signing up for the Good Neighbor program soon."

"What program is that?" 117 asked.

"The LAPD will basically put you in a house in a certain neighborhood hoping to increase relations between the police and the people you protect,"

57 explained. "Seems like a good idea. I just wanted to find a roommate before I applied for that."

"Even houses are expensive," 117 said. "When I'm not on duty, I'm constantly searching for a new place to live."

"Moving into a house?" 57's eyes filled with excitement. "Seems like it would be really good for you."

"Maybe 3 is right," 117 said as he glanced up at the door to her office. "After Audrey graduated from school and joined the military, she's been based in a few different states, but we made it work whenever we both had the time off. I think I should find a more permanent home for us. It might make us happier if we set up proper foundations."

"Well, you better do it before you permanently work as an amborg full-time."

917 had exited the bathroom and was looking at all the photos and books that lined the shelves.

"Out of the Second Group, you and I don't actually have official civilian alter egos," he said, looking at 117. "Have you ever really thought about something that you would have wanted to do if you weren't an amborg? It just seems strange that you've avoided this subject for so long."

"I could say the same about you," 117 replied. "Is there anything you want to do aside from going back to prison after this mission?"

917 smirked.

"I asked first," he replied.

The two of them ended that conversation before either could properly dive into the subject. 57 eyed both of them and decided to rest her head back. 917 went back to looking at the photos on the wall while 117 looked down.

"Being an amborg is what I'm good at," he said softly. "I don't know... if there's anything else for me."

917 turned to gaze at 117.

"You chose to be an amborg," he stated. "I didn't. Remember?"

"917," 57 lifted her head. "We weren't taking a jab at you about that."

"I know," 917 sighed. "But 3 does raise a lot of good points. We should decide what we want to do. But in my case, a coma patient can't exactly choose, can I?"

It was publicly known to many people that 917 was a rather unique amborg in the ranks of A.I. Industries. He was the first amborg to be cybernetically enhanced out of a coma. The official records stated that Dr. Kendrick had found him dying in a hospital. Acting fast in a short amount of time, Dr. Kendrick had taken the risk of enhancing him while he was out. Miraculously, the enhancement and implants that had been built into his body had successfully saved his life. 917 eventually woke up as a member of the Second Group. However, there was a huge drawback to this.

"I don't remember anything prior to enhancement," he said. "I don't know if I chose to be this way or if it was just luck. If I'm being honest, I'd give up my abilities if I could just remember who I was before we became the saviors of humanity over the last decade. Who am I? What am I now? A monster? What was I like before all of this?"

57 and 117 gave each other a concerned look. They had already heard 917 talk about this a few times before. Unfortunately, neither of them had the means to help 917 out of his peculiar issue.

Suddenly, 917 stared off into space, his eyes focusing on something unseen. 57 and 117 quietly watched.

"I'm going out," he said abruptly.

"Now?" 117 asked.

"It's just for a few hours," 917 explained. "You can come with me if you like."

57 gazed at 117. Raising her eyebrow, she looked back at 917 suspiciously.

"Who just texted you?" she asked.

"An old friend."

917 forwarded the text he'd just received.

"Oh," 117 and 57 responded simultaneously. "Her."

"3!" 917 called upstairs.

A text message alert in their heads grabbed their attention immediately.

"Keep it down!" 3 hissed. "It's late and I don't need a noise complaint!"

"Sorry," 917 replied, texting her with his mind. "We're going out for a few hours, but we'll be back in time to head home together."

"Where could you possibly be going at this time of night??" 3 asked. "Weren't you the ones in a hurry to get back?"

"We're stopping by Eternal Enigma," 917 explained.

"Oh," 3 replied. Even before she finished her response, they all knew that she understood their intentions right away. "I guess that's ok then. Say hi to Tessa for me."

"Understood."

"917," 3 texted him with an angry face emoji. "No sneaking off to see Lina."

"I wasn't about to," 917 replied, heading to the front door. "117 and 57 are coming with me."

"Right, be careful out there."

917, 57 and 117 walked out of the apartment and into the hall. Retracing their steps, they followed the signs back to the elevator. When they got in and began their descent to the ground floor, they continued the conversation.

"Tessa texted you?" 117 asked. "What did she say?"

"She wanted to know if I could stop by," 917 shrugged. "Now's probably one of the only times we may get to see her."

After they got out of the elevator, they walked past the caretaker's booth. It turned its gold LED face light in their direction.

"We'll be back in a bit," 57 explained cheerfully. "Just going out to say hi to a friend."

"Please be safe," the caretaker waved at them. "It is late. Stay together as a group. Have a nice rest of your evening."

Eternal Enigma wasn't too far away, but they couldn't walk there in the time they had. Unanimously, they decided to leave 117's car near 3's apartment. A brand-new vehicle like his would stick out like a sore thumb where they needed to go. 117 flagged down a taxi instead. The driver took them to the entertainment district, which was an area that was open 24/7. It had a steady stream of people wanting to visit the clubs, party through the night, and leave all their worries at home. When they arrived, they stepped out and night turned to day.

The streetlights and every building in sight illuminated the bustling streets, a stark contrast to 3's neighborhood. The pedestrians they passed by seemed to be going about their business as if it were still daytime. After a little bit more walking, they found their destination.

Eternal Enigma was an adult entertainment club. It was a very popular place in this district. As the three of them approached the building, 117 nodded at the electronic signs and the holographic display in the front windows. Those looked like recent upgrades.

"The place seems to be doing quite well."

They walked towards the entrance and up to the two bouncers who were conversing with each other. One was a drone, and the other was a human who was texting on his phone. They didn't seem to be putting much effort into their jobs, which made 917 a little annoyed. They had to know that at this time of night, it was dangerous to slack off. Their footsteps didn't quite catch their attention like they should. The drone stared attentively at them, but the man merely kept his eyes glued to his phone. A moment passed until he realized there were guests in front of him.

"IDs please?" the human bouncer held out his hand, not even bothering to look up.

The amborgs stared. The lack of attention and discipline baffled them. Naturally, 917 looked at the two of them and cleared his throat. He crossed his arms.

"I'm pretty sure I didn't change that much in the last four years," he declared. "Still addicted to your phone, Bruce?"

The human bouncer tore his eyes away from his phone and looked at the three of them carefully. For a brief moment, 917's tone made him laugh. Right before he made eye contact, the amborgs could see that he was preparing some sort of snarky response. Once he took a good look at 917's stern expression, Bruce instantly went pale and stepped to the side.

"M-master amborg!" he stammered, realizing his mistake. "My apologies! C-come right in!"

"I'm not your master," 917 said as he moved forward. He turned and leaned in menacingly as he walked past the bouncers. "You're lucky I don't dock you a day's work."

The bouncer looked on the verge of tears as he apologized profusely and bowed to all three of them.

"Was that necessary?" 117 asked when they entered, the door shutting behind them.

"Yup. Everyone in this place is supposed to be properly protected," 917 scoffed. "If every person in here worked like that guy out there, it's going to go to hell. You'd have too many customers in here outnumbering the staff."

"My my... look who's in the house."

A sudden loud announcement interrupted the activity in the main room. The music paused, and all eyes turned to them.

"Ladies and gentlemen, we have some genuine celebrities in the house. Let us please welcome three of our lovely beneficiaries."

The trio was greeted with thunderous cheers from both patrons and employees throughout the entire venue.

"Keep an eye on your wallets," 917 said as he led them towards the bar. "57, I need you to do me a favor."

"What is it?" 57 asked as she politely greeted a half-naked man who immediately grabbed her hand and bowed to her. "Oh, that's so sweet, but we're not here for that."

917 pulled his wallet out of his pocket and extracted a card.

"You mind hitting the ATM for me? I need about... this much."

He transmitted an amount to her, and she quickly grabbed it.

"Why don't you do it?" she asked suspiciously as a slightly intoxicated guest let out a loud whoop next to her.

"Are you currently single?" 917 asked as one of the female dancers hugged him and got very close.

"Yes, but what does that have to do with...?"

"Just keep moving," 917 instructed as he gently reached for the dancer's arms and pulled them away from going too far south. "Another time Betty. Good to see you."

917 urged 117 to stay at his side.

"117, keep your left hand out of your pocket."

"What?" 117 asked, confused, but complied anyway.

Upon seeing his wedding band, a few of the employees politely backed off. The effect was surprising. They were keeping a polite four-foot circular boundary around them.

"What just happened??" 117 looked around. "Do I smell or something?"

"Would you like a drink?" someone asked him respectfully before 917 could reply.

"Or would you like to sit down, and we'll rub your shoulders?"

917 and 117 both made their way to the bar as 57 split away and tried to get to the ATM.

"Seriously, what just happened?" 117 leaned in to whisper to 917.

"I'm keeping your marriage intact," he replied as he placed his hands on the bar. "Audrey probably wouldn't approve of any of these dancers or entertainers putting their hands on you."

"She supports this type of business. We both do," 117 shrugged. "My marriage remains strong."

"Yeah, you weren't there when we got yelled at after your bachelor party," 917 said casually.

117 paused to think for a moment. Instead of having one traditional bachelor party prior to his wedding, there was more than one. All of which seemed pretty hazy once he tried to remember.

"Wait, she yelled at you?" 117 asked, stunned. "Which party? Thanks to you, I had four! How come I don't recall this particular event?"

"Uh, hold that thought."

"You weren't exactly... sober towards the end of the party," 917 replied sheepishly. "Angel and I struggled to get you to the wedding on time."

"That part sounds familiar," 117 thought harder.

One of the big issues he always had with his multiple bachelor parties was the fact that the rest of his friends in the Second Group didn't officially call them bachelor parties. For some reason, every time he thought he was going to spend quality time with the other amborgs and celebrate his pending nuptials, he would get roped into another operation or mission.

After getting his hopes up for a fourth time, 117 remembered very vaguely what happened that night before he was supposed to marry Audrey the following morning. He had stubbornly refused to allow the others to turn his night into another mission and remembered large bottles of alcohol.

"Yeah," 117 turned his head sharply at 917. "That's right! You made me think that we were going to celebrate, I got mad when I realized you and 999 were secretly on a stakeout and you dragged me along! What was the point of labeling it a bachelor party if you were just going to work??"

"We explained it to you afterwards," 917 replied coolly. "We were protecting you and Audrey. You still haven't thanked us for what we did."

"Crashing our honeymoon?" 117 grumbled.

"Postponing it," 917 clarified.

"You threw Audrey off a moving train!"

"Technically, Angel did that," 917 cleared his throat. "It had to be done. You both got married, didn't you? I call that a successful operation."

"Why do I seem to remember... bagpipes? The morning of my wedding?" 117 scrunched his eyes and continued to sift through his memory banks.

"Oh yeah," 917 snickered. "That was one of the funniest wake-up calls ever."

117 lifted a finger and poked 917's shoulder.

"When we get back..."

He started to speak but 917 brushed him aside as the bartender walked up to them.

"Jack! Darling!"

"Hello Crystal," 917 smiled.

117 was a little annoyed that 917 had changed the subject. All of that flew out of his head when he turned and looked at the woman behind the bar. His eyes widened a fraction. The woman that 917 had greeted was absolutely stunning.

"I haven't seen your friend before," Crystal said as she leaned forward. Her breasts were barely contained by a bright green bikini top, the strings fighting hard for their lives. She casually gazed down and winked at 117. "And from the way his eyes have wandered, it's his first time here."

She licked her lips slightly and let out a small seductive laugh. 917 turned to look at 117 who quickly picked his head up and focused. She had clearly hooked him in on purpose.

"Her eyes are up here 117," 917 pointed at Crystal. She leaned on the bar and rested her elbows on the counter. "Left hand. On display. Put it on the bar now."

117 silently obeyed and placed his hands on the wooden counter. Crystal gazed down and noticed the wedding band. She understood right away and nodded.

"Must be a very special girl to have put a ring on this cutie," Crystal sounded a little disappointed, but she smiled politely. "I admire that about devoted men."

"Your features already do an amazing job of selling business," 917 redirected the conversation from 117 so they could get back on track. "Is Tessa here?"

"Out of prison and you want nothing to do with me? I'm hurt."

Crystal placed a hand on her chest and pretended to look crestfallen. 117 was impressed that 917 was able to restrain himself in such a predicament. A half-naked woman was trying to put in the work on him, but he wasn't letting himself become distracted. His focus was quite strong, considering they were in an environment meant to test it.

"News travels fast," 917 smirked.

"Well, we have our ways here," Crystal spoke enticingly to them. "After all, someone who's been one of our most generous benefactors for years suddenly pops in through our doors. It's enough to make anybody excited around here."

"I'm afraid we're not staying long," 917 said as he playfully stroked the back of Crystal's hand. "It has us in a rather urgent situation. We don't have time for fun. Otherwise, I'd be more than happy to check in with a lot of other people here."

"Here you go!"

A massive stack of money was placed on the counter, and all heads turned to see 57 had arrived at the bar.

"Hi," she said as she placed her hands on the bar. "We good up here?"

"Oh my," Crystal looked 57 up and down. "A pleasure. You know, we could..."

"Not interested," 917 interrupted when he saw Crystal's eyes fill with desire. "57 is not here looking for a job."

Crystal sighed, stopping herself from climbing over the bar countertop like some kind of sexy predator locking onto its prey. Before she could hunt, 917 had intervened.

"Aww," she shrugged as 917 grabbed the stack of cash. "All the pretty friends you bring in are never here for me. I still remember that other nice girl... what was her name? Carol?"

"466 was here?" 117 asked, raising an eyebrow. "Why was she in this place?"

"Crystal helped us supply information at that time," 917 explained quickly.

Crystal was still admiring 57.

"Quite athletic," she remarked. "Exactly the kind of girl we need here."

"Thanks?" 57 stepped back a little. Then she stared at Crystal, looking at her more carefully. "Hey, wait, aren't you Layla Amethyst? The former adult film star??"

"You know? That's it!" 117 also perked up. "I knew I recognized her... face! We've seen your content!"

"Oh really?" Crystal seemed flattered. "Well, I haven't gone by my old name for several years now but it's nice to have fans that recognize me!"

"Yeah, Serina once used your videos to deactivate and disarm a bomb," 57 said cheerfully. "You helped save lives!"

"How interesting..." Crystal looked slightly confused. "I once had an A.I. randomly visit me once. She thanked me for saving lives and said I was a big help. Was she with you??"

There was only one A.I. they knew that didn't care about asking for permission to transmit herself outside of A.I. Industries.

"Was she light blue, brunette, and gave off super bubbly personality vibes?" 117 asked.

"Yes," Crystal said thoughtfully, placing a finger to her cheek.

"Yeah, you helped us save lives," 917 nodded. "The time we used porn to stop an explosion. That was quite the report."

"I think I still need more context," Crystal stated.

"Another time perhaps," 917 said as he passed her the money. "In the meantime, please give this to everyone here. You've been working hard so I might as well leave this for you."

"Always so sweet," Crystal gracefully took the money and held it tightly in her hand. "Just remember to stay a little longer next time. Tessa is upstairs in her office."

"Thank you," 917 said as he led the other two towards the stairs. "I'll be sure to say bye when we leave."

"You'd better," Crystal gave them a cute wave and stared lavishly at 117 and 57.

When they got to the stairs, 57 glanced back at the bar and then followed 117.

"So... how do you know her?"

"I don't want to get into that," 917 replied. "She owed me a favor a while ago and we became even when she helped me rescue 501."

"I remember that," 117 said. The day was certainly filled with a lot of trips down memory lane. "What happened to 501? He doesn't talk about it and he sealed that mission file."

"He asked me never to say," 917 answered as he continued climbing the stairs without looking back. "It's his business. Honestly, I'm surprised that he didn't tell you. Considering that you're his mentor."

"This might just be my opinion," 57 said as she looked at the decorations along the wall, "but you are raising more questions than answers ever since you left jail."

917 didn't respond to her comment. Once they reached the top of the stairs, they searched for Tessa's office. 117 blinked as he looked at the group of people ahead of them.

"Well, that's new..."

They saw a few scantily clad entertainers chatting with the custodians. When they saw the amborgs coming their way, they went back to work immediately.

"Alright, have fun in there!" one of them said as a custodian pushed a cart through a door to a small lounge.

Just before it closed entirely, they saw a man sitting on the other side reading a book.

Based on the signs all over the place, they were in a hall filled with VIP lounges and quiet rooms for privacy. The half-naked entertainers greeted the three of them as they walked past to head downstairs instead of entering one of the lounges.

"Hope to see you downstairs," one short girl giggled as she looked up at them.

The amborgs practically towered over most people in the place.

"Hang out with me," a man flexed his bicep as they reached the stairs. "I give better massages."

No one had time to respond as the entertainers descended the stairs and were out of sight.

"I haven't been hit on like this in a long time," 57 said as she glanced behind them. "I find it quite flattering."

"Me too," 117 nodded.

57 and 917 stared at 117, who immediately corrected himself.

"Not that I would do anything to jeopardize my marriage," he said hastily. "These people are quite alluring. Masters of flirtation."

"Well, when it's your job to basically do that to every customer on a daily basis," 917 said. He led them past the room where the custodian entered. "It's what you have to do to earn a living."

"Is it just me or... is the custodian working inside the lounge with a customer in there?"

Through their enhanced hearing, they picked up the sound of vacuuming followed by a polite compliment.

"Oh thank you, any chance you could do the bedsheets next?"

"Are they roleplaying?" 117 asked, perplexed.

"It's called environmental audio fantasies," 917 answered. "So, they're not actually intimate in there. Someone is paying the custodian to literally clean the room while they relax."

"That's a fantasy to some people??" 57 raised her eyebrows.

"Sometimes I fantasize about getting my taxes filed correctly," 917 shrugged. He pointed at the VIP lounge. "If you pay for it, they'll probably act out a simple slice-of-life fantasy that you can't get outside of here. Depends on the entertainer too. Some of them are licensed professionals."

"But why work here?" 117 asked.

"Sometimes, people don't come here for sex," 917 said as they walked down the hall. "They want an escape from their normal lives. And if they have the money, they'll drop it on someone here and pay them to be their therapist for a short time. Some people bring in so much money just to share their mental workload."

"It's quite impressive," 57 admitted. "Tessa seems to be adding a variety of activities every time we visit her."

They found the main office with Tessa's name plate displayed on it. 917 politely knocked on the door. There was a click as they heard the lock open. 917 grabbed the door handle and pushed it inwards. As they stepped in, to their surprise, there was no one seated at the desk. To their left, right as the door shut, they heard two fast clicks. This wasn't a lock. It was the sound of someone pumping a shotgun.

The three amborgs gently raised their hands peacefully. Slowly, they turned to see a woman aiming a Benelli M3 at them.

"Hello Tessa," 917 said as he lowered his arms and signed, "*Good to see you.*"

They watched as Tessa lowered the barrel. Without a word, she made sure it was safely pointed at the ground. She walked over to the desk and put the shotgun down. Once both hands were free, she signed back to them.

"*Nice to see you too.*"

"We don't have much time," 917 declared as he signed back to her. "It's another emergency recall."

"*This is the fourth one?*" Tessa asked.

"*Fourth one,*" 117 signed to her. He nodded his head.

"*You know what I never liked about the recall?*"

Tessa looked annoyed as she hid her shotgun from view. She looked at all of them and signed again.

"*It brings you all back together. But it also opens the door to another bad thing.*"

The three amborgs watched as she signed one word for them all to see.

"*Vultures,*" Tessa spelled it out for them.

"That is true," 917 replied. "So, we might be gone for some time. I suggest that you keep your employees safe by increasing your security. I was also just in contact with your dad before I got out. He told me to tell you that he's looking forward to next week."

Tessa's expression softened and she nodded. She looked relieved at getting this news.

117 and 57 realized why Tessa had contacted 917 earlier. It was because her father was also in the same prison that they had released 917 from. The man they were talking about was Dr. Gene Wildman, the former head of A.I. Industries' medical staff.

"Thank you," Tessa said. *"His parole board made a decision?"*

"We haven't heard any details other than his lawyers managed to move it up," 117 answered her. "But I think the odds are pretty favorable. Dr. Kendrick has continued to keep his promise. Your dad will be ok."

"But the charges of conspiracy and domestic terrorism?"

917 looked to the side and gazed at a photo sitting on top of a cabinet. He could see a few family photos on display. There was a picture of Dr. Wildman, next to a photo of Tessa, and the one in the center was a family photo of Tessa with both her mom and dad.

"Based on his testimony and the evidence uncovered by our A.I. programs, it's been determined that he was forced to do what he did," 57 explained. "So, his sentence should be reduced because the court never found proper intent to attack Dr. Kendrick or A.I. Industries. Unfortunately, when he was taken in and arrested, they treated him harshly at first because he was considered an accomplice in the Dominoe Incident."

"We should have done a better job of protecting him and your family," 917 stated as he turned away from the photos and addressed Tessa.

In 2128, the Dominoe Incident nearly crippled the entire country in less than a week. The amborgs had been there to end that conflict, but it was difficult to say where or when it started. For Tessa and her parents, the most devastating attack on the nation started for them in February of that year. In the aftermath, 117 had received a message from his technician, Mandy, that Dr. Wildman had been taken into custody. It was revealed that he was one of the reasons that the incident had ended the way it did.

Tessa and her mother had been captured by the Assassin after the battle of New York. They had been kept hostage for four months. No one at A.I. Industries had realized that Dr. Wildman, under threat of losing his loved ones, had been forced to become a mole.

When all hope seemed lost, Dr. Wildman had miraculously cleared 43 to join the rest of the amborgs in Pennsylvania for the final battle when they'd all thought that she wasn't going to make it. His actions, even when he had been forced to do so, was most likely the catalyst that allowed 43 to rewrite herself into an artificial intelligence. Unfortunately, when they rescued Tessa, it had severe ramifications.

Mrs. Wildman had died after being tortured nonstop despite Dr. Wildman's compliance. Even after he had carried out what he was ordered to do, Tessa was also continuously abused and left permanently scarred. There was nothing that anyone could do for them.

Tessa had been found in Los Angeles by the police. She had been traumatized to the point that she was now mute and spent the last nine years healing. Gradually, as she grew older, she eventually moved back to New York and opened Eternal Enigma, a safe haven. She had always told the amborgs that what she experienced should never happen again to anyone else.

"It is what it is," Tessa signed to them with a kind smile. *"There was no way you could have prevented what happened to my parents. You didn't know what happened to me. I'm alive, aren't I?"*

"That you are," 117 smiled. "But if we're being totally honest, you know we're always going to be sorry that we didn't rescue you sooner."

"Four months in captivity is a complete failure to us," 57 explained. "We should have done better."

"It could be worse."

The amborgs watched as Tessa smiled warmly at them while she continued signing.

"You don't need to apologize anymore," she said. *"I should be dead. If I had given up, I wouldn't be here. I kept holding onto the faintest sliver of hope that... it was going to be ok. When I came back to A.I. Industries, I knew that I had survived."*

Tessa had made it clear that she wasn't allowing the past to get to her. They all smiled at seeing how happy she was.

"The truth is," she said as she walked up to them. *"I wanted to see you before you went back home. I'm glad I was able to this time."*

Tessa asked them politely if she could send them off with hugs. They all silently embraced her one at a time. When she was finished, she gave them a thumbs up.

"The amborgs will always be family to me," Tessa said as she leaned against her desk. *"You've always taken care of me and my father, and made sure that this business stayed intact. I hope you come home safe."*

Tessa showed them out when it was time for them to leave. She elected not to go downstairs with them. Tessa felt that she wasn't in the right mind space to be seen by the people.

When they returned to the first floor, the music hit their ears as they moved to the bar. Crystal greeted them again.

"Welcome back," she said in a sultry tone. "Did your meeting go well?"

"Quite satisfactory," 917 nodded. "You think you could do me one more favor, Crystal?"

"Well darling, that depends on what it is," she replied as she ran her finger across his cheek.

117 and 57 stared in amazement as 917 kept a stoic gaze. His eyes didn't wander, and he remained focused on her eyes.

"Tessa's dad is going on probation soon," 917 explained. "We're not going to be available or have time to have someone come keep an eye on him. Any chance you could make sure he and Tessa reunite safely?"

"Oh," Crystal nodded immediately. Her seductive glint was replaced with bright cheerful eyes. "For Tessa? It would be my pleasure."

"Then we won't keep you," 917 nodded.

"At least say goodbye to the Yao triplets," Crystal tilted her head towards the corner. "They would love to do another dance off with you."

"I'm sorry, what?"

57 and 117 stifled a laugh. 917 merely frowned at Crystal, as if it was a secret he hadn't planned to share. Crystal, looking quite pleased, pulled 917 close and she gave him a kiss on the cheek.

"When he came in looking for your friend, 501," she explained as she withdrew behind the bar. "He and 466 showed some pretty spectacular moves."

"You know," 117 grinned, "we could spare a few minutes for some more details."

"Nope."

917 left the bar and began to walk towards the corner. The Yao triplets looked excited when they saw him approaching. 117 and 57 realized that the moment he walked away, other dancers and entertainers began to surround them.

"Good luck trying to get details," 917 smirked as one of the triplets hugged him. "While you're fending off the staff."

117 and 57 quickly moved after giving each other a nervous glance. They began to dodge the advances of the people crossing their boundaries and immediately headed towards the exit. He gave the triplets some attention for a few more moments, then excused himself. After all, it looked very entertaining to see them running out escaping the club before they would be forced to stay.

Chapter 8: A Helping Hand

Melissa Carson's Apartment
Emergency Recall plus 16 hours 18 minutes
6:30 AM Eastern Time

"And time to hit... submit!"

3 let out a huge sigh of relief as she watched the taskbar on her computer turn green. A small thank you notification popped up as she finally closed her documents and finance programs.

The payroll checks for all her staff members were finished. She had them ready to be directly deposited for those that had the means, checks were going to be put on priority, and everyone at the restaurant knew who needed the cash tips.

She was also able to submit reports, manage the inventory, order the next shipments of food, draft the schedules for her employees, monitor the latest utility bills, and even look at some of the reviews that were posted online. Several days of electronic data generated from her restaurant; condensed into one evening.

"I feel like I should get a medal or something." 3 stretched as she stood up and walked to her closet. "Finishing all that on your own? Not bad. Not bad."

She opened the set of double doors and pushed aside the hangers. Behind her clothes, she pressed a small square panel in the wall that opened with a click. A keypad appeared and she entered her passcode. Once it accepted, it turned green and then a small compartment opened. Inside was a small "go" bag, which was filled with all that she needed for any kind of sudden impromptu trip. After 3 reached inside and pulled it out, she pressed another button on the keypad and the compartment closed. When the keypad retreated into the closet wall, she grabbed a shirt and pants from the outer closet, then tossed them onto her bed. Before she prepared to switch outfits, she opened her bag and checked inside. The bag contained a spare uniform from A.I. Industries in case she needed it. She gazed briefly at the A.I. Industries logo on the shoulder patch with the number one directly under it. 3 zipped up the bag and changed outfits. When she was decent, she tossed her pajamas from last night into the hamper, picked up her bag, and left her room.

The instant she stepped out and peered downstairs, she immediately had questions. Her eyes widened and she felt her cheek twitch.

117 was lying on her couch fast asleep, but it wasn't in front of the TV where it was supposed to be. Her living room was disorganized. The coffee table was on its side in one corner, as if someone had set it up that way on purpose. As far as she could tell, there wasn't any visible damage. The footstools that went with that particular table had been stacked neatly in another corner. The couch that 117 was sleeping on had been moved next to the dining room table. 917 and 57 were nowhere to be seen. What had the three of them been up to while she was working?

3 went into the living room and looked around more carefully. She was about to wake 117 up from his peaceful slumber, but turned and noticed something outside. 917 seemed to be standing alone out there. It was still pretty dark, but she recognized his silhouette. Curious, 3 walked towards her balcony doors, which were open. When she got closer, she realized that he was in the middle of a phone call. It was public, so she could hear his voice. She lingered nearby, eavesdropping on his conversation.

"How was Portland?" he asked.

"It was normal. You listen and I will speak. I have questions."

"I knew you would," 917 replied softly.

3 instantly recognized the other voice through the phone's speaker. That low-spoken sharp tone and direct use of short sentences could only be one particular amborg. He was talking to his best friend, 999. Now that she thought about it, it made sense that he would be contacting her. 917 hadn't told any of them that he was going away to prison. 3 remained quiet and snuck closer to hear some more details.

"What were you in prison for?"

"Dr. Kendrick punished me for enacting revenge against his orders," 917 replied.

"He should have punished me too," 999 replied.

"Well, it's good that he didn't," 917 replied.

"You ordered me to stay. You left me to find survivors," 999 said in a chilling tone. "You went off. Without me."

"Is there another question in there?" 917 asked gently. "Or are you just going to keep talking about what already happened?"

"You should have brought me. I would have fought with you," 999 stated.

"And then you would have been kicked out too," 917 replied.

"You and I had an agreement," 999 said. 3 could hear a hint of frustration in her tone. "We promised. The two of us. We would fight together. So why did you leave?"

"I'll tell you this, and please believe me when I say it."

917 lifted his head, gazed up at the sky, and leaned forward over the railing.

"Because what I did that day made me a monster," 917 stated. "I didn't want you to be sent away with that."

There was a pause. From behind her balcony door, 3 watched silently and listened. He certainly did sound sincere, but did 999 pick up on that? She hoped that she wouldn't have to step out and provide backup, otherwise the Lone Wolf of the Second Group would know she was eavesdropping on their phone call.

917 spoke again.

"I'm sorry I broke that promise," he let out an exhausted sigh after his apology. "I want you to know that."

There was another brief pause. Was she about to hang up on him? 917 and 3 both relaxed a little when they heard 999 speak again.

"After this recall," her tone sounded gentle, "Are you back for good?"

"I can consult with Dr. Kendrick about that," 917 said.

"I suggest we finish this conversation," she said, "once you get back."

"Sure," 917 dipped his head. "That sounds great."

"Oh, 917," 999 said. "You should know that 723 was asking to see you."

"What did she want?" 917 asked.

"Unknown," 999 replied. "She only wants to tell you."

"Does she just want it to be one on one?"

"She mentioned that if there were witnesses, then it would be helpful."

3 observed 917 pause. He looked like he was straining to get his next sentence out. That statement seemed to put him on edge.

"Ok, I feel slightly uncomfortable now," he said in a nervous tone.

"I predict that since she is ok with others present, more people can validate whatever she wants to talk to you about."

"If things go wrong," 917 said in a wary tone, "bring popcorn because it might be dinner and a show. You don't know 723 like I do."

"Perhaps it won't turn out that way," 999 replied in a neutral voice. It sounded like a poor attempt at reassurance. "I should go. See you later?"

"Soon, yes."

917 hung up the call. 3 opened the door a bit further and stepped out onto the balcony.

917 heard her approaching footsteps and acknowledged her presence without needing to turn and look at her.

"When did you finish upstairs?"

"A few minutes ago. I... whoa!"

3 stopped when 917 turned his head to face her. There were bright lights shimmering across his forehead concealing part of his face, but she had already seen what was underneath. It was evident that 917 was using a hologram to mask his actual appearance.

"That bad, huh?" he smirked.

"No, of course not. I just... well, I never knew that your scars needed to be covered up that much," 3 said as she leaned onto the railing. The two of them gazed down into the street.

"Doesn't matter if I hide it," 917 sighed. "It's what you see if you look at me extra carefully."

The whole right side of 917's face, from what she had briefly seen while he was activating the facial hologram, had scars running from his head down to his cheek. His right eye had been completely replaced with a synthetic one, and it looked like he had been struck in the head with something hard. Based on how large the scars were, it was brutal. It certainly explained how he got into a coma.

"I know it's none of my business and this might be too personal," 3 said, looking fascinated. "Can I ask...?"

"Why?" 917 finished the question for her. "Why do I choose to hide my real face with CGI? I guess I can tell you since you caught me. I think you're the only amborg that's seen my whole face."

917 turned to face 3 again. His holographic disguise was back in place, restoring his face to its usual appearance. There was no indication of any physical scarring, making it seem as though he'd never been injured in the first place.

"When I was about to wake up as an amborg, Dr. Kendrick told me that he set up a recreation of what my face would look like if I wasn't injured," 917 waved a hand in circles around his eyes. "Apparently, I was in bad shape when I was discovered. The only things he focused the most on were my new right arm..."

He raised his hand, opened and closed his fingers a few times, and then pointed at his right eye.

"... and a new eye."

3 reached out as 917 lowered his arm. She pointed at it, prompting him to hold his hand out. He allowed her to touch his wrist, and she inspected it.

"When I woke up and saw myself in the mirror, I had no idea who I was. Gradually, as I healed, I knew something felt off, so I told Dr. Kendrick to remove the facsimile. He actually informed me that I had the ability to do that on my own. When I did, it was one of the worst things I'd ever seen before."

3 looked up.

"But he repaired the damage?" she asked.

"Most of me," 917 shrugged. "I asked him to let me keep this new face over the scarred one. That way, the people I helped wouldn't see me as some sort of monster."

"Your scars tell people what you've survived and lived through." 3 let go of 917's hand gently. "You can choose not to hide it anymore."

"Unlike the rest of the amborgs," 917 respectfully shook his head, "I have the face of a monster, and no one wants to see that whenever I'm in the field. So, a holographic disguise to conceal it makes it easier for everyone else. And think of it this way, for formal events, I don't have to apply makeup!"

"You wear makeup?" 3 asked.

"Well, before I was in jail, I went to a lot of comic cons," 917 said thoughtfully. "You save a lot on makeup if you have a holo-guise."

"Does... Angel know? Or has she seen?" 3 laughed a little as the two of them looked up towards the east.

"No," 917 replied. "I don't know how she'd react."

"You two are quite close, I think she'd be ok with it."

917 let out a small, strained grunt. She knew that this meant that he felt uncertain. It also seemed like the perfect time to change the subject.

"In my 15 years of being an amborg," 3 said as they watched the sun peeking up through the buildings. She nudged 917 in the shoulder. "I think you have got to be one of the most interesting ones."

"Any chance you could do me a favor and not tell anyone?"

"Sure," 3 nodded.

917 and 3 admired the sun as it began to light up the city. It was time for everything to wake up. The amborgs had to leave and head home.

"One last question," 3 said as 917 began to head inside. "So, Dr. Kendrick gave you a new arm and a new eye. Ever since... did you ever find out or remember more about yourself?"

"6 once told me that the more I try to pursue it, it might slip out of my grasp," 917 shrugged. "All the leading experts I've spoken to also said that if I leave it alone, my memories will gradually return. Unfortunately, I might need to accept the fact that there's a chance that they won't come back."

"Well, you never know..."

Once they stepped back inside, 3's look of annoyance reasserted itself, but a mischievous idea popped into her head. She linked up with 117's CPU, established a connection to transmit directly into his head, and cranked the volume up. She inhaled deeply, and 917 stepped to the side. It was about to get loud.

"117," she stated in a commanding tone.

The combined use of her voice in the back of his head and spoken from her mouth had double the effect. 117's eyes flew open as he shot straight up. Startled, he looked around quickly.

"Whoa!" he clutched his head with both hands as 3's ear-splitting wakeup call continued to rattle his head.

3 shut off the transmission and chuckled.

"Good morning to you," she said, using only her normal voice. "Does someone want to explain to me what you did to my living room?"

"Oh, it was a game of rock-paper-scissors." 117 slowly tried to open his eyes and yawned. "Actually, it became a game of coffee table-footstool-sofa."

"For what purpose?" 3 glared at the two of them, pretending her previous conversation in private with 917 hadn't happened.

"We were fighting over who would get the guest room upstairs," 917 explained casually. He seamlessly moved on and added to the flow of the conversation. "57 won."

"By throwing my furniture?" 3 asked.

"No, we threw your pillows," 917 replied. "Quick-draw style with a random timer."

It was a mini game that the amborgs had come up with whenever they wanted to pass the time. They would pick one style to play and then take positions in a room. Someone would set up a timer that was set to go off at a randomly selected countdown. When the buzzer went off, the players were allowed to move. In this case, 117, 57, and 917 had a standoff with the couch pillows. When their timer went off, they would throw them, trying to hit each other. If one of them was struck, they were out. Sometimes the timers were set to go off after several hours if the amborgs felt like killing a ridiculous amount of time. Normal humans found it quite tedious at times, but it was entertaining... when the amborgs finally made a move.

"How many rounds?" 3 sighed.

"We had about nine rounds," 917 explained. "We got back from visiting Tessa at about one in the morning."

3 checked the time.

"Are you kidding me?" she asked. "Nine?"

"I was getting tired after round five," 117 said. "The timer took 49 minutes and 11 seconds to go off."

3 imagined the sight of three amborgs in her living room standing still for that long. If anyone else had been watching, that would have been the most uncomfortable experience ever. They had way too much time on their hands.

"And it never occurred to you that the noise might bother someone?"

"We were extremely careful," 117 said.

A door opened upstairs, snagging everyone's attention. 57 walked out and headed downstairs.

"That was a great nap!" she announced. "That was a great game."

"I need coffee."

3 shook her head and walked to the kitchen.

"Put my furniture back!" she demanded.

117 picked up the sofa and gently walked over to the living room. 57 grabbed one end and helped to steer it into the right position. 917 began to move the footstools back to their former spots.

Once the living room was restored, 117 remained on his feet to do some exercises. 57 took a seat on the couch to relax while 917 gazed out the window. The outside world gradually woke up as the morning went on.

Suddenly, a text message alert chimed from 117's bracelet. It was a generic status update from amborg 18.

"I have good news and bad news. Which one do you want to hear first?"

57 sighed as she looked up. She had her feet propped up on a small square cushioned stool and had tilted her head back, eyes closed, but was now focusing on 117.

"Well, how about the good news considering we've had such a long day." She stretched her arms up behind her head and cracked her shoulders.

"18 has officially responded to the emergency recall and is the last First Group amborg to do so," 117 reported.

"Good," 3 said from the kitchen. "I can't wait until we get back and she puts us through mandatory training again. Once I finish this cup, we need to get back before she does. I set up a meeting with Dr. Kendrick."

"No coffee for us?" 57 asked.

"You rearranged my furniture last night," 3 snapped. "No."

57 grinned and let out a laugh. 117 kept reading the texts.

"Sounds like 501 and 466 didn't mess it up," 917 remarked with an impressed smile.

"That is not entirely accurate," 117 replied.

917's smile faded. It was time for the bad news; a moment which always managed to destroy the small moments of hope and replaced them with fear and dread.

"Spoke too soon. So, they did mess it up?" he asked, tilting his head forward and glancing at 117, who nodded. "What happened?"

"They apparently broke down Alberto Biagino's front door," he replied.

"Of course they cause an international incident when they were given one task," 57 sighed.

117 shared screenshots of the text messages to the others. They all read them thoroughly.

"Oh good," 117 said cheerfully. "Alberto Biagino decided not to press charges or retaliate against A.I. Industries for the inconvenience."

"But a man like him would have demanded retribution, right?" 917 asked.

"He runs one of the world's biggest criminal syndicates," 3 spoke from the side. "Of course he wanted something."

A few more texts came in as 117 got the full story from 18. He was also trying to message 501 and 466 to get their side of it all, but for some reason they had stopped answering.

"Apparently Alberto dropped the damages and was satisfied with watching them fight 18," 117 explained.

Everyone thought the story was quite impressive. Even if the circumstances had been different, they would have had to deal with a whole different set of problems altogether.

"501 and 466 must have had quite an interesting duel with 18," 917 stated as he kept reading 18's messages. "She's saying they fought really well. I wonder if she's sending the footage of... Never mind, there's the video file."

917 immersed himself in the video that 117 forwarded to him. 18 was highly experienced, incredibly wise, and very strict. Not only was she 917's First Group mentor, but she also oversaw their training sessions and exercises. She had trained all of them personally and retained a large amount of information about their preferred methods or styles in the fields. As they watched the video, 117 couldn't help but feel slightly envious of 501 and 466. The two of them had utilized a very effective two-amborg technique in their battle strategy against the First Group amborg, which had garnered a lot of praise. Several others were posting compliments and leaving reviews. He sometimes wished that 18 would approve of his fighting style since he was the one responsible for teaching 501 and 466 how to be self-sufficient. After 43 had passed on, he'd taken care of them as much as possible. Fortunately, he was aware that a large majority of the other Second Group amborgs had taken the time to help him out every now and then.

"They are on a flight home now," 117 nodded his head. "501 just messaged me."

He read the texts from 501 and 466.

Don't worry about me, the text from 501 read, *466 and I had a sparring session with 18 after we accidentally destroyed the front door. The movies we've watched haven't properly prepared us for this, but we are glad that 18 is coming home with us. Sorry for all the trouble. We will accept any or all other punishments when we get home.*

117 then looked at the message that 466 had sent.

I broke down the door. It was my fault, but to be fair, I thought a door that belonged to one of the most powerful families in the world would do a better job of reinforcing it. I think I traumatized the poor doorman, who was doing an excellent job, by the way. Fortunately, this situation was resolved thanks to a flying roundhouse kick to my head, courtesy of 18. I don't know if 501 has mentioned it to you, but he woke up thinking it was the setting from... that one time. He's ok and has gotten better but... he's still suffering. Please check in on him whenever you get the chance. Be home soon!

501's messages were short and vague. 117 didn't think much of it, but once he read 466's detailed account of what happened, he began to feel concerned about 501's wellbeing.

"501 seems to be dealing with some anxiety issues," he said to the others.

"Aww, from that time he was kidnapped?" 57 asked.

"Yes."

"I don't blame him," 57 nodded as she continued relaxing. "What he described in his post-action report was rather terrifying."

117 glanced at 917, who was listening, but still reviewing the footage of 18's duel with 501 and 466. He watched it play on the little display screen from his bracelet.

"Very smart," he muttered. "She's utilizing her agility while he's focusing on a grounded approach in order to get 18 to switch styles to balance."

117 decided to speak up. He remembered one important thing that he never had the chance to say.

"I never thanked you properly 917," he said.

"For what?" 917 looked up.

"You were the one that got 501 out," 117 explained. "Thanks for doing that. I just wish I had contributed more to the rescue effort."

"I was happy to do it," 917 replied casually. "Besides, you contributed plenty. Every person played a significant role in narrowing down where he was being held captive. I'm just glad he was ok, and we got to him before any serious harm was done."

"Hey guys."

3 suddenly came out of the kitchen.

"I'm set. We should probably get going," she said. "We'll go home right away and check in. We should call for a pickup. Now."

57 sprung to her feet. 117 stopped texting and 917 turned off the video footage.

"I thought we were going to take the train," 57 said.

"No, I don't like the idea of being the last amborgs to make it home. We need to get to the nearest A.I. Industries safe house," 3 said as she put on a jacket. "If we hitch a ride, then it'll get us home quicker. We can board the transport based there."

Everyone nodded, understanding the plan. They were all ready to head out the door as 3 prepared to lock up and secure her apartment.

"I'll drive," 117 stated.

"Shotgun," 57 declared.

After they took the elevator down and walked through the lobby, they noticed that a human receptionist had arrived to open the main office to the apartment building. The caretaker drone was giving him an update as 3 bid them farewell. They wished the four of them a good day and they all exited the building to head to 117's car.

"What do you have in your car?"

3 put her go bag inside the trunk and shut the door. 117 recited the inventory to her.

"I have weapons for each of us," he said. "A couple of supplies in case of emergencies."

"Ok, so you, 57 and I all have our amborg jackets," 3 said as they climbed into his car. "What about 917?"

"Sorry," 917 replied, "Mine is back home. I went into prison as a plain-clothed civilian."

3 was talking about the amborg jackets that were actually labeled with their numbers—the ones that the public saw them wear whenever they deployed on their missions. 117 would have had his close by in the car. The same for 57, since she was the one tasked to get them all. 917 was the only one who didn't have his uniform.

"I have two other jackets," 117 said. "One is an unmarked A.I. Industries jacket, and the other is a spare."

"I'll take the unmarked one when we make it to the safehouse," 917 said. "Otherwise, it'll look confusing if I grab your other jacket and people mistake me as you."

They all chuckled as 117 started the car and drove downtown. Two amborgs wearing "117" was going to cause a bit of confusion out on the streets. It was best not to take that kind of action at all.

The journey to the New York A.I. Industries building wasn't far. Once they arrived, they would discreetly report to the staff onsite, wait for the air transport to arrive, then fly straight back home. However, as the drive went on, they encountered a strange sight.

"Is it rush hour?" 57 asked as she put her hand on the dash and leaned forward to look around.

"I'm going to switch on the scanner," 117 said, pressing a button on the display screen.

"Why wasn't it on?" 917 asked curiously.

"I shut it off when I went on vacation," 117 replied. "I didn't want to suddenly drive towards the first sign of trouble if it alerted me."

All vehicles that the amborgs drove were always hooked up to police scanners and secure news networks. This allowed any amborg in the vicinty to immediately respond to a situation that could require their assistance.

When the radio switched on, 57 flipped through the different channels to listen to the news.

"Minutes ago, armed robbers attacked United Credit and Savings..."

57 changed to the police scanner.

"All units, be advised, we have heavily armed suspects barricading themselves inside! Dozens of hostiles in control of hacked drones!"

3 leaned forward and placed her hand on the back of 117's seat.

"United Credit and Savings is one block from where we need to go," she said.

"What a coincidence," 117 said as he switched the display to tactical mode. "Orders?"

3 was the ranking amborg in the vehicle. As a collective group, they all looked to her for directions.

"Blast the siren," she said. "Let's get in there."

117 pressed some more buttons on the dashboard. A red and blue light appeared on the hood and began to flash. The siren began to chirp and wail as 117 pressed his foot down on the pedal. Cars ahead of them began to clear to the side as they weaved their way forward.

"There it is!" 117 declared. "There's a barricade."

As they approached their destination, they encountered a police barricade blocking their path. Metal fences had been erected, and civilians were being ferried away. Armed SWAT officers and NYPD police held a perimeter that they needed to get through. A line of cars was being redirected down another street, but 117 didn't follow them.

"Signal one of those officers," 57 said. "Let's introduce ourselves."

A young-looking officer noticed the red and blue emergency lights on their hood and made his way over. 117 shut off the siren as they watched the man stare at them with suspicion.

"Hey!"

He knocked on the window, and 117 respectfully nodded to him. He promptly rolled down the window when the officer motioned for him to do so.

"Excuse me, but who the heck are you??" the man demanded. "This area is off limits, and I don't recognize this vehicle. You'll have to turn around until we get this situation under control."

"Greetings," 117 smiled politely. He pointed at the barricade. "We're actually trying to get to this building which is about three blocks in that direction. Perhaps we could offer assistance? There are four of us."

"No one's getting through here," the officer replied sternly. He eyed 117's civilian outfit in disbelief. "We have armed hostiles up ahead and the area is blocked off. I'm going to have to ask you again to turn around."

"We're amborgs," 117 answered courteously. "We have a transport that is waiting for us."

"Yeah, right," the officer replied sarcastically. "Can I see some ID? 'Amborgs'. Ha."

The officer chuckled, initially thinking that 117 was messing with him. Without saying a word, 117 pulled up his sleeve and activated his bracelet. The gold material gleamed in the sunlight as the projector illuminated, and he selected his profile. The officer examined the image displayed on the bracelet, carefully inspecting 117's license. Everyone in the car watched as his eyes widened.

"Never gets old," 57 remarked, enjoying the young officer's reaction.

"S-sorry about that sir," the officer stammered as he made eye contact with 117.

"I'm not a sir," 117 replied kindly. "Any chance that one of your supervisors or sergeants is available?"

"One second Mr. 117."

The officer hurried away before 117 could speak again. The others looked on with big grins on their faces.

"Look at that Mr. 117," 57 nudged his right shoulder. "You probably made that guy piss himself."

"How do you do today, Mr. 117?" 917 added in an exaggerated proper tone. "Is the weather to your satisfaction? Perhaps some more explosions or gunfire will bring more excitement to your day."

"Oh, come on, that's not the first time someone referred to me as a 'mister,'" 117 replied, rolling his eyes. "'Sir' also doesn't sound right either. Do I look old to some of these people? 3?"

It was a mistake to ask that to the oldest amborg currently in the car. The moment he realized who he'd directed his question to, it was too late. 3 raised an eyebrow and crossed her arms.

"I'm afraid I don't know what you mean Mr. 117," she answered nonchalantly, feigning ignorance.

117 pouted slightly as the others laughed. Their amusement ceased when they noticed the police officer who stopped them returning with another one clad in heavy body armor. They checked the stripes on his shoulders, confirming that he was a sergeant.

"I definitely didn't ask for any help from the amborgs or A.I. Industries," the man said angrily. "We've got a situation, and we have it contained."

"Are you positive that you don't need our help?" 117 asked politely. "It would probably be quicker if we assisted you. We are on a tight schedule."

It was interesting to hear someone from the police denying help from the amborgs. Four of them happened to arrive on the scene and were ready for action. If he had been in this man's shoes, he couldn't fathom why he would turn away such a generous offer of support. The noise in the background suggested things weren't going well for them.

"I'm positive," the sergeant replied. "You let us deal with those lunatics and then you can be on your way."

"Well, that's unacceptable," 57 leaned over, interrupting the conversation. "There's four of us here that can end this in a few minutes. Like we said, we are trying to get back home asap."

"And I'm telling you I get that," the sergeant crossed his arms. "But we don't need you stepping in for us."

"Look here, sergeant... Humphrey," 57 eyed the man's name plate on his chest and looked him in the eye. "How would your superiors like it if you faced twice the civilian casualties during this particular incident? And, thanks to your body camera footage and ours, how do you think they'd react to seeing actual evidence of you denying four combat-ready amborgs from assisting? Stopping or delaying us from where we need to go is also obstructing us from important business we have. I don't think you want that charge sticking on you. Not a good addition. But by all means, we'll just sit here and let you do all the heavy lifting."

The man's face hardened as he continued to stare angrily at 117 and 57. After a few moments, he stepped back. He took a moment to deliberate and then made his choice.

"Let them pass!" he commanded.

"Thank you," 117 said, rolling up the window and driving forward. "Please allow us to stage our car once we're through the barricade."

Several police officers lifted a fence post that was blocking the road and pushed it outward, creating an opening. 117 drove through and parked the car on the sidewalk. After shutting off the engine, they all swiftly exited the vehicle. The group stepped out onto the edge of the combat zone and began walking toward the back.

"What do you suppose that guy's problem was?" 917 asked, looking back and watching the sergeant bar a news reporter from trying to sneak past. "Pretty big stick he's sitting on."

"I'm not sure," 117 shrugged as they opened the trunk.

57 made her way over to an armored policeman in tactical gear and began to question him about the incident. As she gathered information, the trunk popped open and the other three started grabbing some gear. They hurriedly swapped their civilian clothes for their A.I. Industries jackets, which had their numbers branded on them, with the exception of 917 who donned the unmarked one. 57 returned as they were unloading weapons from their small armory.

"Ok, we have a large group that attempted a botched bank robbery," she reported as she grabbed her jacket out of the trunk. "At least 15 armed hostiles, fully automatic weapons, a few hacked security drones, and two old behemoth drones."

"Behemoths and hacked drones? All that for a bank robbery?" 3 asked. "Who even has the capability to gather all of that together??"

"It's a group known as the Equalizers," 57 reported as she zipped her jacket up. "Former military vets, heavy weapons, and definitely equipped to steal drones to have them do their bidding."

"I know some of them that were in prison with me," 917 said. "Most were discharged from the military because, well, a lot of them are crazy or have a lot of anger. They have advanced training and are not to be underestimated, so this might be a bit of a fight for us."

"And the police didn't want our help?" 117 asked as he reached in and pulled out the weapons rack and ammo. "There's no way they could have finished this by themselves in a short amount of time."

"Let's get in there fast," 57 said, grabbing her gun and checking her ammo. "A few of them retreated into the bank when the police first arrived, and the fighting began. At least three wounded officers, no casualties. The Equalizers are trying to fend us off. It's only a matter of time until they kill someone."

"Who knows how much ammo they still have left." 917 listened to the gunshots in the distance. "They can't sustain a prolonged defense, but if they dig in tight, they're not going down without inflicting as much damage as they can. We need to finish this quickly. Hey, that's my rifle."

917 reached onto the rack and pulled out the same semi-automatic rifle that 117 had seen 57 carrying with her when she picked him up from the cabin.

"I brought your rifle with me when I found out I was supposed to pick you up," 57 smiled. "We kept it clean and maintained it for you while you were gone. No one used it."

"Thank you," 917 said as he picked it up and conducted a quick inspection.

A year after the Dominoe Incident, several amborgs reported one common problem that kept occurring in the field. Any firearms or other weapons that they picked up to use in combat tended to break in their hands very easily. Even if they were to just simply hold something, the amborgs had a strong grip strength which sometimes rendered guns useless. The armory personnel back at A.I. Industries hired a team of specialized gunsmiths and experts to design personalized weapons for each amborg. They could all choose to go into the field with their own unique guns instead of having to use damaged ones during their missions. Most of these custom-made guns were built heavier and reinforced with stronger materials to avoid being crushed.

917's rifle was a restored M-1 Garand semi-automatic. It was now designated the MX-1 after someone had given the classic weapon a heavy modern overhaul. It was originally going to be melted down and destroyed, but it was upgraded and given to 917 instead. It was amazingly accurate and packed a punch with a decent range. Not as far as 297's sniper rifles, but it could help pick off targets from a distance if necessary.

He was the only one in the team that had a semi-automatic. 117, 57, and 3 strapped handguns to their belts and chose automatic rifles as their primary weapons. Once they were loaded up and ready to move in, 117 closed the trunk and they all gathered around.

"What's the plan?" 57 asked 3.

"I want a diamond formation," 3 said as she gazed down the road. "I'll take the lead, 117 goes left, 57 on the right, and 917 covers the back."

All of them moved away from 117's car. He locked and secured the doors as they took their formation.

"They're probably using the behemoths and the hacked drones to distract us while they find a way to escape," 3 said, stepping forward. "Their problem right now is that the perimeter is going to tighten and choke them until there is no way out. When they realize they're trapped in a corner, they're going to fight and take as many as they can down with them. So, we're going to take out the big targets first. Any robber we come across, we try to take them alive. We get to the bank as fast as possible and keep limiting their options."

"Roger," they chorused, acknowledging her orders.

"Let's move. Stay close. Form up! Diamond maneuver."

3 took the lead, with 117 positioned just behind her left shoulder and 57 on the other side. 917 followed at the rear, keeping a lookout for any potential threats from the sides or behind. The group moved in their formation towards the intersection, where the sounds of the escalating conflict grew louder and more intense as they drew nearer.

"Look! Amborgs!"

A few police officers who were pinned down looked their way, suddenly grateful to see them. 3 quickly led the team towards the car where the officers were taking cover. Every window was shattered, and the sound of bullets hitting the other side filled the air as they greeted 3's group. 3 and 57 knelt down to talk to the officers, while 117 and 917 took up firing positions, scanning the area ahead for any immediate threats.

"Is anyone hurt?" 3 asked.

"No hits here," one officer reported. "We're almost out of ammo so we're really glad to see you."

"57." 3 turned and pointed at the three officers. "Take them back away from here. Cover their escape and then move back here to join us."

"Right."

57 swiftly instructed the three officers to stand up and get ready to move. Once 3 gave her the signal, the officers bolted. 57 followed closely behind, doing her best to usher them back towards the barricade they'd initially come from. With them gone, 3 looked carefully over the bullet-ridden car and tried to recon the area. She spotted some targets directly out in the open.

"Ok," 3 said as they all took careful aim. "One behemoth with seven hacked drones surrounding it. No signs of the human robbers."

"I agree," 117 reported. "No human targets in sight."

"What do you think?" 917 asked.

The amborgs physically present hadn't encountered a behemoth-class drone in a long time. A few had made an appearance over the last few years but by then, they knew exactly how to take them down. They were first encountered in Chicago the day that 43 was fatally wounded. They were designed by the one who would go down in history as The Assassin. When he declared war on the US, he had deployed a massive army of these things and given them away as gifts to anyone that wanted to help him spread chaos across the country, striking fear into the rest of the world. They stood over 12 feet tall, were heavily armored, and sometimes were equipped with flame throwers or ice-cold coolant tanks. Standard firearms were useless against their armor, unless you could hit them in their weak spots, which was usually right behind them, in their backs. Aside from that, they needed weapons with armor-piercing capabilities or high-explosive power in order to get past their defenses.

They were in a relatively good spot. The car they were set up behind was right on the corner of the street. Once they stepped out and turned right, the enemy drones would spot them. The behemoth they'd spotted had three machine guns retrofitted on both of its arms, and it was firing down the street, right across from their position. The amborgs spotted more police officers who were shooting back on the other side of the road, but they were in the same predicament as the other three officers they had just sent away. 3 assumed that the behemoth was firing down the street at another barricade. It was quite literally a massive problem.

They remained under cover and kept an eye on the target. The drones stopped shooting at their hiding spot and were now focus-firing with the behemoth at the police. This change in focus was likely due to the drones noticing three officers retreating and not realizing that the amborgs had taken their place. If a drone were to turn towards them and spot them, they'd lose the element of surprise.

"Six 50 caliber machine guns," 3 sighed, eyeing the behemoth. "If the other behemoth shows up, then that's twice the amount of deadly firepower that we're going up against. The police are severely outgunned."

"They probably weren't expecting an amborg to drop in," 917 stated.

"There are four of us," 117 said. "We can handle this easily."

The sound of footsteps were heard from directly behind them. While 117 and 917 faced the front, 3 turned around and saw 57 rejoin them. Now that they were all together, the team could move in.

"917," 3 said as she used her HUD to mark the small drones. "You and 57 will remain here and attack from the right. 57, cover 917. On my signal, he will shoot the hacked drones."

"Got it," 917 said as he took aim at his first target. "And what signal am I waiting for?"

"117 and I will sprint across the street, draw the enemy fire off the police, and have it focus on us."

"We're going to be bait?" 117 asked, widening his eyes.

"Relax," 3 replied. "I'll go first. Unless you'd like to be the one to go up against the behemoth from the front?"

"I think I'm good," 117 replied with a casual smile.

"Good," 3 nodded. "You and I will run across the street into the open. Once they see us, 917, pick off the drones. Once they're down, you and 57 go right and take the behemoth from its left side. 117, you go from the left and hit the right flank. I'll keep its eyes focused on me. Disarm it before it opens fire again."

Everyone acknowledged her orders. 57 took a position next to 917 as he carefully aimed at the head of the closest target. 117 and 3 moved towards the hood of their car and got ready to run. They disengaged the safeties on their weapons and waited for 3's command.

"Go!" she said. "Weapons free!"

917 fired seven consecutive shots as 3 charged out of cover with 117 right behind her. 57 watched in awe as 917 nailed every single shot, taking out all seven drones by hitting their main processors dead center. They fell to the ground like life-sized dominoes, their metallic frames collapsing and clattering all over the pavement.

117 and 3 dashed across the street, drawing the behemoth's attention. 117 made it safely to the other side and took cover, while 3 stopped in the middle of the road. With a clear line of sight to the behemoth, she scanned for the second one while lining up her shot with the rifle. Then, she pulled the trigger.

She emptied her magazine entirely as a spray of bullets struck the behemoth center mass. It didn't appear to do much damage, which was expected, but now she had its attention. 3 quickly ejected the magazine from her rifle and reloaded as the behemoth turned its bright red eyes on her. She remained in place and stared up menacingly at it. It raised its arms, preparing to take aim at her when it realized that she was a new threat.

It didn't get a chance to retaliate. 117 opened fire and hit its right side. As the behemoth turned its head to target him, 917 and 57 closed in and unleashed their attack from the other side. Getting hit from two different sides proved very effective as it struggled to calculate which target to shoot at first. As 917 continued to fire at the behemoth's head and disorient its sensors, 57 slung her rifle behind her shoulder and attacked. 117 mirrored her movements.

As 917 and 3 concentrated their fire on the head, keeping the behemoth distracted, 117 and 57 were able to close in and go for the arms. At the same time, almost in sync with each other, they both climbed onto one arm and punched a square section on the side. Both managed to pry open the armored panel and force it open, revealing an electronic panel underneath. 117 and 57 hacked into the controls and deactivated the system. The behemoth's machine guns stopped firing from both arms. They had successfully disarmed it.

When she saw that the front was safe to attack from, 3 slung her rifle over her shoulder and got ready to sprint. It was time to take it down.

"917!" she called, marking the path she was going to run on. "Give me a boost!"

917 turned, nodding to acknowledge her command, activated the safety on his rifle, and swung it around to carry it behind his shoulder. He quickly ran in front of the behemoth, checked its position, and then faced 3. She saw him squat down slightly, cupped both of his hands, and held them down below his waist and near his knees. When he was all set, he signaled 3.

"Ready!" 917 firmly planted himself and waited.

3 took off, sprinting right toward him. Once she got close enough, she leaped up and aimed for 917. Adjusting a little, he managed to catch her. As her feet landed in his hands, he channeled all his strength and launched her up and over his head.

"Happy landings!" he yelled.

Using the power from his toss, 3 flew at a high speed towards the behemoth's head. As she drew near, she curled her fingers into a fist and hit it, right on target. There was a loud crash and a resounding clang as she popped the head clean out of its socket. Gravity pushed her back to the ground and she flipped forward. 3 managed to land back on the ground successfully and glanced behind her.

The behemoth was still trying to shake 117 and 57 off its arms, its head sparking, but the damage was already done. A moment later, it whined as it powered down and fell backwards onto the pavement. 117 and 57 jumped clear before it slammed onto the road. There was a heavy thud as it crashed down. Right as it lay motionless, 3 saw that it was still sparking and started to leak fuel. The robot immediately went up in flames.

"Cut off the arms and put out the fire!" 3 instructed quickly. "There's still live ammo that could get cooked!"

3 faced forward to check the area ahead. Suddenly, she heard a loud boom. It sounded like cannon fire. Her eyes widened and she realized what was coming. 3 instantly tried to dodge, but it was too late. A massive artillery shell exploded, blinding her with a bright light while striking her right shoulder and sending her flying off her feet. The immense heat of the explosion sent 3 tumbling to the ground, her HUD flashing with bright red alarms.

"Amborg down!" she heard 917's voice call out.

3 landed on her face and tried to focus, her vision clouded. Her sensors immediately began to recalibrate as she struggled to get back on her feet. Then, she felt someone grab her and help her up. Once she got into a seated position, she opened her eyes. 917 had rushed to her and was inspecting her for damage.

"I found the other behemoth," 3 coughed. She grumbled in pain as she looked at where she'd been hit.

"High explosive shell," 917 informed her. "That behemoth has a tank barrel retrofitted on its arm. I guess that explains how they robbed the bank."

917 pointed and 3 followed his line of sight. There was a massive hole where the front entrance of the bank should have been. The two of them spotted the behemoth, which was standing guard in front out in the street. The robbers had mounted a giant gun barrel and had converted the big drone into a walking artillery piece. They guessed that when the bank had tried to lock themselves down, the behemoth came forward and opened the doors. In this case, it had gotten rid of the entrance.

Although the behemoth had taken a shot and hit 3, it had one disadvantage. The gun had to be reloaded manually. They could see a team of robbers lifting another shell to load into the drone's gun port, which was taking up quite a bit of time. Whoever had the idea to modify it like that was either a genius or completely crazy.

3's shoulder throbbed as she tried to come up with a plan.

"It's going to fire again once they reload," she groaned.

"Don't worry," 917 said as he drew his rifle. "I have an idea."

"Are you sure?" 117 asked over the comms.

"Trust me," 917 replied confidently. "You focus on putting out your fire hazard. I got this one!"

It looked like 917 was about to start shooting at the robbers.

"Are you aiming for the shell?" she asked, guessing what he was attempting to do.

917 shook his head and ejected the ammo clip from his rifle. He rummaged in his small bag, trying to find something.

"Negative," he answered as he pulled something out. "If the robbers drop the shell or if I detonate it, the explosion will cause a lot of damage. I've got a better idea."

917 quickly put what he was holding in his hands on the end of the barrel of his rifle. 3 looked closely and recognized what it was. It was a rifle grenade. As he mounted it and checked that it was firmly in place, 917 held his rifle like a mortar and took aim.

"Uh, 917, you might want to hurry."

"I just need them to finish loading," he replied calmly. "Gotcha!"

3 saw that the robbers had successfully finished loading the behemoth's gun and it fixed its gaze on them again, preparing to fire. They were in danger of being shot if 917 was too late. Fortunately, it didn't take him long to launch his preemptive strike.

"Fire in the hole!" 917 yelled once he finished calculating his targeting solution.

He pulled the trigger and there was a loud popping "ptunk" sound as the rifle grenade launched up off the barrel of his rifle and began to arch downwards towards the behemoth. The two of them watched as the projectile hit its mark and exploded.

Right on the port of the big gun barrel, foam burst out everywhere and began to expand around the behemoth's weapon. Inflating like a balloon, they watched the yellow foam cover up the gun. It was an Expanding Gel Grenade or E.G.G. for short.

"Where'd you get that?" 3 asked.

"117 kept some of these handy in his car," 917 replied, watching with satisfaction. "I'm glad he had them available."

The behemoth tried to fire another shell right as the foam covered up the barrel. There was a muffled thump and they watched as the behemoth's arm exploded. The robbers nearby yelled in shock as they were sent flying. 3 realized what 917's plan was.

Sealing the barrel of the gun didn't allow the shell to go anywhere once the behemoth tried to fire it. The attack backfired internally and the immediate implosion disabled the cannon and trapped most of the blast, minimizing the damage. 917 had managed to reduce the blast radius. If he had detonated the shell before it had been loaded or if it had accidentally been dropped to the ground, it would have been worse. Thanks to the E.G.G., the behemoth was properly disarmed.

"Expanding Gel Grenade," 917 grinned, reporting to the rest of them. "Enemy artillery neutralized."

E.G.G.'s were invented a few years after the Dominoe Incident. The brilliant minds from Dr. Kendrick's R&D team at A.I. Industries had struck gold with this particular invention. It had originally been designed for emergency services and environmental use. Construction workers used the foam components to fill in potholes or cracks in roadways, stabilize deteriorating beam supports in buildings, and other temporary fixes. Firefighters and emergency responders used them often to rescue people. Once the foam hardened, it was fireproof and capable of blocking a spreading fire or, if you lowered the concentration, it could be soft and bouncy. Since they inflated quickly, lots of people could fall from incredible heights and land safely instead of waiting for emergency teams to inflate massive airbags. E.G.G.'s could also be used for nonemergencies, like makeshift trampolines for kids and young adults. Over time, the amborgs, along with the military, also helped find more practical uses. Thanks to 917, his idea brought down a deadly weapon.

"Ok," 3 tried to stand up. The pain in her shoulder was dissipating. "We need to bring it down for good. 117, 57, are you two ready?"

"Fire's almost out," 57 reported. "But we need 15 more seconds!"

"Understood," 3 sighed as she tried to flex her injured arm. "We'll take care of... 917?"

3 blinked and realized that 917 had left his position. Her eyes widened when she saw that he had charged for the behemoth on his own.

"917!" 3 cried out in alarm. "Are you nuts?! You can't solo a behemoth!"

917 didn't stop, even though he'd heard her transmission. 3 watched helplessly as the behemoth turned its attention to him and prepared to swing its other arm at the lone amborg. What happened next caught them all off-guard.

"917!"

3's cry was too late. 917 had run up to the behemoth and with his rifle, extended a bayonet from it and prepared to attack. He lifted his right leg and kicked the behemoth's left knee, dislodging a piece of armor. As the plating fell to the road, he quickly stabbed the knee with his bayonet point-blank into the circuitry, and fired several shots. The bullets inflicted significant damage, causing the behemoth to drop to its knees. 917 pulled his rifle out, retracted the blade, switched the safety on, and swung it around his shoulder, unequipping it. With its right arm still functioning, the behemoth tried to lift it, preparing to smash it down on 917's head.

3 watched in horror as it was about to crush him. Amazingly, this wasn't the case. As the behemoth's arm descended, a deafening thud echoed through the air. The ground quaked and trembled slightly upon impact, leaving everyone staring in awe. A small crater formed in the road where the immense force had attempted to flatten him. 917 had lifted both his hands, caught the giant robot arm, and held it firmly in place. He wasn't about to let his head get squashed.

With a massive feat of strength, 917 seized the behemoth's arm and executed a judo shoulder throw. The behemoth was lifted over 917's head and hurled to the ground with a mighty heave. The ground echoed with another earth-shattering crash as it sprawled on the pavement. 917 maintained his grip on its arm, lifting it once more and sending it flying over for a second throw, causing it to land face-first on the street.

117, 57, and 3 remained where they were, still staring as 917 continued his relentless assault on the behemoth. Ignoring its attempts to recover, 917 lifted it for a third time and sent it crashing helplessly into the street once more. The confused drone struggled to stand, but before it could even begin calculating, 917 released its arm and leaped onto its chest, positioning himself at its neck. He lifted his right fist, charging his next attack. Once he'd amassed enough power, 917 struck a fatal blow, decapitating the behemoth. Its head flew off and bounced in the street with a few metallic clangs as the behemoth powered down, becoming still and lifeless.

"What the hell?"

117 was the first to blurt out what everyone was thinking. 3 remained in a state of shock as 57 and 117 took hold of her shoulders, helping her to her feet. The trio stood together with mirrored expressions of disbelief and amazement, processing what had just happened.

"It used to take a minimum of three or four amborgs to knock one down like that," 57 stated as she gazed at the wreckage.

"Not to mention those things are extremely heavy," 117 pointed out.

The behemoth drones weighed several tons each and all of them had just witnessed 917 throwing one around like a ragdoll.

The three of them cautiously moved forward, checking their surroundings. 117 and 57, with their guns at the ready, opened fire at four more drones attem-pting to retaliate. Unfortunately for them, the amborgs had better accuracy and easily took them out.

"Their outer defenses are down," 57 reported as she scanned the area.

"The rest of them are probably trapped in the bank," 3 said.

Glancing towards the bank, she could see people inside running around in a frenzy, likely in a state of panic at the sight of a team of amborgs approaching. 917 jumped off the behemoth and drew his rifle.

The gun crew robbers were easily subdued and apprehended. Once they were secure, the team moved and positioned themselves near some damaged vehicles for cover, maintaining a clear line of sight to the bank.

"How did you do that?" 3 demanded, looking at 917.

"I had to improvise," 917 replied, looking drained. "117 and 57 were busy and you were damaged."

"I know why you did that," 3 sighed. She clarified her statement, "I asked you how you were able to do that."

"It's like that scene from the Avengers movie when Hulk slams Loki into the ground multiple times," 57 stated. "Except in reverse. Big mean robot gets beat up by the little guy."

"Maybe what we all need now is a little guy," 117 said, thinking about what she was describing. "Oh, that scene was funny."

They all understood that reference. 117 was quoting from the same universe but a different movie.

"Captain America: The First Avenger," 917 recited.

"Focus..."

117, 57, and 917 turned to look at 3, who was clearly annoyed. As they all turned their attention back on the bank, he stated the year that Captain America premiered. It was considered a classic film.

"2011," 917 finished briefly as they all stifled a laugh.

"Ok Shang Chi," 3 sighed. "You made your point. Still didn't answer the damn question."

"In theory," 917 explained as they looked at the giant hole in the entrance to the bank. "I used power to temporarily overload my implants, increasing my strength and stabilizing myself in a short amount of time to inflict twice the damage."

"That's a huge loss in power," 57 said. "Are you ok?"

917 nodded. He blinked a few times and they noticed he was swaying a little.

"That did take a lot out of my strength," he nodded while he let out an exhausted sigh. "Someone else should probably go first."

"Well, to give you some time to recover, perhaps we change our approach? Temporarily?" 117 suggested.

"What did you have in mind, 117?" 3 asked, keeping an eye on the shadowy figures frantically scrambling around inside the bank.

117 lifted his head, and yelled as loud as he could.

"Attention!" he boldly announced. "I am David 117 of A.I. Industries! If you lay down your arms and come out peacefully, then we can put an end to this! Will you free the hostages inside the bank and come out?!"

For a brief moment, there was silence. Suddenly, gunfire erupted from inside the main entrance and the broken windows, hitting the amborgs in their heads as they ducked down behind a car. Thanks to their enhanced exo-skeletal bodies, the bullets bounced off like someone had pelted them with marbles.

"I think that answers your question," 57 replied as she massaged her forehead.

"So, it would seem," 117 sighed. "Any other ideas?"

"Well, it wasn't a bad idea altogether," 3 said as she activated her bracelet and pulled up the bank schematics. "We were shot by eight guns in total. We took down their entire drone defense team out on the street and captured the robbers that were reloading the big gun. If our intel was correct, then there's still 10 robbers inside. If there are hostages, we run out of time if they decide to use them as shields against us."

"I don't think they'll resort to killing them," 57 surmised. "Psychologically, it's not something they would do."

"If they become desperate enough," 3 replied, "That could be quite dangerous. We need eyes on the inside."

"Let me try and hack the surveillance cameras," 57 said.

57 tried to wirelessly connect to the bank's network. While she concentrated, 917 looked at 117.

"Hey 117," he spoke up. "You got any more eggs?"

"I have one," 117 pulled out another E.G.G. from his bag. "I don't think it'll be effective if we throw it in there."

"I'm not suggesting that we do that," 917 said as he put his rifle in his lap and held his right wrist.

"I got eyes," 57 reported.

57 transmitted footage that she was now receiving from her bracelet. They watched as the different cameras cycled.

"They've taken cover in various places of the bank," 3 observed the layout. "The hostages were taken inside to the bank vault. Two of them are watching them while the rest are waiting for us now that they've got no way out."

"Any attempt to assault the bank will put the hostages at risk," 117 stated. "If they finished robbing the vault, where's the money?"

"Moved from the vault to the center of the main lobby," 57 said as they switched the camera. "Looks like we came right as they were about to start loading their getaway vehicle."

The amborgs peeped over the car and looked at the bank entrance. They scanned the rest of the area but didn't spot any vehicles that looked like they belonged to the robbers.

"Their escape vehicle probably fled when the fighting started," 3 said. "They're trapped with hostages. I'm open to suggestions."

"Need a hand?"

A sudden pop caught everyone's attention and they turned to look at 917. He'd pulled his right hand off his wrist socket, and he was holding it up for them to see.

"What the hell are you doing now??" 3 stared.

"I can separate the hostages from the robbers."

917 placed his hand on the ground and they watched as it walked around on its fingers like a spider. He was remote controlling his own hand.

"That's creepy," 117 said bluntly.

"I didn't know you could do that," 57 looked fascinated.

"Perks of a robotic prosthesis and having a lot of time to yourself in prison," 917 grinned. "Also when you spend time in the slammer, you get bored. Wipe those looks off your faces, I wasn't *that* bored. Now strap the grenade to the back of my hand and I'll sneak it in there. Remote detonate it once I set it down."

"Wait," 117 said as he pulled out some tape. "If it's on the back of your hand, how are you going to set it down without drawing attention with just the one hand??"

917 looked at them awkwardly and glanced down at his hand.

"I didn't think about that actually..." he muttered. "I suppose you'll have to detonate it when I get to the vault. I can always get it back later."

"And what's to stop them from killing hostages while your hand sneaks past them?" 3 asked.

"We need a distraction," 57 said. "Anyone want to fake a surrender?"

"Why would we do that??" 117 asked incredulously as he finished strapping the grenade to 917's hand and put it on the ground. "We just destroyed all of their drones and their big cannon to just throw up our hands at them and claim we surrender to their terrifying power???"

"I was just throwing it out there..."

"I'll talk to them," 3 sighed. "Here, hold this."

3 passed her rifle to 57 and stood up.

"Buy me as much time as you can," 917 said. "57, transfer the cameras to me."

917's bracelet lit up, displaying the cameras' footage, and looked for the best route for his hand to crawl into the bank undetected. When his hand scurried away, 3 took a deep breath and walked out into the open.

"Hey! They're coming out!" someone inside shouted. "Get ready to fight!"

"Hold your fire!" 3 quickly called out to them, holding her hands up peacefully. "Please! Hold your fire! I have come to negotiate!"

Out of the corner of her eye, she saw 917's hand quietly scuttle across the street and stop under one of the windows.

"Oh yeah right!" the same voice yelled.

"There's no one at that entrance," 917 said as he looked at the interior cameras. "But I'll be spotted if I go in that way."

"I have an idea," 57 said. She quickly transmitted a message on their private channel. "3! See if you can get them to reposition."

3 wasn't entirely sure if this was possible, but she had to try. She kept talking.

"I would like to know what your demands are!"

"Don't think I don't know what you're doing!" someone inside yelled. "You're trying to distract us so those other three can get past us!"

"I am simply trying to find a way we can all walk away from this alive," 3 answered politely. "Would you be able to tell us how many hostages are still inside?"

"Nice try! I ain't falling for that! You want a demand? Fine! I want all of the amborgs on your team to step out, no weapons, where we can see you!"

3 glanced back at the car. From behind cover, 117 and 57 looked at 917, who let out a sigh.

"Let's do it," 917 quickly transmitted to them. "They're getting anxious!"

57 and 917 shut off their bracelets and the live images from the security cameras disappeared. Before they stood up, they transferred the video feed of the bank interior to their own internal HUDs. 3 turned to face the bank.

"Alright! We're all coming out!" she declared. "There are four of us here! Would you be willing to, as a gesture of good faith, release a few hostages?"

"I want all of you to step out! In exchange, we don't kill hostages!"

The leader wasn't budging. The risk was too great and if they antagonized him even further, then this situation would reach a boiling point.

"No need to be hasty!" 3 responded, still holding up her hands. "We're all stepping out!"

If they were all being given permission to step out towards the bank, this would be a good way to get into position while drawing their attention. Unfortunately, that would leave them completely exposed. Even if they were bulletproof, automatic fire would still be quite painful. 117, 57 and 917 stepped out from behind their cover without their weapons and walked over to 3.

"Hold up your hands! All of you!" the leader yelled. "No sudden movements!"

3 shared a look with 117 and 57. If they all did this, no doubt the robbers would spot something unusual. The three of them looked at 917, who sighed again. When they saw him lift his arms up, they mimicked him.

"Hey! What happened to that one?!"

"What do you mean?" 3 asked innocently. "Which one?"

"The Korean amborg on the end! Where's his hand?!"

"I'm Chinese..." 917 muttered, looking slightly annoyed. He raised his voice and called out to the bank. "You had a big gun on that behemoth of yours. It took everything I had to take it down. My hand fell off! It was a pretty good fight! I'd give you guys two thumbs up if I was able to!"

"Shut up!"

"Ok," 917 closed his mouth and began to concentrate.

57 transmitted to him on their private channel.

"They're all repositioning," she said, double checking the camera footage.

"Moving," 917 muttered.

"Ok!" 3 raised her voice. She gestured to the others like they had just been revealed on stage. "We've complied! What are your demands?!"

"We want you to stay right there! We want you to send us an unmarked and untagged vehicle! Once it gets here, we're going to have the hostages load it up with all our money and you're going to escort us past the police checkpoints and barricades!"

"Alright! Give me a moment to call someone, ok?!" 3 nodded her head, making sure the robbers could see her. She turned to others and messaged them privately. "Please tell me you're getting close to the vault."

"I need twenty seconds," 917 replied.

"An unmarked vehicle takes a lot of time!" 3 called out to the robbers. "We can get you one, but we need you to be patient!"

A few shots were fired from the bank, and 3 felt something hit her forehead twice. It was like they had been hit by a firing squad. The others were also hit by two bullets each.

"How rude," 117 grumbled.

The leader yelled at them again.

"You'd better get started on bringing us a vehicle! Or do I need to execute someone?!"

"What a prick," 57 grumbled, feeling the sting from the bullets.

"No need," 3 replied calmly. "Let me try and expedite this!"

"You do that! And you know what?! Start taking your clothes off!"

The amborgs stared, dumbfounded at this request. They all looked at each other to confirm if they had just heard correctly.

"I beg your pardon?!" 3 yelled.

"I heard that without your fancy uniforms, you amborgs are still bullet-proof!"

"We are not stripping our clothes off!" 117 spoke up.

"You're willing to do anything, right?" The leader yelled. "I'll let you have one hostage each if you all decide to take off your clothes! Four in total!"

"We're not actually considering this, are we?" 117 asked nervously.

"If we say no," 57 cautioned them, "They'll probably start killing more people."

3 glanced left and right. The streets had been cleared and she could see the police approaching from both sides to tighten the perimeter around the bank. She had a feeling she knew why this demand suddenly popped up out of nowhere.

"Well, aside from embarrassing us on national television in front of all of these people," she surmised, "They're trying to take the attention off themselves. I've got no problem stripping, but it's a little funny that they think this particular course of action will slow us down in any way."

"I think they're just trying to get some eye candy in before they go to prison," 57 grumbled. "Perverts always try to find a way."

"My wife will find this quite amusing if we go through with it, but I am still very hesitant," 117 fidgeted nervously.

"Hasn't your wife seen you naked before??" 917 asked. "You've been married for 6 years."

"On our personal time, it is visually pleasing for both of us," 117 replied. "But we're in public in front of a bunch of cameras that are connected to the never-ending abyss known as the internet."

"Well, we can definitely avoid any embarrassment," 3 let out a sigh. "But it depends on whether 917 is in position."

"Almost there," 917 replied.

"I suggest you speed things up before these perverts get any other ideas," 57 added. "No pressure or anything. It's just our asses are on the line."

"We're waiting!" They heard the leader yell. "Take them off!"

"You know, I never thought I'd say this during a mission," 917 smirked. "But my right hand is in position."

3 looked at 917 and stared at his goofy expression. His acerbic wit struck once again. Shaking her head, they all glanced at 117, who was rolling his eyes as he activated a connection with the grenade via his neural network.

"Remote detonating the grenade," 117 sighed. "Three, two... and..."

917 and 57 watched the live feed of the security cameras as everyone heard a loud pop from inside the bank.

"Egg deployed," 917 grinned.

3 gave her next command.

"Attack!"

3 took the main entrance and the others each picked one window to leap through. Within seconds, they were able to enter the bank. The robbers had turned around when they heard the E.G.G. go off at the vault entrance, letting their guard down as it expanded and solidified into a temporary defensive barrier.With them distracted, the amborgs managed to close the distance and engage in close quarters.

Without access to the hostages, the robbers had no leverage and the amborgs had nothing restricting them from ending the conflict as quickly as possible.

A few robbers attempted to shoot at 57, who skillfully dodged and took cover behind as many obstacles as possible. With quick thinking, she grabbed whatever items she could find and turned them into improvised weapons. 3 and 117 strolled menacingly towards the others and were quick to force a surrender. Despite having one hand missing, 917 was able to utilize plenty of foot maneuvers and kicks to bring down the last of them.

In minutes, the robbers had been captured alive. 3 sent a signal to the police, notifying them that it was all clear.

"Threatening lives to get us to strip naked says a lot about you," 3 stood over them and gave them an evil stare. "I'd be careful next time if I were you."

57 was delivering the post-action report to the police supervisor in charge while the emergency crews entered the bank. Some of the bank's employees, under careful guard, began to count the money that had been gathered in the center of the main lobby, making sure none of it had left the establishment. Other officers were searching the robbers for any concealed weapons or money they might have pocketed.

117 and 917 were talking to a few firefighters regarding the gel wall that was covering the vault door. They both helped to clear it away so that EMTs could check on the hostages.

"I happen to think that you're quite appealing."

117 stared at 917.

"Can we not talk about this?" he asked as he slammed his palm onto the gel wall.

They paused a few moments when they heard knocking coming from the other side.

"Come on, if we had all been forced to strip, no shame whatsoever," 917 replied as the two of them started punching the gel. "These people would be flattered that you were willing to get naked in order to save their lives. It would have made a funny story to tell Audrey."

Once they had inflicted enough damage, the gel wall shattered like glass.

"So, you would have been fine being embarrassed nationally?"

"117," 917 said. "I was in prison for four years. Being naked in public is child's play in comparison."

"Really?" 117 raised an eyebrow. "What happens in prison??"

"Well, if you're in maximum security, you have quite a reputation. Whenever I was allowed out of there, I was pretty busy. Avoiding gang rape in the showers, looking out for shivs, and poison in my food. Public humiliation? That's less scary."

"I don't know," 117 said. "I don't feel comfortable around people in that situation."

"Speaking of Audrey," 917 changed the subject, a sudden spark of realization in his eyes. "Is she still mad about us ruining your honeymoon?"

"Delayed our honeymoon," 117 corrected him. "No, she's over it."

"Really?" 917 asked. "Because Angel did throw her off a speeding train. Sure, she made it through that alive but you know, I'd still be pissed. You are still mad about not having a bachelor party."

"I said it's fine and it's a good thing she didn't die," 117 glared at him. "Otherwise you would have had to deal with me. I'm actually still annoyed about the botched bachelor party you tried to take me to."

"Good thing we scheduled a few, right?" 917 winked.

"Sneaking me out on official A.I. Industries missions doesn't count," 117 sighed. "You were supposed to take me out to celebrate one of the happiest days of my life, not use me as bait to catch some assassins..."

"It all worked out," 917 replied, blasé.

"That isn't the point," 117 replied. "I got married before I had a chance to really bond with my friends and share one relaxing night with all of you. Your actions could almost have ruined the wedding, and you stand there cracking jokes about it. It was a big moment in my life, and you chose to make it about the next mission."

917 awkwardly fell silent as the EMTs moved in and the hostages were finally let out of the vault. The robbers were all taken into custody by the police. 917 and 117 regrouped with 3, and together they went to join 57, who was wrapping up her report.

"....no casualties," she was in the middle of saying.

"Excellent," the officer writing down notes nodded. "That certainly is a nice way to wrap up the report to the chief. Thank you, Katie..."

The officer glanced at 57's number that was displayed on the chest pocket of her jacket.

"57," he nodded.

"Right," she smiled.

As he walked away, the amborgs gathered together.

"I think that detour kept us for too long," 3 said. "Shall we?"

The four amborgs exited the bank, retrieved their gear, and headed for 117's car. As they passed emergency crews, they were warmly welcomed with greetings, waves, smiles, and thanks. It was a very nice reception. Right as they got to the car, they began to pack everything. They decided to remain in uniform since their next stop was home. Just as 117 was about to close the trunk, an alert suddenly appeared on their display screens. All of them looked at each other.

"It's a public announcement," 57 said. "'Stay tuned for the following announcement... from the President.'"

"That's not good," 117 muttered.

It was a national broadcast from The White House. The President of the United States was about to address the people. This concerned the amborgs. Things were about to escalate.

"Wait, the President is going to publicize this now?" 57 asked, staring wide-eyed at them. "I thought we still had a few hours."

"Should we leave?" 117 asked.

"No," 3 replied. "Just watch the broadcast. Try to act casual."

Advertisements on the sides of some buildings and every billboard switched to a bright red color. The automated announcement spoke again.

"All residents of the nation please stand by. The President will be live in three, two, one."

The screen switched to a man sitting behind the Resolute desk in the Oval Office. It was President Bill Holland in his fancy suit and tie, his Presidential pin clearly visible on his left lapel. He kept a calm and professional demeanor as he began speaking with a familiar opening statement.

"My fellow Americans," he announced, "I am here sitting before you today to share a discovery. A discovery that will go down in history forever. Several hours ago, the United Nations convened an emergency session and after careful deliberation, we have all decided to reveal to you the truth regarding these recent events. The question of whether or not we are alone in this universe has been answered. There are no doubts... and we are preparing a response."

"917," 3 transmitted to all of them privately. "Please contact the safe house. We need to have our transport warmed up and ready to go. Tell them to hurry. We need to get back to A.I. Industries before the people here decide to swamp us. This will be a short announcement."

917 nodded as he discreetly lowered his head to make a call. There were several people on the streets beginning to gasp in shock and looking at each other frantically. President Holland kept a serious expression, which helped him continue the broadcast, but out here, many were confused and starting to worry. The amborgs realized that they needed to prepare for a quick exit.

"I understand that this news will be quite shocking to many and it is in our best interests to remain calm and steadfast under these circumstances," the

President continued his speech. He kept glancing down at the words written on a sheet of paper sitting before him, but continued to focus as much of his attention on his camera. "Please listen carefully to the following current information. Yesterday at approximately 12:20 PM Eastern time, multiple space agencies detected an unidentified object on a direct path to Earth moving at a speed faster than what our own shuttles are capable of. Not long after it entered our atmosphere, it crash landed in Kenya. Local authorities and emergency deployment teams responded quickly to secure the area under the guidance of several advisors working for our space organizations. This was confirmed to not be a meteorite. Upon closer inspection, it was reported to be a spacecraft not of Earth origin with one single occupant inside."

"ALIENS!"

The amborgs looked to see that there was a lone man in the streets pointing at a huge TV screen.

"Invasion! The end is near! They're going to kill us all! We're all dead!"

Many people near the man started to back away in terror, but he started to swing his arms in panic and almost struck some other bystanders. When it was clear that he seemed beyond reason, a few police officers tried to reach out to him. They attempted to calm him down, but it was no use. The man threw a punch, hitting one of the officers, quickly escalating the conflict. Two officers immediately tried to subdue him, who had now become aggressive and out of hand. The scene turned chaotic as they struggled to restrain him and get the situation under control. 57 suddenly ran to help.

"57! No!" 3 yelled, but it was too late.

57 stepped in as the man fought off one officer while another was desperately trying to force him to the ground. 57 snuck behind and grabbed the crazy man in a headlock and in moments, rendered him unconscious. The broadcast continued as the amborgs half-listened while keeping an eye out for any other sudden outbursts.

"The visitor, which was the sole passenger, has been taken to a secure and undisclosed location. The spacecraft they traveled in has also been secured and taken to a top-secret location."

"Want to bet it's Area 51?" 917 asked.

"Transport," 3 reminded him angrily. "Now."

The President was doing his best to communicate important information while also being cautious to not reveal any sensitive details. This was a common practice to ensure that the public doesn't get misinformed. Thankfully, the speech writer deliberately omitted any sensitive material from being disclosed. The amborgs desperately hoped that news of the 43 imposter wouldn't be revealed.

"Until we know more, I have ordered my staff and the Joint Chiefs to recall all military personnel and put them on alert once they report in. Emergency services, law enforcement, and all necessary workers are also to report in as soon as possible. We will be prepared for the events of a potential hostile challenge from outer space and will muster what strength we can gather in order to face what is coming. I would like to encourage the American people to remain calm as we move forward with this unprecedented event. I understand that what I am asking everyone to prepare for is a huge endeavor, but it will be alright, and I want to assure you that we will make it through this. Please travel to and from your homes safely. All transit lines and modes of transportation will do their best to accommodate everyone. Please proceed in an orderly fashion, remain calm, and stand by for more information. God be with us all. Thank you."

It was clear that the President's tone was not filled with aggression, but the fact that he used the words, "potential hostile challenge," would create unrest. It wouldn't be long until some people online would tear apart the speech and twist it around. The media would have a field day with that speech. It was likely that depending on how things went, he was one of the leaders of the world that wanted to resolve this diplomatically. Most people in the U.N. were probably hoping that there wouldn't be an invasion.

The amborgs were now at a disadvantage. They didn't know what consequences they would face now that the arrival of a spaceship had been brought to light. Until they all reported to Dr. Kendrick, they were in trouble being stuck out in public. The broadcast was a major spark that threatened to ignite the situation.

"Hey look! It's an amborg! Are you going to fight aliens?"

"There's a team here! They can help!"

"That's not good," 3 said to 117 and 917.

A few people had noticed 57 when she'd helped the officers subdue the crazy person. Moments after the broadcast had ended, a crowd of people were moving their way. Their uniforms were drawing attention.

"Hey," 57 said in a reasonable tone. "I don't know what's going on either.

"Are you going over to Kenya to find out more?"

"Are the amborgs back? Again?"

"What do you know?"

People began to bombard the police and 57 with too many questions. Many people were talking all at once and trying to get close, causing her to back away slowly. The police officers suddenly realized that there was a crowd building. Immediately, they called for backup on the radio as they moved to help 57. Even though they were also confused and possibly scared as well, they rallied together to try to keep the peace. The amborgs were a little relieved to see them helping.

"We need you to back off!" one officer said to everyone.

"Let her talk!" someone yelled back.

"917, get in the car and start it up!" 3 commanded. "We need to get to our transport! 117, let's go get 57 away from that crowd!"

117 tossed his keys to 917. Catching them, he quickly unlocked the car and climbed into the driver's seat. As he started the engine, 3 and 117 jogged over to 57. A few more officers at the barricade had joined, but more and more people gathered. If things continued this way, and the crowd became too violent or if any of the police made a wrong move, someone was likely going to get hurt. They were about to be outnumbered.

"Everyone!" 3 called out to them as loud as she could. "If I could have your attention, please!"

Several people up front heard her and tried to quiet down, but there were a few others in the back still shouting out questions.

"What are you all doing here when there's aliens landing on Earth?!"

"Aliens?! Here?! Oh hell no!"

"LISTEN!"

57 had grabbed a microphone from one of the officers nearby and had shouted into it. Silence fell over the entire crowd. Clearing her throat, she spoke to them again in a much calmer tone.

"Everything is going to be ok!" she explained.

3 dipped her head to 57. She had made a good move to get them to quiet down. Just in time, too. It looked like the police were getting ready to swoop in. They had officers in armor and riot gear, but they were all hoping they wouldn't need them today.

"Listen!" 3 spoke as loud as she could. "I am amborg 3 of A.I. Industries. As of right now, my entire team and I do not know what is going on. We were all watching that broadcast for the first time!"

"What were you doing here?"

3 turned to face the woman who had asked the question.

"About 15 minutes ago, we stopped a bank robbery," she explained. "Fortunately, we were able to provide some assistance before anyone was hurt or killed. The robbers were taken in and arrested by the NYPD. As of right now, we are returning home to A.I. Industries to try and understand what is currently happening. Please, return to your homes for the time being."

"Is it an alien invasion?"

"Like I said," 3 answered calmly. "We don't have any information about that. Rest assured; you have my word that we will be conducting an investigation. Please return to your homes."

A few people started to leave, but several remained. It was understandable since they didn't get a clear answer. Ignoring them, 3 motioned for 117 and 57 to pull away from the crowd.

"Let's go!" she said to them loudly so that the people nearby could hear her.

"Don't leave!" someone cried out in fear.

"Ignore that! We can't stop to comfort everyone!" 3 whispered in the back of their minds. "There's nothing we can do right now."

The police went from an armed robbery to trying to pacify a panicked as best as they could. This was an unexpected development to everyone's day. The President's announcement was an odd and meager attempt at revealing the truth.

"Why did the President make an announcement?" 117 asked as they hurried to the car. "This is too early."

"I don't know," 3 replied. "We need to find out."

They all clambered inside the car and 917 quickly took them to the safe house.

Chapter 9: Disciplinary Action

A.I. Industries
Dr. Kendrick's Main Office
Emergency Recall plus 12 hours 11 minutes
10:39 AM MT

"With all due respect Mr. President, your timing was extremely bad. I needed 24 hours since the spacecraft landed. Not 12!"

"I know. My entire staff all agree about that."

Dr. Kendrick was video chatting with President Holland on a secure line. He had been trying to update the current situation since the emergency announcement, but this was aggravating him.

"If they agreed, then why did you make that announcement before we were able to acquire any information? Did your staff also urge you to go to the public?"

President Holland maintained a serious expression as he clasped his hands and rested them on his desk.

"Kenya feels that the UFO landing on their territory should have been their jurisdiction," Holland stated. "The only messages we got from their embassy were their demands asking for you to relinquish control."

"Which I recall was made perfectly clear," Dr. Kendrick replied. "My space station discovered the incoming anomalies, and our joint task force with NASA were the first responders. You should have allowed us to handle this."

"I know," Holland explained. "I felt it was necessary to tell the people before Kenya tried to dictate where, when, and how the information was shared."

"Each country, under orders of the UN Secretary General, were ordered to proceed with this announcement hours from now," Dr. Kendrick said, pointing his finger down and tapping it on his desk twice. "You accelerated everything and now the people have more questions than answers. Answers that we do not have. Kenya was trying to put pressure on everyone else just to see who would crack. Bill, you let them play your hand."

"The response from the people probably would have been worse if Kenya had made their announcement first," the President sighed. "I am the first leader of the United States to be in charge during a potential alien invasion."

"Don't even think about using that excuse," Dr. Kendrick replied. "You're busy maintaining your public image and catering to foreign relations while we have yet to interrogate a prisoner that is not of this world."

"Well, how else do you expect us to respond?" President Holland asked, looking annoyed. "Anything that affects the world as a whole causes massive problems. Everything about this is political and it's the only playing field that I can handle. Call it a coping mechanism or whatever you like, but we must face facts! The stock markets, herd mentality, Congress, and everything going on in this country are heading into rough terrain. I was trying to convey strength."

"I admit that I'm not as politically versed as you are my friend," Dr. Kendrick countered. "That's true. But do you remember when the Third World War ended?"

"Yes," Holland nodded. "Of course I do."

"And do you remember where you were when the Dominoe Incident ended? What about the European Crisis? Brazil?"

President Holland nodded silently.

"Every time, this country and the rest of the world recovered from those events," Dr. Kendrick declared. "You will be able to get through this and the country will not fall into disrepair. Don't give in to pressure. You are one of the world's strongest leaders. We may be in for a rather difficult journey, but I need you to promise me that you will continue to trust me. We are doing everything we can about this. Just don't go make any more announcements. Any uncertainty on your end is psychological and public opinion will follow if you panic. Kenya wanted you to make the first move so that attention would shift to us."

"Damn it," Holland looked away and tried to think.

"I need to rally the amborgs and bring our readiness back to full," Dr. Kendrick said. "I suggest you do the same, Mr. President. Use the strength you conveyed to bring the country together and ease the people that are scared."

"What do you plan to do?"

"Mr. President," Dr. Kendrick sighed. "I have a prisoner to interrogate. When she tells us what's going on, then I will get back to you. Until then, I suggest you also tell the rest of the White House to calm down. If they panic, then everyone else will. You need to lead us and put on a brave face for the time being."

"Easy for you to say," President Holland took a deep breath and gulped.

"Yes, it is," Dr. Kendrick nodded firmly. "Do you know why? Because I don't work at the White House. You do your handholding and I'll worry about everyone here."

"You realize that A.I. Industries is based on U.S. soil, right?" President Holland tilted his head and gave Kendrick a stern look. "You sure you want to put yourself up on a higher pedestal than where you're currently standing?"

Without even taking a moment to think of his answer, Dr. Kendrick began to recite a couple of sentences out loud.

"Well, my grandfather's work with the brightest minds of his generation was responsible for cleaning up World War 3's radiation in key parts of the globe. My mother designed medical, biological, and neuro-technology that we use every day, and my father is the reason why 45% of the country's police force are staffed with drones."

He extended three fingers as he listed his parents' and grandfather's significant achievements.

"And somehow," Dr. Kendrick then pointed at himself, "my parents found time to raise me—a third-generation scientist in charge of the world's most powerful family of cyborgs and your best hope for ensuring that your presidency will remain intact after we deal with this."

"I'm amazed someone like you isn't running the country," President Holland chuckled.

"Wouldn't suit me, Bill," Dr. Kendrick replied.

"I can see why my predecessor wasn't kidding about that ego of yours," Holland nodded respectfully. "Well, if this doesn't go south on us in the next few days, I've asked my Chief of Staff and National Security Advisor to draft a bill for you, John. We will start allocating funds and I formally approve for you to seek out volunteers for more amborgs."

"How much?" Dr. Kendrick asked.

"How much do you need?"

"The amborgs currently active are 119 in total," Dr. Kendrick said. "I hope to double that before the end of the year."

"Based on what I know of the budget you spent for the first 90 amborgs..." President Holland stared at Dr. Kendrick through the screen. "I can't authorize that much for 120 new amborgs. Does A.I. Industries even have the facilities to get that many people?"

"Don't underestimate how far we've come," Dr. Kendrick said. "How about three new groups of amborgs, 90 volunteers?"

"Will you concede to allowing me or the U.S. Government to utilize them whenever we want?"

This triggered some painful memories in Dr. Kendrick. Many years ago, he remembered when he had sat on Capitol Hill and was grilled for hours over the course of several days. The U.S. government had demanded that A.I. Industries relinquish control of the amborgs to the military, since the amborgs at the time were the world's strongest individuals. Dr. Kendrick and his senior staff contested for their right to keep the amborgs from being militarized and controlled by anyone seeking to exploit them. His eye twitched as he stared into President Holland's eyes.

"Absolutely not," Dr. Kendrick stated firmly. "Over my dead body. Two groups? And I'll let you select a few candidates?"

President Holland perked up at this counteroffer. No one at the White House had been given this opportunity before.

"Deal."

"Pleasure doing business with you," Dr. Kendrick nodded. "I'll get back to you in a couple of hours."

The video chat ended as Dr. Kendrick shut off the screen. He let out another sigh. Suddenly, a chime came from his door.

"Enter," he called out.

The doors hissed and slid open to reveal a familiar face. Dr. Kendrick recognized her Versace attire immediately. It was a stylish and practical outfit from Italy.

"Reporting in, as ordered."

"It's good to see you Kiden," Dr. Kendrick nodded as he pressed a button on his desk. The video screen folded up and automatically stored itself in a compartment of his desk. "I trust your flight back was alright?"

"It was," 18 nodded as the doors closed behind her. "But then right before we made it home, we saw a rather shocking announcement."

"No kidding?" Dr. Kendrick replied sarcastically.

The two of them let out a small laugh. 18 then lifted the data pad that was in her hand for him to see. She gently placed it on his desk.

"I understand that most of the amborgs onsite have already completed most of their readiness exams and fitness tests," she stated. "With your permission, I'd like to resume control and oversee the others. Right away."

"Done," Dr. Kendrick nodded.

"If you also don't mind, I have another inquiry before I allow 501 and 466 to enter."

"I was wondering where they were," Dr. Kendrick looked up from the data pad. "What is it?"

"I understand that my former apprentice was in prison?"

There was a short pause as Dr. Kendrick set the pad down on his desk and clasped his hands together. He knew that 18 was observing his reaction to steer the conversation in a certain direction. The only move now was to play it out.

"Yes, he was," he decided to tell her the truth. "At his request, it was kept a secret for a few years."

"Four, by my count," 18 said. "What happened?"

"You should ask him."

"I'm asking you."

Dr. Kendrick and 18 locked eyes for a moment. She was trying to stare him down to gain more information. He merely chuckled, and he didn't so much as blink.

"What have I always said about trying to interrogate me?" His smile faded and it became cold and unwelcome. "I'm not fond of it."

18 broke eye contact and shrugged her shoulders.

"I'm his mentor and you were the last person to see him before he was sent away," she explained. "He's my friend... and I haven't been there for him enough."

"If memory serves me correctly, 917 is no longer your apprentice, right?"

After 117 first met his grandfather, Dr. Kendrick had the amborgs adopt a new mentorship policy. Instead of being deployed on missions alone, amborgs would always operate in teams of two or more. Almost all of them after that had an assigned partner. By Christmas, when the Third Group amborgs began their first missions, they were assigned to members of the First and Second Group. Under special circumstances, Second Group amborgs also had the option to apprentice under a First Group amborg.

"After our last assignment together," 18 admitted with a pained expression in her eyes. "I went back to Italy... and he picked his next assignment. I didn't know that you had put him behind bars."

"Well, you've confirmed to me perfectly that we successfully kept it a closely guarded secret. Beyond that, I believe you and your former apprentice can discuss this on your own," Dr. Kendrick replied.

18 tried to speak again but instead looked disappointed.

"Why can't *we* discuss this? I must know."

"My apologies, Kiden," Dr. Kendrick repeated his answer firmly, but in a gentle tone. "Jack will have to be the one to tell you that. Assuming he's even interested in sharing with his closest friends."

"Yes sir," 18 sighed.

"Now where are 501 and 466?" he asked. "They need to report in, too."

"Right... about that."

18 turned to look towards the door.

"Come in!" she called.

There was another chime as Dr. Kendrick opened his office door. When it hissed and slid open, his eyes widened in surprise as 501 and 466 walked in. They were both doing something strange.

"Reporting in!" 501 panted.

"Into the corner," 18 said gently.

Dr. Kendrick was about to ask, but then remembered. 18 was notorious for her punishments.

501 and 466 had a bucket of water in each arm. As they maintained their balance and slowly eased their way into the corner, they both faced Dr. Kendrick with nervous smiles.

"Right," he said as 18 crossed her arms. "How long are they going to hold onto those buckets?"

"Until I say so," 18 replied.

"I didn't get a chance to read your report," Dr. Kendrick sighed. "What happened?"

While 501 and 466 stood obediently in the corner, 18 briefly described what had happened at the Biagino estate. The more that she explained it, the more pain that seemed to emanate from Dr. Kendrick's expression.

"In conclusion to my preliminary report," 18 nodded firmly. "We still have mutual trust in each other."

Dr. Kendrick had also read the data pad she'd given him. He listened and confirmed everything she'd written. Now she was answering any questions that came to mind.

"Well, that's quite a story," Dr. Kendrick nodded. He turned to look in the corner. "Kiden, are you sure this is necessary? Wasn't the fight punishment enough?"

18 tilted her head and looked at where he was pointing. 501 and 466 were standing as stiff as boards, trying not to drop the buckets. They had remarkable endurance, but he was curious to know how long they had been holding them.

"Alberto was ok with not billing you for the damage to his front door," 18 replied. "But they still destroyed his personal property. This is absolutely necessary. Their actions may sometimes have consequences that will weigh them down. They must live with their mistakes."

"Aren't we taking this a little too literally?" Dr. Kendrick asked.

"Do you want to know how expensive the door was?" 18 countered with her own question.

"I guess it's necessary," Dr. Kendrick hastily said, clearing his throat.

501 and 466 looked down in shame. That was that.

"Was there anything else we could do for our friends?" Dr. Kendrick sighed.

"I think Alberto mentioned an apology," 18 replied, grinning.

"I suppose that could be arranged," Dr. Kendrick pondered what she had said and nodded. "I find it interesting that all it took to avoid paying for the door was a... sparring session."

"They did do a pretty good job," 18 gestured at 501 and 466.

"Naturally," Dr. Kendrick smiled. "They had a good teacher."

"I should get back to overseeing the training," 18 said. "I also need to evaluate myself. May I be excused?"

"Of course," Dr. Kendrick replied. "Once the remaining amborgs arrive, just keep in mind that I will be addressing everyone sometime later today."

18 dipped her head and turned to leave. She was about to signal 501 and 466 to follow her, but stopped and turned to glance back at him.

"May I ask one more question?"

Dr. Kendrick silently nodded.

"What made the President suddenly make that announcement? Did you tell him to do that?"

"No. I only told him what we knew, and it wasn't a lot," Dr. Kendrick glanced at the compartment where the secure video screen was hidden away. "Kenya, as it turns out, wasn't entirely happy that A.I. Industries and the U.N. had stepped in to contain the situation. Although they eventually gave permission for us to assume control, a lot of people were starting to ask questions. Fear and paranoia began to spread. Instead of giving us time to start mounting the official investigation, they threatened to leak everything they had."

"But that's insane!" 501 said from the corner. "What were they thinking?"

"It's understandable behavior," Dr. Kendrick answered 501. "People become desperate when they allow their fear to take hold. Unfortunately, President Holland responded by telling the truth ahead of schedule. Kenya was hoping that one of the larger world powers would redirect focus, and it worked. The U.S. is about to deal with millions of terrified people. It doesn't help that we're caught in the middle of it. A.I. Industries needs to hold fast and stand firm. Once they're done protesting on the President's doorstep, they'll come for us next."

"But we still don't have enough information," 466 piped up. "Right?"

"That is true," Dr. Kendrick nodded grimly. "We have an unconscious prisoner downstairs dressed like an amborg formerly in our ranks. We don't have any answers until we can talk to her. If this was just an ordinary imposter trying to play a practical joke, then we didn't need to recall everyone. But the fact that she's from space makes this so complicated. I wanted to wait until we knew more... but now the public is aware."

Revealing the truth to the public did apply a certain amount of pressure. Based on Dr. Kendrick's expression, however, it was probably too much pressure. Even with the limited amount of information they had, this would only calm the people down temporarily. When more questions came to mind, or the masses started to gather again and allow their paranoia to collect all at once, they would be facing this crisis all over again.

"18," Dr. Kendrick politely spoke to the three of them. "Do whatever you need to get ready. A lot of eyes are on us. We're making history right now."

He turned to look at 501 and 466 specifically.

"You two finish up whatever disciplinary action that 18's given you," he said emphatically. "I want you to prepare yourselves. This is probably going to be the most difficult mission that the amborgs have ever faced. I want to be perfectly clear to you two and the rest of the Third Group..."

501 and 466 gulped when they saw Dr. Kendrick tilt his head forward and give them a cold and serious expression.

"There can be no room for mistakes. No more international incidents. It's time for you kids to step up and focus. Understood?"

"Yes doctor," 501 said meekly.

"We understand," 466 squeaked.

"Alright," Dr. Kendrick waved them towards the door. "That'll be all. Don't spill any water on the way out."

18 moved to the door and held the handle. Pulling on it, she allowed 501 and 466 to go first. Both carefully lugged their water buckets out of Dr. Kendrick's office. 18 slid the door closed behind her.

"Disciplinary action?"

The three of them spotted two people wearing amborg uniforms walking up to the office. The LED strips of patterned light designed into their uniforms was iconic. 999 and Lizzy 723 approached. 999's jacket had glowing neon purple stripes and 723's stripes glowed white.

The amborgs were allowed to modify or choose different color schemes when wearing their uniforms. Their personal preferences and favorite colors were a special way of distinguishing themselves from each other and the general public.

"Angel!" 501 and 466 grinned excitedly.

"You look good with purple," 18 complimented her, dipping her head. "But the new girl here doesn't seem to want to accessorize."

999 and 723 didn't respond. 501 and 466 both looked at 18, as if wanting something.

"Ok," 18 noticed their expressions and relaxed her shoulders. "You can put the buckets down for a bit. Mingle."

501 and 466 eagerly set the buckets on the ground. Some water spilled out on the floor and they both opened their arms. Immediately, 999 held up her hand and spoke sharply.

"No," she declared, shutting them down.

"Aww..." 501 and 466 drooped into a state of depression.

723 stood there, puzzled.

"I don't understand," she said, giving them a blank stare that mirrored 999's. 18 thought for a moment that she was looking at twins. "What were they going to do?"

"They want to give 999 a hug," 18 explained. "You know... like when someone tackles you without knocking you over?"

"But if the original purpose is to subdue the target, would it not be more effective to just carry on with the tackle?" 723 asked.

"No," 999 said. "That is hazardous. We are not in combat."

999 looked at 501 and 466. Both looked like they were about to cry. She let out a sigh.

"I suppose due to the long amount of time since we were last in close proximity..." she stated, "And since you've been through a rather difficult ordeal..."

There was a pause as she suddenly saw 501 and 466 perk up. They suddenly looked like puppies. 723 observed everyone's expressions and waited to see what would happen.

"I will allow you to hug me for... four to five seconds," 999 seemed to retract slightly as she sensed the excitement building up across from her.

466 gasped.

"45 seconds?!"

"No!" 999 replied, looking livid.

501 and 466 both rushed forward and had her surrounded. 18 watched in amusement. 999's hands were outstretched as if someone had jabbed her with ice. She didn't hug them back. They held on for about five seconds exactly. Once they were finished, they let her go and turned their attention to 723. As they stepped forward, 723 shook her head.

"Please refrain from touching me," she stated.

The two of them stumbled forward, caught themselves, and stayed in place. As 501 and 466 backed off, 18 cleared her throat. The two of them immediately went over to pick up their buckets and stood in place.

"You know that you're supposed to hug them back, right Angel?" 18 snickered.

"That has never been a requirement," 999 replied coldly.

"I'm pretty sure society would disagree," 18 shook her head as she laughed. "Other than that, ten out of ten."

999 shook her head at 18's rating of that hug. Before she could respond, she was interrupted.

"Permission to speak?"

723 had straightened up in front of 18.

"We're not in the military," 18 nodded her head. "Go ahead."

"I would like to request your forgiveness," 723 stated bluntly.

Everyone was caught off-guard by this statement. 18 raised an eyebrow.

"For what purpose?"

723 turned to glance at 999, who gave her a slight nod of her head. Turning to face 18 again, she spoke in a bland and monotonous tone.

"My recent etiquette lessons for human behavior fell into the category of apologies and forgiveness," she explained. "I was the cause of several incidents in the past. I would like to apologize."

"Well, when you put it that way, how could I refuse? That was just so moving," 18 replied, adding a bit of humor in her tone.

723 stared with a blank expression. 999 glanced at her and shook her head, rolling her eyes slightly.

"Did I fail in this particular instance?" 723 turned her eyes to 999 again.

"No," 18 laughed. "I'm trying to tell you that I accept your apology."

"Very well," 723 responded neutrally. "Thank you for your time. This matter is now closed."

"How many other people are on your list?" 18 asked curiously.

"Approximately 32 remain on my list," 723 stated.

"Have fun with that," 18 smiled.

"Amborg 18," 723 interrupted. "The purpose of my actions is not for fun."

"18. You can just call me 18. You need to work on your sense of humor," 18 replied casually. "Try and put in a little more emotion if you're having this particular conversation with 32 other people. You can repeat your apologies to them all you like, but if you think that grants you 100% forgiveness, then you have a long way to go."

"I don't understand."

18 walked past, dipped her head to 999, and motioned for 501 and 466 to follow.

"You will someday," she said to 723. Then, she turned to speak to 999. "I'll see you both in the gym later for training."

"We won't miss it," 999 replied.

They went their separate ways. 999 and 723 headed towards Dr. Kendrick's office. As 501 and 466 followed 18 with their water buckets, they couldn't help but ask a few questions.

"What's that forgiveness list that 723 is talking about?" 501 asked.

18 glanced at the two of them.

"You don't know? She's a Third Group amborg and hasn't told you?"

501 and 466 shook their heads. 18 faced forward and continued to lead them down the hall.

"That's kind of surprising." 18 said without glancing back.

"Not really," 466 answered. "Sometimes she acts so introverted. I think she could be a Fourth Group amborg. It's interesting that she apologized to you. What could she have done to offend you?"

"And 32 other people?" 501 added.

"Well, she tried to kill me," 18 replied.

501 and 466 both stopped in their tracks. They almost lost their grip, and more water was spilled. After they managed to steady the buckets, they

straightened up. 18 turned around to see their horrified expressions. She smiled, finding their reactions quite amusing.

"Wait," 501 looked behind him. "723? What do you mean she tried to kill you?"

"I mean she attempted to take my life," 18 replied. "About four times, actually."

"Four times?" 466 exclaimed. "How did we not know about this??"

"Well, if you stop repeating everything I'm saying, I'll get to that," 18 tried to calm the two of them down. "Do you remember over the last ten years that there were rumors of amborg-killers?"

501 and 466 both nodded quietly.

"723 is one of them," 18 sighed. "Or to be accurate, she was one. We didn't tell anyone who she was when she was rescued because we knew that this would be a likely reaction if one of you discovered her origins."

501 and 466 both stared at each other. It was quite interesting. If 723 didn't want them to pry into her personal life, she could have avoided the whole public apology she gave to 18 earlier. Their curiosity had gotten the better of them.

"But now that we know," 501 said, "What do we do??"

"Just keep acting like everything is normal," 18 replied. "The past is the past. 723 is obviously making an effort to reshape her personality. It was probably why she was willing to do all of that openly in front of you two."

"I just assumed that she was a really quiet girl," 466 said. "I think that was the first time that I ever heard her act more... human."

"Well, I highly doubt that she would go around introducing herself with this icebreaker..." 18 straightened up. She spoke in a forced monotone, imitating 723. "'Greetings, my name is 723 of the Third Group. I have been instructed to kill you. Prepare to die.'"

18 then spoke in her normal voice.

"If I had to give you an estimate," she informed them, "she has the most combat experience in your group."

"Why would she end up being an amborg?" 466 asked.

"Let me put it in words both of you will understand," 18 explained. "When the time came for us to hunt her down and kill her, we spared her life. She never asked to be put through what she's seen. She was brainwashed and void of all aspects of her humanity. Once she was caught, we decided to give her a chance to come to A.I. Industries."

"What made you decide not to kill her?"

"It took some convincing but... I looked her in the eye and didn't think that this was how her life was supposed to end."

When they got closer to the gym, 18 allowed 501 and 466 to set their water buckets down.

"Every amborg deserves that chance, right?" 18 smiled. "Now, you two get the chance to go through your physical evaluations. You ready?"

501 and 466 shrugged their shoulders and swung their arms around. They both felt relieved to not have to carry those buckets anymore, and were now eager to begin their training tests.

"It's going to be very exciting to see 117 and 917 again!" 501 smiled. "I missed them!"

"I agree," 466 nodded.

18, 501 and 466 made it to the entrance of the gym. The doors opened and they stepped inside.

There was plenty of activity going on. Several staff members of A.I. Industries were either using the gym for personal training or helping to evaluate the tests of the amborgs that had returned home. Preparations due to the emergency recall were underway as every amborg present went through a very strict fitness routine to be cleared for duty.

"Just remember," 18 reminded them from behind. "Don't get too ecstatic when you see them."

"Why not?"

"Because every international incident that you cause, I genuinely fear for your lives," 18 muttered.

Upon completion of their evaluations, they would submit the results. This was done so that each amborg could immediately identify any weaknesses and correct them as soon as they came up. There were plenty of exercises that had to be done over the next two days until Dr. Kendrick provided them with more instructions. He couldn't do that until all the amborgs were onsite.

"Alright," 18 instructed. "Let's go to the range. They have some spots available for us."

501 and 466 agreed and they walked across the gym. Amborgs from all four groups were spread out performing their tasks. They passed two Fourth Group amborgs doing push-ups with heavy cargo containers leaning against their backs. 501 was glad that he'd already done that test before they left to

pick up 18. The three of them ended up picking three booths for themselves once they reached the firing range.

"Look who's here!"

The three of them turned to see Johnny 5 of the First Group overseeing the range. He smiled at them as they arrived.

"Bring any souvenirs back from Italy?" 5 asked 18 as they greeted him.

"Yeah," 18 gestured to herself. "Me. Now, will you get on with our session?"

"Alright alright," 5 chuckled as he hit the green button at the control desk. "You just want your job back. I get it."

A buzzer went off as the amborgs in the range saw targets appearing at the furthest end. Each amborg went to the weapons rack, selected handguns, and grabbed some ammo. They all made their way to individual booths.

"We start with small firearms only. Great! Everyone is good to go," 5 instructed. "As always, there are three tests. Accuracy, Speed, and the Combo! Standby to begin the accuracy test! Round 1 will commence once all amborgs on the line have selected and loaded their weapons!"

501 inspected his weapon carefully. When he was ready, he loaded it and switched the safety off. The light surrounding his booth shined green as he waited for the next set of instructions. Once all the other booths switched to green lights, 5 continued the test.

"Keep your weapons downrange and your fingers off the trigger until ready to shoot!" 5 called out to all of them. "All targets are stationary and in the center! You are being assessed based on how many points you acquire. Please do not fire your weapons at someone else's target on the range, otherwise your scores will be instantly disqualified."

"Question?"

501 heard another amborg speak.

"What happens if I shoot 501's target, as an example?" they said. "Could 501 just shoot my target in return and we'd still be able to submit our scores?"

"Your bullet, your target," 5 stated his answer firmly and enunciated each word. "You must aim at your own target and not someone else's. I will be watching."

"But what if we miss our bullet to our target, hit the other person's, and then they shoot ours? Wouldn't that still be the correct number of bullets?"

"Some of you have a tendency to miss when distracted," 5 answered. Suddenly, the buzzer went off and they heard him joyfully yell out, "Ok, begin!"

501 took notice of the other targets in place, then redirected his focus to his own as 5 initiated the round. Carefully, with both hands, he steadied his grip and took aim. The sound of gunshots filled the range as the others began firing at their targets. Gently, he anticipated the recoil and squeezed the trigger.

His first shot hit the target in the center. Ignoring the other shots from everyone else, he focused and fired his gun until he ran out of bullets. He was glad that he wasn't the last one to finish. Everyone was firing their weapons at their own pace. Gradually, the noise died down as the last person used up their ammo.

"Reload!" 5 commanded.

Everyone grabbed another clip from the ammo box next to them. 501 ejected the empty one, placed it on the table, then reloaded a fresh clip. Once he heard the click, he slid the barrel forward and it snapped in place. It was ready to fire again. However, the next test hadn't begun.

"Safety your weapons! End of round one! Standby for round two!"

The targets moved forward as mini spotlights illuminated them, allowing everyone to see the results.

"The winner of the round is 501 of the Third Group!" 5 announced. "Good shooting!"

Satisfied, 501 pumped his fist excitedly. He couldn't wait to tell 117. Then he heard 5's next set of instructions as their targets lowered out of sight and were replaced with new ones. Five smaller targets appeared at different parts of each person's lane.

"Round two! Setting up! You have five targets to shoot. You may hit each one in whatever order you like. You must hit all of them in order to finish the round! Multiple shots or misses of any of the targets will be a penalty on your score."

501 picked up his weapon again and looked at the first target he wanted to shoot.

"Shooters! Disengage safeties! Take aim! Begin!"

Unlike the accuracy test, this one was about hitting the targets quickly rather than being patient. In round one, each amborg had taken their time to shoot the target. Now, there were multiple consecutive gunshots as all of them rapidly fired their weapons.

501 aimed at his first target and pulled the trigger. Without even waiting to see if it hit, he took aim at the next and fired his weapon. Quickly, he shot

three more times. His heart sank when he noticed that one of the targets at the very back of the lane was merely grazed, not even registering his shot as a hit. He took aim and fired one more shot. He wasn't the only one. He heard a few of the others take one more extra shot at a missed target.

"Cease fire! Safety your weapons! Standby while we calculate results!"

It took a minute for 5 to calculate the scores. 501 saw the lights in the lane on his right illuminate brightly. It was 18's lane. She had won round two.

"Kiden 18 of the First Group takes this round!" 5 announced.

Everyone politely clapped and cheered as the range darkened and they began to reset it for the next round.

501 received a chime in his HUD and saw that 18 was trying to send him a voice message. He opened it and found himself in a group chat with her and 466.

"Hey 501, 466," 18 said, "Would either of you two like to make this interesting?"

"What did you have in mind?" 466 responded.

501 also listened intently. He was eager to know where this was going.

"If either of you win in the last round," 18 stated, "You get to pick the next exercise for me to be evaluated in, and I'll also treat you to lunch. As thanks for coming to get me."

501 felt his mouth salivate at the thought of food. He maintained his composure, despite the fact that he was the only one in his booth, and spoke.

"What about if you win?" 501 asked politely.

"Other way around, I pick your next training exercise and you two would owe me a favor," 18 replied. "No questions asked. Deal?"

"I think that's satisfactory," 501 declared.

"Are you sure?" 466 asked. "You don't know what her favor could be if we lose…"

"Well, then let's avoid losing," 501 shrugged as he picked up his gun.

"That's the spirit."

18 sounded pleased as she ended the group chat. They then heard 5 announce the start of the next round.

"Round three combines speed and accuracy!" he explained. "You have 20 seconds to shoot all the targets that appear in your lane! Pay attention and do not accidentally shoot your neighbor's targets! Points will be tallied at the end of the timer! All shooters, disengage safeties!"

501 raised his gun and pointed it down the lane. There was nothing there, but once 5 started the round, they would pop up fast. He mentally prepared for where they would spring out as he switched the safety off.

"Begin!"

Right on cue, the targets were thrown out into the open and the entire range lit up. Everyone began to shoot their targets as fast as they could. 501 took aim at the ones moving and spinning at the back. One target was rotating in circles. One second, it would show itself to him, and the next, it would flip 180 degrees around, and the backside would be exposed. If he hit the back, then it wouldn't count as a hit, so 501 fired as the front began flipping towards him. The bullet hit the target just as he had hoped. It stopped spinning, and then ducked out of sight. 501 aimed a little higher at two targets that were bobbing to the left and right. Timing the motions, he put two perfect shots at each target and those next two were removed from sight.

It got easier as he worked his way backwards. Every shot hit its mark, and he felt a rush of excitement when he finally reached the last one, which was closest to him.

"Gotcha!"

501 pulled the trigger and the target was hit in the center. Right as it was stored away, he looked at the timer and heard 5 giving a countdown.

"Four! Three! Two! One!"

A loud buzzer sounded and everyone stopped firing.

"Ceasefire!" 5 commanded. "Safety your weapons and put them down! Let's see who the winner is!"

Everyone had managed to hit their targets within the time limit. To determine the winner, it was now a matter of seeing how accurate they were. Speed was an important factor when trying to finish in under 20 seconds, but more points were allotted if a shot hit as close to the center as possible.

501's heart sank when he saw the lane to his right light up again and a sequence of bright rainbow colors started glowing. It looked like someone had started a rave.

"A bulls-eye in every target for round 3! That's a perfect score! Congratulations Kiden 18! She's the winner for this group of shooters!"

Everyone clapped and cheered as they all stepped out. 18 waved her hands to them with a smile on her face. 501 and 466 both knew what this meant, however.

"Please return your weapons! We have another group doing some testing! Standby to reset the range again."

Everyone followed 5's instructions and emptied their guns. A few drones walked up and collected the empty clips and the guns as another team of amborgs selected weapons from the storage rack.

"So," 501 said meekly. "What do we owe you?"

18 laughed, giving him a light punch in the shoulder. 501 rubbed it gently.

"I'll tell you after we get your evaluations done," she smiled. "For now, you two are coming with me."

"Oh," 501 eased up a little. "That doesn't sound too difficult."

"I just hope it isn't anything weird," 466 looked crestfallen. "What training exercise did you want us to do?"

18 grinned again.

"My personal favorite," she beckoned for them to follow. "Reflex training."

There were a few other Third Group amborgs that also got roped into the same session as 501 and 466. Reflex training was a straight-forward training exercise. Unfortunately, whoever was overseeing it could decide to increase the difficulty levels whenever they liked. Since this particular activity was 18's personal favorite, they were probably not going to come out of this unharmed.

The exercise took place against a wall where a line of security drones would be the opposition. The amborgs had to stand with their backs to the wall and dodge all the incoming projectiles thrown or shot at them. There were a wide range of weapons that they used for this training. Some drones carried non-lethal rifles that fired either rubber bullets, which could sting and bruise, or taser rounds which could stick to any part of the body, incapacitating someone. Others threw weighted medicine balls, and a few drones even came equipped with small arm cannons. Fortunately, the amborgs had a strong tolerance to pain. The drawback to reflex training was the fact that anyone who went into it unaware would probably risk receiving severe injuries.

"Everyone ready?" 18 asked.

The line of amborgs against the wall nodded.

"Yes!" they replied in unison.

501 and 466 gazed carefully at the drones opposite them. They both hunched down and raised their hands like they were about to tackle someone charging at them.

"Stand by!" 18 commanded. "Avoid all incoming projectiles until the timer ends! Begin! Commence firing!"

In seconds, the drones unleashed a massive arsenal of weapons. 501 dodged a rubber bullet as he ducked to the right. Then, another drone threw one of the big medicine balls at him. With quick reflexes, 501 leaped upwards and slightly to the left, narrowly avoiding it. Unfortunately, this maneuver put him directly in the path of a taser heading straight for his chest. As he landed on his feet, he felt it connect and stick to his jacket, discharging a surge of electricity into him.

"Yeoww!"

He wasn't out, but it began to hurt really badly.

"Hang in there!" 466 said quickly as she ducked to the left and avoided a drone that had tried shooting a beanbag at her.

501 glanced at the timer 18 had set and saw that they were only given one minute for this session. Not even 10 seconds had passed, and he'd already been shocked. It was only going to get much more difficult from here.

"Concentrate 501. We taught you better than this."

501 blinked and he side-stepped another rubber bullet. He glanced over and saw that 917 and 999 had appeared next to 18. They sure loved to make an entrance.

"What are you doing?"

501 and 466 both turned their heads to see 917 and 999 reprimanding the drone that had hit 501.

"You've stopped firing," 999 stated, pointing at the timer, "during an active exercise."

"I apologize," the drone responded as its bright blue faceplate turned to look at the wall, then at them. "Amborg 501 and 466 were injured."

"And if this exercise was real," 917 interrupted sternly, "the enemy wouldn't just let us recover. You allowed 501 and 466 four extra seconds. Resume firing now."

After a moment of contemplation, the drone turned to face 501, who gulped.

"Yes sir," the drone lifted his weapon and took aim.

917 and 999 were both correct. In an actual mission, their adversaries wouldn't give them a moment to breathe. Since they were all training and trying to prove that they were ready for duty, they had to be subjected to extreme measures.

Swallowing, 501 took a breath and focused on the next incoming projectile. Eventually, one minute passed by and the buzzer sounded off.

"Cease fire!" 18 ordered. "Recover!"

The amborgs along the wall instantly relaxed. Many of them leaned against the wall or simply sat down. 466 remained standing, but she looked winded. 501 felt 917 staring hard at him and pretended to hide how much pain he was in.

"Piece of cake!" he said.

He watched 917 lean in to whisper something to 18. She returned a smile that worried 501. What were they up to?

"I agree," 18 said, a cheeky smirk appearing on her face. "Drones, prepare to fire! Increase difficulty!"

Everyone along the wall groaned as they all prepared to get back on their feet. 501 and 466 were both about to assume their defensive stances when 917 approached them.

"I want you all to picture the drones as your enemy," 917 instructed. He pointed at the line of robots standing in line across from them. "They are not A.I. Industries. They are not friends. Let's pretend that they are out to kill you. Keep your eye on them and anticipate! Pretend that I am not here to help. Pretend that 466 has just been killed and you've been backed into a corner."

917 turned his gaze to 501.

"Don't allow yourself to be distracted," he said. "Focus. If the enemy manages to overpower you, you're dead. Do not allow that to happen."

"Understood," 501 dipped his head meekly. "Can I say that I'm really glad to see you?"

"You may," 917 nodded. "Good to see you too. But, later. You, focus. Now."

917 turned around and walked back to 18. 466 spoke to 501 briefly on a private channel.

"He hasn't changed a bit," she said. "But... if I'm being honest..."

The two of them stood up and prepared as they saw the drones taking aim at them again.

"It's-good-to-have-him-back!" 466 said hastily, remembering that they were still about to be shot at.

"I agree!" 501 was barely able to say as he leaned into his defensive stance.

"Begin!" 18 called out to the drones. "Focus, everyone!"

One more round later, every amborg finished and passed the test with flying colors. 501 and 466 both let out a heavy sigh of relief when they heard

18 happily announce that this evaluation was successful. That is, until they heard a familiar voice express their disappointment.

"Let's change this a little."

501 looked up. Even after beating the increased difficulty, 917 didn't look satisfied. Looking over at 999 didn't help at all, since she always looked unsatisfied.

"What is it?" he asked as the others also listened attentively. "Didn't we pass?"

"Per the requirements of A.I. Industries? Yes, but it's not good enough," 917 shook his head. He turned to look at 999. "I say we run your program."

"No," 999 stated, without taking her eyes off them. "That program is extremely difficult."

"And that's exactly why they should participate," 917 replied, ignoring her argument. "Everyone, to the center ring! Drones included. Bring your weapons."

The Third Group amborgs and the drones gathered everything and followed 917. 999 and 18 gazed at each other, but silently walked with him.

The ring was a huge circle towards the center of the gym. It was mainly used for team sporting events, duels, sparring sessions, and battles between each other. The Third Group amborgs were feeling a bit anxious, but there was a hint of curiosity since it didn't seem like they were going to be fighting each other.

Once they arrived at the ring, 917 motioned for the Third Group amborgs to stand in the center. Then, he signaled for the drones to surround the outer ring. It was clear to everyone what was coming next.

"I have asked a few A.I. volunteers to help us out for this test," 917 announced. "All of you will remain in the center circle. If you fall or step outside of it, then you're out for the round. Do not exit the center of the circle. This is advanced reflex training. The program was written and authored by our own lone wolf of A.I. Industries. You will be surrounded from every direction. Work together as a team to avoid being hit. That's all."

"Hold on!" 466 said as she frightfully watched the drones moving to surround the outside perimeter. "There are 12 of us in the center! There's under half the Third Group here..."

"A correct but obvious assessment," 917 nodded. He turned and gave 466 a stern gaze. "What's your point?"

"The center of the circle has a 14-foot diameter!" 466 exclaimed nervously as she watched multiple weapons being readied. "We can't fit and avoid being shot at the same time!"

"Excellent," 917 stated, folding his arms. "I didn't realize all of you started slacking off while I've been away."

"No, I didn't mean…"

The more that she looked at 917's gaze, the more that 466 lost her motivation to reply. The cold and angry look of disappointment overpowered her protests. 466 became silent as she readied herself. 501 meekly raised his hand and 917 nodded his head, signaling that it was ok for him to speak.

"Why are the A.I. volunteering for this training session?"

"I'm glad you asked," 917 replied. "The drones will be operated by our very own artificial intelligence friends. Their accuracy, reaction times, and speed will be increased tenfold."

"Oh boy," 501 gulped.

"All weapons, set to stun!" 917 commanded. "Ready!"

Every drone on the perimeter raised their weapons and took aim. There were four A.I. programs, including Serina, floating outside. Each operated a team of 5 drones at a time. 501 suddenly realized what was going on. In the previous test, they had the advantage of being able to see when the drones were preparing to fire because they were positioned on opposite sides. This time, they had to anticipate which drone would initiate the attack. An A.I. would have the means to randomly choose and set specific shots for them. Since they were surrounded, they would have to pay attention to every direction. It was like a herd of sheep being corralled together while facing a firing squad ready to unleash hell.

"Begin!" 917 shouted.

Silence fell as everyone hesitated. The drones, still aiming their weapons, remained still. Each A.I. in charge of their group waited, but 917 knew that they were transmitting to each other. Who would be the first to fire the first shot?

"I didn't design the test for a group," 999 whispered to 917. "It was only meant to train one or two amborgs at a time."

"Well, then this is perfect," 917 replied. "They might as well find out their flaws now rather than later."

999 turned and looked at 18 and 917.

"They're not ready for this," she urged the two of them.

"999," 18 replied softly. "It will never be fair... especially when they face the worst kind of missions. Your objection is noted but this is 917's test. I will allow him to take charge this time."

999 fell silent. The others couldn't tell if she was complying or sulking. Maybe both. They continued to monitor the center of the ring. Suddenly, someone made a move.

One drone fired its rifle, and a stun bolt flew towards the center. The Third Group moved to duck out of the way, but the rest of the drones began to fire in a random sequence. All 12 of them in the center kept an eye on the perimeter. With all of them linked together, they attempted to coordinate as a team to dodge the incoming attacks.

"According to the official A.I. Industries minimum test requirements, I believe they are ready," 917 glanced at 18 who nodded in agreement. "If they're not ready, according to you, then when will they be?"

The Third Group amborgs continued to duck and weave as a team. It seemed to be going well for the first few seconds. 917 then pointed at the circle.

"Sometimes, you have to apply a bit of pressure to properly motivate them."

"Someone will get hurt..." 999 responded.

As if on cue, a mistake was made. They watched as 786, a timid looking amborg with shoulder length black hair, accidentally collide into 901. Her hair clip was knocked out, causing her hair to fall in front of her eyes, and making her an easy target for a stun round to hit her in the shoulder. 786 yelled out an apology as the two of them collapsed on the ground. The remaining amborgs started to panic.

"Everything hurts," 917 said. "Anyone that says otherwise is selling something."

"999," 18 cleared her throat. "He does make a very clear argument. I'd like to see how this goes."

The drones were much faster, thanks to the A.I. who were in control of their actions. One by one, the Third Group amborgs in the center of the ring were hit, dropping like flies. After less than a minute, 501 and 466 were the last two standing. There was almost no room to stand with ten other amborgs scattered around the inner circle. Both were clearly exhausted as they panted heavily, their eyes darting frantically in all directions, trying to anticipate the next incoming shot.

"I got to admit," 917 nodded, slightly impressed. "They lasted longer than I thought they would."

"How long exactly are they supposed to last?" 18 asked, looking concerned. "You didn't set a timer. Did you?"

"Yeah, about that, no I did not."

501 successfully dodged another shot. Unfortunately, when he moved to the left, he almost stepped on amborg 261's butt. He quickly tried to correct himself, but one of the A.I.'s took advantage of the situation. Two rounds hit him in the chest, and he tumbled on top of someone.

He heard a yell as he felt someone else topple on top of him. 466 was the last person standing, so he assumed it was her that had fallen on him. The electricity from the stun rounds blocked out the pain, but he knew that he was probably going to have a large bruise on his back from where she landed.

"Test complete!" They heard 917 call out to them. "Recover!"

The amborgs in the center groaned and slowly began to stand up. A bunch of mechanical footsteps moved towards them as a few of the drones stepped forward to help them up. Once everyone was back on their feet, the drones resumed their positions, and then the complaints began.

"This is impossible!"

501 and 466 watched as one of the Third Group amborgs spoke to 917. It was amborg 249.

"If the difficulty continues to increase, we can't pass," he said.

"That is why we constantly practice and train, Roland," 917 replied. "Like I said before, you already passed the minimum requirements to enter the field. But you can be better than that."

"Can I take a break?"

917 almost looked like he was about to refuse, but nodded.

"Of course," he answered. "249 is requesting a short break. Anyone else?"

"I actually would like one too," 466 raised her hand weakly. "I'll do this again when I'm not so tired."

Everyone else decided to raise their hands and follow suit. When 501 and 917 made eye contact, however, he felt a strange urge to stay in place.

"No thanks."

Everyone looked at 501. 466 glanced back, as if asking him silently what he was doing.

"Could I try the next round on my own?" he asked.

"I would like to remind you that you can rest for a bit," 917 said. "I am pushing this test on all of you, but it doesn't mean you need to kill yourself."

"Well, if we want to get to your level," 501 said as he remained in the center. "Then this is what I need to do."

"Are you sure you want to do this by yourself?" 466 asked. "This isn't mandatory."

"We've seen other amborgs pass the test by themselves," 501 nodded. "I should try to as well."

"I know," 466 gave him a worried look. "But I'm asking if you're sure that you want to try and do this yourself. 501, according to the rankings, you're the second worst fighter in the Third Group..."

"I'm getting better!" he protested. "You can't believe what the rankings say. Do you really think I'm the second worst?"

"I was being nice," 466 sighed. "You're easily the worst, but you do make up for it with a really kind heart."

"How can I call myself an amborg if I don't push myself?" He shrugged his shoulders for emphasis, making sure everyone could see.

466 smiled as they all stayed clear of the ring and held position at the perimeter.

"Just don't push yourself to a point of no return, ok?"

466 gave in and withheld her reservations. She crossed her arms together and mimicked 917. Instead of looking relaxed, she clenched her arms nervously as the test was about to begin.

"Be advised," 917 announced. "501 has elected to undergo advanced reflex training alone."

The drones readied themselves and took aim at 501, who stood in the center.

"Because you're alone for this round," 917 called out to him, "You are in fact outnumbered and out-gunned. I am signing off on your records that the Third Group participants today have made significant improvements to their reflexes and evasion. However, for this particular set of circumstances, you are allowed a shield to defend yourself. We'll add different tools the more that you do the test."

501 looked slightly confused.

"Are you just making more and more challenges as you go?"

"Not everything we encounter will be the same," 917 snapped. "We all must adapt. Someone get him a shield."

"Can you throw it to me?" 501 asked eagerly.

"No!" 917 declared. As 501 sighed dejectedly, he looked at the rest of them. "You are not Captain America. Don't throw equipment around. Remember to always practice safety with weapons."

917 leaned over to 466.

"Do not let him touch any more grenades."

466 merely nodded quietly.

One of the drones walked up to 501 with one of the training shields. It actually was circular and did have a design that Steve Rogers probably would carry around. A big bright "**A**" was painted in the center instead of a star. These shields that they had in the gym were modified with increased durability for the amborgs due to their higher-than-normal strength.

"We're not playing a game of Electro-Shock," 501 asked, sliding his left arm into the brace. "Are we?"

"Just imagine you're playing the part where all of the projectiles are flying directly at you," 917 explained. "You're just defending yourself and not trying to score any goals."

"Sounds easy enough!" 501 grinned optimistically.

917 looked at all the drones and gave the command.

"Begin!"

The drones began to open fire. 501 started to dodge and use his shield to deflect the incoming stun rounds. 466 took the opportunity to tug on 917's sleeve.

"917?" she murmured. "You do realize that 501 doesn't play defense in the Electro-Shock games. He plays better on offense."

"Well, I missed out on the last four years of games," 917 replied calmly. "I understand that he is a good fighter, but that's meaningless unless he practices how to defend himself. How bad could he be?"

"Aaaaaargh!!!"

466 and 917 gaped, eyes widened in terror. 501 had been hit from behind by two stun rounds, causing him to writhe in pain. He fell face-first onto the ground with a tremendous thud.

"Ok, that was bad," 917 stated as 466 rushed to 501's side. He turned to one of the A.I.s floating next to him. "What was the time you got?"

"Oh…" she flashed and blinked a bright red. "I was supposed to time that?"

"Yes," 917 stated. "I needed to double check."

"I'm just kidding 917," the A.I. laughed. "501's time before he got hit was 8.72 seconds."

917 checked his own timer and let out a sigh. He had hoped that his conversation with 466 would distract him into thinking the session had gone on longer. According to the A.I. and his internal chronometer, the results were accurate.

"I really hoped that he would last longer than that," 917 shook his head as he marched towards the center of the circle.

When he got close enough, 466 was kneeling beside 501's prone body.

"501? Come on back to us now," she said in a soothing tone. "You're ok."

After a few more seconds, 501 picked his head up off the ground and groaned. He gently rolled onto his side and managed to get into a sitting position.

"I got hit twice," he mumbled. "It was so fast."

"When you feel ready 501," 917 said, "Get back up."

"Let's have the medic check on you," 466 said.

"No."

501's response surprised them. He slowly got to his feet, and he addressed 917.

"Can I try again?" he asked as 466 rose up next to him.

"No!" 466 exclaimed. "You need to take a break! 917, please tell him!"

917 looked 501 in the eyes and didn't say a word. 501 gave him a firm nod, his expression unwavering.

"Reset for another round," 917 conceded.

"Thanks!" 501 did a little dance with his feet as he pumped himself up again.

"What are you doing?!"

917 walked out of the circle with 466 following him at a rapid pace.

"He can't go through all of that again," she said.

"I can't stop him 466," 917 replied as they reached the outer perimeter and turned to face the center.

"You can order him to stop," 466 said as the drones checked their weapons.

"If I ordered you to stand still while someone killed you," 917 replied in a soft voice, "Would you follow the order?"

"No," 466 answered. "But I know you wouldn't say anything like that to us."

Everyone outside the circle became quiet as the A.I. programs signaled to 917 that they were ready.

"Take aim!" he commanded. "Begin!"

Once again, the training sessions went on. As the rest of the Third Group amborgs rested and observed 501's techniques with each round, they began to mentally envision how they would carry out this test. The second test yielded better results than the first. 501 had survived 19 seconds, which was over twice the amount of time than the first time. Two rounds later, he had managed to make it to 32 seconds. At that point, signs of exhaustion began to show on his face. 501 was drawing more and more air with every breath, panting like an animal who had just succeeded in eluding the predator hunting them after a lengthy chase. The sweat forming from his forehead trickled down as he continued to push himself. Finally, the next time he was stunned, 917 and 466 approached him in the center of the ring.

"I can get this!" 501 boldly declared as he struggled for air. They lifted him up and put him back on his feet. "Let me go again!"

"501," 917 gazed down at 501's feet and inspected him. "You already got this. Take a break. The whole reason why I kept you all training in this test was to test your resolve. It was never about making it to a certain time limit. It was about seeing how committed you were."

"No!" 501 stated firmly. "Again! Please?"

"You need a break!" 466 stated. "At least rest for a minute and let someone else take the test!"

"No," 501 answered as he clung onto the shield. "This time, I want to do the test with someone else!"

501 stayed rooted to the center of the circle as 917 and 466 glanced at each other.

"You want a partner?" 917 asked with a nod. "Well, I don't think that's a bad idea."

"Ok," 466 sighed. "I'll get ready."

"Actually," 501 cleared his throat. "466, could you wait on the side? I do want to do this test with you but... I actually wanted 917 to partner with me."

917 and 466 looked taken aback. This was a surprising request.

"You're the one running the test," 466 looked up at 917. "Are you allowed to participate?"

"Well, if we were actually scoring this to clear him for duty," 917 answered, "Then no. However, 501 does have the right to choose whomever he likes as a partner since we've already finished submitting the official results. Everyone in the Third Group has exceeded expectations."

917 walked forward and waved to the drone guarding the weapons rack. He transmitted his request and the drone selected something out of the various items. It came back and 501 stared with a stunned expression at what it was holding.

"You do this test with a sword?" 501 asked as the drone handed 917 the training weapon.

"It's easier this way," 917 replied. "One day, you'll use whatever tool you like whenever you practice."

"But it's so thin," 501 pointed at it. "Are you trying to defend yourself like a Jedi?"

"A sword is much quicker than the training shield," 917 explained. "I sacrifice a large surface area for faster movement. When surrounded and using the sword to block the stun rounds, it forces you to aim carefully and to be as precise as possible."

917 and 501 stood back-to-back as the drones prepared for the next round. 466 was the one who would call out the command to start. 18 and 999 both observed silently. Now that this wasn't official, it was just a free practice round.

"I can't wait to see how you do," 501 said. "I've never seen you pass this exercise before."

"Take aim!" 466 called out.

Everyone fell silent as 917 and 501 prepared themselves. 466 hesitated, then called out once again.

"Fire!"

This time around, everything felt much simpler. 501 concentrated on what lay ahead while 917 covered him from behind. Everyone outside the circle looked on in disbelief. 917 was swinging the sword with one arm like it was nothing, keeping all the stun rounds at bay. His movements were so quick and precise that the sword looked like it was dancing as it spun like a fan. But for 501, things were a whole different story.

He was already exhausted from being stunned repeatedly, and he had yet to take a break from this particular test. 917's energy and speed showed no signs of wavering. 501 was close to his breaking point.

501 realized how different their two styles were. For a moment, he only caught glimpses, but he was in awe of how skilled 917 was. The older amborgs had more combat experience than the Third Group, and it was truly a marvel to witness it up close. 917 was right, they hadn't made any

advancements at all. Reaching the bare minimum requirements wasn't enough.

Eventually, 501 must have reached his limit because as the incoming rounds from the drones became too much for him, he felt himself moving slower in response. His HUD was signaling a fatal warning and an alarm in his head went off.

"Uh-oh," he muttered as he read a bright red '**danger**' sign that appeared in his eyes.

Another flash of light caught his attention. He looked up and noticed a blue light coming from the drone ahead of him. It had fired a shot, and he saw a spark of electricity as the stun round flew straight for his chest. He tried to move his left arm to block it, but nothing happened. Realizing his strength was failing, 501 knew it was over right before he was hit.

The electricity caused his entire body to seize up and he fell to the ground. The last thing he saw before everything went dark was 917, still fighting on. How was he able to keep going, even after losing the person behind him? He wanted to see more but fell unconscious.

"501!"

501 opened his eyes groggily. As he tried to focus, he noticed his HUD wasn't in the red anymore. He felt someone helping him up as he gazed upwards at the two people standing in front of him.

"I got hit again," 501 shook his head in order to reorient himself. "What was my...time?"

917 was looking down at him. He could see that his soft black eyes were filled with concern, but that wasn't what 501 was looking at. He was looking at the person standing behind his right shoulder.

A woman with long brown hair, blue eyes, dark hair, and fair skin was gazing down at him with a smile. It couldn't be.

"Hey. Don't worry about your time. Focus. Can you hear me?"

501 could hear 917's voice, and then he felt someone holding onto his shoulders. He turned his head to see 466's face in front of him.

"I told you!" she chewed him out instantly. "You should have taken a break sooner! Now you've hurt yourself!"

"Well, I just..." 501 faced 917 again and blinked.

Once his eyes were able to adjust and focus, 501 didn't see the pretty woman anymore. Instead, he saw Vanessa 6 of the First Group with her medical bag slung around her shoulder appear behind 917.

"Uh," 501 was confused for a moment. "Has 6 been there the whole time?"

"I just got here 501," 6 looked around, swinging her brown hair as she checked the area. "Good thing 999 called me. I'm not surprised to see that you're up to your usual shenanigans."

"But there was..."

"No buts," 6 interrupted as she knelt in front of him. "What were you thinking? Everyone here says you haven't taken one break for the last couple of hours."

She then turned to look at 917 and 999 angrily.

"And what were you both thinking?! Weren't you watching his vital signs?"

"Of course I was," 917 replied, backing away when he heard 6's tone.

"I really am fine," 501 tried to speak again. "It's not any of their faults! I wanted to keep going."

6 turned around and shined a light on his face. She investigated each of his eyes, checked his pulse, and read his medical scans from her data-pad.

"I know you try to push yourself 501," she said as she pulled out a bottle of water, placing it in his hands while 466 undid the straps of the training shield and removed it from his arm. "But if you go overboard, you risk putting your own body in danger. I want you to rest for one hour before you resume any other physical activities."

"You're the doc," 501 nodded. After taking a sip of water, he politely spoke again. "6, when you have a minute? I wanted to talk to you about something."

6 glanced at 501 and 466.

"Did you want to talk about something between the three of us?" she asked, "Or one on one?"

"One on one please," 501 turned to look at 466.

"You seem to be in a very productive mood," 466 remarked.

Once they helped him up, she nodded and became silent. 6 pointed a finger at 917.

"Please take it easy on the rest of them. 117 will be back soon and I'm sure he'll want to know what his apprentices have been up to," she ordered. 6 then turned to look at 466. "The rest of you should get ready. Dr. Kendrick might be announcing a meeting soon. Anyone not finished with their assessments should plan on taking care of the rest afterwards."

917, 999, 18 and 466 remained at the circle and arranged another round of training. Many of the Third Group amborgs, who had watched the whole thing transpire, were motivated to get back in the center. As they all eagerly prepared, 6 and 501 walked over to a bench along the wall of the gym. She set her bag down and took a seat. 501 sat next to her.

"Alright," she sighed. "What's up?"

"Just a few minutes ago, I thought I saw someone," 501 nodded towards the circle and 6 followed his gaze. "She was really pretty."

"I think that's your exhaustion causing a minor hallucination," 6 replied bluntly as she watched the next round of the reflex test. "What did she look like to you? If you're so sure you saw her?"

"Before I saw you appear beside 917," 501 stated, "I thought I saw Amara 345."

501 glanced at 6, who paused. She turned her head and looked at him with a serious expression. 6 leaned forward and slid a bit closer so that they could talk a little quieter.

"You haven't talked about her in a while," she spoke softly. "Did you mention her in front of 917?"

"No," 501 answered. "Not since the funeral."

"Are you sure you saw her?" 6 asked. "Because you could be trying to express some unresolved emotional issues that you've kept to yourself for a while."

"I am definitely sure," 501 insisted. "Amara 345 was half-Indian right? This girl definitely looked like her."

"Is it possible that one of the A.I.'s appeared nearby and just happened to look similar to her? Because the rules state that no one is supposed to be running around looking like one of us. Don't forget Halloween eight years ago, that was a nightmare. Maybe another one of the amborgs that had a similar color of hair or hairstyle?"

"No, I actually saw her in the flesh," 501 said firmly. "Not a holographic image and not one of the A.I. programs. I know it sounds stupid but... do you think that she's still around?"

"Paranormal activity or ghost sightings have always been a gray area 501," 6 sighed. "I don't know what you're seeing. An after-image of 345? Maybe an old recording that activated when you got stunned? She continues to live on in our memory. Sometimes our brains just allow us to see what we think we want to see. Were you thinking about her during the reflex test?"

"I think so," 501 lowered his head, suddenly feeling sad. "I wanted to keep doing the test for 917. It seems really important to him."

"I know it is," 6 nodded. "He's always used more practical methods. Sometimes I wish he would open up a bit more about why he pushes you."

"He's not a bully," 501's eyes widened in alarm.

"I didn't mean that," 6 chuckled. "He pushes you to be better. But I think that he still..."

A loud bell suddenly chimed overhead. Everyone stopped and looked up as an announcement began over the speaker.

"Attention all amborgs," a man's voice echoed across the entire gym. "Dr. Kendrick has convened a meeting. Please proceed to Auditorium One for a mandatory briefing. Once again, all amborgs are to proceed to Auditorium One for a mandatory briefing. The meeting for all other personnel onsite will proceed afterwards. Please stand by."

"That's us," 6 said as she stood up. "Let's go."

The amborgs that were present in the gym stopped their current activities and began to leave. Anyone handling weapons properly stored them before following the others. Many of them simply put a pause on their exercises and left the security drones and other staff members to handle the cleanup.

"What were you about to say?" 501 asked as he began to follow 6 to the exit.

"Remind me later," she replied. "I have to go join the First Group. I'll see you at the briefing!"

"But...!"

"501," 6 replied sternly without looking back. "This is the official briefing for the Emergency Recall. Do not be late."

"501!"

466 and 917 were walking up to him.

"What are you doing?" 466 asked. "Let's go!"

"Ok sure!" 501 nodded as he glanced at her. "Let's..."

He paused when something caught his eye. Very briefly, 501 looked over to the ring and saw 18 and 999 coordinating with people walking around them. A few feet behind 999, he blinked. The same woman that he saw standing at 917's side earlier was there again. She appeared to be listening intently to 18 and 999's instructions, but they didn't seem to notice her. She turned to gaze at him and smiled gently. This time, he knew for sure that he could see her. Before he could say anything, another amborg walked past his field of vision.

When they'd passed, 501 looked again and the woman was gone. 18 and 999 were the only ones standing in the center of the gym.

"Are you alright?" 917 asked.

466 was concerned as she put a hand on 501's forehead. She checked his temperature while 917 turned his head and tried to follow 501's gaze. He turned back and focused his attention on him. Clearly, he didn't seem to notice what 501 had seen. 466 removed her hand when 501 gently moved his head away.

"Yeah," 501 kept looking over their shoulders, but eventually shook his head. "I don't know. It's been a rough day."

"Maybe you need more rest after the briefing?" 466 suggested as the three of them began to leave the gym. "We can have 6 give you another checkup. You were stunned a total of 29 times."

"A normal human being would have been incapacitated for a month based on how much electricity hit you," 917 remarked.

"I'm ok," 501 replied. "I think I'm just distracted."

"Well, you definitely don't want to lose focus for the briefing," 917 shrugged as they followed the other amborgs.

501 nodded as he and 466 walked side-by-side. As they fell silent, he decided to peruse the footage of what he had seen. To his surprise, when he looked at the footage he had recorded ten minutes earlier, he saw nothing. He carefully examined it again to double-check. 466 and 917 had walked up to him just after the announcement had been made. Then he looked over their shoulders a few feet. Behind 917, there should have been a woman that looked like Amara 345 but, in the footage, he had seen nothing but an empty part of the gym. No one had been there.

Why do I still recall seeing a woman standing there? It definitely looked like 345, but that's impossible.

501 decided that he would start to investigate this after the briefing. That is, assuming he knew what it was he was looking for. Halloween wasn't coming up soon, but were there ghosts at A.I. Industries now?

Chapter 10: Me, Myself and Serina

Auditorium One
Emergency Recall plus 14 hours 17 minutes
12:45 PM MT
Total Amborgs Present: 119

Here we go. Another family reunion.

David 117 glanced around and couldn't help but marvel at the sight before him - all the amborgs were back home. He followed the line, eventually reaching the section designated for the Second Group. Whenever there was a briefing that required all of them to attend, the auditorium was set up with one section for each group of Amborgs. Each section was arranged with five rows of six chairs, 120 seats in total for all active amborgs. There were only 29 amborgs on the official list for the Second Group, but there were still 30 seats set in their section. 117 proceeded to the first row and took the second seat right next to Carter 297.

"117," he smiled. "Good to see you."

"Likewise," 117 shook 297's hand. "How are you?"

"Pretty excited actually," he replied casually. "I got a firsthand look at what we're probably dealing with."

"You were there?" 117 asked.

"You bet," 297 nodded. "I got a front row seat by accident and then I saw the emergency recall after Dr. Kendrick's space marines cordoned off the area and denied all outside access. He couldn't believe it when he gave me a call and asked me why I was there. It took a few minutes for me to explain that it was a total coincidence."

That part sounded quite entertaining. The entire matter of someone dressed as Serina 43 arriving from space had everyone on edge. 117 could only imagine the shock Dr. Kendrick must have felt upon discovering 297's beacon near the crash site secured by the Space Jumpers.

"You avoided getting spotted?" 117 asked curiously.

"Well, I had a bit of fun first," 297 snickered. "I stepped out of cover and waved at them."

"You didn't."

"Of course not," 297 gave 117 a light punch on his shoulder. 117 shook his head at 297's joke. "But I am curious what their reaction would have been. Alien spaceship crashes on the ground. They come in to secure it and then all of sudden, I pop up out of the bushes. They probably would have arrested me for being a witness or something."

"So, you didn't actually get in close to see for yourself?" 117 let out a disappointed sigh. "Even though you were actually the closest amborg there?"

"Sorry 117," 297 placed an arm around him and gave him a quick hug. "When Dr. Kendrick informed us that somehow Serina 43 made a comeback and was the passenger who landed on Earth, I knew, after watching them haul that alien ship away, that if you had been in my place, you would have tried to get in there to figure out what's going on. If I had gotten close enough, I would have definitely tried to confirm it for you."

"Thanks 297," 117 nodded. "I appreciate that. However, I guess now we wait for Dr. Kendrick to confirm it to the rest of us."

"We'll get to the bottom of this," 297 smiled. He brushed his hand across his chest pocket. "Besides, I missed being in our uniforms. It feels so nice to be back here with everyone."

297's jacket displayed the same patch insignia as 117's, both bearing a "2" for the Second Group under the A.I. Industries logo on their shoulders. His stripes, however, were a darker shade of green, whereas 117's neon stripes were a lighter hue. The other amborgs settled into their seats, each with their own different colored stripes, an impressive sight to behold. It was a rare occurrence for them all to come together like this, having only happened a few times in the past.

"Speaking of which," 297 spoke up as Ryan 35 walked in front of them and sat on his right side. "Have you gotten a chance to talk to Serina about all of this?"

"I haven't had time, it's been pretty hectic since we got back," 117 sighed. "We tried to but then she got called away. She seemed really serious."

297 glanced towards the back of their section. "I see that we're all here. I heard you and 57 picked up a certain friend from... prison?"

"Yes, we did," 117 nodded.

"Peacefully?"

"Naturally," 117 replied. "It would have made headlines if the amborgs broke into Fulton Federal."

"So, what was he doing in there?"

"You'll have to ask him for the full details, but he was involved with the Cypress Syndicate after Silhed," 117 answered quickly.

"You're kidding," 297 exclaimed. "That was him? Whoa. Cypress was a huge organization that the military didn't even dare to go up against."

"Apparently," 117 shrugged. "57 thought that Dr. Kendrick put him in there and exiled him for four years."

"You know I almost believed those rumors," 297 said, crossing his arms. "I mean, you remember when Thomas 227 was exiled from A.I. Industries for several months? And I thought that was bad."

"Yes," 117 looked to the third row at 227, who was in a conversation with one of the twins, Steve 92. "But he went after a target that wasn't sanctioned by Dr. Kendrick. As a result, that man accidentally died. 917 essentially confessed to me that he destroyed an entire mob sect all alone."

297 paused, staring off into space. 117 knew that he was thinking and processing some data.

"Silhed," he muttered. "The most recent headline about a town named Silhed was in Ohio when Cypress destroyed it. There's no mention of A.I. Industries or of 917 being involved in that incident. I assume Dr. Kendrick kept that hidden from the public?"

"Pretty much."

"Can't blame either of them," 297 let out a shudder. "Man, I just got chills. I can see where both of them are coming from but damn, that's pretty intense."

"I don't know," 117 sighed. "My grandfather called me recently and told me about what happened in LA. They discovered a prison ship filled with orphans and dead civilians."

"What?" 297 blinked. "When was this?"

"Right before the Emergency Recall," 117 replied. "Oh look, I think you can ask about it now."

117 turned his head and saw 777 enter the auditorium. The timing was perfect. Before he could wave, 777 had already spotted him and was making his way over.

"Luis!" 117 greeted him with a smile. "Good to see you."

"I'm glad to see you too David," 777 nodded to him and 297. "Carter."

"117 was telling me about LA," 297 waved. "How are you holding up?"

"I'm ok," 777 sighed. "It was really rough. I finished a quick session with 6 to share my thoughts. I just wanted to come over and thank 117, actually."

777 addressed 117 and bowed his head respectfully.

"Your grandfather is really wise and helped me get through quite a bit of emotional turmoil too."

"He's a great man," 117 smiled sympathetically. "Thank you. Let me know if there's anything I can do for you, ok?"

"Same to you," 777 answered. "This whole situation is... unprecedented."

"How many?" 297 asked. "If you don't mind sharing?"

"153 children were safely rescued from the cargo ship," 777 answered. "There were 213 dead civilians aboard the ship, possibly more missing if the investigation turns up any more victims. If I had to estimate, this gang somehow managed to gather 500 people or more and were trying to sell their kids to the slave trade."

"A few people, I can see that," 297 pondered. "But how did they manage to kidnap families and kill hundreds without this getting out? However they kept it under wraps, they sound like a new level of evil."

"I agree," 117 stated. "I can see why you were one of the last amborgs to return after the Emergency Recall. Did you find anything else out?"

"LAPD is working with your grandfather's vigilantes to figure out how they did this," 777 reported. "The prisoners we captured are refusing to give up any information. Their loyalty is hindering our progress which makes it difficult to identify who is behind this. They had fake shipping manifests, military grade weapons, and a lot of hired guns. That's not even including the fact that this gang just had a fully fueled cargo vessel, and they were legally docked in Los Angeles. If not for this outer space incident, I'd still be out there trying to figure this case out."

"Well, when she gets a second," 117 brought his hand up to his chin and started thinking. "Maybe Serina can spare a moment to help."

"Someone say my name?"

A small flash of light appeared from the chair on 117's left, and the three of them turned to see Serina floating there.

"Hey," 297 waved. "There's the bravest *little* sister we know."

117 smiled as he lifted his hand and held it up for her. She stuck her tongue out at 297's comment.

"Good to see you guys," Serina said as she leaped onto it. "Finally, I can have a few seconds to rest."

Since she didn't have a physical body, she didn't technically have to "sit" down on 117's hand. She was merely a holographic projection that could float around, but still enjoyed behaving differently from the standard programs at A.I. Industries. It also made the connection between them more human-like. Serina never liked conversations to be dull or strict. She always felt that if everyone involved in a conversation with her could relax, then they could forget about her being an A.I. and talk to her like normal.

"I got to tell you, this is turning into one logistical nightmare," she said as she held out one hand and put it forward, as if trying to signal someone to stop. "Thankfully, all the amborgs are capable of getting back here efficiently, but ever since the news of what happened in Africa leaked, the whole world turned into a Black Friday sale. Now every mode of transportation is fully booked and everyone who failed to get back on time is stuck in worldwide traffic."

Serina turned to look up at 117.

"By the way, Mandy should be back in about 31 minutes," she smiled cheerfully. "She and Palmer were on the first flight back from Paris immediately after the Emergency Recall was initiated."

"How were they?" 117 asked.

"I'm a little concerned," Serina's smile faded. "Mandy sounded really excited. More so than usual. I think being on vacation was starting to bore her."

"I'll ask her when I see her," 117 shrugged. "She does hate being forced to use her vacation days. Dr. Kendrick is probably never going to hear the end of it."

Serina stood up and her hologram flashed brightly. Her usual articles of clothing had changed on the spot. She had switched from a normal hoodie and pants into a skirt and button-up shirt. She had also given herself some high heels and was putting on a holographic blazer. The amborgs watched in amusement as she modified her voice.

"I told you Dr. Kendrick!" Serina imitated Mandy, increasing her pitch slightly. "If the world ends when I go on vacation, I'm going to say, 'I told you so!'"

Another flash of light and Serina reappeared wearing a white lab coat, a tie, and slacks. She put on some holographic spectacles and cleared her throat.

"The world is not going to end Mandy," Serina declared in a deep voice. "Now go enjoy your vacation. Nothing bad is going to happen whatsoever, so you just go ahead and relax. Otherwise, I will have an amborg serve as your escort."

Serina swapped back into Mandy's outfit.

"I don't need an escort!" she stated in a huff. "I can take care of myself!"

She switched back to Dr. Kendrick's clothes.

"On the contrary, you do," she spoke properly and in a formal manner. "The amborg will make sure that you don't return until all of your vacation days have been fully utilized."

"I really missed hearing her imitations," 297 chuckled as the rest of them were breaking out in fits of laughter.

"It's good to be home," 117 agreed. "I think you were quite accurate, Serina. Nailed it. But, if we could get back to what we were talking about, 777 needed your help with something."

"Did you not hear me when I said I needed a few seconds to rest?"

Serina let out a sigh and in another flash of light, she was back in her usual attire.

"Anyway, I just finished reading Luis 777's after-action report from Port Hope," she stated as she gazed up at them. "Geez, that's terrible. What can I help with?"

Serina's advanced processing abilities never ceased to amaze. In less than two seconds, she'd already read all of 777's report and was ready to assist. From her perspective, time worked a little differently, which was why she and the A.I. were very resourceful.

"Any chance you could help me put together a list of suspects? Specifically, anyone who would have the resources to pull off what we uncovered?"

Serina nodded as she listened to 777's questions. After a moment of pondering, she answered.

"I'll start with examining the shipping manifests from the docks," she nodded. "I'll forward the LAPD some intel which they could use to get through to the prisoners. Every person has a weakness. When discovered, they will squeal. But what we'll focus on is where those kids were being smuggled to."

They watched as Serina pulled out a holographic tobacco pipe and paced around the palm of 117's hand. Mimicking Sherlock Holmes, she voiced her thoughts to them.

"Assuming that this gang doesn't have strong security on their computer systems, I could figure this out in minutes," she stated. "However, the shipping manifests are heavily encrypted which means that whoever drafted the fake ones is no amateur. Once we find out where the ship was dropping off its cargo before your raid on the docks, we could potentially start getting some suspects. Oh."

Serina's eyes widened.

"We should all take a seat!" she suddenly exclaimed as she threw the pipe over her shoulder and disappeared into several pixels. "Dr. Kendrick is coming!"

"To be continued," 777 nodded as he walked away to his seat.

A chime got everyone's attention and the entire auditorium became quiet.

"Attention, please take your seats."

Everyone took their seats. All conversations were put on hold or switched to private channels.

"Duty calls," Serina said, disappearing in an instant.

Out of the corner of his eye, 117 saw Serina suddenly appear among a group of A.I. programs that were gathering in the corner. Despite the fact that the briefing was set for amborgs only, he could only assume that they were here at Dr. Kendrick's request.

117 heard doors open and he turned to look. On the opposite side of where most of them entered, Dr. Kendrick came in, followed by a few of his colleagues. He recognized Mr. Ramirez at his side and two security guards serving as an escort for their group. One guard remained at the entrance they'd come through and stood at attention. The other one proceeded to the entrance on the other side and blocked it off. Mr. Ramirez followed Dr. Kendrick to the front of the auditorium and took a seat while Dr. Kendrick walked up to the podium with a data-pad.

"Good afternoon," he declared.

All the amborgs returned his greeting simultaneously in one loud chorus.

"Good afternoon, Dr. Kendrick."

A dozen chimes rang out and lights flashed all over the room from every amborg's bracelet. Some even spoke in their real voices. Dr. Kendrick smiled happily at all his children. Each one of them had returned, completely aware of the developing situation. There was little time, but at least Dr. Kendrick was able to look over each section of amborgs.

"Everyone," he said, slowly sweeping his gaze over the crowd. "Thank you all for returning. It was indeed short notice and I apologize ahead of time to each of you."

He looked at 3, 18, 35, 92, 93, and 917, each of whom stood up in acknowledgement.

"Especially the amborgs that were in no position to respond immediately," he continued. "You have the United Nations and another potential world crisis to thank for your expedited journey home. Please be seated."

The First Group sat back down, but they all remained at attention. They were the originals: calm, wise, and preparing themselves mentally. Hopefully if things went wrong, Dr. Kendrick could count on their experience and charismatic leadership.

He looked to the Second Group, specifically to the one vacant seat next to 117, which wasn't a surprise. It would always be there as a reminder and tribute to their fallen sister. Fortunately, this had no negative effect on the First Group at the moment because they were more focused on anxiously waiting for the next command. It was likely his imagination, but Dr. Kendrick could have sworn many of the younger amborgs appeared more laid back and relaxed.

Especially the Third Group, the ones still considered to have the combined curiosity of a pack of children. Many of them were flashing smiles of extreme excitement. A few of them showed some anxiety, but all of them seemed glad to be back in each other's company.

Lastly, the most recent group of amborgs, The Fourth. Not one of them flashed a single smile, but their whole party made the number of amborgs in the room seem staggering. None of them had participated in the Domino Incident, yet all were remarkably skilled, just like their older predecessors. They were special amborgs created during the era of peace, which meant that they were still learning about human etiquette. Dr. Kendrick didn't blame them one bit for not being more invested. They were completely oblivious of the significance of what had happened in the last few hours. All of them merely responded to the call to return home and were waiting for an explanation.

"Alright, I shall be brief. All of you know by now that something tremendous has happened," he spoke calmly as he opened some images on the screen. "This is a short recap. At 10:20 AM MT, a little over 14 hours ago, Ziggy 2 was the supervising amborg aboard the Apogee Station. An anomaly was detected, and we confirmed that it was a tear in space, an interdimensional rift of some kind. Before we had a chance to properly grasp what we had witnessed, we detected an unidentified flying object hurtling towards Earth. It touched down and landed in Kenya shortly after. The space-jumpers secured the crash site very quickly and we attempted to take the ship and the single passenger inside to acquire more information. Naturally, those of us who were first on the scene were surprised to see that the passenger was a woman, in her mid-40s and wearing an A.I. Industries number. A number that should have been retired. Now to get to the bottom of this, we must be vigilant. Amborg number 43 has returned to our lives, and we are going to figure out what circumstances led to this event. The First, Second and Third Groups knew her personally, whereas the amborgs of the Fourth Group would have heard about her by reputation only. One of our closely guarded secrets is the fact that our artificial intelligence Serina here holds 43's memories, personality, and is a perfectly revived form of the girl that she used to be."

117 glanced at Serina, who stared back solemnly. Normally, she'd be giving an encouraging smile, but he could see that she was worried about what was going on.

"We were hoping, under cooperation from all the space agencies worldwide, to reveal what had transpired at the end of the day. Unfortunately, due to some political issues and bad luck, the secret is out now, and everyone wants an answer."

Dr. Kendrick brought up the images of the woman who was the occupant of the crashed spaceship. Several in the audience hadn't seen these and were looking closely at the glowing "43" in the photos.

"To solve this mystery, we need to know what this woman knows. I want the following representatives from each group to go to interrogation once she regains consciousness. These amborgs knew her the best to my knowledge, so they will be the ones to speak directly to our guest from space. As for the remaining groups..."

A list of their names appeared on the wall behind him.

"Each group shall select two pairs of leaders, one for a trip and one to remain here onsite, followed by a second in command of each leader's choice. I know that many of you may have a hard time readjusting to the order of command, but it is necessary if we are going to figure this out quickly. So, for this operation, establish an organizational structure. In the meantime, I shall prepare for a voyage to Apogee Station. I want reports from each representative within the hour. Leonard, please take over. Dismissed, and good luck to us all."

As Dr. Kendrick was about to step out the door, he turned to face them again.

"I'm going to be honest with everyone," he said. "This is a spectacular moment in history. I apologize once again if it seems like there are very few answers. We must all prepare for the fact that everything, from this point on, is changing. I ask that everyone remain calm, and we will get through this. Don't be surprised if the rest of the world doesn't feel the same. People are counting on us. We will be ready to respond when they ask for our help. Thank you."

The doors closed behind Dr. Kendrick and his escort. Serina glanced back at 117. Then she turned towards where they had left and disappeared in a small flash of light. 117 and 297 exchanged glances.

"He's pretty shaken up," 297 remarked.

"He has to constantly update every single world leader on the situation," 117 replied. "I'd hate to be in his shoes right now."

The sound of shuffling quickly filled the room. Amborgs 1 and 2 made their way to the front while everyone else grabbed their chairs and turned towards their respective groups. It was quite an interesting sight to see each group huddle together in their own unique styles.

The Fourth Group quickly and efficiently reorganized their chairs into a flawless circle formation. It looked as though they were about to play some sort of game, but in reality, they were silently communicating with each other on a private channel to select their leaders.

The Third Group was a different story entirely. Instead of arranging themselves in a neat formation, they were completely disorganized, their chairs scattered but still close to one another.

The Second and First Groups appeared the most relaxed, but slightly dysfunctional. They weren't in an arbitrary formation like the Third Group, instead everyone just turned around and faced the center. They purposefully left 43's chair alone.

The First and Second Group amborgs were all experienced and comfortable with each other. It felt more like a family reunion as they all greeted each other warmly and excitedly. According to most of the after-action reports over the last decade, the Second Group had spent more time together in the field than the First Group.

That was the big difference between them and the older amborgs. The first 30 amborgs of A.I. Industries combined had the highest number of solo missions completed. In the early years when they were so few in number taking on the world's challenges, they relied mostly on themselves in many situations. They shared strong mutual bonds and showed a high level of respect for each other. It was just less touchy-feely for them.

As they quickly began to vote for their leaders, 1 and 2 signaled for everyone's attention.

"Ok," 1 said. "Who is to appear in interrogation?"

The amborgs who were chosen by Dr. Kendrick all raised their hands: 3, 5, 6, 297, 117, 917, 999, 57, 35, 501, 466 and 280. A few Third Group amborgs stared at 280 with surprised expressions. Ignoring them, 1 looked at the team and nodded.

"Very good."

"It's interesting that 280 was selected," 18 remarked. She immediately followed that up when she noticed several of the Fourth Group looking at her. "I just meant that for a Fourth Group amborg to participate in the interrogation is strange since you're the only one who has never known 43 personally. I meant no offense."

"None taken amborg 18," 280 replied in the neutral tone that they were all too familiar with. He maintained eye contact as he spoke up, "Dr. Kendrick selected me because he believed that I needed to get more experience on the job. I have studied 43's records extensively during my training period so I can provide a perspective that is objective and not personally biased."

"Sounds... legit?" 5 said, raising an eyebrow. "How extensive do you mean?"

"Extensive," 280 repeated the answer.

"5," 6 nudged him in the side.

"Hey, don't blame me for trying to get him to open up a bit more."

"Anyway," 1 interrupted. "We are also establishing our chain of command. I am here for the First Group, the votes call for me to be a leader. If there are no objections, then I want Ziggy 2 to be my second. He has been in space personally and has the best experience with what we have seen so far."

"No problems there," 2 replied as he looked at the other First Group amborgs, who were all nodding in unison. "I'd rather Leonard be in charge instead of me. He's always got the leadership role down."

"Only because you never want to," 1 replied with a smile. "Alright, do we have a second leader to keep an eye on things planet-side? 2 and I are already spoken for."

"Yes!"

The rest of the First Group chanted simultaneously as Amborg 4 stood up. She looked around a little nervously while they practically pushed her up to the front. She took a spot next to 2 and waved at everyone.

"I guess it's me," she replied with a modest chuckle.

"Who else were we going to pick?" 2 snorted. "8 and 9?"

The First Group started to laugh as amborgs 8 and 9 both shook their heads. The two of them were notorious for being the pranksters of A.I. Industries.

"Hey," 8 held his hands up in plain view. "Last time I was in charge of something... 9 blew it up."

"Because you were being an idiot," 9 replied as she slapped him on the shoulder. "And I only set fire to the objective, it just happened to explode when it got out of control."

"Which is what happens when you mix it with hazardous chemicals," 8 scoffed.

"Alright!" 1 announced, interrupting the conversation before 8 and 9 could have a go at each other. "4, who is your second in command?"

"Give me 8," 4 smiled.

"What?!" 1, 2, 8, and 9 all exclaimed at the same time.

4 laughed. She shook her head, making the rest of them relax.

"I swear, you guys are too easy," she chuckled. "I would actually like to nominate 18 as my second in command."

Everyone turned to look at 18, who nodded her head.

"I won't let you down 4," she said as the surrounding amborgs nodded in agreement. "Even if there are other options available."

"You're just bummed you can't go to space," 297 called from his section.

"Yeah," 18 snapped back as she lifted her feet up and rested them on the chair across from her. "Keep talking, eagle eye, and I'll toss your ass up into orbit."

297 chuckled while the rest of the amborgs continued laughing. The Fourth Group merely stared silently while 1, 2, and 4 sat down with The First Group. Now it was the Second Group's turn. After a quick vote, 117 stood and walked up to the front, which didn't come as a surprise.

"I don't think I should automatically be the leader," he protested as the Second Group motioned for him to stay put. "There are others more qualified. Almost all of you are capable!"

Several of his colleagues continued to heckle and ignore his protests. 117 laughed and found himself a leader once again.

"Are you kidding?" 57 called out to him. "You're the obvious choice for this one. 43 is an A.I. now. So, remember to choose someone alive as a second, ok?"

"And the prisoner in our basement doesn't qualify," 92 stated. He turned to look at his twin brother, 93. "Because...?"

"...She's an imposter until proven otherwise," 93 finished the statement.

"Very funny," 117 sighed.

117 had already thought it through extensively before anyone could even ask. He'd only been given a short time frame to consider the options and he felt that his decision would almost certainly grab some attention.

"I would like to nominate 999... as my second-in-command."

A hushed silence fell over the room. The laughter died in an instant, replaced by wide-eyed stares and nervous looks in response to his statement. Taking in the reactions of the members of the Second Group, 117 could feel a palpable sense of unease. Slowly, they all shifted and turned towards the very back of their section. A cold and familiar female voice spoke up. It had been a while since he'd heard her voice in such a chilling tone, so long that it was making him wish that the 43 he knew was still alive.

"Wouldn't you rather have 917 to be your second in command?"

The rest of the Second Group stared apprehensively at Angel 999, who had her arms crossed.

"Doesn't he sound like the better choice?" she asked casually.

917, who was seated right next to her, gave her a sideways glance. Though he appeared cautious, he remained silent. The rest of the Second Group exchanged awkward glances, their eyes darting uncertainly between the front and back of the room. 117 looked at 1, silently questioning whether or not he made a good choice. 1 merely gave him a shrug.

"An interesting choice," 1 transmitted to 117 privately. "You sure you want her as your backup?"

117 nodded, showing his commitment to his decision.

"Well, I did say if it was alright with you," 117 cleared his throat as he saw the Third Group huddle closer. "I've decided to state my reasons at a later time."

999 looked up at 117. She turned to glance at 917, who didn't respond. He gave her an encouraging smile, which made her sigh.

"I never said I wasn't alright with it," she declared as she closed her eyes. "I'll do it."

"Then it's settled," 117 tried to focus the attention back up front. He optimistically smiled and clapped his hands together. "999 is officially my second-in-command."

117 saw 35 nudge 57 and she quickly stood up. She walked up to the front and joined 117. At least this broke the tension as everyone started to refocus.

"Hey everyone," she announced. "I have been voted the on-site leader of the Second Group. I would like to choose Ryan 35 to back me up."

"Me?" 35 looked up in surprise. "I guess I could... I mean, it's the first time in years since I've been in a command position with so much responsibility. Sort of."

Once 117 and 57 were confirmed as the two leaders of the Second Group, she placed a hand on his shoulder as they walked back to their seats.

"I wish you luck," she said. "Whatever you have planned, I support it. Even if I do have some concerns."

"Noted," 117 replied. "But what's done is done."

After 117 sat back down, they all shifted to the Third Group quickly before 999 could change her mind. 501 stepped up to the front with none other than 466. The second pair of leaders ended up being August 95 and Kayla 53. They were also equally as experienced as 501 and 466, so the Third Group had picked them. Unlike the slight awkwardness left by the Second Group, they quickly voiced their decision and sat back down without another word.

This left the Fourth Group. Without any hesitation, four of them stood up and marched up to the front of the room. Alex 280 and Ally 113 stepped forward and announced that they would be the first pair of leaders. Riley 65 and Morgan 224 were the second pair. Their vote was quick, and the announcement was efficient. It was almost as if they were watching a police lineup of drones.

"Alright then, we have our chain of command," 1 said confidently. "Sort of. If there isn't any form of internal conflict."

He looked at 999 carefully, but continued listing out their assignments.

"Alright, this is a list of specific duties that I'm assigning to everyone except the interrogation team. Move out. I want reports from each leader and their second in command ready for Dr. Kendrick about our readiness levels and who we've designated as the amborgs in charge. 18, please keep everyone working on their fitness evaluations. Get them all cleared for duty in four hours."

Everyone exited in an orderly fashion and split off to begin their work. 65 and 224 quickly received congratulations from 501 and 466 for being voted as leaders of the Third Group. The Fourth Group amborgs left without so much as a goodbye to anyone. 57 and 35 walked up to 117 as they prepared to head to the interrogation wing.

"Is it wise for all four of the designated leaders of the Second Group to be a part of the interrogation?" 35 asked. "It may be counterproductive since this might be too personal for a lot of us."

"On the contrary," 117 replied. "All of us together is the best way to figure out who the prisoner is. Whoever she is, we all will be witnesses. We'll make this fast, 35."

Just as they were about to leave, they were blocked. The door hissed and slammed shut with a loud click, locking itself tight. 117, 35, and 57 froze for a moment, glancing to their right to see 999 with her hand on the lock.

"Are you going to tell me why you picked me?" she asked.

Her tone was soft but there was something chilling in her voice that made them all shudder. 117 got goosebumps and assumed the other two also felt the same thing.

"Oh! Look at that!"

They all glanced back to see 5 raising his hands and backing up uneasily.

"I'll... um... go out the other exit," 5 gave them all a wave and walked another way.

Several other amborgs also followed him and they proceeded towards another door. 117 noted a mix of fear in their hasty retreat. 6 was right next to him, grinning in amusement. She eyed them all and politely backed up. Before she turned away, 117 thought he caught a glimpse of concern on her face as she looked at 999. Suddenly, he heard footsteps and turned his head, his whole body freezing up as he found himself face to face with 999.

"Why did I pick you?" 117 stammered. "Oh that's simple!"

35 and 57 walked up to the door. 999 glanced at the two of them and pushed a button on the panel. It unlocked and slid open.

"We'll..." 35 spoke fast. "We'll just head to the interrogation room first."

35 and 57 rushed out while 999 continued to stare at 117. 917 was already out of sight, which seemed to make her presence feel scarier. The amborgs only felt comfortable around 999 when 917 was around to keep her from... being alone with a target.

She didn't close or lock the door again as she stepped out first. That was 117's cue to follow her.

"I asked for a recommendation, and I agreed to it."

999 grabbed 117 by the shoulder and directed him to the side. A couple of people walking by noticed but didn't say anything. Retracting her hand, she glared up at him.

"An A.I.?" she asked. "Why?"

"You were the top option that came up," 117 replied.

"Liar," 999 replied in a low voice. "Choose another amborg to be your partner."

"Wait!"

999 began to walk away, so 117 quickly confessed.

"Serina asked you to do it!"

She stopped, slowly looking back at him in suspicion.

"Serina picked you," 117 said. "I agree with her decision."

"Why would Serina pick me?"

"Because I trust you. You're my first choice? That's just a couple reasons to start off this conversation."

There was a flash of light and Serina appeared, floating in between the two of them.

"After I died, there were a lot of things that I had started but didn't get to see to the end," she explained. "Everyone stepped in to follow through on everything that I never got a chance to finish. You were the one that helped the most, Angel."

"There are more qualified individuals," 999 replied, shaking her head. She glanced at Serina and at 117. "You both know that I'm not a leader."

"Yes, but you're one of the best amborgs I know," Serina held her hands together, pleading. "I know you don't like comparisons but 117 and I were also close to each other just like you and 917 were. Both of you were practically joined at the hip for a long time! Well... except for him being in prison for the last four years, which I had no idea about, by the way. No offense to 917, since he's actually one of the coolest guys I know, but the Second Group didn't vote for him at all."

999 looked at 117 and narrowed her eyes. He could tell that she really wanted Serina to get to the point.

"You're right," Serina sighed, bowing her head. Her illuminated figure seemed to dim as her mood changed. "There are other qualified individuals. But if 917 isn't someone that they want, even if he is a close friend to 117 and I, then I want my bestie to protect him. I guess you could say that I wrote you in on the ballot."

"What ballot? We aren't running for office," 999 replied. "And we are not besties."

Serina looked up at 999 with wide eyes. She flashed a bright yellow as she put her hand on her chest, as if she couldn't fathom what she had just heard.

"But what about all the time we spent together??" she asked as she looked at 117. "Those moments we bonded."

"Serina," 999 grumbled. "Whatever free time the two of us had was spent dueling with each other. We were always trying to see who the best fighter was."

"Look," Serina chuckled nervously as she shrugged her arms to 999. "It doesn't matter who was the better fighter..."

117 knew she was speaking modestly. When she was alive, Serina 43 was A.I. Industries' best fighter, but it was probably not a good idea to mention that, since Serina was trying not to upset 999 even further.

"...All that matters right now is this," she said, pointing at 999 and 117. "I am dead! You're not! That means, I'm asking you, my bestie, to protect my best friend! Please? I just want to make sure that you protect each other. Will you be his partner for this mission?"

999 took a moment to think as she looked away. When she turned back to them, she let out a sigh.

"I still think you could have picked someone else," she conceded and nodded her head. "Fine. I'll do it. But if for some reason, I'm the one who has to take over when 117 is unable to do his job, whatever consequences come from my actions are on you."

"I can live with that," Serina nodded. Then she looked away in confusion. "Wait, I'm still dead... so... I can accept those conditions."

"Serina," 117 groaned.

"I'm kidding!" Serina looked up at 117 and shrugged. "Look, there is an imposter dressed just like me in our basement and we have to interrogate her... me. Let me cope, alright?!"

With a bright flash of light, Serina disappeared into the panel, and they saw her light moving down the hall fast. 999 and 117 turned to each other after watching the light fade away.

"She's under enough stress," 999 said softly. "I shall set my issues aside and uphold her request."

"What issues are you dealing with?" 117 asked.

"Need-to-know," 999 replied. "That information is need-to-know and you aren't qualified."

"You realize that I outrank you for this mission," 117 suggested. "I could order you to..."

117 stopped when he saw 999 frowning.

"Never mind," he said.

"Wise choice," 999 muttered.

"Can I ask you one more thing before we go to interrogation?"

999 let out a groan as she rolled her head back and stopped walking. 117 braced himself, turned, and saw her glaring at him again. He really wished he had backup right about now.

"No," she declared. "But based on how chatty you are, I assume you're going to ask anyway."

"I apologize for making you step out of your comfort zone..." 117 started to say.

"Like making me your second-in-command?" 999 muttered. "Forcing me to abandon my preferred introverted solitude?"

117 pointed down at her bracelet which had been broadcasting her voice the entire time.

"You... uh, haven't actually spoken an actual word from your mouth," he observed. "You've been speaking from your bracelet the entire time..."

"State your damn question already," 999 crossed her arms impatiently.

117 nodded and stopped rambling.

"You were the last person to see 917 before he left to go see Dr. Kendrick four years ago," he stated. "You were with him when Silhed was attacked. What happened to you both?"

999 unfolded her arms but continued to gaze at him skeptically. He knew she was trying to figure out if it was safe to trust him. He decided to voice the other troubling issue on his mind.

"Look, I'm in charge of the entire Second Group again," 117 said. "This is not a personal investigation. I just need to know what you saw and if this is something I must be concerned about."

"No," 999 said quickly.

117 lowered his head and fixed her with a stern look. Her glare had softened, and he could see the hurt behind her eyes. Surprised, 117 examined her facial tics closely, realizing it was probably the first time he felt she might be lying to him.

"Don't lie," he said.

"I'm not," 999 replied, shaking her head uncomfortably.

"Look," 117 sighed. "I feel terrible about the fact that he was in prison and none of us knew. He was my best man when I married Audrey, and I didn't know how much pain he was in. But you're his closest friend."

"And I'm telling you that Jack 917 will do his job without any issues," 999 replied firmly. "Yes, he went on a rampage when we found Silhed burning down. My hands are as dirty as his, but you want the truth? He took full responsibility when we returned to A.I. Industries to face the consequences."

"What? But that would mean that you would have also been imprisoned or exiled too."

"Yes. But he didn't let that happen. And that's the truth," 999 looked down. "My best friend went to prison and accepted punishment. He left without me. The one person who taught me to trust other people again. I don't know the full details. My instincts tell me, despite all these issues, that 917 is still going to do his job properly. He's not crazy."

117 figured that this conversation was a dead-end.

"You both took down a crime syndicate by yourselves without backup," he said dimly. "Based on what information 917 felt like sharing and since you're vouching for him..."

117 glanced around, noticing a few people going about their business. Nobody seemed to be eavesdropping on their conversation. He looked back at 999 and let out a sigh.

"I'm sorry," he said.

"What for?" 999 asked.

"I personally picked you to partner with me on this mission because I wanted to know if I could count on my friends. I know that having doubts isn't ok and I understand if you don't want the job."

999 pivoted and walked away. 117 turned his head but didn't follow. After a few steps, 999 glanced back over her shoulder.

"Come on," she said. "Let's go to interrogation."

"Uh," 117 stammered as he sped-walked over to her. "You're not quitting?"

999's bracelet flashed as she pointed two fingers at his face.

"Allow me to be clear," she said. "You didn't need to ask me to be your partner just to get information on 917 or on me. Just ask. You know that we will back you up under any circumstances... but not like this. Please understand that we... I... am asking you to keep trusting us. The moment that we start doubting each other, we destroy the very reason why we became amborgs. Understood?"

117 nodded silently. This was the first time he had ever heard something so meaningful from her. The Lone-Wolf attitude had always kept 999 closed

off from him and 43 back then. Actually, that wasn't correct. It kept her closed off from almost everyone.

"Besides," 999 said, "I can't quit being your partner for this one. Serina asked me... and you accepted her recommendation. I'm not about to back out now."

117 smiled slightly.

As they headed to the elevator that would take them down to their destination, another question formed in his mind. Had he misheard or did 999 actually say something wrong?

She had said that if they started doubting each other, then it would destroy the whole purpose of becoming amborgs. But there was one tiny flaw with that reasoning: 917 hadn't chosen to become an amborg. He had been saved by Dr. Kendrick and was changed involuntarily.

Before he could properly ask, something grabbed their attention. 501 and 466 were both awkwardly watching a conversation down the hall. Their eyes were fixed on 723 and 917, who were chatting.

"Not good," 999 said cautiously.

As they approached 501 and 466, the conversation could be heard more clearly.

"What course of action do you recommend?" 723 asked.

"I already said it's fine," 917 said politely.

"Your tone of voice is not expressing genuine satisfaction."

501 turned to face 117.

"Do I want to know?" he asked, and the two Third Group amborgs shook their heads frantically.

"723 was insistent on apologizing to 917," 501 informed them.

"Except, she's kinda pushing the matter even further which might be aggravating him instead," 466 added nervously.

"Why?" 117 asked as he looked at 723.

"Because to her, forgiveness is too much of a priority."

Before 117 could even ask what that meant, the three of them saw 999 rush forward. Shocked, 117 leaned in with 501 and 466 to watch.

"723," 999 announced her arrival. "Enough. You've apologized. Please return to your duties."

"917 is not accepting my apology," 723 reported casually.

"Because I keep telling you that it's fine," 917 raised his voice.

"I attempted to murder you."

723 continued to speak in a neutral tone and that, combined with her declaration, didn't seem to make things better. 917 stepped forward menacingly, making 723 retreat a little. 999 noticed this and immediately stepped in between them, raising her hands for them to stop. 501 and 466 gasped as 117 stepped forward, prepared to intervene if necessary. Fortunately, no one laid a finger on each other as 917 glared at 723.

"Yes, you did," 917 said with an angry huff. "I told you it was fine."

"You are not fine," 723 said in a lower voice.

"723," 999 interrupted them. "Back off. Don't you have a few evaluations to finish?"

"Yes," 723 nodded.

723 turned and left without looking back. 999 put her hands down and looked at 917. She got cut off when 917 made to walk away.

"It was under control," he said.

"Sure, it was," 117 cleared his throat, announcing his presence.

"Relax," 917 said, noticing his small audience. "I wouldn't put a hand on her."

"Are you ok?" 117 asked.

"I don't know if you want me to answer that honestly," 917 replied. "You have a girl who was brainwashed into trying to kill us over the last decade that's trying to seek forgiveness after becoming one of us. I don't know if that pisses me off just because it's ironic or because I can relate."

"Umm..." 501 gulped as he and 466 moved with the rest of the group. "What do you mean by that?"

917 glanced at 501 and sighed. He allowed his anger to fade away as he shook his head.

"Don't worry about it," he said. "Let's go. We have a job to do, and we still need to finish our reevaluations."

They watched 917's back get further away. After a moment, 117 glanced at 999, who looked slightly crestfallen. He gently placed a hand on her shoulder.

"Nothing to worry about?" he asked.

"Nothing to worry about," she declared.

999 gently lifted her hand and smacked his off her shoulder. 117 retracted his hand hastily, wincing in pain from the hit. He had forgotten that she hated being touched without consent. Still, she'd made some notable progress in her

emotional development. If it had been years ago, she would have judo-thrown him to the ground before his hand would have even felt the fabric of her jacket.

999 proceeded after 917. 117 turned to look at 501 and 466, who both looked a bit anxious.

"You two realize that if you're the leaders of the Third Group for this mission, you need to try and deescalate the situation," he said, massaging his hand.

501 and 466 glanced at each other and shrugged.

"We'll keep that in mind, 117," 501 said.

They made their way to the elevators and headed downstairs. The ride was quiet and a little uncomfortable. It was awkward, but they all got off on the right floor and made their way to the security room with the mirrored window.

Inside, the other selected amborgs were already there. Once 117, 501, and 466 joined the group, they all began a brief discussion as they looked through the glass window. In the other room sat their prisoner, locked up and tied down with custom built chains. She was awake now and the only occupant on the other side.

"If I had not seen this for myself, I would never have believed it," 297 said with a grave look. He was putting on a brave face, but he was still shocked all the same. "117, I know you're going to refuse anyway but I'm just putting it out there, you don't have to be here for this if it makes you uncomfortable."

117 felt 297's hand pat him on the shoulder.

"I appreciate it 297," 117 answered as he felt the hand retract. "But I think I'll stay."

"So. Uh. Does anyone want to…? I don't know. Go in there?"

57's question didn't get any responses from anyone else. They were all too busy staring.

Everyone looked through the security glass. Inside the fortified prison box, the woman wearing the specially designed jacket of A.I. industries was sitting quietly. Apparently, she hadn't spoken a single word since she woke up, but had silently complied with the security guards when they chained her to the table. Although the number 43 glowed bright red, printed on her back and shining across her chest pocket, the woman appeared to be older. Much older, which was enough to make anyone suspicious.

The first thing that 297 did was activate a scanner on the display screen. On the window, the scanner pulled up an image of her face along with a few photos and a live video feed on the top of the screen.

"So, the facial recognition says it's her," 57 said, pointing at each photo and the live video feed. She looked at the files that were left for them on a nearby desk. "It's either correct or it's malfunctioning. The Space-Jumpers performed DNA testing and it also came back as an exact match to Amborg Serina 43. I guess we'll know more if one of us is going to try and talk to her."

"Who's willing to try?" 917 asked. "It'll be difficult since we have no idea what this person is thinking."

"Not it," 999 bit her lip. She stared intensely but she didn't step up. "Someone else should go first."

"I volunteer."

Everyone turned to see 280 come forward.

"Perhaps someone who has never been affiliated with the accused imposter can provide objectivity to the questioning process."

All of them looked at the Fourth Group amborg, considering the idea.

"Not a bad idea actually," 6 replied as she viewed the medical files. "35, I want you to observe the prisoner with me. Psychoanalyze her and get a good read while 280 talks to her. Let's see if we can figure her personality out, piece by piece."

"It'll also allow us to see a Fourth Group Amborg in action too," 5 said with a smirk.

"I don't know," 999 said with concern as her icy gaze peered through the glass. "Someone who has known her for a long time would have a better chance. I'm putting you on the spot in this case, 117."

"The lone wolf has a point," 57 nodded in agreement, but her smile suddenly faded. "Did I just agree with 999??"

"The only problem is," 117 crossed his arms, "I feel if I go first, my personal feelings may interfere with my judgment."

"Well, that brings us back to the original plan," 5 heaved a sigh and walked up to the glass. "I mean, 280 can help us establish a clear picture. Then perhaps we can slowly work our way to sending in a familiar face. Assuming she actually knows any of us."

"Are there any objections?" 3 asked politely.

No one said a word. 117 glanced at 280 and gave him a signal.

"It's settled," 117 declared. "280, you're up."

280 looked back at him and tilted his head.

"Up on what?"

His question made all of them, except 999, grin and chuckle lightly. Several of them sighed and started to shake their heads. 501 merely patted 280 on the back and urged him to proceed. Without another word, he moved towards the door.

"Wow," 35 grinned. "Did we all sound like that?"

Everyone raised their hands. They all laughed again but 999 merely shut her eyes and shook her head. They all stopped, though, as they saw the door inside open and 280 walked in.

"Good afternoon, ma'am," he announced.

The woman had looked up when the door opened. Through the window, they saw her raise an eyebrow.

"Afternoon, eh? Thanks, I was starting to wonder when I should get ready for bed."

The moment the first words came out of her mouth, the amborgs immediately began to analyze her voice. Recordings of their 43 were in their databanks and they were already trying to compare this woman's tone, inflection, and vocal patterns to 43's audio files.

"Oh wait," she raised her wrists, rattling the chains. "Can't do that because, what do you know? I'm kinda tied down. Be a dear and let me go? As a gesture of good faith?"

"I'm afraid I cannot comply," 280 replied, but was immediately interrupted.

"Look, I'd love to chat but I'm real short on time," the woman sighed as she glanced towards the window. "This is for whoever is behind the glass. I am Serina 43, of the Second Group, A.I. Industries. However, I'm not from here and you'll find that I'm not lying. Get my other self here to confirm it if you have to know for sure."

All the amborgs tensed up. There was a good reason why. Everything she was saying in the vocal analysis was coming back with positive results. As far as they were concerned, there were no hints of deception in her voice that they could pick up on. Her voice was a perfect match.

117 stared silently along with everyone else as 280 maintained his composure.

"I am afraid I don't quite understand," 280 replied. "Your other self?"

"I'm talking about the Serina 43 that you know," the woman said. "Get it? It's really not that difficult."

She turned her head, eyes once again fixed on the window. The rest of the amborgs on the other side saw her eyes flash a bright blue, then revert to normal. Her eyes had been upgraded with scanners, too. Did she just see through the mirrored glass?

"Well," 6 said in a soft voice, "she certainly has similar cybernetics like us."

They watched as she returned her attention to 280. She smiled.

"I suggest you decide quickly on your next move... Alex Two-Eight-Zero of the Fourth Group."

"I never told you my first name," 280 stated. A hint of surprise spread across his face. "How could you...?"

"My equipment may seem outdated, but I know exactly who you are," she spoke again as she stared at 280. "There's been plenty of evidence ever since I got here. You can see that I am cybernetically enhanced and an amborg of *my* Dr. Kendrick's design."

She then lifted her hand and pointed at the window, rattling the chains as she did so.

"Still don't believe me?" she said. "Including you, there are 12 of you outside of this interrogation room. There are three amborgs from the First Group, six from the Second Group, and two from the Third. I'll even take it one level further. Their names, with some possible differences, are Missy 3, Jonathan 5, Vanessa 6, Carter 297, David 117, Theodore 917, Alicia 999, Katie 57, Ryan 35, Dominic 501, and Carol 466."

"Get him out of there!"

5 transmitted a quick message to 280, who received the signal. Everyone else was taken aback. 501 and 466 hid behind 117 in terror.

"Excuse me," 280 said calmly to the prisoner. "Please wait a moment."

"I'm not going anywhere," she replied playfully. "But please... There is little time."

As he excused himself from the room, the woman smiled and wiggled her fingers in the chains in reply. Outside, everyone else stood in shocked silence. They had definitely not expected to hear that. All of them switched to a private channel.

"That... was terrifying," 297 stared at the prisoner.

"She just identified every single one of us," 57 said. "How did she do that?"

"It really is her," 501 trembled. "Isn't it?"

Gradually, everyone got a grip and began to come to the realization that it was true. The interrogation rooms were built to keep people isolated on the inside. This woman dressed as 43 had somehow figured out how to see past their screening process entirely.

280 rejoined them. 6 looked at him closely.

"Are you alright?" she asked.

"I feel... afraid," 280 replied in a neutral tone. "I was identified, even though no one outside of A.I. Industries should know my first name."

"Then let me in there."

There was a flash of light and suddenly Serina appeared in the room.

"If she wants me, then she'll get me."

"No," 117 declared. "You can't give her what she wants."

"What choice do we have? We don't have any information, she does."

Serina looked up at each of them. 117 eyed her questioningly.

"Besides, I know I can do this," she nodded her head confidently. "I have a technique I've been wanting to try."

"Ok then," 917 said. He looked at 117 and Serina. "So, do we send in another amborg and risk dragging this out or do we comply with the prisoner's demands and send in Serina with her... new technique?"

917 laid out each option and let the others ponder. The more time spent considering each one, the longer this would all remain at a standstill.

"I say we send Serina in there," 297 cast his vote. "We can't keep doing this over and over. She recognized 280. I think she is who she says she is."

"Maybe we shouldn't be treating her as hostile."

Everyone turned to look at 57. She shrugged her shoulders and waved at the glass window.

"If she has the strength of an amborg, then she would have tried to break out by now," she said. "Or she's biding her time. Either way, if Serina goes in there, what's she going to do? Try to punch a hologram that has control of the weapons in there?"

"Actually, there's another issue I'm thinking about," 6 said cautiously. "I'm more concerned about whether she has the ability to hijack an A.I. program if she comes into contact with Serina."

"How likely is that?" 297 asked curiously.

"It's likely but we shouldn't rule it out," 6 shrugged. "Remember, Serina was in my brain for a while when she was reconstructing herself."

"Well, in the interest of speeding things along," Serina sighed as she raised her hands and cracked her knuckles, "I'm taking the lead on this."

Bright lights emanated from her fingers, accompanied by a popping sound effect as she began stretching. 5 politely raised a hand and asked a quick question.

"So, what kind of technique is this?" 5 asked. "You planning to hit the gym or what? A holographic good cop, bad cop?"

"Very funny," Serina stuck her tongue out cheekily.

She swiftly leaped into the wall, creating a flash of light that made the panels along it glow, and she zoomed out of sight.

"What's she up to?" 501 asked.

"I have no clue," 117 replied.

After a few moments, they got their answer. The door of the interrogation room slid open, and a figure walked in. They all gaped in disbelief at who it was.

"Alright, you wanted me. Here I am."

Serina 43, their Serina 43, sauntered over to the table and the other 43 glanced up at her. 117 couldn't believe his eyes, it was like he had gone back in time to ten years ago. Serina had somehow appeared inside the interrogation room in her original body.

"Whoa," the older 43, still chained up, said in awe. "What kind of beauty regime are you on because I need some of that. Does everyone here look... young?"

"I think we can skip the pleasantries," Serina cleared her throat and crossed her arms. "Please answer our questions. Who are you?"

"Well, now that we've got this on record," 43 said as she lifted her hands and shrugged. "I'm you."

"Impossible," Serina replied. "Where did you come from?"

"The answer to that kinda depends," 43 replied. "From your perspective, after I've explained it, I came from pretty far away. But in my opinion, I came from... next door, if I had to choose an accurate description. Whatever you want to use to interpret it."

"Parallel universe?" Serina raised her eyebrow skeptically.

"You got it," 43 gave Serina a playful finger gun. "You've probably already had plenty of time to figure out that I am not from here. I'm glad that it was somewhat obvious when you discovered me."

"And if I were to suggest that you could be lying?" Serina asked. "That this is some sort of elaborate scheme to undermine us?"

"Will you be realistic? Come on," 43 scoffed. "You understand that I didn't spend all this time and resources just for fun. A lot of lives were sacrificed to get me here in order to successfully land on your planet. I was hoping that you'd be the one to find me. I had questions too when I volunteered for this. What would I look like? What would my home look like? And what would my friends...?"

43 glanced at the window and looked desperate as she waved her hand at the others watching.

"...what would they look like?" she finished as she put her emotions on display. "How's Dr. Kendrick? Where's David 117? Is he out there watching us right now?"

Serina became quiet as she looked towards the window. 43 rattled her chains and put her palms on the table.

"I didn't just put on this red amborg jacket to impersonate you," 43 sneered, but she gazed at Serina and nodded approvingly. "You have a nice blue one. Nice color choice. It suits you. But let's move past that and get serious for a moment."

43's eyes narrowed as she leaned forward and looked up at Serina. Everyone could tell that she appeared a little nervous.

"I risked a lot to get here so don't suspect me of lying," she said coldly. "You're lucky that I haven't..."

43 rattled the chains tied around her wrists.

"...broken these," she said. "Because if you piss me off, I will resort to extreme measures in order to get my point across."

"Is that a threat?"

"Even if it was," 43 sighed, "it's nothing compared to what's coming."

Serina unfolded her arms. She clasped her hands together and fidgeted slightly. After a moment of silence, she glanced towards the window. 117 recognized her expression immediately. She had an idea brewing.

"Do you want to see him?"

43 looked up, appearing confused.

"117?" Serina offered. "I can bring him in here. Maybe you'd like to talk to him?"

Both women inside the interrogation room turned towards the window. 117 looked at everyone else, awaiting instructions.

"Well," 297 said, "looks like Serina just made a choice."

"Good luck," 57 said, smacking 117's back.

"It might help if you just ignore the fact that inside the room, you have your dead ex-girlfriend and a... self-proclaimed alternate older version of your ex-girlfriend," 917 stated.

"Thanks a lot," 117 sighed as he exited the room.

117 left the room and entered a side hall. He walked over to the door and allowed the scanner to see his face. Taking a deep breath, he entered the passcode into the lock and the door clicked. It slid open, revealing the whole room. 117 stepped across the threshold and waited as the door hissed and shut behind him. For extra measure, he locked the door.

"Oh, my gods..."

117 glanced at Serina, who had turned around to watch him enter. He summoned his courage and gazed at 43. She sat there, stunned.

"Y-you almost look like..." 43 stammered, "you look exactly like you did when we started out all those years ago."

"Enough out of you!" Serina snapped.

43 recoiled slightly, looking annoyed as she glared up at Serina.

"What is my problem? Or in this case, *your* problem?"

Oh no. 117 began to worry. *Was this how everyone was going to start talking??*

43 and Serina glowered at each other. 117's eyes widened and he turned to look at the mirrored window, only seeing his reflection and that of the two women in the room. He realized there was no way for him to pick up on any signals from his colleagues. He returned his focus to the conversation. Hopefully, with all the stress that she was under, Serina wouldn't blow this up.

The more he thought about it, the more he realized that the tension in the air was sending chills up his spine.

"My problem?" Serina pointed at herself and scoffed. "You've seen him. David 117. Just like I promised. Now you keep your end of the deal. What is going on?"

"Feisty," the older woman remarked. "Reminds me of myself."

"Look," 117 said as he stepped forward, drawing her attention. "How about this?"

117 transmitted the clearance codes from his mind to the cuffs. There was a beep as the light turned green and they unlocked.

"What are you doing?!" Serina asked, dismayed.

"A gesture of good faith," 117 said, not taking his eyes off 43. "So, you were saying?"

43 looked at Serina carefully and then started massaging her wrists. She leaned back comfortably.

"I'll admit I was a little apprehensive to wake up from my trip as a prisoner and in chains," she said. "I guess it makes sense now why you did it. But, it was a terrible idea and now, we've lost precious time."

"Precious time for what?"

"Your universe is in danger and I was sent here to tell you that help is on the way to fight against the looming threat," the old 43 spoke. "I am indeed, in a sense, from outer space. But technically, not *your* outer space. I am an amborg belonging to an organization known as the Space Command Enterprise, an organization devoted to space exploration, peace, and the hopes of searching the unknown expanses of the stars."

"You are from a parallel universe?" 117 asked. "Because we have found no scientific evidence that those theories are true."

"Correction," 43 explained. "No scientific evidence... so far. At least in your universe."

"It's a likely story," 117 said, looking her over a few times.

He glanced at the window and pretended to look doubtful for his team on the other side. Suddenly, an idea popped into his mind that could help them verify 43's story.

"At first, we couldn't lie properly," he explained, looking at Serina. "But over time, based on experiences or enough trauma, we've matured beyond our original programming to where we have a better use of our original people skills. You could be successfully concealing lies that we are unable to detect."

"You need to trust me," 43 replied. "I can't describe everything to you in words alone."

She paused as a look of realization spread across her face. 117 gazed down at her and a small smirk formed at the corner of his mouth.

"A data transfer," he said.

The tension in the room rose instantaneously, reaching an intensity level that could be rated on a scale of one to ten, with one being everything is fine and ten signifying the end of the world. The reaction to 117's statement went from a one to an instant 12 in less than three seconds.

"No!" Serina exclaimed.

43 suddenly yelled.

"WHAT THE HELL?!"

117 saw it out of the corner of his eye. In her hastiness, Serina had tried to slam her hand on the table but instead, something shocking happened. 117 and 43 both witnessed her hand phase through the table. With wide eyes, Serina looked at 117 and snapped her hand back. She straightened up and began stammering. Her hands were distorted but slowly returning to normal.

43 leapt to her feet, causing the chair to crash to the ground. She and 117 both assumed defensive stances while concentrating on Serina. That's when he realized what she had done to make herself appear so lifelike. He'd first suspected that she had utilized some sort of holographic projection when she entered the room with a "body," but now it made perfect sense seeing it brought up to... literal light. Everything about her physically was an illusion.

"Oops," Serina bit her lip.

"You're... not real?" 43 stared.

"No, I am," Serina let out a sigh. "Just not the way you're thinking."

Serina turned and gave 117 a look of sorrow.

"I'm sorry," she said. "Damn it."

Serina turned and faced 43.

"I'll show you mine..."

In an instant, the projection dissipated and dissolved as the pixels forming the image of past Serina 43 disappeared. In seconds, Serina reappeared in her holographic A.I. form and stood on the table. The older 43 cautiously looked down, her mouth hanging open.

"... if you show me yours," Serina finished, shrugging her shoulders.

43 closed her mouth and stepped forward. She leaned in and looked at Serina closely, who was back to being only a foot tall.

"Oh wow," 43 said. "I have a whole bunch of other questions..."

117 cleared his throat loudly, causing 43 to look at him and quickly straighten up.

"...which I will set aside to get back on topic," 43 nodded her head firmly.

"117. If we're getting back on track, can I speak?"

It was 6's voice being transmitted over the speakers. 117 looked towards the glass and nodded.

"What is it?" he asked.

"Look. First, Serina," 6 announced. "Nice hologram. That was a really nice job. We're all impressed."

"Thanks," Serina nodded her head awkwardly.

6 continued voicing her concerns over the speakers clearly for everyone to hear.

"Second," she said warningly, "I don't care if she claims to have amborg abilities or if she is from a universe next door. This woman is requesting your consent to perform a process which requires our highest level of trust. She may claim to be 43, she may know which of us are watching right now in this room, and she may be very convincing, but I need to speak up about your rights."

"6," 117 sighed. "It's a data transfer. Not a marriage proposal."

"I am speaking for your health and security," 6 said sharply. "A data transfer from a woman like this is dangerous. It could be an attack on your CPU waiting to happen. I won't allow any contact between you and a complete stranger just because she claims to be your old ex-girlfriend. Alternate universe or not, these are your cybernetics we're talking about here."

"Then I'll do it."

43 and 117 looked down at Serina, who was gazing back up at the two of them with a serious and determined expression.

"You?" 43 asked. "You can do a data transfer? Even though you're..."

"Dead?" Serina asked.

"I was going to say A.I., just for the record," 43 said. "Hold the phone. Rewind a few seconds... you're dead? *I'm* dead?! In this universe?! How are you even existing?!"

"This is going off the rails," 117 muttered, turning his head to look at the window.

"Yes," Serina replied smugly. "I'm dead. But at least I know how old I'm supposed to look, give or take in a few decades. I'm just glad I aged... so well."

Serina's sarcastic comment was apparently the tipping point. 43 lunged forward and swung her right fist. It was clear that she didn't appreciate being called old by a tiny A.I. like Serina. Unfortunately, her attack didn't work. Serina vanished on the spot as 43's fist passed through thin air. She reappeared unharmed in an instant.

"Yeah, nice try," she said. "Still a hologram, by the way."

43 backed off and took a breath.

"117," 3 said over the speaker. "Do we need to intervene?"

117 glared at 43.

"Do we?" he asked her.

After taking a moment to calm down, 43 raised her hands and surrendered.

"No," she muttered as she went to pick up the chair.

Serina turned to look at 117.

"If 6 is not ok with you doing a data transfer, then let me do it, and then I'll filter whatever she was sent to tell us to everyone else," she said. "I'm an A.I. I can do this."

117 glanced at the window and shrugged.

"She does have better security and processing power than we do."

"I suppose so," 6 replied grudgingly. "Without an actual amborg body, she does have the means to take care of herself."

Serina nodded confidently.

"Who better to understand me than... me? Right?"

"Yes, we agree on that," 43 sighed. "I'm willing to go along with this plan, if anyone wants to know. If you're all in favor of it, then please, let's do this. I'm really running out of time."

117 looked at Serina, who gave him a confident grin.

"Ok then," he said. "Go ahead, Serina."

"Alright," Serina said, giving a thumbs up. "Time to get to know... other me and have a good look at what I've got."

She looked at 117 who returned her gaze with a bit of skepticism. The older 43 twitched slightly when she heard that, betraying her discomfort and causing her to cringe just a little.

"Yeah, yeah I get it!" Serina sighed to break the tension. "That did sound weird."

43 decided to take a seat back at the table and Serina moved closer.

"You need to look at my visual data and archived materials which I carried with me on file as well as my orders," 43 explained. "We were fortunate to discover your universe, the Epsilon universe, had amborgs like me. Which is helpful considering you're the universe next door. I'm ready when you are."

"Sounds like a plan," Serina replied.

She suddenly leaped into the air and disappeared in a flash of light. In seconds, 43 froze and seized up. Her muscles tensed as she struggled to remain upright. After a few brief seconds, there was another flash of light as the A.I. reappeared sprawled across the table as if a bouncer had just booted her out into the street.

43 fell forward but managed to slam her arms on the table to keep from face-planting. She shook her head repeatedly in an effort to focus. The surge in power from the transfer had knocked her out of balance.

117 quickly rose to check on the two of them.

"Are you both alright?"

"It was weird," 43 said woozily. "But she wasn't exaggerating about her computational speed. I think she makes a better A.I. than an amborg. That was fun."

"I'm still one of the best in this universe!" Serina snapped groggily as she stood up, flashing a bright green color. "If you're here to help us, then great! But what are we supposed to do with our outdated technology? Oh what a great universe..."

"I suppose that means you believe her?" 117 asked.

"Of course I do!" Serina turned to face the interrogation window, a look of sheer terror written across her face. "Everyone! She was right! Or I was right! We lost a lot of time putting her in chains! We need to get her to Dr. Kendrick! We must warn the governments, the people, everyone! Oh. Not in that order... wait! We need to... to..."

"Calm down Serina!" 117 said frantically. "If I believe you, then we all do. Hopefully. Now, take a second. What are we warning everyone about?"

"War," the little A.I. said with huge, frightened eyes. "We need to prepare."

Chapter 11: To Infinity...

A.I. Industries Launch Facility
Emergency Recall plus 1 Day 12 hours 32 minutes
11:00 AM MT

"Dr. Kendrick, we are now approaching the launch facility."

"Thank you."

The launch facility was based deep in the mountains. It used to be one of the military's secret installations, but A.I. Industries found that they could convert it for their own use. Cape Canaveral in Florida was still in use for sending things up into space, but thanks to a business deal, Dr. Kendrick was able to reconstruct this location. It was in a secluded area, far enough away from prying eyes. Overall, many of his senior staff and members of the board agreed that it was a good business deal, but also felt like he was rubbing it in their faces with how wealthy he was. Now that there was a possible alien invasion, they were all grudgingly acknowledging how right Dr. Kendrick was about owning a personal launch site to expedite the delivery of parts and supplies to his space station.

"We've been preparing for launch as soon as we received your instructions, Dr. Kendrick."

Dr. Kendrick was in a video call with one of his site supervisors. As the bus traveled along the road, he transmitted information to him. The screen displayed a steady stream of data detailing the inventory being sent up to the space station, allowing him to easily keep track of everything being transported.

"All of the supplies that you asked for are secure and ready to go," he said.

"Thanks to our new friend," Dr. Kendrick stated, "we have an idea of what's coming. I will contact you again once we're in orbit."

"Looking forward to it," the man nodded. "Good luck. Safe trip!"

As Dr. Kendrick shut off the screen, another phone call was taking place a few seats away towards the back. 117 was in a private call with an old friend.

"I can't believe you're already off on your next mission. We barely had any time for catching up."

Mandy Palmer sighed, but she smiled at 117 through the video screen. She had finally managed to get a few minutes to herself, and they quickly called each other for a brief reprieve.

"I'm just glad that you made it back home without any issues."

"More like we got lucky," Mandy replied, groaning slightly. "It was a nightmare trying to get through the terminal once my flight landed. Tom had to hide his military uniforms in our luggage, and I couldn't wear or carry anything with the company logo."

117 guessed why.

"Otherwise, people would have kept stopping you to ask questions?"

"Bingo," Mandy nodded. "I'm glad we were able to get through the crowds. One of the A.I. Industries staff members met us at a tram station, and we had to take a lot of back alleys and side roads to make it out of the city. Remind me again why the amborgs couldn't send us their drop-pods or heli-transport?"

"It would have drawn a lot of attention," 117 casually remarked. "Did Tom make it back to base?"

"He's all squared away and reporting in with his superiors," Mandy smiled confidently. "Wherever he goes, he gets to be deployed there via helicopter or jet if necessary. And his wife gets to hunker down here with everyone else."

"What does Dr. Kendrick want you to do?"

Mandy gazed at 117 and paused, staring at him inquisitively.

"What is it?" 117 asked nervously.

"Nothing," Mandy snickered. "I just remember the days when you would ask me that question in a different way. Remember? You would always say something formal like, 'what are they requiring you to do' or 'what is your current assignment?' But look at you! You've come a long way from that lost little boy who needed guidance."

"Thank you," 117 smiled proudly. "Being married for about 6 years has also taught me many things."

"Oh, don't get me started on when you started dating Audrey," Mandy scoffed as she held back her laughter. "You and the other amborgs kept trying to calculate her emotional satisfaction after every date and seeing those spreadsheets gave us a lot of headaches. To be fair, one pro to Dr. Kendrick ending the technician program did mean I didn't have to witness those dates live from your video feed."

"Do you miss being a technician?"

"Sometimes," Mandy sighed. "Yeah, it gets rough knowing that you're working in the field without me being your second pair of eyes. But it is what it is. You and the other amborgs needed us less and less with every mission. Whenever one of you decided to go incognito, we didn't need to be all up in your business. Now Dr. Kendrick has me assigned to a communications team. We're most likely going to be on call and keeping in regular contact with The White House. The President has been requesting updates."

"It is an important job," 117 nodded in approval.

"Important? Yes," Mandy sighed again. She sounded bored. "But not as entertaining. You can't tell President Holland's cabinet members to punch the bad guys like I used to tell you. It's not as fun anymore."

"I can understand that," 117 replied. "About things being less fun. Do you think I could ask for a favor?"

There was one thing that had been on his mind ever since the briefing and the awkward selection of leadership for the Second Group. 117 felt it was better to acquire as much information as he could. Mandy silently nodded and gave him a friendly smile.

"I selected Angel 999 to be my second in command when we go into space," 117 explained.

"Uh, I already knew that? Thanks to the notice board?" she chuckled. "Interesting choice. Good luck with that. Not that you asked for my opinion but... go on. Why are you repeating old news?"

"She made a comment suggesting that I should reconsider," he continued as he glanced over his shoulder at the back of the bus. He turned back to his phone. "She put down 917's name."

"Well, he's definitely a good choice," Mandy perked up, eyes hopeful.

117 paused, which was a dead giveaway to her.

"Unless he's not a good choice?" she suggested. "Let me guess, am I one of the lucky few that share this particular viewpoint?"

"You'd be right."

"Since we're on the subject of our good friend," Mandy said, "there's a rumor going around here. Is it true? Prison?"

"Yeah," 117 said. "Dr. Kendrick sent 57 and I to pick him up from Fulton Federal Penitentiary."

"Do tell," Mandy said excitedly.

He quickly gave a short recap of what they had encountered. 917's confession during his outboarding process, the trip to visit Tessa Wildman at the club, the fight in New York, and also how every single person that was involved didn't seem to have anything to say about what happened four years ago.

"I had no idea..." Mandy muttered as she tried to process it all. "But since we all didn't know, well... that's not really a bad thing, David."

"I just don't think he's telling the whole truth," 117 sighed. "He's a great amborg. But Dr. Kendrick kept it all a secret from us, and we're supposed to be a family. We're all supposed to count on each other. If 917 did all the things that he admitted, is he a good choice to help me lead the amborgs?"

"I don't think I'm able to answer that," Mandy shook her head. "My gut tells me that when you met with him and had your little catch-up session, he was genuinely telling you the truth. Maybe it was just difficult for him to come to anyone else at the time. You know, when he was about to be sent away, there was probably a lot of tension, and the time away probably helped him cool off."

"Can you get in touch with his former technician?"

"Meilin?" Mandy asked. "Sure. I think I still have her contact info. But why?"

"You're one of the few individuals that knows me quite well," 117 said. "So maybe Meilin can provide some insight about 917. I would like to know more about him as I reconsider."

"You got it," Mandy said cheerfully. "Just remember, it'll be ok. I'm sure that things will work out."

"You're just saying that. You don't know if that's true."

"You're right," Mandy responded bluntly. "But it's what you needed to hear. Call me when you're aboard the station."

117 smiled as they ended the phone call. Even when there were no guarantees, he did have to admit that she was usually right under these circumstances. Hopefully, Meilin could spare some time from her retirement to contact him soon. He would have to wrap up this leadership situation quickly before they ran out of time.

The bus slowed down, and he looked up and saw a large gate with the A.I. Industries logo on the front of it. The gate sank into the road, as if it was on quicksand. Once the way was clear, the driver took them through.

The bus maneuvered in front of a small outpost that almost looked like a small airport terminal. 117 could see the small tram that would take them over to the launch pad. Once the bus came to a stop, they were allowed to stand up and disembark.

The amborg teams followed Dr. Kendrick outside. Some of them grabbed their bags and small belongings. Making sure that nothing was left behind, everyone gathered outside. The luggage compartment underneath opened up and they all began to pull the heavier bags off. From the terminal, a few drones and employees came to them with empty carts. In a timely manner, the carts were loaded with their footlockers and other travel cases designed to protect their luggage during the trip up into space.

After a quick headcount, Dr. Kendrick led them all inside, wheeling everything towards the outpost. Once they passed through the doors, they arrived at a desk for processing. When they were cleared, they made their way towards the tram.

As they all gathered in the waiting area, 117 noticed another group already there. He recognized their uniforms immediately.

The Apogee Space Jumpers were also returning to orbit. Dr. Kendrick and the amborgs would be joining them along with 43 to make the necessary preparations. 117 noticed a mix of smiles and laughs among the group. Their camaraderie was noticeable, much like the amborg groups. They appeared eager to get back up into space for their next assignment. Unfortunately, the amborgs and other volunteers going up with them felt differently.

Most of them harbored concerns about whether the small ragtag group of volunteers would be sufficient for this mission, considering they were literally traveling out of this world. The limited number of amborgs currently active wasn't enough to watch over the entire planet, and now they were planning to launch a fraction of them into space. If it wasn't obvious enough, space is huge. One individual, cybernetically enhanced or not, would feel incredibly tiny once they left Earth's atmosphere.

"It's just like a normal flight," 117 said as they loaded their baggage onto the tram. "It's just going to be extremely bumpy and then we all become weightless."

"Do you need something for the ride?"

117 turned to find 2 standing behind him, who tossed a small canister to him. 117 caught it easily and glanced down at the label. They were motion sickness pills, based on the description.

"6 says to take one of those now," 2 instructed, "and then one more before we board the shuttle."

"I think I'll be ok," 117 replied.

He tossed the pills back to 2, who nodded in response.

"Alright," he chuckled. "Just have the vomit bags ready in case you feel queasy."

2 walked away to rejoin the First Group amborgs. 117 heard a bag drop onto the spot next to his and he turned to see someone else next to him. He awkwardly smiled when he realized who it was.

"It'll be my first time in space," 917 stated as he glanced up. They looked through the ceiling window at the sky. "They don't really have any zero-g training facilities in prison. Don't be surprised if I accidentally float off."

"Well, we can't have that, can we?"

117 and 917 chuckled briefly. 917 then left to join 999.

"You ok?"

117 turned and saw 43 walk up to him. Since she wasn't from their universe, she didn't have any belongings. Everything in her pockets from when she crossed over to their world was all she could carry in the small craft she'd flown in. Instead of replying, he glanced at her suspiciously.

"What?"

117 blinked and dipped his head apologetically when he noticed 43 looking at him inquisitively. Her pleasant expression was replaced with immediate skepticism as she came to a halt before him.

"Sorry," he said, shrugging it off. "A lot on my mind."

"Ok," 43 smiled nervously. "Because you were the one who convinced the rest of the amborgs to let me walk around freely back during my interrogation. I sure hope you're not reconsidering."

"Reconsidering? Yes. But not what you think," 117 replied.

43 glanced at him and then shifted her gaze over his shoulder. He didn't need to turn around to sense that she was looking at 917 and 999. She returned her focus to him, figuring it out in seconds.

"Dissension in the ranks?" 43 asked curiously.

"Not really," 117 shrugged.

"Well, I'd volunteer for the job. Unfortunately, I don't think I qualify."

"Because you're from a different universe?" 117 replied with a cheeky grin.

"Well, there is that. I was actually going to say I had no jurisdiction here," 43 shrugged. "I doubt everyone here would be supportive of someone who was, by your standards, dead for years. Leadership from a ghost, especially a ghost of Christmas past, is probably not in the cards."

"Well, at least Christmas is still celebrated in your universe," 117 replied. "Scratch that off my list of personal inquiries."

Both shared a quick laugh as they exchanged jokes, relieving the tension and distracting 117 from his thoughts momentarily. As he continued securing his bags, someone else approached and spoke to them.

"Excuse me? 117?"

117 turned around and saw Sergeant Harrelson standing in front of him. He reached out to shake the sergeant's hand, and they greeted each other.

"Sergeant," 117 shook his hand firmly. "Good to see you."

"Likewise," Harrelson smiled. He let go and then turned to address 43. "Ma'am."

"Oh great," 43 sighed as they shook hands. "I've become a 'ma'am.'"

"Meant no disrespect," Harrelson said. "I just thought I should say hello before anything else drew your attention. I didn't get a chance to really chat with you before."

"Oh right," 43 nodded. "Harrelson? I recognize your name now. You led the ground team that arrested me while I was out."

"Yes ma'am," Harrelson nodded firmly. "We extracted you and your vessel as fast as we could before Kenya authorities could arrive. We were told to protect you at all costs."

"Well, at least you're honest," 43 let out a sigh. She massaged her wrists where her bindings had been hours ago. "Mind if I ask you a question?"

Harrelson nodded.

"How exactly do you feel about... all of this?" 43 gestured at nothing in particular. "Alien invasion? Important news from me? Not of your world?"

"Sounds like one hell of an adventure."

"Pardon?"

43 lowered her head and stared. Even 117 was curious about Harrelson's casual response.

"I've been dreaming about first contact scenarios ever since I was a kid," Harrelson explained. "My family have been astronomers for the last three generations. We always believed that something was out there and now I'm looking at it right in front of me."

Harrelson dipped his head to 43, who appeared stunned.

"This is going to be one of the biggest moments in history and I'm honored to be part of it," he grinned. "Looks like we're all going up together."

"Well, that was an unexpected response," 43 replied when she regained her composure.

"We have a saying onboard Apogee Station," Harrelson smiled as he clasped his hands behind his back. "Expect the unexpected."

"Thank you, Sergeant," 117 nodded.

"No problem. I just thought I'd let you know something important. It's an honor to be fighting alongside the both of you again. Just like old times."

"In that case, we'll see you up there," 117 said. "Catch you later."

"Don't get sick on the ride up."

He gave them a salute and turned around. As he walked away, 43 watched as he rejoined the other space-jumpers.

"I don't think I know him, not from my universe," she said quietly. "I've also been getting a lot of that lately."

"You don't see a lot of familiar faces?"

"Aside from the amborgs?" 43 shook her head. "No. But I think I can get used to one thing."

"What's that?"

"If seeing me inspires that much hope, then that's something that'll motivate me," 43 smiled. "It's quite refreshing seeing a few people acting like that. You know, after they get over the initial shock of alternate universes. It feels less lonely the more I'm here."

"Was it always that bad? Where you're from?"

"Not really," 43 shrugged as they walked towards the tram. "Before we decided to launch this operation, it was just pretty normal. Served aboard starships, one by one, and eventually, they asked me to be part of this. It was quite an unusual type of mission, but a great opportunity. I couldn't say no when command tasked me to come over here."

"You mentioned that you weren't supposed to come alone?"

"I was supposed to have a group of marines to escort me around but they didn't come through with me," she said. "They stayed behind to distract the Tandeeri so I could make it through. I hope they're all ok."

"Well, we'll find out once they get here," 117 smiled.

It was probably extremely difficult for her. Every person who recognized her would have been taken aback to see her standing right there in front of them, solid and real, and not a ghost. After fighting and living in space for a long time, it seemed very strange to be back in a bustling society. Not only was she alone, 43 was also probably thinking about the people who had sacrificed everything to get her here. The best thing that they could do was to make sure it was not in vain.

"Let's make sure that we roll out a welcome mat," 43 smiled as they followed everyone and got in line.

They all entered a miniature three-car subway tram and took their seats. Drones were seen loading the last car with their luggage. Once they got comfortable, they waited for their departure notice.

"I wanted to ask you about me," 117 said quietly to 43.

43 turned. He noticed that she had shifted her legs, even though there was nothing hitting her feet or ankles. Was this question a sensitive topic or was she not allowed to answer it?

"I had a feeling you might."

"Back when I first met you," 117 recalled the moment the interrogation doors had opened, and they were face to face. "You said I looked just like him. The 117 from your universe?"

"You all do," 43 replied. "In this universe, you all look really great for a bunch of... 30 to 40 year olds??"

"I'm actually 28," 117 remarked.

Suddenly, they heard the engines start up on the tram. The doors hissed and closed shut.

"You look great," 43 smirked.

The tram was just a few minutes away from the launch pad. Everyone on board turned to look out the windows as they neared their destination. The journey was quite beautiful, with views of lush green forests that eventually gave way to expansive fields of solar panels.

Once they stopped, everyone stood and filed off the tram in an orderly manner. Everyone else was chatting normally, cracking jokes or making bits of small talk to ease the tension. 117 remained quiet as they all made their way to the transport.

"Attention, Echo flight will launch in 15 minutes. Attention, all passengers bound for Apogee Station. Echo flight will launch in 15 minutes."

As the crowd approached the shuttle, Dr. Kendrick approached the flight crew.

"Captain Hicks," he greeted them warmly. "Lieutenant Frye."

"Whoa," Frye muttered from the side, slowly going into fanboy mode. "He knows my name??"

"Cool it," Hicks whispered out of the corner of her mouth. She then addressed Dr. Kendrick normally. "Doctor, it's a pleasure to be taking you up for this flight."

"You and Planck are our best pilots," Dr. Kendrick replied. "I'll give you raises if you can get us all up there in one piece."

"Can do."

Dr. Kendrick then pointed at the dropships on the launch pad.

"So, can you give me a quick report on why there are four ships prepping for launch? I thought it was just the two ships that came down to investigate 43's spacecraft."

"Yes sir," Hicks nodded promptly. "Those other two shuttles were originally scheduled to depart with supplies and new personnel to the station. When 43 arrived from the whole anomaly thing, we scrambled and now we're launching ourselves back up there in the next transfer window."

"Ah, I see," Dr. Kendrick nodded. "Thank you, Captain Hicks. We'll finish boarding."

The boarding process was simple. Their luggage was loaded and everyone slowly marched onto the transports, promptly taking their seats.

"Good morning, everyone!" Captain Hicks' voice resonated over the ship's speaker system.

From his seat, 117 saw Hicks walking by, talking into her headset.

"This is your captain speaking," she said as she strolled by and headed towards the cockpit. "Once the doors are closed, you will feel a few jolts as the ship sets in motion for a brief period. Nothing to be worried about. For those of you who are flying to Apogee station for the first time, we will be taxiing to a mount that will then be attached to a booster which will give us the kick we need to reach orbit. From there, it will be about 22 minutes of flying and floating. So please sit back, relax, and welcome to our bumpy stairway to heaven."

Minutes after the ramp closed and sealed shut, they heard the engines whining as they started up. A noticeable rattle shook the ship as it began to move, exactly as described. Without window seats, they could only feel the movement. Of course, they all knew this wasn't a normal passenger liner experience.

"You know," 117 gulped. "It does feel like we're taking an international flight."

"David 117," 43 said, gazing at him with a fascinated look. "Are you afraid of flying?"

"No, it's not that," 117 replied as he gripped the harness straps that held him to his seat. "I just prefer to do my flying while on the planet. It gets quite disorienting once you remove gravity altogether."

"Take it from someone who spent half her life in space," 43 said gently. "It takes a bit of adjusting but you'll start to treat outer space like going on a boat. Once you're out there, it feels like you're floating through water."

"Huh?"

"That's what my instructors always told me," 43 shrugged. "I don't actually have an official way to deal with space anxiety."

The ship abruptly came to a halt, causing them to be shaken again. After a moment of silence, they could hear hydraulics whirring outside. Then, several loud metallic thumps reverberated through the hull, as if someone were firing a nail gun at them. This was the booster rocket being attached.

"Attention all passengers," Captain Hicks informed them. "We're prepping for launch. The ship will be raised vertically, and the boosters are being juiced up. Stand by and hang out for a few. Please make sure your seat backs and tray tables are in their upright position. If not secure, then good luck because you're probably screwed."

"I have a question," 501 transmitted from his seat. "Has anyone ever fallen out of their seats during a launch?"

"Yes sir," Sergeant Dean Hammond spoke up. "We lost one passenger before. Fell out of their seat after lift-off and they dropped to the back of the transport. Shattered every bone in their body."

"Oh..."

117 couldn't turn to look at 501's seat, but he could hear his breathing rate spike. However, despite the fact that he had given such a serious answer, he could have sworn he heard Hammond stifling a laugh.

"I'm kidding, sir!" he snorted suddenly and burst out laughing.

The rest of the space-jumpers let out a chorus of laughter. 501 sighed in relief.

"Uh, sergeant," 117 spoke up. "Is that the truth?"

"Yes sir," Hammond answered with a nod. "It was a crash test dummy that was purposefully designed to fall out of its chair during test launches. Had that been an actual person..."

117 saw Hammond hold up both hands and mash them together, as if crushing an invisible soda can.

"But we haven't lost anyone so far," Hammond finished in a reassuring and confident tone.

An alarm went off, causing them all to shut up. There was a loud whirring and the next thing they knew, the entire inside of the shuttle began to tilt backwards.

"Are the shuttles or transports in your universe like this?" 117 asked.

"No, they have enough power so they don't have to be boosted off-world," 43 replied reassuringly.

"Must be nice," 117 said as the entire ship stopped moving, and they all found themselves seated at a 90-degree angle. "The future in your universe sounds so much more convenient."

"Hey, I think I just thought of a coping mechanism for us."

117 glanced at 43 as they waited. He nodded his head quietly, signaling her to continue.

"There's stuff I don't know about your universe and there's stuff you don't know about mine," 43 said. "How about we play 20 questions? Except, we just keep going?"

"Uh, sure?" 117 nodded again. It did seem like an intriguing way to distract him from his nerves. "Actually, sure. That sounds nice."

"Attention all passengers," Hicks made another announcement. "Ignition will kick off in two minutes. Get ready to hold on for dear life."

In a desperate attempt to avoid freaking out, 117 quickly turned to 43.

"So uh, the shuttles where you're from?" he asked. "How do they work?"

43 gave him a calming smile, clearly sensing his growing anxiety.

"The shuttles from my universe don't need all of this preparation," she explained gently. "They can just enter and exit the atmosphere, touch down, and then fly again in less than half an hour."

"I know that the chances of us visiting or seeing your universe are highly unlikely," 117 smiled. It was calming for him, having this conversation. "Hearing your perspective is unique. Do you feel like our universe is completely different? Since your home is 75 years ahead of us?"

"Well, the obvious answer is yes. It certainly looks and feels very different," 43 nodded. "I mean, there's a lot of variations. It feels strange being an inter-dimensional time-traveler. Everything feels old-fashioned, but most of it is still familiar."

43 then tapped him on the shoulder.

"Also, you asked two questions..." she scoffed. "My turn. So, I think my next question to you is about me."

43 pointed ahead and 117 peeked over the top of the seat in front of him. He spotted Dr. Kendrick's head near the front row, close to the cockpit. 43 directed his attention to the glowing blue light next to him. Serina was up front as well.

"So, she," 43 said, "I mean, me. You're telling me that I reconstructed myself into an A.I.?"

"Yes," 117 answered.

"None of you helped me... her?"

"Serina did it all by herself."

"Nothing like that has ever happened in my known history," 43 replied. She looked impressed and continued to ponder how it was even possible. "Humans can model A.I. programs and a few have built them from scratch. As far as I can remember, no one has ever died and reincarnated as one. It's so fascinating."

The sound of an automated voice over the speaker interrupted them.

"This is launch control, we are t-minus 15 seconds to launch. Ignition sequence priming. Echo flight, godspeed."

For 117, he had only gone up into space twice. This would be the third time. Every single launch was always as nerve-wracking as the last. Each time someone asked, he could never put it into words. Someone had once told him that it was like they were being strapped to a huge explosive and you had to hope that it was put together correctly, and the next thing you knew, you were in the air.

Throughout Earth's history, there have been no accidents or catastrophes since the heartbreaking stories of all the incidents that occurred in the 20th century. Even with this information in mind, 117 still felt his heart pounding. There was only one thing he could do to distract himself until the shuttles reached space.

He closed his eyes and tried to retreat into his mind. It was like hitting pause and browsing the main menu of a movie. Only, he needed to kill enough time so he could ride out the violent shaking of the boosters firing a bit easier. He focused on his wife and sifted through a ton of pleasant memories. He literally began to watch parts of his life flash before his eyes, using his cybernetics to display the images.

The interior of the shuttle was built strong enough to muffle the noise from outside. Fortunately, the shaking subsided after a few minutes. Once he felt it going upwards, the force of the launch pushing him back into his seat, the jolting became less and less severe.

Then it was over.

117 opened his eyes slowly and listened. Like magic, the interior of the shuttle fell into quiet stillness. It seemed as though time had frozen inside the

entire passenger compartment. With the sensation of weightlessness now that they'd left Earth's gravity, it felt like he was on the verge of floating out of his seat. Thankfully, nobody did, since they were securely held in place by their seat straps.

As he reoriented himself, he saw the door leading to the cockpit open and Lieutenant Frye entered. He appeared to arrive backwards, as if climbing down a rock wall. 117 watched as the lieutenant hooked his foot onto a rung and pushed off the wall to swing upright to align with the passengers.

To avoid feeling nauseous, 117 continued to observe Frye who was communicating with sergeant Hammond about the shuttle. In null gravity, there was no up or down. No matter what position he picked, Lieutenant Frye could be hanging upside down, sticking straight out from a side wall, or standing on his head. It began to feel fun for 117 as he watched with a smirk.

"Glad to see you starting to enjoy yourself," 43 whispered from the side.

"It's entertaining," 117 admitted.

"Yeah, it is."

117 and 43 both grinned as Frye suddenly did a backflip and caught one of the rungs next to Hammond's seat. Doing a handstand, the floor was both down and up as he seemed to dangle there. They watched as he used his hands to "climb" back towards the cockpit and when he reached the door, he pulled himself inside to join Hicks up front.

"This is Captain Hicks," she said over the announcement system again. "Booster separation in three... two... one..."

There was a brief hollow rumbling, then followed by more silence.

"And we are clear," Hicks said cheerfully. "You may freely roam about the cabin if you like. We are now enroute to Apogee Station."

"Shall we continue?" 43 asked.

It was the best way to pass the time. They threw questions back and forth, from the simplest ones to the most complex. Sometimes, if there was a question that prompted a long response, they would switch back to an easy one. Although, even a simple question generated fascinating and unexpected answers.

When he asked what her favorite food or drink was in the Alpha universe, 43 admitted that it was difficult to narrow it down to just one or two items. When she was able to, he was baffled to hear that her favorite cocktail was a rainbow Al-suaria Keento sorbe. Whatever that was. He didn't even know if he could even pronounce it. At least one of her favorite foods was spaghetti. He decided to give an easy response off the top of his head and tell her his favorite dish was chicken marsala.

Then, they asked each other about family. 117 talked about his grandfather. 43 surprised him by sharing about her dad. As it turns out, both of them had one living relative in their lives. 43's father had been in the audience when she had successfully become an amborg, but for 117 and his universe's 43, it was not that public of a ceremony. When the war broke out in her universe, 43 discreetly had him relocated someplace safe. It felt ironic because in Epsilon, 117 and 43's parents had been killed trying to keep them safe and had asked Dr. Kendrick to take them in if anything happened to them. The rest was how it all turned out.

Another bit of irony that evoked sympathy in 117 was the fact that 43 and Serina seemed so alike. Despite technically being the same person with similar alternate universe personalities, it felt like the more he got to know the older Alpha 43, the more he saw a significant copy-paste aspect in both of their lives with some differences sprinkled in. Serina and 43 were both alone.

She hadn't mentioned anything in their line of questioning, but what made 117 confused and more invested in their little game was the fact that 43 seemed reluctant to talk about her universe's amborgs. It seemed like, the closer he got to an answer, she would avoid giving a direct answer.

Before they could continue, they heard another announcement. Time seemed to fly by quickly.

"Attention all passengers, we are now on final approach with the station. Thank you for choosing Echo Flight sponsored by A.I. Industries! We hope you didn't vomit inside the cabin. Please wait until we have touched down and are at complete stop before getting up and disembarking. Have a nice day and don't hesitate to call us for pick up. I am in fact a 5-star rated driver on Uzoomly."

The Space-Jumpers burst into laughter and let out a chorus of whoops and cheers. The amborgs, though, were filled with relief and smiled.

"Also, please give a special thank you to the man, the myth, the legend himself," Hicks finished her announcement like a gameshow host. "Dr. John Kendrick for being with us today. Everyone remember to take good care of our most beloved VIP for this trip."

Everyone unfastened their straps and harnesses, ready to exit the shuttle. After a moment of waiting, the ramp hissed and began to lower. 117 watched as the Jumpers nonchalantly made their way off the ramp, and once they were clear, the rest of the group was given the go-ahead to disembark. Technically, according to military regulations, the civilians and VIPs were supposed to go first, but Dr. Kendrick preferred it the other way around. If there was ever a time that he would be caught in an actual firefight, he had always explained that having trained professionals at his side was better than leaving him alone with a gun.

117 texted Mandy really fast to let her know that they made it aboard the station. Her replies came back instantaneously.

As long as none of the satellites are destroyed or conveniently put out of commission, I have a good line of sight for communications. Signal me if anything goes wrong though, ok?

He smiled as he texted a thumbs-up emoji. That was something 501 had actually taught him to do. She texted him again.

If you stick with Angel as your partner for this one, tell her to stay vigilant. Also, here's Meilin's contact info. Text her before you try calling. B.T.W. Nice use of the emoji. Good to see that you're not slacking off on those.

117 saw Meilin's phone number and email address appear on his phone. He quickly drafted an introductory message and sent them to both as he focused and joined the crowd.

The drones in the hangar had begun unloading the ships. Echo flight had flown up from Earth with two other transports that had brought other personnel and supplies for the station. Dr. Kendrick waved for all the amborgs to follow him.

"Good luck sir," Sergeant Harrelson said as he walked by. "Space-Jumpers! Fall out!"

Everyone watched the marines move out and head to a different part of the station. The amborgs and a group of A.I. programs under Serina's supervision gathered around Dr. Kendrick. 20 amborgs had come up into space. The First group was composed of 1, 2, 3, 5, and 6. The Second group had 117, 999, 777, 297, and 917. 501 and 466 led 249, 593, and 49 of the Third group. 113 and 280 made up the Fourth Group team along with 63, 100 and 378. They figured that this would be a suitable team for an outer space mission while the remaining 99 amborgs oversaw any situations on the surface. If need be, the amborgs there would serve as a last line of defense should things in space go wrong. This was a rather grim aspect that the 20 volunteers had accepted when they made the collective decision to travel to Apogee station. If needed, reinforcements could be summoned within a couple of hours. Unfortunately, based on 43's intel and reports about the possible threat, they probably wouldn't even last that long if Earth's outer space stations came under attack.

"I hope 95 and 53 are going to be ok running the rest of the Third Group by themselves," 501 sighed.

An A.I. was quickly taking roll to make sure everyone was accounted for. 466 patted 501 on his shoulder and gave him a positive grin.

"They'll be fine," 1 said reassuringly. "A real test of leadership always goes to someone who faces uncertainty. Once they overcome that, they'll understand what it means to lead. There's only so much a theoretical approach can teach you when a lot of pressure can practically push you to guide others looking up to you."

"Yeah, right, "2 chuckled. "4 is living proof of that. Instead of lecturing, she just throws everyone into the deep end. Even going on sabbatical doesn't do much to help you get away from her watchful eye."

"Katrina 4 has been very exceptional at monitoring the whereabouts of each amborg since the days after the Domino Incident," 280 interrupted. "She is a capable leader no matter how many unnecessary feelings of anxiety all of you are exhibiting. The mission will come first and be fulfilled despite how much negativity there is."

The First Group amborgs all sighed.

"Ok we get it," 5 continued in a bored voice. "Sheesh. What a mood killer. Want to know how stupid we sounded originally? Look at the Fourth Group amborgs."

"There's no possible way to kill or murder a mood," 280 countered. "All one can do is make it go away temporarily under certain circumstances."

"It was a joke little bro..." 5 added. "Man, now I know how our technicians must feel."

"It certainly does make sense considering how many times my technician used to say how much she hated me," 777 smiled.

Once they finished taking attendance, Dr. Kendrick called out to everyone.

"Alright everyone," he said. "Let's head this way."

The Third Group amborgs, having the least experience in a zero-G environment, were beginning to look queasy. The space enthusiasts in the amborg family were primarily centered in the First and Second Groups. Even the Fourth Group amborgs seemed to be zoning out a little as they adjusted to the new environment. It was probably extremely nauseating for them, even if the gravity was artificially simulated.

"Remember kids," 5 instructed. "Point your mouths away from the group should you feel like letting loose. That's why we all brought barf-bags in case someone feels like remembering what it's like to throw up."

"That's not funny 5," 6 said angrily as she checked everyone's life signs and monitored the readings carefully. It was obvious why she volunteered to come along. "Outer space may seem like a really exciting thing to most people, but it can be equally bad as well. If all you're going to do is joke around, you could at least help the inexperienced spacers to relax."

"But that's supposed to be your job," 5 whined. "I'm perfectly fine with my comedic relief."

"Dr. Kendrick," 6 sighed. "Would you please back me up?"

Dr. Kendrick turned around, stopping at the mention of his name. He instantly lifted a finger. They all remembered what the fore finger gesture meant. Take him seriously or suffer the consequences.

"Without a doubt," he said, "Vanessa happens to be right. Comedic relief does help sometimes but only when appropriate, Johnny. Outer space seemed like a grand adventure until we found out that alternate universes existed. I think we can save the jokes until after this is won and done."

"If that's what the doctor wants," 5 held up his hands, "I will be happy to oblige. But a good joke does ease the tension even if the end of the world is around the corner. You'll pardon me for remaining just a little rebellious."

"How optimistic..." 999 gave a look of contempt. "He's going to die first at this rate."

"Yeah, let's not talk like that," 917 said nervously. "It's taboo. I want to try and enjoy the fact that we're going to be living in space for some time."

"It is also perfectly alright to be optimistic under the circumstances," Dr. Kendrick replied, looking at 999 and 917. "I know that recent events have made everyone tense and the stress level is really high. But we will get through it. Space is a marvel for anyone willing to set foot out of the gravity of our home. After all, humanity has always been fascinated with exploring the unknown."

"Except the unknown is coming to us," 297 remarked.

"True but take a good look at where we are."

Dr. Kendrick pointed out the window. The earth was in full view, spinning at a steady rate. It was almost hard to believe that there were many important eyes on them now. Eyes they couldn't see but were there, nonetheless. Dr. Kendrick made sure everyone could hear his next statement.

"Have any of you ever imagined that you would be standing here?"

The question made everyone pause, their gazes going straight to the window. The Fourth Group amborgs almost had an answer for Dr. Kendrick but the others hushed them, signaling for them to remain quiet.

"Most members of society criticize or judge me for doing so many extra-ordinary things," he said. "They say that this station is unnecessary and a waste of money. Every time someone doubts me or you, I say they're wrong."

Dr. Kendrick turned to look at the amborgs following him. He smiled.

"I say that every single moment that we are up here, looking down at our home planet, is completely worth it. It makes me think that there is hope and that we can clearly see the next day, even if 43 tells us that the biggest fight of our lives approaches soon. This is where the world will be looking to when it all takes place. You are the ones that stand here, beacons aboard one of my crowning achievements. This space station."

"I just got chills," 777 whispered in awe.

"But if you do not take the environment outside of this station seriously," Dr. Kendrick warned them, "the people's lives onboard as well as yours will be in danger. While we get to the bottom of this, I want you all to promise me that you won't do anything stupid."

"Aww, but sometimes stupid does help."

Everyone looked at 501, who shifted nervously. Everyone knew, including the Fourth Group amborgs, about his clumsy tendencies. Dr. Kendrick eyed him, but smiled encouragingly.

"Ok. Err. Maybe not stupid," Dr. Kendrick changed his choice of words. "Stay out of trouble while we're up here. Do I need to remind you how expensive this station is?"

"Umm," 501 raised his hand. The Third Group all looked curious. "How much?"

"If we all individually sold our parts," 297 estimated bluntly. "Probably wouldn't even cover a single power outlet…"

"Actually, it's about three times more expensive than the First Group's cybernetic enhancement, integration and rehabilitation," 1 answered promptly. He paused and then added, "That's without adding taxes."

"Wow…" 466 gulped. "I had no idea we were so expensive. The economy must love us."

"Focus children," Dr. Kendrick interrupted. "This is not the same type of environment as back on Earth. It's a whole new playing field. Serina has a routine of what needs to be done. Learn it and then get to work as soon as possible."

Serina nodded and flashed out several commands to the amborgs. Many of the amborgs in the group had actually been in outer space before, but they were all given the same standard protocols for living on Apogee Station. The first step was Zero-G reinforcement training for the less experienced amborgs.

"Ok amborgs," Serina said. "We will divide equally into groups... again. I have made a rather brief but hopefully clear schedule for everyone. We will have one amborg from each group down in the science bays. They will be working on the anomaly the station detected. Just in case the weak-minded of the amborgs don't get it, we're trying to figure out if a portal sent a hallucination of 43."

"Hey, I'm right here..." Alpha 43 said in an offended tone. "Hallucination my ass."

"It's just to confirm that we're still sane," Serina explained. She was trying desperately not to sound like she was throwing a fit. "All of us can see you, hear you, and know that you're real. But we still need a quick test to make sure that the universe as we know it hasn't begun to collapse in on itself. You know, quantum breakdowns and paranormal collapse of the space-time continuum? The stuff we don't want to happen, basically."

Fine," 43 replied with a huff. "Just point me in the direction where everyone who believes me are gathering. We can actually deal with all the relevant information and prepare our defenses while you keep wasting time."

"Second..." Serina said with a grumble. "We need to get started on training in the gravity room. Crash courses on how to fight and travel in Zero-G will be held in there at all times. It will also be available for anyone who wants to just participate in open practice. Then there's the matter of guarding Dr. Kendrick."

"Wait what?"

Dr. Kendrick looked at Serina with a worried expression.

"Like I already told you Serina," he said. "I don't need a bodyguard or any other form of protection. We don't have enemies up here."

"Even if we don't," Serina scoffed as she glanced at 43, "if we do come under attack under any circumstances, then it would be a good idea to make sure an amborg or two are at your side. If war is coming, then it's time we prepared ourselves for it. I also seem to recall how much you wanted us to take this mission seriously, doctor. Am I right?"

Dr. Kendrick bowed his head sheepishly.

"Yes you're right," he admitted.

"Damn right I am," the little A.I. flashed a bright blue. "Now then, if anyone doesn't have any questions, we can begin getting used to this place being our temporary home."

"That's it? We're being let loose on the station just like that?"

297's question was met with a stern look from Serina. His gaze faltered and he looked down at the ground.

"Sorry," he muttered. "It's just that we weren't meant to travel in space. At least, not this soon. The transition from Earth to here is so surreal. It just feels weird not being certified and then being told to just get used to a situation we know little about."

"You're an amborg," Dr. Kendrick said. "Accept the fact that you aren't like normal humans. Consider yourselves certified astronauts. Speaking modestly, I may be the one of the smartest individuals on the planet, but I am envious of all of your abilities. What I have in terms of knowledge, you more than make up for in physical ability and strength. It is ok to be scared, too. But being scared is one of the only ways to have courage to face the unknown. Right?"

"I think that's actually in the S.C.E. manual too," old 43 smiled. "Courage for the unknown is a great adventure."

117 looked at 43 and remembered the period of time when the amborgs decided to enjoy the world after the Dominoe Incident. Although it wasn't in outer space, it did take courage for them to leave home and seek out new adventures on their own. Perhaps there really was nothing to be afraid of. Life had merely provided them with the opportunity to come back and face something together.

"Well, I don't know about you guys, but I want to go for a spacewalk!"

501's enthusiastic interruption brought 117's attention back to the present. It suddenly seemed as if the tension had disappeared.

"What did we just tell you about doing something stupid?" 466 joked.

117 had an idea.

"If it's alright," he suggested, "I think before we all separate, we should have a briefing from 43."

"She's already explained everything to us," 3 stated.

"I think it'd be best if we also share with her everything we saw when she arrived. We should put to rest any doubts still lingering about her."

Dr. Kendrick stared at 43, who didn't look like she was against this particular idea.

"We did interrogate her," 6 informed them. "I think 117 has a point. It'll be easier for us to trust each other if she knows about our perspective."

"I guess that is acceptable," Dr. Kendrick nodded. "Serina, let's delay your itinerary for a bit. I think we should go to the observation room, where it all started."

The observation room was just a short walk away. Once they'd all arrived and settled in, 117 stood with Serina while 2 presented a detailed report about what he and the technicians witnessed when 43's ship arrived. 117 kept looking at 43 and noticed that she was fully invested in the report. Telling the story chronologically was effective from here since the station had full recordings and readings of the entire event. It was a perfect place to start.

"So, you were able to boost the resolution on the camera by powering the link yourself from your own energy reserves?" 113 asked 2, who was replaying the video logs from the Jupiter probe. "That is quite remarkable but rather risky on your own energy, isn't it?"

"Yes."

They watched as the fuzzy screen temporarily cleared. This was the part where 2 had amplified the power briefly. They all examined the images of the wormhole.

"It's really interesting," 2 replied to the Fourth Group amborg. "The anomaly had enough power to distort the Jupiter probe when we realigned it to try and get a visual. What I did was send a boost of energy on a direct path to the probe and that was enough to clear the image for a few seconds. The distance from the station to there was quite significant so... no wonder it didn't work for long. It was a risk but my instincts took over."

"How did you know it would work?" 280 asked as the image on the recording returned to a fuzzy state.

"I didn't," 2 answered with a slight cough. "It was a stressful situation and I had to think quickly before we lost the opportunity."

"Well," 117 said as he cross-examined the records and data from NASA and the station. "It looks like it all checks out. All the sources say this anomaly did happen. 43 says it was an artificial wormhole. Really interesting."

They heard someone clear his throat. Everyone turned to see Jacob raising his hand.

"Scrambled up our readings pretty good and then we detected an object hurtling planet-side seconds afterward," he explained. "We've been trying to find out new ways to boost power from our relays to the probes. We can easily detect where the anomalies are, the only problem is if they keep scrambling our monitors, then we can't identify friend or foe."

"I take it that means all the station personnel now know about the supposed alternate universe?" Serina asked Jacob. "Did everyone get the report?"

"It was a little rushed and sounded impossible," Jacob shrugged. "A few of us didn't take it so well. Multiple reactions are what comes from something so out of this world... or universe."

"What was your specific reaction?" 117 asked.

"To be honest?" Jacob grinned. "Smells like a pretty great adventure if you ask me."

"Again?" 466 asked softly. "How many people aboard the station are space nerds?"

Dr. Kendrick had unfortunately heard this comment and stared at her sternly. 466 instantly shrunk down and closed her mouth.

"You find the experience fascinating?" 280 and 113 both looked at each other in confusion. "That's not an emotional response we expected you to exhibit."

"Well, of course!" Jacob smiled as he turned to look out at the stars. "Some people go about their whole lives wondering what might have been if things were different. I grew up believing that there was always the possibility that an alternate version of me was doing something other than working in space. Maybe I was an accountant, maybe I was obese, maybe I became an evil person, or maybe I was head of the Olympics committee."

Jacob looked at the amborgs. 113 and 280 stared at him as if what he was saying made absolutely no sense. 117 smiled.

"Those possibilities do sound interesting," he spoke thoughtfully. The very subject made him think about what his Alpha universe version was like.

"I don't mean to be so negative about this next comment, but what do we do if this station gets ripped apart?"

Everyone looked at 297. The technicians working at their desks all stopped and looked up. His words had caused everyone in the room to tense up.

"We don't have much of a defensive position..." he observed. "Considering the station is revolving around the Earth constantly, and we have no clue where the next anomaly will appear. How do we stop an invasion when they could just bypass us and land anywhere on the planet?"

"Remember," Jacob said meekly, "our space budget from NASA and Dr. Kendrick's financial backers only totals about two hundred billion dollars. It only allows us to maintain this station, equipment, and research about six percent of the outlying space surrounding Earth. Begging your pardon but it's a big ass galaxy to monitor out there."

"Do we even have weapons?" 777 asked. "Weapon emplacements on the station?"

"Well," Jacob muttered. "All experimental."

"Crap," Serina said, changing into a pale white color. "I think we all just acknowledged the fact that the station we are on could easily be destroyed before we could finish breakfast. Way to go guys, we're probably all going to die like a sheet of paper going through a shredding machine."

"Well, everyone dies anyway," 113 said casually.

"Not helping!" 5 groaned.

"Suddenly the adventure just became really grim," Jacob shuddered as the amborgs began arguing amongst themselves. "I'm going to grab some coffee."

After the report from the observation room, they went to the cafeteria and began sulking. It was the Fourth Group amborgs' lack of a simple vocabulary that was annoying the older amborgs. They really were like shadows, completely void of basic human interaction.

During their meal, which 3 had volunteered to cater, 43 was bringing them up to speed. This presentation was being recorded and after some post-production editing by the A.I., they would draft and send this to everyone around the world.

"Hmm, do you think you can add a bit more desperation?" Serina asked. "You sound too rigid."

43 groaned as she stood at the head of the table with a data-pad. Her hands clenched in annoyance, but she smiled.

"I'm sorry," she replied sarcastically. "I'm not exactly an actress here. I'm trying to talk normally. If you want genuine emotions, why don't you lock me up again?"

"That won't be necessary."

Another A.I., a red one, had popped up next to Serina and Dr. Kendrick.

"Look, if we use the footage of her interrogation, it won't exactly send a positive message to the people."

"Thanks Rose," Serina sighed.

Everyone eating watched in silence. Rose disappeared in a flash of light and reappeared next to 43. Her red outline matched the stripes on 43's amborg jacket. 43 casually dipped her head to greet the little red A.I.

"Hi," Rose waved her hand. "I'm Rose!"

"I kinda guessed," 43 nodded courteously.

"I know that it is frustrating having to do what you're told in a slightly condescending manner," Rose stated.

"I can hear you! I am not being condescending!" Serina protested.

"This has got to be one of the most hilarious things I've ever seen," 5 whispered.

"I hate to admit it, but you're right," 6 replied, both of them falling into quiet laughter. Rose ignored Serina and continued to look up at 43.

"Whatever issues that you have going on with each other, please consider resolving them soon. All that matters right now is everyone here, and those down on the planet need to know what you know. May I ask why you volunteered to come to our universe?"

"Simple," 43 replied. "I needed to get here. A lot of people sacrificed everything to send me across universes. All so that you could have a fighting chance and know what was coming."

"Great! Think about that and let those emotions fuel this presentation!"

Rose then disappeared and returned to Serina's side. 43 looked taken aback at being directed by an A.I., but it did help. She took a deep breath and spoke again. Her tone of voice became serious, and she spoke at a moderately fast pace so that she could still be understood.

"The race that we are at war with is called the Tandeeri," 43 stated. "I'm here to try and train everyone up with lessons from where I'm from. Data transfers at my age are very painful and I can't do it all the time. So, look at the data pads I've compiled for you while I explain."

Each person's data pad, as they ate their meal, revealed what appeared to be a set of images. 117 looked down at his as Serina curiously flew over the table. She was recording footage for the film. She hung over his shoulder like a parrot. The image appeared to be a timeline of sorts.

"Based on what we know of our universes," 43 explained, "Alpha universe is approximately seventy-five years ahead of yours in the future. But time is continuous at the same rate. One year here, one year there as well. No time discrepancies of any kind. I hate to brag but... our technology and advances are a lot more significant than Epsilon universe. No offense."

"None taken," Dr. Kendrick said immediately. "Politics, a third world war, and chaos really set us back. Having a seventy-five year advance is quite an advantage."

"We fortunately never had a third world war of any kind," 43 said in a teasing manner. "Imagine a universe where you guys didn't have one. The possibilities are endless."

None of the amborgs seemed to be amused, which prompted her to clear her throat and continue the presentation quickly.

"The S.C.E. was an organization formed when we discovered the ability to travel faster than light," she continued as they all read the presentation. "We established outer colonies on habitable planets, discovered alien species friendly to us, and expanded our perspective of the galaxy."

"You discovered hyperdrive?" 3 asked as she ladled out more soup for everyone. "Or just... a standard F.T.L. technology?"

"Yes," 43 nodded. "Our organization is probably what you'd consider to be NASA two point oh."

"And you call it the 'Space Command Enterprise'?" 917 asked as he swiped a finger across his pad. "Are you going for a Star Wars or Star Trek motif?"

"What are those?"

Quite a few of them looked up at Alpha 43 apprehensively. 117 cleared his throat, but 43 merely smiled.

"I'm kidding," she said, holding up her hands. "Star Wars and Star Trek exist in my universe. I know what they are."

"How can you have a universe of space fleets if you don't have Star Wars or Star Trek?" 917 muttered angrily.

"Shh," 999 nudged him. "Now's not the time to be a fanboy."

"Look who's talking," 917 retorted. "Who was it that begged me to buy a rare, autographed poster signed by Carrie Fisher on Imazoom for her birthday?"

There wasn't anything else from 917. 999 swiftly brought her hands up behind his head and pushed him headfirst into the table with a loud crash. It wasn't enough to knock him out, but it did shut him up as 999 looked away. 117 could have sworn she was blushing.

"I never would have pictured Angel being a Star Wars fan," 501 muttered in amusement to 117 on a secret channel. Everyone silently pretended the commotion hadn't happened. "It's rather neat."

"Anyway."

43 stared at 917, who was now sitting back up.

"Wow," she muttered cautiously. "Just like what Alicia used to do. The Tandeeri. They showed up about nine years ago near one of our outer colonies in the far reaches. We dispatched an ambassador fleet to contact them when we believed them to be from a deep unknown expanse of unexplored space."

"Right," 297 sighed. "Unknown alien fleet, unknown part of space, no point or historical sign of origin... Sounds legit. So they were hostile when you contacted them?"

"The colony they were near ceased all communications and no one was heard from again," 43 said. "Well... I don't really know about that since I wasn't there. I don't believe they were hostile at first. We tried to make contact but the only thing we heard back from them was gibberish. Not even the amborg assigned to the fleet could make out what their language was. The only discernible word that was repeated in the first response we received was Tandeeri. And according to every archaeological, historical or even linguistic record, we have no hints or even a description of what this species is. Energy weapons from their fleet were used to overload the systems on our ships and they were ripped apart. We've been at war with them ever since. We've outfitted every ship at our disposal with weapons. Anything to give the colonies a chance. But every encounter we have engaged them in has always ended badly. We don't even know if we're making a dent in their numbers to be significant enough to give people the impression we're at a good standing in the fight."

"What does all that have to do with us?" 1 asked the question all of them were silently pondering. "Even if you have no laws forbidding the sharing of this information, you could have left our universe alone to make these discoveries ourselves. Eventually, our population would be at a point in time where this sort of science is plausible. So why risk it all and come here?"

"Because we strongly believe that they're not native to my universe. The S.C.E. believes that the Tandeeri aren't a species that originate from Alpha."

The room erupted in a mix of confusion and surprise. The A.I. programs immediately circled the table and recorded their reactions. Rose looked like she had hit the jackpot as she zoomed around excitedly with Serina.

43 continued the presentation.

"Before we encountered the Tandeeri, one of the alien races we had first encountered had developed a new technology. A form of transportation that they claimed would make our hyperspace travel obsolete. This was the concept of artificial wormholes. At first, the idea was supported among the scientific community. The ability to travel across light years within seconds instead of weeks or months was an achievement that deserved recognition. But unfortunately, we encountered a very bad side effect when you consider making an artificial portal instead of letting it happen naturally."

"So, you discovered alternate universes because of an accident?" 6 asked curiously.

"A lot of people were there during that accident," 43 replied, nodding to 6. "Artificially creating Einstein-Rosen bridges was looking to be a reality. But we discovered that instead of traveling to different parts of the galaxy, these wormholes had the ability to take us great distances out of our own universe. Way beyond our universe. The test results were chaotic, and we realized that stumbling into other universes where we didn't belong was very unwise. Ultimately, we outlawed the use of artificial wormholes. Instead, we now only use them to study where we could go, where we should avoid going, and explore as much as possible without exposing ourselves. The S.C.E. figured that wormholes would be a way of learning about other universes, except it had to be very carefully monitored."

This had everyone leaning forward, their interest piqued. 1 raised a hand, but 43 noticed and motioned for him to lower it.

"I know," 43 said. "So why am I here if it sounds like we don't condone artificial wormholes? The answer to that question took months to settle. In our studies of this technology about a year and a half ago, we discovered that the Tandeeri also can travel between universes."

117 grew nervous. If it took the S.C.E. years to develop this technology, then the Tandeeri already having access to wormholes was a huge problem.

"Around the time we first used them for observation purposes, we sent stealth ships to your universe secretly to acquire information about your time period and technology, and we designated your universe as Epsilon and never came back again. But the Tandeeri were apparently here on several occasions, which led us to suspect that they were planning on setting their sights here. Not close enough to the Sol system to be detected by you, but we have found traces. That's when the S.C.E. board brought the matter to the alien races of the Interstellar Council, one of the leading governing branches in the Alpha galaxy. We petitioned to disregard the law forbidding travel into alternate universes and wanted to send help."

"That's so nice of you guys," 3 smiled as she looked over the information.

"Yeah," 43's smile faded. "Nice of you to say so but there were a lot of people that advised against it. It really took a lot of debating and discussion to figure out whether it was worth saving all of you."

"Well, hey!" 297 replied sarcastically. "An alien invasion is coming to destroy an entire universe's population. We'll just hold them off with our meager technology and die slowly without ever knowing why these Tandeeri wanted to destroy us."

"Actually," 43 said, "that was one of the arguments we used to gain favor."

297's face perked up, but he still frowned.

"A lot of species on the council believed it wasn't right to leave you to die to an enemy you know nothing about or had no prior knowledge of whatsoever," 43 explained. "Basically, it didn't seem fair to the people of Epsilon universe. We've been at war and in an effort to reorganize their strategy or possibly establish a foothold, we suspect the Tandeeri are using Epsilon as their staging ground for another attack on us that could cripple the S.C.E. and the Council. We also believed we had an obligation to protect you since this is an enemy we've failed to protect others from. The S.C.E. was given the task of drawing the line in the first place. Having millions of lives lost in other universes is a tragedy, even if it isn't our universe. If the Tandeeri travel to a countless number of places, then we argued strongly that we would be the universe that drew the final line."

"It's a declaration saying, 'stay out of innocent universes,'" 1 affirmed. "Very bold move."

"Admirable too," 917 nodded. "Out of all of the millions of universes, it takes guts for just one to stand up to a threat to all of us. I think we can all appreciate the Alpha universe deciding to risk everything for us."

43 smiled as the rest of them nodded.

"You can thank us once the supporting fleet crosses over here."

43 brought up an image of some very sleek and futuristic looking ships. In comparison to what they had, the starships from the Alpha universe were much more advanced.

"Any day now," 43 said. "Elements of the S.C.E. fleet will arrive sporadically. The only reason they haven't done so sooner is because it's been difficult locating safe places to send our ships over. Generating wormholes takes time and we believe the Tandeeri are aware of our plans, since they've been harassing our fleets every opportunity they get. I was merely sent ahead to warn your Earth and the necessary individuals."

"But if you were already aware there were amborgs in our universe," 6 asked, "Why not just send the whole fleet at once? It's not like we have the technology to fight you off. If you were planning to warn us, and help us defend the planet, then wouldn't showing up with a lot of equipment be the right move?"

"Yeah..." 3 said nervously as she set a few plates of cookies on the table. "I'm sure every planet wants to see a giant fleet of starships jump out of hyperspace, tell us that everything we know is wrong and create massive planet wide panic. If that happened, I'd hate to think how normal people would react."

"I wouldn't put it that strongly," 6 replied with a grumble. "I'm just saying, have the S.C.E. fleet or whatever arrive in our universe outside of our solar system or something. Then they could plan out what they wanted to say to us in the safety of our universe. Instead of all the trouble we caused with arresting 43, we could have possibly saved a bit of time."

"Arguably yes," 43 replied. "But the S.C.E. on my end wasn't going to just allow ships to cross over like that. Once wormholes collapse and close, we're cut off from our home universes. So, I can only rely on the fact that they will be on the way over in a couple of days. Mistakes were made, I got arrested, but what's done is done. Even the best laid out plans can hit the fan no matter how much time is invested in them. All that matters now is the fact that you know what's coming and I will do everything in my power to help."

"We can argue how this should have ended another time," Serina said. "I personally would feel a lot better knowing when the first defense ships arrive."

"I was given two days to do everything to inform you," 43 replied. "The S.C.E. will be sending the first group of ships after that. I was incarcerated for a great deal of time so... if my timer is correct, then they'll be here tomorrow."

"That sure is awfully fast," 466 said.

"It's giving me chills," 501 replied. "Well, maybe we don't have to just sit around."

Everyone turned to 501, who looked down meekly. Then, he glanced up and noticed everyone staring at him attentively as if something strange had happened.

"Oh wow," 501 said in amazement. "You guys aren't telling me to shut up?"

"Why would they?" 43 asked curiously, looking at the rest of them.

"No, it's just..." 501 said nervously. "This is the time when I usually say something stupid, and everyone tells me to shut up."

"Well... in case you haven't noticed 501," 466 sighed. "You haven't said a stupid thing yet. If anything, you didn't even finish your thought."

"Oh..." 501 looked at everyone again, who returned his gaze with inquisitive looks. "I guess I was about to contribute, but stopped myself. I was going to say that... until the fleet gets here, maybe we can keep acting as if we still have hope."

"He does bring up a good point," 6 smiled. "All that matters is that we're all together preparing for the fate of the planet. We can still do everything that is possible and when the time comes, we hope it's enough."

"We always used to rely on luck for most of our accomplishments anyway," 297 nodded in agreement. "Sometimes it's the best we can do."

117 clasped his hands together and laid his arms on the table. He was extremely nervous but at the same time, felt an unusual sense of excitement. It was something that he hadn't expected to feel again after so many years. Everyone was attempting to stay optimistic even though they were all deeply scared about the possible threat.

"Can you promise that help is coming?"

He phrased his question clearly and as loudly as he could, doing his best to keep the fear from his voice. Everyone turned to face him, and the smiles all faded once more. 43 stared back at him. She bit her lip and then spoke.

"Help will be here," she stated firmly. "I believe in my friends in the S.C.E. I know they won't abandon this universe. Until then, we can be strong."

"Well, here's an idea... who's still hungry?"

After dropping off the last of the cookies at the table, 3 smiled warmly.

"I think I can cook up a feast for dinner tonight using the meager resources aboard the station," she said grinning. "If we fight, then we fight well-fed."

"I'm interested in the Zero-G room," 297 stated. "I think the sooner we start practicing, the better we can hone our skills. After all, we spent so much time planet-side, we need to get used to flying. So to speak. I think that some of us have a date with zero gravity before dinner."

He looked to the rest of the amborgs as if he was already assembling a small team. 1 and 6 both nodded, indicating they were going with him.

"We'll go too," 999 said looking at 777 and 917, who both also nodded. "501, 466. You and the Third Group need to learn space travel too."

"Can't I help make dinner?" 466 asked. "I don't know if I want to be sick before a meal."

"I'll be right there taking care of you," 6 replied confidently. "The exercise will help you digest better. Besides, we have tons of research and studies from all the space agencies on Earth at our disposal aboard the station. You will be fine."

466 smiled, but slumped her shoulders down. The Fourth Group amborgs sat silently as they all looked to each other and the senior amborgs for guidance.

"What is it you would like us to do?" 280 asked.

"Why don't you pick an assignment?" Serina asked, leaping off 117's shoulder onto the table. "There's plenty of work to do."

"We are confident in our abilities in space," 113 responded. "We just need mission orders."

"You can choose for yourselves," Dr. Kendrick said. "You don't always need to ask what to do every time you don't know. Do what you feel like is worth doing."

"We would rather follow instructions," 280 said rather bluntly. "What we feel is close to irrelevant."

"That's your problem."

917 let out a sigh.

"If you sit around waiting for orders all the time or someone to give you instructions," he said, "you'll never be more than just a blank and cold machine."

"Jack. That's enough."

Dr. Kendrick spoke up before the conversation could get any more awkward. 917 dipped his head towards him and instantly fell silent. The First, Second and Third Group amborgs shifted uncomfortably. The Fourth Group amborgs stared at each other with their neutral expressions, but didn't respond. 43 looked around curiously but didn't question the matter. It almost seemed like she had retreated into the background.

"Right," Dr. Kendrick said, putting on a game face smile. "Ally, Alex, why don't you two stick with me? I could use your help with research until dinner. The rest of the Fourth Group, you all participate in the Zero-G room with 297's party for now. We will be here for some time so be prepared to offer services and adjust accordingly to anything that needs doing on this station. Are we all in agreement?"

All of them held up their gold bracelets, green lights flashing. Everyone nodded and rose to their feet.

"Good," Dr. Kendrick nodded as he, too, stood. "Alright my children, let's get to work. I expect everyone to be here when 3 informs us dinner is ready."

As they all left, Alpha 43 walked over to 117 and Serina. 999 tipped her head to 117 and left to join 297. With his second gone, 117 looked at Serina.

"You don't want to go with Dr. Kendrick?" he asked her kindly, extending his hand forward.

"No thanks," Serina sighed as she jumped into his hand. "I need a few minutes. This is a lot to process. The information from myself is pretty cool, but a lot to work out. We're going to be editing all of this gradually. I'd rather stick with you guys if... 43 is going to be with you."

Both he and 43 heard how uncomfortable she sounded. It was understandable, since Serina was literally referring to herself, who also wasn't exactly herself.

"Ok," 117 said, nodding and giving her a reassuring grin. "Well, I still had a couple of questions about the Alpha universe. You're welcome to be a part of that. If you like."

"Yes please."

"Ok then," 117 said. "Well, I wanted to ask... What is A.I. Industries like in Alpha universe?"

"It's pretty much the same," 43 replied. "Big company all run by Tom Kendrick."

"Tom?" Serina asked. "His Alpha version's first name is Tom?"

"At least it's easier to distinguish between the two of them," 43 replied.

"I know you're supposed to ask a question next but..." 117 felt excited. "Actually, I really wanted to know if there were any laws against meeting our Alpha universe selves."

43's smile seemed to fade. She gazed at the two of them.

"Well, obviously not," 43 said, eyeing Serina. "I willingly came here expecting to meet myself, right? Well... not exactly like this. As far as I know, there aren't any rules about wanting to meet... you? Yourself? You get the idea."

"Wow," 117 said, looking at Serina in fascination. "I have so many questions. Like what my job was... er... is. I want to know what I'm doing, and all sorts of things."

Serina stared at 117 as if meeting his Alpha self was the craziest idea ever. But her silent stare didn't seem to deter his enthusiasm. He failed to notice 43's smiling expression wavering. She seemed to be uncomfortable.

"I..." she said. "I could tell you all about what he did."

It was the past tense that got 117's attention.

"What do you mean?"

43's face became solemn as 117 flashed a confused smile. Serina also looked at her Alpha version with a curious look. She turned a cautious yellow-orange color.

"There's something I haven't been able to tell the rest of you," 43 admitted softly. "The truth is, I was very happy to see almost all of you again. But the fact that you asked about your Alpha versions...well..."

"What's the matter?"

117 and Serina were now looking at the middle-aged amborg with concern. The silence was enough for them to suspect what she was about to say. It almost felt like a giant force of wind was going to strike but still, they had to hear her exact words. Then came the truth, and they found that they weren't prepared for it.

43 looked at 117 and sighed.

"I'm sorry 117. There's a reason I was avoiding answering that question. But the 117 I know is gone. Your Alpha version is dead."

Chapter 12: ...And beyond!

I'm dead? I'm dead. No. Wait. She said that he was dead.

"117? 117?"

He's dead? He's dead. But there are so many things...

"117?"

I always imagined that it was possible but... there were so many things I didn't get to ask... that I wanted to say to him.

"117! You're drifting!"

117 felt a strong grip on his arm, pulling him forcefully. He jerked his head down and looked around frantically in a quick attempt to adjust. When he turned to the right, he felt a sharp flick on his forehead.

"Ow!"

Wincing in pain, he saw 999 glaring at him.

"Are you alright?" she asked.

117 and 999 were both floating in the zero-gravity training room. A few other people were using it to conduct practice maneuvers, but they were in an isolated spot hanging onto a floating prism. 117 had apparently let go and began drifting away. He would have been stuck floating around aimlessly at a snail's pace if 999 hadn't grabbed him.

"6 says it's mentally unhealthy to drift in space without any response for a certain period of time."

The room was filled platforms and various floating geometric shapes, creating a tremendous obstacle course for them to play around in. Unfortunately, in 117's case, he was doing the opposite of play, which was a first. 999 had decided to take it upon herself to try to do the responsible thing and attempt to console him... in her own way. As his second-in-command, she couldn't just sit by and let him mope.

"Sorry Angel," 117 sighed. "How long have I been in here?"

"You entered this room 15 minutes ago," 999 replied. "I assumed you just wanted to practice alone since I didn't see Serina or 43 with you. But after you started moving for a short time, you just stayed here in place. What were you thinking?"

"I just got some bad news," 117 answered.

"You couldn't have done that in a room with gravity??" 999 asked. "There aren't any park benches in an obstacle course. I only came over to grab you because you literally started to space out."

As a result, he had accidentally drifted. Normally, that meant that one had lost focus. In outer space, that was rather dangerous.

"Don't do that."

"What?"

999 smacked 117's shoulder hard. He almost floated away, but she grabbed his arm and pulled him back to the prism they were hanging onto.

"Don't be like me," she said angrily. "Don't shut yourself out. If you do, then everyone else will worry. You're one of our leaders. What happened to all your enthusiasm about the Alpha universe?"

With one arm firmly clasped around the bar of a nearby platform, 999 watched as 117 floated a few feet away, his arms crossed and a distant look in his eyes. It appeared as though he was slipping back into a mindless trance. Were her words even reaching him?

"If you don't say anything in the next five seconds," 999 warned, "I'm going to grab my sword and cut your clothes off in zero gravity. Make you fish for them naked while the rest of us laugh."

117 suddenly perked up and looked at 999.

"Since when do you laugh?" he said as he reached an arm out and snagged onto the platform she was hanging from. "I'm sorry, Angel. I was a little shocked."

"Go on."

"How would you feel if you were told your alternate universe version was killed?"

999 blinked twice and then dimmed her eyes.

"Sounds like a good start to the day," she responded quickly.

This made 117 fumble.

"What?!" he exclaimed, then sighed. He took a moment to regain his composure, then looked away. "Ah, I had that one coming I guess. Look who I decided to seek comfort from."

Even though his head was turned, he could feel her cold gaze drilling into the back of his neck.

"117, if you were seeking comfort, go cry to your wife," 999 stated bluntly. "However, if it's any consolation, I felt that your topic of conversation was interesting enough to warrant a response. If you would like to continue making use of my generosity, which I am still willing to offer, would you like to know why I responded the way I did?"

"Is this how you talk to 917 all the time? You have a rather odd form of speech."

"No... I'm usually the quiet one. He does all the talking," she said with a grumble. "It's actually really uncomfortable when he's silent like how you were."

"Fine... why are you so fascinated about my dead Alpha version?"

"Simple," 999 pulled herself in and kicked off of the platform. She propelled herself to another nearby obstacle and leaped towards another. "Your alternate universe version is dead. And Alpha is next door to our universe. If you really are as tough as I know you are 117, as we all know you are, don't you find it curious as to why you'd be killed? If it was my Alpha version that I discovered was dead, I certainly wouldn't feel sick to my stomach. I'd want to know everything I could as to why there was a universe where I didn't make it. Whether it was by accident or fate... maybe it's my destiny to die if parallel universes or the multiverse have some cosmic galactic connection. But you can still do something about it, learn while you're still breathing."

Even though her words were severe, she was correct.

"So don't just sit around moping," 999 said. "Life continues and it never stops just because you don't feel good. Take every opportunity that comes your way. Smash it, grab it, brush it off, or embrace it. Whatever you want."

117 looked at his second in command in wonder. This was a side of Angel that very few amborgs got to encounter. It was probably thanks to 917. He had most likely rubbed off on her over the years.

"Wow, Angel," he said, beginning to smile. "That was really moving."

"Enough of that!" she snapped. "Get back to work!"

The meager compassion in her voice vanished, and her face suddenly burned with annoyance. A clear definite sign that he had to start running. Or in this case, floating. Away from her.

"Hey! Hey!" he cried out as he felt her gaining on him, causing him to frantically try to move faster towards the next obstacle. "Give me a chance to catch my breath!"

"The enemy won't allow you to hesitate!" 999 spat at him. "Hesitation is death! Death is what awaits those who are stupid and not vigilant! We're in space and we train, train, and train!"

"Alright Mad-Eye I get it!" 117 panicked as he extended his hand to the closest hand hold.

Suddenly, 117's momentum came to a jarring halt as he felt her hand grab onto his ankle. Before he could react, he was swung like a bat and collided head-first into a nearby platform. It was exceptionally amazing how quick she was despite the lack of gravity.

"You must refocus!"

I wonder what Audrey's doing right now, he thought as he felt his head begin to throb from the impact.

The next thing he knew, 999 had kicked him in the stomach and he was sent coasting off again.

■ ■

A.I. Industries Communications Room

"I'm sorry but that is classified, and protocol forbids me from revealing any sensitive information."

"You do know that I'm married to an amborg right? I could just give him a call if you won't be the one to update me."

Carter the A.I. flashed an annoyed shade of orange. He knew perfectly well of his former caretaker's relationship with the amborgs, but it was still no reason to leak classified information. He crossed his arms and looked at the screen.

Audrey was smiling back at him from the other side. She'd changed into her dress uniform and was ready for action. Or in her case, the large amount of paperwork being sent her way. She had taken a breather to give Carter a call.

"Since you have secondary means to acquiring classified information, why don't you call your husband?"

"I can't always play the nepotism card," Audrey shook her head, laughing. "Besides, I wanted to give you a call and see how you were doing."

"Well, I didn't get to be with Serina's group... oops."

"Why?" Audrey eagerly jumped in on that statement. "What group?"

"Nothing!"

"Carter? Did you get kicked off another project for some sort of trouble?"

Carter fidgeted nervously, but Audrey noticed that he had changed color. He turned slightly pale before reverting to full orange.

"Carter..." Audrey took a guess when she saw his tell. "You didn't get grounded again?"

"Temporary suspension," Carter muttered.

"Which means you got grounded," Audrey let out a derisive laugh. "What did you do?"

"Hostile malware attack," Carter admitted embarrassingly. "Three weeks ago. I thought I could handle it myself, but I needed a lot of help."

"What was the damage?"

"No access to restricted or classified data," he reported. "It did play havoc on the electrical for a short time while I tried to take care of it but unfortunately, there was still a bit of trouble since I failed to properly catch it."

"Seems a little harsh to put the blame on you."

"Well, I have to take responsibility, otherwise the whole A.I. Industries network will collapse."

Audrey nodded and then paused. Suddenly, a mischievous grin appeared on her face as she stared at Carter, making him feel slightly unnerved.

"What?"

"So, you're saying that you're not busy at the moment?" Audrey asked.

"No," Carter replied.

"You sure?"

"I'm sorry Audrey!" Carter said in a hushed tone. "I cannot tell you anything! Even if you are my former caretaker, I had to swear an oath when I was sent to A.I. Industries. I promised to never violate company policies!"

"You and I both know that your record isn't exactly spotless."

"It makes me wonder if you two are planning something shady."

Carter and Audrey froze. He turned on the spot and saw 18 looking down at him with her arms crossed, gazing at the two of them inquisitively.

"Carter? You know you're not supposed to be in here unsupervised."

18 walked over to the console he was on. Carter looked down in shame and even Audrey lost her cool confidence at the sight of the First Group amborg. The two of them let her continue talking.

"I am perfectly aware of your relationship with 117, Ms. Wright," she stated. "It is nice to see you again but unfortunately, we are operating under maximum secrecy. It is not that we personally doubt your ability to keep secrets, and we are aware of your clearance level. However, any extremely sensitive information must be carefully reviewed before we share it."

She gazed at Audrey on the screen.

"Every person..."

18 glanced at Carter, who turned a bright shade of red.

"...and every program at A.I. Industries must adhere to the rules."

"Yes, but isn't it our right to also know what's happening since it affects all of us?"

18 turned her head sharply and raised an eyebrow.

Realizing what she had blurted out, Audrey immediately hunched over as if she was afraid of getting hit.

"I can agree to that. I understand, knowing your position in the U.S. military," 18 replied casually. "The only reason I am slightly disappointed is the fact that Carter is here operating a video call unsupervised."

"What's wrong with that?"

"Because he's grounded," 18 replied.

"I knew it!" Audrey exclaimed.

Audrey immediately shut up and mouthed an apology over the videochat.

"And because he's grounded," 18 smirked, "he's technically not supposed to be doing anything without someone else present. So, Carter... an unauthorized transmission without supervision? That's three more days added to your sentence."

"I can explain..." Carter stammered.

"Should I also add in another three days?" 18 looked at the console to Audrey. "For failure to notify the department head of whom you're contacting?"

"When did communications get this strict?" Audrey asked. She looked shocked. "I don't think the last emergency recall had you tied up like this. Carter?"

Carter looked up at 18, and in that exchanged glance, Audrey immediately knew that there was something else on their minds. Before she could ask, 18 nodded to Carter. Once he had permission, he turned to face the screen.

"Umm, Audrey," he mumbled. "I also didn't mention this but... I recently got put on the A.I. watch list by the Fourth Group amborgs... because they think I'm a terrorist."

Audrey's reaction was pretty much what he had calculated. He saw her eyes widen to the size of two large dinner plates and then she buried her face into her hands.

"Oh my god," she said. "What did you do? You're telling me this now?!"

"Nothing!" Carter replied. "They keep an eye on me because I am considered to be a foreign artificial intelligence."

"They called you a terrorist?" Audrey exclaimed. "I wish I was told about this sooner! No one thought to tell me!"

"It's not that he's dangerous," 18 replied reassuringly. "The other A.I.s here are friends with Carter and we all like him. The points that the Fourth Group amborgs brought up, unfortunately, are valid and not disregarded, which is why we are still debating them. However, until we can manage to get the Fourth Group to stop hassling Carter, we felt it necessary to always keep someone with him. Any moment he's unsupervised doesn't look good for him."

"But that's terrible! How can Carter's dream job be labeling him like that?! He is my father's creation and I'd trust him with my life! Uh... most of the time."

Audrey looked at Carter.

"Carter," she said. "You can always come home whenever you like! I'll send a first-class package for you to ride in!"

"It's ok Audrey!" Carter replied. "I know I haven't done anything wrong. Running home away from work would hinder my progress! I have an important thing I'm trying to do! Very secret!"

"Carter..." 18 groaned.

"Oh... oops again."

Carter looked annoyed with himself as 18 shook her head. He had accidentally leaked some more information, getting Audrey hooked back in. Regrettably, it worked, because her complaints dissipated, and she refocused her attention to her former A.I.

"What secret?" she switched gears and spoke calmly. "Is it... legal?"

"Serina thinks it is," Carter replied, but this only made Audrey press him even further. "But I promised not to talk about it."

"How is it that the Fourth Group labeled you as a terrorist, you got grounded, and now you're working on a secret project with Serina?? What are you trying to pull??"

"18?"

A security guard had arrived to check on them.

"My apologies," she said. "I heard raised voices over here. Is everything ok?"

"Yes, thank you," 18 nodded. "Would you mind doing me a favor?"

The guard nodded. 18 looked down at Carter.

"Supervise this A.I. please. Carter?"

Carter turned to look up at 18.

"Wrap it up in three minutes," she directed. Facing the guard, 18 spoke to her. "Once it gets to the end of that time, remind him to end the call. Got it?"

The guard nodded as she turned to watch Carter. 18 walked over to a console that was further away and activated it. She entered the number she wanted to call and heard the ringtone. It was answered immediately, and Alberto Biagino's face appeared on the screen. She quickly encrypted the call once he had made the connection.

"Hello, my friend!" he greeted her warmly. "You're a little late."

"I'm sorry," 18 replied. "When you're in charge of overseeing everyone's training, it gets extremely busy."

"You're the best person to whip them into shape. My prime minister made an announcement on behalf of the United Nations. Is it true?"

18 looked up and scanned the room. No one was monitoring her.

She felt a little bad about the fact that she had just been standing over Carter and giving a lecture about sharing classified information. Here she was, sitting a short distance away and contradicting herself.

"I can most certainly not tell you that," 18 answered softly. "I cannot tell you whether or not we spoke to our visitor, and they most certainly didn't tell us that more were coming."

"Is there a reason you're talking like that??" Alberto asked.

"I was just messing with you," 18 chuckled as she checked that the line was secure. There was no way for anyone to hack into this conversation. "I suggest that you prepare yourselves."

"Prepare what exactly?"

18 let out a sigh. She looked to where Carter and the security guard were. He was still in a deep conversation with Audrey. Hopefully, the guard was keeping track of the time until she had to remind Carter to end the conversation.

"18?"

18 glanced at the screen again.

"Everything," she said. "Prepare everything at your disposal."

"That's still too vague..."

Alberto let out a disappointed sigh.

"Our new friend has given us quite a story," 18 explained. "She was sent here to warn us of some kind of military invasion."

"From space?? An invasion?"

"Si," 18 nodded.

"An invasion from outer space usually ends one of two ways," Alberto said. "With our destruction or a fight big enough for the history books."

"We have a team up there now," 18 said. "With our new friend."

"You didn't go with them? I'm surprised."

"There are still some amborgs here and I must help lead them," she explained. "We're trying to help the planet prepare the welcome mat. That and there are other situations popping up now that the world is panicking and trying to maintain order. You can help us by trading information."

Alberto nodded his head.

"I'm listening," he replied.

■ ■

A.I. Industries Gymnasium

To ease the tension, every employee and amborg at A.I. Industries were readjusting to their original lives as best they could. For the ones remaining on Earth, this was slightly easier since they had gravity. The halls and different buildings of the entire company were home to them, making the transition back to the amborg lifestyle simpler.

The last ten years had given them many opportunities for character development and to create a lot memorable experiences. After the Dominoe Incident, half of them had left to learn what it was like to live normal and peaceful lives, but every time there was an Emergency Recall or if any other situation called for it, they would return to do their jobs as amborgs. Many of them had developed exceptional living habits outside of A.I. Industries. However, to the older amborgs, or those with more old-fashioned mindsets, this had made them seem sloppy. Even though 18 had cleared everyone for duty after they passed their evaluations, she'd still authorized that every person should continue their training and continue to implement their skills and knowledge. Whatever was coming, due to Serina 43's warnings, it required them all to be at their best.

"Fire!"

The command echoed through the air, immediately followed by the sharp sound of various weapons and firearms discharging. A rapid flurry of bullets hit the targets on the range.

57 oversaw the training session as each person fired their weapons, creating a cacophony of gunfire from handguns, rifles, and automatic weapons, nearly drowning out all other sounds. Every amborg diligently practiced with their own custom-built weapon. Once their ammunition ran out, the range fell silent as they waited for the last person to finish.

"Put your weapons on safe!" 57 commanded when she saw the lights on each person's booth switch to green. "Set everything down!"

35 stood next to her and called out to the control booth located in the observation room on the second floor, where a pair of security guards and a few scientists were monitoring the gym.

"Exercise complete! Let's see the results and prepare to reset!"

Unlike the evaluation tests, this was just a free-for-all type of practice on the shooting range. Each booth only had one big circular target sitting at the end. Up in the control room, one of the scientists acknowledged 35's words and hit a button on the console. Each shooter on the range watched as their targets rolled up to them.

"Oh, come on! Really?!"

57 pointed at 92's target when it stopped.

"Jon 92! Steve 93! Are you kidding me with those scores?!"

The twin amborgs of the Second Group, 92 and 93, stepped out of their booths as 57 marched up to them. Both gazed at each other and shrugged while bearing identical cheeky grins when they turned to face her. 57 wasn't amused at all.

"You lowered your scores on purpose! Look at these groupings! Everyone else was on target!" she exclaimed as she pointed at both of their targets. "Can I get an overlay?! Standard human outline?"

She glanced up at the observation booth, where the scientist who had rolled the targets back to them nodded in acknowledgment. He input her next command, and they all focused their attention on the targets. In an instant, the circular target was overlaid with a new background image. The circle disappeared, replaced with the shadowy outline of a human figure. The bullet holes remained visible, and 57 was now able to provide feedback on what they had done wrong.

"Both of you landed two shots in your opponent's arms, missed the neckline completely, put a shot in the lungs, missed the heart, and only put two out of four into the head! Are you trying to give the bad guys a fighting chance to return fire or try to kill you?!"

"To be fair, all our bullets that hit the 'enemy' are accurate," 92 held up finger quotes as he pointed at his target. "The misses were just meant to be funny."

"Come on 57," 93 added. "We were only joking around. Just because the only reason we got back together as a family is because a reincarnated alternate universe version of 43 tells us an invasion is coming doesn't mean we can't provide a little bit of comic relief."

"Appreciated, but being annoying in order to feel better about the problem isn't setting a good example," 57 rolled her eyes. "Next group of amborgs! Grab your weapon and prepare new targets!"

As everyone equipped themselves and got ready for the next round, 57 walked back to 35, who was calculating each of their results.

"Relax sis!" 92 called after her. "You're letting the pressure get to you! Take a break when you get a chance. Even our leaders can afford to laugh every now and then!"

57 whirled around and almost argued back. When she took a moment to register his words, she realized she didn't have a response. He was right, even if she didn't want to admit it out loud. Closing her mouth, 57 made a strange motion with her hand and then turned to head back to her partner. 35 looked up from his data pad and gave her a light chuckle.

"How can I take a break when all of this is happening?" 57 muttered.

"Take it easy 57," 35 said calmly. "You're too wound up. We're not saying that you're doing a bad job of being a leader. You can just dial it down."

"Do you think I'm putting too much pressure on myself?"

35 stopped working and looked at her.

"Let me put it this way. Yeah."

He pointed to the twins who were now making jokes with a couple of the Third Group amborgs. They seemed to be in high spirits despite everything that was going on.

"Look, we're all dealing with a fair amount of stress," 35 explained. "But there's no harm in decompressing whenever we have the opportunity."

"Do we have the time?"

57 crossed her arms and exhaled. She lifted her arm and activated her wrist bracelet. The number of amborg requests was increasing rapidly. Her bracelet displayed a long list of tasks, requests, and missions that they had to sort through.

"Ever since the President's announcement," she stared grimly at the flowing list, "everyone has been asking for help. Once we start prioritizing and deploy, there's no way we can help all these people."

"You don't have to sort through that," 35 said. He realized why she was so devoted to working now. "The A.I.s and every available employee onsite are sorting through every phone call and request we're getting. Police and the military across the country are rallying together to help too."

"Before and during the Dominoe Incident," 57 said, "the military and the police struggled. But then we came into the picture. After the Dominoe Incident, they said they didn't need us anymore. Only after an Emergency Recall, they rallied together and yeah, they helped us get through a lot of distress calls and requests for help. But now? We have an alien invasion, and everyone is terrified."

35 fell silent.

"Even if they're highly trained, the police and military are going to panic. When that happens, when they need us, we have to be ready."

"57," 35 replied, holding up his hands. "Katie. I get it. The rest of us do too."

"Have you found out anything? From the tier-one priorities?"

57 was asking about the amborg requests and missions that had been flagged to tier-one, which meant that they required immediate attention. 35 nodded as he flipped his data pad around for her to see.

"Our little Los Angeles escapade?" he asked. "I don't think we have much to go on."

57 took the data pad and read it. She shook her head and tilted it forward in frustration.

"How can we not have any leads?" she asked. "There are 153 kids... Orphans! Many of them! And 213 people dead! Most of them are their parents! Their families! How can this be?"

"Well," 35 shrugged. "That's why this is at the top of the list. 777 left us with quite a discovery. I think that one of Dr. Kendrick's assistants even suggested that we might need to have the President in on this one."

"And... why would we be going to the White House about this?" 57 asked.

"Oh right," 35 said. "You barely passed your geopolitical classes."

57 glared at him, which prompted him to continue his explanation.

"When 777 and Mark's vigilantes discovered this cargo ship, it was planning to sail into international waters with a falsified destination in the manifest," he said. "LAPD has the jurisdiction and the authority to pursue any connections in the U.S., but homeland security and the F.B.I. are leading the international task force. President Holland might need to bring this matter forward to the U.N. security council."

"Hey guys, want some dessert?"

92 and 93 strolled over with some popsicles for them. 35 happily accepted a red cherry one and 57 grabbed an orange one without batting a smile.

"Thanks," they both said.

"Hey," 92 said when he noticed their expressions. "We were just messing around earlier. We didn't mean to annoy you."

"No," 57 sighed. "There's just a couple of problems weighing on me. 35 was giving me a crash course explanation about how the LA cargo ship incident is going."

"Oh that?" 93 asked. "I heard 777 got kicked off that assignment."

"Huh?"

57 and 35 stared at the twins. What did that mean?

"Yeah," 92 said. "He found out just before he and the team went up into space. Commander Bradley told him that the feds wanted him out. They asked for a different amborg."

"They asked him to stay out of this?" 35 raised an eyebrow. "The amborg who discovered the entire enemy operation?"

"He got exposed," 92 explained. "This gang or organization that was trafficking people. They know that an amborg spearheaded the attack on the docks."

"Those kids he saved," 57 brought her hand up and massaged her forehead. "He told them that he was an amborg when they were rescued. Damn it."

After the attack on the docks, even if he hadn't talked to anyone about it, it would have been easy to guess that a cybernetically enhanced human was the reason why the cargo ship had been publicly exposed. This incident became a major news story right when 43's arrival shocked the entire world.

"That's not the worse part," 93 said. "777 got greenlit."

"He has a bounty on his head," 92 showed them a photo from his bracelet. "It was posted anonymously online on social media."

"Oh yeah," 35's eyes widened. "That is worse."

57 looked at the photo. There it was. Luis 777 of A.I. Industries. Wanted dead or alive. Total bounty to the amount of...

Everyone collectively paused. There was a loud pop as 35 pulled his popsicle out of his mouth. 92 and 93 both nodded in sync with each other. 57 nearly spat out the ice in her mouth.

"Yikes!" she said as everyone looked at the price. She took another huge bite out of her popsicle and let the icy cold flavor cool her off. "We really pissed off whoever owned that prison ship."

"Hang on a minute," 35 said, not taking his gaze off the bounty. "This was posted online? What if we had cybercrimes trace this back to where it came from?"

"We could," 92 nodded. "Might take some time."

"It's a lead," 57 said. "No matter how small or insignificant. Someone has marked 777 as a target and we need to make sure he's protected."

"Well," 93 shrugged. "He is in outer space. So, unless the bad guys find a way to kill him from down here, he's probably in the safest place ever, aside from being here at home."

"But that's so strange," 57 lowered her head to think. "Why take him off the assignment? If he was marked as a target, 777 has volunteered to be the bait. He's done it before. Putting himself out there so that he can draw the attention off the rest of us while we swoop in and help. You'd think that he'd be the best choice to stay on the planet and see this through. Who convinced him to go up into space and leave this matter to the rest of us?"

"Uh-oh..."

Everyone turned to look at 35. The trauma was apparent in his eyes as a look of realization spread across his face.

"There's only one person," he said slowly. "One. Who would be that convincing. The question now is, who wants to try and bring this up with... her?"

■ ■

Conference Room

The person mentioned by the Second Group amborgs at the gym happened to be in a very important remote meeting. Despite having a lot on her plate, she was always busy calculating and thinking about multiple contingencies.

"Katrina? What are you looking at?"

4 glanced at Dr. Kendrick on the wall screen, engaged in conversation. She'd suddenly shifted her gaze to the side, as if something had just darted across her vision. She snapped her attention back when he had called out to her.

"Sorry Dr. Kendrick," she replied casually. "I had a strange feeling just now. Please ignore that. Continue."

"Ok, then..." Dr. Kendrick said. "What I want you to do is carefully help review these recommended protocols. Everything marked in red is for the amborgs, blue is to the governments around the world, and green are my notes and suggestions to President Holland. This should be a good amount of preparations."

4 nodded with a smile. Using the information that he had acquired in outer space, Dr. Kendrick arranged a video conference to provide more instructions. A terminal on the wall was hooked up to the screen, and a data pad inserted into it glowed green, indicating that it had received information from the Apogee station. 4 extended her hand, prompting the sensor to eject the data pad. Once she read it, she nodded and passed it to 95, the Third Group leader. She needed a second pair of eyes to confirm the information Dr. Kendrick had sent.

"Very straightforward," 4 replied. "May not be popular or well received by certain government officials, but it is better than nothing. When do you think we should tell the world about alternate universes?"

"At this rate?" Dr. Kendrick sighed. "I was debating about whether I wanted to make the call to President Holland myself."

"It's your decision then," 4 nodded.

"Hmm," Dr. Kendrick placed a finger on his chin. He then looked up and turned his gaze to 95. "What do you think, August?"

"Me?" 95 blinked.

95 looked at 4 and Dr. Kendrick. He wasn't usually the one asked to give an opinion. Dr. Kendrick and 4 were both staring at him intently now.

"I think people tend to understand and believe in what we tell them if we don't hide anything," he struggled to state his words. "We're not covertly trying to strike into the hearts of people. We're just hitting them and trying to cushion them in case they fall. Maybe we should tell the whole truth. That's just my opinion, though."

"If I interpreted that correctly... 95 is right," 4 attempted to decipher the young amborg's words. "Keeping this a secret is not good. However, it is also dangerous depending on how receptive the world will be. An alien invasion changes a lot. But revealing the multi-verse will upend everything we know."

"It means that no matter what we do or say," Dr. Kendrick shook his head, "the response will be very good or also very bad."

"You did a great job though sir," 95 said. "There are few who could summarize what you just recently learned into a presentation fit for government figures within the time frame you had. Without cybernetics, you are the genius that everyone believes you to be."

Dr. Kendrick perked up and smiled. It was exactly what he needed to hear.

"Thank you for the kind words and your opinions."

He inhaled and let out a deep breath.

"I'm very grateful to have all of you helping me while we work together on this," he said. "Now, I must prepare to address the U.N. Everyone back home should get ready for another worldwide announcement afterwards. Once the other nations review and reveal what I'm about to share with them, then society will respond. Be prepared."

"Good luck sir," 4 nodded as the transmission ended and the screen shut off. 4 sighed as she allowed her shoulders to droop.

"That was very well said," she said turning to 95. "You seem to be taking to your role as leader very nicely."

"All part of the job, right?" 95 smiled nervously. "Usually, 501 is here to help, but now I'm on my own."

"Not entirely," 4 replied. "Hey 95, do you think you can go have some food sent here? I'm a little hungry."

"Sure."

She stood still as 95 promptly left. When the door hissed and slid shut, 4 smirked.

"Well done," she said out loud. "I almost didn't hear you."

There was a sudden thud on the floor as someone dropped from the ceiling into a crouch. Kayla 53, 95's second in command, straightened up and dusted herself off with a smile.

"Aww," she said bashfully. "I was hoping you'd leave before I was caught."

"Since when have you been practicing ninjitsu?"

"Well, when I found out I was one tenth Japanese and distantly related to a clan of ninjas, it became a phase," 53 admitted. "It's really relaxing just hanging up there."

"You taught yourself how to do all that?"

"Almost," 53 said, lifting a finger and began to twirl her hair. "I've been mimicking several videos from the older amborgs."

"Hmm I see," 4 said, bringing a hand up to her chin. "53, you heard 95 just now, right?"

"Yes. Every word."

"How do you think he's doing so far?"

"He's acclimating to the role really well," 53 smiled. "Much better than the last Emergency Recall."

"I agree," 4 nodded. "You ready for the next part?"

53 nodded eagerly.

As the two of them sat down at a table, the door opened again and 18 walked in. While 4 was beginning to ask questions to 53, 18 joined them and rested her elbows on the table.

"I swear," she groaned as she propped her head up on her perched arms, "if I have to clean up after another developing problem, I will quit being a leader, Katrina. I swear I'll..."

18 decided to leave it at that, shaking her head and looking at the other two amborgs in front of her. She didn't want to talk about what happened earlier.

"What are you two doing?" she asked.

"Ah!" 4 said, pausing from her note taking. "Sorry 18. This is good stuff. You want in? I don't think you heard about this since you've been with the Mafia all these years."

"I guess I'm hearing about it now."

"It's something the girls set up," 53 explained. "I imagine the guys have something similar, but ours is pretty sophisticated."

"It's a voting system," 4 said as she continued writing. "Combined with opinion polls. We're ranking each individual amborgs to a set of categories that we came up with. For recreational purposes."

"Ranking? In what?" 18 asked.

53 began to list off a bunch of different things.

"Like who's the best fighter, has the fastest computational speed, rational thinking, the most charm, who we'd like to see drunk, who could give the best inspirational speech before battle, the best L.A.R.P.-er, the best video gamer, the best at sports at a human level, master of disguise, best driver, who would be gay or straight, who could be president, most likely to be arrested. The list does go on."

"Why is this sort of thing necessary?" 18 asked suspiciously, even though she was already imagining several amborgs that would fit the roles of a few of the listed categories.

"I like information," 4 said. "It's how I maintain connections with everyone so I can formulate the best plans."

"I think you're obsessed with information," 53 said.

"Is that any way to talk to your mentor?"

"No wonder people label you as some overachieving perfectionist," 18 said. "Because you actually are."

"I've known that I've been like this my whole life," 4 replied casually. She didn't take offense at being labeled. "If you don't want to see it as me indulging in keeping tabs on everyone, then just see it as a simple social experiment. Most people conduct surveys, rate others on a performance level, and so forth. Some of us have gone through some changes in the time they've been away. 6 studies everyone's mental health. I study their social lives."

"95 had a really good speech earlier when Dr. Kendrick was indicating signs of depression," 53 smiled. "We should make note of how well he is getting over his shyness in certain conditions."

"I was getting to that," 4 said. "18, did you want to add someone to the list?"

"How about 501 as the biggest idiot?" 18 said without even hesitating. "Breaking down a door to the Mafia sounds like him even without context."

"Well, that's a nice contribution," 4 said with a look of skepticism. "But 501 has held the title of 'idiot' for several years in a row. He may even retire the category based on his victories. Anything else?"

18 looked down for a second. There was one person on her mind that she had worked with before that fit the bill. It was probably best to ask 4, who pretty much knew everything.

"917?" she asked. "I don't have a category to put him in. Do you think he's ok? Mentally?"

4 and 53 paused. They fell silent and looked at 18, who returned their gazes with a serious expression.

"Worried about your old apprentice?" 4 asked.

"Always," 18 replied. "He saved my life once. He's a good man."

"117 is the one who can relate to him the most," 4 sighed as she pondered. "But the one who knows him the best is 999. They are best friends. To answer your question, I think he'll be ok. But he did go through a very hard time, so it's very difficult to talk about his mental state. What do you think 53?"

"He misses her," 53 said softly. "We all do."

"345," 18 replied. "Yeah, it was a terrible time."

18 then looked at 4. Her lip curled in anger.

"And then you replaced her," she stated.

"I did," 4 replied bluntly. "Does 917 still dislike 723?"

"Well, it's pretty understandable since 723 has tried to kill the two of us before," 18 said.

"Making her an amborg was the best way to gain access to information," 4 replied coldly. "She's an asset and she has contributed."

"Are you going to acknowledge how hurtful that could be to 917?"

18 suddenly slammed her palm on the table. 53 jumped in fright and quivered, but 4 merely sat there. She didn't even flinch as she narrowed her eyes.

"I suppose you're about to state the obvious?" she said in a boorish tone.

"917 and 999 lose 345, their apprentice amborg," 18 snarled. "And you have 723 take her spot. You replaced her number completely."

"And I suppose you wanted me to just keep a seat in the Third Group vacant? For her? Like 43? A dead girl? 345 wasn't a perfect little angel like Serina."

"Stop!"

18 and 4 turned to 53, who decided to interrupt their heated conversation before it could get out of control.

"Don't fight!" she said.

18 stopped talking and slunk back in her chair. 4 looked away, avoiding eye contact.

"My point is..." 18 muttered, "you didn't even tell 917 or 999 that a new amborg was going to take her spot. 345 died alone on a mission. And before they could even finish grieving properly, 723 came into the picture."

"I am not trying to make an excuse," 4 replied softly. "But 723 needed to be taken in. Everyone else wanted her gone. Having her join A.I. Industries as an amborg, with her background, was the right thing to do. At the time, I focused on the long-term benefits."

4 projected an image from her bracelet. It revealed 917's profile to 18.

"I predicted that 917 would come to terms with 345's death and move on," she declared. "And he did. So, I will reiterate that he is ok."

53 raised her hand meekly. 18 and 4 both saw and nodded their heads.

"What is it?" 18 asked.

"I am curious," 53 said. "Is an amborg such as 917 capable of having a mental breakdown? He was in jail after destroying a gang all alone. After being away for so long, could he be dangerous out in space?"

"No," 4 replied. "It is my opinion that he is one of the best amborgs we have on the team. He is not a danger out there. We must trust each other."

18 added to her answer.

"Yes, show sympathy and compassion for him. But at the same time, he is just like all the rest of us. He won't let the past distract him until after we finish the job. He doesn't quit when he's passionate about something. I think that if 6 was still down here, she'd agree with me when I say that 917 still fights on even after all the losses sustained. 345 was a great amborg. She wouldn't want us to waste time moping."

"Yeah," 4 nodded. "We've talked about this long enough. I think we should get back to work."

It was probably the best time to end their short break. As 4 continued to read more information on the data pad, she spoke up again.

"If I'm being completely honest," 4 said. "I'm more concerned about 999 than him."

53 gazed curiously at her mentor.

"I don't understand your meaning."

4 looked at 53, then to 18.

"Let's just say," she said ominously, "the quietest of the group is usually the most dangerous. There's a reason she's a lone wolf."

Chapter 13: Deadlock

Apogee Station
Medical Bay

"I was expecting an injury to happen but certainly not to you, 117. At least, not this soon."

117 held an ice pack up to his head. It was still throbbing painfully from when 999 had hit him.

"999 always did have a rather brutal way of making us snap out of it," he groaned.

999 sat next to his bed and merely scanned the room. Turning her head like a security camera, she eerily kept watch, keeping an eye out for any possible threats. 6 and 117 eyed her suspiciously and shared awkward glances.

"That's not terrifying at all," 117 muttered.

"It is for your safety," 999 replied.

"I don't feel safe!"

6 stifled a laugh as she examined the bruise on his head. 999 only crossed her arms and closed her eyes. Was she pouting?

"6," he groaned. "What did you teach her when you were her mentor?"

"Oh, I'm sorry 117," 6 chuckled. "Doctor-patient confidentiality. You understand, right?"

"Confidentiality?? What does that have to do with this? 999 was your apprentice! Not a patient! Right?"

6 just gazed at 999, who had opened her eyes but was still looking away. She was intentionally avoiding the conversation and trying to find solace in her silence. 6 sighed and stood up.

"So," she said, "999 told me that you had quite the shock. Aside from the physical damage to your head."

"It's nothing to be concerned about," 117 replied.

"Don't forget something."

6 motioned towards the entire med bay and 117 followed her gaze. There were a few other people on duty who were busy working, but he didn't see anything that stood out to him.

"You may be the leader of the Second Group, but this is my med bay," 6 declared proudly. "I answer to 1 and 2. But, when you're hurt and here while I'm on duty, I outrank you. So... let me ask you the question again."

6 stood over him and looked down at him. Even though she was smiling, he could feel her stern gaze burrowing into him. 117 wished that he could sink under the covers to hide from her watchful eye.

"What's going on?"

117 felt the ice pack lift off his head. He blinked and saw that 6 was now holding it. After a few more moments of uncomfortable silence, 117 decided to give in and answer the question.

"I really... I really wanted to... uh... I wanted to meet him."

117 reached over to the side of the bed and hit a button. As it started to lower, he hit another button, making the bed whir and raise him up to a sitting position. Once he was upright, he leaned forward. 999 and 6 were both looking at him quietly, listening intently to his responses.

"Do either of you remember what happened the day after you became cybernetically enhanced?"

999 stayed quiet, but 6 slowly nodded.

"It was a long time ago," she answered. "I remember how cold and empty it felt. If I stopped thinking or calculating anything, it felt like my mind was hanging over the edge of a dark and vast abyss."

"It was like that for me, too."

117 had shoved that particular set of memories to the back of his mind and tried to forget them. Now, they were resurfacing, dragging his emotions with them. He felt as though he could hear the pounding of his heart, echoing in his ears, and his stomach felt like it was sinking with the weight of it all.

"Suddenly waking up, all of my memories and emotions prior to the enhancement were suppressed. I couldn't feel anything anymore. Even when 43 was there... Things always felt so cold and alone when we weren't working. I was hoping that if Alpha 117 was there in the other universe or if he was coming to help us, then I could learn so much more."

"And then 43 told him that his other version was dead."

6 turned to 999, who'd spoken up, then looked to 117 and nodded.

"Well, that explains quite a bit," she observed. "999 was trying to get you out of some sort of funk."

"Yes."

"Well, then there's a simple solution to this! Go talk to her again."

"43?" 117 asked.

"No," 6 replied sarcastically. "Talk to Angel here. See how many more injuries she decides to dish out on you. Of course you should talk to 43."

6 turned away and crossed her arms. 117 noticed that she appeared to be focusing on something. Then she glanced back at him.

"It's ok to be upset and shocked by the fact that you didn't make it in an alternate universe," she said kindly. "But think about this, 117. If the multiverse didn't exist, we would all be doing our own self-reflections. We do this all the time. If you wanted to learn more about what kind of person you were in the Alpha universe, don't be sad that your Alpha is dead. From my perspective, there's one person aboard this station who can probably tell you all that you need to know."

"And you ran away from her and left her alone," 999 added. "Very cowardly."

"Oh, come on," 117 sighed. "Even you must have experienced total shock and battled depression of your own."

"This isn't about me," 999 said.

"Anyway!"

6 clapped her hands once, interrupting the conversation before it could escalate. The two of them shut up at the sharp sound.

"That's why I thought I'd call them here."

In a flash of light, they all saw Serina appear at the bed stand next to 117's head.

"What were you thinking?!" she yelled. Then she turned to 999. "And what were you thinking?!"

"Cognitive recalibration," 999 replied quickly in a soft tone.

"She hit me," 117 replied.

"It worked," 999 finished.

"There you are! Look, I know that A.I. don't have physical bodies, but you need to remember that some of us still need to walk to get to..."

43 suddenly appeared from behind a curtain.

"...where we need to go," she finished, all eyes now on their unexpected guest. "What happened?"

43 noticed 117 on the bed and her eyes widened.

"What happened to you?" she exclaimed.

"Already asked," Serina crossed her arms and grumbled.

"She hit me," 117 gestured to 999.

"Cognitive recalibration," 999 repeated.

"Did it work?" 43 asked.

"Yes," 999 replied.

Serina and 117 shouted, "no", simultaneously. 43 pivoted and appeared ready to reprimand 999, but before she could, she got cut off by someone stepping in her way.

6 seemed like she was having the time of her life. She looked at 43 and held out her hand.

"Hi! Alpha 43, we met after your interrogation," she greeted cheerfully. "Vanessa 6!"

Baffled, 43 took her hand and nodded courteously.

"Uh... hi. What's going on here?"

"Well, the good news is that 117 can be cleared for duty again," 6 replied. "I think you all have some things to catch up on."

"Yeah," Serina turned to 117. "You ran off so fast. Are you ok?"

"I just... froze up," 117 admitted. "I wanted some time to think."

"We went to the Zero-G room, but that's when we heard from the marines training there that 999 had sent you to the med bay. We were worried."

Serina gave 43 a suspicious look.

"Well, I wasn't," she added.

"Right," 43 scoffed. "Considering you zoomed all over the station looking for him."

"Look, you're not in the clear either!" Serina protested. "You told him that he was dead!"

43 sighed, glancing at 117 with a bit of remorse, and nodded.

"You're right. 117, I'm sorry I didn't tell you," 43 bowed her head. "I didn't know how to tell all of you. How was I supposed to just directly say that my partner, my best friend... was dead?"

"That's kind of an important detail," 6 replied from the side. "Isn't it better that we found out now rather than later?"

"I would have said something sooner," 43 sighed. "But it's kind of diffi-cult to really think about the delivery of that story when you've just been released from amborg custody, and then we had to make a trip into space."

"Are we going up against a species that could kill us?"

999 asked her question directly.

"Alpha 117 is dead," she said. "Am I dead? 917? 297? The rest of us?"

43 fell silent. 999's look of disdain worsened as she continued talking.

"The S.C.E. has been battling the Tandeeri for years," 999 stated. "This is the information you provided. Care to be a little more honest with us? Are we all going to die?"

"No!" 43 replied. "Absolutely not!"

"Then how are you still here? How are you alive? Are you hiding anything else from us?"

"You know? I'm not sure I like your tone... or what you're implying."

6 cleared her throat loudly.

"Not in my med bay," she reminded them gently. "Take this somewhere else if you're going to start an argument."

"She's right," 117 immediately spoke up. He was quite alarmed at the dark turn this conversation had taken. "999, what's done is done! All we should focus on right now is the next step!"

"Let's talk about something else, shall we?" Serina suggested. "We're already dealing with a lot of issues."

"Yeah," 117 nodded eagerly, smiling at Serina. "Maybe we could go back to the 20 questions game we were playing!"

"43."

43 turned to face 999, who was looking up at her.

"What is it?" 43 asked.

"Are the conditions in your universe dangerous? If so, how often?"

"Ok," Serina tilted her head in surprise. "I guess Angel is starting first."

"Apparently," 117 raised an eyebrow.

43 looked confused. Moments ago, 999 had displayed a rather unsettling mood. Now, it seemed like she had decided to change it up. It felt like she was trying to make a connection. 43 pleasantly shrugged her shoulders as she thought of her response.

"I would have to say that there's a fair amount of danger," she replied with a kind smile. "Space travel or living in space is almost always dangerous. Why do you ask?"

999 didn't immediately respond, which caused everyone to look at her. They remained silent. She had a very strong and intense poker face, making it difficult to know what was on her mind at times. It was quite a surprise to hear her ask a question, that was for sure.

"I would like to request a duel," 999 suddenly declared. "Fight me. One on one."

"Huh?" Serina blurted out, changing to a pale blue color.

43's smile faded and 117's eyes widened. The gleam in her eyes faded as she locked her gaze with 999. 6 observed everyone carefully, seeming slightly more interested than concerned.

"Uh, 999," he cleared his throat. "What are you doing?"

"She looks like Serina 43," 999 stated. "I want to know if she fights like her."

999 nodded to Serina, who looked shocked.

"I really don't think we should go there," 117 said nervously.

"We should," 999 replied. "117, if you won't, then I will. This isn't the time to be a gentleman. She can persuade you with her words and make you think that she is who she says she is. You had your chance to get to know her this whole time. It's my turn. I'd like to confirm my theory with something a little more practical."

"I didn't come to your universe to fight you," 43 replied calmly. "This was not the plan."

"Well, what if it is the plan now? We're just waiting around for your reinforcements or the enemy, aren't we?" 999 crossed her arms. "If you think that you can't handle a duel, then there's no harm in refusing."

"999, stand down," 117 said. "This isn't necessary."

"Are you ordering me to?"

"I'm in charge of the Second Group," 117 replied sternly. "So yes, I am ordering you to..."

"Then I challenge you for the role of leadership," 999 stated. "If I win, you let me carry on with this duel."

"This is quite the power vacuum," 6 muttered.

"You're not helping!" Serina hissed, turning bright red.

"I'm not fighting you!" 117 protested. "You would most likely win!"

"Since you concede and agree to that outcome," 999 continued to stare at 43, "then my challenge still remains in effect."

Then 999 did something that crossed the line. She stood up from her chair and glared at the older amborg.

"What'll it be old lady?"

Everyone fell silent. A few people in the background gasped. 117 figured that this conversation would attract some attention, but this was really bad.

999 rarely insulted anyone, but Alpha 43 didn't know that. 117 glanced at her and fear instantly struck. Her eyes had narrowed, clearly showing that she'd taken serious offense to being called old. It was difficult to know what her reaction would be and if it turned out to be bad, then he hoped that he would be able to calm her down quickly. Except for the Fourth Group, 117 remembered a long time ago when their universe's 43 had single-handedly wiped the floor with them. They all weren't strangers to her wrath and if it was the same for the Alpha universe, then 43 was royally pissed.

"Bold talk," 43 scoffed, curling her lips into a malicious grin. "Especially for someone far from home. You sure you want to do this? Prepared to lose?"

"Let's go. I challenge you to a deadlock," 999 replied. "Fighting one other amborg must be easier by comparison. Unless you need to take a nap?"

"Alright, my child," 43 brought her hands together and rubbed them menacingly, as if plotting revenge. "I accept."

She turned to glance at 117, and he backed away slightly.

"Why don't we grab some of the others and have them prepare for a show?" she smiled. "You want to know more about me? I think now is a perfect opportunity to show you how we take care of business in my universe. Where do you want to do this? When?"

"Training room," 999 replied coldly. "Be there."

"Already on my way."

43 didn't storm off or rush away. She merely lowered her gaze on 999, turned, and walked away. Silence fell over the med bay, every footstep loudly echoing off the walls.

Once she was gone, 117 immediately got out of his bed and grabbed her shoulder.

"What do you think you're doing?"

999's answer was immediate.

"Are you going soft?" she asked.

"No," 117 replied, feeling confused. "What does that have to do with this?"

"You chose me to be your partner on this mission," 999 said. "That means, if I feel that you're most likely going to lead us into disaster, I have an obligation to steer you back on track."

"I suppose you're going to tell me what you mean by that? Because you're not making any sense."

"I will. You're being an idiot."

999 looked at 117 sternly.

"That sounds a little harsh," Serina muttered.

"Most of you are wasting time asking 43 all of these questions," she said. "If there's an alien invasion coming our way, as she's described, I want to learn what her plan is. I want to know how she's going to help us fight an enemy we don't even know whether or not they exist. Is she going to save us and prevent the destruction of Earth by herself? We're just supposed to trust her?"

"I trust her," 117 replied. "Why is that such a bad thing?"

"Maybe that's why you are dead in the other universe. That exact way of thinking."

117 paused. He was about to try to interrupt and tell her that she was wrong. 999 even stopped and gave him a look so he could respond. Instead, he found himself mulling over what she said carefully, considering the validity of her words.

"This is an opportunity to see how an amborg from her universe fights," 999 stated. "What happens if we're invaded and we're unable to fend them off? If things are as bad as she says they are over there, do you really want to talk your way out of the coming battle?"

"It's because things are bad over there," 117 sighed as they began to walk down the hall. "That's why she came here. She's scared and wants to help."

"She's helping me now," 999 cracked her knuckles. "I want to get a little more training in before the Earth comes under attack."

999 made her way to the door, with 117 trailing behind. Serina floated alongside them as they left the med bay.

"Be right there!" they heard 6 say. "I got to wrap up a few things here!"

117 followed 999 to the training room. Advertisements and announcements lined the walls and display screens. The deadlock duel had been scheduled, and everyone was welcome to come watch. 117 was impressed with how quickly the other A.I. programs had prepared everything. He glanced at Serina, who was shaking her head.

"Don't look at me," she replied. "I'm against this fight."

When they arrived at the training room, they noticed that a small crowd had gathered. One of the technicians even brought a camera to broadcast the fight to the rest of the station. Word had traveled fast. 999 proceeded to the center of the ring to explain the rules to 43.

"Is this really happening?" Serina said from 117's shoulder. They settled into the bleachers among the Second Group and the rest of the amborgs who'd come to watch the duel.

"Yup," 117 replied. "I got to be honest, this mission has turned into quite the show."

"What was she thinking? What is she thinking right now?"

"I'm afraid I can't answer that," 117 replied helplessly.

"I was talking to him!"

917 turned his head when he caught a glimpse of Serina's sudden movement, and his eyes widened when he realized that she was in his face. Due to her small size, she looked like a pissed-off Tinkerbell, which caused 917 to instinctively lean back. Meanwhile, 777 and 297 glanced between 117 and Serina, curious about which fight to watch.

"Oh, m-me?" 917 stammered.

"If I had a physical body, I'd slap you! Yes! You! Why is Angel about to fight... me?!"

Serina pointed a finger at the ring. 917 merely shrugged in response, which only seemed to frustrate her more.

"I wish I made popcorn," 297 whispered.

"I heard that!" Serina spat, flashing an angry red color. "Why didn't any of you have the sense to try and stop her?!"

"I was with her and you the whole time!" 117 answered.

Serina gave him a look of haughty derision.

"Uh, have you tried stopping her in the past?" 917 asked. "Because that hasn't really gone well for most of us."

Serina continued to glare at them silently.

"Are you that worried about them?" 917 asked. "I could have sworn that you had some unresolved feelings directed at Alpha 43. Aren't you curious to see how this resolves?"

"It's not them I'm concerned about," Serina said as she clasped her hands tightly and brought them up to her head. "Do you remember when I was the one who would duel occasionally with Angel?"

117 and 917 both nodded. Even 777 and 297 looked at each other, reminiscing about their sparring sessions many years ago.

"Do you remember how those matches usually ended?" Serina asked in a very stern tone.

"Oh no..." 917 suddenly looked worried.

"Exactly," Serina put her hands on her hips. "If Alpha 43 is just as strong and fast as I once was when I still possessed a body, and she's about to have a one-on-one duel with the Lone Wolf of A.I. Industries, who happens to be the deadliest amborg in our ranks, what exactly do you think will prevent the complete and total destruction of the space station? You know, the big glass Christmas ornament with a fragile sticker floating in the vacuum of outer space??"

The guys looked horrified as her words sunk in. Serina was raising some really excellent points regarding their current situation.

"Why didn't you bring this up the entire time we were walking here??" 117 asked under his breath.

"Because I won most of our duels back then!" Serina replied. "You bring that up around Angel and see how well she responds! Like I'm going to be the one to piss her off even more before a big fight."

"Yeah, that's very bad," 917 muttered.

"Well, we already tried," 117 gestured at 999 as he looked at Serina. "Maybe you'll have better luck?"

Serina considered this for a moment and nodded.

"I'm putting a stop to this, right now."

Serina suddenly disappeared. They saw another flash of light as she reappeared next to 999 and 43. Unfortunately, this didn't seem to yield the desired results. With another flash of light, 117 and 917 watched her vanish and reappear again at their sides in an instant.

"She 'shooed' me!" she exclaimed outrageously. "She actually 'shooed' me!"

Serina looked like she had been slapped in the face while the guys were trying not to laugh at her failed attempt.

"Nice negotiating skills," 917 snorted.

"Shut up..."

"Someone here better put a stop to this fight if it gets out of hand," Serina let out a frustrated sigh.

A moment later, they heard a chime from overhead, followed by an announcement broadcasted throughout the entire room.

"If you are a non-combatant, please exit the floor. Duel commencing soon."

"We might be a bit late for that," 777 muttered.

"You want to know what I think is weird?"

Serina and the Second Group amborgs turned to look at 501 and 466, who were seated nearby with the Third Group.

"Not that anyone asked," 917 replied with a shrug. "But what's weird?"

"Serina is here," 501 pointed down at the bleachers they were sitting in. "But 43 is there. It's pretty weird that she can provide commentary on herself."

"I never thought we'd get ringside seats to a 43 versus 999 duel again," 466 said. She was quite fascinated. "It must be so surreal for you, Serina."

"I'd rather put an end to this than just be a spectator..." Serina groaned.

"Cat fight," 917 sang in a soft voice.

"Actually, we don't call them that anymore."

917 stared at 117 blankly.

"What? You changed the name?"

"A couple of years ago," 466 added.

"They're called 'deadlock' fights," 117 explained. "You know, if two amborgs are unable to resolve a situation through peaceful means, then they can fight it out if their problem is in a deadlock."

"Is there anything else I missed in prison?" 917 asked curiously.

Everyone thought for a moment.

"Jackie from accounting married Anthony from R&D," 501 said excitedly.

"Really? Good for them," 917 nodded in approval. Suddenly, he started to laugh. "Wait, Anthony Chan? So, her married name is now..."

"Jackie Chan," everyone said altogether.

"Nice," 917 chuckled.

"Yes, yes, there's still a few things you need to catch up on," Serina grumbled. "Terrific. We'll set up a tea party. Can we please focus?"

Everyone hushed and turned their attention to the middle of the room. 43 and 999 were engaged in some opening banter before the starting signal.

"I assume that there's something you want from this fight?" 43 asked as she rolled her sleeves back.

"Why assume that?" 999 responded, unfolding her arms and began pacing. "Perhaps I simply wanted to fight."

"There's more to it than that," 43 replied. "Tell you what, if I win, you tell me why you're making this such a big deal."

"I will agree to that... if you win," 999 said coldly.

"And what do you want?" 43 asked. "This is more than just a fight for you."

"Whether or not I want something out of this," 999 leaned forward and assumed an attack stance, "...is not your concern."

"Fair enough," 43 shrugged and readied herself.

Everyone watching fell silent as the two amborgs from two different universes prepared to fight. They watched in anticipation as a timer on the display screen circling above them started a ten second countdown. 999's style of fighting was quick and efficient, but what about 43? She was from an alternate universe and lived through completely different environments and settings in comparison. Would her experience and methodology be similar to how they knew her Epsilon version or was she going to be a totally different kind of fighter?

117 looked at Serina and studied her face. Even though she'd said before that she didn't want to see this fight happen, it was obvious that she was curious to see herself in action.

"Combatants," the announcement declared. "Good luck. You may begin in five... four... three... two... one."

The timer hit zero and the buzzer went off.

999 and 43 cautiously approached each other, keeping their eyes locked as they anticipated each other's next moves, strategizing and planning their tactics. The air crackled with tension as they stood there staring menacingly at one another. After a suspenseful moment, 999 made her move.

She dashed forward and attempted to deliver a high kick to 43's head. 43 sidestepped, dodging the kick with ease. Allowing her to reset, 999 took a step back and repositioned. Then, 43 advanced and threw a right cross. 999 also sidestepped, effortlessly evading the attack. 43 smirked.

"Alright then," she said as she cracked her knuckles. "Shall we?"

"You have extensive military training," 999 observed.

"Space is more dangerous than you think," 43 replied. "I trained with the best."

"So did I."

"What are you waiting for? Show me."

Both resumed combat right away. The fight progressed at a rather slow pace. It looked like they were focusing on strength rather than speed from the spectators' point of view. 117 assumed that 999 was attempting to gauge just how strong 43 was.

Their reflexes were impressive. 999 and 43 were easily outmaneuvering one another, dodging punches and kicks. It was like they had just begun a well-choreographed dance. After a few seconds, however, things weren't progressing the way either of them would like. Eventually, 999 moved in and aimed for 43's head. 43 responded by deflecting 999's punch and they both stepped back.

For a moment, the two amborgs stared intensely at each other. Finally, at the height of everyone's suspense, 999 charged.

999 lunged forward and attempted a flying kick. 43 stepped aside but couldn't completely avoid it, so she deflected her foot with her hand. As soon

as she landed, 999 unleashed a series of kicks that 43 managed to block. After a brief flurry of attacks, 999 resumed a crouching stance.

117 noted the contrasting fighting styles they had chosen. 999 went out of the gate with kicks and foot techniques, whereas 43 took a defensive stance, relying on hand techniques. It was agility against a stable and grounded opponent.

999 swung her leg, missed, and then spun around. 43 expected another leg sweep, but realized it was a feint. 43 attempted a leg check down below, but 999 spun and aimed a kick to 43's head. She barely had time to duck when 999 closed the distance and tried to throw a few punches, but it was no good. 43 stumbled back slightly and quickly raised her hands to defend herself. For a second, everyone thought that she was completely on the defensive. Then, in the next moment, she made her move.

Suddenly, 43 advanced and lifted her right arm. Bringing it downwards, she attempted to land a punch in 999's face. When her counterattack was blocked, she followed up with a right and a left punch. Although 999 managed to defend against the strikes, the audience noted the variation in their fighting styles.

"She really does have Serina's style," 917 said in fascination as his eyes remained glued on the duel.

117 noticed that Serina was analyzing Alpha 43's movements. She looked at him and nodded to confirm.

"Her strength and speed are an exact match," she said.

Her tone was a mix of awe and surprise. If they hadn't seen it for themselves, they might never have believed it. 117 definitely felt a sense of nostalgia sweeping over him as the fight went on.

43's combat style had a lot more power. Once she deflected a few of her punches, 999 really started to focus on evading and picking up the pace. 43's punches grew more powerful with each strike, overpowering 999's defenses. 999 was slowly wearing down, struggling to find a way to fight back. Despite her strong punches, 43 seemed to have the upper hand.

"Angel is wasting too much movement trying to set up her kicks," 917 commented. "43 is keeping her directly in front of her and slowly wearing her down."

"I thought she's as good as you?" 501 said with a frightful expression in his eyes.

917 gazed at 501.

"Yeah," he admitted. "But the two of us never stood a chance against 43."

999 attempted a couple more kicks. Instead of spinning, she managed to land a side kick to 43's chest. It didn't have much effect as 43 continued to move forward as if she were merely hit with a slow-moving beanbag. 43 crouched, brought up her fists like a boxer, and attacked with a triple combo. On the third strike, her fist managed to break through 999's defense, landing a hit to her ribs. She staggered back a bit, but she remained on her feet. As 43 advanced, 999 refused to back down and straightened up to meet her.

43 stooped forward and grabbed onto 999's jacket. 999 nearly stumbled forward as 43 lifted her off the ground. With a loud shout, 43 suddenly flung Angel straight down and slammed her into the floor. Fortunately, 999 didn't allow this to stun her. She quickly rolled away as 43 strode confidently towards her.

999 looked up and saw that 43 was still coming at her. 43 attempted a spin kick to her head, but 999 dodged it, then saw her chance. As 43's leg passed over her head, 999 spun around and struck out with her left palm, hitting 43 in the left eye. 43 stumbled to the side and 999 stepped back defensively, giving 43 a moment to recover. She may not have done much damage with that last attack, but 43 still needed a second to blink and refocus.

"Fine," she smirked. "You want kicks?"

999's eyes widened as 43 suddenly surged forward, raising both legs to kick her. Moving faster than anticipated, 43 caught 999 off guard, putting her on the defensive once again. She had to come up with something fast before 43 overwhelmed her in an endless flurry of strikes.

999 threw her right fist forward, but 43 quickly grabbed her wrist, pivoted, and pulled her over her shoulder. Rather than flinging her, 43 held on and tried to throw her directly onto the floor. 999 managed to bend and land on her feet first, preventing her from slamming onto her back. 43 realized what she was doing and adjusted. She hunched over, wrapped her arms around 999's waist, and lifted her up again. Everyone watched in horror as 999 was thrown over 43's shoulder in a powerful suplex maneuver. With a mighty roar, 43 threw 999 to the ground with a massive thud, sending a huge tremor through the whole floor. 999 bounced on impact and laid prone, but the fight still wasn't finished. 43 knelt down and brought her fist into the floor, inches from 999's nose, creating another loud boom and causing everyone to flinch in terror. She'd intentionally missed 999's head and then stood back up. When they thought it was over, 43 whirled around and kicked 999 in the stomach. She cried out in pain as she curled up in agony.

"That's illegal!" one of the station technicians yelled out. "Foul!"

"It is not," 280 replied calmly. "The match isn't over yet."

"It's 999's decision now," 297 trembled. "Look!"

While curled up on her side, 999 coughed as she suddenly raised her right fist and aimed it at 43's ankles. Her hands were shaking, but she refused to back down.

280 had to explain a few more details to the spectators that weren't familiar with amborg deadlock duels. The fight wouldn't end until one side conceded to the other. If one side had fallen down, they were given a total of ten seconds to get back up, like in wrestling or boxing events. In this case, however, 999 had signaled that she was continuing the duel.

"Is that it?!" 43 yelled. "Is that all you got?!?!"

Her voice echoed throughout the entire room. 117 glanced at 917, who looked furious. It was probably taking a lot of strength not to suddenly leap into the center and interrupt the match. Even though his best friend had been thrown to the ground, he showed no intention of making a move. 43 continued to yell her taunts as she turned to look at the audience members.

"You see this?!" she roared. She pointed at 999 and kept going. "How dare you?! How dare you think that I came here with some untrustworthy plan?! How could you all lock me up the moment you saw me?! At first, I was happy!! Before I came here, I hoped... I wished... and I prayed!!! That I would get to see my friends again!! Even if they weren't the same ones I knew!! Then I wake up, find out I'm dead, and you all treat me like an imposter!!!"

999 had her fist still hanging in the air like she was waiting for a fist bump that would not be reciprocated. She had stopped shaking and was firmly staying still as 43 continued to rant.

"You know what?!" her voice trembled with rage. "I don't care what you wanted if you had won!! I don't care why you did this!! Do you know what I want?!?! I want my friends!!"

466 let out a squeak of pain. 117 glanced over and noticed that she was holding hands with 501. He had most likely squeezed too hard, which caused her to react. Everyone silently listened as they watched 43's rage dissipate and turn into sadness.

"I want my family!" she yelled. "I want them back!! And I want this war to end!!"

999 coughed on the floor, shifting everyone's attention. They watched as she slowly put her feet under her and managed to get back up into a standing

position. The entire time, her fist was still held out and aimed at 43. She panted and tried to avoid falling down as she attempted to focus.

"Let's go," she said.

117 noticed that Alpha 43 was on the verge of tears, but the instant 999 stood back up, refusing to surrender, her anger simmered back to the surface. 43 sniffed, reached up to her face, wiped her mouth with the back of her hand, and readied another combat stance. 999 also raised her fists.

"Fine," 43 replied.

999 leapt forward, raising her right foot for a front kick. 43 sidestepped it and threw a few more punches, but Angel evaded them easily. Backing up a few feet, 43 advanced towards her aggressively, but 999 had a plan. She lifted one leg and kicked 43 in the chest, causing her to halt in her tracks. It didn't do any damage, but that wasn't what she was going for. 999 took that split-second opportunity to move in and throw a punch. 43 immediately grabbed her right wrist and tried to push back, causing her to tilt and lean back. 43 subdued 999's right arm and put her into an elbow lock, preparing to throw her down once more. Thinking quickly, before she could be thrown, 999 leaped up and executed a backflip. Stunned, 43 couldn't maintain the hold as 999 flipped out of her grip and landed back on her feet.

999 took advantage of this surprise maneuver and swiftly turned so she was back-to-back with 43. Extending both arms behind her, she quickly wrapped her arms around 43's neckline, spun her around, pulled her head back, and bent forward. With a powerful heave, she lifted 43 and flipped her onto the ground. 117 stared in amazement as the tables were turned. As 43 struggled to get up after the impact, 999 raised her right leg high and brought her heel down on the back of 43's head. The moment her head hit the floor, 999 crouched down and began delivering a flurry of rapid punches.

43 managed to raise her hands and shield her head. In a swift move, she lunged forward and grabbed 999's ankles, causing her to fall on her side. As 43 got back on her feet, she straddled over 999 and unleashed her own series of punches. Despite being on the ground, 999 defended herself well against the onslaught. 43 attempted to grab her by the shoulders, but 999 skillfully evaded her grasp.

Furious, 43 seized 999's elbows and hoisted her up, only to drop her on the floor again. 999 kicked 43's left leg, causing her to kneel. She latched onto 43's right arm and wrapped her right leg around it to prevent any escape. With 43's arm locked in place, 999 jerked her foot up and kicked her in the face, disorienting and blinding her momentarily. She managed to break free from 999's hold and retaliated with a powerful kick to the ribs.

As 999 curled up into a fetal position, 43 stomped on her right side, pinning her arm underneath her shoe. She cried out in agony as she took damage. Without hesitation, 999 managed to slip her pinned arm around 43's ankle, curled up her leg, and kicked 43's left shin, causing her to fall into a split. She let out a shriek of pain, giving 999 the chance to slide out from under her shoe. 999 pushed herself up and punched 43 in the eye.

She suffered severe damage to her left temple, and she started to bleed. The two amborgs quickly backed away from each other. 999 struggled to stand up and attempted to raise her fists in a defensive position. Unfortunately, her right arm was trembling, making it difficult to keep it level with her left arm.

Across from her, 43 brought her hand up to her eye and felt the warm, sticky blood trickling from the wound in her head. She kept her other fist up and her good eye trained on 999.

"They're still going?!" 777 exclaimed.

"Shh!" 297 hushed him. "This is the best part!"

No one could really respond as they were all left speechless by how this fight was progressing. 999 and 43 began to attack each other again. Now that each of them had taken a significant amount of damage, their movements were slower, and their attacks suffered a loss of power. The two of them kept landing hit after hit, as it was now a fight to the finish. They were trying to see who would outlast the other. The only problem was, did one of them have to die in order to finish the duel?

43 and 999's punches weren't as effective as before, so they decided to switch things up and focus on throwing kicks instead. As they mirrored each other's movements, they concentrated on using their legs to try and gain the upper hand. In a last-ditch effort, they charged at each other and leaped into the air, aiming flying kicks at one another. The two combatants collided in midair, striking each other in the stomach. The impact sent them both crashing to the ground, where they lay motionless on their backs. Everyone watched in stunned silence as neither 999 nor 43 made a move to get up.

"They're alive right?" 501 asked, after a suspenseful moment.

They all got their answer ten seconds later when a loud beep echoed across the room and the announcement was made.

"Both combatants incapacitated. The duel has finished."

"Medic! On the floor! Now!" 117 yelled out across the room.

A few of the station medics who were observing the fight sprinted out to the floor to examine the two injured amborgs. From the look of it, they were in fact still alive, but now they needed to assess the damage.

"Well, the station hasn't blown up," 297 said, breathing a sigh of relief.

"Ok, that was awesome!"

Everyone turned and saw 6 hurry past them to join the medics.

"I got distracted watching the live video feed on the way here," she explained hastily. "Duty calls!"

117 was sure that 6 was more interested in examining 43's injuries. Being from a different universe, she probably wanted to see if there were any physical similarities or differences. Hopefully, she would prioritize 999 as well. He turned to look at Serina, who had kept quiet the entire fight.

"Are you ok? Serina?"

"I almost froze," she stammered. "If I still had a physical heart, it'd be beating like crazy."

He couldn't imagine what seeing that fight must have been like for her.

"It's nice to see that I still got it," Serina chuckled nervously. "But yikes, I don't think I want to see that ever again."

Everyone left the bleachers and strolled over to the center of the ring. They kept a certain distance at the request of the medical team, but tried to sneak glances whenever they could.

"Let me through! That's my best friend."

One of the medics had stopped 917 from entering the ring. She looked to 117, silently requesting confirmation. He immediately nodded, giving her the go-ahead. She stepped aside and allowed 917 to rush over to 999.

"It was a draw," 999 coughed. "She's good."

"So are you," he replied reassuringly. "Anything broken?"

"No," 999 muttered. "It hurts like hell."

117 and Serina decided to join the medical team taking care of Alpha 43.

"43?"

43 opened her eyes and glanced up at him and Serina.

"Hey," she groaned, giving them a faint smile.

"That was quite a fight," Serina muttered.

"Not gonna lie," 43 grinned and let out a laugh. "It's been so long since I felt an ass-kicking like that. I was about to get serious."

The sudden change in her mood began to concern them. Serina cautiously floated next to 43's head and hung over her. She gazed up at her small holographic form and focused.

"You sure sounded serious... Quite an emotional performance included too," she stated. "A little too emotional by our standards, if you want my honest opinion."

"I'll be fine," 43 replied softly as she tried to sit up. She eyed the two of them with concern. "If you still had doubts about me..."

"No," 117 replied. "I don't doubt you. Not anymore."

"And you?"

Upon hearing 117's response, 43 briefly smiled before turning her attention back to Serina. Serina's stoic expression didn't waver as she looked off to the side.

"I guess," she said. "I've just never heard myself yell like that before."

"Oh?"

"I overreacted one time a while back," Serina glanced at 117. "Once with 117's grandpa. But I never really screamed or cried like that before."

"Ok, I didn't cry," 43 smiled.

"Kinda felt you were about to."

Serina and 43 both chuckled. The medics saw that she was ok to stand, and they slowly helped her to her feet. 117 decided to go and check on 999 as 6 eagerly rushed to 43's side. He had to see if his second-in-command was still alright. He hoped that she was ok.

"How is she?" 117 asked.

He wasn't really speaking to anyone specifically. Anyone that was checking up on her could hopefully give him a straight answer.

"Sir," one of the medics stood up and addressed him. "She's got some bruises. Nothing broken. If she was a normal human, maybe, but so far, she's going to recover."

"If that's the case, I'd like to speak to all the amborgs present. When she's ready, I'd like Alice up on her feet. *Now.*"

117 immediately recognized the voice behind him without even needing to turn around. Chills rode up his spine. The medic that had addressed him glanced over 117's shoulder, his eyes widening in horror as he took a step back.

117 boldly turned around, along with many others. Dr. Kendrick stood there, his presence demanding immediate respect as a wave of silence fell over the room.

"Dr. Kendrick," 117 stated nervously. "We didn't see you."

"Well, if you want me to continue pausing for dramatic effect, then by all means, let me know when it's convenient to have this discussion," he said, glaring at everyone.

"I can explain," 43 spoke up.

"No," Dr. Kendrick said sharply.

"Ok then," 43 lowered her head and quickly shut her mouth.

917 began to help 999 to her feet. When she realized that Dr. Kendrick was in the room, she hastily asked him to pull her up. Dr. Kendrick looked directly at her once she stood up.

"Are you alright?" he asked politely with a look of indifference.

"Yes doctor," 999 replied.

"Then go to the medical bay," Dr. Kendrick replied with a firm nod of his head. "You and 43. Vanessa, please treat them immediately."

"You got it," 6 replied with a smile. It quickly faded when she noticed that he wasn't smiling back. "Let's clear out!"

6 led the medics away from Dr. Kendrick's stern, watchful gaze, with 999 and 43 following closely behind. Right before they stepped through the door, he called out to the two of them.

"Keep this in mind," he declared as they walked past him. "I don't care what universe you're from, but you're aboard my station right now. You will follow my commands while you are on my property and you will not, under any circumstances, not... risk all our lives in the middle of outer space."

43 and 999 both dipped their heads quietly and left the room. Dr. Kendrick began to describe his perspective prior to his arrival.

"I was wrapping up a nice conversation with the entire U.N. security council about our activities out here. Pretty big presentation, I might add. Then, less than a minute after I step out of that private meeting, I see a bulletin all over the station feed of a deadlock duel. Naturally, I was absolutely shocked and then furious to see that the two participants also happened to be two very important people that we can't exactly have attempting to murder each other."

Dr. Kendrick gazed at all of the amborgs present, looking extremely displeased. It was probably incredibly stressful maintaining global diplomacy while also having to deal with the fact that two of the strongest human beings decided to mess around. If it wasn't for the fact that they were aboard his space station, then he'd probably be more lenient. Even though he had arrived right after it ended, he didn't hide his disappointment.

"What were you thinking?" he asked in a grim tone.

He looked at 117, who immediately stepped forward.

"I take responsibility," 117 dipped his head apologetically.

"I didn't ask you that," Dr. Kendrick snapped. "What were you thinking prior to or when this duel was enacted?"

"I was hoping to go back to calmly asking Alpha 43 some more questions," 117 explained. "But 999 decided to initiate the challenge."

"She insisted," Serina replied. "She used a rather direct way of figuring out Alpha 43's motives."

"Couldn't you avoid a physical confrontation?" he asked, glancing at everyone else. "Anyone? Are you telling me that she challenged her to a fight simply because she wanted information or an excuse to satisfy her own personal vendetta?"

"It wasn't a vendetta," 917 replied. "She told me while she was on the floor."

Everyone turned to look at 917.

"Angel said that she wanted to know how powerful the Alpha universe was," he said. "While we still had time, she wanted to see how strong 43 was. She can explain whatever she needs us to know. But even if we accepted her statements, we still don't know anything about her universe. The only thing that she was worried about was whether or not we could be ready against an invasion. So, the deadlock was a way to sample the kind of power we could expect."

Now it made sense to 117. He nodded to 917, indicating that he wanted to add something.

"999 was worried about the fact that my Alpha version and most of our other versions are also dead," he turned to say to Dr. Kendrick.

Dr. Kendrick looked slightly taken aback.

"43 didn't mention this..."

"Well, it's understandable," 117 shrugged. "If the war in Alpha universe is capable of killing us, the strongest people alive, then we really need to work on our weaknesses and focus on our strengths."

"She wanted that duel because she wanted to show us how bad it is over there?" Serina asked skeptically.

"43 moved, fought, and stood on equal footing with Angel," 917 replied. "We might need to step up our training if we're going to be facing the biggest fight of our lives soon."

Dr. Kendrick let out a sigh.

"Alright," he said. "Send me the footage of the duel. I didn't get a chance to see it. I suppose reviewing it might highlight some important details of the Alpha universe. The rest of you go back to your duties. 117, Serina, you go back to the medical bay and check on Alice and 43. If her theory and what you're all saying is true, then I really hope that you're right."

Everyone left the room and went their separate ways. As they said a quick goodbye to the others, 117 walked with Serina back to the med-bay.

"Does she look like she could go berserk?"

117 looked at Serina. Unfortunately, he had no idea who she was specifically asking about.

"Who?"

"Me? Alpha 43?"

Serina was probably referring to the outburst that they had witnessed 43 display during the deadlock.

"I've never screamed that loud before," Serina shuddered as her holographic form fizzed a little. "It felt like I wasn't looking at an Alpha version of me. It genuinely felt like listening to a woman who had lost everything."

"I know that feeling," 117 replied. "It was the same for me the day I lost you. It was on my mind for a long time ever since you were killed."

Memories of when she had been struck by a knife ten years ago flooded back in his mind. Seeing a blade pierce deep in her chest was traumatizing for all of them. It didn't help that Serina was beyond saving.

"I mean," 117 shrugged, "losing Audrey or any other members of my family would probably be the end of my world."

"Losing you already broke her heart," Serina mumbled. "I can't exactly say I don't feel the same as she does."

"Well," 117 tried to be encouraging. "I'm glad in this universe, you made it. With just a minor physical difference."

"Excuse you," Serina sputtered and began to laugh. "I call it the best upgrade of my life."

When they reached the med-bay, the entire staff on duty were abuzz. Everyone was talking about what they had just seen on the live feed of the fight. 117 and Serina made their way over to where 43 and 999 were resting. Both their beds were placed next to each other. A few Space-Jumpers were standing guard and they perked up as soon as they noticed 117 approaching.

"At ease," he said, and they all fell into parade rest. "What's with the marines?"

"The whole time we were heading here, a handful of staff members grilled us with questions like paparazzi," 6 answered as she spread lotion on 43's eye.

"Ow!" 43 cried.

"Oh, calm down," 6 replied. "This isn't the worst thing ever."

"Yes, it is," 999 muttered. "Your experimental ointments have a tendency to burn."

"They do not! They are cleared by the medical board."

6 pouted as 117 and Serina shared a nervous glance.

"Anyway," 6 sighed as she set the ointment down. "Did Dr. Kendrick chew you out?"

"I don't know," 117 shrugged as he glanced at Serina.

"His speech patterns were full of disappointment, but he seemed pretty understanding after talking to us," she said. Then she gestured at 43 and 999. "I think that these two not destroying the station also made him feel better.

"That's for sure," 6 laughed.

"Since we're supposed to watch you," 117 sighed. "I think he'll be here shortly. He may want an explanation."

"43 is strong," 999 looked at Serina. "Her Alpha version is just like her. I sparred and trained with her for many years. I apologize."

43 looked at 999, whose eyes were downcast.

"I'm sorry for riling you up and pushing," she said. "It wasn't me trying to see how strong you were. I wanted to feel your full emotions about this war that's coming to our universe. We've survived a few conflicts, but what you've described to us is quite terrifying."

117 and Serina shared another look. They were amazed to hear 999 opening up like this.

"I don't want to lose my friends either," 999 muttered as she looked 43 in the eye. "But I kept doubting you because I couldn't believe this was happening. When you hit me, hurting me back, I felt the real you. I don't know how else to describe it."

"Watching the fight opened all of our eyes," 117 said. "I think 999 was trying to prove to us that we needed to step it up and get to your level. Otherwise, my Alpha's death would have been in vain."

"I'm sorry too," 43 smiled. "But truthfully? Before we get scolded by Dr. Kendrick, I just wanted to say, it was a really good fight. Seeing everyone training and getting ready gives me hope. Coming to the Epsilon universe and seeing all of you alive... is the chance I always wished for. The chance to make sure I'm here to protect you all this time."

999 waved her hand at 43.

"I'd shake hands," she mumbled without batting a smile, "but you did step on my arm."

"I'll let it slide this time," 43 let out a laugh.

"So," 6 eyed everyone with a cheeky smile. "Out of curiosity, the duel ended in a draw. I'll just come out and ask you both directly. Who would have won if you had kept going?"

999 and 43 immediately perked up.

"Me," they both declared simultaneously.

"Yeah," Serina let out a giggle. "That definitely brings back some fun memories."

Chapter 14: "What am I supposed to do?"

LAPD SWAT HQ
Emergency Recall plus 3 Days 2 hours 3 minutes
11:31 AM Pacific Time

"Listen up! I need everyone's attention!"

Every officer gathered around a massive table in the middle of the operations room of the command center. A few had come in casual attire, but most were in full uniform. It wasn't a regular occurrence for them all to mobilize, but when it was an emergency, they knew the drill.

Commander Bradley walked over to the center of the table and addressed her personnel.

"I'm glad you were all able to make it here!" She spoke loudly, securing a small microphone to her collar and linking up to the PA system. "As you can imagine, we are on high alert."

The amborgs had their own problems to deal with, meaning they had much higher priorities. The police and military had to help as much as they could.

"I understand that many of you got called away from your families or have already been here for your shifts," Bradley declared sympathetically. "So, as always, if you need to go back to them, your loved ones, I won't hold it against you. Go home, no problems. If you come back, great, if not, just be safe. But if you're all going to stay here, I need your help. Now more than ever. The city needs us at our best."

A few officers politely raised their hands and stepped out of the crowd. Bradley acknowledged them and watched them exit the room. For the majority that remained, she nodded as she continued the briefing.

"I've been getting calls from almost every single office belonging to the Feds," she said. "We've confirmed with A.I. Industries and the White House. We have a pending alien invasion possibly on our doorstep."

Everyone started murmuring, but Bradley continued to speak over them to ensure they caught every word she'd scraped together. If they fell out of line, then it would absolutely be devastating for morale.

"Keep it together!" she yelled. "You're all officers, for crying out loud! The point is, we need to get out there on the streets and help however we can. Ever since the President made that announcement, people are panicking! Crime sprees are on the rise! We need to get ready for a lot of disorganized chaos. If there's one thing that thugs and criminals love, it's the opportunities that pop up when we have global catastrophes on the way!"

Bradley surveyed each of her squad leaders and best sergeants. She needed to count on them to be strong and inspire the rest.

"We need to protect the city. Now, whether or not this whole invasion announcement is real, the people are panicking. Anyone with a badge needs to get out there now. First priority, help the other divisions secure sensitive targets and then protect the community. Ignore petty crimes, focus on people, not property."

"Commander? Are we going to get backup from the amborgs? The last time we had a big emergency like this..."

"It'll be exactly like the last time we mobilized," Bradley replied. "Don't count on them to help. They've got bigger problems, so we're going to handle what they don't have time for."

Bradley glared at everyone.

"Look, I know you're scared. So am I! But if any of you feel like calling those glorified tin heads for help, forget it! It's no longer their job to babysit you kids! They're in the major leagues whenever an emergency affects the entire planet. We handle what's left! You're SWAT. The best in my command. The people count on us. So, get out there, help where you can, and continue acting like the world isn't going to end. Maintaining public order is society's top priority and our best chance at saving lives. Stay safe!"

As everybody dispersed, Bradley made her way back to her office. Once she arrived, she saw someone sitting in one of the lounge chairs.

"Captain! It's good to see you!"

Bradley cringed when she recognized the voice. She let out a sigh and marched around her desk to face the man, who sprung to his feet.

"Harrison," she sighed. "I could have sworn you were retired. Last I saw you."

Harrison smiled as he held out both of his arms. Bradley shook her head, declining the invitation for a hug.

"I figured you'd enjoy seeing a friendly face," he said, lowering his arms.

"For once, you're right."

"Whoa," Harrison looked stunned as he smiled brightly. "Did you just admit that I was right? I've been on the force for 50 years!"

"Stow it," Bradley snapped, glaring at Harrison.

"50!" Harrison enunciated. "Fif-teeee... and I'm finally being told I'm right... from my old boss?! The one person who always had a huge stick up her..."

Commander Bradley drew her sidearm and placed it on her steel desk. It made a loud clang, causing Harrison to chuckle as he stopped himself from finishing his statement. As an extra precaution, he held up his hands.

"That's more like it," Commander Bradley said, retrieving her weapon and holstering it. "You've certainly allowed retirement to make you more candid with your words."

"Part of the reason I thought you kept me around in your division was because of my charm."

"Shut it. I also didn't say that now was a good time for visitors."

Harrison held up a thumb and pointed over his shoulder at the door to her office.

"So I've been told," he smiled.

Bradley gazed at Harrison suspiciously. Then she groaned, realizing why he was probably here.

"No," she declared.

"You haven't even heard me say anything."

"No," she repeated.

"Come on Commander Bradley," Harrison stood his ground defiantly. "I've been retired for a week and then all of sudden, we got an announcement that an alien invasion is potentially happening? You need every hand on deck for this! I still have a badge to protect and serve this city!"

"I retired you because you've done enough for our city and the LAPD," Bradley replied in a strict but sympathetic tone. "You should be at home with your family."

"I know I can still be of some use to you," Harrison replied. "If you let me help you out, then this will be the last thing I do for you."

"You can't join SWAT," Bradley answered. "You handed in your retirement notice, cashed on your pension, and you were officially out."

She maintained a stern gaze on him as he continued to plead with his eyes.

Harrison was one of the few veterans back when they were still on patrol. After she had been promoted as the commander of SWAT, he had stayed at their old station as a training officer for all new recruits. Things went well as mortality rates dropped and things in the city improved. Several months ago, Harrison had hit her with the news. He'd put in his notice and was planning his retirement. His final end-of-watch shift had symbolized a heroic 50 years on the job and they had all said their farewells a few days ago.

"That was then," Harrison argued. "Now, the world is at risk."

Bradley wasn't so pleased about this. She was annoyed that Harrison was back, trying to undo one of the biggest moments of his life.

"I can't un-retire you," she sighed. "This isn't how it works! Even if I wanted you back, what happens if you get killed?"

"Retirement is killing me. If you're short-handed, send me back to the central station," Harrison spoke insistently. "I can still do a great deal of work instead of lounging back at home. Let me help supervise back there. Lewis and the other youngsters could use the help running things."

"What about your family?" Bradley asked.

"They'll be fine," Harrison nodded enthusiastically. He then glanced to the side and thought carefully. "At least, I think they will. My kids are more into this crazy futuristic science phenomena than I am, but they'll know what to do if things go wrong."

"You're no longer a police officer," Bradley sighed. "This is only a visit."

She grabbed a datapad off her desk and booted it up. Once the screen was active, she scrolled through her files.

"You understand that because you're no longer an employee, I can't re-hire you?"

"Yes," Harrison replied.

There was one option that she could technically approve. However, everything that the old man had to do would have to be off the books.

"You can only act as a consultant and volunteer your time?"

"Yes, ma'am."

"Well then," Bradley sighed as she swiped upwards on her pad. "I suppose with my recommendation, I'm appointing you as my liaison to the central division. They know you're on the way."

"Thanks commander! Want me to say hi to Lewis for you?"

"Make sure he doesn't do anything stupid," Bradley grumbled.

"I can't promise that."

Harrison dipped his head and gave her a big grin as he turned to exit her office. She let out a sigh.

"I hope you know what you're doing," she grumbled. "I better not regret this."

After Harrison left, Bradley closed her office door and grabbed her phone. She went through her contacts and dialed the number to reach Mark. He picked up right away and his face appeared on her computer screen.

"Marsha!" he said cheerfully. "It's good to see you!"

"Ok, moving on from that," she snapped. She was getting tired of people saying how nice it was to see her. "Any latest intel?"

"I'm afraid not," Mark replied. "My contacts in Europe are still looking for leads. Wasn't the FBI supposed to take over when you reported the cargo ship to your superiors?"

"Whoever set up that entire operation probably already has countermeasures in place for that," Bradley muttered.

After 777 and Mark discovered the orphans and victims at the docks, the FBI swooped in and practically took over the investigation, since it had been deemed an act of terrorism to murder a large group of civilians. The motive was unclear and the gang members in custody had kept their mouths shut. The police and SWAT were sidelined until they were asked by federal agents to assist with any leads local to Los Angeles. There was something quite sinister at work and it was being camouflaged by the whole outer space drama that had monopolized the world's attention.

"Whoever is running this has to be smart enough to know how we're going to respond," Bradley guessed. She pondered her thoughts and brought her fist up to her chin. "They'll know every move we make and when the FBI task force moves in, they could be gone before we find any shred of evidence."

"Or it could be an ambush," Mark said. "Maybe they left the cargo ship for us to find so that they'll try to have us eliminated at the next engagement."

Commander Bradley paused, squinting her eyes, then glanced at Mark on the screen. He chuckled at her reaction.

"What?" he said. "I didn't think of that, my grandson and his friends did."

"That makes more sense," Bradley nodded cautiously to him. "But based on that, it means that they know we're coming after them. Do you think you'd be able to find out how to shut this enemy operation down before I lose officers or any FBI agents get ambushed?"

"Are you unofficially asking me to take the lead on this particular mission?"

Bradley leaned on her desk, looked down, and exhaled. She wanted to lash out at him like usual but, under their current circumstances, she didn't have a choice. Every high priority task needed someone to oversee it and she was tied down due to conflicting jurisdiction.

"Yes, I am," she said. "Los Angeles, along with every single town and city, is getting flooded with chaos. I don't have the manpower to finish what we started at the docks."

"Well, I thank you for asking me so nicely," Mark replied. "I can also exchange a few favors with A.I. Industries and see if there are any consultants available to back me up."

"Just be careful," Bradley nodded. "I owe you a bottle of whiskey if we get through this."

"I will collect on that," Mark nodded as he pulled his hood up. "*When* we get through this."

The call ended, and the screen on her desk switched off. Bradley picked up another data pad containing the emergency protocol guidelines. She had to distribute them to the rest of the captains and division leaders across the city. They were all going to need as much support as they could get.

■■■

Apogee Station
Vanessa 6's quarters

"Authorizing amborg meditation program. Please confirm passcodes and access personal memory banks. I need a refresher."

Her quarters were almost identical to the room she had at A.I. Industries, except this one undeniably had a much better view.

6 was kneeling on a mat on the floor. Surrounded by candles and other objects that represented relaxation from her travels, she took a deep breath and accessed her memory files. She closed her eyes and began to remember.

The procedure to access personal memories was very easy. Usually, an amborg could bring up something forgotten instantaneously and recall it word for word as if it had never disappeared into the maze of their long term memory. 6's technique was a slightly modified version. A lot of science-fiction and classic pop culture films often depicted scenes where characters could access and replay their memories. She had created a new interactive version to watch them like a home movie. In this case, she was able to act as a non participating third party as the sessions played. The sensation of being your own ghost had proven effective for several counseling sessions from previous patients.

"Go to October 17th of 2132 please," she stated.

As the selected memory began to play, she closed and then reopened her eyes.

There was no written title for the memory of this particular day. In place of where it should be, it simply stated the location of where she had been and the date. A time stamp icon appeared and she stated her next request.

"1:23 PM please," she said.

The time index fast-forwarded to where she had requested.

"2132 October: A.I. Industries Medical Bay" floated in front of her eyes before fading. 6 nodded confidently and played the memory.

As the surrounding environment came into focus, she soon found herself standing in the medical facility back home on Earth. It was remarkable to see how the place looked in the past. Then, she grimaced slightly. It looked a lot messier than she remembered.

"Ah yes," she said as she looked around excitedly. "This was after I returned from 'Doctors Without Borders' in the Middle East. I remember now."

The sound of a book closing made her turn towards the desk. In front of her sat her younger self, Vanessa 6 of the past, who was sifting through a stack of books.

"Wow," 6 leaned forward and stared. "No offense but methinks that my hair looks better now than it did before…"

The other 6 didn't respond, which was to be expected. This was only a memory. Her current self couldn't be seen or heard. Just to humor herself, 6 smirked and hopped up and down like a bunny. She laughed when her younger self went about her business, completely oblivious to the silliness ensuing invisibly in front of her.

All of a sudden, the door burst open and a wave of chaos rolled in. 95, 501, 5, 92 and 93 practically flew in and crashed onto the floor of the sickbay. The younger 6, slightly startled, stood and walked around her desk to see what the fuss was about. 6 watched and followed herself. Now she remembered why there was always some kind of mess.

"What are you all doing?" 6 of the past spoke to the small crowd of amborgs.

"Was my voice always that pitchy??" 6 commented as she gazed at herself.

She was ignored as the two of them stared at the amborgs struggling to get back up.

"Don't look at me, it's not my fault," 5 replied as he untangled himself. "I was on my way here to have a routine maintenance check for my leg when these pranksters thought it'd be funny to steal my leg. I'm not kidding 501! 95! Give it back!"

"Come now Johnny," 92 smirked. "It may have been carried out by our dear younger brothers..."

"...but we were the masterminds," 93 finished with a laugh.

"Hence, that's why I'm killing all of you right now."

"But 5," 501 replied innocently. "We only wanted to see you hopping around without it."

"Yeah it's really hilarious," 95 snickered. "It makes for good times. We got a lot of it on video, too."

"I'll show you a good time..." 5 snarled as he rolled and put 92 in a chokehold. "When you're all dead! That leg is a gift from Dr. Kendrick, our dear old father. Anyone who steals it will pay!"

"Boys! Hey! Quiet! Can't a girl get a word in?"

All of them turned and looked up at 6.

"You tell them girl," 6 said encouragingly to her younger self.

"If you boys are through trashing the place," the younger 6 said sternly, "I have a patient. OUT!"

Everyone except 5 scrambled to their feet and ran off laughing like a group of miscreants. It was odd to see amborgs not behaving their age. It was even rarer to see 5 not being humorous and carefree about it.

"Thanks 6," he sighed as he grabbed his leg and tried to sit up.

"My goodness," 6 knelt down and picked him up. "Come on. Into the bed."

"Oh you're so forceful," 5 smiled as she carried him bridal style. "Please be gentle with me."

This comment, however, prompted her to drop him. He fell with a loud plunk onto the mattress. 6 turned on her heel and went to go pick up his leg.

"I thought doctors took the Hippocratic oath..." 5 grumbled in pain as she pulled a cart next to his bed and propped his leg onto it. "You could be a little nicer."

"It doesn't apply to family members who are stupid," 6 said as she grabbed a screwdriver and began opening compartments. "I have to make this fast. I'm seeing 117 and Serina in a moment."

"Ooh a quickie then?" 5 eyed her seductively with a very bad smolder. "Before your threesome with another amborg and an A.I.?"

"Do you ever stop?" 6 said without batting a smile. "I liked you when you were serious. However short a time that was. If you want to be a test subject for the new settings on the restraining straps, you are more than welcome to be strangled."

"I'm sorry, I can't seem to stop thinking up funny comments to everything you're saying," 5 chuckled as he raised his hands behind his head and leaned back.

"Then don't say it."

"Ok. You like serious?" 5 sat up and leaned towards her. "Will you marry me?"

6 turned and gave him a blank stare. Seconds later, she smirked and began to laugh.

"Now that's funny," she snorted as 5's face recovered from the rejection.

"Oh come on," he said with a hopeful smile. "At least have a dinner date with me. Like that time we went out."

"We weren't going out... that was an amborg party, which was a terrible decision. Why should I go out with you? I don't see you being serious enough to properly share a meal with."

"Look, I'll prove it," 5 said seriously. "You know how I don't let anyone else but you do maintenance on my leg? Well, I let you help me out, even when I don't really need it, because I want to find time to be alone with you. Would you consider that to be a little romantic?"

"Why are you completely ignoring the fact that 917 also has a prosthetic limb? He would have the knowledge to fix your leg, too."

Older 6 raised an eyebrow in disbelief at what she was hearing. She watched on with a smirk. She was enjoying the show way more than her past self was.

"I wish I had popcorn for this," she muttered as she watched herself look into 5's eyes. "Because I've forgotten how hilarious this was."

"Come on," 5 said. "I'm being serious now and I'm legitimately making a pass at you. What do you do, oh great doctor?"

"I have a patient coming any minute," 6 replied firmly. "Can't we just talk about this another..."

"That's more than enough time for me to..."

"Johnny," 6 suddenly declared, cutting him off. She waved a finger sharply in his face. "One more word out of you and I activate the restraints."

"What?"

"That's a word."

6 began to cackle as her past-self hit a button on the console next to 5's bed. The mechanical bed's harnesses snapped into place, wrapping around his waist, arms, leg, and his neck. A metal arm with a mouth guard appeared and instantly shut him up. His eyes were filled with surprise as he found himself completely immobilized.

"Crap," 5's voice said dejectedly from his bracelet.

"Umm, we can come back later."

Everyone looked towards the entrance of the medical bay to see 117 standing there with a wide-eyed expression. On his shoulder sat Serina with an equally stunned look.

"Y-yeah," the little blue A.I. stammered. "I think they need some privacy. How about locking the door next time? You know... if you're planning to do that?"

"It's really not what it looks like," 6 replied calmly.

5's eyes said it all as he groaned. It looked like he wanted to evaporate on the spot as 6 casually turned back to his leg. The real 6 was practically about to roll onto the floor laughing.

"Yeah, this ain't exactly the most comfortable hospital bed I've been in," his bracelet lit up as he transmitted on an open frequency. "If it was what it looked like, I'd be much happier."

"Shut up," 6 said. "What did you two want to talk about?"

"Dr. Kendrick got an urgent message. The weather station from Brazil sent a transmission," Serina replied. "It looks like they'll have a category eight hurricane hitting from the east within four days."

"What?" 6 looked alarmed.

5 listened silently, his eyes showing the same level of alertness. He glanced at everyone in the room.

"Their last report stated that they were expecting it to die down," his brace-let flashed. Even though his robotic tone was apparent, they could hear a faint sign of emotional distress. "It's increasing?"

"Exponentially," Serina nodded.

6 and 5 exchanged silent glances. She hit the button next to the side of the bed and the restraints unlocked.

"He's going to enact another Emergency Recall?" 6 asked.

"He wanted to let all amborgs on site know first," 117 replied.

"That's a good idea," 6 muttered. "Gives us time to plan it out. What do you need me to do?"

Serina changed from blue to a bright green color.

"All amborgs will be called in for immediate deployment. We need our best doctor with us, but that also means we have to reschedule our session."

6 chuckled as she quickly examined 5's leg. She handed him an electric screwdriver, quietly asking him for assistance. He complied and helped her get to work on fine tuning his leg.

"I think the more accurate question is what do you need us to do?"

"We need triage zones," 6 answered. "A lot of them. Safely across South America and well out of the areas that will be hit. I need to reach out to every hospital, every charity organization, and alert all medical stockpiles. 117, can you let me borrow 501 and 406? Serina? Could you help me contact the amborgs with most medical experience? I need a team to help me."

117 and Serina both nodded.

"6, we need you to help oversee a medical base being temporarily established," 117 said. "Will you do it? We know you just got back."

"Of course I will," 6 nodded. "The best place for us all to be is right there. Here 5, I'm done with the leg."

5 and 6 finished the checkup and set their tools down. She handled his leg delicately and he allowed her to place it in both of his hands. He grinned cheekily at her.

"Help me put it on?"

"Not falling for that," 6 scoffed. She looked at 117. "What about everyone off site? There's a lot of us incognito, right?"

"4 is getting ready to handle the arrangements," 117 nodded. "But we're down to half strength."

"Well, Dr. Kendrick needs to hit that red button asap," 6's eyes widened. "We can't fight the aftermath of a hurricane with a handful of amborgs."

"Even at full strength," 5 said, stretching his legs and hopping a few times in place. "Four groups of amborgs are going to be spread thin."

"Then we can't waste another second," 6 replied.

The four of them turned to exit the medical wing while the older 6 watched them go. When the door opened, they saw another person standing in the doorway.

"Oh," 117 stopped. "345!"

"Amara!" Serina said excitedly with a smile.

The older 6 perked up and looked towards the doorway. She had forgotten about bumping into the Third Group amborg here. She leaned to the side and watched her younger self, 5, 117 and Serina interact with her.

"Hey!" 345 said cheerfully. Her long silky brown hair flowed with her movements. "I was wondering if I could ask 6 about something? Is now a bad time?"

"Actually," 6 sighed, "it is. But if you can walk and talk, that's good. Is it personal?"

"No," 345 replied.

"Then walk and talk it is," 6 commanded. "Let's get to work! I need a full inventory count and we got to get it ready before the emergency recall! I need two teams...!"

6 didn't follow her younger self. Instead, she folded her arms and then some words appeared in front of her face. It was a warning sign that stated that the primary subject of her memory had left. Which meant that unless she followed, there was no reason for her to hang around. 6 sighed and ended her trip down memory lane. As the scene around her disintegrated, she blinked and saw her quarters aboard the Apogee Station fade into view.

As 6 stood up, she closed her eyes, took a few deep breaths, and allowed her perception to return to the present reality. Once she opened her eyes, she was alone again.

"Brazil," she muttered, feeling thirsty. She went to get a cup of water. "Even as amborgs, we still failed."

Before she grabbed a plastic cup from her cupboard, she suddenly realized something.

During her little memory trip, something had caught her eye. She turned on her phone and placed a call, linking it up to a private channel in her head. There was one amborg in particular who would be able to answer the questions forming in her mind.

"Contact 501," she stated.

A chime at the door snagged her attention. Right as 501 answered the call, 6 found herself torn between what to respond to.

"Hello?" he asked. "Hi 6! Everything ok?"

"Y-yeah!" 6 stammered. "Just a second!"

6 walked towards the door and paused.

"Who is it?" she asked loudly.

His confused voice mistakenly answered her.

"It's 501?"

"Not you!" 6 said hastily. "Give me a second!"

"You said one second... and now it's been two?"

501 had waited a literal second. It was adorable and funny, but bad timing. Slightly annoyed, 6 was about to respond when she heard someone faintly speak on the other side of her door.

"It's me."

That didn't help at all. 6, unfortunately, had no idea who it was. The voice was too faint and she couldn't tell if it was a man, woman, or a drone outside. She ruled out it being a drone since they usually answered who they were upfront. Letting her curiosity get the better of her, 6 opened the door with 501 still on the line. Once her door slid open, she was face to face with 999.

"Oh!"

999 stared silently as the two of them stood awkwardly looking at each other. 501's voice in her head got her attention.

"Hello?" he asked.

"Call-you-back," 6 said quickly, placing her hand up to the side of her head and disconnected the call. She casually smiled at 999. "Hey! Angel! Good to see you!"

999 tilted her head skeptically and didn't say anything.

"Come on in," 6 stood aside and welcomingly gestured for her to step inside.

"Busy?" 999 asked.

"I was just finishing some stuff," 6 replied. "So what's up?"

"Are you talking about up or down in outer space?" 999 asked. "Or are you asking how I am?"

6 let out a sigh. Ever since she had become 999's mentor, this was how their conversations would typically go.

"Well, you thought I was making a joke before I did, so specifically, I'm asking how you are," she replied.

"Then I am not fine," 999 nodded, responding bluntly. "I am requesting a counseling session."

6 lowered her gaze. She felt like she needed to do another memory replay of the last ten seconds to make sure she had heard correctly. When she saw that 999 was serious and not messing with her, she spoke again.

"You? Requesting a session?"

6 was stunned that 999 had actually said it. The only times that she had participated in any form of counseling or attended her appointments was if she had been instructed to do so. It was rare to hear her take the initiative.

"You've never requested one before," 6 felt intrigued.

"Is it that strange?" 999 looked slightly hurt.

"No! Not at all," 6 said as she motioned for her to have a seat. "Sit down and relax! Why don't you tell me what's on your mind?"

"I think I'm on the verge of a mental breakdown," 999 admitted as she sat down.

"Ok, look," 6 said. "You had a very intense deadlock. Once I listened to the way that 43 was screaming and yelling throughout that entire thing, it felt like a huge vent session for some unspoken issues. Why don't you get some more rest and in about an hour, I can evaluate you and clear you for duty? Take you off the injured list?"

"I don't want that," 999 replied.

6 continued to tilt her head and scanned 999's neutral expression. There was definitely something bothering her underneath her cold and almost lifeless exterior. One reason why 6 had requested to be her mentor so many years ago was because her personality was extraordinarily unique.

"Do you want to use your actual voice?" 6 asked.

999 shook her head. Her mouth remained shut, and her voice kept projecting from her bracelet.

"I'd rather speak to you nonverbally."

999 wanted to text her thoughts to 6 privately. Unfortunately, this didn't seem like a proper way to deal with whatever was making her anxious.

"A lot more will be taken off your shoulders if you let out your actual emotions with your speaking voice," 6 refused the invite to the private channel, shaking her head firmly. "I want you to speak freely about whatever is bothering you. Now, why do you think that you're about to have a breakdown? Do you suspect a burst dam?"

"I feel as if everything I do," 999 said as she fidgeted with her hands, "everything is about to explode. I've been trying to rest, and I've been trying to de-stress. What should I do?"

"First, breathe. Deep breaths. Well, I'd say that maybe a nice session in the simulator might be a good..."

"Already done."

"Ok then... what about taking a nap?"

"Done."

"Well, I can only assume it's one other problem that's weighing down on you."

6 grabbed a pitcher of water, poured a cup, and brought it over to 999. She grabbed it politely and took a sip. 6 poured herself some water, too as she eyed her carefully.

"You've kept your emotions bottled for too long," 6 stated her diagnosis. "Longer than any amborg that I've ever seen. It's not good, Angel."

"But there are others who have also managed to avoid a burst dam for the same time period," 999 replied.

In 6's mind, she almost wanted to be tragically honest with her. Instead, she kept some of her thoughts private.

Technically, she was correct, but those other amborgs were born with unsuppressed personalities. It wasn't that 999 didn't have one, it was the fact that she had everything about her past concealed.

With her normal emotions also locked away after cybernetic enhancement, the lone wolf attitude made her look cold in the eyes of the public and the other amborgs. Unfortunately, 999 never properly learned how to express herself. Everything she felt and all of her thoughts were kept under wraps, and she was most likely feeling this way because those feelings wanted out... and they didn't want to come out the peaceful way. One trigger and 999 would violently lash out with everything she had contained. Since she was still in control, 6 was concerned if this mission would prove too much for her.

"You're unique," 6 stated. "Just because it hasn't happened for some people doesn't mean that you'll manage to avoid the matter entirely. I did have one question that suddenly popped up."

"What is it?"

"Why did you agree to be 117's partner when you knew that you were struggling?" 6 asked politely. "It seems quite risky to put yourself in a leadership role if you're also dealing with your mental health issues."

"117 and Serina asked me to."

"I am aware of that," 6 sighed. "But why did you agree? That's my question. That's what they wanted you to do. My question is why say yes to them in the first place? You could have just passed it on to someone else and they would have respected your choices."

"I want him to see me. For the longest time, all I've ever wanted was for him to see me again."

6 paused as she looked at 999. One look and she was instantly able to decipher what she was saying. Angel was thinking of her best friend.

"Again," 6 crossed her arms, "you don't need to push yourself this hard. You don't need to elevate yourself on this pedestal that you've built in your mind. 917 has always looked at you the same way he always has."

999 got up and took a seat in one of her chairs, setting her cup on the table. 6 joined her and grabbed one of the other seats.

"He cares about you a lot and he has always seen you as his best friend," 6 smiled. "You have never needed to change yourself or do anything outlandish to know how he feels."

"That's not completely true," 999 replied. Suddenly, she looked up and saw that 6 had her hand outstretched, like she was about to put it over her face. "What are you doing? Are you scanning me?"

"Yeah, I'm checking your brain activity," 6 nodded. "I needed to see how you were doing since we left Earth and... oh God!"

6's eyes widened as she withdrew her hand. 999 had no change in her expression and continued to sit still. The scan was going off the charts, according to her readings. Alarmed, 6 transferred the data she had acquired onto a datapad that was sitting on the table. She picked it up and looked at it carefully.

"I feel fine," 999 replied calmly.

"First, you and I both know that is not true at all," 6 said with an incredulous look. "Because second, these readings are higher than your last check-up! One deadlock caused this?! Or is it because we're in simulated gravity?"

999 didn't have a response.

"These results are just above mentally stable but I could still put you on medical leave," 6 explained as she turned the data pad for her to see. "What is wrong?"

"What's it like? Carrying secrets about us?"

"You mean doctor-patient confidentiality?" 6 asked, shrugging casually. "It's like when someone tells their sins to a priest in one of those confessional booths. I can't repeat anything you tell me."

"Does knowing all of our secrets cause any moral dilemmas?" 999 asked.

"I'm not sure I enjoy where you're going with this," 6 said suspiciously. "Mind if I turn up the lights in my room?"

999 rolled her eyes, but nodded her head. 6 eagerly transmitted a command to her light switch. The lighting in her room increased, and they were able to see each other a bit more clearly.

"I don't have anything that bad to share," 999 grumbled.

"Oh, I believe you," 6 said confidently. "I just felt like making my room a little brighter... cheerier... and safer."

"I interrupted a phone call when I knocked, didn't I?"

"Oh," 6 waved it off like it wasn't important. "I was just in the middle of talking to 501."

"He once made me a promise," 999 said, a faint smile forming on her face.

"Oh yeah?" 6 asked as she leaned forward intently.

"After 345 passed away, he promised us he'd be there for us no matter what."

"That's nice of him," 6 grinned. "He's always been keeping an eye on you. I imagine it's because he looks up to the Second Group a lot."

"It's my fault she's dead."

6's smile faded. Her cheerful and calm expression was replaced with immediate dismay.

"No!" she burst out unexpectedly. "How could you say that? Why would you...? No. Don't say that like I wasn't there. Because I was there and you couldn't have known what would happen."

"She was my responsibility," 999 said, glancing down.

"We were all equally responsible for taking care of her," 6 sighed. "Do you know what I was doing before you knocked on my door?"

999 looked at 6 blankly, which was her cue to keep talking.

"I was looking at old memories," 6 replied softly. "I looked at all of the past Emergency Recalls we were summoned back home for. All three of them. Remember the third one?"

"I can't forget it," 999 shuddered.

"Brazil," 6 nodded grimly. "You realize that we were unprepared for that, right? But despite the odds, 345 did her job. You did too. We all had to make our choices then."

"We were supposed to stay together," 999 replied. "Then she got hurt. If it hadn't been for Brazil, then she would have stood a chance."

"She wouldn't want you to blame yourself," 6 said. "I'm telling you that too. I take it 917 doesn't know? Since you've bottled this up for years?"

"Everything that's happened in my life is all my fault," 999 declared. "It's what I deserve."

"Angel... what are you talking about?"

"917 first joined the Second Group after he woke up from being enhanced out of a coma," 999 muttered. "The first person he became friends with was me."

"Yeah? What's that have to do with anything?"

999 stared 6 dead in the eyes.

As she studied her expression carefully, 6 was bombarded with a flood of memories. She recalled being away on an assignment when Dr. Kendrick brought in a boy with a severe head injury. Days later, they'd received word that the boy had been cybernetically enhanced while in a comatose state. Although she hadn't been on the medical team that saved this particular boy from his fate, she had always found the story fascinating. The only issue was the lack of information leading up to it.

Suddenly, her eyes widened when she realized what her apprentice was saying. The implication was obvious and too good to pass up.

"Consent," 6 muttered before pondering a little longer. "How did 917 give consent to become an amborg when he was unconscious? Dr. Kendrick kept that a secret and no one ever really knew the answer. Unless, you were there?"

999 leaned forward.

"I need to tell you what happened. Just promise you'll tell me if I made the right decision."

"Well," 6 decided to lean back and make herself more comfortable. "Like I always say, there's no judging until after you share the story."

6 grabbed her cup of water.

"And I do love stories. Especially the ones that you share."

Training Room

"Here's what's really crazy."

466 turned to look at 501.

"What is it?" she asked curiously.

"If that was how strong and fast Alpha 43 could fight," 501 said slowly. He turned and gazed at 466 with wide eyes. "Imagine how she would fight us in zero-gravity."

"It's understandable," 466 shrugged. "She's been in space longer than any of us."

The two of them continued to watch as everyone else on the bleachers began placing bets. 43 and 999's deadlock duel had ignited a spark of excitement among the others. They started organizing more sparring sessions and smaller bouts after their normal training schedules.

"Ok, are we taking bets?"

"I'll bet three thousand on 297."

"Ha! You're so on!"

3 and 5 sat together, enjoying the sandwiches they'd made from a plate filled with a variety of other foods. The natural ingredients from the bio-dome section of the station caught 3's attention when they first arrived. Being a chef and a food-lover, it was only natural for her to be curious about the taste of space-grown food.

Those who weren't participating were relaxing, watching as other amborgs brushed up on their combat skills. 43 and 999's duel had also inspired several of them to challenge each other. Instead of actively trying to kill each other, everyone focused on having fun and gauging each other's capabilities. No zero gravity or floating around in space for now. It was just a grounded, so to speak, time of sparring and hanging out.

917 and 297 were standing several feet across from each other in the center of the room. The amborgs eagerly waited in anticipation. Both of them wielded practice swords that were designed to electrocute the other upon making a wounding or killing blow. This particular pairing for the fight was generating a lot of hype.

"Look I'm telling you," 3 argued as she munched on her piece of sandwich, "917 is the best swordsman out of all of us. All of A.I. Industries. He has patience and the strong mental discipline that makes him the fastest. In theory, I think he can take this fight on for months if he has to."

"I'm still betting on 297 because he was in the Special Forces," 5 huffed. "He went through the basic training regular humans had to go through and only the top twelve percent of all applicants can survive the year of training they do to graduate. Have you seen what they're forced to do in the first week? Sheesh. I'm counting on 297 because he's willing to take that first shot, and strike hard and fast. He trained to kill flawlessly."

"Guys! Shh!"

501 and 466 leaned forward in anticipation as 777, who was refereeing, politely motioned for everyone to quiet down. 3 and 5 quickly swallowed the

mouthful of food they had and held their breaths. In the back, 224, 365, and 378 from the Fourth Group observed silently.

"Keep your wallet out 5," 3 muttered. "I'm winning this bet."

917 and 297 gripped their blades firmly and readied their stances. A hush fell over the room as the two fighters stood perfectly still. Then, simultaneously, they stepped forward and a superhuman duel began.

A regular human would have had to replay the video and watch it in slow motion to begin a proper analysis of what the amborgs were witnessing. They could see it perfectly, but it was like watching a pair of knights who had each downed ten Redbulls all at once.

297 lunged forward, 917 blocked and countered the attack. After a brief pause to assess their moves, they both swung their swords and struck again. The swords clashed repeatedly as they skillfully deflected each other's strikes. This transitioned from fencing to broader, more powerful motions. When stationary attacks weren't cutting it, 917 and 297 began to incorporate more footwork into their duel. They sidestepped and lunged again, making sure their swords never remained locked longer than a second. Not once did the two amborgs take their eyes off each other. It almost felt like the duel had transformed into something else entirely.

501 watched in fascination. It felt like watching a beautifully choreographed dance. It was more civil and less violent than 999 and 43's deadlock.

"Why are they fighting left handed?" he asked, leaning over to 466 as the strikes of their swords rang loudly throughout the entire room. "Why not start out using their right hands?"

"I think the fight would be over too quickly if they used their dominant hands," 466 surmised. "I think it's impressive when someone is ambidextrous."

"Oh," 501 said, a little crestfallen. He looked down at his left hand and flexed his fingers. "I'm not good at left-handed tasks."

"I didn't mean it that way," 466 giggled.

"Hey! Out of bounds!"

777 yelled at 297 and 917 who were still sparring with their training swords. Their movements led them dangerously close to the bleachers, causing some station techs in the audience to quickly retreat to safer seats to avoid getting caught in the whirlwind of blades.

Fortunately, they heard 777's warnings and they started to move back towards the center of the room.

"You know?" 297 grinned as he swung downwards at 917's head. "You're pretty good!"

917 raised his blade and blocked horizontally. He smiled back.

"Thanks," he politely responded as he reset and swung at 297's right side. "You know something I find interesting?"

297 crossed his left arm over his chest and aimed his blade downward to intercept 917's swing. They focused on a box technique, visualizing a perfect square in the center of their bodies and taking turns striking at each other on all four sides consecutively. Their swords were trying to find an opening.

"What is it?" 297 asked, blocking an underarm swing aimed at his leg. "Nice one."

"For someone that likes using firearms," 917 chuckled as he alternated between attacking 297's head and sword arm in a triple slash swing. "You've kept up with your knife techniques."

"You gotta keep that up, considering if someone manages to get in close," 297 said as he tried to stab 917's chest two times, but he was countered quickly. "I mean you're not so bad yourself. Considering, whoa, that you were in prison for a while."

"It's not so bad," 917 grunted as the two of them swung high and low. "Plenty of time to myself, healthy meals, and when not in maximum security, nice hit-by-the-way, just avoiding shivs on a daily basis."

"I have no idea how to respond to that," 297 panted as he tried to use his height to intimidate 917.

297 stepped forward with two large steps and tried to swing overhead. Since 917 was slightly shorter than him, he merely ducked down and somersaulted to the side. 297 stopped his advance and lowered his sword when he saw that 917 was preparing to swing lower, aiming for his shins.

"Don't worry so much about that," 917 chuckled. "You deal with international insurgents. I'll deal with the domestic ones with double life sentences. Also, need a second to catch your breath? You sound tired buddy."

"I can still kick your ass," 297 smiled confidently. "Especially when I do this."

917 had backed 297 up to wear 3 and 5 were sitting. Unlike the station techs that had scrambled away, the First Group amborgs cheerfully stayed put. Once 297 got too close to the bleachers, he swung his sword in a circle and in one fluid transition, switched to his right hand. 917 began to back away

as 297's dominant hand began to attack with more speed and precision. 917 continued blocking with his left hand as the fight began to speed up.

"Pretty amazing," 917 said as he concentrated on defending himself. 297's attacks were getting closer and closer. "You have kept up with your training."

"Ten years with Special Forces," 297 said with a grin as they locked swords.

"Just one more thing," 917 said as the clanging stopped for a few seconds and gave him a mischievous smile.

"What's that?"

"You may be good with knives," 917 shoved 297 away with his right arm, "but not the sword."

917 then switched his foot placement. His right foot moved forward and he tossed his sword into his right hand. After a quick practice swing to reset his weapon in his hand, 297 watched as 917 changed styles, now wielding his sword with both hands. He went from one-handed fencing to two hands gripping the blade.

Everyone looked on as 917 sped up with his strikes. 297 also used both hands to grip his sword, but they noticed his combat routine seemed to be faltering. Surprisingly, they watched as 297's rigid style was overwhelmed by 917's speed and control.

Finally, after a couple of minutes, 917 delivered a strong blow that deflected 297's blade to the left. 297 fumbled, and that was opening 917 needed. In one fluid motion, 917 raised his blade above his head and struck 297 in the neck, much like a samurai's precise strike. The electricity surged into 297, stunning him and bringing him to his knees. He cried out in agony as he writhed in pain on the ground.

"Wow," 501's mouth hung open.

"Wow indeed," 466 nodded in approval. "It's our turn now. Oh, 3 looks really happy."

3 held out her hand, grinning as 5 groaned. He clapped his hand into hers and made a wire transfer from his personal account. 3 cheerfully pumped her fist up, feeling a few thousand dollars richer.

"A pleasure doing business Johnny," 3 smiled as she checked her online accounts from her HUD. She waved at the center of the ring. "Thanks 917! I'm rich!"

917 merely smirked and nodded. 297 lay prone on the ground with a look of defeat, silently pouting while the electric shock continued to prevent him

from standing. 917 stepped forward, kicked 297's weapon away, and extended his hand.

"Cautious as ever," 297 sighed and put on a smile. "How'd you know I was going to try for my weapon?"

"Body language," 917 smirked as 297 grabbed his hand and was helped back to a standing position. "Knowing you, I just knew that you weren't accustomed to losing and always try to take every advantage that comes your way."

"I joined the world's strongest military," 297 said as he massaged the place where 917 had struck. "You're right about me disliking defeat. All I want to know is how..."

The two moved off the floor as 501 and 466 stepped into the center for their turn.

"How is it you're so good with a sword when it doesn't seem like you've been practicing?"

297 and 917 took a seat beside 3 and 5, who looked on with curiosity as they all reached for different sandwich pieces and started snacking away.

"My secret is," 917 said as he bit into his food. "Wow this tastes great, 3. My secret 297, is that I always try to act like I don't know how to fight, but my desire deep down is to kill you until I win."

Everyone stopped chewing and stared as 501 and 466 began to spar in the background.

"This coming from the guy that studied martial arts because it teaches benevolence and preservation of life?" 5 asked.

"Dark thoughts are motivating," 917 said casually as he winked.

"Are they?" 5 asked nervously.

"He has a point," 3 nodded.

917 chuckled and patted 297's shoulder.

"Especially since 297 is one big muscular amborg who is a Special Forces soldier," he explained. "10 years with Special Forces? Doesn't compete with a lifetime surviving on the streets."

"We're... uh... *all* from the streets??" 297 asked.

"Anyway," 917 said as they all laughed, "I simply put... sixty percent of my strength into beating him. Because we all know..."

"Strength at ninety percent and above guarantees death," everyone said simultaneously.

"Alright!" 917 clapped his hands. "We all remember that!"

"I can understand that," 297 nodded.

"What, killing insurgents to fuel your dark desires?" 3 looked at 297, who rolled his eyes.

"Well since my insurgent kill count the last two years has been... zero," he said in a mocking tone. "My dark desire right now is not being bored."

They all laughed again when a loud slam and yelp caught their attention, drawing their focus to the fight. They all looked in time to see 501 flying in the air and body slamming into the mat. 466 was on his heels and tackled him when he got back to his feet.

"What happened to their swords?" 5 asked.

"Hang on, let me replay the footage," 3 responded as she activated her bracelet.

"Well, as I was saying," 297 smiled. "About boredom. Isn't it nice killing time by hanging out with family?"

"Aww how sweet," 5 smiled and batted his eyes, causing them all to snort. "Love you too little bro."

"As much as I can't believe that I'm saying it," 3 replied, rolling her eyes with a developing smile. "I did miss all of us together."

"Yeah it is pretty nice," 917 nodded. He suddenly looked up and prepared to stand. "I see that 501 is still struggling. Also, we should move."

"ARRRGHH!"

In a fast fluid motion, 917, 297, 3 and 5 grabbed their plates and moved a few seats to the right. As if on cue, 501 was sent barreling into the chairs they were all just occupying a moment ago. 466 grabbed her practice sword and walked up to 501.

"You know 501," 917 said as they all got comfortable once again. "Swordsmen are supposed to be light on their feet, but isn't this a little too much?"

"Yes," 501 groaned.

"Why do you still continue to hold back?" 917 asked sternly. "Before we launched and came up here, you were up all night for hours continuing reflex training. You were improving. So what the hell is this?"

"No excuse," 501 replied.

"Oh that's how it's going to be?" 917 scoffed. "Well, I did miss your over explanations but... glad to see you have some self-restraint. But I don't seem to recall that this is how I trained you. Furthermore, Angel would be extremely displeased."

"I would rather take 466's punishment than 999's," 501 grumbled.

"Oh look at that," 297 said, pointing eagerly. "Wish granted."

"YARGH!!! NOO!!"

466 was giggling almost a little too gleefully as she stabbed the sword into his abdomen. As 501 twitched and convulsed violently in the wreckage of the chairs from the sharp electricity, 777 blew his whistle.

"Come on 466!" he said. "That's enough cruel and unnecessary punishment."

"It's cruel and unusual punishment," 466 replied.

"Correct!" 777 said angrily. "And also unnecessary so, cease and desist."

466 smirked as she withdrew the sword from 501. Everyone continued laughing as 501 kept writhing on the ground. The door opened and 117 walked in. He looked down at 501 and at the others, then nodded.

"You ok Donut?" 466 asked in a sweet tone. "I didn't hurt you too badly did I?"

"Only my pride and solar plexus," 501 muttered as he continued twitching. "Did anyone take bets during... that particular match?"

"Oh yeah we all did," 3 said without even blinking. "We all bet 466 would win. No brainer right there."

"What did I miss?" 117 asked.

5 sent the footage of the sparring session to 117 to review. As he caught up with current events, everyone else began to criticize 501 and 466's performance.

"You believe in being a gentleman during a fight," 297 added his notes to the review. "Admirable in the movies and other forms of pop culture sometimes, but there are people who take advantage of that."

"That is why you fail," 5 responded in his best Yoda impression. "Mmhehehehe."

"I'm pretty sure that doesn't sound like Yoda..." 117 muttered. "Wouldn't his character say it like this? 'why you fail, that is,'??"

"He is directly quoting from the movie," 3 shrugged as 5 chuckled with a cheeky grin. "You're still debating this after how many years?"

"If Yoda was supposed to remain consistent," 117 replied, "he's supposed to always talk backwards."

"He talks like that because it's by choice," 5 replied.

"Yes," 501 mumbled as he struggled to stand up. 466 grabbed him and helped him into a chair. "Yoda speaks like that because it's to honor the master who trained him."

"Doesn't sound right," 117 looked at the floor curiously. "You don't talk like me."

"Imagine that," 466 eyed 501 with a cheeky grin.

501 shrugged and casually glanced at 917.

"What?" 917 asked.

"Nothing. Is there ever going to be someone who'll bet on me?" he asked with a small whine.

"Wow, he looks like a puppy," 3 observed. "A poor emasculated puppy."

"I don't look like that when I lose, do I?" 117 asked.

No one answered this. Instead, they were interrupted when 917 stood up. "I would."

501 and 466 perked up.

"Really?" 501 asked with a hopeful gleam in his eyes.

"Sometimes, you interpret your failures as mountains," 917 explained. "But I've seen you follow a pattern over and over again. You try climbing the mountains, sometimes you try flying over them, or you can dig underneath. Whatever method you come up with, you always try and eventually, I know that you'll succeed. When I know you will, I just might bet on you."

"That was cool," 466 said.

"Did you pull that out of nowhere?" 5 asked. "Because that sounded like you've been waiting to say that for a long time."

"Well, in prison," 917 eyed 297, who smirked. "I also had a lot of time to think about things I wanted to say."

"Aww, and what did you want to say to me?" 297 asked.

917 smacked him upside the head.

"Ow!" he laughed.

"That," 917 chuckled.

"I recognize the handwriting," 297 grinned.

466 gave 501 a reassuring pat on his shoulder. 917's words brought huge smiles to their faces.

"Thanks 917!" 501 said with relief. "I won't let you down!"

"You may be an idiot," 5 said. "But your 'sensei' at least will always fight for his student. Distant, but he does care."

"Naturally. I hope to see him succeed just like 117 and 43. Ever since she became Serina the A.I. and he went off to court that girl Audrey from the Academy, someone had to offer a hand to help take over mentoring 501 and

466," 917 explained. "And 5, I'm Chinese. I am 501's 'shi-fu.' 'Sensei' is the Japanese title. Get it wrong on purpose and you'll suffer 297's fate."

After the sparring sessions were over, they bid each other farewell and went off to perform their own duties. 917 decided to rest back in his quarters while 501 and 466 followed him to listen to his wise rambling. 117 and 297 wanted to go back to the Zero-G room, which left 3 and 5 to clear the dishes. Fortunately, 777 was the only other amborg remaining there.

"Hey 777," 3 said. "Are you doing anything? We want to ask you something."

"Sure."

777 helped them clean up. Then they all left the room, each with a stack of dishes in hand.

"I like to think that 917 is right about 501," 3 stated with an admiring nod.

"Yeah," 5 agreed. "I think that he's gotten a lot more serious over the years. But I do miss his sense of humor sometimes."

"It's just a difficult time," 777 said. "He'll be ok."

"Well I was wondering if 917 had a thing for 999," 5 said bluntly. "I think the two of them seeking solace in each other would be healthy."

"Well she doesn't really express feelings like a normal girl," 3 said.

"We are amborgs," 777 chuckled. "I don't think normal is the right word."

"Well you must know something right? 777?" 5 asked. "Do you think they should be a couple? Give us a little Second Group gossip."

"I wouldn't exactly know," 777 shrugged. "They never seem to talk about it in any context when we aren't deployed. A unique relationship, yes, but not one we can really gossip about. If I had to guess, I'd say the chances of them dating is on the same level as 5 getting 6 to marry him."

"Oh ho ho ohhh," 3 burst out laughing. Now it was 5's turn to be angry. He looked like he was about to blow a gasket as 3 continued to chortle. "That's funny because it's true! Ah ha ha ha!"

"Also, why do you ask?" 777 wondered as the three of them arrived at the cafeteria.

"Well everyone is so tense," 3 shrugged as she caught her breath. "I miss all the gossiping and rumors. I was curious to see the progress of all of our friendships or relationships while I was gone. It's such a relief just talking about what humans do to ease tension and live their lives."

"We all want what's best for each other," 5 added with a grumble.

"And in your case," 3 snickered, "It isn't working out too well."

- -

David 117's quarters

"So, in your expert opinion, what do you think?"

"First, before I answer, this is not what you should be doing as a leader."

117 and 297 had both left to hang out with each other after the sparring sessions. Instead of going to the Zero-G room, they decided to take a break in 117's quarters so that they could do some catching up. After they sat down, the conversation seemed to hit a dead end, or did it?

"I know," 117 sighed.

"Why don't you just sit down with 999 and 917?" 297 insisted as he took a sip of water from his canteen. "Together? You know? Like the old days?"

"Before I had the chance to bring it up," 117 sighed, "999 challenged 43 to a deadlock, and there hasn't been a proper moment to talk to 917."

"Well, we get hit with unexpected things all the time," 297 replied with a casual shrug. "But if you're asking me for my opinion, then I think that 917 is of sound mind. He seems to have his head in the right place, even though he spent time in prison."

117 paused and glanced down.

"What?" 297 leaned forward. "You wanted something to be wrong?"

"No," 117 answered.

297 stared and took a deep breath. He really wanted to help figure out 117's dilemma.

"117," he said cautiously. "Spill."

After taking a moment to think, 117 revealed what was on his mind.

"Why won't he tell us?"

117 clenched and unclenched his fist out of mild frustration.

"That's what this is about?" 297 let out a sigh of relief as he leaned back in his chair. "You do realize that he doesn't have to tell you everything. What you're doing right now; this vetting process is wrong."

"So do you think I should do what 999 recommends?" 117 asked. "Demote her and put someone else in charge? She's nominated 917 to take her place if I choose to allow it. What if I asked you or 777 to take the job?"

297 chuckled.

"I can't decide for you," he smiled sympathetically. "But, if it makes you feel better, I can tell you with absolute confidence that they'll do their jobs right, no matter who you take on as your partner."

117 still didn't feel convinced.

"Alright," 297 decided to take another swig from his canteen. "Let me share something with you. I have only told Dr. Kendrick this story and now I'm sharing it with you."

117 looked up and nodded. He began to listen attentively.

"Do you know why I joined the Special Forces?"

117 shook his head. 297 handed his canteen to him, which he accepted graciously. 117 took a sip and then his eyes widened. There was a small amount of alcohol in the canteen. Was this even allowed aboard the space station?

"Relax," 297 smirked when he saw 117's surprised reaction. "We can filter out alcohol really fast."

"Dr. Kendrick allowed you to smuggle alcohol here?"

"What he doesn't know won't hurt him," 297 replied. "He always told me to just make sure to stay responsible."

"Let's refocus," 117 handed 297's canteen back. "Can we do that please?" 297 smiled and took it.

"After the Domino Incident," he said, eyeing his canteen and turning it in his hands. "We witnessed many lives get destroyed. We received a lot of threat assessments across the world, so I knew I wanted to contribute more. One of the first places I transferred myself to was Ramstein."

"Oh yeah," 117 remembered. "Enemy insurgents attacked Ramstein Air Base."

"There were a lot of casualties," 297 stated, taking a sip from his canteen. "Most of them were just trying to rotate home as soon as they could. Their families and homes were destroyed while we fought desperately to retake our own country. I put myself on the team that was assigned to track down whoever was behind the attack."

"How did it go?" 117 asked.

"Honestly? I still have nightmares," 297 replied casually. "Not because of the fact that we succeeded in capturing the targets, but of what happened afterwards. Most of the people I fought alongside had a rough time coming home. A lot of trauma and hard issues that they had to bring back."

297 downed the rest of his canteen and set it on the table. He wiped his mouth and looked at 117.

"Yeah, we fought and succeeded," he said. "But at what cost? It wasn't coming home that made my friends broken. It was what we did and what we saw that kept us from properly sleeping again. So I stayed with Special Forces."

"Because you liked it?" 117 asked.

"Because every mission I came back from was good," 297 explained. "Every soldier that made it back with me was a victory for me. I did what I did so I could keep sending more and more of our bravest and finest soldiers home."

That certainly did explain why 297 was barely home. In fact, aside from the previous Emergency Recalls, 117 could hardly remember when 297 had visited or come home over the last 10 years.

"The first Emergency Recall was when the Global Security Conference was bombed and we responded," 297 said. "The second one had us responding to a war, then Brazil, and now this. And every time I come back to A.I. Industries whenever Dr. Kendrick calls for us, you know what I see?"

117 tilted his head as 297 answered his own question.

"The best people I would give my life for," he smiled. "I do the job and fight as an amborg because we have to. To ensure that our home and the planet is a better place through our actions. My hands aren't clean, 117. I killed a lot of people, I won't deny that. And if someone wants me to answer for that; perhaps if the circumstances are brought up, then I will face the consequences. But whenever I was feeling low, when I felt like an absolute piece of shit, I had you and everyone at home."

117 blinked and noticed 297 still smiling, but he also saw that his hands were trembling slightly. 297 noticed as well and gripped his left wrist with his other hand to steady himself.

"Dr. Kendrick encouraged me not to dwell on the past," 297 said softly. "It was actually refreshing to know that everyone in our family didn't see me as a monster. You didn't care about what I did when I was away from A.I. Industries. I just know that whenever I did come back, you all welcomed me cheerfully and pulled me out from a dark place."

"So how come you never visited or returned home more often?" 117 asked.

"Well, for one thing," 297 chuckled. "It's hard requesting time off or sneaking away from the army. Aside from that, I just continued doing my job knowing that everyone back home had my back."

"You still have nightmares?"

"Yeah," 297 nodded. "I know that once this mission is over, whenever that may be, I'll be back on Earth, doing what I do best. Being a soldier. That's what I look forward to after this."

297 then leaned backwards in his chair. He stretched his arms upwards.

"So, back to your current problem," he said. "917 went to prison for taking down a criminal syndicate. Big deal. From the moment I've seen him back at A.I. Industries up to now, he looks happy to be back. My honest opinion is that I totally get what he was probably going through."

117 listened and started nodding.

"I lost a lot of good soldiers," 297 explained. "And I was ordered to hunt down the enemies that killed them. It was a vicious cycle of endless killing and fighting. So, I'll ask you for an honest answer, 117. Do you think I'm dangerous? Or do you still think I'd be a good candidate to be your partner?"

"I didn't know that you went through all of that," 117 replied softly.

"Well, I chose to bear that alone," 297 shrugged. "Most of you probably wouldn't be able to handle what I've got on my shoulders when everyone is dealing with their own demons. Isn't it fair to also assume that 917 has been doing the same thing? 999 too? Hell, 777 uncovered a cargo ship of dead people with your grandfather. We're all dealing with a lot of high stress."

117 bit his lip as he looked at 297. He was right. Prior to the Domino Incident they had shared a brotherly type of relationship. Every amborg had a special kind of friendship with each other. Although 117 wasn't a soldier like he was, he had always looked up to 297. His perspective was also as unique as the other amborgs in the Second Group.

"I guess," 117 said. "I should make a final decision on this matter."

"You should," 297 nodded. "Also, I'm stating for the record that I'm not taking the job if you want me as your second in command."

"Why not?" 117 asked.

"Because it's much more entertaining watching you agonize about it."

297 stood up to leave.

"If I may," he said as 117 also stood up to properly show him out. "I think there's a third option that could settle this for you, once and for all."

"What?"

"Make Alpha Serina 43 your partner," 297 suggested.

117 stared.

"I don't think I could do that," he replied.

"Why? Because she's not from this universe?" 297 raised his eyebrows. "Are we going to ignore the fact that she fights, thinks, and acts just like our own 43? She's an ideal choice!"

"I don't think Dr. Kendrick would go for it..."

"That's your problem 117!" 297 sighed. "You never know unless you try. 999 already proved during her rather violent deadlock that 43 wants to see this mission, her war that she's fighting, to end. She's totally committed. Talk to Dr. Kendrick and let him know what you decide."

297 walked to the door and it hissed open. He stepped outside and 117 remained in his quarters.

"No matter what you decide," he said with a reassuring smile. "It's not like the rest of the amborgs would mind. There's only 20 of us in space with you. The rest are on Earth. So if you make this choice, it's not even affecting all of us. Aren't you the one blowing this out of proportion?"

"I just like getting as much information as I can," 117 replied. "Is that wrong?"

"Not really," 297 shook his head. "But come on 117. We're training up here and planning for an invasion. Not a presidential election."

297 then shut the door in 117's face. When it clicked shut, 117 turned away from the door and went to sit down in his chair again. He took a moment to ponder 297's advice and then, after making a quick deliberation, he turned on his phone.

It was time to resolve the problem, once and for all. Otherwise, he wouldn't be able to concentrate on moving forward with the task at hand.

Chapter 15: The Calm Before the Storm

Apogee Station
Zero-Gravity Obstacle Course
Emergency Recall plus 5 days 1 hour and 4 minutes
12:35 PM Pacific Time

"Nicely done!"

117 returned to the starting area and grabbed onto the railing. Once he managed to wrap his fingers around it, he used his strength to pull himself onto the platform and his feet magnetized to it. Floating through zero gravity was like trying to swim through an endless ocean.

"You're getting faster."

117 looked up at 43 and 999, who were observing him.

"Not as fast as either of you," 117 let out a laugh as he tried to catch his breath.

"She's more experienced," 999 pointed out.

"I'm just glad that you two are getting along," 117 smiled. He looked at 999. "My partner..."

Then he gestured to 43.

"And my former partner who is from Alpha universe."

"We just needed to fight each other out," 43 grinned as she gave 999 a light fist bump on her shoulder.

"Touching me," 999 said warningly.

"Sorry," 43 retracted her hand when she saw 999's eyes narrow.

117 continued to smile as 999 side-stepped from 43. It was nice to see them acting friendly towards each other. It didn't matter whether or not they were genuinely feeling that way, but it was certainly good for morale. The last thing they needed was another duel, which would probably trigger another terrifying and gut-wrenching vent session.

"It feels great today, doesn't it?" 43 said optimistically.

"She seems happier," 117 transmitted to 999 privately.

"Agreed," 999 replied in a reluctant tone.

It had been two days since their deadlock duel. 43 was behaving like someone who'd just visited a spa or something. It was understandable, considering she had gotten the chance to spend time hanging out with everyone. Sure, she was still taking her job seriously and training them as she was instructed. What kept their hopes and spirits up was the fact that she was eagerly having fun while doing so.

Unfortunately, she was likely putting on an excessive show of positivity to mask how worried she actually was. When they arrived aboard the space station, 43 had stated that she'd been given two days before the S.C.E. would send the support fleet to back them up. It had already been double that amount of time.

Two days ago, 43 had reassured them that they would show up then. Yesterday, her answer had changed to that day. Today, her answer to 117 earlier that morning had been hopefully any time soon. Despite her warm sense of camaraderie, 117 knew that she was no-doubt freaking out internally. All they could do was keep passing time. The best way to keep her mind occupied was to keep training and preparing with the time they hopefully still had.

"You weren't by any chance thinking of challenging her to another duel, were you?"

999's silent look gave him the answer he needed.

"Right," 117 nodded. "Didn't think so."

Quickly, he switched back to a public channel and spoke out loud so that 43 wouldn't notice that they were secretly talking about her.

"What's 917 up to? Are you both ok?"

43, who had been observing the Third Group amborgs soaring across the room, turned around and stared at them curiously. 999 glanced at the two of them, looking as stunned as a deer caught in headlights.

"He's fine!" she replied immediately. Her sharp tone caught him off guard. "We're ok."

117 and 43 exchanged a look. They turned back to 999, who was concentrating on her data pad a little too hard.

"Uh," 43 chimed in innocently. "You don't sound ok."

43 pointed at 117 and 999.

"This isn't about the leadership thing, is it? I thought we resolved that two days ago? That whole meeting the four of us had?"

The meeting she was referring to had taken place shortly after 297 dropped his words of wisdom with 117. He had summoned 917, 999, and 43 to one of the private conference rooms to confirm his decision.

He'd started the conversation by saying that he would stick with what he had. 999 was who he picked based on Serina's wishes and she would continue to be his partner on this mission. At the time, back on Earth, he admitted that he had concerns about the decision but after reflecting and gathering more information from his peers, he felt that the decision was the right choice.

The meeting had been a short one because he needed to confess to 917 and 43 that they'd both been considered as the prime candidates to take the job if he had decided to switch partners. When he informed them that there wouldn't be any changes, they carried on like normal. Although, if the leadership job wasn't still on her mind, there was something else bugging 999.

"I think it's a 917 issue," 117 surmised.

43's interest was suddenly piqued. She lowered her gaze inquisitively and started to gently probe.

"You two aren't..." she carefully started. She eyed 999 curiously with an awkward inflection in her voice.

"What?" 999 looked up and glared at 43.

"...ahem, sleeping together?" 43 finished her sentence slowly as she cleared her throat. "Sorry, I thought that I was being explicit."

"No," 999 replied in an annoyed tone.

"Ok, are you annoyed because you actually aren't with him?" 43 asked, "or are you annoyed because, yes, you want him to hook up with you but he's not?"

"I swear, the more you hang out with us," 117 shuddered, "the more it really seems like 43 came back to life."

"Yeah, and she's just as nosy," 999 scoffed.

They watched as 999 disengaged her shoes from the platform and she kicked off. As she floated towards the entrance to the room, 43 and 117 did the same and tried to follow her. He activated a private channel to 43, and she accepted the invite instantly.

"What's 999 like? Her Alpha version? Are she and 917 a couple?"

"Oh I can spill the tea on that," 43 replied eagerly. "They're married."

"Really?"

117 and 43 landed at the doorway and started following 999.

"All the files I brought with me are available to the public," 43 replied with a smile. "You should look into your Alpha selves a bit more."

"It feels weird though," 117 shrugged. "Reading about yourself that lived a completely different life? I take it 999 knows?"

"Of her alternate universe's marital status?" 43 nodded. "I'd guess from her mood, she found out and she's a little jealous."

"Of who? Herself?"

"Let me put it to you with me as an example," 43 placed a hand on her chest. "I'm jealous of you but I've accepted that there's nothing I can do about it."

117 stared at 43. There was only one thing about him that he suspected would be the reason why she would admit this.

"You spoke with my wife?" 117 asked.

"No," 43 shook her head. "I didn't want to pry. Serina was very insistent on telling me though. I think she was subtly trying to tell me to back off if I had any thoughts about trying to rekindle a lost relationship."

"Are we talking about the same thing?" 117 glanced ahead, making sure that 999 was still in sight.

"Let me put your mind at ease, David 117," 43 chuckled. "Yes, I was in love with your Alpha version. We were together and then he was gone. I've accepted that. I won't deny that seeing you again has revived a lot of positive memories from where I come from. But, you're the 117 of this universe. I have also accepted that your life here is not the same as the 117 I knew. I have no intention of trying to interfere or inserting myself into some sort of multiverse love triangle. I think, if you'll agree to this statement, that we're better off being friends."

"Well," 117 nodded with a confident smile. "I'm glad we got that out of the way. But what about 999?"

"You really do need me to spell it out for you, huh?" 43 chuckled.

"I'd really appreciate it."

43 put a hand on his shoulder as she pointed at 999's back.

"Picture this," she explained. "999 discovered that in the Alpha universe, she was happily married. My guess is, her jealousy comes from the fact that she wants that in this universe too."

"999?" 117 asked. "She's never said anything like that before."

"She still has human emotions," 43 smirked. "They're just suppressed. That's why I find her so interesting in this universe. Her story is so mysterious and intriguing. She closes herself off. She has a few friends, but I can tell she wants someone to love her. It would appear that she wants love from one person conveniently aboard this station, too."

"917?"

"Bingo!" 43 winked and nudged 117 in the rib. "Now, all you have to do is figure out what seems to be holding them back. There's definitely something on both their minds that's stopping them from going all in on a relationship. It's a shame, they look good together."

"What do you suppose it might be?"

117 turned his head and stared eagerly up at 43. She politely shook her head and shrugged.

"I don't know," she smiled sheepishly. "Hey, I never said I had all the answers. Everyone here is not from my universe! Different stories and different events than what I remember from Alpha. Do I have to remind you that I'm the interstellar tourist here?"

"Right," 117 said, looking a little crestfallen.

"I don't think it's that big of a deal," 43 guessed. "But put yourself in her shoes for a second. If the Tandeeri get here and they start the biggest fight of our lives, wouldn't you want a few moments alone with the person you care about?"

"Ok, enough! What are you two talking about?"

43 and 117 flinched. 999 had stopped walking and turned to look back at them.

"Nothing important," 117 replied hastily. "I was just thinking of calling Audrey!"

999 lowered her gaze and appeared to grow more irritated by his answer. 43 closed her eyes and shook her head. 117 realized he'd just put his own foot in his mouth.

"Congratulations," 999 muttered. "Don't keep your wife waiting. At least you have someone to call."

999 stalked off, her footsteps sounding loud and hollow.

"Oops," 117 brought a hand up and palmed his forehead.

"Why don't I talk to her later?" 43 asked.

"If you think it'll help," 117 sighed. "Maybe I'm the one that needs to be replaced as the leader."

"Nah, that's not happening," 43 chuckled. "We just need a bit of damage control. Uh... Serina?"

"Yeah?"

A flash of light and Serina appeared in front of them.

"Boy, you got to lower the lights on your entrances before someone gets a seizure," 43 grinned while holding up a hand to shield her eyes.

"Funny," Serina stuck her holographic tongue out at her. "If you wanted me to inflict damage, you should have used the codeword 'flashbang' when you called me."

"What happens with a flashbang?" 43 asked.

"Oh you know," Serina shrugged her shoulders. "It's like a flashbang grenade. A grenade that goes 'flash' and 'bang.' My version is ten times more flash and I make a loud eardrum-shattering bang. It's much deadlier."

"I never thought I'd hear my sarcasm come from an A.I.," 43 snickered.

"What can I say, I get it from you," Serina dipped her head. "So what did you need? I have to get back to Dr. Kendrick and work on some tests."

"How about the codeword, 'matchmaker'?" 43 asked with a grin.

Serina glanced in the direction that 999 had gone, then looked at 117. A smile slowly formed on her face as she began to catch 43's meaning.

"You know, I thought Angel seemed a little upset about something when I was passing by," she said. "Say no more. I'm going to find 917."

With a flash of light, Serina disappeared. 117 peered at 43.

"And what was she planning to do?"

"An invite for 917 to actually start paying attention to her," 43 grinned. "Maybe 917 will get off his butt and take her to dinner or something."

117 looked slightly alarmed.

"What?" 43 asked, noticing his reaction.

"A dinner date?" 117 responded nervously.

"Yes," 43 nodded, looking confused. "You know, a date that involves dinner?"

"No, that I know about," 117 said as he leaned closer. "Serina definitely knows the right way to handle this but we cannot try and set up a dinner date!"

"Why not? What does that mean??"

"It reminds them of the day that..."

Suddenly, a phone call began to ring in his head. 117 glanced to the corner of his HUD and saw Audrey's face appear. This was interesting timing.

"Oh, it's Audrey," 117 said. He held up his index finger to 43. "Hold that thought?"

"Sure," 43 nodded.

He quickly answered the call and heard her voice. Her sweet and soft tone seemed to elevate his spirits slightly.

"Audrey? I was actually thinking of calling you later today."

"I'm on break, hi honey," Audrey replied. "How are things?"

"We've been training hard and waiting for help to get here," 117 replied. "How are things at work?"

"Everyone here is on edge," Audrey replied. "The defense committee just reported to the President. Our military forces are at about 86% ready."

"That's impressive considering it's been less than a week since 43's arrival," 117 smiled.

"Well, you can thank the threat of invasion for having everyone rushing around and scrambling to get things taken care of," Audrey said. "The President and the Joint Chiefs have declared DEFCON three."

"I'm glad they haven't escalated to two," 117 shuddered.

"They just might!" Audrey sounded nervous. "According to 43's reports, we may need to respond with nuclear weapons!"

"That can't happen," 117's eyes widened. "If we use them, then everyone else who has them will also launch them. It'll be the end of us."

The loss of life if the entire world decided to retaliate with their nuclear arsenal would be catastrophic. The fact that someone from either the Pentagon or the White House actually suggested it as an option was a terrible idea. Even if to avoid an invasion from space, what if this strategy failed? They would destroy the Tandeeri and potentially incinerate themselves in the process. Or worse, if an alien species from an alternate universe was coming, would their most lethal and powerful weapons of mass destruction even do any sort of significant damage? Alpha 43 didn't come from a universe that primarily used nuclear-based weapons.

"You need to keep Dr. Kendrick alive and protect him at all costs," Audrey stated. "If something happens to him, you didn't hear this from me but... President Holland will have no choice."

"I thought the President was on Dr. Kendrick's side," 117 said.

"He is," Audrey answered. "But remember, the President still has a bunch of staff members and the military officials under his command that don't fully agree with A.I. Industries."

"Audrey," 117 cleared his throat. "Are you sure you're even allowed to share this information with me?"

"I asked Joey to encrypt this line," Audrey stated, dropping her voice to a whisper. "I'm sure President Holland will try to warn Dr. Kendrick as soon as he can, but if anything happens to them, the defense committee will take over. I heard one of the Generals talk about the 25ᵗʰ amendment!"

"The vice president and the rest of his cabinet wouldn't go through with that," 117 replied reassuringly. "President Holland is of sound mind and is physically capable of carrying out his responsibilities as our leader."

"People do crazy things when they're afraid!" Audrey said. "There's a lot of tension and discord here at the Pentagon!"

"Are you safe?" 117 asked cautiously.

"I don't think it's safe to go to my apartment," her voice dropped back into a hushed tone. "When the invasion starts, I wouldn't be surprised if a major power vacuum occurs far from the public eye. I would personally feel better if an amborg or two got assigned to the White House to make sure there's no funny business."

"Alright," 117 made up his mind. "Then it's a good thing you're a valuable contact with information at the Pentagon. Thanks for sharing this."

"117," Audrey nervously warned him.

"Right, thank you for **not** sharing what you just told me," 117 corrected his statement.

"Do you think I should try to take a few of my allies here to A.I. Industries? Or should I go to the White House?"

117 tilted his eyes towards 43. She had been standing quietly off to the side and stared curiously when he looked at her.

"I think you should stick close to your friends," he said out loud. "Go to the White House, one of us will be there and assigned to protect the President. You should bring Joey and anyone else you trust. And if... something goes wrong, Audrey..."

Audrey remained quiet as he took a deep breath and closed his eyes for a moment.

"Go to A.I. Industries. It'll be the safest place for you. If you can't make it there, then I want you to go to our safe house," he instructed. "The one I built for you. Stay there, you know who to call."

"Do you really think it'll come to that?" Audrey asked.

"Hopefully not," 117 said. "I'm unable to physically stop you from doing what you want to do but I trust your judgment. Just promise me that you'll run if things go horribly wrong."

"I will."

"You know I just want you safe, right?"

"Always. I love you."

"I love you too," 117 nodded firmly as he looked at 43 again. "Audrey, the phone lines are probably still slow and jammed up. Call Mandy on our emergency line if you can't reach A.I. Industries."

"I will. You come back home to me."

"I plan to."

As 117 hung up the call, 43 crossed her arms.

"That sounded intense towards the end there," she remarked.

"I have to hope that the amborgs on Earth can stop any power-hungry individuals from taking over once this war starts," 117 stated.

"Is your wife ok?" 43 asked.

"Yeah," 117 nodded. "We have contingencies planned. We just never thought an alien invasion would be the reason why we would have to act out on them."

"You're smart," 43 nodded. "You've planned better than most."

"Let's hope it keeps us and everyone we care about alive," 117 shuddered.

They both began to walk down the hall. He quickly drafted a text message for Mandy as they proceeded to meet with Dr. Kendrick. According to the schedule, he should have been in the mess hall getting lunch.

Mandy, he wrote, *Send an urgent priority message to Tom and all of his friends. The people he trusts need to know that tensions within the chain of command are high. If President Holland or Dr. Kendrick falls, you must identify any interested parties that want to take over if it comes to that. If all else fails, make sure Tom gets to safety.*

He sent the message and confirmed the delivery, then looked at 43.

"The only thing that makes me nervous about this situation is that we're up here and everything else is down there," he said. "It doesn't feel right that my family is out of my reach."

"I haven't been home to Earth in a long time," 43 replied. "I've been in space fighting this war. But I have hope that one day the war will end. I am here on behalf of my universe to protect yours."

43 pointed out the window at the Earth.

"Isn't that worth fighting for? Isn't all of that worth dying for?"

Before 117 could answer, he received a text message ping in his head. Mandy had read his text and sent a reply.

Thanks for the heads up, she wrote. *That makes sense, considering the planet is about to make contact face-first with an alien species, and the fact that they are hostile is enough to put the fear of God in everyone down here. I just texted Tom and I'll give Audrey a call, too. Your grandfather also contacted me. He was checking in on you. Let him know how you're doing when you get a second, ok? Sincerely, the woman not in your head anymore.* ;)

117 smiled as he texted a quick thank you, then turned back to 43.

"Yes," he said determinedly. "Absolutely."

"So, do you think that you have time to explain where we left off?"

117 was about to nod in agreement when suddenly, there was another call from across the station.

"Oh," he said as he looked at the caller ID. "It's 1. Hello?"

"Hey 117! Do you read me?"

"Loud and clear," 117 replied. "What's up? Give me your nonliteral response."

"It's very cold right now," 1 responded cheerfully. "But I'm good. What's up with you?"

"I'm with 43 right now. Can we put her on?"

"Sure! Go right ahead."

117 looked at 43 and nodded. He sent her a group invite, which she accepted. As she did so, there was a crackle in the transmission. Odd, it should have been clear if 1 was in the vicinity.

"Hey 1," 43 said as she and 117 kept pacing down the hall. "How are you?"

"One of the technicians and I are on a spacewalk towards one of the relays," 1 reported. "It needed a replacement part."

"You're outside?"

"It's pretty cool, right?" 1 chuckled. "2 suggested that someone else take care of this, but I figured an amborg would be able to expedite this."

"Well, I can see why 2 would be worried," 117 said. "It doesn't sound like a good idea, especially since you're the leader of the First Group up here."

"Don't worry 117," 1 replied without any hesitation. "I know what I'm doing. I've logged plenty of spacewalk missions in the last two trips I've been to Apogee. It's a piece of cake."

"So how is the atmosphere out there?" 43 joked.

"What atmosphere?"

43 rolled her eyes and gave 117 a shove. Their laughter died down, ending in a collective sigh. After a quick breather, they continued with the discussion.

"Anyway, I'll tell you why I called," 1 continued in their heads. "Kelsey and I are just about finished with the repairs to this relay. We were about to head back inside when some of the station techs asked us to take a look at one of the sensors nearby. We're going to start walking over there."

"What'd you do?" 117 asked.

"They said that since I was out here anyway, I should test its functions. Apparently, the control room picked something up just beyond Pluto and asked me to confirm the readings."

43's face fell, amusement replaced with pure shock. She immediately placed a hand to her ear and began to speak again in a harried tone. Her other hand shot up and gripped 117's shoulder, causing him to wince in pain as she tightened her hold on his jacket.

"What kind of readings, 1??" she asked urgently, concern clearly displayed across her face. "What was it? When did this happen?"

"A few minutes ago. Some high level of gravitational anomalies," 1 replied. His tone also shifted to one of concern upon hearing her reaction. "We were actually about to divert a probe to get some eyes on it and inform you when we were sure. And from the way 43 just said that, I think it might be a good idea to head back inside now."

43 looked at 117 apprehensively.

"Call 2!" she said desperately. "Add him to this call! 1! You need to get yourself and Kelsey inside! They're coming!"

"Your reinforcements?" 1 asked nervously.

117 dialed 2 and waited for him to accept the invite. He glanced at 43 anxiously, who met his gaze with terrified eyes.

"Worse," she replied softly.

"Hello? Can you hear me?"

They heard 2's voice enter the call almost immediately.

"2!" 43 stated. "It's me! Listen! Where are you?"

"I'm in the main control room with Jacob and the other techs," 2 replied quickly, recognizing the urgency in her voice. "I'm keeping an eye on 1's camera footage of his spacewalk. What's going on?"

"Exactly what time did the station sensors detect that anomaly past Pluto?" 43 asked.

117 glanced to the side and looked out the station window. He could have sworn he saw something moving. As he tried to focus, 2 answered.

"11 minutes and 42 seconds," he said. "Exactly."

"12 minutes," 43 gasped. "2! The station needs to go on red alert now!"

"I copy that," 2 replied. "Is it happening now?"

"Yes! Yes!" 43 answered, becoming increasingly more distressed by the second. "Listen to me! The Tandeeri fleet! Once detected, it's a pattern! They always arrive in between 12-13 minutes!"

"But we haven't detected anything," 1 replied. "Even when we reconfigured the station sensors to 43's recommended specs."

"1! Just get inside!" 43 exclaimed. "The sensors not picking up anything after an anomaly might mean that your sensors are broken, but I'm pretty sure that they're not! The Tandeeri fleet are camouflaging themselves!"

"Going to red alert," 2 reported. "Standby."

"43!"

117 stopped and grabbed 43 by the arm. Pulling her back, he kept his eyes fixed on the movement that he'd caught sight of. There was definitely something out there. He watched stars vanish and reappear as something invisible moved their way.

"43..." 117 said in a very nervous tone as he pointed. "What is that?"

The stars were no longer being blotted out. Instead, he could make out the shape of an approaching object, followed by a distinct sound. There was a loud rumbling noise, and 117 saw lights flicker to life. It took him a moment to realize that he was looking at the windows of a spaceship. This vessel was unlike anything he'd ever seen before, resembling the futuristic designs often depicted in video games and science fiction movies. It appeared to be equipped with some sort of cloaking technology, gradually revealing itself as it moved closer to the station. Clearly, it was not of this world, or even their own universe for that matter. Just as 43 had described, the Tandeeri were now right there before their very eyes.

43 gasped in horror.

"Too late," she whispered. 117 felt her arms pushing him, urging him to run. "We need to go now!"

The lights in the hallway switched to a dark shade of red as the klaxon alarm went off. Another heavy rumble shook the floor as they felt it vibrate beneath their feet. A yellow bolt of light soared from below them towards the enemy ship. 117 immediately recognized it as one of the main guns stationed there. Originally designed to perform tests by shooting objects into sections of space, with 43's assistance it had been modified into a laser pulse gun. As the bolt traveled towards the Tandeeri vessel, it made contact but was absorbed by a strange barrier, causing it to dissipate. The enemy ship, still intact, started to retreat slowly, with the front of the ship glowing ominously.

"Who gave clearance to fire?" 117 exclaimed as the alarm kept ringing. "What's going on?"

His eyes met 43's, who stood there completely frozen. She immediately began calling out as the Tandeeri ship generated what looked like an orb of light. The energy weapon was getting ready to fire.

"1! Get inside now!" she yelled as the orb instantly shot towards the station. "Brace yourselves!"

Suddenly, an emergency announcement echoed through the corridors, carrying Dr. Kendrick's voice throughout the station.

"Attention! This is Dr. Kendrick! Station hands! Brace for impact!"

They barely had time to register the announcement as the orb collided with the station, sending 117 tumbling to the ground. The orb hit with enough kinetic force to destabilize his footing, but what really caught his eye was the sudden glow of the electrical panels. With a quick scan, he noticed the power levels were reaching critical levels. Before he could warn 43, who was barely getting back to her feet, an explosion erupted from the panel behind him.

"Let's GO!" he cried as they crawled back to their feet and took off running. As they passed each corridor, they could hear the cries and yells of nearby station members. "We got to get to the main observation room!"

"Are there any other weapons the station might have?" 43 yelled as they stopped.

The electrical overload had damaged some of the wall conduits. They had burst open and some small sparks had ignited an electrical fire. The station fire safety equipment activated and a drone was seen trying to extinguish the flames. 43 and 117 quickly went to a nearby console, turned off the power, and contained the fire to assist in putting out the flames. Dealing with fire in space was no joke, even with the station's emergency protocols in place. The drone thanked 43 and 117 for the assistance and continued monitoring the damage.

117 stared back at 43 with concern.

"I don't think we have anything else..." he said grimly. He desperately tried to rally his team. "We have to try and warn the planet. This is 117, checking in, can anyone hear me? I need every amborg to report in! 999? 777? 917? 297? Anyone from the Second Group? Anybody?!"

"Hey!"

43 grabbed 117 and shook him.

"Stay calm!" she instructed. "You panic and it's all over. I know you're scared. I'm scared, too."

There was a crackle of static, and 2's voice came through.

"Attention! This is amborg Ziggy 2. All amborgs and station personnel, if you can hear this, switch to the emergency channel. This is amborg 2! I repeat, switch to the emergency channel!"

117 and 43 both tuned their communications and tried to respond.

"2! This is 117! 43 is with me! Are you ok? Status report?"

"117! We took a huge hit!"

"Yeah, we felt that one... What's happening?"

"The electricity levels aboard the station skyrocketed like crazy, but we managed to prevent the main systems from exploding," 2 reported. "We got hit by a massive energy blast! Definitely not like anything we've seen before."

"Yeah, that'll do it," 43 nodded with terror written across her expression.

"Look, we have to try and reorganize," 117 replied. "I need to find 999! Can you get everyone else's location?"

"Well, in the event of an emergency, all personnel are to rally to the designated safe zones on the station," 2 said. "I've got another problem!"

"What kind of problem?" 117 asked.

"I've lost 1!"

"What?!" 43 and 117 both exclaimed.

"He got Kelsey inside the airlock when the energy blast hit! Now his beacon isn't registering on the sensors!"

117 looked at 43.

"Did he... um," he stammered at the thought of losing his friend. "Did 1 get incinerated?"

"If he was hit directly by the blast, yes," 43 replied. She quickly waved her hands reassuringly to 117. "But I'm sure he's fine!"

"His beacon isn't registering on the sensors!" 117 said frantically.

"Sensors are down," 2 replied. "Doesn't mean he's dead."

"Well, if he's lucky, he's still alive... and still outside."

43's reassurance didn't help. The two of them exchanged another look and took off towards the main control room.

"Is this what it's like back in your universe?" he asked.

"I've had worse," she admitted as they both ran down the hall.

Outer Space
Distance from Apogee Station: 598 meters and climbing

"Hello? Mayday, mayday. Is anyone receiving me? Anyone copy??"

1 was desperately trying to establish radio contact with Apogee station. While tumbling through space, he struggled to engage his emergency thrusters. Once he managed to get them working again, he used them to try to slow down. Unfortunately, the thrusterpack shorted out after a few bursts, making it impossible for him to fly back to the station.

After successfully shoving Kelsey inside the airlock, 1 hoped that she was safe. Just as 1 was about to follow her, he saw the energy blast heading towards the station. He closed the door as fast as he could, hoping it'd be enough to prevent her from being electrocuted to death, but the floor panel that he'd been on had suffered an electrical overload and exploded. 1's boots were still magnetized to it and he was sent careening into space.

"This is amborg Leonard 1. Can anyone hear me? Scratch that. Can anyone read me?"

Despite the fact that 1 was now a human satellite hurtling through space, he was able to properly focus. His thruster pack was still malfunctioning, but every now and then he was able to fire a really short burst, preventing him from spinning out of control at a speed that would've probably made a normal human sick by now.

It was very difficult for him to fathom that minutes earlier, he'd been talking casually with 117 and 43. Then, he had witnessed something truly awesome and terrifying. He even managed to take photos and videos of it, too, before he was sent flying away.

Three enormous ships had materialized out of nowhere. They were completely invisible until that moment, blending seamlessly into the surroundings. The instant they appeared, someone had fired the main cannon at the closest ship, triggering a fierce retaliation from the lead Tandeeri vessel. Truly, it was quite a spectacle that he couldn't believe he had witnessed and survived, but now, surviving was probably going to elude him. Stranded in the endless void of space and dying alone was going to be his fate unless help arrived soon.

1's anxiety was increasing by the second. With each passing moment, without working thrusters, he was only drifting further and further away.

"Yeah," he sighed in the back of his head. "First amborg in space to complete multiple spacewalks. Now I'm going to be the first amborg to die. Lost in space... Safety line snapped. Malfunctioning thrusters. And one piece of a floor panel magnetized to me. End of the universe and I got a front row seat..."

Finally, after the sixteenth attempt to restart his thrusters, 1 was finally able to orient himself into a fixed position. At this rate, perhaps he would be able to point his thrusters and fire a short burst to start pushing himself back towards Apogee station. He had a lot of distance to cover. The problem now was, would he even be able to make it back in time?

Over four and a half minutes passed since he was launched into the unknown. Under normal circumstances, five minutes is nothing. It usually goes by in the blink of an eye. Except, in outer space, it could mean the difference between life and death.

1 stared in the direction of Apogee station and watched everything unfold. It didn't look like it was going well. He desperately tried to fire the thrusters again, hoping that he could start his journey back.

He saw the same ship, the one closest to the station, fire a few more shots. Each time an energy blast hit, the station took on more damage. 1 noticed that there were additional ships in the Tandeeri fleet, approximately thirty-seven more, lingering a short distance away. The three sitting at their doorstep were probably the main ships, assessing the situation to determine if the Apogee Station posed a threat. The sight of the vast fleet in the distance raised concerns - they were likely gathering their forces for an impending invasion of the planet.

Strange, he thought, *why would only one ship continuously fire but not shoot to kill? Are they actually allowing us a fighting chance? Since the rest are all lying in wait?*

1 couldn't quite believe that the Tandeeri had that much power, but weren't wiping them from existence. All of his friends were still aboard the station. Were they being spared or did the Tandeeri want to take them prisoner? There was something odd about their attack pattern. If they were here to invade the planet, then why mess around and waste so much time? It was like they were toying with them for their own amusement.

The station was slowly sustaining damage, yet they were holding out fairly well. Dr. Kendrick certainly spared no expense into making it quite durable, but it was clear that they weren't going to last much longer. There was only one turret reconfigured to defend the station, and since the first energy blast, it was now out of commission, rendering the Apogee Station defenseless against the enemy onslaught. 1 tried to remain optimistic by viewing the situation as a possible victory, since the station hadn't been totally destroyed yet, but the odds were quickly turning against them.

"Not as bad as the Domino Incident," he pondered. "But this time, we're all probably going to die faster and fail everyone on Earth."

He turned his neck and looked around. The good news was that he hadn't been launched towards Earth. If he had gotten caught in the gravitational pull, then he most likely would have been incinerated to death while trying to hit that window to begin atmospheric reentry. The bad news was he was still slowly drifting away in space. Then, he spotted something with his enhanced vision and got an idea.

It was a satellite zooming around the orbit of the planet. He recalled 43's briefings from a couple of days ago. She'd mentioned that it took massive amounts of energy to generate wormholes, and that energy was strong enough to disable and knock out their best sensors. Maybe the reason that he wasn't able to reconnect or establish communications with the station was because they had no means to do so. At the very least, perhaps he could try broadcasting a distress signal to a working satellite down to Earth.

In theory, maybe it was possible. In space, the Apogee station was orbiting the planet at a certain speed. Since satellites were smaller man-made objects that were also traveling around Earth repeatedly, maybe he could make a connection.

"This is amborg Leonard 1 of the First Group, A.I. Industries, transmitting in the blind."

He tried to activate a communications channel. He heard static and a chirp as he tried to send out a message. There was no response, but he hoped that someone would receive his transmission.

"This message, if anyone is receiving a warning to the planet, if all communications from Apogee station have been cut off, then NASA and every space agency on Earth need to warn their governments and the entire planet."

As he continued explaining the situation, he could only watch helplessly as the battle of Apogee station continued to go downhill. Suddenly, he heard a chime from his display. He looked down at his arm and saw that his thruster pack had finished resetting again. The green light shined brightly. Immediately, 1 fired his thrusters.

A quick two second burst and he felt himself moving back towards Apogee station. With his magnetic boots still stuck to the floor panel that had launched with him, he imagined he must have looked like he was surfing on a ridiculous square board. His display suddenly turned red as the thruster pack stopped functioning. 1 tried to reset it again.

"This is 1, transmitting in the blind," he declared. "The Tandeeri fleet has arrived in full force. Please notify all commands that they have arrived at Earth. Apogee station has made contact and we are unsuccessfully holding out. I've fired my thrusters and I'm attempting to return to the station. If I make it back, I will find any survivors and hopefully a working shuttle to get us back planet-side."

As he continued moving, he managed to get his thrusters back in the green and fired another two-second burst, which increased his speed. He had to be careful not to add more, otherwise he would reach the station too fast. Once he got control again, he would need to course-correct or fire the thrusters to slow down.

The Tandeeri ships had stopped firing on Apogee. It looked like they were sitting there, waiting for a response of some kind. Based on how damaged the station was, 1 wasn't sure if there was anybody alive to even try and fight back. For all he knew, he was the only survivor of the attack.

"No," he muttered, "don't think like that. Everyone is ok and I got to get to them. I won't die in space!"

He cleared his throat and tried broadcasting again.

"Amborg 1," he said, not taking his eyes off of Apogee station. "Transmitting in the blind. The Tandeeri ship that was closest to the station fired some big energy blasts. It caused an explosion during my spacewalk and I got launched off of the station. I drifted about four minutes and 32 seconds before I could reset my thrusters and start returning to the station. I have lost contact and am continuing my attempts to reestablish communications. If anyone is listening, you must prepare for invasion."

1 took a deep breath. He checked his oxygen levels, which were still in good shape. In case he ended up stranded for a while longer, he had to remain calm and ration his air supply wisely.

"Transmitting in the blind... again," 1 declared. "I need someone to tell my family that I love them and I'm sorry. If I don't make it back from this, then

I'm really sorry. But, every mission that involves protecting people and saving the world is something I won't regret doing. I love who I am and what I do. I am an amborg that..."

1 fell silent when his eyes caught sight of something. A crackle of light appeared a short distance from the Tandeeri ships. Had he imagined it? Another crackle, much larger and more intense than the first, flashed like a lightning bolt streaking across the sky, or in this case, space. Last he checked, that shouldn't be possible.

What happened next made 1's jaw drop. He gaped as another giant burst of light appeared, revealing a huge crack in the fabric of space itself. A ring of energy emerged from the crack, followed by a small circular portal opening at the center. The portal expanded rapidly, swirling like a vortex. From where he was, it looked as though someone drilled a hole...in space.

An enormous portal, which definitely looked like a wormhole, appeared in his line of sight. It bore a striking resemblance to the anomaly captured in the footage of 43's arrival. Except, this portal was different - it continued to expand quickly, growing larger by the second. As he was trying to estimate its exact dimensions, he soon understood why.

An enormous object was hurtling through at an alarming speed. It was like watching a pair of floodgates opening. 1 suddenly realized that it was a futuristic-looking starship barreling his way. As it exited the portal, the wormhole slowly began to collapse. Drifting towards Apogee station, he marveled at the sheer size of it. If he had to take a guess, it looked to be about a quarter of the size of one of the Tandeeri ships. In comparison to Apogee station, it was massive. Lights gleamed from every corner of the ship.

The Tandeeri ships near Apogee station swiftly changed direction to confront the ship that was now maneuvering to intercept them. It almost looked like a pack of wolves encountering a bear. Instead of opening fire, the Tandeeri turned and steered back towards their own fleet.

"Holy mother of God," he stammered. "That's a big ship."

Apogee Station
Five Minutes Earlier

"This is Apogee Station! Attention! The Tandeeri fleet is here! They've begun an attack on the station and we've taken substantial damage! Does anyone copy?! Houston, do you read?!"

2 stood in the main control room as he attempted to fix their communications with NASA. Unfortunately, with the way things were going, he wished for anyone to hear his transmissions at this point.

"The Tandeeri fleet has arrived and we've been attacked," he declared as he tried to transmit their distress signal. "Massive energy blasts have overloaded our systems, but the station is not completely destroyed! If anyone copies, Earth needs to prepare for invasion! Situation deteriorating rapidly up here! We have casualties onboard!"

2 scanned the system and tried to get a damage report from the station's computer, which was barely functioning. Several systems throughout the station had been severely damaged or utterly destroyed. The internal sensors were picking up life signs across the entire station, but it was difficult to identify who was dead or alive. Dr. Kendrick's ingenious design of the structure was the only thing preventing the station from plummeting out of orbit, but each energy blast threatened to push it over the edge. There were several small fires crackling around the control room and many screens had blown to pieces. Amidst the chaos, a few people were desperately trying to reorganize while 2 kept performing system diagnostics.

He looked up and shouted a command to one of the drones.

"Get over there and put out the fires!"

Without a word, the drone turned its head and promptly followed his order. It jogged over to the fire that 2 was indicating and put it out with its built-in extinguisher.

"Anyone still able to get to their feet should tend to the wounded!" 2 instructed.

"Help me..."

2's console started to fizz and display static. He looked over at Jacob, who had called out to him. He was lying under a desk, bleeding from the side of his head and clutching his stomach. 2 curled his fist and gently hit the table furiously, then quickly made his way over. He raised his hand and activated his medical scanner to check Jacob's condition.

"Hey, I got you Jacob," he said soothingly. He knelt down and pulled a rag from the emergency kit. "I'm right here, ok? Communications are dead but help will find us. 6 or someone will be here soon to get you to the medical bay. We'll have you safe and secure in no time."

It was a meager attempt to keep Jacob reassured, but he was worried all the same. The energy emanating from the Tandeeri weapons were interfering with their communications. They were completely jammed. With the station's systems damaged, the interference was cutting deep, even into the Amborg's communications channels, which meant that their foes were very powerful. To make matters worse, the station could explode at any moment if it couldn't hold out any longer.

Jacob suddenly began to cough, which prompted 2 to cradle the technician's head. He wasn't sure when 6 would arrive, but the least he could do was apply as much of his medical training as he could while continuing to supervise the other survivors.

"I need someone over here to help me!" 2 commanded. "Davison! Keep trying to contact the others! Carla! Leave her! She's dead! We'll take care of the dead later! Wounded come first! Anyone uninjured please focus! We're still alive but we need to work together!"

Davison quickly took a seat at his console to assess the damage. He put on his headset and attempted to reestablish communications. Meanwhile, Carla had been trying to perform CPR on one of her colleagues. Unfortunately, after a few minutes of trying to resuscitate her friend, 2 could already see that her life signs had flatlined on his scanner. With a solemn nod, she followed 2's order to move on. Rising to her feet, she went over to another tech and aided in securing a bandage around their arm.

"Ugh... let's just face it 2," Jacob coughed. Burn marks marred one side of his face that extended down to his neckline, while blood seeped from his left shoulder, causing him plenty of pain. "Even after we get through this, I guess I'll always be ugly like this."

"What are you talking about?" 2 said confidently, forcing a laugh. "You were always ugly. These injuries are an improvement. You look pretty cool."

They both laughed softly as another technician crawled over to them. 2 saw that it was Carla and she was in tears.

"2," she said frantically. "We have most of the fires near the remaining systems put out. But I think we only managed to save our skins for another few minutes. How are we going to warn the planet?"

"We keep trying Carla," 2 replied, putting a hand on her shoulder reassuringly. "I'm sorry I ordered you like that, but you froze. We'll get you through this. Both of you and everyone else here are going home as heroes."

"We can't... 'cough,' all make it home," Jacob groaned weakly. "Not when most of us are dead."

"That isn't what I meant," 2 said as he checked Jacob's vitals and motioned for Carla to sit. "I was saying that…"

A loud crash cut him off. He turned to face the entrance to the observatory. Suddenly, he saw two pairs of hands reach in from the other side and pull the door open. He watched as Amborg 6 and 999 ripped the door open and staggered inside. Both of them wrapped their arms around each other and hobbled over to 2.

"You're alive!" 2 exclaimed as 6 fell to her knees while 999 struggled to stay standing. "You're both hurt?"

"There was a system overload," 6 panted as she massaged the bruises on her head. "Both of us were hit by it as we tried to get out of the way. We treated as many as we could on our way here."

"Here, help Jacob."

6 wiped her forehead and blinked a few times. She immediately maneuvered over to Jacob and Carla and began to examine their conditions. She looked both of them over, finishing her examination in seconds.

"No physical injuries," 6 stated. "But she is in danger of going into shock. Remember to breathe Carla."

Carla appeared to be in a daze, oblivious to everything going on around her. 6 and 2 exchanged a glance before turning their attention back to Carla, who was staring off into space, completely lost in her own thoughts. 6 reached out and grabbed her shoulder.

"Carla!"

Carla gasped, blinked, and then her eyes found 6.

"You with us?" 6 asked firmly.

"Yeah uh… Yes!"

"Focus!" 6 replied and repeated her instructions. "Breathe! Keep breathing. We're going to get you out of here."

"Shell shocked?" 999 asked, observing from the side.

"It's understandable," 6 sighed. "Now, for Jacob."

6 placed a hand on Jacob's wounds. He winced when he felt her touch.

"Severe electrical burns all across the body. Physical damage but no internal bleeding," 6 diagnosed as she reached for her medical kit. "Burn lotion and painkillers applied. One syrette of morphine. Well done, 2. Good job treating him. I can probably have him moved to the medical bay."

"I was going to see about applying more medicine," 2 stated.

"No," 6 replied sharply. "This is enough. Too much and it might have been bad for him. All we can do is let him rest, but I really need to get him stabilized somewhere safe."

"Dangerous," 999 spoke up. "Getting to the medical bay might be fatal."

"And we're all probably going to die before we make it there," 6 grumbled. "Is the station going down?"

"Not yet," 2 answered firmly. "But we will if the attack continues."

"999..."

2 and 6 turned to look at Jacob, who lifted his hand and pointed towards something. They followed his gaze and saw that 999 was attempting to leave.

"Hey Angel," 6 said in an alarmed tone. "What are you doing?"

999 staggered with each step as she made her way to the door. She ignored them and kept going, which worried them more.

"999," 6 spoke sharply. She quickly struggled to stand and called to her once again. "You're still injured. Stay here!"

"I'm fine," 999 replied coldly. "Everyone is ok here. We finished helping all of the survivors we found. I need to find... 917."

"He'll be ok!" 2 said. "Don't go running off by yourself! It's not safe to be alone."

"I can't lose him!" 999 replied. "I made... a promise..."

Suddenly, she ran off through the doors before anyone could stop her. 2 and 6 glanced at each other. He looked confused, and she let out a sigh.

"What did she mean by that?" 2 asked skeptically.

"Let her go," 6 turned and went back to tending Jacob. "There's no way we can stop her by ourselves. Let's focus."

"Even after all these years," 2 sighed. He glanced at the door before turning to help 6 stabilize Jacob. "I still don't understand their relationship."

"Their friendship," 6 enunciated softly in a quick attempt to correct him. "Their partnership. Their... relationship is unique in and of itself. Words can't even describe how strong their bond is."

"What does that mean?" 2 asked, raising an eyebrow.

"Sorry," 6 answered. "Doctor-patient confidentiality. I can't say any more."

More footsteps echoed through the room as another group of people showed up. 117 and 43 arrived, carrying Dr. Kendrick who appeared a bit disoriented. Serina trailed behind them from the station projectors that were apparently still functioning. She flashed and whizzed around the room as they all regrouped.

"We need assistance!" 117 shouted, and 6 immediately hobbled over.

They helped Dr. Kendrick to sit down as they all hovered over him protectively.

"I'm fine everyone," he said reassuringly, waving his hands. "I was just taken by surprise."

"More like a panel blew off and smacked you in the face," Serina snapped as she landed near a computer and tried to access it. "Just be glad that 117 and 43 arrived to help carry you. I wanted an escort for you... but NO... you had to go running off alone."

"I was coming back from the bathroom!" Dr. Kendrick exclaimed. "But yes, you're right! I'll be sure to be escorted every time I need to use the facilities. So, can we get back on track? Did we contact the surface?"

We've been trying but unsuccessful," 2 reported and shook his head. "We could make a break for the escape pods?" he asked, suggesting an alternate plan.

"They aren't escape pods," Dr. Kendrick replied. "They are retrofitted drop-pods that act like escape pods, but are good for quick travel around the world instantaneously from orbit."

"That's what an escape pod is," Serina reminded him.

"Rest Dr. Kendrick," 6 commanded as she took a look at his medical readings. "Or I'm going to sedate you."

She turned to look at the others.

"He might be concussed," she said. "We need to get him to safety, but I don't think a shuttle or an escape pod would be the best option right now. How hard did the panel hit him?"

"If it hit his neck at the correct angle, it would have decapitated him or impaled him," Serina answered. "I'd say he's lucky that it only smacked him."

"At that speed, it would definitely cause a concussion," 6 muttered.

"I can't rest," Dr. Kendrick said determinedly. "My amborgs... my life is scattered all over the station. We are the first line of defense for Earth and we can't even make contact. We can't rest now. Not while we are facing the threat of an attack."

"We can deal with that in a bit," 2 interrupted. He turned to Serina and pleaded. "Listen, Serina. 1 was outside the station when we came under attack. Can you go to the hangar and have them scramble the emergency shuttle? He's still outside!"

"Oh shit," Serina looked alarmed. She nodded and turned around. "I'm going to try and contact the hangar!"

"Wait a minute," 117 said as he looked around suspiciously. "Now that he mentions it... Hasn't it been a while since the last attack?"

Everyone paused and glanced upwards. Straining to listen, they heard... nothing. Some of the consoles continued to fizz and spark, but it sounded like the battle was over. 43 turned and walked bravely towards the window.

"It has, oddly enough, gotten very quiet," 2 agreed.

"Well, that can be answered if you look outside."

Everyone turned to 43, who was pointing outside with a look of relief on her face. The others who were able to stand followed suit, gazing out the window alongside her. Even Serina turned a pale and timid shade of blue as she peered outside.

"Ok that wasn't there a few minutes ago," she said meekly. "Damn."

They all turned their heads and spotted a new ship resting within full view of the station. It was shaped differently than the Tandeeri vessels, and the color scheme was remarkably different. This definitely had to be one of the ships that 43 said would be coming to help.

"It's the S.C.E. Firestar," 43 breathed in relief. She held up her hands as if offering a prayer of thanks. "I thought they wouldn't but they did. It's the flagship."

The name of the new vessel was printed on the side of the bow, confirming the truth in her words. They saw several gun batteries and cannons mounted on top of the deck. There were rectangular shapes protruding from the side and windows all along the length of the ship. Several of the guns were firing blue bolts into the distance towards what they imagined was the enemy fleet. Suddenly, several hatches towards the stern opened up and about ten or twenty smaller ships flew out. They instantly clumped in a formation and flew towards the station. The new arrival was finishing off the Tandeeri and driving them away.

"Ok..." 6 said staring. "I think I just died for real now."

"Don't go dying yet Doc," 2 breathed. "My heart attack might be beating you to the punch..."

They all stood silently as a transmission came through on one of the damaged consoles. Despite the static and the crackling electricity, the signal broadcasted quite clearly.

"This is Admiral Ra'aiah of the Second Colonial Defense Fleet of the Space Command Enterprise aboard the starship Firestar."

The monitor was hijacked and a woman appeared. Every monitor still functioning displayed her clearly. Her short brown hair was neatly tied up in a bun as she sat upright. She wore a uniform with a design that was definitely not from their world. To be exact, it wasn't a uniform that existed in their universe. Her serious and stoic expression seemed quite intimidating but they could hear the concern in her voice.

"We detect large amounts of damage. Your station is in danger of collapse and we are sending rescue teams. Is anyone able to respond?"

"I think this call is for me," 43 said.

She made her way over to the damaged console while everyone, despite being in a dazed or wounded state, continued to gape at the large ship docked in front of the station. There were indeed several small formations of small lights, which they realized were smaller ships approaching. Everyone else who was wounded, including Jacob, were all trying to get help in order to catch a glimpse of what the rest of them were seeing.

"Firestar," 43 said into the console. "This is commander amborg 43. We're all ok right now and it is good to see you. Please send medical emergency crews as well. We have many casualties and wounded."

"Understood," the woman on the screen replied. "It is good to hear from you 43. I am sorry we weren't able to arrive sooner. I take it your mission was a success?"

"More or less. You've arrived just in time," 43 smiled. "We could also use some counselors and first contact tacticians, too. Please send them at your earliest convenience."

"Counselors?" the Admiral asked with a confused tone. "Did the Tandeeri affect everyone's minds that badly? Are the inhabitants of Epsilon vulnerable to their energy attacks?"

"I think the shock is from your epic arrival. It was a psychological attack that has affected everyone's minds. But, at the same time, their dreams are being fulfilled as well."

Admiral Ra'aiah raised an eyebrow and nodded slowly. It didn't seem like this was the answer she was expecting, but she decided to go with it.

"Ah. I see," she paused. "I might need clarification on that last detail though. Sending the counselors and first contact advisers. Stand by for assistance."

Chapter 16: Friends
in High Places

S.C.E. Firestar

"Shuttle flight 230, this is Firestar. Pattern is open. Begin approach."

"Roger that Firestar, this is shuttle flight 230. We are on approach with several vital passengers aboard. Permission to dock?"

"Shuttle 230. Permission granted. Proceed to bay 12. Checkers red. Call the ball. Slow to one quarter throttle. Prepare for final landing sequence. Hands-on approach."

"Roger, Firestar. One quarter throttle. I have the ball."

117 was concentrating hard on trying to obtain information as he heard the conversation from the shuttle cockpit. Unbeknownst to 43, he was probably the one amborg out of all of them feeling very insecure about boarding a starship not of their own universe. Everyone else seemed to be enjoying themselves as if their favorite adventures were about to begin. As a result, he had decided to take a seat where he could promptly eavesdrop on the conversations within the cockpit of the shuttle. 43 sat across from him while 999 sat calmly next to him.

"Dr. Kendrick looks years younger," 917 said from 999's right side.

"He certainly does."

117 looked over at Dr. Kendrick who was in deep conversation with 43. He gestured at all of the many consoles and technologies in the shuttle and kept asking what they were or what they did. Naturally, because of his earlier injury, he was closely monitored by the glowing figure of Serina on his shoulder. 117 and 917 couldn't help but chuckle.

"Like a little boy receiving candy," 999 observed from between them. "Quite unsettling…"

"Just imagine all the things we're about to see," 917 said in wonder as he looked at a nearby console. "We've been given permission along with the rest of the amborgs down on the surface to board the flagship."

"Maybe we shouldn't be so excited about it," 117 pointed out softly.

"Are you nervous 117?"

117 looked at 999 who had turned her head in his direction. 917 was also leaning forward in his seat curiously. He figured that they had picked up on how anxious he was feeling.

"Probably as nervous as you were when the station was attacked Angel," he admitted glumly.

"I wasn't nervous," 999 replied softly. This was interesting. 117 had never heard her sound so… agitated. But before he could analyze her tone, she immediately spoke again. "917 was fine thanks to 501's actions. I can't believe I am thanking him of all people."

"You know, I am curious," 117 said, a thought suddenly occurring to him. "917, what did 501 do?"

"Well, he and 466 split up," 917 explained.

"I'm pretty sure I have rules advising against that tactic," Dr. Kendrick said without looking at them.

117, 999, and 917 stared at Dr. Kendrick. Without even glancing in their direction, he continued to pay attention to 43 as she awkwardly stared between every one of them. When he noticed that she had stopped her presentation unexpectedly, Dr. Kendrick politely smiled.

"I hear very well," he explained.

43 nodded and then resumed her presentation about the shuttle.

"I swear, he has amborg hearing," 117 remarked.

"He created us," 917 nodded in agreement. "I'm not surprised."

"Please continue before we go off-topic," 117 smiled.

"Right," 917 snickered. He looked at 117 and smiled cheerfully. "501 and 466 saved us. She went looking for you. He came looking for me. Right around the same time that Angel here also found me with my Fourth Group trainees."

Prior to the appearance of the Tandeeri, 917 had actually been coordinating a self-defense class with the Fourth Group amborgs. All of them had studied and trained in the same martial arts courses and fight classes but now, there was always the possibility of encountering an alien species in combat. This meant that some of their fighting techniques had to be upgraded. So, he had coordinated with 18 on the surface and they put together an improvised curriculum. 917 had been running a session with the Fourth Group about thinking outside the box right before the station was attacked.

"Before the attack. A little bit before," 917 explained, "we were by one of the station power generators. We had some down time and thought it'd be good to learn about how they worked."

117 felt uneasy, uncertain if it was from the way the Alpha universe shuttle pilot was flying or the fact that he wasn't sure he liked where this story was going. With "Donut" 501, it was sure to end in a rather interesting way.

"We only realized something was wrong when we weren't able to reach anyone else," he continued the story as 117 listened intently. "At first, we thought it was because the power levels in the room were blocking our signal but the engineers told us that there was no way any power source aboard the station could cause such a powerful interference. We figured something was wrong when their radios were out."

"Then the station was attacked," 117 said.

917 nodded. As he continued sharing the story, he'd begun to pull up his left sleeve. 117 noticed that it had been bandaged.

"We assumed we were under attack when the generators began to overload beyond what they could handle," he said. 117 could see the traces of anti-burn ointment that had been applied. "We knew that the equipment couldn't have been malfunctioning all at once so we all had to do some quick thinking. 501 had the idea of engaging an override which would... well, he tried to manually flush the energy from the generator to other systems in order to prevent it from being overloaded entirely in one spot. He figured opening the energy pathways to other sections of the station would relieve the pressure."

"That sounds like 501," 117 replied with a nod of understanding. "Only he could think of something that ridiculous in such a short time."

That explained why 501 wasn't among them in their shuttle. 6 had actually put him, Jacob, and several other wounded people from Apogee Station on another shuttle coming in with their flight. The Firestar was supposedly preparing for their arrival and had the facilities to assist them. The wounded would have to delay returning to Earth for a little while longer, it seemed.

"The only problem was," 917 continued his story. "The power coming from the Tandeeri weapons, if I understand this correctly, wasn't just overloading the generator, it was overloading everything. Like catching lightning without a harness. So his idea was useless. It probably only bought us a few more seconds and we did have to evacuate the room. As the Tandeeri kept shooting us, he thought he could prevent the station's destruction by trying to absorb all the power that he could before a system would overload and explode."

"He did what?" 117 asked in alarm.

"I'm surprised he didn't explode," 917 nodded to confirm 117's shocked expression. "But before we could stop him, he hooked himself into the power grid and took on an energy blast almost head on. I got the least of it but we got shocked pulling him off of there."

"Well," 117 breathed a sigh of relief. The shuttle suddenly rattled, making his hands jump to his seat harness. "At least that didn't happen. I should have checked up on him before we left Apogee."

"Well, we're about to have that chance in a bit."

"Sorry," 117 said as he unclenched his hands. "I think I'm just nervous. Excited, too. A little tense because of how fast everything is happening. Everything is too surreal. Even with all the information we've already been given."

"As your second in command," 999 spoke. "I hold the responsibility of ensuring teamwork and preventing our cooperative efforts from collapsing by making sure you do not break."

117 and 917 both stared at 999. He felt a little better hearing that.

"Wow, Angel... that was really..."

"Shape up right now or I pummel you."

917 laughed as 117 sighed.

"And..." he chuckled enthusiastically. "There's the Angel I know."

A loud clank reverberated through the compartment, and everyone felt a brief shudder as it shook, then settled back into stillness. 117 heard the pilot speak again.

"Skid down. Maglock secure."

"Shuttle flight, Firestar. Welcome back."

"Roger that. Thanks for catching us. Attention all passengers."

Despite already being quiet, everyone gave the pilot their undivided attention.

"We have touched down and are secure," the pilot declared cheerfully. "Opening bay doors momentarily. Prepare to disembark. You may disengage your seat harnesses and gather towards the exit. On behalf of the S.C.E., it's an honor to have flown the amborgs and Dr. Kendrick. Regular shuttle personnel, look sharp. The Admiral is organizing the welcoming committee herself."

Everyone glanced over at 43 who hit the center button on her harness. The belt around her waist came undone and retracted into the seat while the upper restraints unlocked and lifted up into a cabinet just above her head. The rest of them followed her lead, pressing their own center buttons. When 117's harness was released, he stood up, prompting everyone else to do the same.

Suddenly, the lights turned red and everyone jumped when the alarm went off. The deafening screech only lasted a second before stopping as abruptly as it started.

"Sorry," the pilot announced. "Hit the collision alarm. Hand slipped."

"Pilots like messing around with us sometimes," 43 winked as she led them all to the back of the shuttle. "It's their way of showing us they have a sense of humor."

"A warped sense of humor..." 117 felt his heart pound as he laughed nervously.

"If it wasn't for the fact that we were in space..." 999 grumbled, glaring at the cockpit.

"Easy," 917 cleared his throat.

Hopefully, 999 wouldn't be angry enough to commit a murder.

There was a whirring noise as the back of the shuttle opened up. The door fell outwards towards the ground and a ramp extended, much like one on a military cargo plane. The engines roared once and then immediately shut down. 117, along with the rest of the Epsilon passengers, peered out to see what was happening outside.

The hangar bay looked almost unreal. It resembled a three-story warehouse back on Earth, except it was bustling with activity. Smaller craft and tons of crewmen were busy working like a swarm of bees. Once the door lowered, a booming voice cut through the chaos.

"Company! Fall in!"

All activity in the hangar came to a halt, and then in one swift movement, groups of people lined up. A central aisle was created for them to walk down, while rows of crew members gathered on either side.

117 turned to see people in silver jumpsuits wearing or carrying helmets. He looked carefully at their insignias and shoulder patches, and confirmed they were pilots by the cool artistic designs. Their helmets were also decorated with small artistic decals and aesthetics.

A different set of crew members gathered in formation dressed in a mix of orange and yellow jumpsuits. Some were wearing protective helmets, headgear, radio headsets, and carried tools along their arms and beltlines. They resembled construction workers from Earth, but 117 guessed that they were engineers or perhaps part of the hangar deck crew, probably in charge of maintenance and repairs.

On both sides, lining up closest to the ramp, were armed troops. They wore helmets with fastened chin straps, dark armor padding, and gear all over their bodies. Soldiers or marines, from the look of it. Many of them were carrying what looked like advanced rifles and had similar sidearms holstered. There were a few that seemed to carry other gadgets as they lined up at attention. Most of them were putting their weapons away or swinging them around to point them upwards.

The final group that stood out appeared to be officers. They looked the most uniform in comparison to the massive crowd of people. Although they were fewer in number to the pilots, marines, and engineers, it made sense. Their shiny uniforms gleamed under the light, with silver stripes adorning their wrist sleeves. Some of them had two or three, but most of them only had one silver stripe. While they didn't glow like the amborg's jackets, they still managed to catch 117's eye.

117 looked ahead and spotted a single figure waiting at the end of the aisle. A female officer was surrounded by three other officers and flanked by a squad of six armed guards. These were the only ones that had gold stripes on their sleeves. They had to have higher ranks.

"Here goes nothing," Dr. Kendrick said slowly, adjusting his posture as everyone prepared to disembark. "Let's greet our new friends, everyone."

"Company! Attention!"

Every single crew member instantly straightened up. One of the gold-striped officers at the head of the formation stepped forward. He raised his arm and 117 noticed that there was something in his hand. He brought it up to his mouth and blew into it. The sharp sound of a boatswain's whistle pierced the air. It sounded synthetic, nothing like a natural one at all, but it was loud enough to call everyone to attention. Anyone carrying a weapon or rifle held it pointed straight up, presenting their arms carefully and rather beautifully as they stood motionless. Those that were unarmed raised their right hands and saluted. 117 noticed that they saluted differently in their universe.

A standard military salute is done with the right arm raised, elbow straight up and parallel to the floor, and the forearm bent at a 45-degree angle with the palm outstretched. The tip of the fingers are positioned right at the eyebrows. The military in the S.C.E. did everything except keep their palms parallel.

Instead, they were kept perpendicular. Their style was similar to the British salute, just backwards. The British military salute is done with the palms perpendicular to the floor and facing whomever is directly across from them. The S.C.E. had their palms facing the other way with the backs of their hands facing outward.

"117, you going to stay on the shuttle?"

117 blinked and saw that 917 had stopped to wait for him. He realized that he'd been focusing too long on the formation, and he quickly moved to catch up. After a few quick steps, he was back at 999's side. 1, 2, 117 and 999 flanked Dr. Kendrick from behind, with the leaders of the First and Second group escorting him. 43 walked ahead of them as their group exited the shuttle and headed towards the Admiral.

117 glanced back and saw 297, 5, and 777 bringing up the rear, followed by Captain Harrelson and a squad of his space jumpers. Everyone walked up the aisle like the red carpet had just rolled out for them. It was like meeting with royalty.

The other shuttle had landed off to the side. There was another crew making their way over to meet them, but 117 could see out of the corner of his eye that they had red cross patches on their uniforms. Medical personnel were meeting with 6, who was unloading the wounded from Apogee station. He noticed that 501, 466, and Jacob were on stretchers as many of the injured, but able-bodied, helped each other off the shuttle. 280 and 113 were also hurt, but managed to keep their composure as the Fourth Group amborgs stayed close together and guarded 6's patients.

The group from their shuttle was quite the contrast to the welcome party. 117 turned his head when he realized they were being greeted.

The Admiral and her ensemble stopped in front of them, seemingly ready to bow. Everyone followed suit and leaned forward, including Dr. Kendrick with a slight nudge from 43. 117 and 999, who were then joined by 1 and 2, stood in formation as Serina's glowing figure peeked out from behind Dr. Kendrick's ear. They all watched carefully as the S.C.E. officers straightened up.

Admiral Ra'aiah stepped forward and smiled. 117 immediately noticed something odd about her. Although she appeared human, he caught a mysterious glint in her eyes, there and gone in an instant. Perhaps this was just how people looked in the other universe. Dr. Kendrick coughed once before extending his hand.

"High low," he said confidently, but fell silent when he realized he botched the greeting.

Admiral Ra'aiah continued to smile curtly, giving Dr. Kendrick a moment to salvage the conversation.

"I-I'm sorry," he stammered. "I was attempting to say 'hi there' but then I tried to switch it to 'hello' halfway and... here we are."

She let out a soft laugh. Behind her, the other officers smirked slightly, but maintained their composure.

"Well, on that note," she answered. "It was unique. High low to you."

She gently placed her hand over her heart, linked her right thumb with her pinky, and brought it up to her eyebrows in a salute. Unlike the traditional military salute, she opted for a three-finger salute with the back of her hand facing them. After lowering her arm, a nearby officer took a deep breath and shouted.

"At ease!" the man behind her ordered.

In one swift motion, the entire formation lowered their salutes and switched to parade rest.

"Nice discipline," Captain Harrelson muttered behind 117.

117 glanced back. Harrelson shrugged and gave him a smirk, looking perfectly at ease. 117 returned his smile, then faced forward again.

"Dr. Kendrick," Admiral Ra'aiah said, lowering her salute and offering her hand. "It's been a long time. Please. Allow me to properly reintroduce myself. A video screen hardly does us any justice. I'm Admiral Ra'aiah. Commander of the Firestar. This is my first officer, Commander Ulgo."

"Um... I'm sorry. Again?"

Dr. Kendrick shook her hand firmly, then lifted his own hand to wipe the sweat off his forehead. The Admiral immediately caught what she'd said and began to chuckle.

"Oh pardon me," she replied. "I'm still thinking that we're in Alpha. I met you. Uh, I mean your Alpha version, a few years ago."

Her attention drifted as she glanced over Dr. Kendrick's shoulder. She noticed the wounded from Apogee and her smile faded.

"Get the wounded to the medical bay! Now!" she commanded. "Let's pick up the pace!"

The crew members hauling the stretchers technically hadn't stopped, but their pace seemed to quicken as they rushed towards the exit of the hangar. Admiral Ra'aiah motioned for everyone else to follow.

"We can continue this conversation as we heal your injuries," she offered kindly. "Please, follow my marines. Ulgo, please return to the bridge. I'll be there soon."

Commander Ulgo nodded and headed another different direction as Admiral Ra'aiah led them out of the hangar into a corridor. As they all walked towards the door, another officer yelled at everyone in the hangar to disperse and go back to work.

The medical team was given clear passage as the hangar resumed its activities. The crew members expertly maneuvered around them to ensure the wounded weren't impeded.

A couple of minutes later, they were all packed in the ship's medical bay. It was far more advanced than theirs back home. 999 had to punch 6 in the shoulder to snap her out of her daze. She was completely out of her element, but paid close attention to how the doctors were treating their injuries.

"You can't even begin to imagine how much there is that I want to ask," Dr. Kendrick began bombarding them with questions. "Is that an epidermal regenerator of some kind? What kind of power does this ship run on? What species are aboard this ship? How should I behave around them?"

Once he was sitting on the bed, being examined by a medic, Admiral Ra'aiah came over and stood next to him. She watched in amusement while the medic kept trying to perform a simple medical screening, but kept getting interrupted by all the questions.

"Admiral," the medic mumbled. "Requesting permission to sedate the patient?"

"Denied," Admiral Ra'aiah replied with a laugh. She turned to look at Dr. Kendrick with a kind smile. "Dr. Kendrick, if you don't mind, please let my staff give you a clean bill of health before you get too excited."

Dr. Kendrick nodded and snapped his mouth shut. He continued to fidget like a child, eager to hop up and down. 2 stood behind him like a protective shadow. Over by the next bed, 1 was guarding 280 and 113.

5 and 6 were in deep conversation with a doctor, who was absolutely fascinated with 5's prosthetic leg. Everyone realized this doctor had a robotic eye implant, which was designed solely for medical purposes. 6 kept trying to ask questions about, to no one else's surprise, the various medical fields but was constantly ignored by the doctor who was inches away from fondling 5's leg. For some reason, he had been asked to take a seat on the bed despite having minimal injuries.

"Oh look at that use of the alloys," he said as 5 smiled uncomfortably while 6 pouted. "The connection from the leg itself maintains a strong connection to the central nervous system without any signs of neurotransmission decay, allowing for the same movement, maybe better, than your original biological leg! How extraordinary! Would you be willing to donate this to the cybernetic philosopher's organization?"

"I don't think so," 5 gulped nervously. "This is one of a kind."

The doctor's face fell in disappointment, which allowed 6 an opportunity to start asking him some questions. 5 was able to gently sneak away and hid next to 117. The two of them walked away and found the Second Group amborgs badgering some of the marines with Captain Harrelson's squad.

"What's the range for this particular kind of rifle?" 297 asked as he admired a rifle that one marine was carrying. "How many rounds per clip? What kind of rounds do you use? Are they called rounds? Semi or fully automatic? Do you have any shielding equipment for extra protection? What kind of combat techniques can you show us? Do you guys use hand held rocket launchers of some sort?"

While the marine started answering his questions, the squad of space jumpers were quietly listening close by. 999 was questioning another marine who had a sword attached at their hip.

"That's an interesting sword," 999 pointed curiously. "What is it made of? Can I have one?"

917 was hanging out with a pilot who was watching over their wingman. As the doctor performed a post-battle medical exam, 917 cheerfully asked his questions.

"I'm actually interested in what kind of fighters you have," 917 said with a gleam in his eyes. "How fast can they go? How agile are they? How many weapons can they carry? Any of them transform? Can someone take me up for a ride if possible?"

"My questions are the same as 917's," 999 added as she called out to them.

Even Serina was taking a shot at examining the different pieces of technology. She flew from console to console and was traveling out of various conduits excitedly.

"What's the calculating speed of your best computer?" she would ask anyone who had the time to look at her. "What kind of artificial or virtual intelligence components do you use? Anything like us or better? Are they like Jarvis from Iron Man? EDI from Mass Effect? How smart are they? Do they like videogames or long debates about programming? Are they sentient? Programmed? Or raised like kids? How much equality do they get?"

117 couldn't help but feel a little left out. True, he was thinking about what his Alpha version must have done in the other universe. But the truth of the matter was, he was feeling so overwhelmed that he had no idea where to start. Everyone else seemed to be acting on their nerdiness and their own dreams and hopes. It only made him think of the fact that he had no idea what he wanted.

"117, come here."

He looked at Dr. Kendrick, who was motioning for him to sit down next to him on the medical bed. As he sat down, another doctor began checking on 117 while Admiral Ra'aiah waited for them to finish the exam.

"What's the matter?" Dr. Kendrick asked. "Even while the rest of us seem to be enjoying ourselves, you're choosing to distance yourself. Are you alright?"

"I don't know what to feel excited about," 117 replied with a sigh.

"Oh trust me, after I started my company, my wife used to say that to me quite often."

"What?"

"Nothing," Dr. Kendrick smiled, waving it off. "This reminds me of the time you failed your career prospects examination. You always did seem to have a lot of things on your mind that prevented you from moving forward."

"I don't know," 117 shrugged. "Maybe it's the fact that we almost died? Now things seem like they're normal again? How do I even begin to address that?"

"117, what of this universe do you think would just give an answer to such a complicated issue?" Dr. Kendrick pointed to the rest of the amborgs. "Everyone here is choosing to forget about their responsibility and explore for fun. But as an amborg, you'll be ready to leap into action when the moment calls for it. Right?"

117 sighed. He wasn't sure if this was what he needed to hear. He looked over at 777 who was reading a medical bulletin.

"I'm going to go out on a little bit of a whim here but," Dr. Kendrick eyed 117 inquisitively. "Are you feeling lonely?"

"Out of place," 117 replied quickly. "I'm not sure if I can get used to this."

"Well, there's plenty of time now," Dr. Kendrick smiled. "These people aboard this massive starship saved us. I think our odds have improved significantly."

117 looked down at the floor. He then glanced up and gazed at Admiral Ra'aiah. She met his eyes and smiled before resuming her conversation.

"You spent the last few days preparing for the end of the world," Dr. Kendrick said. "We all did. Now that we have a fighting chance, what else is bothering you?"

117 turned his head and looked at Dr. Kendrick. The first thing to come to mind was Audrey. Then Mandy popped into his mind, along with thoughts of all of his friends back home on Earth.

"You're worried about Audrey?"

117 nodded. Dr. Kendrick knew them all so well and was very acquainted with their individual lives.

"Everyone back home, too," he added. "What if we fail them?"

Dr. Kendrick glanced at Admiral Ra'aiah. 117 followed his gaze.

"What if you don't?" he asked confidently.

Admiral Ra'aiah wrapped up her conversation with the doctor and then strolled over. She smoothly brought her hands forward from behind her back, gesturing politely as she invited herself over.

"See anything interesting?" she asked.

Dr. Kendrick nodded and nudged 117 with his elbow.

"Everything," he said happily.

"Thank you," Admiral Ra'aiah grinned.

"Oh, I mean..." Dr. Kendrick's eyes widened, and his smile was replaced with a look of terror. "Your ship is fantastic! You being in charge of the whole thing is amazing! Very interesting!"

"Well, I'm glad you approve," Admiral Ra'aiah nodded. "It was difficult to get our ship through to your universe."

"May I ask something?"

117 raised his hand, drawing their attention. He politely stood and spoke up.

"Do I look like my Alpha version?"

Admiral Ra'aiah blinked, paused, and gave him a quick once-over. Sadly, she began to shake her head.

"I'm afraid," she said, "there's not really enough context to your question. But I think I know what you mean. I don't think you do."

She noticed his crestfallen expression and instantly tried to salvage the conversation.

"But I think that's a good thing!" she said awkwardly. "In this universe, you look fantastic and unique to yourself!"

117 raised an eyebrow. Admiral Ra'aiah tilted her head slightly and let out a sigh.

"Actually," she admitted, "the truth is, I haven't met your Alpha version before. I've only heard stories about him. I'm sure we could pull up photos of him in our archives, if you wanted to learn more about him."

"Maybe," 117 said with a hopeful look, "they're in Alpha."

"Who?" Dr. Kendrick asked.

"My parents?"

Admiral Ra'aiah's face fell when 117 looked at her eagerly.

117 caught a glimpse of Dr. Kendrick's solemn expression from the corner of his eye. Neither of them likely expected that, but the Admiral boldly stepped forward.

"I don't have the answers that you are seeking," she replied, but she quickly added more information to make her answer sound more helpful. "But I expected to hear that type of question when I hoped to meet any of the Epsilon amborgs. I'd very much be willing to help you find them. However, that is not a question I have an immediate answer due to present circumstances."

"Then what can we do to help?" 117 declared firmly. "I speak for the Second Group. We're ready."

The other amborgs weren't paying attention. They were all focused on pestering the visitors from Alpha with their questions around the medical bay. 117 awkwardly nodded.

"Well, I'm ready," he finished his statement.

Admiral Ra'aiah looked at him and then at Dr. Kendrick. The doctors who'd finished their examinations were staring, too, their attention having shifted to the conversation. Admiral Ra'aiah smiled and turned to the doctors, who were nodding their approval. 117 realized they were nodding because they'd apparently passed their unusually fast medical exams, but the message couldn't be any clearer than it already was.

"I can see that," Ra'aiah nodded. "Well, it looks like all the medical staff are finished and well, would you all like to accompany me? Those of you cleared for duty are welcome to follow. We would like to show you the ship. My crew is at your disposal and will continue to answer whatever questions any of you have."

"Won't the Tandeeri attack again soon?" 297 asked, raising a hand. "You managed to beat them back but we didn't destroy them. Are we safe?"

"Unfortunately, that is correct," Ra'aiah replied grimly. "They will be back, but we are monitoring them and we will have reinforcements soon. I felt it necessary that the Firestar arrive first because we felt that you couldn't wait any longer."

She stood aside and gestured for them all to follow.

"Until then," she said, "you are welcome aboard the ship and her facilities. There's no way of knowing when the Tandeeri will attack, but if you'd like to see any specific part of the ship, I can send someone to take you there. I can't split myself into multiple copies, unfortunately, and the party remaining with me will be heading for the bridge."

"May I remain here?" 6 asked. "I would like to oversee and observe my patients."

"Translation," 5 added after shooing the obsessed doctor away again. "She's really turned on by all of the futuristic technology and wants to see how everything works."

Several crew members burst out laughing at his expertly timed joke. Unfortunately for 5, 6 brought a fist to his face while brandishing a very bright smile.

"Please take this idiot with you too," she said politely.

"I think my face is broken," 5 sputtered with a cheeky grin.

After that, even though the Admiral offered to give them a tour of the various parts of the ship, they all opted to stick with her because of its immense size. 5 stayed back, having been injured by 6's antics. 501 and 466 were still being kept under observation, so the Third Group stayed behind to monitor them. Ra'aiah continued her conversation with Dr. Kendrick as she guided them out of the medical bay.

"Rest assured doctor," the Admiral spoke reassuringly as she led their group down the corridor. "Your crew aboard your station will be remembered for the courageous defense you put up. And we will rebuild it just the way it was."

"My thanks, Admiral," Dr. Kendrick sighed. "I only wish that the lives we lost could have been avoided. But how are we handling this diplomatically with the world?"

"I have ordered communications to be transmitted to all your high government officials," she explained. "We will hold our position up here while my people contact the planet. If your leaders wish, I can send delegates down to Earth utilizing first contact protocol. They are trained diplomats and will help with the transition of your citizens."

"We're very grateful for that," 1 casually thanked her as they kept walking.

"Yeah," 2 agreed. "4 is going to love this. Experienced interstellar travelers with a lot of training and experience? It's a dream come true."

"Some people could still respond poorly to all of this, right?"

"There is always that possibility," Admiral Ra'aiah said. She turned to look at Dr. Kendrick. "I noticed that some of your amborgs are requesting backup. If I send my crew down to Earth, I could have them offer any other amborgs or volunteers the chance to come up if they like."

"Maybe we should hold off on that until after you contact my leaders," Dr. Kendrick said. He turned to look at the viewport and watched the many shuttles and fighter patrols flying around Apogee. "You have my thanks for breaking it to the world nicely. Everyone deserves to know the truth and they need to be aware of the threat. Let's hope that the people of Earth can cope."

"In my experience," Admiral Ra'aiah said, "coping is never easy. Be prepared to face a lot of questions that won't be easily answered. Still, we must brace for the coming chaos and confusion from the masses. A forced first contact such as this isn't easy."

"Oh, we've had reports of many incidents across the world," Serina spoke up. "A lot of people are still acting out of fear and causing a lot of problems."

"It is understandable when it comes to human nature. Especially since a few thousand years ago, we thought we were the center of the universe," Dr. Kendrick explained. "Several hundred years ago, we knew the Earth was flat. And a few days ago, we thought we were alone in the universe. I can imagine everyone's expectations being completely shattered to the point of chaos."

Before Admiral Ra'aiah could respond, someone spoke up from behind, stopping them all momentarily in the hallway.

"Excuse me Admiral," 297 raised a hand. "Would it be too much to ask if I could see the armory?"

"Yes, it would 297," Serina sighed, rolling her eyes. "It's not like they're just going to let us have access to their space guns..."

"Well, as long as you are under supervision?"

Dr. Kendrick looked at Admiral Ra'aiah, who was eyeing 297 skeptically. After a moment of pondering, she waved to one of the marines that was escorting the group. He was wearing full body armor that looked like it weighed two tons, and carried a massive rifle with a glowing orange band of light running from the trigger to the nozzle. The type of power or ammunition it used was a mystery to them. Serina was likely worried about the potential consequences of using weapons from another universe.

"If you'd like," the guard spoke in a deep and gruff tone, "we can go now. We just need to make a turn down the next hall that's coming up."

"Yes," the Admiral nodded to 297. "Be sure to allow the commander an opportunity to become acquainted when you get there."

"Which commander am I looking for?" 297 asked curiously.

Admiral Ra'aiah looked at 297 and grinned. The group watched curiously as she pointed at him before taking the lead down the hallway.

"I was referring to you," she said. "Welcome back. Commander 297."

297's eyes lit up as his jaw dropped in surprise.

"Did you hear that?" he nudged 917. "I'm a commander! Wow, back on Earth, in this universe, I'm just a sergeant!"

"A weapons sergeant," 917 replied. "Still a pretty good rank."

"Do we... all have ranks?" 999 asked.

"Some of you do," Admiral Ra'aiah replied as the whole group moved forward again. "Marine, take care of 297 and see to it that his questions are answered. They all will require weapons for the foreseeable future."

"So, you have marines aboard?" 777 asked as 297 left with the soldier that had offered to take him. "Seems pretty standard for a space fleet. How is the military command formatted in Alpha?"

"They are standard," Admiral Ra'aiah nodded. "Each ship in our entire fleet doesn't fly without a complement of marines."

"What are their main tasks aboard your ship?" Serina asked curiously.

43 was the one who answered this question.

"For security reasons, diplomatic asset protection, ship-boarding offense/ defense, and the occasional ground assault missions. My personal favorite for when the fighting gets up close and personal."

43 winked at 117. As an amborg, it was probably more fulfilling for her when she got a chance to charge into battle. They had the advantage when dealing with close-quarter situations.

"And for the Admiral," 43 gestured to Ra'aiah and the officers that weren't in body armor. "She delivers hellfire with her heavy weapons when there's something our fists can't take down. From what I heard, this ship can bring down a sledgehammer of justice on our enemies."

"I don't say that at all," Admiral Ra'aiah shook her head and stared at 43. "No one aboard my ship says that."

43 snickered as she took over the explanations again. She maintained decorum and obviously didn't care for 43's disregard of professionalism. There was definitely a difference in their attitudes that was hard to miss.

"Marines adhere to starship protocols at all times," she said sternly. She turned to Dr. Kendrick. "They undergo the same basic training that my officers and regular crew go through. The S.C.E. offers a lot of career opportunities. After you enlist and take the primary courses at the academy, you're free to choose your specialty. Whether it be a space marine, pilot, combat medic, starship specialist, engineer, operator, however you want to serve aboard a starship."

"Well, that certainly explains all the different uniforms we've seen," 917 remarked.

They watched as a group of officers walked past. They stopped, stepped aside, turned, and saluted Admiral Ra'aiah as she and the group walked past. She saluted them, which prompted them to silently continue on, allowing them to head back to their duties.

"Silver stripes are junior officers," Admiral Ra'aiah explained. "Fresh out of fleet command school and on track to be the next captains and commanders of their own vessels. If you see more silver stripes, they're higher ranks and you can refer to them as senior officers."

"May I take a guess and assume that silver stripes are then promoted to gold?" 917 said, gazing at Admiral Ra'aiah's uniform.

"Correct," she nodded proudly. "Gold stripes can command this ship if anything were to happen to me or my bridge crew. These officers are upper etches."

"Etches?" 777 asked.

"Upper echelons," 43 replied. "Department heads, supervisors, and usually in charge of large sections of crew, decks or the toughest leaders aboard."

"Admiral?" 117 raised his hand. "If I may?"

"Go ahead."

117 glanced at their marine escorts, the officers with them, and at the people walking by. So many details and so many crewmembers with specialized tasks and responsibilities.

117 pointed at a silver striped sleeve that was next to him.

"I see two stripes," 117 pointed out. "This officer has been here for some time?"

"Eight months, sir," the officer nodded her head. "I get my next stripe in four."

"Then you become a senior officer?" he asked for clarification.

"When I get my fifth stripe," she answered politely. "Five or six stripes are eligible to go gold."

117 then turned to another officer standing behind 917. He had gold stripes.

"You've been serving for... two years?" 117 guessed.

"Yes sir," the officer nodded, and he grinned cheerfully. "Before I was posted here on the Firestar, I served on two other ships."

117 looked at Admiral Ra'aiah curiously.

"These officers must serve for a minimum of a few years to be able to command. May I ask how long you've done this job?"

"I became the captain of my own ship after my fourth year," she answered with a smile. "It took another three for me to qualify for my admiral."

"For a ship this size, you must have a large crew complement to keep her running."

"Indeed, we do," Admiral Ra'aiah said. "The Firestar carries four companies of marines in the garrison, which is two times that of a regular troop transport. The rest of us, aside from the officers, include engineers, technicians, R&D science divisions, pilots, the bridge and tactical crew, medical staff, battle-bots, mess hall civilians, and the families aboard too."

As if on cue, a bunch of children came running through, startling everyone. They all cleared the way as they playfully dashed by. The amborgs watched them in fascination. Their presence reinforced the Admiral's point.

"Aboard the flagship?" 117 asked curiously. "Like Star Trek?"

"Indeed," Admiral Ra'aiah beamed. "It's nice to know we share the same recreational lore. The crew operates at maximum efficiency because of the close support and comfort of their loved ones. Anyone who has no family aboard enjoys being part of a population the size of a small city in this ship. Some species claim that bringing our children with us is a distraction. But many believe it is a reminder of the good things we bring with us as we explore space. Feel free to disagree though."

"I doubt we can. Considering it's too late to send all these families back home," Dr. Kendrick chuckled.

"For many crew members, this ship is home," she replied as they arrived at an elevator of some kind. The guards all stopped following and left the group. "It is the first of its kind to be built. Heavily fortified with new shielding technology from a combined research initiative. I'm proud to say that we've survived on more than one occasion. Every encounter we get through is a victory that generates hope. It's something we definitely need in this war."

117 glanced at a few people walking by in the same bright orange and yellow jumpsuits that were in the hangar.

"Engineers?" he asked politely.

"Correct," Admiral Ra'aiah turned and dipped her head at 43. "You certainly taught them well."

"Well, I did have some time on my hands," 43 answered.

"So, is this kind of ship a deep-exploration ship as well?" 3 chimed into the conversation. She had been observing and soaking in everything in her surroundings. "It seems like it'd be perfect for colonization or expanding your influence across the universe. A moving city in deep space."

"Yes, it is," the Admiral responded again with a grin as they waited for the elevator. "We have enough provisions and power to survive a decade away from any colony or major S.C.E. star base. There are all sorts of crewmen aboard with different backgrounds and cultural values. The diversity in the species aboard is notable as well. It's probably one of the first ships where I've witnessed all of us, human and alien, coexisting peacefully."

"Most of the alien species that are a part of the S.C.E. tend to stay with members of their own race when it comes to other ships in the navy," 43 explained. "It's easier for them to maintain their unique living conditions. The Firestar is equipped with a lot of special accommodations to generate ideal housing for some of the people you'll see as you explore the rest of the ship."

"Interesting," 3 said in amazement. "Speaking of cultural and diverse backgrounds, any chance I could see your mess hall?"

Admiral Ra'aiah looked a little taken aback, but it was no surprise to the rest of them. When there was food around, 3 was always lured straight to a kitchen no matter where it came from. They saw it coming, especially since 6 was glued to the medical bay and 297 had gone looking for a space gun.

"Oh... of course."

The Admiral gestured to a passing guard, gave him quick instructions, and 3 headed in another direction with her escort. Meanwhile, the party remained behind to wait for one of the elevators to arrive so they could proceed directly to the bridge. While they waited, a crewman walked by and accidentally stumbled into 917.

"Oops!" she exclaimed as she straightened up and adjusted her cap. "I'm terribly sorry, please excuse me sir."

"Hey!"

The gold stripe officer that was behind 917 snapped at the crewman. He looked furious.

"Be more careful!" he said. "Do you know who this is?"

The silver striped junior officer turned to face 917. There were two silver stripes on her sleeve, just like the officer standing next to 117. 917 merely raised his hands and laughed it off.

"Please! No need for that!" he quickly stated, hoping to defuse the situation. "No one got hurt!"

The officer that had bumped into 917 dipped her head. The gold striped man nodded his head and politely backed down.

"As you were, ensign," he grumbled.

The girl bowed her head and turned to leave.

"Lieutenant," Admiral Ra'aiah said sternly.

"Ma'am," the officer halted and stood at attention.

"As good as your intentions were," she said in a soft tone, "you don't get promoted to commander by embarrassing your fellow shipmates or our special guests for minor infractions. I think we can overlook those small issues, wouldn't you agree?"

"Yes, Admiral. Sorry ma'am."

The elevator arrived and the doors slid open without a sound. The elevator was huge. Admiral Ra'aiah allowed the amborgs to go first with Dr. Kendrick. As they boarded, 917 took 117 by the arm and they settled into a corner, then signaled 999 to stand in front of them. As the Second Group huddled together, 1 and 2 stood with 280 and 113 to protect Dr. Kendrick in a square formation. Admiral Ra'aiah stepped into the elevator with 43 and her officers.

As everyone continued to chat, 917 sent 117 a request to speak on a private channel.

"What's up 917?" he asked after accepting the strange and random invite.

917 returned his gaze with a slight frown. Obviously, something had happened that had caused him to be suspicious.

"It's most likely nothing," he shrugged, "but it was interesting how that crewman weaved her way through the group and conveniently tripped on me. Strange footwork if you ask me. I just figured out why."

"What do you mean?"

"I replayed the footage that I recorded of her walking through us," 917 smiled to look casual in case anyone looked in his direction. "She bumped into me on purpose."

"To do what?"

917 reached into his chest pocket and pulled something out.

"She was trying to tell me something."

He held a tiny slip of paper in his hand. 117 quickly looked at it, blinked to take a photo of it, and 917 discreetly put it back in his pocket. The two of them pulled up the image in their HUD to examine it without anyone noticing.

I need your help. Please come to the corridor next to the entrance of hangar three in one hour. Storage room. Hope has returned with you.

There was a faint whirring noise that began to wind down. If he had to guess, 117 believed that the elevator was about to come to a stop. The technology was impressive. The ride was so smooth that they hardly felt any movement.

"What are you going to do?" 117 asked as the elevator doors opened and everyone began exiting. 917 tilted his head as he thought about what to say. "How do you know this isn't a trick?"

"It's usually always a trick," he sighed. "It always gets the nice people. Chances are, she knew the other me. Then again, it could be a trap. Amborgs probably fetch a high price on the black market where they're from."

"You're actually considering this?"

"Well, it's the best way to figure out what's going on," 917 admitted. "Information on their end is what's got me curious. Gathering as much knowledge as we can could be useful. Might as well take a chance. I'll see about being discreet when we're allowed to roam around the ship. If we're allowed to. Let's end the private channel and get back to everyone before they realize something's going on."

They exited the corridor and entered the bridge. Several computer consoles lined the walls, each one manned by an officer. The windows gave them a perfect view of Apogee station. The S.C.E. shuttles were zooming around, slowly repairing the damaged sections.

The person sitting in the center of the room turned around, saw the Admiral, and rose from his seat.

"Admiral on deck," the officer announced. "She has the conn."

"Thank you, lieutenant," Admiral Ra'aiah smiled courteously and dipped her head. "As you were."

The officer walked away and took a seat at another console, resuming his work as if nothing had happened. The silver and gold striped officers in the group politely excused themselves and headed to their own stations.

"Dr. Kendrick?" Captain Harrelson said, looking around the bridge with wide eyes. "This has to be the most amazing thing in my entire life. Thank you for letting me be part of it."

"Captain," Dr. Kendrick grinned, nodding in agreement. "The feeling is quite mutual."

Admiral Ra'aiah smiled as she walked to her chair and pressed a button.

"This is the admiral," she spoke formally. "All hands will maintain battle readiness. Please begin first contact protocol."

The Admiral sat down and brought up a couple of holographic screens. After skimming them, she brushed them off and they disappeared from view. Meanwhile, Dr. Kendrick was looking around in awe and trying his best not to run over to one of the consoles. 117 noticed he kept stepping forward but would then quickly retract his foot. He almost looked ready to hijack the Admiral's seat.

"This is very impressive Admiral," Dr. Kendrick said as calmly as he could. "I was wondering if I could..."

Admiral Ra'aiah glanced at Dr. Kendrick and noticed how much self-restraint he was showing. He was doing his best to maintain his professional demeanor, yet she could tell that he was on the verge of bursting with excitement.

"Go right ahead doctor," she said, lifting her hand and waving at nothing in particular.

And he was off.

And he was off. He ran up to a sensor console and immediately began pestering the person on duty, who was taken slightly by surprise. As they began to share a deep overview of their station with Dr. Kendrick, Serina chuckled nervously and glanced at the others.

"I'm going to make sure he doesn't get too excited," she said. "6 told me to monitor his vitals. He did get hit in the face during the attack."

"Didn't they say that he was alright?" Captain Harrelson asked. "Wasn't he concussed?"

"They had some sort of scanner that fixed him up almost instantly," 1 replied.

"This ship has it all," Harrelson nodded.

He walked off to join Dr. Kendrick, and Serina blinked and reappeared hovering over his shoulder.

Except for 280 and 113, the amborgs present grinned at the sight of their creator showing his inner child. Since they hadn't really received any orders or figured out their next move, they decided to hang around where the Admiral was sitting. It took Admiral Ra'aiah a second, but she soon realized that she had only allowed Dr. Kendrick off the metaphorical leash. She noticed that they were hovering around her and quickly addressed the amborgs as if she suddenly had taken command over them.

"If you have any further questions," she informed them, "my staff is available as well. You don't need to primarily stick with me."

"I did have one question Admiral," 117 asked. "Where are the Tandeeri now?"

The Admiral nodded and brought up a screen that projected from her arm rest. She then spoke to the entire room.

"Get me a location on the Tandeeri."

"Aye ma'am," said the sensor officer sitting next to the person being questioned by Dr. Kendrick. "Displaying location."

A small screen appeared in front of Admiral Ra'aiah. She lifted her right hand and enlarged it with an upward swiping movement. Dr. Kendrick noticed and attempted to copy her, but his screen disappeared instead, leaving him standing there with a puzzled expression. The amborgs, all silently snickering, focused on the Admiral's screen while the sensor officer explained how it worked to Dr. Kendrick.

It was a map of their solar system, from what 117 could see. At the center of the circle on the screen was a blue arrow, which represented the Firestar with the initials in bold letters. **S.C.E. DF1**" floated above the triangle and the name **"Firestar"** floated below that. The arrow was in close proximity to Earth and a gray diamond off their port bow was the radar depiction of the Apogee space station. 117 looked closely at the map and saw that it was bigger than it seemed. The sensor range was remarkable as it extended all the way past Pluto. Then, the map immediately highlighted a group of red arrows clustered around Saturn.

"The radar shows that the enemy is massing just off the fifth planet in the system," he reported. "No other movement, Admiral."

"Keep me posted," the Admiral replied. "They're regrouping for another assault soon. Or they may have established a staging ground for reinforcements.

I want four squadrons deployed to establish a patrol perimeter. I want to know which direction they'll come from now that they know we're here. Send one squadron to protect the station. Engineering, continue monitoring main reactors. Keep running drills with E-weapons tactical. Weapons details, begin diagnostics of the point-defense guns. Stand-by to recharge the R-batteries on all decks. Load payload hotel-echo alpha-potato, all cannons. I want launchers to ready MVA clusters. All departments stand ready at yellow alert."

There were several calls of "Aye" and "Yes ma'am" from the various bridge members.

Admiral Ra'aiah sighed and then turned to 117. The map on the display disappeared.

"There we have it," she said as she leaned on one arm. "Not much to do now until they make another move."

"Ok that's very good news," 117 nodded, but he was wondering about what he had just heard. "But there's an S.C.E. code that uses the word potato?"

"Oh. Ha ha," Admiral Ra'aiah said as she clasped her hands together. "No. I was using the standard military alphabet. But I never liked how the letter 'p' stood for papa. He was... intense. I substitute the word with potato. They're very delicious by the way."

"Do you dislike your father?" 999 asked quietly.

"No," Admiral Ra'aiah replied bluntly. "I just have a hard time saying papa sometimes. Personal preference. What about your parents?"

"Dr. Kendrick is a great parent to us all," 999 said, watching as every other amborg nodded in agreement. "Our real parents... we've never known them."

280 and 113 looked on passively as the rest of the amborgs bowed their heads solemnly. Admiral Ra'aiah realized what she had just asked.

"Oh right. I see," she said, dipping her head. "I didn't mean any offense."

"It was a legitimate question," 280 said. "Personal but legitimate."

"And, we're changing the subject," 917 said, giving the Fourth Group leaders a glare. "Admiral, do you have any way of contacting the rest of your fleet?"

Technically, even with the presence of the S.C.E. flagship now serving as the new line of defense for Earth, they were still outnumbered by the Tandeeri fleet. Admiral Ra'aiah looked thoughtful for a moment and then answered.

"It's dangerous for ships to jump between universes in the first place," she explained. "Once a wormhole is closed, communication is lost since we technically crossed through another door and closed it behind us, so there's no signal. We could generate a wormhole now and send in a few communication buoys, but we don't know if that will do any good. When the Tandeeri get wind of a wormhole generation, they practically swarm us."

"What do you know of them?" 117 asked, sneaking a glance at 43, who shook her head.

"Unfortunately, we only have theories," the admiral sighed. "In other words, we don't know much. We don't know what the Tandeeri tactics are when they travel from different universes. All we know is every time we have activated and created a wormhole, they're always there."

"So, everything we know of the Tandeeri is pure observation?" 117 asked. "It's very strange that you've never seen a single one of this species."

"In a manner of speaking, yes," 43 nodded solemnly. "When we first encountered them, there was an attempt to communicate which told us they were intelligent. But we had no idea how smart they were. They actually contacted us first, but then we were attacked without warning. They pretty much declared war and they've been beating us back."

"Including us," 2 said. "They have some rather powerful energy-based weapons. What do you know about those?"

"Their weapons are definitely unlike anything we've developed or seen in any of the universes we've deemed safe to travel to," Admiral Ra'aiah answered his question promptly. "High energy blasts that overload and rupture our components. We've been pushing for faster and more agile ships, but it's expensive to manufacture and it takes too much time. Not to mention the Tandeeri defenses are equally powerful as well. Their shielding is extremely difficult to get past and we've only been able to replicate that technology for temporary moments in battle. A useful advantage but not good enough. The Firestar is one of the only ships that carries actual energy shielding for extra defensive measures. Our top scientists then theorized that the Tandeeri are actually not from our universe. This is based on what we've observed about their technology."

"Why is that?" 777 asked.

"Our weapons and technology cannot be matched to the Tandeeri at all," she said. "And this is just a guess… It's because they use materials and resources not of the Alpha universe. Nothing in our universe could match initial scans of their ships. To be honest, we've never been able to properly scan a Tandeeri ship since they aren't really that welcoming. Any attempt at salvaging or even foraging for a sample, whenever possible, is moot.

Several pirate organizations have put out bounties for whoever even catches a live Tandeeri, which so far hasn't been collected. We don't know their language. Colonies are utterly destroyed and razed to the ground. No witnesses. Our stealth ships then discovered they were making wormholes and found that they could travel across to different universes as well, which is the main reason why we don't think they are native to both our universes."

"It's just like you said," 117 said to 43.

"Even with our best ship in the fleet," 43 stated, "we're still fighting an uphill battle."

"Admiral," 117 said thoughtfully. "Have there been attempts to find the Tandeeri home world? Perhaps there is the possibility of locating a source and figuring out ways to deal with it."

"Without knowing which universe they're from," Admiral Ra'aiah sighed and placed a hand on her forehead, "we have no way of pinpointing exactly where they live. It's hard enough that your universe and ours are vast and unexplored. It's even more difficult pooling resources to search a million other possible realities."

"Well, maybe we can focus on what we can do to help instead of what we can't," 999 said. "May we look around the ship?"

"Yes of course," Admiral Ra'aiah nodded. "43, if you could accompany or direct them, they're to be given full access to anything they need. Any help or inquiries about certain areas of the ship, you can use the computer terminals if you get separated from each other. Also, we have crewmen in specific departments who'd be able to help, too. After all, the engineers probably know more about the engines than I do."

"I'd very much like to go to the hangar bay," 917 said. "Your ships are quite amazing."

"I guess the armory might be a good idea," 117 shrugged, having no idea what to do. "Or maybe I should check on 501."

"Let's check out the equipment," 777 suggested. "I think it'd be smart for us to try to learn about their gadgets and tools so we can be of use during the next engagement."

"Is there a library?" 999 asked.

All the amborgs stared at her. Admiral Ra'aiah eyed each of them curiously, unsure of what to say in the midst of the immediate awkwardness surrounding her chair. 999 looked back at all of them and rolled her eyes.

"It's not that surprising..." she muttered and looked away. "I read... Occasionally."

"The elevator can take you. Just follow the signs," Admiral Ra'aiah replied courteously. "Oh. Is there something I can help you with?"

280 and 113 were still hanging about. They were the only ones who hadn't requested to see anything.

"Yo!" 917 said. "Spock and Saavik. Don't just stand there like the Admiral's shadows... You don't always need to wait for someone to give instructions."

"Fourth Group amborgs," 117 explained to the Admiral.

She looked oblivious, having no clue what that meant as Dr. Kendrick rushed over.

"I see," she replied with a look of bewilderment. "Well, if you would like to stay on the bridge, then maybe something of interest will catch your eye?"

"Alex. Ally," Dr. Kendrick interrupted. "The Admiral has work to do. Why don't you do your sister Vanessa a favor and help monitor my condition? Maybe you can just observe me while the nice crewmen of the bridge give us a tour?"

280 and 113 both nodded silently.

"If they're going to escort you," 1 said with a smile, "perhaps 2 and I could go exploring?"

"6 wants at least one amborg watching me," Dr. Kendrick eyed the Fourth Group leaders. He then turned and nodded to the others. "Go ahead."

43 led the six amborgs to the elevators for the next part of their adventure. Several crew members actually moved out of the way for them, which was quite surprising. Their Alpha versions must have commanded great respect. When she pressed the button, the doors opened. They entered and 43 spoke again as the elevator smoothly began its descent.

"What did you want to look in the library for?" she asked curiously.

"It's personal," 999 replied with a shrug. "I'm actually curious about... myself."

999 gazed at 917.

"What did you want to see in the hangar?"

"It's personal," 917 said casually. "Not really, I mean... I actually really want to see the fighter craft they have. Some of the designs looked cool! Maybe if they're not looking, I'll commandeer one."

"Oh, there's no need for that," 43 smiled. "Just ask for permission and someone will let you take a look. Just remember to give it back to the pilot when the next fight begins."

777 looked at 1 and 2.

"Where did you guys want to go?"

"I was very curious about their engineering department," 1 replied. "I'd love to see how this ship is run."

"What about you, 117?"

2 had turned his gaze to 117. Everyone else also looked his way, which caused him to start sweating.

"Well, so far," he started, "the armory seemed like a good idea. Maybe checking on 297 would be wise."

"Ah yes," 43 nodded. "We can stop there after 999 gets off at the library deck and 917 at the hangars."

The elevator stopped moving and the door suddenly opened. One crewman walked in. He noticed that they were all amborgs and hesitated for a moment. 117 smiled and waved politely. The crewman timidly asked that the elevator go to a certain deck. Seconds after the door closed, the elevator resumed its journey. They all felt a jolt as it shot to the right, stopped, went left, then shot backwards, sending them lurching forward. It almost felt like a throwback to Willy Wonka's glass elevator.

"This is definitely a weird elevator," 917 said. "999, what floor did we ask to go to?"

"I didn't," 999 replied. "It just automatically went down when we got in. I don't think I recall any of us actually making a request."

"It was probably me."

The crewman spoke up confidently, but then cowered down a little.

"I called for an elevator, and you probably happened to be in it and because you didn't actually ask to go anywhere, that's what happened."

"Oh good," 917 sighed. "I almost thought this elevator could read our minds."

"Umm, excuse me."

The young junior officer, who had one silver stripe on his sleeves, had taken out a notepad and a pen. They immediately understood what the man was asking for.

"May I get an autograph from all of you?"

They all glanced at each other and smiled. This officer was apparently a fan, and they were happy to indulge him. 117 took the notepad and the pen and tried to write his signature, but another problem popped up, which had him stymied. The amborgs eyed the pen and realized it wasn't a normal one. The problem for 117 was, there wasn't a clicker or a button of any kind... or an extendable pen tip. He turned it over in his hands, trying to figure it out.

"Um. This will be a stupid question but... How do you use this pen?" 117 asked, coughing embarrassingly. "I'm unfamiliar with how to use this..."

"Oh, that's a new ink discharging pen," The crewman explained. "Just push the red button and the pen activates. Press the green one to dispel the ink and then you write with it."

"Sounds like a regular fountain pen if you ask me," 917 said.

117 pressed the red button and then the green one without hesitating. 43 watched in silent amusement.

A laser-like light shined brightly onto the notepad from the pen. 117 clicked it off and looked at the pad. A moment later, a spot of ink appeared where the light was shining a moment ago. Amazed, 117 gazed fondly at the pen. He enthusiastically pointed, pressed the buttons, and began scribbling his name without touching the paper while the crewman continued with the explanation.

"It's one of the best pens designed," he explained. "It can be used like a regular pen, but it's so much better. The green button dematerializes the ink, sending it along the laser. Wherever it's pointed, it goes. And then it rematerializes on any surface. It can go up to at least half a mile away."

"Any surface?" 117 looked up curiously with his fingers clenched tightly on the pen.

"Hey!"

Everyone stared at 777, who'd jumped up like a frightened cat. 117 had forgotten to let go of the green button. The instant he looked up, the laser shot out, and 777 happened to be in the line of fire. Everyone watched as he lifted his arm and inspected his sleeves. Ink lines and blots were materializing all over his chest and upper body. Somehow, the laser had also shined briefly on his face and now there was a dark line across his right cheek.

"I can actually feel the ink!" he exclaimed. "Whoa!"

"Oops," 117 chuckled nervously as he quickly passed the pen over to 917.

The crewman fumbled in his pockets and grabbed a handkerchief while 917 signed his signature carefully. Once he was done, he passed it to 1.

"Oh, that tends to happen a lot with people just beginning to use those," he muttered apologetically as he wiped the rag over 777's arm.

The ink disappeared from his clothing instantly, vanishing like an eraser on a whiteboard.

"An ink removing handkerchief?" 117 asked. "Talk about washable wipes."

"There were a lot of flying colors going around when these pens were first introduced to the public," the man explained.

"Nice play on words there," 2 smiled politely.

777 wiped his cheek and the ink disappeared. It was like it had never been there. Once they had all finished signing the notepad, the crewman eagerly took it back into his hands.

"Thank you very much! My kids are going to love this! Thank you for your time! Well. Good luck for both of our universes!"

As the elevator stopped and let the man off, the amborgs then turned to figure out where each of them was headed.

"Ok well, I guess I'm going to the archives..." 999 said. The minute she spoke, the elevator immediately began to move. "Unless we get another giddy crewman asking us if they can cook us dinner."

"I wasn't expecting to meet a fan," 117 said. "But you know what? If there are a bunch of them backing us up on this ship, it makes me think we're going to be ok."

Everyone in that elevator agreed that his words made sense. It seemed to boost their morale significantly. Even though she looked reluctant to side with 117, she nodded in silence, which spoke volumes.

Chapter 17: Staying down to Earth

A.I. Industries

"How bad is it up there?"

4 and 18 were on one of the communication terminals with 1 and 2. The leaders of the Earth Amborg teams were also participating, so 35, 57, 95, 53, 65 and 224 were watching the meeting as well.

"Hilariously bad," 1 answered on the screen.

"This terminal is really cool though," 2 muttered.

1 looked at 2 who wasn't looking directly at the camera. He seemed to be more fascinated at examining the screen. Everyone on Earth watched as 2 kept moving in and out of the frame as he was paying attention to everything else except the meeting.

"Can you focus?" 1 asked.

"Why? You're reporting in enough for all of us," 2 replied. "Just let me examine this high-resolution terminal."

"Ziggy!"

"Ok! Fine!"

2 straightened up and let out a disappointed sigh. 1 shot him a look and then turned back to the camera, and the two of them faced the screen normally.

"Sorry for going off-topic but where are you?" 18 asked as the rest of them all stifled their laughter.

"The big Alpha universe starship," 2 answered. "In outer space?"

"No, I know that," 18 rolled her eyes. She gestured to everyone. "We know that! Where are you even speaking to us from? Is this call safe?"

"It took us a while to hook up a secure connection to A.I. Industries," 1 explained. "But these communications terminals are available to the crew. We just grabbed a private room on the way to engineering to check in. It took us a few minutes to call you guys."

"Ok!" 4 clapped her hands excitedly. "Leader of all of the Earth amborgs here!"

"Of the First Group," 57 raised an eyebrow. She felt it necessary to leave a reminder. "Don't just forget about us."

"Back on track," 4 turned and gave the rest of them serial killer eyes. "Please?"

57 maintained a strong and stoic expression while 35 winced in fear. 95 and 53 both bit their lips and hunched down as far as they could in their seats. As usual, 65 and 224 of the Fourth Group kept staring blankly. 4 faced front and looked at 1 and 2, who were both watching apprehensively.

"Yes," 1 agreed cautiously. "Back on track."

"You were saying?" 18 sighed.

"As I said before," 1 continued his report. "Things are bad. Hilariously bad. We were outgunned, outmaneuvered and not as prepared like we thought. We didn't stand a chance and people aboard Apogee station were killed in the hopes of braving the new frontier of space exploration."

"Meaning," 18 glanced at 4. "If the S.C.E. Firestar should fall... One ship, against the enemy fleet which has about 40 of them... If you are destroyed in space..."

"We'll die making a much better stand than Apogee station," 2 nodded his head. "But Earth will fall if the Tandeeri land on the planet itself."

"It is conceivable that if they successfully touch down on Earth," 224 said bluntly, "they will face the full might of our military strength."

"Which is why I don't doubt that we can put up a fight and make a valiant stand," 1 glanced at 2 nervously. "But based on what we've all seen up here, Earth will fall within weeks if they get their hands on home."

"What about our current casualties?" 57 asked.

1 and 2 exchanged glances, then their eyes drifted to the floor. The atmosphere in the room shifted as everyone lowered their heads, allowing for a moment of silence to honor the people that had lost their lives.

"Too many," 2 replied when they all lifted their heads. "Some station techs, engineers, and crew were killed instantly. I'm sending the exact numbers."

"We took a bad hit," 1 added. "We were hit like a sudden heart attack."

"And the wounded?" 95 asked curiously.

"501 and 466 are recovering from powerful energy attacks that overloaded their cybernetics," 1 reported and nodded to 95 and 53. He knew that the Third Group Earth leaders were worried. "Thankfully, they both survived."

"Except now," 2 interrupted the positive vibes with a dash of realism. "249, 593 and 49 won't leave their sides. The Third Group team up here are scared, which means that this interstellar war might be too much for them to handle."

"They'll have to adjust," 4 protested.

"Not finished," 1 cut her off sternly. "5 and 6 are both working together in the medical bay to care for the survivors and the injured. 224, 365, and 378 were also damaged but they contacted us and said they wanted to explore the ship when they were cleared. Everyone else just went to the bridge and we've separated."

"Aside from that," 2 added, "we're seriously understrength. The new technology and reinforcements of this ship is reassuring but... this is way beyond what we handled before on Earth."

"I have an odd feeling I know what it is you're going to ask us to do," 4 stated.

"The Admiral was very clear," 1 said with a nod. "First contact specialists and diplomats will begin contacting all of our world leaders. We go from the top to bottom. Everything changes once those dialogues open. Once they get permission from our President, as an example, a few shuttles will be sent to Washington D.C."

"And you want us to get ready to send another team of amborgs to reinforce you?" 18 asked.

"It would help a lot."

"99 amborgs on the planet Earth," 4 looked at the other leaders, "and you want us to pluck another team of volunteers from them and send them up into space. You realize that the 20 of you already up there are the most experienced and qualified for outer space travel and activities?"

"4, what did I tell you?"

4 and 18 exchanged glances. 1 was talking about a conversation that they had before Dr. Kendrick took them to the launch facility. He stared at her sternly through the screen and crossed his arms. 2 looked at him and then the rest of them with a somber gaze.

"Right," 4 nodded. "You're the boss. Wasn't doubting you. We'll get on it right away."

"Should be easy to rearrange the roster down here," 18 said as the rest of the amborg leaders nodded. "But we can probably only spare a few volunteers. If we send too many up, we won't be able to handle this if it all goes south."

"Some will be fine," 1 answered as he gave them a thumbs up. "Do what you can."

"Don't worry about it 1," 18 said. "Each amborg up there is capable of handling this fight. You're giving a lot of people hope already."

"One can only hope it's worth it," 1 said, looking down. "Thanks 18. Let us know if help is coming."

"See ya," 2 waved.

The transmission ended. As the screen went dark, the amborgs all quietly glanced at each other.

"What was 1 talking about?" 18 asked politely. "What did he tell you?"

"He told me to remember the first mission we teamed up for," 4 replied. "I didn't trust his judgment at the time and he told me to trust him. When I told him that going up into space was not the best option, he reminded me again."

The other leaders stared. Most of them were shocked to hear 4 admit something like that. She had been against the mission to space?

"Don't look at me like that," 4 stated. "I seem to recall us being in a similar predicament when we voted to determine the fate of the Assassin."

"But, you didn't tell us you disapproved of 1's mission," 57 stated.

"Because I knew it would have halted the decision-making if I had spoken out against him," 4 answered, impatiently tapping her foot a few times. "It had to be unanimous from all of us to approve the mission. Otherwise, we would all be here on Earth."

"He vetoed you?" 18 raised an eyebrow. "Is he insane?"

4 glared angrily at 18. It was one thing to judge the very first amborg's decision, but she wouldn't tolerate them besmirching or desecrating his character. Even if 1 overruling her opinion was true, he had done so because he felt it was right.

"We all know that 1 is not insane," she snapped. "He did it because he believes in 117, and 117 believes in 43. They felt that was enough."

After taking a moment to calm down, 4 looked at them all and shrugged.

"So, what do you all think?" she asked, speaking to no one in particular.

"Before we send help up there, there's something bothering me. I feel this is going to be worse than the Domino Incident," 57 replied. "Something about the S.C.E. dropping in so conveniently makes me uneasy."

"At least they get to fight," 35 said, crossing his arms. "We're the ones down here who have to deal with the public relations and other problems."

"Our tasks are of utmost importance," 65 declared.

"Yeah, thanks buzzkill," 35 retorted.

"You would think that all the science fiction in our history and other cultural references and frames of lore would better prepare our society for first contact," 53 muttered to 95.

The two Third Group amborgs looked worried while the others exchanged looks. 4 and 18 walked over to their seats and sat down with them. 4 raised her arms and clasped her hands behind her head, while 18 reclined in her seat and gazed up at the ceiling.

"Well, when the real thing happens in real life to people who have only seen this stuff in movies," 18 said, "then it's pretty damn scary."

"Fear is irrelevant," 65 spoke bluntly. "All we need are the tools and necessary plans to succeed."

The First, Second and Third Group leaders gazed at 65 and 224.

"For once," 18 scoffed as she looked at them sternly. "That is a good point."

"Easy," 4 said, narrowing her gaze on everyone. "Remember, if the public could see us now, they wouldn't exactly be thrilled at seeing us at each other's throats."

"What do we do?" 53 asked.

"I'll put together a list and talk to some amborgs," 4 answered her promptly. "In the meantime, let's get ready to adjust and cover each other's tasks. 57, where are we at with 777's mission of special circumstances?"

"I've been in touch with 117's grandfather and the LAPD," she replied informatively. "We have reason to believe that whoever owned that cargo ship is in Tangier."

"Morocco?" 18 asked. "I haven't been there in a while but..."

"No," 4 said loudly, which caused everyone to stop.

"I can make it there and find the one who's responsible!" 18 protested.

"This conspiracy was discovered by an amborg from the Second Group!" 57 pointed out casually. She rapped her fist on the table twice. "It's my mission!"

"First things first," 4 replied quickly. "The leaders of this particular situation are not going to abandon their positions!"

"Are you kidding?!" 57 looked furious. "Dead civilians were discovered in my city!"

"And may I remind you, Katie 57," 4 interrupted sternly, "you are an amborg and your skills apply to the entire world as a whole. Not just the city of Los Angeles!"

"So why won't you...?!"

4 slammed her fist on the table and there was a resounding crash. When she lifted her fist, they all stared quietly at the newly formed dent that she had created.

"Interrupt me again and I swear I will restrain you," 4 snarled.

35 looked at 57 nervously. Her eyes were twitching with anger as she held back and sulked in her seat.

"Amborg leaders are not to go gallivanting off on their own," 4 declared. "That's why we have each other. I suggest that we send someone else. Not only are you the leader of the Earth Second Group amborgs, but you are too emotional for this mission. I'm sorry 57, but that little demonstration of your feelings was more than enough to disqualify you."

"Damn you and your calculated thinking."

4 pointed at her head for all of them to see.

"This calculated thinking, young lady, is why you're alive! Like it or not, you take orders from me, first and foremost," she said menacingly.

4 looked at 18.

"There is someone that I would like to see take command of 777's mission."

18's eyes widened. She knew instantly. If it wasn't her, then 4 had one specific amborg in mind. She couldn't believe it.

"No!" 18 shook her head firmly. "You can't use her."

"Why not?" 4 asked.

"She tried to kill me," 18 responded immediately.

"And where did this attempted murder take place?"

18 bit her lip and shook her head. She threw herself back in her chair and let out a grumble.

"Morocco," she muttered. "You can't assign her to this."

"Last I checked," 4 turned to look at 95 and 53, "she just finished an assignment and has returned home for a breather. The Third Group can spare her, she's available, and she has plenty of experience operating by herself in shady spots. Besides, she's not that well known to the public like we are."

"Oh!" 95's eyes lit up with recognition. "You mean...!"

4 transmitted instructions to the two of them. Once they received them, they nodded.

"Go get her please," 4 nodded. "Tell her we have an assignment for her. Priority one."

95 and 53 stood up. They hesitated, but when no one spoke up or tried to stop them, they quickly moved from the table and left the room.

"You're pinning the success of this mission," 57 spoke softly, "on a Third Group replacement."

"An accurate title but I believe that 723 can accomplish this," 4 said as she began to draft the mission parameters in her mind. "She'll be able to handle it."

"You want her to go in alone without backup," 18 shook her head again.

"Well, based on the number of times that she hunted you and your apprentice before," 4 raised an eyebrow and stared at 18. "I'd say she's more than capable of doing this even if you were to dislocate two or three of her limbs before sending her out."

Before 18 could respond to this, 57 stood from her seat and pushed her chair into the wall. It crashed hard, which caused the ceiling lights to shake. 35 also got up, but 57 waved at him to not follow her.

"I'm leaving for a couple of hours," she scoffed. "35, please take over."

"Uh, sure," 35 nodded his head, but he looked at her with concern. "Where are you going?"

"L.A.," 57 replied. "Maybe stop by Giuseppe's."

18 rose from her chair. She didn't look happy at all.

"I don't think that's a good idea," she murmured. "We need all hands on deck."

"It's fine."

18 was interrupted when 4 merely waved a hand casually.

"We can manage without you for a bit," 4 nodded. "We'll call if something happens. Just be safe. Two hours. Understood? Be back by then or we will come get you and force you back here."

"Understood," 57 repeated as she nodded respectfully. "I might just be an extra ten minutes if that pleases your royal highness."

"Why are you leaving during a crucial moment? This is quite possibly the establishment of one of the most profound and pivoting moments in Earth's history."

65 was staring at 57 with the same neutral gaze that they used to display when they all first started out. It was almost as if a mirror was placed between the new generation and the old.

"Because," 57 said to them. "If the end of the world does happen, I want to have my favorite food one last time. And if it doesn't, I want to remember what it feels like to have something I enjoy before everything changes forever."

57 walked over to the two Fourth Group leaders.

"I want to do it because I'll feel good and happy even if it's just temporary," she said. "Then... I will make fear irrelevant if aliens come and try to destroy the only place I can call home. Even the Fourth Group has something deep inside that they want to preserve and cherish, right?"

Both of them didn't respond. They were analyzing her words carefully. Even if their expressions remained vacant and unchanged, all of them knew that 57's words had made a significant impression. That was the end of that discussion.

The door opened and 723 walked in. She was followed by 95 and 53. Everyone stood up to greet her.

"57, 35," 4 dipped her head. "Dismissed."

She looked at 65 and 224 and also nodded to them.

"If you don't mind," 4 turned to look at 723. "We'd like some privacy. 18 and I will explain this mission to the Third Group."

"Uh," 35 lifted a finger. "You realize that because they're also leaders, they're just going to tell us anyway. Right?"

"I am directly ordering you to leave," 4 said. "Only the Third Group and my partner, 18, will know what it is that I'm about to say to 723. A handful of people who know will guarantee her success. I'd prefer it that way while the rest of you, concentrate on any other important priorities."

■ ■

S.C.E. Firestar Armory One
Deck Ten

"You should take this 117."

117 held his arms out forward as he and 917 watched 43 rummaging around a few boxes. She had opened a cabinet, revealing a bunch of devices neatly displayed on some sort of tray. These special gadgets appeared to be new additions to their weapons inventory. 43 handed him a small hand-held item that resembled a Rubik's cube.

"What's this do?" he asked curiously, turning it over.

"It's a transformorph," 43 explained. "It's yours. Or it was yours. A few years before the Tandeeri showed, you met with some natives on the Orellian belt past Garda point. Although they chose to be isolated and restrict themselves from space travel, they had the ability to create devices that could morph into certain things to trade with off-worlders. A sickness had appeared among the native population and you saved them by offering them our medicine and information. As a reward to show their gratitude, they gave you one of their sacred tools. It is loyal to you. See if it recognizes you."

"Recognizes me?"

"An inanimate object that can recognize 117?" 917 asked with a puzzled look.

"Yes. I hope it works."

43 examined the cube in 117's hand, appearing concerned at first, but then relief washed over her as a change occurred. Within his fingers, they all witnessed a series of markings begin to emerge on the cube, arranging themselves into some sort of sentence. 17 stared in fascination, except he didn't recognize the language at all.

"It should automatically recognize you as 117 despite the alternate universe barriers," 43 murmured. "It's matched to your DNA, so you are its master. Let me see, you did teach me how to read the language when you were finished with your mission with the Orellian natives. It says, '*a new wielder seeks the power of the tool on hand... a power that is forbidden for those that would abuse it or who are unworthy.*'"

117 looked at 43 as she continued translating the marks. 917's eyes widened. She was speaking to an inanimate object that appeared to be sentient. All in the palm of his hand.

"*... But this new wielder feels familiar,*" 43 recited as the marks continued to shape into sentences, "*as if a long lost memory suddenly revived. This tool believes that the master has returned. Now the power inside shall be available to you from now on.*"

43 paused and turned to 117, who knew that this was the end of the translation. With a vague idea of what to do next, he looked at the now dormant cube and spoke up.

"Umm," he pondered quickly. "Can you speak English? Or... write English?"

It seemed like a ridiculous thing to do, but 43 nodded encouragingly. The cube shined once and then words began to appear across one of the surfaces again. Instead of the squiggly lines and hieroglyphs of the language 43 had translated, the words that appeared next were now in English.

It apologizes, the words on the cube now said, *this unit is unable to speak the English language due to the lack of organs capable of producing comprehendible noises, so it is resorting to a visual display of the language requested as the appropriate alternate solution. Switching from previous default language to requested one. Shall it confirm this action as the correct setting from now on?*

Taken aback, 117 stared at 43 and then at the object in his hand. This cube was reminding him a lot of a computer or something a mobile device would usually say when it underwent a first-time setup.

"Umm sure?" he said to the shining cube. "Default setting as English for now is very convenient. Uh let's see, what can you do?"

"I never thought we'd be having a conversation with a cube," 917 said with a smirk. "We are still sane right? Back then, we would have been in the asylums diagnosed with schizophrenia for this type of thing."

43 grinned at 917 and nodded in answer as the words on the cube rearranged themselves into a coherent reply.

This unit, it wrote, is capable of morphing and altering its shape to suit your needs within certain parameters. A couple of examples include handheld tools, uncomplicated weapons, safety features, etc.

"So can you turn into a gun, for instance?" 117 asked curiously. "What are some of your examples of uncomplicated weapons?"

Replicating a firearm is simple, he read. *Upon transformation, generation of an infinite supply of ammunition is possible. However, propelling or shooting ammunition shall literally separate pieces of this unit from itself. This unit has the capability of mimicking normal firearms, however, after a certain amount of shots have been fired, the unit shall revert back to its dormant state. The same is said with explosive devices. Bombs require too many pieces, but this unit can actively turn into one. However, if given the order to destroy itself, this unit will self-destruct and cease to exist. Asking this unit to convert to an explosive is a last resort and it suggests that it doesn't be ordered to do so. The previous owner's preference was always for it to become a sharp object. For instance, knives, swords, and stabbing articles were very widely used on several occasions.*

"You keep calling yourself 'it,'" 117 said observantly. "Is that your name?"

"It" is always the default name whenever this unit's owner's previous owner has passed on or handed it to a new worthy master, it replied. *This unit has had many names as it passed through time and was used by many others. You may choose a new name for this unit or even request a name it has used before.*

117 thought for a moment, then looked at 43 for assistance. She immediately shook her head and pointed a finger at him silently. Evidently, he would

have to do this himself, which was what she was basically saying. If he was to assume his role over this... cube... then he wanted to treat it fairly. Then an idea came to him.

"Do you remember your previous owner? Or master...? The owner before you met me?" he asked politely.

The owner before you is long gone, it said. It almost sounded like it was sad. *This unit misses him because he was always kind. Yet, you bear a remarkable resemblance. It feels familiar somehow and the way you hold this unit makes it seem as if you have used its power before.*

That was something 117 never expected to see.

"You missed me? You can feel emotions?"

It is partially empathic. It has had many owners and was able to understand their feelings through a way of seeing. This unit is happy to be in the hands of a capable owner again. It has sat in the dark for a long time waiting for the master's return or the arrival of a new one that is worthy. It was sad when 43 informed it that 117 had been killed. It wishes it had been there to help but it was left behind to help the needs of others.

"Looks like you inherited a puppy," 917 said. "A small square one."

"You think so?" 117 shrugged. He looked down and asked politely, "What was your name? With the 117 before me?"

The words then rearranged themselves. They all got a good look at what it was writing to them.

He described this unit's physical appearance as intriguing. After we met, he named it Argentum. The explanation he gave was that the name was the word for "silver" in your language of Latin.

"Well in honor of the one before me, and to pretty much just go with the simplest way, I'd also like to call you Argentum," 117 smiled, but he wasn't sure if the cube could see. He just wanted to appear pleasant. "It suits you and I like my own creativity."

It is pleased to take upon this name. From now on, it will respond to you with the name Argentum. 117 is Argentum's new user. For future use, speak Argentum and this unit shall be ready and at your disposal. Excuse Argentum, master 117. Argentum must rest now. It does not like to talk too much. Call upon it when the need is dire.

The words disappeared, leaving the cube blank and dormant. 917 and 117 both stared at each other. Not only did they finish a conversation with a sentient cube, it literally ended the whole discussion on its own and left them hanging.

43 smiled cheerfully as 117 gently put Argentum into his jacket pocket. It would definitely take a while to get used to its intriguing behavior.

"So is it a weapon or a tool?" he asked, looking at 43 questionably.

"It is what you want it to be," 43 shrugged. "Remember though, as long as it's with you, use its name as much as possible. Even if it does acknowledge you as the master, you need to develop a bond with it so your teamwork becomes more effective. Now then, 917, I have something for you."

43 pulled a handheld silver object from another drawer. It seemed similar to Argentum, but it looked slightly different. It resembled much like the hilt of a broken sword.

"This is your favorite weapon," 43 smiled as 917 took it from her hands.

"What is it?" 917 asked as he pushed the button immediately.

"It's a sword," 43 answered as the device suddenly opened. She quickly reached out and pointed his hand upright. "Careful. Aim it away from you!"

A metallic sound rang out as a blade shot up and out of the slot. 43 swiftly directed it away from them, keeping everyone safe. Excitement flooded his eyes as he gazed at it.

"Oooh," 917 nodded approvingly while 117 looked at the blade in awe. It appeared to give off a faint glow. "I got a Percy Jackson sword!"

"But it doesn't turn into a pen..." 117 pointed out. "It looks like someone mashed a samurai sword and a lightsaber together. How is it so shiny?"

"It's so light," 917 swung it away from them and gave it a few practice swings. "Feels like it might shatter in my hands."

"That was 117's most powerful sword," 43 explained. "It was also designed for him on one of his classified adventures a few years back. So far, according to the files he left behind after he died, the sword only works for him. He also mentioned a few times that it somehow senses your soul."

"That doesn't make... sense? My soul?"

917 and 117 both stared at 43, who shrugged again. This time, her smile was gone.

"Some of these items are hard to explain," she admitted. "All I know is, they're yours and you deserve to carry them."

"Well, that's pretty cool," 917 nodded, nudging 117 in the side. "I'll be sure to keep this safe then. Looks like we both got some silver charms to keep on us at all times."

He pressed the button and the blade snapped back into the handle grip. Suddenly, 117 remembered something important.

"Didn't you want to go see the hangar bay?" he prompted. 917 looked at him with wide eyes.

"Right!" he exclaimed. "Sorry guys, I wanted to go see what the hangar bay was like! Thanks for the sword 43!"

"No problem," 43 smiled as 917 walked out towards the elevator. "Oh wait! You'll need this!"

She tossed a gun his way. 117 quickly dodged out of the way as it flew over his shoulder. 917 turned and caught it in one fluid motion.

"Standard issue," 43 said as she also tossed him a holster. 117 avoided it again. "Don't get caught by the enemy without it. You always told us how the creation of gunpowder ended the need for swordplay. But now, with shield emitters and personal deflectors, swords have been revived in our futuristic era of combat."

"Thanks," 917 said appreciatively. "I like the sound of that. Swords getting a fair shot at fighting against lasers and firearms."

He quickly made his exit. 117 smiled. He was curious as to what the mysterious crew woman wanted with 917, but he decided that staying with 43 was his best link to the Alpha universe. He cast a hopeful glance her way.

"Can I have one too?" he said, pointing at the display of firearms.

"I wasn't going to let Argentum be your only weapon," 43 chuckled as she tossed another handgun to him.

Another door hissed open and 117 saw 297 and 777 rush in cheerfully.

"I LOVE the Alpha universe!" 297 yelled triumphantly.

"I guess you two enjoyed the shooting range?" 43 smiled.

"These weapons are incredible!" 297 exclaimed as he set his sniper rifle down on the table. "They're so lightweight but they pack a punch!"

"Switching ammo types for certain weapons is also quite effective," 777 remarked as he put his rifle on a shelf and examined another one. "Kinetic bullets cause more damage, but plasma and laser-based weapons can carry more charge to them."

"It depends on how much ammo you want," 43 explained. "If you use lasers or charged weapons, then you have higher ammunition counts. Increasing your damage output with bullets, HV rounds, or slug-throwers means you should definitely avoid missing your targets."

As 117 turned his gun over in his hands and familiarized himself with how to use it, he got a call. He picked it up and allowed everyone else to hear. They continued following 43's instructions and were making adjustments to their weapons when 117 heard a friendly voice.

"117," 6's voice spoke over the channel. "Are you there?"

"Go ahead 6," he said as he put on the holster that 43 gave him.

"Hey," she said. "Umm, there's no easier way to put this... But I wanted to let the amborgs and Dr. Kendrick know as soon as possible."

"What's wrong?" 117 asked as 43 stared inquisitively at him.

"Jacob's dead."

117 stopped and looked up. 43 paused, staring at him wide-eyed. 297 and 777 froze on the spot, listening in shocked silence.

"What?"

117's voice fell into a whisper as 43 walked over.

"The injuries from when the Tandeeri attacked," 6 said. There was tension in her voice, attempting to avoid revealing the break in her tone. "If the Firestar had gotten here sooner, maybe... maybe... We were too late. 5 and I lost him."

"I'll be right there 6," 117 said, but he was interrupted.

"It's alright 117," 6 replied softly. "I'm... going to ask if I can have Jacob be prepared properly. Maybe a shuttle could take his body back home soon once communications are complete with Earth. Someone needs to bring him back to his mom. I just... needed to let everyone know."

"Even so, Dr. Kendrick will want to say something," 117 replied.

"Yeah. I'll call him. Don't worry. In the meantime, I'm learning about medicine all over again. But I think what's really important is that I don't want to let any more of us die under my watch. I've got to be better prepared. So, this is 6, out."

"Wait!"

But it was too late. 6 had hung up and the line ended as the four of them stared at each other in silence.

"Damn it," 297 mumbled. "I liked Jacob."

"I only spoke to him a few times," 43 looked at 117 in concern as she moved close to him. "He seemed like a good man."

"He was one of Mandy's friends," 117 replied. "He was our friend."

"Oh yeah?" 43 nodded.

"Yeah," 777 said. "He had been my technician for a couple of weeks."

"Me too," 297 nodded.

"Hold on," 43 glanced at the two of them curiously. "Jacob was both your technicians?"

"Before the technician program was dissolved and retired, each amborg always had one assigned," 117 explained. "But, sometimes, we found ourselves short-staffed every now and then. So technicians had to switch to other amborgs if their assigned ones were unavailable."

Before Jacob had applied and been accepted onto Apogee Station for a tour of duty, he had been an amborg technician. To be accurate, he wasn't assigned to one amborg, he had been assigned to almost the entire Second Group and a handful of Third Group amborgs, too. He and many other technicians had several amborg notches on their resume which definitely elevated his career at A.I. Industries.

43 readied a rifle. She added a belt and inserted some glowing blue clips, which 117 assumed were ammunition clips.

"I'm so sorry," she said.

117 looked down at the new gun that he was holding. A weapon of the future from a universe that wasn't his own. He turned it over a few more times and pretended to inspect it more than necessary.

"One more family to write a letter home to," he said. "Hopefully, his death won't be in vain."

"Are you alright?" 43 asked.

"Yeah," 117 nodded as he holstered his weapon. "Let's go. We've got a fight to win."

117, 297, and 777 walked out of the armory with their new arsenal of weapons. Slinging rifles over their shoulders, they now had suitable protection if they entered combat.

"Just be careful though."

"Of what?" 117 looked at 43.

They approached another elevator and she hit the button.

"You suddenly developed the same look as Alpha 117, before I never saw him again. It was full of motivation but... also dangerous at the same time."

There was a loud ding and the elevator doors opened. They stepped inside.

"What happened to Alpha 117?" 297 asked.

43 looked at them all nervously. She opened her mouth, but didn't know how to answer. Fortunately, 117 spoke up.

"I don't think I want to know."

As the elevator doors closed, 117 looked up.

"We should go to the medical bay," he said. "I want to go check on the injured."

As the elevator whirred and began to move, 43 nodded in agreement.

"Sure thing."

Chapter 18: Hidden Conspiracy

S.C.E. Firestar Medical Bay

"Well, the electrical damage wasn't permanent. Your implants and internal organs are all functioning normally now. I can clear you two to active duty without any problems."

466 beamed happily as 501 reached for his jacket and began to put it on. The rest of the Third Group amborgs had already left when 501 told them to go explore. It was the first time he had actually been elected as a leader of the Third Group and he wanted to make an impression despite his injuries on Apogee.

"Thanks 6," he said smiling. 6 returned his smile, but they both knew it wasn't the same usual smile. "You're the best doctor ever."

"Thank you 501," 6 said as another doctor walked by. "But to be honest, there are much more qualified individuals here. See that doctor? He's half human and half of a species that has excellent hearing. He can hear the sound of your heart when you're about to have a heart attack. I'm not sure if that's true but I'd love to be able to hear what your cells are saying. He could tell us our exact heart rates without even using a monitor."

"Are you going to be ok?" 466 asked as she helped 501 to his feet. They both sympathetically glanced at 6, who was trying to distract herself. "We know how you feel right now. Even doctors don't always have to be brave."

"It's ok," 6 smiled, averting her eyes when she noticed their expressions. 501 and 466 thought she was hiding her face so they wouldn't see her composure slip, but then they realized she was looking at 5. "Even if I don't feel alright at the moment. I have the best amborg comedian right there who can... provide me with entertainment and the will to laugh."

5 was chatting with a crew member who was having difficulties with their own prosthetic. They had a robotic left leg, which was cool, but its mobility was much slower than his own artificially built leg. Medical technology from an alternate universe was quite fascinating to him, regardless.

"I didn't hear any sarcasm in that, did you?" 501 leaned towards 466. "She just complimented 5! Without hitting him!

"Right!" 466 grinned confidently. "That's probably the first time I've heard 6 admit to liking 5, and then he wasn't immediately incinerated, cut, blown up, or restrained with those creepy medical restraints back home."

"Very funny you two," 6 turned around and waved for them to leave. "Now go! I want to learn how to save people now. You go out and have fun saving the universe and enjoying yourself."

501 looked at 466, who met his eyes with a smile. They both instantly lit up with excitement and exited the medical bay like a pair of school children eager to get to class on time. 6 watched them leave and then felt someone slap a hand on her shoulder.

"Hey," 5 smirked as she turned to face him. "How's my favorite doctor?"

"Can I ask you for a serious favor, Johnny?"

6 shrugged off his hand. She put down the tablet she had been given earlier and dipped her head. She hesitated and took a deep breath. She was glad that 5 understood that it wasn't the right time to make a joke. When they both knew they were on the same page, 6 raised her arms and held them up.

She didn't look him in the eyes, but she saw him nod and move in for a hug. He felt really warm, completely blocking the cold atmosphere of the room.

"What's up?" he said as she rested her chin on his shoulder.

"I don't want to lose any more patients," 6 declared. "Once this war is over, I want to stay here and learn everything they know. Because I can't stand losing people who need a cure more than anything."

"What's the favor?" 5 asked.

"Will you help me? I can't do it all by myself."

"Amborgs don't progress alone anymore," 5 said as he looked at a pair of doctors moving Jacob's body away on a stretcher. "117 taught all of us that. Help will be there for anyone who needs it. Our family has never been one to go back on our word."

5 let go as 6 cleared her throat and reached for the tablet, but 5 picked it up first.

"Come on," he smiled. "Let's see what they have in store for us."

Port Side, Hangar Bay Three

917 strolled through the halls of the starship filled with awe. There were so many things to learn, but there was no time to stop. With only about four

minutes until the meeting, he hoped he was heading in the right direction. So far, he estimated he had covered around six percent of the deck. If he took a moment to linger, even for a minute, time would slip away from him.

During the trek to the hangar bay, he wished that he hadn't accidently walked into the section where the pilots resided. They all looked very intimidating, but he felt relieved when they weren't treating him as a hostile. Afterwards, he found what appeared to be the barracks and local command center. After some pointers with a few of the officers at their posts, he was able to find the place where the storage rooms were. Presumably, if he had read the note correctly, then he was in the right place.

"Or..." he muttered, "if it's not right, then there are only four other hangar bays to go to including this one, as well as at least sixty other storage rooms just on this deck alone..."

"Psst."

917 whirled around. The door to the storage room swung open, revealing the crewman from before. He quickly scanned and examined her measurements to confirm it was the same person he had run into earlier. She stood quite normally, just as he expected a disciplined member of the crew should act aboard a ship. In all honesty, he was attempting to search for something out of place, but there didn't seem to be anything wrong. Except, that was what bothered him. There was no harm in looking into the situation further... was there?

As he stepped into the storage room, the crewman quickly held up a hand, stopping him. There was a word scribbled on a small paper in her hand that said, "*remain quiet.*" Dumbstruck, 917 watched silently as the crewman looked left and right down the halls. There were a few other people walking around, so she silently leaned back. The paper in her hand suddenly sparked and caught fire. It disappeared without a trace. No odor or any type of ashes.

Flash paper? 917 wondered as she opened her mouth to speak.

"Oh, you're an amborg?" she said in a surprised tone, which made 917 lift an eyebrow. She looked around again. "This is perfect timing. Some crates have fallen over in the corner and I cannot put them back in place by myself. I could use your expertise in this matter."

"Of course," 917 replied as he followed her. "So... secret notes on combustible and untraceable paper? Very analog."

"You don't really get the concept of a secret meeting... do you?"

917 chuckled when she turned back to give him a skeptical look.

"No no, I do," he said as she led him into a corner. "I'm all too familiar. It's just that you and I are from different universes and today has kind of been a rather weird day. I'm choosing to use my sense of humor to hide how uncomfortable I am."

"Very specific... but honest, too. I appreciate that. Now tell me..."

When they reached a hidden corner, completely out of sight of any other crew members, she turned to face him and frowned.

"Is there a reason you look like you're about to spring towards the entrance?" she asked.

Apparently, there was nothing that could get past her. She was definitely very perceptive, and not to be underestimated at all. There was still something funny about her that made him uneasy, but he couldn't deny that he felt intrigued.

"Oh I don't do it all the time. It's only when someone asks me to meet them in private, I always feel like it's a trap," 917 said as humorously as possible. "Every encounter except for one has ended badly for me."

"An amborg of your caliber?" she replied. "Worried that I led you into a trap? I guess the rumors were true. It was wrong of me to hope you'd remember..."

"Uhh," 917 stammered. "You're not seeking child support or anything like that, are you?"

"Hell no," she said immediately as she looked up at him. He could see that her eyes had widened. "We worked together before."

"Right," 917 sighed with relief. "Just checking. Because I can't afford to pay for child support at the moment. To be fair, you are from Alpha and I don't remember the last time a woman asked me to do something like this."

"Relax," the woman said as she reached up for her hat. "If we had children, I'd tell you. But my priorities right now are not focused on a relationship with anyone at the moment and you need to be brought up to speed right away."

She removed her hat and her hair fell down. It was a strange sight, and 917 could have sworn that her hair was glowing. It was a dark-brown red color despite the way it practically lit up. Or was it red-ish brown? He settled on mahogany, going more towards brown but combined with the rest of her face, she looked practically out of this world. She didn't seem like a woman anymore, he almost felt like he was gazing at a princess. The humans of Alpha probably had access to some really spectacular beauty regimens.

"I'm actually glad that you're noticing where my eyes are," she said, tucking her hat into her belt. She tilted to the left, but 917 kept staring. She then tilted right when she noticed the slightly dazed look in his eyes as he continued to follow her movements. "Uh... hello?"

917 blinked and cleared his throat.

"Sorry," he said.

"No, I should apologize for the discretion and how we originally met, but you have to help me," she shook her head. "Believe me, the worst case scenario was knocking you out, tying you up, and forcing you down here in a crate. Speaking honestly."

"I believe we all are helping," 917 gulped nervously. "This war involves all of us doesn't it?"

He glanced at one of the crates she stood next to and imagined being shoved inside one. He was sure that they were half his size. She noticed and chuckled slightly.

"Yes," she replied. "And it will require all of you to resolve it as soon as you can. This war. The one that you and your friends have been dragged into is wrong. You can't believe every story that the S.C.E. gives you."

"Wrong?" 917 looked at her in disbelief. "What do you mean? Trying to defend against an invading fleet from destroying our home? Who are you?"

"I'm sure that somewhere deep down in your mind, you have questions about how convenient it is that most of you can't speak to your Alpha."

917's heart suddenly began to pound as his emotions took over. He was already aware of the fact that the war had claimed the life of his other self, but now this random mysterious officer was speaking to him in such a condescending manner. He definitely was not enjoying the complete change in her tone.

"Where are you going with this?" 917 lowered his eyes in a glare and reached into his pocket.

"You don't need to draw your sword," she said. "I'm not here looking for a fight."

"I must have missed something," 917 replied. "Like the part where you implied that our Alphas are dead. It's a little strange that a..."

He glanced at the silver stripes on her sleeves. There it was, the same two stripes that he'd seen when he had bumped her.

"...Junior officer would go out of their way to randomly bump into me, almost cause a scene, and covertly initiate a meeting like this. Who are you?"

"In my defense," she answered, holding up her hands, "Lieutenant Bulla is an egotistical self-righteous moron trying to do everything by the book. He almost blew my cover with the Admiral right then and there."

917 changed his mind and reached for his holster. As he got ready to draw his gun, the officer remained calm and collected, not flinching at all.

"I'm not asking you again," he said.

"Easy," she warned him. "If you kill me, then everyone dies. You really want your girlfriend suffering before the end?"

"She can handle herself. Don't threaten her," 917 said, his voice trembling and filled with violent promise. "And now I'm pissed. Who are you?"

917 drew his weapon and aimed it at the woman's head. She narrowed her eyes and stood firm. She showed no signs of fear, even with the threat of certain death staring at her down the barrel of his gun.

"If you're willing to risk the end of your world," she replied calmly, "then go ahead and pull the trigger. Should you choose to end my life, then I will graciously accept my death, while you seal your own fate."

917 steadied the grip on his gun and made sure that if he pulled the trigger, the shot would be fatal. Both of them locked eyes for what felt like an eternity. Finally, he decided to lower his gun, but he kept it drawn in his hand.

"Fine," he said. "Who are you? A spy?"

"A friend," she replied. "My name is Braelynn."

917 watched as the officer suddenly reached for her belt.

"Hey," he warned her cautiously.

"Relax eagle eye," she said as she grabbed her hat and pulled it into her hands. "I'm just getting out of your hair."

She unfolded her cap and lifted it up.

"Literally," she winked. "I know you can convince your friends to help end this conflict."

Once the hat was over her head, her hair vanished into it, like it was sucked up by a vacuum. It was all perfectly concealed, making it seem like she'd just shaved it all off on the spot. 917 stared, eyes wide in disbelief.

"How did you do that?"

"This is my favorite hat," she smiled. "Amazing how technology is right?"

"Hey," 917 replied. "You're not just going to leave now are you?"

"I'll find you again," Braelynn answered as she tipped her hat to him and pulled it down over her eyes. "The more time I spend with you, the worse it makes things for me. I'll be in contact again. I promise."

"What are you up to?" 917 asked. "You drag me down here for the most angry introduction of my life and you just expect me to pretend I didn't see you?"

"Ok," Braelynn looked up at him and nodded. "I'll give you one moment of honesty. Would you mind putting your gun away?"

917 nodded as he holstered his weapon.

"I'm listening."

"I can see it in your eyes," Braelynn said as she tilted her head up and gazed at him. "You can see it in mine too. Both of us have survived wars, killing, and been to hell and back. I'm doing what I'm best at and that's making sure that the amborgs make it through this. Be honest with me, you don't want this war to end up on Earth, right?"

"Yeah," 917 tilted his head.

"Then I've got your back."

Braelynn stepped past 917 and he instinctively stepped aside. He called out to her as she walked away.

"How do you know my nickname?" he asked. "Only my closest friends are allowed to use it."

"I know you better than you think," Braelynn replied casually. "I hope you don't shoot me just for saying it to you, eagle eye. Take a moment to think really hard about who we are."

"Alright," 917 nodded cautiously, falling into step beside her. "Friend. You're not actually an ensign are you?"

"Let's just say it's easier to do my job if I hide my actual rank from everyone."

"No," 917 decided to take a poke at her. "I held a gun to an Admiral's head?"

Braelynn laughed.

"Nice try," she said. "Until our next meeting."

She led him back to the entrance. Once they reached the door, it slid open with the press of a button. A few other crew members passed by as they stepped inside. 917 glanced back and saw that she had somehow gotten ahold of a data pad without him noticing. Like a magician, she carried on as if nothing out of the ordinary was happening at all.

"Thank you so much for your assistance," she said, increasing the pitch of her voice enthusiastically while looking up to him, beaming. "Perhaps you could help me again sometime if you passed by?"

917 decided to go with her performance.

"You're welcome," he dipped his head with a smile. "Hopefully we'll bump into each other again."

The sudden shift in her speech and demeanor left him with no choice but to play along. He looked at the people behind them as they continued about their business. If someone was following this girl, whoever she was, then she was definitely trying to keep a low profile. She had to be some sort of specially trained operative or undercover agent of some kind.

"Thanks," Braelynn said as she turned and walked away. "But it was only professional. I wasn't asking for a date."

917 glared at her, irritation etched on his face. Although she was mysterious and elusive, she didn't have to be insulting. Just as he was about to respond, momentarily forgetting that she was trying to keep a low profile, the alarms suddenly went off.

917 raised his eyes as the deafening alarms rattled his ears. He lowered the volume on his hearing to buffer the noise, then turned to Braelynn. To his surprise, she had vanished into the throng of crew members that had begun to move. She was fast.

The corridor was suddenly flooded in a blaze of red warning lights. The blaring klaxon echoed relentlessly, triggering an instinctual rush among the crew—human and alien alike—who sprang into action with remarkable speed. 917 couldn't help but admire their impressive coordination, getting to their destinations in such an orderly fashion, and how well they were able to respond with such rapid alertness. In the midst of the chaos, the Admiral's voice resonated through the speakers.

"Action stations! Action stations! All civilian personnel, red alert!" Admiral Ra'aiah declared. "Condition one! Enemy contact confirmed. This is not a drill. All hands, this is not a drill."

"917!'

917 turned to see 297 and 777 running towards him. 297 carried a rather interesting looking sniper rifle, whereas 777 had his rifle slung on his back. 917 gazed down at his weapon and nodded approvingly. It suited him with the way he wielded it so fiercely.

"Good to see you two," 917 smirked. "What are you guys doing?"

297 and 777 both glanced at each other sheepishly.

"We got lost," they said simultaneously.

"Oh?" 917 almost laughed. He composed himself and cleared his throat. "Well, here's one of the hangars and a storage room."

The three of them positioned themselves against the wall and stood still. The crew bustled about as they stayed back and watched. They weren't combatants in this battle, making waiting around all the more challenging. Although the alarm had stopped ringing, the red lights in the halls continued to flash.

"You know what sucks about not being on the bridge crew of a ship?" 297 asked them on a private channel.

"What?" 917 replied casually in his mind.

"Every one of these crewmembers could die instantaneously," 297 said. "It takes the bridge and the captain of a ship to give orders to protect the ship and fight. Yet, the irony is that a ship requires everyone onboard to function the way you want. You could die, in space, even after who knows how many years of training they spent just to serve aboard a ship. Especially since we're in a war."

"We can't protect this many," 777 sighed, watching everyone move with fierce determination. "Years of training... only to have the possibility of dying in seconds. Hardly seems fair."

"Indeed," 297 nodded. "I don't wish to see all of these people dying for a war that they probably didn't ask to be a part of."

"You take pride in being a soldier, Captain America?" 777 asked.

"I want to fight so that people don't have to," 297 replied. "Too many good soldiers were killed when we first started out and a lot of bad ones rose into places where the good could have brought the changes that the world needed. The more I fight on distant battlefields, the better I can act as a shield or strike from a distance."

"I know somewhat of what that's like," 917 replied. "I guess. At some point, I didn't want to be who I was anymore and just tried to run away from it. Until this happened to the world, I just wasn't up to it."

"No offense, 917 but... I call bullshit on that."

917 and 297 pivoted to 777. He was staring at 917 intently, like he had just discovered something off about his response.

"You didn't want to be who you were anymore?" 777 shook his head. "I don't believe that for a second. Running away to hide in a prison from the rest of us as a form of exile is a weird way to pass that across to the rest of us. Wouldn't it have been easier on you if you just took a sabbatical?"

"I technically did," 917 replied nervously.

"Bull," 777 repeated. "Your behavior and your actions ever since you came back have been completely different to what you've been saying. You've been acting like you weren't locked away in maximum security."

"Hey," 297 interrupted. "He doesn't have to answer to you. We all still have our basic rights to privacy."

"Thanks 297," 917 said. "But, 777 is right. I have been acting quite dismissive about... prison."

917 raised his hand and put it on 777's shoulder.

"I appreciate you calling me out on how I've been acting," 917 smiled. "I can't go into detail about it, but it was related to an assignment."

"Assignment?" 777 raised his eyebrow and crossed his arms. "What assignment?"

"After 345 was killed in the line of duty," 917 replied, "it was a difficult time. When Silhed was destroyed later, Dr. Kendrick approved a top secret assignment which required that I leave for some time. No one could know."

"But, a top secret assignment from Dr. Kendrick," 297 gazed at 917 with a mix of curiosity and anxiety. "That would mean it's classified and on a need-to-know basis."

"And I think," 917 sighed, "it's time for you to know. But uh, don't tell Dr. Kendrick I said anything."

"Ok, for once," 777 perked up, his interest piqued. "I'm just going to say, spill the tea."

"Alright, after I went on a rampage after Silhed was destroyed, I was..."

A deep, rumbling noise reverberated from above, signaling that the Firestar was firing its weapons. Simultaneously, several loud whooshing sounds emanated from below and down the corridor, drawing their attention. The amborgs recognized this noise as the ship launching its fighter craft into space like a catapult on an aircraft carrier. The Firestar's fighters and bombers were loaded into massive tubes and fired into space like bullets from a gun.

"Man, I wish we could watch this on TV or something," 297 groaned. "It feels so boring just standing here."

"Dude!" 777 glared at 297. "Let 917 finish the story!"

"Dr. Kendrick exiled me into prison," 917 said on the channel. "If anyone at A.I. Industries decided to go looking for answers, the cover story was that I was banned from home for a period of time. Never to return for breaking the rules."

"But," 297 focused his attention back on the conversation. "Does that mean that the attack against the crime gang was sanctioned?"

"Oh no," 917 replied, "it wasn't. Not on official records. Dr. Kendrick used that as a pretense and a way to covertly get me into prison."

"And that was your assignment? You were intentionally there?" 777 asked.

"Dr. Kendrick received information from a secret friend that something was going to happen."

917 used his eyes and did a small interpretive dance with his head. He tilted left and right uneasily and looked at the two of them, hoping they would understand or recognize his facial cues.

"A recon mission? Behind bars?" 297 asked.

"No you idiot," 777 sighed. "I'm guessing you were there to protect an inmate or try to prevent some big incident."

"Sorry 297," 917 snickered. "777 is slightly more on the nose than you are."

"Hey," 297 grumbled. "There's a lot of black market knowledge that you can gain access to from criminals. Even the big ones that run their own little kingdoms in prison."

"And you would know this, how?"

917 and 777 both stared at 297, who looked slightly flustered.

"I thought we were talking about 917," he retorted.

The three of them laughed. It died down quickly as 777 jabbed 917 in his shoulder.

"Alright," 777 smiled. "What was your mission?"

"You need to promise not to be mad," 917 stated. He glanced at the two of them. "Both of you."

"Ok?" 297 responded cautiously.

"No," 777 refused the request.

"Fair enough," 917 sighed. "I was assigned to monitor everything inside Fulton Federal Penitentiary and investigate a few things. The biggest one of all was guarding one really important inmate."

"Who was it?"

917 turned and fixed his gaze on 777. After a moment, he awkwardly tried to form the right words to 297. They could both sense that this question stirred some inner turmoil. 777 felt skeptical, but he scrutinized his expression, searching for clues to understand the situation.

"There was a reason I asked if you wouldn't be mad," 917 stated.

297 and 777 looked at each other. Neither of them could figure it out, until 777's eyes widened.

"No," he exclaimed. "You don't mean..."

A phone call interrupted their conversation, causing all three of them to pause. They checked the caller ID and saw that 999 was calling.

"To be continued?" 917 asked as he picked up.

"Sure!" 297 nodded.

As 917 answered 999, 297 looked at 777 and mouthed, "*who?*" 777 just glared back.

"You mean you don't know?!" he replied.

917 awkwardly stepped away from the two of them and spoke to 999.

"Hello?"

"You are carrying one of the most sophisticated space rifles from an alternate universe!" 777 was yelling behind him. "How can you not know?!"

"For your information," 297 replied grouchily, "if you repeat the words, 'alternate universe,' then you might understand the fact that some people are focusing on other matters at hand!"

917 was trying not to laugh at the argument that he had unintentionally started.

"What is happening?" 999 asked in the call. "Are 297 and 777 fighting?"

"Yeah, you might have just interrupted a private conversation," 917 answered.

"I'm sorry but I needed to contact you immediately," 999 stated. "I just found something."

A sudden explosion cut her off, and 297, 777, and 917 were sent staggering forward. The blast came from the hangar behind them. It shook the halls, sending crew members sprawling to the ground and stumbling over each other. A voice echoed across the hall, cutting through the chaos.

"Enemy ship in the hangar bay!" someone said. "Security details to the hangar! Intruder alert! Enemy ship in the hangar bay!"

"What just happened?!" 999 said urgently on the line. "Are you alright, 917?!"

917 whirled around. 777 and 297 had stopped arguing and were now in bladed stances. They exchanged glances, nodded, and prepared for action. 297 charged his rifle while 777 and 917 drew their weapons. 777 swung his rifle forward, checking his ammo, and 917 drew his pistol. Together, they advanced towards the hangar entrance.

They quickly got into a formation. 917 took the lead with 777 directly behind him and 297 bringing up the rear.

"Yeah I'm fine," 917 said. "297, 777 and I are going to check it out! Notify 117! Enemy contact in the ship's hangar!"

"Copy that," 999 replied. "Call me again. Please."

"You know I will," 917 responded. He hung up the call. "Well, 297. You did say you wanted action."

"Hell yes," 297 declared. "Ready!"

"Ready," 777 added.

917 opened the door.

"Move in!"

The three of them entered the hangar, with 917 taking the lead down the center. 777 positioned himself to the right while 297 faced left. They quickly stepped into a wedge formation to cover a 180 degree field of vision. As they scanned the entire hangar, their eyes locked onto the action unfolding before them.

"Get those wounded out of the hangar!"

"I need help over here!"

"Where's the fire crew?!"

Amidst all of the screams and yelling, the amborgs caught sight of a large fire that was quickly spreading. They didn't see or hear any weapons being fired in the hangar, which meant that there were no intruders. At least, none that they could see, as the hangar was in complete disarray.

"Hey!" 917 shouted to a nearby engineer. "What happened?!"

"Sir!" he replied as he dragged another officer away from the flames. "Tandeeri fighters slipped past our defenses! It came in here on a suicide run!"

Fire crews and flying drones were already on the scene putting out the flames before they could spread to fuel tanks and other combustible materials. 917 ordered the engineer to proceed to safety as the amborgs moved cautiously towards the center of the hangar where the commotion was concentrated.

"Move those munitions away from the fire!" someone yelled. "Put it out before they get cooked off and kill us all!"

There was a ship, fully engulfed in flames, and people were rushing to get as far away from it as possible. Firefighters fought tirelessly to keep the inferno contained. From what they could tell, its unusual shape suggested that it was not something that originated from Earth or resembled any of the S.C.E. fighter crafts.

"Officer!" 917 called out to a man who looked to be in charge of the situation. "How did this ship slip through?"

"Some pilots needed to do emergency landings!" he replied fast. "Enemy fighter just flew in from behind them! It came in and dropped into some fuel tanks! It blew up and now we're roasting in one giant oven!"

917 turned to 297 and 777, who put away their weapons when they realized there was no battle to engage in. Instead, they picked up some firefighting gear and moved closer to the burning wreckage of the enemy fighter. 917 holstered his weapon and helped some engineers pick up a hose. Together, they worked as a team to extinguish the flames.

"Guys!" 917 yelled. "We've got to get the fire out, otherwise we lose a possible lead to the Tandeeri!"

777 and 297 both acknowledged his instructions. They had also acquired fire suppression equipment, and the hangar crew gave them a quick crash course. The drones flying above released extinguishing agents, and with their equipment, they started to successfully combat the flames.

"Did you get any pictures?" 917 asked.

"Yeah," 297 called out. "But they're all just pictures of it on fire! Probably useless at this point."

"I think it's working!" 777 shouted.

He was wrong. An explosion erupted from the burning wreckage, sending them all flying backwards. 917, 777 and 297 landed on their backs. 297 managed to roll back onto his feet, but 917, who'd been closest to the blast, was still sliding slowly away from the ship. They hadn't felt that kind of destructive force in an explosion since the Dominoe Incident. What made it interesting, though, was that this time they actually took some damage.

917 groaned in pain. He could feel warm blood dripping from his head. The shockwave from the blast had hit his core really hard.

"917!" he heard 777 yell.

The next thing he knew, he felt hands grabbing his shoulders and he was dragged across the floor.

"Agh! What the hell?" 917 coughed.

He realized that 777 and 297 had moved him away from the wreckage, which was still on fire. 777 crouched in front of 917, shielding him as 297 did an emergency medical scan.

"Your amborg implants..." 297 said. "They're damaged. Mine too... 777, are you ok?"

"Yeah, I'm fine!" 777 responded. "Might have a bruise tomorrow but it's nothing I can't handle."

"Can you let go of me please, 297?" 917 grumbled as he shook off 297's hand, which was still clutching his shoulder. "Stop that! That hurts!"

"Are you kidding?" 297 said, retracting his hand. "You just promised to call 999 back a few minutes ago! If you die, I am not going to face her when I break the news!"

"Don't forget!" 777 added. "You still need to finish spelling out everything to 297! He still hasn't figured it out!"

"That's not important right now!"

"Stop it! Both of you!" 917 said. "Help me up!"

297 and 777 helped 917 get back on his feet as they each checked their scans. Then they surveyed the smoldering ship behind them. The flames were nearly out, thanks to the addition of several more drones flying overhead, supporting the crewmen. Everyone was slowly picking themselves back up and diving back into firefighting. The heat had subsided enough for the amborgs to look out from the hangar bay, taking in the ongoing battle outside. They spotted a few Tandeeri capital ships, with both friendly and enemy fighters zipping around and weaving through the chaos. The shimmering edge of a blue force field kept them safe from being sucked into space, just like in very sci-fi movie they could think of.

"I think the Alpha universe has weapons and natural elements capable of killing us," 917 stated.

"Yeah," 777 muttered. "We need armor and protection. This isn't good."

"Yeah," 297 groaned. "Things suck a lot more now."

"Is my right arm alright?"

"Yeah," 297 looked at 917 briefly. "It's fine."

"Then let's keep looking."

The three of them made their way back over. All the flames had disappeared, and the drones zoomed off to tend to other small sparks and contained fires the rest of the crew were managing to settle. Things were starting to feel normal again, despite the lasers and missiles whizzing by outside while the battle raged on.

"Well," 297 said. "It looks like we could light it on fire again and then barbecue. Maybe grab some marshmallows and make some s'mores."

297 was right. 917 looked at the blackened wreckage of the ship and attempted another scan. The fire had been so hot that there was absolutely nothing to salvage or worth examining. He sighed.

"Damn it," 917 mumbled. "It doesn't look like there's anything to salvage."

"Well," 777 pointed up towards the top of the wreck. "The explosion opened a hole. Why don't we climb inside?"

"Is that safe?" 297 asked.

"Uh," 917 quickly stopped 777 before he could move forward. "Let's see if they have some protective space suits."

"Right," 777 replied. "That might be the safest option."

"I definitely didn't come all this way to die in a fire," 297 said cautiously. "I really hope it doesn't catch on fire again."

The three of them coordinated with the officers and the surviving hangar crewmen. As they helped to clean up, the ship's security detail arrived and they requested some equipment. A Tandeeri fighter ship, even if burnt to a crisp, was definitely something that could help them gain some much needed insight. There was no way that the amborgs would allow this opportunity to slip by.

Deck Seven
Residential Area, Infant Care

"Are you a parent of one of the children here?"

466 looked back at the receptionist with curiosity. The receptionist was not human, so her attention was definitely focused on their physical features. The receptionist blinked its four eyes, and 466 noticed it was smiling at her. She quickly looked into one pair of eyes and greeted them.

"Oh goodness. No," 466 chuckled. "No, I was exploring with my friend and we got separated. The ship is pretty big."

"It is, is it not?" the receptionist replied. "There is a map outside the door. We are in the bow, section two of the residential area on deck seven. Chances are, your friend might still be here in this section."

"I can always find him," 466 smiled. "Just point me in the direction of the screaming as that's usually the best way."

"You are not married to this friend are you?"

"No."

"Good, because the kids are all down for their naps at the moment. Screaming would be counterproductive. I need this job."

The receptionist grinned as 466 snickered. Unfortunately, she couldn't tell if the receptionist was actually laughing, too. Finally, she decided to ask a question that had been weighing on her mind for the past few minutes.

"If you don't mind me asking," she said, "what alien race are you from?"

"Ah yes," the receptionist replied, putting down a pen. "There have been rumors that visitors from Epsilon Earth were touring aboard the ship. I am one of the matriarchs of the Brakovish Arklashi. But before you comment on what a mouthful that is, the humans find it easier to refer to us as the Kovark for short."

"Oh. I wasn't going to comment on that," 466 replied cheerfully. "In fact, you said... Bra-koh-visshh... Ark-la-she. Did I say that correctly?"

"That was spoken very nicely, miss. Thank you for hearing and putting special emphasis on 'vish' and 'lashi.' I am Breya. Happy to be of service."

"Hello Breya," 466 said, extending her hand.

The Kovark receptionist stared and blinked all of her eyes back. She paused, leaving 466 hanging.

Oh, she thought, *do they not shake hands? Probably wasn't one of their customs.*

Before she could lower her arm, the receptionist extended two right arms. She apparently had four arms. 466's hand reached out and grabbed one hand and met a total of eight long fingers.

"Humans love shaking hands," Breya declared as 466 grabbed her other right arm. "How interesting."

"Nice to meet you," 466 gazed down, fascinated at the skin pattern on the two right hands. "Did you say you were a matriarch?"

"Yes," Breya replied, lowering her arms back to her side. "Normally one would assume that this certain title, in your culture, refers to a woman who is the head of a family or tribe, or maybe an older woman who is powerful within a family or organization. That is partially accurate as I belong to the Kavachin-pama. A specific organization which literally translates to your word, 'care-givers.'"

"It must be an honor to be a matriarch of that group you are part of," 466 said as the receptionist walked around the desk.

"Not really," Breya replied, which caused 466 to stare questionably. "When a member of our species comes of age, we have the option of choosing a field of study or an occupation. Then and only then do we obtain the rights and authority of the matriarchy or patriarchy."

"There wouldn't happen to be any... gender issues that your people have to deal with... Are there?"

"Our society is considered to be one of the few successful egalitarianism races in the universe," Breya explained casually. "We seek to better society with our knowledge instead of seeing limitations that do not exist. In fact, there are many of us that see other races, especially humans, sometimes have better qualities than our own. We do have minor courses in the art of being badass though."

"You think humans are better?"

"Well, for one thing," Breya said with a smile. "Your eye exams are cheaper since you only have one pair. Some of us have two or three pairs."

The two of them laughed.

"What was that about the art of being badass?" 466 asked as their laughter died down. "So you teach your young how to...?"

"...make a name for themselves and look awesome at the same time," Breya finished her sentence and winked with the two eyes on her right side. "But enough about me, I believe the history of my race can be taught at a later time. I am very curious about what being someone like you is all about. Specifically why you decided to become an amborg."

"Oh, there isn't that much to say," 466 said. "I imagine we're pretty similar to our Alpha versions."

"It is a pity," Breya said. "Amborgs as strong as you are... almost all of you being killed. It seems very interesting."

"What makes you say that?"

Breya brought her hand up to her cheek as if pondering what to say. 466 was amazed at how direct and quick the subject changed with every question and sentence they spoke.

"Before I was part of the Kavachin-pama," she said in a hushed tone. "I served under your brother, 117."

"Oh really?" 466 said in astonishment. "He would love to meet you if you'd like."

"Maybe I will," Breya said. "I remember when he once told me to leave the S.C.E. military and focus more on what I wanted to do. I chose to be a caregiver."

Breya had served with Alpha 117 in the S.C.E. military? She was a combat veteran? The questions that were forming fascinated 466.

"What made you decide to leave the military?"

"I figured it was a way to balance out the mistakes I made," Breya sighed. "I was ashamed and went through terrible times whenever I returned to both home and the battlefield. My anguish was... hurting my heart heavily and my shoulders bore the weight of the people I lost and killed. I originally became a soldier because I didn't want to remain trapped on my home planet, but I ended up separating myself from my family. You don't see many of us aboard starships."

"Every fighter carries that," 466 said sympathetically. "So you became a caregiver? Now you're here taking care of the future generations."

"I believed that my goal in life was to protect and care for orphans and children," Breya smiled. "Not make them. 117 supported that decision even after I retired from military service. I was asked to reenlist though. Many of us were. There was definitely a lot of backlash directed towards people choosing not to fight when the Tandeeri showed themselves."

"Being a caregiver to children is just as important," 466 replied. "In our universe, they don't get paid enough."

"I see. Well, I'm sorry to cut it short but I have to begin my rounds soon," Breya replied as she walked back to the desk and picked up a data-pad. "If you see 117 before I get off work, tell him it's very good to hear from him. Also, I'm sorry that I wasn't there to die at his side when he fell in combat."

"I will," 466 nodded as she held up a hand in farewell. She felt slightly unnerved at the dying comment, but she kept smiling. "I feel like he'd be happy that you were still alive."

"Curious is it not?"

"What is?"

466 looked at Breya who was perusing her datapad. She turned to 466 with an inquisitive look.

"A great soldier such as 117," she said. "It's still hard to believe the one I know is gone. Knowing him, a good soldier wouldn't just fall that easily. I hope that you do not suffer the same fate."

Breya walked through a door without waving goodbye and disappeared. 466 stood there, baffled. It was nice that she had wished for them to not die. Still, that was an ominous thing to say out loud. Perhaps the Kovark had a different bedside manner than humans?

"Hmm," she murmured. "Now I'm curious about how we ended up dying. Are the Alpha amborgs weaker? Or are the Tandeeri devilishly stronger?"

466 suddenly felt nervous being alone. She glanced over her shoulder and scanned the area, as if checking for a hidden assailant.

There's something strange in the room, 466 thought.

She couldn't quite determine what it was specifically, but she knew she had to leave. Before she could, the door that Breya had entered opened and a little visitor walked through. It was one of the children from the nursery.

"Aww. Hi there," 466 cooed. "Are you lost?"

The little boy, human, wandered up to her with a finger in his mouth. He nodded quietly, but then lifted both hands. She knew what he wanted and beamed.

"Oh well, you can just climb into my arms," 466 said as she lifted the boy up. "Then we can see about wondering where you came from. Is there anyone here who can take you? Breya?"

The door opened again, and 466 turned to see who it was, hoping it would be Breya. Instead, a little girl burst in, rushing over as soon as she spotted the boy 466's arms. She raised her arms up, and she couldn't help but melt at the sight of the girl's sweet, innocent gaze.

"Aw. You too?" 466 sighed and knelt down. She shifted the boy to her right arm and with the other, she grabbed the girl with her left and stood up with a child in each arm. "I suppose I might as well. Hopefully someone qualified comes in. Oh is that Breya? Or somebody?"

466 raised her head with a glimmer of hope as the door opened a third time. But instead of what she expected, she heard a soft mewing noise. Confused, she looked down to see another toddler who resembled a cat stroll through.

Oh no, she thought, *what did they do? Escape the play-pen?*

The newcomer stopped at 466's feet, looked up, and stared at her with adorable feline eyes. Why did this one have to look up at her? Her face practically melted from how cute it was.

"They have neko-children?? That's so amazing!" 466 said as her heart fluttered. "I'm going die from all this cuteness! I wonder if cat kids are as hygienic as they are adorable."

Her willpower beginning to falter, 466 looked at the two quiet kids in her arms. Then she glanced back down at the neko-child who was sitting on all fours.

"There aren't any available arms," 466 announced. "But you're welcome to hug a leg?"

Without warning, the little cat child immediately bounced up and began climbing up 466's legs... with claws. When it made it up to her waist, it changed direction and crawled around so that the toddler was now climbing up her back. At least it had the decency to avoid her chest. Before she knew it, she felt a big weight resting on her right shoulder as the kitty curled up and perched there. She could have sworn that the little climber was purring.

"You children are incredibly well-behaved," 466 said, standing as still as she could, trying not to drop anyone. "Oh dear."

The door opened again and another eager toddler came through. If Breya had shrunk, then this child definitely looked exactly like her. It had to be a young Brakovish Arklashi boy. Or was it a girl? 466 looked down at the little child, who stared back with four green eyes. It blinked and they changed to a bright blue. She saw the child lift its two right arms and pointed at its chin curiously.

"Unless, you're in the mood for a climb," 466 panted, "be my guest. I sure ain't going anywhere."

The moment she said it, the little Korvak's eyes suddenly glowed, and a bright aura immediately surrounded it. The next thing 466 knew, the small alien flew up off the ground, zipped around, and landed on her left shoulder, perching there and tilting its head on top of hers.

"Or you can do that. Just fly up there and make me both impressed and concerned," 466 sighed. "I feel like a tree... Now I know how an Ent feels. If I have to walk around, kids, I'm in trouble."

As the group of children muttered and babbled quietly, an announcement came over the intercom. She could hear a male voice reporting over the speaker. It was Commander Ulgo's voice.

"Attention. Attention. The Tandeeri fleet has been pushed back and they are in full retreat. Admiral Ra'aiah has set the ship back to condition three. Stand down from combat stations. We are also pleased to announce that a wormhole has opened near our position. The lead elements of our fleet have arrived. They've informed us that reinforcements will arrive within the next two days. First contact protocols are going well and we are sending the first shuttles down to Earth. That is current as of now. Thank you for your time. Please stay safe."

"And meanwhile," 466 muttered, "I've got four kids who have arrived and are occupying my space. This is going to be a long day."

Deck 2
Firestar Archives

999 exhaled, letting out a big sigh as her hands trembled. She took her hands off the computer pad and massaged her eyes. How long had it been since she requested time in the archives?

Too long, she realized when she checked the time.

"What am I thinking?" 999 muttered. "I should be focusing on the Tandeeri. Not my own personal inquiries."

Her search results and images from the various data-pads laid out across the table were anything but the Tandeeri. Most of the information she had found was classified, and she was trying to sort through what was public record and what wasn't. Normally, it would be easy to look into cracking the locks, but at the same time, she kept getting distracted from all the subjects that had caught her eye as she gave herself a crash course in Alpha universe history. There was so much information at her disposal that she couldn't keep up. She wished there was more time.

"345," she mumbled. "With your fast reading speed, all of these would be a breeze."

Suddenly, 999 tilted her head up and frowned. She had detected a new presence in the room. Thankfully, it was a familiar one.

"I taught you better than that," she said out loud. "I still heard you. That is a failure."

There was a slight chuckle as 501 appeared from around the corner. He had managed to open the door and sneak inside the private room, but he hadn't succeeded at being entirely stealthy.

"Hi 999," he said, waving cheerfully. "Are you busy?"

"Mmm."

999 was slightly annoyed at the interruption, but she lifted a finger and pointed at a chair near her. 501 cautiously pulled the chair out and sat down.

"You got lost?" she noted as 501 looked around the archives. "Where is 466?"

"We got lost," 501 admitted with a sigh. "I got distracted."

"So did I."

"What are you looking at?" 501 asked curiously, reaching for a data-pad.

"Information," 999 replied as she continued to read. "If there's anything that the S.C.E. is hiding, then I want to know. Furthermore, it will be useful for us to have every advantage we can find regarding how we can end the war."

"You mean like a tactical advantage?" 501 looked over the data-pad. "Oooh, 'Dark Haven'? What kind of planet is that?"

"Wars can end in multiple ways 501," 999 said. "Only war-crazy action goers seek violence and the eradication of the other side in order to win. I seek a diplomatic advantage."

"Is that even possible?" 501 inquired as he flipped through the data-pad. "Wow, they have modern shinobi organizations? Space ninjas?"

"I believe all options should be considered," 999 replied. She allowed 501 to have fun reading whatever he wanted as she explained. "Perhaps if we lose the war, we can still find a way to compromise where we can and draw where the line ends. Also, I detest getting information that my Alpha universe self was so easily killed."

"It is sad isn't it? Knowing that in another life, we ended on such quick paths."

"Don't be silly," 999 snapped. "Sadness is for children. What I care about is why the path we took ended so fast in the first place."

"Foul play?" 501 guessed.

"There is always foul play in the world or... any universe," 999 said. "I grew up with it and that feeling has never left me. Ever since we boarded this ship. There's something strange going on. I don't know. It makes me... uneasy. Do you feel that there's... a presence of some kind? A dark one?"

"If it's ok for me to admit it outloud," 501 replied calmly. "I kind of agree and know how you feel. Everyone always said I should trust my instincts. I've also never heard you use the word 'uneasy' before. You really have suspicions that something is wrong?"

"Always assume that there is 501," 999 said informatively. "If everything seemed so perfect, wouldn't it make you slightly worried?"

"Are you looking up amborg records?" 501 said as he grabbed another data-pad. "Hey, this is the file for 34-..."

999 stood up quickly and slammed her hand down on 501's data-pad. It fell out of his grasp and she pinned it onto the table, where it made a loud

clunk. 501 looked up, expecting her to be angry, but she merely stared at the table. She had definitely been good at one thing. Speed was her game.

"That's not important right now," 999 said, her breath shaking with building tension. "Go find someone else to harass. I have important things to do and you're making me uncomfortable."

501 held up his hands and stood from his seat.

"I'm sorry," he said meekly. "I just know how you feel! I miss her too."

"You don't!" 999 yelled.

501 flinched as 999 turned to him and glared. Her cold gaze made the blood drain from his head, but he maintained his position firmly.

"I do!" 501 protested emphatically. "At her funeral, do you remember?"

"Stop it."

"You do remember what I told you?" 501 asked. "I told you and 917...!"

"Stop!"

"When he cried and you tried to look strong!" he pressed. "I promised that I would not abandon you!"

"STOP IT!!"

999's scream pierced his ears so loudly that 501 felt tears welling up. He carefully lifted his gaze to her, seeing the agony etched on her face as she fought to breathe and hold herself together. Looking around, he saw that her scream had attracted the attention of S.C.E. crewmen and civilians outside the windows, all of whom had stopped to watch the drama unfolding in the meeting room.

"You have no idea," 999 said tensely as she turned to stare down at him. Her voice trembled as she practically spat out her words. "Don't you dare say you know what it's like. You've never had to watch someone you love, someone you were just talking to earlier that day, never come home! You have never known what it's like to hold on to someone and beg them to stay with you! Don't you ever say that you know what I've been through. We may have the same cybernetics but you will never understand. You remember what I once said to you?"

"You've said a lot of things," 501 gulped, speaking softly.

"I told you the best way to not be me was to be better!"

"But I know where you came from," 501 said quietly. He didn't feel like it was ok to just remain silent. "Your childhood was terrible and that's why you have a hard time trusting people. That's why you prefer being alone. But you're an amborg and a really tough one and I don't think that's what you want. You have 917 as your best friend! And all of us look up to you... even when you don't like having us around. I just want you to know that we all care!"

"Get out."

"999!" 501 protested. "I care! You're my friend!"

"Find better friends. Leave."

999 threw the pad she was holding across the table, sending it gliding toward the door. 501 made a move to catch it as it came to a halt at the end of the table. Just as it teetered off, he hesitated, sensing it was better to let it drop. It fell to the floor with a clatter. When he glanced back at 999 one last time, she had averted her gaze, looking down and away from him. He took that as his cue, and he turned to leave.

"But, you are my friend," 501 said as he quickly departed. "I'm sorry."

He expected 999 to throw another pad at him, but it didn't happen. Rounding the corner, he flung the door open in a rush. A few onlookers he brushed past continued to stare, but he ignored them. He made his way to the archive entrance, hoping to find someone–anyone–who he could hang out with.

As he made his way to the security gate, he missed out on what the receptionist said to him and he got into the elevator. It wasn't until he noticed that the elevator wasn't moving that he realized he didn't know where to go.

"Oh," he said. "I don't know where I'm going. Uhh, 3?"

He called 3 and she immediately answered.

"Hi 501," she replied. "Everything ok? You rarely call me."

"Where are you?"

"I'm trying out some food at the main mess hall," she replied. "It's pretty interesting. This ship has the makings of a military base. Like, there'll be multiple barracks, recreational rooms, and mess halls for sections of the ship. But the residential area has a mini-mall with a shopping complex and some basic needs for families and residents, like a hotel. Do you want to come and have something to eat with me?"

"Yes please," 501 said with a sigh.

"You don't sound ok," 3 replied. "Do you want me to get 117?"

"No," 501 answered. "I don't want to bother him. I made 999 mad. Where are you?"

"Ah I see. Come to deck eight," 3 said. "Someone will show you the right section."

"Ok."

501 asked for deck eight and the elevator began to move. Within minutes, the doors opened and he stepped off. He looked around, but there were very few crew members.

"Excuse me," he said to one stepping onto the elevator as he got off. "Where's the mess hall?"

"The main one is down the corridor and then a few rights and lefts," the crewman answered. "Just follow the arrows, sir."

"Thank you."

501 looked at the walls. It was just as they said. There were displays on the walls with colored arrows pointing out special sections of the deck. There were the bathrooms, then further up were the lounges, and then finally, the place he was looking for.

"Ok," he said. "It's this way. How hard could it be to follow the signs?"

He was in a second corridor when he heard what sounded like a faint crash coming from a room nearby. Confused, he stopped to listen. There was another small crashing sound. He walked slowly towards the source of the noise. Finally, he stood outside the door of a regular storage closet and listened again. Was a crewman doing something private inside or just being a klutz? It was usually his job to cause a scene most of the time.

"Are you alright, sir?"

501 spun around and jumped. An officer in a gold-striped uniform stood beside him. She took a step back and flinched when he yelped, clearly startled by her.

"Geez!" he exclaimed. "Sorry! I..."

"That's alright," she cleared her throat. "Is something wrong?"

"You didn't hear that?" 501 said as his hand flew to his heart.

"Hear what?" the woman asked. "Pardon me, sir. You were just standing there so I was curious if anything was wrong."

Apparently, she wasn't able to hear the rattling noises and the things hitting the floor inside the closet. 501 realized his heightened sense of hearing must have just automatically picked up a suspicious noise. Suddenly, he remembered what 999 had said about things never being right all the time.

"Oh," 501 chuckled. "I guess I was just hearing things. It is a really awesome ship. I just wanted to remember what some things sounded like."

"I see," the woman nodded. "I'll continue with my duties then."

As she walked away, 501 waited anxiously until she disappeared around a corner. When she was gone, he quickly checked the door lock.

"There's got to be a way in," he muttered as he jabbed a green button.

There was a small hiss as the doors parted.

"Voila," 501 mumbled triumphantly as he looked around. "You're a real Houdini, Donut…"

When he stepped inside, he expected a crewman to respond in terror but to his surprise, there was no one inside. Amidst all the shelves and how large the closet appeared, there was no evidence that anyone was or had been inside recently.

"Strange," 501 said as he cautiously leaned on the door frame. "What was going on in here?"

501 wished he still had a technician assigned to him to help provide a second pair of eyes. But unfortunately, he had to do it by himself.

Suddenly, a couple of boxes tumbled from the shelves above. They hit the ground with a loud thud, causing 501 to look over his shoulders. There didn't seem to be anyone around, so what was the worst that could happen?

"I could… do the decent thing and try to tidy up," 501 said slowly under his breath as he stepped inside. "Maybe it's a stray pet or alien Chihuahua? Hehe."

The door closed slowly, and he heard more objects being rattled.

"Or a ghost lives in here?" he said weakly as fear gradually took over. "Oh screw it. I'm getting out of here!"

As he turned to leave, something heavy hit him from behind and he fell to the ground.

"YAARRGGHH!!" he yelled as he landed on his stomach. "Don't eat me! I'm not digestible! Remember to recycle my parts! For the ecosystem!"

With his eyes shut, 501 trembled as the weight on top of him shifted around. Then, he felt something poking the back of his head. Had he actually encountered a space animal of some kind?

501 opened his eyes and blinked in confusion. He rolled over and sat upwards. Once he got a clear look, he froze.

"Ok…" he said as his eyes widened. "What are you supposed to be? Oh no…"

Three things happened. First off, he tried to scream. Second, he realized that nobody can hear people scream in space—or, in this case, the closet that was virtually soundproof. Finally, he got tackled right in the face and was immediately knocked unconscious.

Before he could even wrap his head around what just happened, darkness took over. Talk about rotten luck.

Chapter 19: Soldiering on

A.I. Industries
Emergency Recall plus 8 days 3 hours

"Are you going to be honest with yourself?"

4 paused in the hallway and looked at 18.

"I'm always honest with myself," 4 replied with a slightly confused expression. "Perks of having a mind of my own."

"Then tell me why you insist on antagonizing the others?"

4 let out a light chuckle.

She stopped when she looked at 18 and realized she wasn't laughing.

"Oh, you weren't being sarcastic?" she asked smugly.

"You just think this is a big joke, don't you?" 18 shook her head.

"When the timing is correct, yes, I find certain things funny," 4 replied. Her face fell and she said softly, "May I remind you of one important fact, 18? It is not my fault the others can't keep their own emotions in check."

18 grumbled angrily and crossed her arms. 4 merely patted her on the shoulder.

"Loosen up," she said. "You'll be less stressed."

"You're telling me that you don't feel anything?" 18 asked. "Miss I-never-had-a-burst-dam? 1 may have selected you to remain in charge because you are capable of making tough choices, but you could at least stop behaving so stuck-up all the time."

"It is my intention to make sure that the planet still stands after this war is over," 4 replied firmly. "And if we lose our friends, I have to bear the burden of making sure the fight still goes on. I am fortunate to have you with me at my side, but if amborg morale is better served by my roaming the halls of A.I. Industries crying like a little girl, I shall gladly defer to your expertise."

"We've known each other for over 15 years," 18 retorted.

"Once again, I appreciate your repeated history of stating the obvious," 4 nodded.

"Why do you have to stick to the old ways so much?" 18 rolled her eyes and glared at 4. "Back when we were emotionless monsters. People didn't want us, they feared us! Long before the Second Group amborgs joined us and helped change so many things! Wouldn't you rather show the world that you're not heartless? That even you, amborg Kat 4, cares?"

4 gazed at 18 expressionless. 18 sighed and turned to walk away, but 4 caught her by the arm, making her pause.

"Some people like the spotlight," she explained as she began to walk side-by-side with 18. "I don't. It doesn't suit someone like me. I just happen to think that my emotions are a burden. In 15 years, if you have to ask me why I am the way I am... It doesn't seem like you know me at all."

The two of them walked on in silence. Their footsteps echoed in the halls as they passed by a few human employees. 18 saw 4 acknowledge them, but ignored their questions and kept going. Instead of following in an attempt to continue talking to them, they merely went their own way. This wasn't exactly helpful for a cohesive work environment.

"Would it kill you to at least acknowledge that those people were just trying to ask how you were doing?" 18 exclaimed.

"I don't have the time," 4 stated. "I'm busy figuring out how to keep them all alive."

"That's the problem," 18 mumbled. "You keep acting all high and mighty and you'll lose their respect."

"Well, my strength lies in forming the best laid plans," 4 said, "not for the recognition. I do it so that everyone has an idea of what direction to steer towards. An orchestra that's led by a good conductor is what everyone appreciates. Most of the time, they don't even bother to learn the name of the conductor at all. That's all I need in my life."

They both made their way outside, spotting the landing pad where everyone was gathering. The amborgs and several staff members waited just beyond the safe zone as 4 and 18 walked up.

"How long until they arrive?" 18 asked.

Carter was seen hovering with a few of the other A.I. programs. He turned and floated over to them.

"Captain Hicks just informed us that she is on final approach," he reported.

"Thank you," 4 replied. "Everyone! We have some people coming home! Let's welcome them back!"

The crowd lifted their heads and waited patiently. A few more staff members hurried out of the building, rushing to join the rest of the group. Among them, 18 spotted Mandy racing toward them.

"Sorry I'm late!" she exclaimed. "It's a nightmare trying to organize supply runs with how chaotic it is out there."

"Thanks for doing that," 18 nodded. "Were you close to anybody up there?"

"Yeah," Mandy nodded. "I knew them all."

"Here they come!"

Silence fell over the crowd as they kept their eyes trained upwards. The wind picked up, getting increasingly louder. Then, the thunderous roar of booster engines sliced through the air. The amborgs were able to dampen the noise by muting their ears, while Mandy pressed her hands tightly against her head. Three small dots appeared on the horizon, gradually revealing the silhouettes of the Apogee Station shuttles.

The engines roared as they slowed down and hovered in place. 4 signaled the amborgs with them to get ready. They watched Echo Flight slowly begin to descend, but it wasn't those shuttles that they were being cautious of, it was the third one that was flying in formation with them.

An S.C.E. shuttle, carrying first contact specialists and negotiators, had followed Echo Flight from space to touch down at A.I. Industries. 4 and 18 were tasked by Dr. Kendrick to treat the guests with kind hospitality. Whoever these experts were, they were going to be liaisons to the amborgs on Earth.

The trio of shuttles touched down with a powerful whoosh, sending gusts of wind swirling around the crowd. They hit the ground with a resounding thud, gradually powering down their engines. As the ramps descended, the amborgs made their way toward the waiting shuttles.

"Line up!" 4 commanded.

The amborgs formed a neat line along one side of the ramp, while the scientists and technicians gathered on the opposite side. Mandy joined her colleagues, while the amborgs stood in perfect formation. As the ramp lowered completely, the passengers inside began to disembark.

4 turned her gaze to the first group of people stepping off the shuttle. Four marines from the space-jumpers marched out carrying a coffin with the U.S. flag draped across it. Another four carried a second coffin, then a third, and a fourth.

Everyone who was wearing a hat immediately took them off and placed them over their hearts. Others put their right hands over their chests. Among the A.I. Industries staff, former military personnel, along with the security teams, stood at attention, saluting as their fallen colleagues were carried towards the main building.

After three more coffins were carried out by other survivors of Apogee Station, Captain Hicks and her copilot, Lieutenant Frye, emerged. Once the rest of the crew had disembarked, they allowed themselves to step out onto the ground, too.

"Everyone!" 4 called out to the crowd when she saw Captain Hicks nod to her. "To the other shuttle!"

Captain Hicks and Lieutenant Frye followed the amborgs and the A.I. Industries staff to the second shuttle, where the S.C.E. personnel waited patiently. Mandy and a few of her colleagues glanced back at them, but continued to follow the amborgs. They all lined up again in their groups and they repeated the same ceremony.

The shuttle, Echo 232, under Captain Planck's command, had already lowered its ramp. Another group of marines and Apogee Station personnel began to carry coffins off the shuttle. Everyone at A.I. Industries stood vigil again, sending off their friends with prayers, wishes, and sharing final goodbyes.

Once everyone was off the shuttle, Captain Planck stepped off the ramp with his copilot and nodded to 4.

"Dismissed!" 4 commanded everyone.

"Captain Hicks! Captain Planck."

Both pilots came to greet 4 and 18. They shook 18's hand, but 4 politely declined to touch them.

"Welcome home, captains," 4 dipped her head respectfully. "Night Song and Foe Hammer have safely made it back."

"Thank you," Hicks nodded with a grateful smile. "We'll mourn our friends later. I think our visitors are anxious to meet you."

4 and 18 led a few amborgs and the Echo Flight pilots to meet with the S.C.E. first contact specialists.

"Amborg 4," Captain Hicks gestured towards a man who was giving them a salute. "This is Commander Nelson."

"Amborg 4," Nelson lowered his salute and reached out a hand. "It's an honor to meet you."

"No," 4 looked down at Nelson's hand and politely shook her head. "My apologies, sir. I don't shake hands."

"She's like that," 18 intervened and took Nelson's hand. "Don't take it personally."

Baffled, he shook 18's hand enthusiastically. That sure had to be a rather unusual introduction, especially since they were supposed to be openly communicating and starting diplomatic channels.

"No offense taken," Nelson nodded. "I was trained to respect all traditions, cultures, and personal preferences of everyone I meet."

The officers behind him, about six of them, were carrying small briefcases and equipment off of their shuttle.

"Then I'm sure you'll understand the rules that we have in place?" 4 asked coldly.

"Yes," Nelson dipped his head respectfully. "I received instructions from Dr. Kendrick himself and the documents that you compiled for me."

"We'll summarize it again," 4 stated. "You have another shuttle flying under escort to The White House to meet with the President. They also have the same rules as you do. Your shuttle will be monitored at all times while it is parked here. We have provided you and your crew with your own lodgings onsite here at A.I. Industries. During your time staying with us, we would be honored to strengthen relationships between our universes. However, please be aware that as diplomats from outer space, you will need to remember that you are in our jurisdiction and we will take action if we notice or determine any suspicious activities to be harmful or dangerous to us."

"Understood," Nelson nodded. "Good to be working with you."

"Oh I like him," 4 turned to 18 and smirked.

"Do you have a place where we can set up our equipment?"

18 held up her hand, stopping Nelson's team from proceeding inside the building.

"Please allow us to scan and examine the contents of your briefcases, bags, and luggage," 18 informed them politely.

"If you don't mind following 18 to the security checkpoint," 4 motioned for them to follow the others.

Commander Nelson and his team nodded to her and followed 18. A security team escorted them inside. Captain Hicks and Planck quickly saluted 4 and went back to their ships for a post-flight inspection.

"Whoa, those guys look like they mean business."

Without taking her gaze off of the S.C.E. officers, 4 heard Mandy speaking next to her.

"Mandy," 4 smirked. "I could have sworn you had gone back inside with the others."

"Well, you know me," Mandy chuckled. "I like sticking my nose in certain things. It's much less boring."

"Amborg 4! Mandy!"

The two of them saw George running up to them.

"Mr. Ramirez, how may we assist?" 4 acknowledged him courteously.

"First," he said while trying to catch a breath. "Thank you for helping bring my daughter home from overseas. Second, I need you to bring her home again."

4 merely crossed her arms and looked at him blankly, while Mandy looked worried.

"Uh," she tried to smile, but it was replaced with confusion. "So, she came back but left the premises again? Where did she go?"

"That's why I need to ask for another favor," George sweated nervously and bowed his head. "She said she needed to meet with a friend and would be back soon! But that was an hour ago!"

"I'm terribly sorry sir," 4 replied, shaking her head. "I'm afraid I can't spare anyone. The amborgs are mobilizing."

George and Mandy turned and stared at 4 in shock.

"Please!" he exclaimed. "I'm worried about her!"

"4," Mandy said in a gentle and kind voice. "Isn't there anything that can be done?"

"Retrieving and sending for everyone's family members to be brought here safely has been given high-priority since the start of the Emergency Recall," 4 shook her head. "I am sorry Mr. Ramirez. Thalia shouldn't have left by herself when she knew the rules."

"She helped coordinate the return of three departments in her spare time!" George pleaded. "At least find out who she went to visit."

"You understand what you are asking?" 4 sighed. "You want me to look into her social media? Invade her privacy? When she hasn't been gone long enough to meet the requirements to be declared missing?"

"Actually," Mandy interrupted them. "Maybe I can make a suggestion? Why don't we just ask the last person who saw her? She had to leave by exiting through one of the security entrances, right?"

Mandy had brought up this idea when she noticed that George was looking at 4 in terror. Whether it was because she wasn't considering Thalia a priority or he was about to cross a dangerous line as a parent. Either way, it wasn't going to end well if she hadn't intervened.

"Correct," 4 nodded. "That's footage I can immediately review."

4 paused for a second, glanced down, and then looked up at them again.

"North entrance," she reported. "Audio files from the security camera indicate she went to go see a friend named Wendy. Very fortunate she mentioned it to the guards."

"Wendy?" George blinked. "She's a friend from Vegas."

"That doesn't sound so bad," Mandy said reassuringly. "It's only an hour from here. Maybe I could go look for her?"

4 thought about it and stroked her chin. The only problem that immediately came to mind was the fact that she would be offsite and unprotected. Sending someone with her would probably help but depending on who it was, A.I. Industries would be temporarily without them when she needed every person available.

"You would have to be discreet," 4 reminded Mandy.

"I can do that," she smiled.

"But if someone recognizes you, you'll be in trouble," 4 thought carefully. "You're not going by yourself."

"Can I have an amborg?" Mandy asked with a hopeful look.

"No," 4 refused bluntly. "We're busy."

"Damn it."

Mandy looked at George, flashing her teeth and smiled innocently. She gave him an "I tried," expression as 4 brainstormed the best possible outcomes.

"I think that Mandy going to retrieve Thalia would be best," 4 stated.

"But," George looked at the two of them frantically. "You just said that going by herself was bad and that you couldn't spare an amborg escort."

"I never said the escort had to be an amborg," 4 winked.

4 led the two of them to Echo shuttle 209 and called out to the flight crew. Hicks was talking to Frye and Sergeant Hammond when she noticed them approaching. 4 waved to them.

"Captain Hicks," she said.

"4! Was there something else we forgot about?"

"No," 4 replied. She quickly asked them her question. "Are you returning to Apogee Station relatively soon?"

"Our shuttles need to go through some preflight maintenance, then we'll need to fly to the launch site again and wait until our booster rockets are refueled," Hicks answered with a shrug. "It might take several hours."

"Excellent, I need your help. Would you have time to accompany Mandy and escort her to Vegas?"

The entire flight crew perked up.

"Yes!" Hammond and Frye blurted out.

The thought of going to Vegas under orders from an amborg meant one thing to them—all-expenses paid. Captain Hicks was the only one of the three that didn't immediately agree, but instead looked at them skeptically.

"Hold on," she said slowly. "And what are we doing?"

"Locating and recovering Thalia Ramirez."

"Aww," Frye groaned. "We never get to go for fun."

"You want us to go looking for one girl?" Hicks placed a hand on her hip. "Seems like a waste of..."

The flight crew turned and saw Mandy motioning a hand to them. She tilted her head and nodded to George, who looked flabbergasted at their behavior. With her right hand, she did a horizontal swish across her neck a few times and cleared her throat, signaling for them to cut it out. Then, they noticed George and immediately straightened up.

"Sounds fun! Let's go get her!" Frye nodded.

"What was that about a waste of... I'm sorry, what was it you were about to say? About my daughter?"

Everyone except 4 awkwardly fell silent while Captain Hicks stumbled over his words. George pocketed his hands and shot him a look of frustration.

"Sorry, I misspoke Mr. Ramirez," Hicks replied softly. "I meant, the last time I went to Vegas was a total waste of time. We'd be happy to go and can take off shortly."

"Sorry Captain," 4 cleared her throat. "Low profile. Your ship stays here."

"Ok then," Hicks looked around stiffly. "Boys, let's grab our gear. We should probably change into our civvies."

4 then turned to Mandy as they stepped aboard the shuttle.

"I suggest you also prepare something inconspicuous," she instructed.

"Not my first time going undercover," Mandy nodded eagerly.

4 turned to look at George. She nodded reassuringly to him.

"They'll make sure that it isn't your last."

Mandy turned to pat George on the shoulder. Captain Hicks, Lieutenant Frye, and Sergeant Hammond walked off the ramp with their bags. They all followed Mandy and rushed towards the door inside.

"Thank you 4," George sighed in relief.

"Later," 4 replied. "When we find young Miss Thalia."

George nodded and walked back inside. 4 watched him as he disappeared through the doors, then spotted some familiar faces approaching her. Stuart 8 and Christy 9 were at the front, bringing a small group of amborgs along with them.

"I don't understand why we have to go up into space."

8 grumbled as 9 shoved him.

"Oh lighten up," she said. "Think of all the pranks we could pull off with all the equipment we could have access to."

"It is my wish that you two don't play with fire when we send you into space," 4 declared in a stern tone.

"But it's fun..." 9 whined softly.

"And pretty bad if we blew something up," 8 reminded her in a casual tone.

"Which is why," 4 shifted her attention to the other two amborgs behind them, "I want you two to keep an eye on them."

The Second Group twins, 92 and 93, looked concerned.

"You object?" 4 asked.

"Not so much with your orders. But 4, are you sure you want us to look after them?" 92 answered, pointing at himself and his brother. "We already have enough on our plates taking care of our triplet Third Group apprentices."

"Precisely," 4 said. "We'll take care of the diplomatic proceedings and the media backlash. You take the band of misfits and support the front lines."

"Are you sure that this is...?" 93 spoke.

"...a wise decision?" 92 finished the question.

"I'd prefer if you made headlines up in space than down here," 4 stated.

"You're just asking for us to be killed," 93 said with a huff. "Why can't 274 or 125 come up with us?"

"Both are assigned to protect the President of the United States and the visiting French President," 4 informed them. "In comparison to everyone else standing before me, they have better relations with them."

"Oh come on," 92 said, holding up his hands. "It was one state dinner! We messed up one dinner. Guess that's not going away anytime soon."

"And they didn't find it amusing when the two of you kept fooling around on another certain evening visit," 4 said. "Trading places in the White House may have been an amusing idea but not to the Secret Service."

"The first daughter thought it was funny," 93 mumbled, which made 92 grin cheekily.

"Do I need to remind all of you what happened when a rather intimate scandal almost occurred with another one of the first daughters from a past administration?"

"Oh yeah, that," 8 winced.

"Yeah, maybe don't joke about that," 9's eyes widened.

They all fell silent instantly. If the two pranksters of the First Group weren't laughing, then the joke was over and they had to put a lid on their sense of humor.

"Just get up there," 4 commanded. "Make sure the triplets and the Fourth group volunteers are prepped. You are all we can spare to send up there to reinforce the others. Inform us of any other problems."

"Got it," 92 and 93 answered. They turned to look at the Third Group triplets who were quietly waiting a few feet away. "53, 54, and 55. Go grab our stuff and the two Fourth Group stragglers. We're leaving soon."

As the twins pulled 8 and 9 with them towards Echo shuttle 232, they began chatting with Captain Planck and discussed their plans. The triplets soon followed along with 301 and 365 of the Fourth Group.

"Do you believe that they're the right kind of reinforcements?"

4 turned and saw 723 standing there. Her stealth approach and speed was remarkable. 4 gave her a firm nod.

"I've always felt that their methods were very different from standard protocol," 4 explained. "Space is unpredictable. I think that the amborgs who are the best at being unpredictable can increase our odds of survival."

723 nodded. She wore a backpack with two bags in each hand. 4 examined her belongings and looked at her curiously.

"I am ready to deploy to Tangiers," 723 reported.

"No, you're not. I believe my instructions to you were to keep a low profile."

723 looked confused.

"Please take a little more time to think about your mission, 723," 4 let out a sigh of annoyance. "You are not deploying in an amborg drop-pod and you are not to proceed on this mission in your amborg uniform."

"But this is who I am now," 723 replied. "I am an amborg because Dr. Kendrick gave me this opportunity."

"I understand that," 4 said. "But I'm afraid that for this mission, your old skill set and experience with the criminal underworld is why you were my choice for this. I don't need you as an amborg for this. I want you to get in there, hide in plain sight, hunt down our enemies that evade our watchful eye, and discreetly take them out."

"Are you authorizing a kill order?"

"Not specifically," 4 shook her head. "But you must understand that once you touch down on foreign soil, you are on your own. There is no backup or immediate extraction for you. I am authorizing you to take whatever action necessary to ensure your safety, but this mission must succeed. Otherwise, many people will have died in vain and there will be no way to avenge them."

"I understand," 723 nodded.

"May I suggest a nice leisurely flight?" 4 winked. "One that will get you there fast?"

"The main airport terminals are overflowing," 723 raised an eyebrow. "How am I supposed to get onboard a plane?"

"There's more than one way to fly," 4 eyed the shuttles sitting on the landing pad. 723 followed her gaze and looked at the parked transports. "I suggest an unmarked one. Maybe a friend in the military can help."

S.C.E. Firestar
Ready Room
Four hours later

"To the commanding officer of the S.C.E. Firestar. This message is for your eyes only. However, if the Firestar has been lost, ceased all forms of contact or communication, or been presumed destroyed, disabled or rendered out of commission in action or the line of duty, then all authority and command will be redirected and transferred to the commanding officer of the S.C.E. Alexandria."

Admiral Ra'aiah sat at her desk and read the orders that had been brought over from Alpha universe by their reinforcements. 43 stood at her side and they listened to the message that had been delivered. The automated voice had stopped talking and then another woman's voice spoke.

"Admiral Ra'aiah. If this message finds you, then I commend you for holding the line. I have no doubts that the systems and the technology built into our newest flagships has given you an edge in battle against the Tandeeri fleet. There is some more data included in this set of orders for you and your crew: correspondence, mail, records and data to reconnect them to what has been taking effect since you left our universe. In an attempt to maintain and boost morale for your ship, I hope your crew's spirits are lifted as a result. Back home, efforts across our territories have been calm since your departure to Epsilon. We have every reason to believe that Tandeeri are massing entirely there with you. Therefore, your updated orders are to maintain control and defend the Epsilon universe's Sol system until another batch of reinforcements can be sent over. You are not alone and we will devote everyone we can to assist you. Good luck and may the Gods watch over you. This is Admiral Caldwell, signing off."

Admiral Ra'aiah looked up.

"Well, that's very reassuring."

43 nodded. Admiral Ra'aiah sifted through the datapad and scrolled around.

"Now, onto another matter that we need to get straightened out," she said as she turned the pad and showed it to 43. "Is this correct to you?"

43 leaned forward and read what was on the screen. Her expression immediately turned annoyed and she shook her head.

"Admiral," she said. "That's not right."

"Those are the same orders you and I both received from command," Admiral Ra'aiah turned the pad and looked at it. "Are you telling me that someone sent you the wrong one?"

"Ma'am," 43 protested. "My original orders stated that once I made contact with the inhabitants of Epsilon universe, you would reinforce us within two days! I can show you the recordings I made when I looked at it!"

"Well, according to this, it doesn't say two days does it?"

On the datapad, Admiral Ra'aiah highlighted the section they were referencing. According to these orders, the S.C.E. Firestar was to cross into the Epsilon universe between five and six days. This, however, was in dispute as 43 continued to shake her head.

"That's not right!"

"These are official orders from command," Admiral Ra'aiah stated firmly.

"It's not what it said when I received them!" 43 answered in frustration.

"Careful 43, you're raising your tone against a superior officer!"

"Think about how wrong that sounds!" 43 pointed at the datapad. "You knew I crossed over successfully! And when I volunteered, I was told to expect you soon! Your orders shouldn't have been five or six days! If the Tandeeri had attacked sooner, Earth would have been facing an invasion by the time you arrived!"

"I'll look into it," Admiral Ra'aiah stated. "But it will have to be after the end of this mission. Unless you would like me to utilize the power to send you back home and you can lodge a complaint?"

43 sighed as she lowered her arms to her side. She resigned from her protesting and calmed down.

"No ma'am," she muttered.

"Then you're dismissed."

43 turned on her heel and walked off. Admiral Ra'aiah kept her eyes on the glowing red stripes of her amborg uniform as she made her way towards the door. One small detail bugged her, though.

"What happened to saluting your superior officer?" she said sharply.

43 pivoted, stopping about halfway to the door. The older amborg positioned herself perpendicular to the Admiral's desk, making sure her A.I. Industries insignia was clearly visible. Before Ra'aiah could question the disrespect behind this gesture, 43 slowly lifted both her hands, only to forcefully push them into her pants pockets.

Admiral Ra'aiah scoffed and gritted her teeth. 43 turned, tilting her head back and lifting her nose up defiantly. Then she strode toward the door. As it slid open, she left with a quick and menacing retort.

"Little bat."

The insult caused the Admiral's eye to twitch involuntarily. She couldn't believe that 43 had the nerve to say something like that. It was clear that the Alpha amborgs still alive demonstrated a severe lack in maintaining discipline.

If it were any other officer, she would have demoted them on the spot. If it had been a normal person that she was supervising, then they wouldn't have made it two steps out the door. Admiral Ra'aiah clenched her fists on her desk and let out a sigh. For Serina 43, it was best to leave it alone and drop the matter. After all, in a physical confrontation or battle of the wits, she stood no chance, even if she had a higher rank.

Admiral Ra'aiah reached for her console and a screen smoothly rose on her left hand side. With a swift gesture, she placed a call to the S.C.E. Alexandria. Remembering to send it to the bridge ready room, she waited patiently for Captain Chastain to answer.

He was either on duty or in his quarters, given how long it was taking him to reach a private terminal. After waiting in silence for about six minutes, the screen lit up, and he appeared in the background.

"There's my goddaughter!"

"I swear to gods," Admiral Ra'aiah grumbled. "Please tell me you're in your own ready room or quarters, with no one near you."

"If I say yes, will that make you feel better? Help your complexion? You remember me saying that?"

"Captain!" Admiral Ra'aiah growled.

"Then yes."

Captain Chastain was grinning cheekily as Admiral Ra'aiah regretted every passing second of this call. Nevertheless, she had to get this over with now that he had technically done one step and she had finished the next step in their mission.

"You opened the message from command?" Chastain inquired cordially.

"Obviously," she answered with a sigh.

"Alright then," he nodded as he straightened his collar and sat up straight. "Want to do this here and now? Or do you want me to gather the other captains and we come over for a barbecue?"

"Uncle, if the Tandeeri don't kill you..."

"Nah," Chastain grinned. "You love me."

"Let's just do this," Admiral Ra'aiah glared at him and straightened her posture.

The orders that she had received, along with her reinforcements, meant that she was the new appointed commander of the fleet. She was the ranking officer of the small task force that had arrived to help them. It was the proper time for her to assume control of the battle group in an impromptu ceremony. Despite how small the first wave of reinforcements was, she now had more assets to control and a better chance of mounting a capable defensive. Traditionally, it was how the S.C.E. could distinguish who was in charge. If this mission failed, it would reveal all those who are to blame if they were all killed. She picked up the datapad on her desk and read the message aloud to Captain Chastain.

"To Admiral Ra'aiah, commanding officer of the Firestar, on 17 July, twenty-two er... correction... 2138 of the Epsilon universe. You are hereby requested and required to assume command of the reinforcing fleet commanded by Captain Chastain, commanding officer of the S.C.E. Alexandria hereafter upon receiving these orders upon this date. This fleet merge of the Fourth Expeditionary Reconnaissance Fleet to the Second Colonial Defense Fleet has been signed by First Admiral Belina Caldwell."

"Orders received," Chastain replied promptly. "Reporting under your command."

"Now that we can speak off the record," Admiral Ra'aiah said informally, "You do know that you actually need to obey my orders?"

"What?" A wave of fear crossed Chastain's face. "You mean I have to now? I thought that was just recommended protocol."A

"Yes," Admiral Ra'aiah nodded. "You have to. My first order to you is actually a question about Serina 43."

"What do you want to know?"

Captain Chastain blinked and stopped joking, shifting his attention. Admiral Ra'aiah felt her anxiety flare up again when she remembered her earlier interaction with 43. One look and he could sense her unease.

"Oh," he nodded sympathetically. "Let me guess... pushed your buttons a little?"

"What was she like under your command?"

"She's tough," Chastain spoke bluntly. He lifted his hand to his chin and thought carefully. "Very spirited and eager to get the job done. Quite friendly and she excels at what she does best—protecting and caring for her friends. I know that she was only aboard my ship for a couple of days while we prepared to send her over here to Epsilon but the crew, including myself, really enjoyed her company."

"You don't say," Admiral Ra'aiah groaned. "I can't really attest to all of that."

"I can tell. What happened?"

"After we successfully defended against the last raid," she explained, "you arrived and helped us push them back. 43 suggested that we immedia-tely move out and chase after them. I refused and told her that we needed to hold our position so that we could regroup."

Admiral Ra'aiah leaned back in her seat and sighed again.

"She got mad."

"In front of your bridge crew?"

"No," Admiral Ra'aiah clarified. "I could tell she was angry, so I asked her to wait for me in my ready room. After you transmitted the data package, I listened to it and tried to clarify things. It didn't help at all."

"I think it's because you did things your way and not hers," Chastain suggested.

"The chain of command starts with me at the top!" Admiral Ra'aiah shot him a heated look, her eyes wide in irritation. "I couldn't jeopardize the lives of my crew and Earth if I abandoned my position and went hunting the Tandeeri. Even with you backing me up, if we chase them, their fleet can divide its forces and then circle around and set foot on the planet!"

"You being in charge was not in dispute," Captain Chastain said reassuringly.

I heard that David 117 also had some leadership issues prior to our arrival, she thought. *We're probably not all that different from each other.*

"She's lost everything," he continued as Admiral Ra'aiah refocused her attention to their conversation. "You need to try and see this from her perspective."

"I try to see from as many perspectives as I am able to!"

Captain Chastain stopped and looked at her blankly.

"What?!" she replied. "Why are you...?"

He continued to gaze at her sternly. Without a single word, Admiral Ra'aiah let out another big sigh and nodded.

"Fine," she threw her hands up. "What is her perspective?"

"If you got an opportunity to learn more about her," Chastain resumed his explanation calmly, "you would have learned that she's in a lot of pain."

"I know that," Admiral Ra'aiah said. "I read her entire file."

"The file only shows you part of her life," Chastain shook his head impatiently. "Did you know that she refuses to wear perfume?"

"What does that have to do with...?"

"Because she's afraid that the smell will give away her position," he interrupted in order to keep the conversation going. "Did you know that whenever she decides to sleep, she needs to use heavy tranquilizers, and she can only do it if someone she trusts stands guard outside her room? How about this one? You know why her neon stripes are crimson red? Blood red?"

Admiral Ra'aiah gave her godfather her undivided attention.

"Because she feels that she failed everyone she cared about," Chastain said softly. "Red stripes on one of Dr. Kendrick's amborgs are apparently a mark of shame. After she got the news that the love of her life was killed in action, she switched to red stripes and told me it was because she made a vow to never stop fighting this war."

She hadn't heard Chastain talk like this in a while. His attitude was usually so carefree most of the time that it was different not hearing his humorous inflection in everything he said. He must have had one interesting conversation with 43 before she transported herself to the Epsilon universe.

"She's gone to every colony that the Tandeeri have destroyed," he said sadly. "She's been searching, hunting, and using every ounce of her strength to find the Tandeeri and to make them pay for destroying her loved ones. When the chance to see them again came up, she was the first person to volunteer. She doesn't want to see them killed again. So, she's willing to do whatever it takes... and you dismissed her without even bothering to learn how much this means to her. She's not mad at you for being in charge. She's mad at you for not willing to take the risk."

"And if I lose more people under my command? If I were to lose you?"

"I'm not saying that your decision was wrong either. But we are fighting a war," Chastain spoke gently. "We've already lost enough people. This mission could be won and done! You're in command of one of the most advanced ships in our fleet! And you hesitated. 43 volunteered for this because she has something worth fighting for! Why are you here? What are you fighting for? A promotion? Or are you just going to play it safe and just sit there comfortably in your chair?"

"When we fight," Admiral Ra'aiah fidgeted in her seat uncomfortably. His words were definitely lingering in her mind. "Every person's job is important. From the custodian that cleans the halls to the officers that are department heads. I am in charge of thousands of people. You're telling me that as commander of my own ship, I was wrong?"

"No," Chastain replied. "I'm saying that you should set aside your rank and your ego for a moment... and just understand that you could be doing more. If you think that your actions are enough, chances are, 43 thinks you should be at her level of commitment."

"You got all of that from spending a few days with her?"

Captain Chastain shrugged and smiled sympathetically.

"She got a little drunk at a dinner banquet we held in her honor," he said. "That's why Riley and I listened to her ramble. When she got sober, we knew what was at stake if the mission failed."

Admiral Ra'aiah looked at the datapad with her orders. Then she looked at the viewscreen. After taking some time to ponder, she thought about her next move.

"Captain," she said.

"Yes Admiral?"

"Ready your fleet and have them take up defensive positions," she ordered in a soft tone. "While you defend the planet, I will prep my ship to get underway. I'm going to take the fight to them."

"Bold move," Chastain nodded with an admiring gleam in his eyes. "You want to try taking on the enemy fleet alone?"

"The Firestar is our best ship," Admiral Ra'aiah pondered. "If we engage the enemy, they could divide their forces to cut us off and attack your position. Hopefully, we'll keep as many of them occupied for as long as possible while you try to pick them off, one ship at a time."

"Sounds like a good plan," Chastain nodded. "Think it'll work?"

"I don't know," Admiral Ra'aiah said, "but I do agree with you. We can't just keep sitting here and waiting for something to happen. I'm going to deploy scouts to do some recon. I'll call you in 30. In the meantime, deploy your fleet."

"Sounds good. I'll get things underway immediately."

Chastain nodded to her and shot her a flashy smile before the view screen shut off, ending the call. As it lowered itself into her desk, Admiral Ra'aiah sighed, then activated her communicator.

"Commander Ulgo?" she said. "Can you come to my ready room please?"

A few moments passed, then the door opened with a soft hiss. Ulgo entered, hands clasped behind his back, and made his way to her desk. He halted a few feet away, standing at attention with his hands at his sides. He offered her a quick salute, which she returned, and he relaxed slightly.

"Aye sir?"

"Give me regular reports from the hangar bay," she said. "I want to know as much as we can about the fighter that broke through our lines. It's the closest we've ever gotten to getting one without it disintegrating in battle. Perhaps... 43 would be interested in examining it with our forensics team?"

Ulgo nodded courteously.

"Also," Admiral Ra'aiah added, "please inform our guests that we will be on the move soon. Could you ask Dr. Kendrick and his group to come in here, too?"

Ulgo nodded. He left the room and she waited patiently. Within minutes, he returned with everyone she had requested to see. Dr. Kendrick entered with Serina perched on his shoulder, trailed closely by 280 and 113. Commander Ulgo brought up the rear as the door slid shut, and they all assembled within the space.

"Perfect!" she said, nodding to all of them.

"How can we help?" Dr. Kendrick asked.

"I'm drafting a battle plan with the rest of our fleet," she answered amiably. "I'll be scheduling a meeting in half an hour, but I wanted to brainstorm with all of you and keep you in the loop."

"Is 43 ok?" Serina asked.

Everyone looked at Dr. Kendrick's shoulder, where Serina was waving her hand.

"There was a slight disagreement earlier," Admiral Ra'aiah admitted. She smiled softly to convey empathy. "But, I had her go down to the hangar to investigate the crashed fighter."

"She was happy to accept that assignment," Ulgo reported. "She moved fast."

"Thank you Ulgo," she dipped her head to him. Then she looked at Dr. Kendrick. "What I have planned might work, but I wanted to tell you now instead of later when we moved out."

Everyone paid close attention as she brought up her ideas and began to share them.

"I was thinking about using my ship as bait and try to attack the Tandeeri fleet," she said. "Now I know that sounds risky but I've thought about it and I want to hit them first before they attack us again."

"A very bold idea. You said you wanted to become bait for them. Are you trying to see what they're going after first?" Dr. Kendrick asked.

"So far, we've managed to keep them away from Earth," Admiral Ra'aiah nodded. "But there are a lot of different outcomes that we should consider before the next battle."

She rose from her chair and showed a holographic display of the planet. Her fleet was highlighted in a position near the Apogee Station.

"If I concentrate my forces to defend the planet, we could wait it out until more reinforcements arrive," she explained. "The Tandeeri could send their entire fleet and we could fight them back. But if we lose that engagement, then we all die and they land on the planet. We would lose the last line of defense."

Without the S.C.E. fleet, the Earth would face an invasion.

"So I think a preemptive strike will force the Tandeeri to change their approach," Admiral Ra'aiah pointed at the display and highlighted the red markers. "Obviously, if all of our ships leave this position, the enemy could split up their forces and the Earth would be vulnerable. The mission would fail and we would die. So, our best option is to take charge while Captain Chastain holds the line here."

"Isn't that risky?" Serina asked. "My calculations say that either option might be catastrophic."

"I know that taking my ship out there to attack is quite dangerous, but it could possibly buy us time," Admiral Ra'aiah answered confidently. "If the Firestar attacks the Tandeeri fleet, we can see what they'll do next. They might split their forces and send some of their ships past us and at that point, Chastain will engage them. Or if they manage to avoid us, they'll go for Earth directly and we'll quickly return. How long would a trip back take?"

"Four minutes," Ulgo replied. "At maximum speed."

"If I may?"

Everyone turned to look at 113, who had raised her hand.

"There is another problem," she said. "What happens if you attack and the Tandeeri fleet decides to surround us and destroy us? We would be outnumbered and annihilated quickly. After we're dead, they'll just go and begin the invasion of Earth, and you will have sacrificed this vessel and everyone onboard for nothing."

"A very excellent point," Admiral Ra'aiah nodded. "Which is why I want to engage the Tandeeri in as many hit-and-run attacks as possible and try to take them out one ship at a time."

That got their attention. The amborgs and Serina appeared genuinely intrigued by this plan. A smile crept onto Dr. Kendrick's face, but it quickly faded when he glanced at Commander Ulgo, who appeared quite sullen about the idea.

"Uh, I don't think you agree," Dr. Kendrick mumbled respectfully.

"Correct," Ulgo nodded. He looked at Admiral Ra'aiah in concern. "Ma'am, this ship isn't exactly built for speed. We do have the proper weapons and defenses but... hit-and-run tactics would be very difficult to pull off, considering that the Tandeeri ships are faster and more agile than us."

"This is the only move I can think of in order to draw them in. They've had a lot of time to regroup, and I'm wondering why we've been waiting here for so long. Chastain will hold one final defense and block any attempt for them to land on the planet. If they choose us, however, then we will keep the fighting away from Earth. I'm sorry to say that now it's a matter of seeing what move they make next. If our fleet had more ships, I'd already be after them."

"I don't mean to sound rude," Dr. Kendrick raised his hand. He cleared his throat and shifted uncomfortably. "Especially since I'm just a guest aboard your ship."

"Not at all," Admiral Ra'aiah said. "I welcome your criticism."

Dr. Kendrick looked at the display and focused on the little flashing markers that indicated their position.

"Do you think it's wise to chase them?" he asked.

"No," Admiral Ra'aiah shook her head. "If I'm being honest, it's probably what my dad would do, and he's smarter and more ruthless than I am. My mom would probably wait it out until we received more help."

"Well, if I may speak bluntly again..."

Admiral Ra'aiah took a deep breath. With a slightly strained smile, she looked at Dr. Kendrick politely and braced herself again for more criticism.

"Yes doctor?" she asked, trying to hide how nervous she was feeling.

"I'm not asking what your parents would do. What would you do?"

The entire group fixated on Admiral Ra'aiah. She could almost feel their eyes piercing into her chest. If their stares had been lasers, she would have been incinerated. Instead of freezing up, she decided to say something—anything to get out of this tense brainstorming session.

"Hence why the Firestar will be committing a string of hit-and-run attacks," Admiral Ra'aiah said as confidently as she could. "We'll begin assaulting the enemy fleet. I leave Earth under the protection of Captain Chastain."

"Is he reliable?" Dr. Kendrick asked. "Who is he?"

"Oh right," Admiral Ra'aiah remembered that everyone from Epsilon didn't know her colleagues. "Captain Chastain is the commanding officer of the Alexandria."

Commander Ulgo cleared his throat. Everyone turned and looked at him. He leaned in slightly, casting a meaningful look at the Admiral. Her eyes widened in response, and she shook her head. As Dr. Kendrick and Serina turned their gaze back at her, she froze, forcing an awkward smile, but they had already noticed her reaction.

"What's that all about?" Serina asked kindly. Her tone slowly turned into one of caution. "Something wrong?"

"Captain Chastain... is my godfather."

"Oh," Dr. Kendrick took a second to process this information and nodded. "So he's like family. That doesn't sound so bad."

"Well, I have faith in his abilities," Admiral Ra'aiah stated.

"Ahem," Commander Ulgo coughed.

"But he has a tendency to be... unpredictable," she said under her breath.

"I'm checking the records," Serina said. "I knew his name was familiar. Isn't he the one who oversaw the battle that got Serina 43 to cross to our universe?"

"Yes," Admiral Ra'aiah nodded.

"That sounds good enough to me," Serina gave them all a thumbs-up. "I think he sounds great."

Admiral Ra'aiah glanced at Serina, her gaze lingering on her for a moment.

"Maybe it's because we're in a less crowded environment," she said, pointing at Serina. "But have we met? Because I feel like I know you."

"You might have seen me around," Serina smiled cheekily.

"Ahem!"

Admiral Ra'aiah tilted her head up towards the ceiling and rolled her eyes. If she had to hear Commander Ulgo one more time, she would snap.

"Yes," she turned to look at her first officer. "Ulgo. Is there something else I'm not telling our guests?"

"Permission to speak freely?" he asked.

"Do I have a choice?" she mumbled as she waved her hand invitingly. "Yes, go ahead."

"I didn't tell you to inform our guests that Captain Chastain was your god-father," he explained.

"Yes you did!" Admiral Ra'aiah said incredulously. "You gave me a look!"

"I did ma'am," he admitted bluntly. "But it was not that kind of look."

"Then what kind of look was it??"

Commander Ulgo looked at Dr. Kendrick and cleared his throat again.

"Stop clearing your throat and get to the point, please?"

"Well," Ulgo motioned to Dr. Kendrick again. "Is it alright for me to disclose S.C.E. protocol in front of our guests? The guests who happen to be... civilians?"

"Oh," Admiral Ra'aiah held her mouth shut when she realized what he meant. "Um. Yes. Go ahead."

"Admiral... I gave you a look because it wasn't about your godfather," he stated. "But you do need to relinquish your command of the fleet."

"Great," Admiral Ra'aiah brought her hand up to her face.

"What are we missing?" Serina looked at Commander Ulgo and Admiral Ra'aiah with an eager expression. "This sounds like the start of a great punchline."

Dr. Kendrick shushed Serina, and she snickered.

"If Admiral Ra'aiah wishes to separate the flagship from the fleet in order to begin an attack against the Tandeeri fleet," Ulgo explained, "she must transfer her command to the next ship in line."

"Which means the Alexandria would be in command," Admiral Ra'aiah groaned.

"Chastain?" Dr. Kendrick asked.

Admiral Ra'aiah nodded and Commander Ulgo subtly smirked from the side.

"And I just assumed command a few minutes ago," she mumbled. "I have to go through that entire process again. And we're not scheduled to call each other for another 27 minutes."

"Ah," Dr. Kendrick nodded. "So, we should just wait?"

"Oh, no!" Admiral Ra'aiah activated her viewscreen. "I'll just try and get him on the line right now."

They watched as she activated her transmitter and started a phone call. There was a chime, indicating the call had gone through.

"Admiral Ra'aiah?"

It was a woman's voice this time, and Riley's face appeared on the screen.

"Riley," Admiral Ra'aiah smiled. "Where's Captain Chastain?"

"He's not on the bridge," Riley answered. "He said he wasn't expecting you for another half hour so he went to grab a bite to eat. Is it an emergency?"

"Not exactly," Admiral Ra'aiah replied. "But please have him call me as soon as possible."

"Yes ma'am."

She ended the call and let out another sigh. Dr. Kendrick and Serina exchanged amused glances.

"Should we come back later?" he asked.

"Yeah, go ahead," Admiral Ra'aiah nodded stiffly.

"Dr. Kendrick," Commander Ulgo said politely. "Are all of your amborgs properly equipped?"

"As much as they can be," Dr. Kendrick nodded, then realized that Ulgo was looking at 280 and 113. "Oh. Uh... Alex, Ally, perhaps you two should acquire some weapons from the armory? We are about to go into battle soon."

280 and 113 acknowledged him silently. Ulgo smiled and thanked Dr. Kendrick for picking up on his subtle indicators. He led 280 and 113 towards the doors and showed them out.

"Serina," Dr. Kendrick said cautiously as they decided to wait with Admiral Ra'aiah. "Let's keep tabs on all the amborgs aboard. I think that if we're split up all over the ship, we should maintain contact with each other. I don't want to lose anyone. Where's 117?"

"Down at the medical bay with 5 and 6," Serina replied, checking their beacons.

"I think we should initiate the buddy system," Dr. Kendrick replied. There were a lot of bad experiences from the past that fueled his next decision. "It feels rather unnerving for some reason, but I'm starting to think it's better if we didn't wander off alone."

"Right," Serina gave a brief salute. "Checking their positions."

She turned and stared at the wall. At first glance, it looked as though she was zoning out. Then, she began to report her findings to Dr. Kendrick while looking like a zombie.

"Oh interesting," she murmured, tilting her head. "917 is alone, and going up. His beacon is on the same deck as 3 and 501. I'll have him get those two. 297 and 777 are together, which means they can cover each other. 466 is in one of the ship's... nurseries? That's not good. I'm going to signal 117 and have him go find her."

"Where are the Third Group amborgs and the rest of the Fourth group?"

"249, 593, and 49 are exploring the residential areas where the crew's families live," Serina answered. "365, 100 and 378 are heading towards engineering to meet with 1 and 2."

"Is Angel still by herself?"

"In the archives, yes," Serina nodded.

"Let's have someone go and stay at her side," Dr. Kendrick said. "Wait a moment. Where was 501? His emergency beacon is on. I thought you said he was with 3 and 917."

"No, I said he was close to 3 and 917's current position. His beacon puts him in a supply closet," Serina answered with a sudden confused look. "It came online... a few minutes ago."

Dr. Kendrick lowered his voice as Admiral Ra'aiah glanced their way. The last thing they needed was 501 accidentally creating conflict aboard this ship. They were guests, but it would be really bad if they caused trouble for the people of the Alpha universe. He didn't want anyone to think of the Epsilon universe negatively.

"Oh wait," Serina said, baffled after a second. "He just switched it off."

"Serina," Dr. Kendrick muttered. "Why is 501 separated from 466?"

"I don't know."

"Then let's find out and reestablish contact with him before he gets in trouble with our new friends aboard this ship."

"On it," Serina replied.

Chapter 20: Oreo

S.C.E. Firestar
Medical Bay

"Find 501? Or 999?"

117 stood in a corner of the bay talking to Serina. She had called to tell him that Dr. Kendrick wanted every amborg to initiate the buddy system protocol. Aboard this massive city-sized ship, it was decided that they shouldn't be on their own. 117 thought it was a solid plan.

"Honestly?" Serina replied. "999 can take care of herself. 501's emergency beacon was active for a short time and then he shut it off."

"Yeah, I saw that. I'll be sure to look for him," 117 said.

The amborg emergency beacon was designed to alert any amborg nearby to respond. However, 501 had willingly shut his off on his own accord. It was either an accident or a way to communicate something important to just the amborgs. Whatever it was, 117 agreed with Serina that finding him was a priority.

First, he needed to have some company. 117 walked over to where 5 and 6 were relaxing.

"Hey," 5 smiled. "Who was that?"

"Serina," 117 replied. "She just told me that Dr. Kendrick initiated the…"

"Buddy system," 6 interrupted. "Yup, I got the notification."

"Is it really necessary?" 5 asked. "Not that I'm complaining or anything but this ship seems to be pretty safe."

"Well, that's why I felt you should have these."

117 pulled a pair of guns out of a small travel case he had borrowed from the armory. He set it on the table and opened it.

"Some weapons to give you an edge."

5 and 6 pulled the side-arms out of the case and examined them. 5 eagerly grabbed one of the gun holsters and slipped it around his shoulders, but 6 held the futuristic weapon in her hands, seeming hesitant.

"You ok?" 117 asked gently. "I do have a short tutorial video on how it works."

"No, I was just thinking about Jacob."

5 and 117 paused to look at her sympathetically.

"6, I know this is rough for you to hear but you have to let him go," 5 looked down as he tried to console her. "It wasn't your fault."

"I know," 6 shook her head. "I just keep hearing his last words in my head. He was so excited for this mission, even though he was clearly terrified. He said 'thank you' to me... right as he died."

"Even till the end," 5 shrugged, "he died happy."

"I should have helped you guys escort him on the honor walk," 6 said.

"No, it's ok."

When Jacob had passed on, the doctors and the medics helped make the final preparations to transport his body and the other Apogee Station casualties down to Earth. Instead, 6 put in the request to have their bodies taken over to the station first so that Jacob's friends, the coworkers that survived, could gather his personal belongings. Then, Captain Hicks volunteered to transport him back home to A.I. Industries so that his next of kin could take possession of his body. It would be his final trip home.

"I still have to call his mom," 6 muttered.

"I think she'd like to hear from you," 5 smiled encouragingly. "She'll want to hear about how Jacob was doing."

"You know what's really crazy?" 6 sighed, continuing to hold the gun steady in her hands. "There were a lot of people that we couldn't save in the past. The Dominoe Incident and every Emergency Recall since? I don't have a clue why Jacob's death and the other casualties are affecting me this much."

"I think it's because they were our friends," 5 replied. "You know? Most of the people that we couldn't save before were people we didn't know."

He had a point. Most of the people the amborgs interacted with in the past were easy to move on from. Yet, some of them had the power to leave a lasting impact, evoking emotional responses and memories that could bring about feelings of nostalgia or profound sorrow. The closer they were, the harder the loss when they were gone.

Before they could continue their discussion, 117 received an incoming phone call. He checked the caller ID and saw that it was 917.

"Hello?" he said.

"Hey 117?" 917 spoke softly. "What are you up to right now?"

"I'm in the medical bay with 5 and 6," 117 answered.

"Great!" 917 replied. "Could you loop them in on this call?"

117 glanced over at 5 and 6 and invited them into the call. They both immediately accepted, except 6 was still slightly distracted. She had set the gun down and picked up a datapad.

"They're looped in," 117 said.

"Do you happen to know where 501 and 466 are?"

"No," 117 stated. "I was on my way to check on them after meeting with 5 and 6. Why do you ask?"

"Can you come to where I'm at? Please? Follow my tracking beacon," 917 instructed. "3 asked me to go look for 501 and I found him. Now... um... Well... I'm not sure how to explain it."

117 was already feeling uneasy about this. 5 listened quietly, a concerned look crossing his face at 917 spoke. 117 felt a headache coming on as dread began creeping in. 6 continued to work, seemingly oblivious to the conversation.

"What has he done now?" 117 groaned.

He crossed his fingers and hoped that no one had forced him out the airlock. The last thing they needed was to mess something up for the crew of the Firestar. 5 tensed up, making 6 look up from her datapad and sneak a glance at 117. The three of them were immediately on high alert, anticipating the first signs of trouble.

"Well, 3 told me that he was wandering around," 917 sighed. "He apparently went to see Angel, but she told him to leave, politely. Then he was supposed to meet up with her at the mess hall but never showed. So she got worried and called me to ask me to go look for him. And after that, Serina advised us to stick together. Dr. Kendrick's orders."

"That's when you found him?" 117 said.

"Yup," 917 replied firmly. "He would have called you himself but... uhh... he's a little occupied at the moment."

"With what?" 117 asked nervously. "Can't you just tell us over the channel?"

"I could," 917 said annoyingly. "But, I think this should be kept off the air. Because A, there are no words I can use to describe this particular... thing and B, I really don't want to say this over the channel even though we have secured communications. You're going to have to come and see for yourselves because that's how important this is."

"That's ridiculous," 117 stated. "You can just tell us."

"No, I think showing you is way better," 917 replied. "Please bring 5 and 6 with you. 6, if you can hear me, 501 needs medical attention. That ought to get things rolling for you."

"What's the damage, 917?" 6 asked gently.

As soon as there was a call for medical assistance, 6 was back in on the action.

"We're talking about 501 here 6," 917 answered. "He's always getting in trouble. Just please come over... Come on! No questions! I'm hanging up."

"Alright alright," 5 shrugged to 117. "We're on our way man. Sit tight."

"Hurry."

The channel closed as 917 hung up. 117 looked at the other two amborgs.

"I wonder what he needs with me," 6 said curiously as she grabbed her bag of medical supplies. "Hmm. I think I'll take this doohickey too. This looks fun to use."

"Uh," 5 glanced at the tool nervously. "Are you sure?"

"Yeah," 6 nodded eagerly.

"Ok then," 5 forced a laugh. "Then I would like to point out one odd detail about that phone call."

"What's up?" 117 asked as 6 loaded more stuff into her medical bag.

"You know how most of the time when 501 gets involved in something?" 5 asked. "There's usually alarms and stuff that are going off in the background? Well, I didn't hear anything that time. No sounds."

Right," 117 responded. Then, all three of them nodded.

"Trouble," they said simultaneously, and hurried towards the door.

They covered the distance to 501 in no time at all. It must have seemed strange to the crew how fast they were moving, but they really didn't want to put this off any longer than necessary. Considering that these people had never witnessed any of 501's antics before, they had to take action now before things spiraled out of control. Letting 501 go unchecked was a recipe for disaster.

After they found the nearest elevator, they quickly made their way to the deck where 501, 3 and 917 were located. As they followed the trail, they soon found the storage room. Outside, they heard 501 speaking oddly, which made them stop dead in their tracks.

"Aww," they heard him babble. "3 will be here very soon and we'll see what you like ok? Who's a good boy? Who's a good boy?"

After confirming that 917 and 501's beacons were inside, they noticed that 3 wasn't with them, according to what they just heard. The three of them were still trying to wrap their heads around whether they'd actually heard all that correctly. What the hell happened in there?

"501," 917's voice spoke up. His tone sounded pained. "Just stop. This is already creepy enough. Oh, they're here."

They heard footsteps approaching, followed by a faint tapping on the other side of the door. 117, 5, and 6 glanced at each other as 917 addressed them.

"I saw your beacons," he said on the other side. "Are you guys absolutely positive you're alone and there isn't anyone that is not an amborg accompanying you?"

"Yes?" 117 replied as 5 and 6 checked the hallways for any sign of activity. "But if we're interrupting something personal..."

"Very funny 117," 917 said with a frustrated sigh. "Answer these questions I have for each of you."

They each received an incoming text message alert requesting a security check to confirm their identities. It seemed a little excessive, but they had no choice but to go along with it.

"Is this verification process really necessary?" 6 asked.

"For your sake," 917 said angrily, "this is where a lot of personal information comes in handy. 117, what did I once decide to make for 999 during the Dominoe Incident? What was the ID number on my prisoner uniform at Fulton Federal Penitentiary? And what did I do at the bank before we went back to A.I. Industries?"

117 realized that 917 was asking them things only they knew. If the correct answer to the question was provided, it was proof. Whatever was behind the door, he and 501 were trying to keep it well under wraps.

"It was a scarf," 117 answered as he recalled the failed idea. The answer to the next questions came easily. "The number on your prison ID was 387796. You detached your right hand at the bank."

"I'm sorry," 6 spluttered out a laugh. "He did what? Why wasn't that in the report?"

"Why do you think?" 5 snickered. "Dr. Kendrick was definitely not putting that on paper officially. He has to send those to the President whenever the White House audits us."

"Guys," 117 mumbled.

The three of them shut up when 117 got another text message alert in his HUD. It changed from red to green, indicating he had passed the test.

"Correct," 917 said from inside. "Now for the other two."

117 waited patiently, watching 5 and 6 prepare for their questions. 6 was the next one to receive hers because her expression shifted from confusion to sorrow in a matter of seconds. 917 read the questions he had come up for her.

"6," he stated. "Although it was Dr. Wilder who appointed you as a doctor's assistant during Christmas that one year, you once told me you wanted to do something else for a living if the medical field didn't work out. What was that job? I would also like to have you think about our second Emergency Recall. What were the exact words you told me when I woke up in the hospital at A.I. Industries? 345 was also there at my side during my recovery, but another mission had her steal something from a crime family with sensitive information. What did she steal?"

"Honestly," 6 sighed. "My backup job was to be an ecological conservationist. During the second Emergency Recall in the history of A.I. Industries, the amborgs deployed to resolve a terrible conflict in Europe. The unit you were attached to was massacred and you came home with severe injuries. When you woke up, I said that the war was over and you had succeeded. You told Dr. Kendrick that you wanted to go back as soon as you were able but instead, I argued against that. Finally, for the last question, 345 had to steal a vase. It was a 20th century hand-molded vase that had an international banking account number etched onto it. Once we had access to that account, the authorities were able to seize that gang's assets."

"Very good," 917 said approvingly.

"Those sounded difficult," 5 mumbled.

"Good. Now 5, it's your turn," 917 said. "Which character do you and I relate to the most? Your second question is also meant to tug at your heartstrings. What did you say to me at 345's funeral?"

There was a brief pause. 117 and 6 turned to 5, who wasn't smiling anymore. Before he could answer, 917 spoke up again.

"There was a woman that you and I were once assigned to," he said. "She was in the country living in asylum under protection by the feds. She asked the amborgs for help. Remember? What was the name of her son?"

"Actually," 5 nodded. "Not too difficult at all. The first question is actually a trick question. It isn't one singular character, but two. The characters we relate to the most are the Elric brothers from FullMetal Alchemist."

He placed his hand on his prosthetic leg when he shared his answer.

"When I went to 345's funeral," he sighed, "I knew how upset you were and I also knew then that nothing I said could help extinguish the pain of what you were going through. That was one of the only times where instead of saying anything, I gave you a hug."

117 remembered that. At the funeral, he had been seated while everyone walked up to pay their respects. 5 had asked 917 to stand and the two of them shared a compassionate embrace.

"Trick question?" he asked 5.

"Kinda," he answered. "When I hugged you, 917, I told you that even though she was gone, you still had us and that we would cry with you, laugh with you, and share the pain together so you wouldn't feel alone."

"Answer the third question."

"Well, come on," 5 looked at 6 and 117. "Did those words ever make you feel better?"

"Please answer the last question."

5 sighed and gave his answer.

"Franklin," he said. "The name of the woman's son that we went searching for was Franklin."

"Nice," 917 replied. "The instant I open the door, you get in here as fast as you can and then I'm going to lock it."

The door hissed open before the three of them even had time to acknowledge his instructions. They saw 917 standing inside the door motioning for them to hurry on in. The three of them tried to squeeze in at the same time and they all painfully tumbled in. 6 squealed as 117 and 5 crashed on top of her, causing them to toppled onto 917 in a chaotic heap.

"That was well done," 917 snapped, quickly worming his way out of the dog pile and hitting the door controls.

"Ow," 6 muttered as the door hissed shut. "5, I have a question now... Who are the Elric brothers?"

"I told you to come watch it with us that one night we binged," 5 grumbled. "You need more anime in your life, sweetheart."

"I'll just look them up online later," she muttered.

"Alright," 117 said, feeling a pain in his stomach where 6's bag had hit. "917, enough with the elaborate security measures. What on earth is going on?"

"501? You have the floor."

The three of them looked at 501, who was staring back at them in surprise. All of them froze when they saw what was in his hands.

"Yeah," 917 said as the three of them remained frozen on the spot. "I had the exact same reaction too."

There was an alien creature in 501's hands. It didn't look like a dog or a cat. In fact, it didn't even look like it was supposed to be a pet of any sort. 501 had an actual alien child in his arms that he was happily caring for. They were left speechless, having never encountered a species like this the entire time they were aboard the Firestar.

501 held up the little bundle in his hands for them to see. It squealed happily, causing the three of them to jump back. 501 smiled nervously.

"Say hi to Oreo," he said, shrugging slightly.

The creature looked like a shiny bipedal toddler in some sort of cybernetic suit that fit its form quite nicely. The outer layer looked smooth and organic, like it was part of its body, and it seemed to possess an opalescent sheen. It had small glittering eyes that sparkled as it opened its tiny mouth and cooed at them.

"Uh," 117 stammered. "It looks like..."

"Yeah," 917 said. "It looks like Grogu stole Optimus Prime's armor."

The alien looked about two and a half feet tall. It was hard to properly examine it since 501 was holding it so enthusiastically. Despite 917's comment, they didn't see any pointy ears or green skin. The creature's skin was dark grey but combined with whatever its outfit was made of, it looked shiny in a relaxing and soothing way.

"Tetradactyl." 6 observed with a fascinated look in her eyes. "Its hands... are almost as big as mine! And it's so small!"

Everyone looked at the creature's hands and saw that she was right. Humans had five fingers, whereas this little creature had four digits in total. It had three middle fingers with one opposable thumb. It was also opening and closing its right hand at them like it was waving.

"Ok," 5 managed to say after catching his breath. "What did you do, 501?"

"I didn't do anything," 501 protested. "Honest!"

"That's a bunch of bull," 5 snapped. "It's uh... It's uh... What is it?"

"Its name is Oreo," 501 replied casually.

"May I... take a look?" 6 asked, gulping.

501 held it up for her and 6 crouched close to it. She took out her scanner and began to scan it with trembling hands.

"117?" 501 said. "Please say something. I can't tell if you're about to faint or kill me."

"I-I don't have anything to say..." 117 stammered, merely shaking his head. "It's uh... I... Where did you find it?"

"In here," 501 answered, glancing around the room.

"Ok... Then... Where did it come from?"

He realized he'd asked a question that 501 was able to answer literally. 117 quickly corrected his mistake and waited. There were still tons of questions flooding his head, along with doubt, anxiety, and his continuing need to wake up from whatever this was.

"We don't know," 501 replied as he glanced at 917.

Both of them shook their heads. This answer didn't help at all.

"What do you mean, 501?" 117 asked.

"Well," 501 said. "I don't really know. That's what I mean. I thought about telling someone their kid was stuck in here but then I realized that... well I hadn't seen any of this kind of alien before. So... I looked after it."

"And then 3 sent me to find him when he disappeared for a bit," 917 explained.

"Yeah," 501 chuckled. "I got so wrapped up looking after this little guy that I forgot."

"Are we sure that this is definitely..." 5 said, with a hand on his head. "I mean, we're sure that this doesn't belong to any of the species aboard this ship?"

5 was doing exactly what 117 and 6 were thinking. They were checking their visual memory databases for any traces of any alien species with similar or identical features as the one that 501 was holding. But the more that they checked, the more 501's story seemed to be accurate.

"Ok," 5 said, biting his lip. "I retract my question."

"I can confirm, too," 6 replied. "Out of the seventy-eight races that have sworn allegiance to the S.C.E., there is no alien that looks like this one. And that's just fresh off of my briefly rushed overview of the different species across the Alpha universe."

"Alright," 117 said, waving his hands to get all of their attention. "Now the big unanswered question I still have is, where did it come from?"

"We don't know!" 917 and 501 repeated.

"Ok!" 117 sighed as he wiped the sweat off his head. "How did it...?"

"Oreo!"

"What?"

117 gazed at 501.

"Oreo," 501 repeated with a firm and encouraging nod.

"Fine, Oreo..." 117 sighed. "How did Oreo get here??"

"We're really calling it that??" 5 asked, shaking his head in disbelief.

Everyone ignored 5 as 917 tried to answer the question.

"This seems like a long shot," 917 interrupted, stepping forward. "But this is the theory that we came up with. We think Oreo was on the ship that crashed into the hangar bay. The one that 297, 777 and I saw."

"But didn't that ship explode?" 5 raised an eyebrow. "According to what you reported?"

"Yeee-ah," 917 muttered slowly.

"But if Oreo was fast enough," 501 chimed in, "he could have snuck away!"

"Now you know why it's an educated guess," 917 shrugged. "We would have seen this little creature escaping from a burning ship, but we didn't. We reviewed the footage and saw nothing."

"Ok, so it teleported?" 117 asked.

"That ship crashing into the hangar is the only recent point of entry," 917 replied. "Unless you're going to tell me with a straight face that Oreo's been hiding and living aboard this ship for months, then a little stowaway crash landing here is where I'm betting my money. It's only a theory."

Suddenly, a knock sounded at the door. All of them perked up and scanned the outside for another amborg's beacon. They relaxed when they recognized it as a friendly one.

"It's 3," 501 said cheerfully.

"Wait," 917 said cautiously. He walked up to the door. "3? Answer the following questions please?"

"I brought food," 3's annoyed voice answered.

917 looked at the rest of them before hitting the lock on the door. That was pretty conclusive.

"Ok," he said as the door immediately opened.

"How come she doesn't get three security questions?" 6 asked with an outraged look.

3 stepped inside as 917 shut the door. When it closed, the two of them turned to each other.

"You brought food?" 917 asked.

"I brought food," 3 replied boorishly.

917 quickly tossed out a couple of questions.

"Ok... how about these ones? 3, what did 57 do after we got to your apartment in New York? And... What happened when I made you a chocolate lava cake?"

"57 kicked out a creep that made my neighbor uncomfortable," 3 replied immediately. "And eight years ago, you tried to make a chocolate souffle. You called it a lava cake after you panicked when you saw it fall. I laughed when I saw it because a total collapse meant something went wrong."

"Correct," 917 turned to look at 6. "Satisfied?"

"Yes," she replied.

"Anyway, I brought food so that we could all take a break," 3 said sternly. "Food is important."

She held up a tray that consisted of the strangest looking snacks they'd ever seen. 3 set it on the floor. 501 examined it while Oreo stared at it curiously. 3 selected a snack and held it up close.

"Try some Algora strawberries," she said in a gentle sing-song voice. "You're so cute. Aren't you the sweetest?"

What caught their eye was how these strawberries were totally different from the ones they knew. Instead of the usual round shape with seeds, these berries were long and thin, kind of like straws. Actual straw berries. It almost looked like 3 was holding a piece of red vine candy. Oreo quickly grabbed the red snack, opened wide, and chomped down on it.

"You like those?" 3 looked surprised. "I can't taste any flavor from them. By the way, is it official that we're calling the little guy Oreo?"

"I think so," 501 replied. "Oreo could be a girl too. Just saying."

"Regardless of gender," 6 interrupted. She examined Oreo and shared her observations. "It displays a lot of child-like behavioral traits. Pretty common to adolescence. I'd say this little Tandeeri is about a year old? Maybe two human years old? Definitely an infant. It has responded to verbal and visual cues but doesn't seem able to reply to our conversation. But, there's a lot that we still don't know that could surprise us."

"Anything else you can figure out?" 5 asked.

"I just did my first alien health examination," 6's breath trembled as she smiled with excitement. She looked at Oreo and nodded in fascination. "I'll have to continue observing and write everything down."

"Are you guys mad?" 501 asked nervously.

They watched as Oreo snuggled up in 501's arms. It squeaked and whined gleefully as it grabbed two more of the strawberries and slowly chewed on them. 501 looked like a breastfeeding mother.

"Well I'm not mad," 117 sighed. "I'm just concerned about the crap we're about to deal with. This is a Tandeeri which the S.C.E. is at war with. Now we have in our custody a baby, who's already been named, under our care where we could be discovered and be killed almost instantly."

"And if we don't suffer consequences for this," 5 pointed out, "then a lot of the crew may decide to take it out on Oreo. We may be at war, but it'll look bad for us when we just up and decide to defend it."

"I can see it now," 3 said as she took a bite out of a piece of cheese. "'Excuse me fellow shipmates, we hold in our hands a baby Tandeeri. We respectfully ask that you do not attack it because it is the cutest thing ever.'"

"Ok," 117 interrupted. "Attacking it and displaying it publicly was not what I had in mind. But the truth is, we're not qualified to deal with this."

"We never know unless we try," 501 argued. "It's true that none of us have degrees in interspecies diplomacy or running an alien nursery. But all I know is, we can't just leave Oreo alone and hope this all goes away. And I don't think it's a good idea for someone else to try and take over my job."

All of them silently pondered as Oreo looked around at them with bright, curious eyes. They didn't know for sure if Oreo was aware of how serious the problem really was. Hopefully, it stayed that way.

"Well what do we do?"

117 glanced at 5, but had no response to give him. He recapped the issue briefly in his mind. Somehow, in the midst of the war against the Tandeeri in the defense of Epsilon Earth, Oreo had managed to sneak in and run right into the amborgs. Now that they were involved this deeply, what were their best options? Tell someone trustworthy and hope nothing bad happened, or continue hiding this secret? The first people he thought of talking to were Mandy, his grandfather, Audrey, and Dr. Kendrick. Only one out of those four individuals were aboard the same ship they were on, and he was being closely watched by Admiral Ra'aiah.

"If we do decide to tell someone," 501 spoke slowly, snapping 117 out of his thoughts. "I think it should be the Admiral and Dr. Kendrick. She is the commander of a badass starship and the one in charge. She could be compassionate and nice enough to help us."

"I have to agree with that," 917 said. "If other people aboard this ship discover Oreo, then that will create problems. We have to bring this directly to the Admiral's attention."

"Does anyone know what kind of consequences we could be looking at?" 5 asked.

"I'm not too familiar with S.C.E. protocol," 6 replied. "But harboring an alien child that belongs to the species that the S.C.E. are at war with is probably a conspiracy charge. We've fed and taken care of Oreo and already formed an attachment to it. At least, 501 has. It's not going to end well if this goes public. Our chances for a good outcome are fading with every passing moment."

"People are going to think Oreo is dangerous," 5 said.

"Oreo isn't dangerous!" 501 protested. He cradled Oreo, who looked up and blinked a few times.

"I believe you 501," 5 held up his hands defensively. "But others won't. Not like we do. In war, people lose lives. In the aftermath, survivors want to blame it on the ones who carry the legacy of the war—winners and losers alike. People always want to blame something when they're scared and desperate. Oreo is not going to be treated well by the S.C.E. military if they come crawling around finding it for target practice."

There was one other detail that 117 didn't want to keep quiet about any longer.

"I am curious though," 117 said. "Why did you name it Oreo? Aside from having your own odd nickname, it seems so random."

"Easy," 501 shrugged. "I had a pack of oreos in my pocket when I found 'em. It's a suitable gender neutral name I just picked and stuck with. Oreo likes the name."

Oreo gave a little gleeful squeal, which made 501 grin and hug him tightly.

"Just remember," 6 said as she pulled out a small scanner and held it up to Oreo. "Once you name it, you start getting attached to it. Just be careful. Hey! Let go!"

Oreo had snatched 6's scanner, resulting in a bit of tug-of-war. It was interrupting the scanning process, which was beginning to frustrate 6. It looked as though she was engaged in a game with a pet that wouldn't let go of its favorite toy. Despite being so small, Oreo was stronger than they originally thought.

"Perhaps this is the chance for us to be diplomatic."

The room fell silent as everyone focused on 917, who kept his gaze fixed on the floor. He cleared his throat, trying to shake off the weight of their stares.

"Maybe it's like 501 said," 917 continued. "About the Admiral, I mean. Maybe there's a segment of people aboard the Firestar who believe in diplomacy as a possible end to the war. Maybe the Tandeeri aren't barbaric like we've been led to believe. We just need to find out what their white flag is and call a truce. It's not a popular opinion, but a surrender, or a ceasefire would definitely put a halt on the war and get everyone to stop and listen."

"Any sentient species is peaceful at some point," 3 said thoughtfully. "Even though we crave war, we do try to make the truth known so it clears up the misunderstandings. I still remember how much bad publicity we got after the Dominoe Incident."

"Yeah," 5 nodded solemnly. "Taking the assassin in was a good plan though. People knew who the real culprit was and didn't just blame us entirely. Maybe we can do something."

"Yeah! That's why I think we can do this," 501 said excitedly. "People hold us accountable for our actions all the time. It's because we can do what normal humans can't."

"If Oreo could speak," 117 said, "it might be less awkward. I mean, if it was a grown child, it could communicate to us and help us understand the Tandeeri. Imagine what his family is like."

"Right?" 501 sighed as Oreo gazed up at 117. "It'd be easier to explain all of this if Oreo was able to back us up."

"Was that why we were all included?" 6 asked while checking Oreo's vital signs. "You wanted all of us here to collaborate and figure out how to explain this if necessary?"

"To the right people, yes," 501 said. "I was afraid of what would happen if I was the only one who supported taking care of this little one. I know I mess up a lot. I don't talk well under pressure and people won't listen to me because I'm the 'donut.'"

Everyone glanced at 501, who appeared visibly anxious.

"I'm an idiot," he admitted. "I've made a lot of mistakes before. Earlier, I made 999 upset."

501 looked at 917 apologetically.

"But people look up to you guys," he said as his eyes swept the room. "They know you. They respect all of you. I figured that people will listen to you guys because they trust you more than me."

6 looked at 117 and gave him an encouraging smile while 501 continued to speak his mind.

"All I want to do is just get Oreo home," he stated. "He doesn't deserve to see all this fighting. I know it's the right thing to do. This is my mission. Or... a mission I want to take charge of, if that's ok."

"You know," 5 nudged 117 proudly. "That's a leader talking right there."

Hope began to rise in 117. Donut's little speech was definitely inspiring.

"He is the leader of the Third Group," 117 nodded.

Oreo squirmed out of 501's arms and ran over to 3. As 3 lifted Oreo into her lap, he cheerfully put his hands on her cheeks. She puffed them out, which elicited a strange trilling noise from it. Oreo was laughing in some unique way.

"Then we do just that," 3 said, continuing to puff out her cheeks for Oreo. "The Admiral will understand once we talk to her. And gradually, her influence will spread to her crew. We deal with it slowly and assume all the good and bad outcomes. No probabilities, percentages or calculating the odds. Just focus on protecting what's rightfully innocent from any harm."

"Well, from the sound of it," 6 grinned, "it looks like everyone in this room is slowly getting attached."

"Dr. Kendrick and the rest of the amborgs aboard have to know," 917 added. "We have to be discreet."

They collectively began to brainstorm. The tray of food that 3 had brought turned out to be a feast solely for Oreo. The amborgs left it untouched as they focused on their strategy, allowing the little one to happily indulge itself.

"Dr. Kendrick doesn't want any of us to wander alone," 117 said. "So 3 and 501, you stay here. Keep an eye on each other. 917, you go find 999. 5 and 6, you inform the amborgs who weren't here. I think I'll go speak to Dr. Kendrick and the Admiral."

"Sounds good," 917 nodded. "Simple for now."

"How exactly should we tell the others?" 5 asked gently.

"Do what 501 and 917 did," 117 replied. "Just give everyone else a call and have them come here."

"This will be one heck of a powerpoint," 5 chuckled. He turned and nodded to 501. "Hey buddy, I'll call 466 and have her come here. You need your partner to keep you company for something as important as this."

"Thanks 5."

917 cast a look at 117 as he walked with him to the door.

"Let's move out. I'll message 297 and 777 to look for 43. We should tell her about this."

They left the storage room discreetly as 5 and 6 began to make the appropriate calls to the other amborgs. 501 and 3 made sure that Oreo was hidden when the door was opened.

Once it shut, 117 looked at 917.

"You remember the deadlock duel, right?"

917 nodded.

"Yeah, but what does that have to do with this?" he asked.

"43 lost everything that she cared about to the Tandeeri," 117 suddenly had a terrifying thought. "If she encounters Oreo, what do you think she'll do?"

"I know she's been through a lot," 917 replied. "I highly doubt 43 would do something that extreme."

"Right," 117 forced a nod. 917 had brought up an excellent point. "Yeah. She wouldn't do anything risky like that."

Their smiles faded as they took a moment to think. 917 had meant what he said, but 43 was an Alpha universe amborg with a long history of warfare. They were uncertain about what she was truly capable of. Deciding how to approach her with the news would prove to be difficult.

Main Engineering

"How's it look in there?"

1 leaned forward and peeped inside the maintenance duct. It was definitely a lot cleaner than he originally expected. The service ducts back at home were very dusty and not a good place to crawl through. Then again, why would they be the ones crawling in them? The S.C.E. Firestar was absolutely tidier in comparison, which was definitely leaving a good impression for him and 2.

"Can you hear me?" he spoke into the shaft.

"Look 1," 2 called from inside the duct. "If you told me this morning that visiting the engine room was going to be enlightening, I would have been skeptical, but ecstatic. Now, I just hate you. I mean, really? How did I end up having to crawl inside this maintenance shaft to look for one broken component? A component I haven't seen before? While you get to chill with the sexy engineering chief?"

1 turned to the chief, who was laughing softly. She had twisted her ankle coming down the ladder and he was now wrapping it up.

"It is true," he said, winking at her. "You are sexy."

1 then looked into the duct again and yelled back.

"You're doing the engineers a favor, 2!" he called. "You go search for the component that's roughly the size of a kit-kat bar, replace it, and I get to look at the lovely Chief Hayes' sprained ankle."

"I really do appreciate the help," Chief Hayes nodded gratefully. "Also, if he likes, I have some single friends who'd be interested in meeting him. It's not everyday we get to meet an amborg."

"Ah, he's fine," 1 said cheerfully as he waved a hand casually. "He'll decide if he wants to take up that offer. For now though, we'd very much like to learn about how this ship runs. Perhaps you could teach us as we escort you to the medical bay?"

"Deal," Chief Hayes chuckled. "Only if you promise to help me get in touch with a few amborgs. I want to see if they act exactly like the ones I knew in Alpha."

"I'm guessing you were friends?" 1 asked, hearing the sound of 2 making his way back to them.

"You might say that," Hayes replied as 2's head poked out of the duct. "Some of them were my mentors at the academy."

"Imagine that," 1 said in amazement. "To think that we became instructors."

"Yeah, sounds terrific," 2 muttered, holding up a small component. "What do you know? It actually was the size of a kit-kat bar. It's all fixed in there."

"Thank you," Chief Hayes smiled.

"I was able to successfully replace the part," 2 reported with a huff. "Perhaps you should send someone to double check just in case I didn't do it right."

"Here give me the part," Hayes stuck her hand out. "I want to try and fix it."

"But it is blown out," 2 said. "There isn't any point in trying to do such a thing."

"Well I have to do something to occupy myself in the medical bay," Hayes replied, keeping her hand extended. "How do you know something is broken unless you try?"

Hayes looked over to where the rest of the engineering staff continued to monitor the equipment.

"I'm terrible with a weapon," she said, "but I can work with my hands when it comes to fixing or making things. It's what I do best because this part of the ship is important. It's my job to make sure that everything important keeps everyone alive. So before I recycle or throw away what I don't need, there's no harm in trying to see if I can put something small back together again to help the bigger things."

2 passed the small component and she turned it over a few times.

"We all fight a war together," she said. "Even if soldiers work behind a desk or on the life support systems. That's the part in the structure that I'll be happy with. Fixing, building and maintaining. It's your job to give insignificants such as myself and many others a future to look forward to."

"It is a future that all of us are seeking," 1 smiled.

"I wasn't trying to say you were insignificant," 2 dipped his head politely.

"Well I am," Chief Hayes said cheerfully. "Compared to the amborgs, obviously. You have more important jobs. I find my own ways of being significant when I can be of assistance."

"I don't think we give enough credit to all of these people helping us," 1 said to 2.

"Indeed, I suppose we should figure out a way of correcting this," 2 replied. "Are you thinking what I'm thinking?"

"I am," 1 nodded. "Chief Hayes."

"Yes?"

1 and 2 transmitted their confirmation to each other before 1 asked his question.

"Do you think it's possible," 1 gestured to himself and 2. "We were wondering if we could submit a proposal to…"

Suddenly, all of the lights shifted from bright white to flashing red as the deafening alarms drowned out 1's question. Hayes tried to stand, but only fell down thanks to her ankle.

"YEOW!" she yelled as 2 caught her in his arms. "I'm afraid that will have to wait! Engineering! Battle Stations!"

"You're injured Chief!" 2 yelled as chaos erupted around them.

"Never mind that!"

"Engineering!" Admiral Ra'aiah's voice echoed over the intercom. "Enemy fleet approaching! Send power to main deflectors and give me all the juice out of the core!"

"This is Hayes! Stand by!" Chief Hayes said into her wrist communicator. She looked at 1 and 2 and pointed. "You're going to have to get to the console and do it for me! I'll tell you what to do!"

2 carried Chief Hayes towards the console she indicated and 1 took control.

"To transfer power to the deflectors," Hayes instructed as a loud rumbling shook the room, "you need to open a line to the controllers at weapons command! Swipe and then press those two buttons!"

She then turned to another engineer.

"Karrol! I need you to confirm!"

"Aye Chief!"

1 obeyed without hesitation. They heard a slight humming noise, followed by a thunderous boom from outside that sent vibrations through the area, rattling them around. The engineer named Karrol manned another station and helped initiate the power transfer.

"That was a shield failure on the rear port deflector," Hayes said, looking up and listening. "Get me a damage control team to section five, deck ten!"

"Aye Chief!" someone answered.

"This is Commander Ulgo!" Ulgo's voice said over the intercom. "All hands! Evacuate section five in deck ten! Structural breach of the outer hull imminent!"

"Whoo! Called it!" Hayes said, pumping her fist triumphantly. She spoke into her wrist communicator again. "Damage control! Get those suits on and get to work!"

As 1 manned the console, more explosions struck the ship.

"If you can listen to how far away the explosions are," Hayes said to 2, "how quiet and loud they are, and how many happen in an instant, then you can tell which part of the ship took the most damage! Engineer's ears are the best for this! Like when someone calls for a medic on the field. Just got to know where the sound came from."

"That's amazing," 2 said in the midst of several more loud booms. "You could tell where everything is happening before we could!"

"Well, I had to train to be as fast as an amborg," Hayes chuckled. "Learned from humanity's best."

"This is Admiral Ra'aiah!" the Admiral's voice rang out again from the intercom. "Engineering! I need all power from shields to the engines! We have a problem!"

"This is Hayes!" Hayes said into her communicator once more. "With all due respect ma'am! That's a terrible idea! You want me to take power from the shields?! That's a greedy tactic that will get us killed!"

"The Tandeeri are retreating," Admiral Ra'aiah said forcefully. "But we have to go after them now!"

"We would definitely like to know why, Admiral!"

"The shuttle carrying the amborg reinforcements has been taken."

1 and 2 turned to each other, eyes wide as saucers. The hell did she just say? They stood frozen in silence, staring in disbelief. Undeterred, Admiral Ra'aiah continued to give orders.

"Chief!" she said urgently. "I won't repeat myself! Give me more power to the engines!"

"I need three minutes!" Hayes replied. "Getting underway soon!"

In the midst of the chaos, 1 and 2 remained in a state of shock while Hayes continued to restore order. She caught sight of their stunned expressions as she took charge of the entire department.

"I'm sure everything is ok," she said breathlessly. "I'll get everything situated here. But bypassing shield control... Grr. Do you want to go to the bridge?"

"Are you alright here?" 2 asked quickly, his breathing coming in quick, ragged gasps.

"It's ok!"

1 helped 2 as they gently leaned Chief Hayes against the console. Balancing on her uninjured leg, she flashed them a thumbs up. When she was secure, 1 hurriedly began to speak.

"Come on 2!"

The two amborgs ran for the nearest elevator.

Chapter 21: Emergency Recall Priorities

Amborg Personnel Files: Fourth Emergency Recall
2138 July
High Priority Missions

File 40012
Objective: Locate and Secure A.I. Industries VIP codename "Nova"
Responding Amborg (s): Clint 11 (First Group) & Keith 66 (Second Group)

"Please tell me why we are out here? In the middle of nowhere?"

"You'll find out once we get to our destination."

11 continued hiking up the trail, glancing back to check on his partner. 66 jogged after him and the two of them kept up their pace.

"I just don't get why anyone would like to live out here in the middle of a huge forest," 66 sighed. "Zion National Park is a great place to visit. Living here? I can't imagine."

"Some people appreciate hiding in the wilderness," 11 replied with a laugh. "Little to no reception, fresh air, nice weather, and nothing but nature surrounding you."

"So who is Nova?" 66 asked. "What are they like?"

"I can't exactly share full details but," 11 sighed. "I suppose since we're out here, and no one is monitoring us at the moment, the short version is that Nova was there when the First Group amborgs made their public appearances."

"Nova was a technician?" 66 asked.

"Let's just say that they were a key figure in our lives," 11 smiled.

"So why the secrecy? Why retire from A.I. Industries?"

11 turned and gave 66 a kind look.

"Because employees of A.I. Industries are like any other normal human beings," he explained. "They get old. Retirement is just something that has to happen eventually. So, when it was time for Nova to leave, Dr. Kendrick paid for them to pick anywhere in the world to settle down and collect their pension. Nova picked here."

"Seems like an odd choice," 66 replied.

"When Nova said they wanted to get away, they really picked a nice place to get away," 11 remarked.

This was 11 and 66's first time visiting Nova's home. When it came to the VIPs, the classified employees, allies of the amborgs, or specially designated individuals, they would send someone to check on them annually. Even though they had chosen retirement or to leave A.I. Industries, they were still considered to be family. During an emergency recall, it was natural that the amborgs would want to perform these check-ups.

"I'll say," 66 muttered as he turned and looked back the way they came. "We passed a corner store that had a promotion for half off on turkey gizzards."

"Hey, those looked like pretty fair prices."

"So, Nova was a friend to the First Group?"

"Oh yeah," 11 replied. "They witnessed our first missions, stood by our side for many years, and then just before you happened, Nova decided to disappear."

66 figured that 11 was talking about the Second Group. It sounded like Nova decided to get out of dodge right before his generation of amborgs made their public debut.

"I don't mean to sound disrespectful," 66 called out.

"Which means that you're going to sound disrespectful anyway," 11 laughed.

"Why is every guy's dream to retire and live as far away from people as possible?" 66 asked. "I mean, come on now. I might enjoy living out here for like a week, but then I'd be bored off my ass. If this place is haunted, you can bet I'm running."

"Never figured you for the superstitious type," 11 remarked.

"Look, we can handle ourselves," 66 shuddered. "But I still get nightmares about the time we caught those cultists in the woods. That mission was insane."

"Why?" 11 asked. "Your team succeeded without any injuries or casualties."

"I know," 66 replied with a terrified expression. "But I couldn't believe it and I still can't believe that people are capable of doing that messed up stuff."

"Well, Nova is definitely not like that."

"Didn't you say that this was the first time that you'd be doing a checkup?" 66 asked. "When was the last time you spoke to Nova? Or saw them?"

"15 years," 11 said thoughtfully.

"Oh great, 15 years," 66 rolled his eyes. "Someone definitely doesn't want to remember their time with us. Or maybe, they're just really paranoid."

They continued on until they eventually reached a clearing. A log cabin came into view up ahead, and they hurried toward it eagerly. It wasn't as big as 117's cabin, but it looked inhabited. As they approached, they noticed a motorbike parked in a small shed nearby.

"Ah," 11 smiled. He glanced at 66, who looked around skeptically. "Reconsidering your retirement?"

"Just myself, the birds, trees and nature?" 66 said suspiciously. "Nah, I think I'm ok."

11 walked up to the front porch of the cabin and called out.

"Nova! Are you here? It's amborg 11! We're..."

They paused when they noticed that the door was hanging open slightly. Sharing a wary look, they advanced slowly. 11 opened the door and peered inside.

"Maybe Nova is just super comfortable with leaving their door open?" 66 suggested.

"No," 11 said grimly. "Not Nova."

11 stepped into the cabin while 66 cautiously turned around and surveyed the area. The birds were chirping and the wind blew warm air through the trees. Seeing nothing out of the ordinary, he followed 11 inside.

The two of them looked around. It was pretty standard for a one room cabin. A couple of recliners and couches filled the space, while coffee tables held a collection of books. In the corner, a single mattress lay topped with a comfortable sleeping bag. Opposite them, the kitchen and dining area featured a compact fridge and freezer, a sink, a wooden stove nestled in the corner, and a small table with two chairs. It was a very nice set-up for one or two people that wanted to live out here.

"Out hunting?" 66 asked.

"No," 11 looked at the stove and turned his head to scan the entire interior. "The stove is on. Gear duffel is sitting there on the table. Deer drag hanging on the wall."

11 then looked above the fireplace at the mantle. There was a wooden rack where a rifle was supposed to hang.

"But Nova's rifle is missing."

66 noticed a cup lying on its side on the table. There were liquid stains on the tablecloth.

"Nova must have gotten out of here in a hurry."

"Nova's motorcycle is still outside," 11 said carefully. He shifted his gaze to 66, who was turning to go out the front door. "If they left in a hurry, they hightailed it on foot. This doesn't feel right."

"I saw a transmitter near the log pile," 66 said. "I'll use that to boost our signal. Let me go call it in."

66 ardently walked out on the porch and headed to another small shed with stacks of logs. Beside it stood an advanced communications transmitter similar to one back at A.I. Industries. As he approached it, 11 scanned the area.

"Hold on," he transmitted to 66 through a private channel.

"What is it?" 66 replied.

"You hear that?"

"Nothing," 66 said. "I don't hear anything."

Both amborgs paused. That was the problem. The wind had died down, making it easier to focus on the surrounding environment. The silence was unsettling; the usual chirping of the birds and rustling of wildlife had vanished, as if someone had hit the mute button on the world. Suddenly, 11 caught sight of several flashes of light sparkling from the bushes and greenery a few dozen yards out.

"66, watch out!"

The flickering lights he'd spotted were actually scopes from weapons. There were at least six trained on him, and he could make out several shadowy figures clad in camouflage jumping out. They opened fire, and the sharp crack of automatic weapons filled the air.

Without hesitation, 66 pivoted and sprinted back toward the cabin while 11 drew his gun and returned fire.

"Get inside!" he yelled as he pulled the trigger.

One of the assailants collapsed onto the ground. When he didn't get up, 11 attempted to shoot the other attackers, but the spray of gunfire slowly forced him back to the cabin. 66 drew his own handgun and fired some rounds while retreating. Once safely inside, 11 ducked in after him.

They quickly shut the door as the enemy fired at the cabin. The walls shuddered under the relentless assault, the sound of splintering wood echoed around them. 11 immediately grabbed the dining room table, flipped it on its side, and barricaded the door. Crouching low, they braced themselves as bullets whizzed past. They took a few hits, but thanks to their cybernetics, they ricocheted off of them without causing any damage. In fact, they could identify the type of ammo the shooters were using every time they got hit.

"Whoever these guys are," 11 said as he felt a round hit his shoulder. He shrugged it off while performing an ammo check, then looked over to 66 who was doing the same. "They must have been sitting in this cabin, waiting for Nova. Let's grab whatever supplies we can and get out."

66 looked around for any useful items nearby. 11 noticed a box of 300 Win Mag bullets and quickly swiped it. He crawled over to the wood stove and opened the door. 66 grabbed a flare gun off the same table and some duct tape, and threw it into his pouch.

11 quickly tossed the ammo into the stove and slammed the door shut. Then, he sprinted to the back of the cabin, unleashing a flurry of punches to the floor. After a few hits, he tore off the floorboards, exposing a passage beneath the foundation. They now had a way to slip out from the back.

"Come on!" 11 commanded. "Those rounds are going to pop any moment!"

66 raced over and ducked through the hole. Once he was clear, 11 dove in after him, and together they took refuge under the cabin. Just as they were about to emerge from the other side, a series of loud pops erupted as the heated ammunition began to detonate. The moment it did, they could hear the enemy shooters start firing at the cabin again.

Hoping that would distract them enough, 11 and 66 both sprinted into the woods as quickly as they could. After a few minutes, they stopped at some trees, took cover, and watched the path behind them.

"I have 18 rounds," 66 reported.

"I have 10," 11 replied. "And... one more mag with eight rounds. What do we have to work with?"

"No reception, our radios are not getting through, so no way to contact anyone," 66 panted. "What's the plan?"

"We need to find Nova," 11 said. "They wouldn't have been setting up an ambush back there if they had them. Nova is out here somewhere. What did you get when we got out of there?"

"Tape and a flare gun," 66 reported, then shook his head. "Not a lot of time and I only have one shot."

"Ok," 11 nodded. "If Nova is out here, maybe there's a good chance they're hiding in their hunting blind."

"How do we find it?"

66's question prompted 11 to immediately scan the area. He looked up at the trees and activated his infrared vision. Then something caught his eye.

"There," 11 pointed at a tree. "Trail markers!"

There was a letter "A" drawn in ink on the tree. It looked very similar to the design on their shoulder patches for the amborgs.

"Pretty standard for a woodsman. You got to know where to put your markers and how to find them."

They followed the markers with their enhanced vision and ran as fast as they could. After about twenty minutes, they found themselves in front of a small shed built next to the side of a tree. Stairs led up to it, and as they neared, they noticed a tarp draped over the entrance.

"Any life signs? I'm not seeing any," 66 said.

"Me neither," 11 replied.

As they moved in closer, they suddenly heard the sound of footsteps. They whirled around and heard weapons clicking. However, 11 lowered his gun.

"Drop it!" he called out.

66 also lowered his arms as they both stared ahead. Just a few feet away on the high ground stood two A.I. Industries security drones. These ones didn't look like the standard models back home. Instead, they looked old and worn, and appeared to have undergone some serious renovations. Some parts had clearly been replaced, and the drones showed signs of weathering and prolonged exposure to the elements. Despite their appearance, it was obvious that someone had done an excellent job maintaining them.

"Those are older generation drones," 66 exclaimed in awe. "I thought those had been retired."

"They were."

The drones were bigger and bulkier as they walked cautiously towards them. Years ago, when the new model had been deployed, the old ones were scrapped, deactivated, put in storage, or repurposed for different jobs.

"Drop your weapons," the first one demanded, pointing its weapon menacingly. "Please identify yourselves."

Both amborgs quickly spoke up.

"Clint 11, A.I. Industries, First Group!" 11 stated.

"Keith 66, A.I. Industries, Second Group," 66 added when the drones turned their gazes on him.

"Confirming."

The two drones paused, their faceplates glowing brightly. After a rapid beep and a single flash of light, they both nodded in unison.

"Confirmed. Friendlies identified."

11 looked closely at the drone that had first spoken to them.

"Jim?" he asked. "Is that you?"

"Yes," the first drone nodded again. "It is wonderful to see you, old friend."

66 stared, baffled when he saw 11 walk up to the drone named Jim and shook its hand. The other drone behind him turned to look around and survey the area for any signs of enemy movement.

"Hold on," 66 said. "Nova is an older model security drone? It lives out here in the wilderness?"

"No," 11 laughed. "Jim is one of the drones that watches over Nova. *He...*"

11 turned to look at 66, putting emphasis on Jim's pronoun.

"...has been out here the last 15 years."

"Correct," Jim stated as he pointed at himself and the other drone. "Our model was obsolete when the newer generation rolled off the assembly lines. Dr. Kendrick allowed us the opportunity to choose to do whatever we wanted."

"So who's your friend?" 66 asked, eyeing the second drone.

"My name is Leo," it introduced itself. "Pleased to meet you."

"I missed these guys," 11 smiled brightly. "These drones always had more personality than the ones that are working today."

"Isn't that because Dr. Kendrick... I mean, his father, Dr. Ethan Kendrick, liked treating them as individuals and programmed them with simple emotions?" 66 asked.

"Correct again," Jim nodded. "We were given more free will and the Kendricks always treated us like family."

"Do you remember the story when Dr. Kendrick... I mean, John was kidnapped?" 11 asked 66.

"Oh yeah, that story from class?" 66 nodded. "I remember that."

"Well, Jim was one of the drones on the security team that helped the police save him."

"I'm sure we can catch up another time," Jim said. "What are you two doing out here?"

"We were up at Nova's cabin," 11 stated. "Came looking for you because we had a request to come check in. But we didn't find anyone when we got there."

"Except the team of mercenaries camped out?" Leo asked.

"Mercenaries? What happened out here?"

The drones looked at 66, then exchanged glances.

"Nova had gone into town to purchase a few supplies," Jim reported. "Unfortunately, there was a shootout at the local tavern. Two motorcycle clubs began a territory dispute. Somehow, we got in the middle of it."

"Actually, I accidentally dragged them into it."

The group turned around as they heard more footsteps approaching. From behind a tree, a middle-aged woman appeared, carrying a hunting rifle and dressed in camouflage. She wore a cap and her dark hair tied in a short braid, and she greeted them with a warm smile.

"Clint!" she beamed cheerfully. "Nice to see you again."

"Nova," 11 dipped his head politely.

"Oh, come on," Nova said as she opened her arms. "Don't just stand there boys, you're family!"

11 and Nova shared a hug while 66 hung back, examining her.

"A Second Group amborg?" Nova let go of 11, noticing 66's uniform.

"You can tell?" 66 asked.

"You have a much more rigid posture," Nova said discerningly, indicating 66's foot placement and stance. "What are you two doing out here?"

"There's a lot of things going on right now," 11 replied.

"Does it have anything to do with those rumors I heard in town?" Nova asked curiously. "I heard Old Bob talking about some weird alien invasion announcement from the President."

"You guys don't have radios out here?" 66 asked. "It's been almost a week since that announcement. What about that transmitter back at your cabin??"

"I use it only in case of emergencies," Nova replied. "Even when it's used, I don't download full news articles. It's just to signal A.I. Industries if I'm in trouble."

"So, you didn't get to it? When the mercenaries arrived at your cabin?"

Nova shook her head.

"I'm afraid not," she sighed. "Jim was able to see them coming and warned me. Leo and I grabbed what we could and made it out here."

"We must have walked right into the cabin when the mercs were waiting for Nova to come back," 11 said. "Your bike was still outside, making it look like you were still at home."

"But what was the reason they were hunting you?" 66 asked.

"These clubs are all the same," Nova replied. "Egotistical and desperate to topple the other gangs in order to establish control. The gang that ambushed you is called Vengeance Front. Most of those members are ex-military."

"Which explains the automatic weapons," 11 muttered.

"For a few months, Jim, Leo and I disrupted their operations at any opportunity we could," Nova said proudly. "I fed intel to the police and a lot of their members were arrested. If I had to venture a guess, I think they figured out it was me putting a wrench in their operation."

"Well, what do we do?" 66 asked.

"Well, with one amborg, our odds of surviving are great!" Nova said eagerly. "Two are a godsend! I was going to wait for cover of darkness, but I think the five of us can make it to the nearby ranger station and inform the authorities about our predicament."

"But we can take them," 66 looked at each of them with a confused expression. "Right?"

"As much as I appreciate that," Nova pointed a finger at herself, "I'm the only normal human out here among you four bullet-proof bodyguards. I'm worried the bad guys might miss you and hit me. I'm not exactly as young as I used to be."

"Right," 66 shut his mouth and nodded. "Fair point."

"Let's get moving," Nova chuckled.

As she began to lead them towards a path, she looked at 11.

"By the way," she said. "How's Leonard? How is he?"

"He's just fine," 11 replied.

"Why didn't he come to see me?"

"You know why," 11 cleared his throat awkwardly. "It would violate the agreement you two have."

"Right," Nova looked crestfallen.

"Am I missing something here?" 66 asked.

Nova turned and looked at the Second Group amborg, then shifted her gaze to 11.

"Is he good at keeping secrets?" she asked.

"Yes he is," 11 nodded. "We all are."

Nova faced 66 and held out her right hand. He politely took it and they exchanged a formal handshake.

"66," she took a deep breath and spoke. "Try not to be too shocked but... My real name is Daphne Smith."

66 looked at 11, who was grinning from ear to ear. 66 just stared blankly, trying to figure out who she was. The name sounded pretty common, but he'd definitely never heard it mentioned before. He pulled up the employee database of A.I. Industries, but didn't find any matches.

"You're going to want to check the redacted files," she added amiably. "I'm Leonard 1's wife."

66's eyes went wide, letting his hand fall back to his side. What did she just say? No, he had heard her correctly. 11 cleared his throat, and Nova sighed.

"Ok," she mumbled as she bobbed her head around slightly. "Actually, I'm his ex-wife."

"I have a lot of questions," 66 blurted out.

Nova, or Daphne, started to laugh. She figured that there would be a lot to talk about after dropping that bit of information.

File 40172
Objective: Pennsylvania Police Hunt for two "Bonnie & Clyde" armed robbers. Trending on social media. Dozens injured, zero casualties.
Responding Amborg (s): Tiana 19 (First Group)

"Thank you so much for agreeing to help us!"

Tiana 19 walked up the steps to the police station just as several patrol officers were leaving. She looked back at her drop-pod to make sure that it was still secure. Satisfied, she smiled as she shook hands with the detective in charge.

"Detective Lily William," the woman in a suit introduced herself. "Amborg 19?"

"Yes," 19 nodded. "Can you describe to me what happened?"

"Ever since the President announced this whole outer space thing, it's been one crazy day after the other. Businesses were shut down temporarily but some people decided to reopen their doors. It's like they were all scared at first, but then with each passing day, they just encouraged everyone to keep on going like nothing is happening up in outer space."

19 could already see it in the officers as they went about their business. No one was in a panic, but the atmosphere was thick with tension. Every officer was clad in full armor, just doing their thing.

"Let's just cut to the chase," 19 stated. "I took this mission because you wanted to shut down robbers that are going viral?"

"Pretty typical case of Bonnie and Clyde thinking, they go around stealing and hurting people for personal gain," Lily explained as she showed her data pad to 19. "Janelle Tak and Marcus Lindham. Our two lovers turned criminals."

"A boyfriend and girlfriend?" 19 asked. "An actual couple?"

"I told my watch commander that I would have this case wrapped up by the end of the day," Lily nodded. "I'm betting you can help us cut that time in half."

"Tell me what happened?" 19 asked as she looked at the files. Marcus and Janelle both had a criminal record in their early teenage years, but nothing as serious as the crimes they had just committed in the last two hours. "Who are they?"

"Marcus was a valet as of this morning," Lily explained. "Some nice rich person's club, you know? According to coworkers and eyewitnesses, someone told him to move his ass faster and he snapped. Assaulted the guy, stole a Porsche, and basically quit. Janelle worked for a catering company in a film studio. One of the celebrities freaked out when she got their food order wrong so Janelle trashed the entire buffet table. Pretty much threw a lot of stuff everywhere."

The start of this sounded like two different crimes with a developing pattern.

"Then the icing on the cake?" Lily's face fell, as if a dark shroud had been pulled over her head. 19 could feel the anger radiating from the detective. "These two forced me to come in on my day off after they robbed me and my parents."

"You were robbed?" 19 raised an eyebrow. "My condolences."

"Thanks."

"But how did that happen?"

"Pretty typical actually," Lily replied with a huff. "I've been working the last two weeks non-stop. When I finally got a day off, I took my parents out to brunch. It was a good moment, getting to see them in the middle of all of this chaos. Then those two showed up at the restaurant and robbed a lot of people of their jewelry and miscellaneous items."

"You chose not to fight?" 19 asked curiously.

"I was by myself, off-duty and unarmed," Lily shook her head. "I couldn't risk a gunfight in the middle of all of those people. I came back into work, my parents are safely here at the station, and Marcus and Janelle have been racking up the criminal charges. Now they've started injuring people that have been fighting back. A few families have been hurt. No casualties so far."

19 and Detective William entered the station. As soon as some of the officers spotted her uniform, they quickly stepped aside. Some saluted 19, and she returned their gesture with a cheerful smile as they made their way past the front desk and into the main office. The detective went to her desk and picked up the phone.

"What are you doing?"

Detective William looked back up at her with a grin. She held up a list of numbers she pulled from an open folder next to her computer.

"Stolen cellphones," she said. "I've been calling each of them, trying to reach Marcus and Janelle."

19 nodded. She knew what Detective William was up to. She was trying to establish a connection so that they could potentially run a trace. If they answered one of the stolen phones, they could ping their location and narrow it down.

19 took a look at the list and began to dial some of the numbers to help reduce the workload. After a few unsuccessful attempts, one of the calls went through. Detective William shot 19 a sharp look to indicate that she had made a connection.

"New phone! Who dis?" someone laughed on the other line.

19 glanced at the detective as she hooked into the phone system to start running a trace.

"This is Detective Lily William," she spoke into the phone. "We met this morning."

"Oh yeah, the cop from the restaurant," they heard a woman say. It was Janelle. "What's up detective? You uh, calling to arrest us? I don't think you can do that over the phone."

They heard a man laughing in the background.

"What do you want?" Janelle asked.

"I'm calling to let you know that this is your one and only chance to turn yourself in," Detective William kept a professional tone as she stated her demands. "If we look past all the people you've hurt so far, you've committed armed robbery. Now half the Pennsylvania police are hunting for you."

"Yeah, that's not going to happen."

A man's voice spoke back to them. They assumed it was Marcus.

"You see, we got this whole crime spree planned out," he bragged. "Isn't that right, baby?"

"Hell yeah," Janelle replied.

Lily and 19 suddenly heard a faint sucking noise on the other end of the line. The detective grimaced and rolled her eyes while 19 simply shrugged. The couple were making out in the middle of the call.

"I know that you two have been through a lot," Lily stated.

"Oh please!" Janelle snapped at them over the phone. "If you think reading our files tells you anything about who we are, then you're a terrible cop!"

"I've read enough files to know enough," Lily answered calmly. She didn't appreciate being interrupted, but she had to maintain her composure. "I know you and Marcus both live in a halfway house and never caught a single break in your lives, which is why I'm guessing you decided to turn to crime. Spur-of-the-moment type of action to spice it up."

19 listened as she connected to a computer terminal and searched the internet.

"I know that you two did jail time," Lily said sympathetically. "When you got out, you tried living straight and getting back on track. You got real jobs and worked hard."

"Yeah!" Marcus grumbled. "But we still got treated like scum! Not even worth an ounce of respect!"

19 suddenly got a hit on the internet. She had begun a search for anything on social media that could help them out and noticed something interesting. She found a livestream of Marcus and Janelle.

"Detective," 19 said, turning the computer screen towards Lily. "They are live streaming this conversation."

Detective William, hand still holding up her phone, focused intently on the screen. There they were—Marcus and Janelle, live on camera. As she watched, comments and emoji reactions flowed rapidly along the bottom of the screen. Without a doubt, the couple matched the images 19 had reviewed in the police files.

"You can save your false empathy," Janelle sneered at the camera. "Today, detective, is for all of the mistreated and disrespected workers out there. This is for everyone that has ever wanted to walk out of their job and save themselves from arrogant rich pricks."

"Yeah," Marcus nodded, prompting Janelle to shift the camera to focus on him. "For anyone that believed the lie, that if you just tried to work harder, you could achieve your dreams!"

"We are done begging for scraps!" Janelle looked into the camera and made sure everyone could see her anger. "We are taking what's ours!"

"Let's take it all, baby," Marcus turned his eyes on Janelle and looked at her seductively.

"Let's take it!" Janelle turned to him and grinned.

"I love you."

Detective William heard enough. She took the phone in her hands and hung up. 19 also decided to stop watching the livestream. The comments from the online supporters were filled with so much toxicity that it didn't feel worth it.

"You know what I said to them when they took my mom's pearl necklace? And my dad's wallet?" Lily asked calmly.

19 nodded quietly, giving her permission to answer her own question.

"I told them that when I saw them again, I would have a new kind of bracelet for them," she snarled.

"You said that you were robbed too," 19 said. "What did they take from you?"

"A silver bracelet that was my husband's anniversary gift to me," Lily replied. "I want it back."

"Well, I should join the hunt," 19 declared, turning on her heel and heading straight for the door. "We will notify you when we have caught sight of them."

19 walked out of the station and headed to her drop pod. Instead of opening the door to climb inside, she entered a passcode, and a compartment on the side hissed open. She grabbed the contents inside and set it out on the ground.

It resembled a travel case with two unusually large motorcycle tires in it. When 19 pressed the deploy button, onlookers stopped and stared as it opened up. The massive wheels sprang forward and backward, gradually positioning themselves on the ground, while a kickstand extended to stabilize the bike. The front fork and hand clutch twisted outward as the bike unfolded and assembled itself. When it was ready, a little chime rang out, signaling that it was ready to be ridden.

19 mounted the bike and hit the ignition switch. The motor roared to life as she tied her hair up and put on a pair of safety glasses. She revved the engine and sped out of the police station parking lot.

Behind her, the thrusters of her drop-pod roared as it lifted off the ground. It rocketed up and out of sight as she sped down the streets.

Based on a quick internet search, 19 decided to head towards a few churches. There was a possibility that she knew exactly where Marcus and Janelle would go.

If they were smart, they would try to leave town, but the fact that they had decided to livestream themselves demonstrated not just arrogance and self entitlement, but how ridiculously short-sighted they were. By revealing to a police detective the intention to instigate more public unrest and commit more crimes only confirmed that they were going to come crashing down hard. It certainly wasn't going to help that 19 didn't even need to track the cellphone that Detective William had called. When she saw their location the instant she tuned into the livestream, she already knew where in the city the crazy couple was or most likely to be headed.

"Detective William," 19 stated, initiating a call back to the police station.

The call was immediately picked up.

"Go for William," Lily's voice responded.

"Detective," 19 said as she weaved through traffic and activated her siren. "Please search for any weddings in the area happening around this time, please."

"That shouldn't be too hard," Lily answered skeptically. "What are you looking for?"

"Marcus and Janelle are on a power-trip, which is inflating their egos," 19 informed her. "All of the jewelry and the stolen possessions they robbed will get them a lot of money, but they have to go to a pawn shop or reseller to earn some money for their special getaway."

"So you want me to station units at pawn shops?"

"No," 19 answered. "For them, it's all about the attention. Their social media following is proof of that. They'll get flagged if they try to start selling their possessions in the city. Their best chance to escape would be to run right now. They've already forfeited their head start."

"Yeah, they're not the brightest," Lily grumbled. "Why am I looking for wedding events today?"

"In the livestream video," 19 turned right at the intersection, "Marcus and Janelle wore wedding rings that seemed way too expensive from what I could see. When they robbed you earlier this morning, did they have those rings?"

"No," Lily answered confidently. "They definitely didn't have them."

After a few moments, 19 heard the detective confirm her question. An alert appeared in her HUD as she continued to ride through the city.

"I have a wedding ceremony taking place right now at St. Patrick Church! The couple getting married decided not to cancel their plans, apparently."

"I'm heading there now."

19 rode her bike for about 15 minutes. She was just about to reach the church when she caught the police dispatch from Pennsylvania emergency services on the radio.

"All units, be advised. I have a code 415 unknown at St. Patrick's church."

19 heard some police officers respond. A few units nearby were en route and let dispatch know they were being redirected. 19 promptly alerted Detective William.

"Detective," 19 stated. "Code 415 at St. Patrick's. Marcus and Janelle are there."

"You sure?"

19 pulled up to the church entrance and parked next to the police cars that were already there. The doors were closed, and she noticed that no one was out there to meet her. The officers must have already gone inside.

While she dismounted, she heard gunshots coming from inside the church.

"I'm positive," 19 sighed as she ran up the steps.

As soon as she stepped inside, the sounds of gunfire and terrified screams hit her ears. She saw a crowd of people huddled in the pews and ducking down, trying to stay hidden. She had just enough time to spot a few officers disappearing in the far back corner.

"Everyone! Exit the building! Go, go, go!" 19 yelled as she sprinted up the aisle.

Several people, including a distraught bride and groom, quickly stood and made a break for the entrance. 19 thanked them as she ran head-on toward the sound of gunshots.

"Show me your hands!"

More gunshots echoed through the corridors as 19 activated her beacon and moved carefully down the halls. She scanned for the radio frequencies of the officers onsite. When she found them, she joined the comms and spoke up.

"Attention officers, this is amborg 19 of A.I. Industries. I am onsite and here to assist. Please do not shoot me."

As 19 rounded a corner, she saw two officers waiting at an intersection. When she approached, one of them turned to look over her shoulder.

"Holy shit!" she exclaimed. "An amborg!"

"What happened?" 19 asked.

"Those two nutcases had stolen someone's suit and a wedding dress," the officer in front stated without turning his head. "They forced the priest at gunpoint to marry them and stole the real bride and groom's special day."

"When they saw us, they started shooting," the female officer added. "We got him in the shoulder, though. He's around the corner."

19 immediately walked up to the corner and peeked around. She saw Marcus, the man from the livestream, sitting on the ground. He was wearing a formal dinner jacket with a lot of unnecessary bling, and he was clutching his right shoulder, which was bleeding through. 19 approached cautiously, noticing that Janelle, his bride, was nowhere to be seen.

"Abandoned on your big day?" 19 mused as she crouched down and pulled out her first aid kit.

"I told her to leave me," Marcus groaned. "I saved her."

"No you didn't," 19 replied as she signaled to the police to call for an ambulance. "You should have listened to Detective William and turned yourselves in. Tell me where she is."

"I don't have to tell you shit," Marcus spat. "I have rights. I am unrepentant."

"I shall be sure to pass that along to the judge," 19 replied coldly. "See how well someone with actual authority responds to your disrespectful wiseass."

When the ambulance arrived, the police launched a search for Janelle. They located the car Marcus had stolen, but it was abandoned and Janelle was nowhere to be found. 19 was surprised that she had managed to get away on foot. It couldn't be that hard to miss a woman in a dress with guns, desperately trying to hide from what they had done.

When they arrived at the hospital, Detective William was already there to greet the ambulance. Once inside, she spoke to the doctors who were examining Marcus while he was being transferred onto a gurney.

"How is he?" Lily asked one of the nurses.

One of them answered immediately as Marcus was set down.

"GSW through and through to the upper back. We're prepping the ER right away."

Detective William turned to 19 who stood off to the side, watching patiently.

"You already talked to him?"

"Tried to," 19 nodded. "He's stubborn."

"Then maybe it's my turn to put some fear in his mind," Lily nodded in confirmation.

She approached Marcus, who was still in a lot of pain, but the moment he noticed her, he instantly recognized her.

"You made a mistake with your spontaneous honeymoon getaway," Lily spoke sternly. "I told you this morning that I would find you and arrest you. Now tell me where Janelle is and we just might be able to save her."

"Let me guess," Marcus spoke through gritted teeth. "You want me to tell her to give herself up?"

"Damn right I do. You think that what you're doing is noble? You think that this gets you a happy ending? Grow up!"

19 observed in silence as Detective William bore down on Marcus with her sharp words. Around them, the doctors and nurses continued to work, seemingly unfazed by the charged conversation nearby. 19 was impressed at how effortlessly they managed to tune out the tense exchange between an injured criminal and a police detective while maintaining their focus on their jobs. Everyone in the room were highly underrated professionals, all of them.

"You shot at cops!" Lily snapped at Marcus. "I have hundreds of officers hunting your wife. And when we catch her, if she decides to try shooting her way to freedom, she will die. For all of the people that you robbed, the families you hurt and the kids you traumatized for your selfish gains, you will lose her!"

19 stepped forward and put a hand on Detective William's shoulder. She had angrily stepped up to the gurney, nearly leaning into Marcus' face. 19 noticed that the man's expression was beginning to falter. Fear crept into his eyes as Lily painted a rather morbid picture.

She straightened up, turned, and thanked 19 for gently pulling her back. She reached in her pocket and pulled out her cellphone.

"You will record a message," she demanded. "Tell her to surrender or you're going to wake up from surgery and learn that you became a widower."

One of the nurses placed a bandage on Marcus's shoulder, not bothering to be gentle, as if they were helping the Detective drive home her point as painfully as possible. He groaned in pain and his breathing became labored.

"Forget it!" Marcus managed to say, shaking his head defiantly. "Our entire lives, we've been ordered around. I'm not going to be another person telling her what to do."

Detective William and Marcus both fell silent as they stared angrily at each other. One of the nurses grabbed the edge of the gurney.

"The O.R. is ready," they said.

"Go ahead," Lily nodded. "I'm done with him."

As they wheeled Marcus away, 19 looked at Detective William, who looked peeved.

"I think you did scare him slightly," she complimented.

"Not enough," Lily let out a frustrated huff. "Now we have to keep looking for Janelle."

"You may be done with him," 19 said. "But I don't think Janelle is. Let's set up a trap for her. Use Marcus as bait. Let's see if she's crazy enough in love to want to break out her dear husband."

"There's a very slim chance," Lily looked at 19. "You think it'll work?"

"How long have you been married to your husband?" 19 asked.

"One year, why?"

19 smiled.

"I've been in love before too," she said. "Haven't you ever done something crazy and stupid for someone you were in love with?"

Lily tilted her head and thought for a moment. a wave of painful memories washed over her, and she nodded uncomfortably. 19 chuckled as she strolled over to the nearest vending machine.

"I'll buy you a snack," she said. "It's on me."

Lily was slightly reluctant, but 19 insisted that they take a breather. While they grabbed some coffee and snacks, they set up their trap for Janelle. The hospital security and police would vacate their stations at the hospital entrances. If Janelle tried sneaking in, the hospital workers were instructed not to intervene, otherwise she'd probably start shooting.

Sure enough, after they finished their snack break, Detective William received word from an officer that Janelle had been seen strolling into the hospital. The police planned to let her walk right into their decoy room, where 19 would be waiting.

19 waited patiently, peering through the blinds. Switching off the lights, the room was plunged into darkness, illuminated only by the sunlight streaming in. Her gaze fell on the officer standing guard outside. After a moment, he

stepped away, pretending to answer his cell phone. Seconds later, 19 caught sight of Janelle, who emerged cautiously into view, glancing around before she opened the door.

"Come on baby," 19 heard her whisper as the door opened. "Let's get out of..."

19 flipped the lights on and Janelle stopped in her tracks, her eyes widening in pure shock.

"Oh shit!"

"Hi!" 19 smiled. "I suppose congratulations are in order. For your wedding, and your arrest."

The door was flung open as Detective William and two other officers burst in.

"Hands above your head!" she bellowed.

As Janelle was put in handcuffs, Lily stepped forward, looking her straight in the eye. With a swift motion, she reached around and unclasped a silver bracelet from Janelle's left wrist and took it.

"I told you I'd be there to get this back," she said smugly, while Janelle glared at her furiously. "And look at that, brand new silver bracelets to go with you to jail. I told you I'd be the one to slap them on."

Janelle pivoted to 19 and glowered.

"Why the hell are you working for them?" she spat.

"I don't work for them," 19 replied casually. "I work with them occasionally. There's a difference."

19 followed them out and watched as the officers escorted Janelle down the hall.

"I work for the people that you hurt," 19 explained. "One of the victims you stole from is a friend of mine."

Detective William clasped her bracelet back on her own wrist and admired it. A wave of relief washed over her, and she let out a satisfied sigh.

"Thanks for your help," she said.

"I don't think I did anything really," 19 shrugged. "You handled this quite well."

"Nah," Lily replied. "You were the one who found their live stream, and right away, you pinpointed their location."

"Even before I got to the church," 19 smiled, "your officers responded fast."

"Well, I'm sure they had to," Lily replied, "considering they had no idea an amborg even took this mission. Did you really have a friend who got robbed by Marcus and Janelle?"

"Yes," 19 nodded as she began to walk away. "Kid named Samuel. He's 17 now. I saved him during the Dominoe Incident. Promised him that if he needed anything, I would be there."

"You got his name off one of our police reports?"

19 turned, but kept walking. She nodded.

"Also, I made a new friend today who also got robbed by Bonnie and Clyde. You."

Detective William laughed as 19 confidently strode away.

"I owe you," she called out to her.

"See you around, friend."

19 left the hospital and made her way to her bike. She quickly packed it up, lifted it, and stored it in her drop-pod as it landed in the hospital parking lot. She climbed inside and got ready to fly to her next destination. There were still several other missions on her list, and they weren't going to take care of themselves.

File 40293
Objective: Escort Senator Leera Alden and staff to LAX Airport. Discretion Highly Advised
Responding Amborg (s): Katie 57 (Second Group)

57 stood at attention, eyes fixed on the doors of Los Angeles City Hall. The path leading to the line of vehicles in front of her was clear, allowing her to scan the perimeter without any obstructions. As she confirmed there were no visible threats, a text message popped up. 57 rolled her eyes when she saw it was 4 trying to reach out.

I highly suggest that you abort this mission, 4 wrote. *Your attachment to Senator Alden is understandable, but you are wasting time and resources. Please return to A.I. Industries as soon as possible.*

57 typed her reply mentally and made sure it was sent.

I am already here in the area, she replied. *I can take care of this task and be on my way back in no time.*

I can see that you're obviously not going to abandon your current mission, 4 wrote back. *Please be safe. Also, the next time you want a lunch break, at least tell us beforehand that you're going to be late getting back home.*

57 sighed and shook her head. Technically, when she accepted this assignment, she figured that would be enough notice for the other leaders back at A.I. Industries. They should be able to take care of things while she took on a simple escort assignment.

"I really appreciate your help."

57 turned and noticed that the driver of the car in front of her had lowered the passenger window to talk to her.

"It's fine," 57 smiled courteously. "But please stick to protocol and roll up the window."

"I got to be honest," the driver ignored her request and continued to thank her. "When her security team tried to ask for more help for the senator, it was a relief to hear that A.I. Industries took the request."

"We're just here to help as best as we can. Now roll up the window."

The driver gave a quick nod and complied as the window slid up and locked into place.

In the last week, every state in the country had mobilized the reserves and national guard. The police and military were on high alert while the President kept them posted about the events taking place outside of the planet. A.I. Industries was working heavily with the government to make sure that the people were taken care of and that all protective measures were in place.

All of the requests and concerns from the people were now being addressed and prioritized. When 57 saw this particular mission pop up, she took it immediately. Not only was Senator Alden a bright and young upcoming politician that needed to return to Washington, she also had a personal connection with 57. The driver and other members of the senator's staff didn't need to know this, though.

The doors to city hall opened and 57 watched as an escort of secret service agents and police marched down the steps. Between them was a woman, surrounded by a few aides, who was deep in conversation with them.

"It's really great to see the initiative taking root, but even with all of the problems in outer space, people are still counting on…"

Senator Alden looked in 57's direction and paused. Her entourage came to an abrupt stop the moment she recognized the amborg uniform.

"...us," she breathed.

"Senator Alden," 57 dipped her head politely in greeting.

"Katie 57," the senator remarked as she approached, eyes fixed on her. "You're the amborg escort?"

57 nodded. She turned and opened the back door to the vehicle nearest to her. Senator Alden turned to her aides.

"Ride in the other cars," she instructed.

Her aides nodded and followed the police and agents to the other vehicles in the caravan. Senator Alden climbed into the car and 57 shut the door. She then made her way around to the other side and slipped inside. After settling into her seat, she closed the door behind her.

The voice of the head agent crackled over the radio, issuing instructions.

"Sparrow is secure. We are beginning the drive to LAX. Move out."

Up front, the driver started the ignition and the van roared to life. 57 immediately felt the chill of the air conditioning and quickly closed her vent.

"Sorry," Senator Alden said, reaching out to lower the settings. "Usually, a bunch of us ride together. A cramped car plus the LA weather heats up everything so fast."

As the car began to move, another announcement came through the speakers.

"Sparrow is moving. ETA 23 minutes."

Senator Alden turned to look at 57.

"You look great," she said. "Have you been well?"

"Thank you," 57 replied. "I'm doing ok."

An awkward silence fell over them, and 57 felt a growing sensation of unease.

"I'm the leader of the Second Group for this," she shared enthusiastically.

"Oh! A promotion?" the Senator asked excitedly.

"Not really," 57 replied. "There's a team up in space and I'm the leader of the Second Group down here."

"Oh," Senator Alden smiled. "That's still exciting. Does that mean... Hold on... Are you allowed to be here?"

"Yeah," 57 nodded. "I was in the area and I saw this mission request. Well, I saw that your head of security filed a request to have an amborg escort you to the airport. I, uh, jumped on the opportunity."

"Thank you," Senator Alden said, appearing touched by her altruism. "I do enjoy reading your emails, but seeing you in person is very reassuring."

"I'm sorry we don't get a lot of opportunities to hang out," 57 said. "It's not really in the cards for a senator to hangout with an amborg."

"Well, publically, yes. But at least we find a way to catch up when eyes are not on us. I hope you don't get in trouble when you get back. What if I'm keeping you from doing your job, Katie?"

"This is the job, Senator."

"You can call me Leera when the paparazzi aren't watching."

"Sorry," 57 replied. "I'll be sure to remember that."

"Does anyone ever ask you that question?"

57 looked at Senator Alden. She had a mischievous glint in her eyes, causing them both to start laughing.

"Yeah," 57 nodded. "Some people at A.I. Industries have asked. 'Hey 57, did you know you look like Senator Alden?' It springs up occasionally when I'm chatting with friends."

"What do you usually tell them?" Leera asked politely.

"I just deny it," 57 smirked. "But I can't keep it a secret any longer. A lot of my friends are already working it out. What about you?"

"One of my chief analysts was rescued by you about four years ago when I started running for office," Senator Alden replied. "They swore that they thought it was me who put on an amborg jacket and swooped in to save the day. I managed to convince him that he was exaggerating."

"I think that if I get more assignments with you," 57 said, "I need to bring a disguise, otherwise people will notice us if they look more closely."

"Of the two of us," Leera chuckled, "you're more famous than I am. My entire security team couldn't take their eyes off you."

"No, you're just as famous too," 57 shook her head.

"Did you ever manage to find out about how we got separated?"

57 turned to Senator Alden, whose expression was solemn. Unfortunately, she shook her head, and they both fell silent again.

"I wonder," Leera sighed. She gazed out the window, watching passersby on the sidewalk. "Do you think things would have been different? If I was an amborg and you were a senator instead?"

"If I wasn't an amborg, I definitely wouldn't have chosen to be a politician," 57 stated honestly.

"What about if both of us were found by Dr. Kendrick? Another pair of twin amborgs?"

"You'd make a fantastic amborg," 57 smiled.

"Katie," Leera's smile faded as her eyes caught sight of something. "What's that?"

57 looked over to the left outside the vehicle. She immediately turned on her radio and spoke urgently.

"Stop!"

The moment her command was issued, the driver slammed on the brakes, bringing the car to a sudden stop. The rest of the vehicles behind followed suit and halted. Hearing the order a little late, the police escort ahead came to a stop a few moments later when they realized the convoy had stopped moving.

57 and the senator looked out the window at the roof of a four story building. There was something going on up there and it didn't look good.

"Driver, redirect us to that building," 57 commanded.

The driver replied on a special intercom from the front.

"Ma'am, that's not on the designated safe route," he replied nervously.

Senator Alden took charge right away.

"It's ok," she said. "Please take us over there. Can you also ask the police escort to shut off their sirens and lights?"

Following the senator's orders, the driver made a turn and headed in the direction of the building they'd seen.

"You have good eyes," 57 stated when the driver parked the vehicle. "Stay here."

Without waiting for a reply, 57 stepped out of the car and gazed up at the roof. The sight that had caught the senator's attention was, to some extent, quite terrifying.

A line of people, about eight of them, were standing on the edge of the roof, all holding hands and wearing white robes of some kind. The senator had noticed them from a distance and alerted 57, fearing they were about to leap off together. Now that 57 was out of the car, she could hear them repeating an ominous and disturbing chant.

"The worthy servants will be rewarded and ascend!"

"All hail, children of the stars!"

"We will be welcomed warmly by the celestial beings!"

"All hail, children of the stars!"

57 could tell it was a cultist group or a gathering of fanatics devoted to something seriously messed up. As she strained to hear the chant and searched for the building's entrance, a voice cut through the eeriness, causing her heart to plummet in terror.

"How do we help them?"

57 spun around, her eyes widening in shock when she saw Senator Alden standing next to her staring up at the roof. She watched in horror as the convoy safely parked their vehicles, while her police escort and team of secret service agents cordoned off the area. Many of the officers had also noticed the figures perched on the roof's edge and were urgently calling it in.

"What are you doing?!" 57 shouted. "Get back in the car! Someone will see us together!"

"I know," Leera nodded firmly. "I don't care if we get seen. I care about helping these people! So how can we help?"

"Politicians do not speak to cultists about to commit mass suicide!"

"This is what you do," Leera replied calmly. "I want to help!"

"You can help me by following my orders!" 57 said. "Get in the car or I will force you!"

"Do that and I'll scream," Leera replied cheekily. "I could have you arrested for assaulting a senator."

"Ok, just follow me! And tell your escort to stay down here!"

57 and Senator Alden found the entrance to the building and went inside. As she looked for the stairs to the roof, the senator ordered her police escort and secret service agents to remain outside and not to do anything that could spook the people on the roof.

The building they were in appeared abandoned, and 57 guessed that it was being repaired and repurposed. Since no one was there, 57 then rounded on Leera for her rash actions.

"Now everyone with a camera is going to know about us!"

"And what's wrong with that? I'm not ashamed! Are you ashamed of me, little sister?"

57 lifted her finger and pointed at her sister, but she grumbled as they climbed the stairs.

"I have never been ashamed," 57 stated. "But look at us! Think about how it looks that a U.S. Senator has a twin who is an amborg!"

"Of course I've thought about it!" Leera replied. "I've thought about it every day since we first met!"

57 couldn't forget that evening. Dr. Kendrick had been invited to attend a congressional banquet filled with influential people. The politicians and the government officials had always bored 57, but that night, when she was on Dr.

Kendrick's protective detail, a chance encounter in the bathroom had rocked the foundation of their lives right down to their core being.

57 and Leera found themselves in the women's restroom at the same time, and when their eyes met, they froze on the spot. At first, they suspected they were victims of some kind of elaborate mirror prank. Then, after talking to each other for a few moments, they both got out of there and avoided each other the rest of the evening. After that, 57 had reached out and discreetly learned that they both shared the same DNA. The revelation that they were twins filled them with joy, as they realized they'd been separated at birth, unaware of each other's existence for years.

"You've thought about us, right?"

Leera's question interrupted 57's train of thought.

"Of course I have," she replied honestly.

"What's wrong with wanting people to know that this entire time, I've had an identical twin sister?" she spoke softly. "What's wrong with me sharing how thrilled I feel knowing that someone like you exists and that we're related?"

"I get it!" 57 said sharply.

"No you don't," Leera stated as they reached the last flight of stairs. "I've wanted to say that I love you for a long time! Both of us were alone for so many years and I'm tired of having to walk on eggshells around you! I'm tired of our differences always causing a rift between us! You do that calculating thing you amborgs do and tell me what's wrong about that? What's so wrong with wanting a sister I can connect with?"

"A-alright alright!" 57 stammered. "We'll talk about this later!"

This didn't seem to satisfy Senator Alden at all, but she nodded as the two of them made it to the roof.

"Geez," 57 muttered. "You've been holding that in for a while, haven't you?"

"A few years," Leera replied. "Wow, it feels good to finally say that to you."

57 opened the door to the roof and the two of them stepped out. The chanting grew louder and seemed to be getting worse.

"Let our souls be harvested and the worthy will be free!"

"All hail, children of the stars."

57 led Senator Alden towards the group, which appeared to be made up of teenagers who were all facing away from them. She called out to them. "Hey!" 57 initiated contact. "How about we get off that ledge?"

One of them, a boy who looked to be in his mid teens, turned to them and smiled. He shook his head politely.

"No," he said. "It's ok! This was all prophesied!"

"This takes 'he is risen' to the extreme," 57 turned to her sister, who was staring fearfully at the group.

"Not even my church gatherings are this intense," Leera whispered.

The boy continued to wave his hands and plead to 57.

"The star harvesters will descend and take us on a pilgrimage! The great journey!"

"All hail, children of the stars."

57 was growing a bit tired of the chanting. It seemed as though this boy was the leader of this particular small group. They had to figure out a solution, and fast.

"This great journey will lead us to salvation and our souls will be healed, so sayeth the prophet Elijah."

"Oh great," 57 sighed. She whispered to Leera, "Some nutjob thinks himself to be so high and mighty..."

Leera stepped forward to speak to the boy.

"So, you don't think that the alien invasion is an alien invasion?"

"It is our salvation that comes!" the boy smiled back at her. "We will be free once they arrive on our planet. Then we step out at the appropriate time to be embraced and welcomed into their interstellar arms."

These teens really thought the Tandeeri were basically the same as God? It was a combination of science-fiction and religion morphed into some twisted delusion.

The boy's eyes twitched, and his unsettling grin continued to scare the crap out of 57 and Leera. They watched him link up with his friends again, and they resumed their chanting. Fortunately, it didn't seem like they were about to jump, so they huddled a few steps away to form a plan.

"What are you thinking?"

"I don't know," 57 shook her head. "I can't leave until we get them off the ledge. The nearest fire crew might not make it in time."

"What if we kept them talking?" Leera asked. "You know? Stop them from their weird creepy chanting and get them to think for a second?"

57 tilted her head but nodded. She decided to let her sister take the lead. Leera straightened her jacket, took a deep breath, and stepped closer to the group again.

"Excuse me?"

They stopped chanting and turned their heads to glance back at her.

"Uh," she paused, then spoke optimistically. "I have a question!"

The same boy, the supposed leader, glowered at them.

"The time for questions is done," he said sourly.

The entire group faced forward. 57 and Leera's eyes grew wide as they noticed their feet shift slightly.

"Wait, wait, wait!" Leera exclaimed. "Whoa, whoa! Listen! I... uh... whoa! Uh... my question was, who's Elijah?"

The boy looked over his shoulder while the others continued to face forward. He smiled at the mention of Elijah's name.

"Yeah," Leera nodded when she realized she had gotten through to him. "You mentioned him earlier! Elijah? Tell me about him?"

"He is the prophet! The one who taught us to cast away our earthly possessions!"

"Did he by any chance keep your possessions away from you?" 57 asked.

The boy looked at 57.

"No," he forced out immediately.

57 could instantly tell that was a lie.

"Their prophet is a scammer," she muttered to Leera.

Leera and 57 listened as the boy spoke again.

"He has taught us the truth!" he exclaimed.

"About... the aliens?" Leera asked with a puzzled expression.

"They are souls from another universe!"

"That's not entirely wrong," 57 muttered. Then she had an idea. "So where is Elijah today? Is he here?"

"No," the boy answered with a huge, crazed grin. "He's joining us when we ascend to the heavens!"

"Oh," 57 nodded, making sure that the boy could see her expression. "Is Elijah the prophet on another roof then?"

"No," the boy shook his head and looked down. "This is the one true spot where we all ascend!"

"And yet, he's not here," 57 argued. "Believe me when I say, I've ascended from better rooftops and that says a lot."

The boy's smile faded as he shook his head again, appearing confused.

"What's your name?" Leera asked gently.

"David," the boy said.

"One of my brothers is named David," 57 nodded. "Mind telling us how old you are, David?"

"I'm 16," David replied. "It's the age of the chosen."

"Are you scared?" 57 asked.

David shook his head a third time. He wasn't smiling anymore, but they could see that the conversation was getting through to him.

"N-no," he stammered. "I-I'm at peace! It's that..."

David peered over the edge and then quickly turned back to them.

"I just don't like heights," he said nervously.

"I don't blame you," 57 held up her arms and shrugged. "It is a long way down. Can I ask you kids something? Why does one need to step off a ledge to ascend?"

Her question seemed to hook the rest of them in. The group, still holding hands, exchanged puzzled looks. No one was chanting anymore. Now that they had a moment to think about 57's logic, they began to grow nervous. David, in a last-ditch effort, attempted to argue against them again.

"Because this is the right way," he said. "That's how it must be!"

"Why?" Leera asked.

He paused as he struggled to come up with an answer.

"The spirits love you, right?" Leera asked in a kind voice.

"Right," David nodded.

"They're traveling all this way to see you!" she waved a hand up at the sky, then pointed at the floor. "Do you really think they care how you meet them, as long as you do it with open arms?"

David looked at his group, who all shared the same expressions of concern. He turned to 57, a tear rolling down his cheek.

"It's a test of our faith!" he said weakly.

"There is no doubt that you and your friends have a lot of faith!" Leera nodded sympathetically. "I can feel the devotion! So... why don't you all come down now?"

57 stepped forward and reached her hand out to David.

"Come down from the ledge and we can wait for them together," 57 said softly. "You and I can wait for them on solid ground, ok? I promise, all of you will be ok."

David glanced at 57's hand and then his friends. They were all beginning to turn around. 57 felt a sudden flicker of worry. Would they have to try to reach out and force them back off the ledge? Was it a mistake to have even allowed them the choice to decide? Leera was not a trained specialist and couldn't try to save them if they fell. At the most, 57 had time to maybe grab two of them and dive off the roof after the others if they jumped, but either way, it would be dangerous.

Her worrying quickly turned into relief as David reached out and grabbed her hand. 57 gently led him off the ledge, and the others followed suit. 57 and Leera both gently offered their hands to the kids and pulled them back.

"That was really scary," David shuddered.

"I know how you feel," 57 empathized.

Once the kids were persuaded to head down to the street, the authorities arrived to help secure the area. The delay had taken a bit of time out of Leera's schedule, but she wasn't too worried. Her flight wouldn't leave until she got to the airport, so it was ok for her to be late.

"That was exhilarating!" she said as she clutched her chest. "My heart is pounding! You do stuff like this all the time!"

"I really hope you don't decide to leave office and become an amborg," 57 muttered. "You being a normal human up there with me was terrifying."

"Yeah, but if I was an amborg, we both would have been fine!"

"Leera," 57's eyes widened. "You have to survive the cybernetic enhancement surgeries first!"

"Oh," Leera's face fell. "I forgot about that."

"Just get in the car…"

57 and Leera got back in the same car they'd arrived in. In minutes, they would reach the airport and she would be on a flight back to Washington D.C.

"You did great," she complimented 57.

"Thanks," 57 replied with a grim nod. "You were pretty cool too."

"Ever since the day we met and then you and I had our first private meeting," Leera said softly, "I thought it was so cool that you were one of the strongest human beings in the world. I knew that if I continued serving my country, I could also save lives and affect change the way you do. You're my hero."

"You think I'm a hero?"

"Of course."

Once they reached the airport, the driver pulled into the parking lot and Leera exited the vehicle. 57 also got out to say goodbye to her.

"Well," Leera sighed. "I'll see you around."

"Yeah," 57 smiled.

Neither of them wanted to hug each other in public, so they merely exchanged a courteous farewell.

"You really think I'm a hero?" 57 asked again.

"Yes, of course. Why?"

"You're mine," 57 stated. "You're my hero, too."

Leera had never felt so happy to hear that before in her entire life. Laughter bubbled up from her as 57 cracked an identical grin. Several onlookers and their police escort couldn't help but stare at the sight of the two women, their smiles perfectly in sync. It was an indescribable level of happiness.

Chapter 22: Improvise, Adapt, Overcome

S.C.E. Firestar
Bridge

"With all due respect doctor, if you don't calm down, you will be removed!"

"You're not moving fast enough! Those are my children out there! My amborgs have been kidnapped!"

Commander Ulgo and Dr. Kendrick were engaged in a heated argument. Serina was floating in between them, but her lack of a physical body was not enough to keep them from yelling in each other's faces. All she could do was awkwardly float there and observe.

"Gentlemen!" Admiral Ra'aiah cut in furiously, stalking forward. "Not on my bridge! Security will keep you restrained if necessary!"

"Please Dr. Kendrick!" Serina pleaded. "You're not strong in your condition! Don't fight! You need to calm down!"

Captain Harrelson and his marines stood by with their weapons safely holstered, ready to intervene if necessary. The bridge crew of the Firestar appeared anxious, but ready to defend Commander Ulgo. It felt as though a serious skirmish between two universes was imminent, but Admiral Ra'aiah's commanding presence brought everything to a standstill.

"I'm sorry," she said to Dr. Kendrick, who looked to be on the verge of tears. "They've been taken."

Shortly after laying the groundwork for the Firestar's hit-and-run operations that she'd proposed, the Tandeeri had made another swift move against them. It wasn't until they'd come in dangerously close, still cloaked under their invisibility shield, that they realized it was too late.

The shuttle that arrived at A.I. Industries had been making its way from Earth to rendezvous with them. Unfortunately, squadrons of Tandeeri fighters had appeared out of nowhere and surrounded the shuttle. Before they could fully comprehend the gravity of the situation, the Firestar and the other S.C.E. ships leapt into action to drive the Tandeeri back. By the time Admiral Ra'aiah deployed her fighters, it was too late. The Tandeeri had slipped away, taking with them a very valuable prize.

They were all on the bridge when they received confirmation.

All of them had been on the bridge when they received confirmation. Dr. Kendrick was shocked and outraged. He couldn't believe it was true—his amborgs had been captured by the enemy.

The lack of action taken against this particular discovery was what ignited Dr. Kendrick's angry outburst. But Serina's voice and consistent flashing in front of his eyes made him take a few breaths.

"This was my fault," Admiral Ra'aiah explained as he calmed down. "I didn't think that the Tandeeri would avoid us entirely and intercept the shuttle. Those are my pilots and crew members with your amborgs. Now we need to restrategize. Hopefully we can find some way to get them back alive."

"They aren't... just... amborgs, Admiral," Dr. Kendrick said, breathing heavily through his nose. "These are kids. My. Kids!"

"Your blood pressure, Dr. Kendrick," Serina said anxiously. "Please, let me call the others! We can figure this out!"

"I understand that," Admiral Ra'aiah replied patiently. "But with all due respect, you should let someone who knows how to command this ship to help you."

Dr. Kendrick looked as if he had been punched. Commander Ulgo turned and actually moved to stand side-by-side with him. Serina flashed a pale pink.

"What is going on here?"

Everyone glanced over as 43 step onto the bridge. Shortly after, 117 ran in as well.

"Admiral!" 117 exclaimed urgently. "I have something really important to tell you! But... is what we heard true?"

The large crowd of people gathering around the Admiral's chair made the situation difficult to contain. She fell silent and looked at everyone.

"Ahem. Admiral," Commander Ulgo coughed. "Perhaps?"

He gestured with a slight nod of his head towards her ready room. Admiral Ra'aiah nodded back and let out a sigh. This was getting out of hand, and they needed privacy.

"Thank you Commander," Admiral Ra'aiah responded, then motioned for the entire group to follow her. "Please take over the conn. Let me know if there are any movements. Dr. Kendrick, have you and your friends come to my office. Please?"

"Aye ma'am," Ulgo responded. "Ship-wide reports within ten minutes. Find out who was in that shuttle. We need to prepare emergency rescue plans.

Jensen, find out if there are any family or relatives to the shuttle crew. We have to prepare something. Just in case we need to tell them what's happened."

The group slowly ambled back to Admiral Ra'aiah's ready room. This was the first time that 117 had gone back there. He was impressed with how spacious it was, enough to fit their large group with room to spare.

Dr. Kendrick was still being escorted by 113 and 280. This time, Captain Harrelson and his marines entered the room as well. Serina quickly sent a text to 117, recalling that during the last meeting, the space-jumpers had stationed themselves outside the room to secure the entrance. 43 led 117 inside while Admiral Ra'aiah made her way to her desk.

To 117, her ready room resembled a medium-sized living room. It looked comfortable and cozy, like a CEO's office. It housed a desk and a pair of chairs in front of it. It was always two chairs... Why was it always two? A couch and coffee table lent a homey touch, making it easy to overlook the fact that they were in space. His attention was drawn to the eight-foot scratching post in the corner.

"Uh," 117 opened his mouth, but Serina whispered in the back of his mind.

"Don't ask," she said quickly.

He switched to a private channel.

"Why?" he asked with his mind.

"Now's not the time!"

"Oh, so you're also curious?" 117 asked while everyone settled in.

"I'm-always-curious! Shush!" Serina answered hastily.

This was their cue to pay attention to the matters at hand. As Admiral Ra'aiah spoke to Dr. Kendrick, he transmitted another private message to Serina.

"What kind of cat would need a post that...tall?" he asked.

"Uh, are you talking to me?"

117 turned and saw that 43 was looking at him. She realized that he'd sent his message to her by mistake and smiled.

"You were about to say 'big' weren't you?" she asked with an amused look in her eyes.

"And invite a sexual innuendo?" 117 replied casually while keeping a straight face. "I think not."

"Well, I was curious about it, too since I was in here earlier," 43 replied. "But on duty, I don't think it's appropriate. Since you're not under the admiral's command, maybe she'll be lenient to you if you ask."

"No thanks," 117 said. "I choose life."

"What do you mean there's no plan?!"

43 and 117 ended their private conversation as they snapped back to the current situation.

"I'm sorry, Dr. Kendrick," Admiral Ra'aiah replied. "I don't have an immediate solution to rescue your amborgs and my crewmates."

"That's unacceptable!" Dr. Kendrick slammed his hands on her desk, causing her to lean back slightly. "You have this advanced ship! You have the means! Please!"

"I can't!" she shot back in a futile attempt to calm him down. "The plan I had originally has gone out the window! We need to come up with something else!"

"Send someone to go after them!"

"I meant something else besides that!"

"Hey!!!"

Serina unleashed a bright red flash of light, instantly capturing everyone's attention. The room fell silent as she looked frantically between Dr. Kendrick and Admiral Ra'aiah, whose argument was getting out of hand.

"This isn't helping!" Serina shouted anxiously.

"She's right."

43 cleared her throat.

"Admiral," she declared. "I know that both of you were on the bridge. Would you mind describing what happened? The Tandeeri kidnapped our shuttle?"

117 nodded his head in agreement. Hearing the announcement across the ship was shocking, but how did this happen? There was also something strange about this particular move by the Tandeeri that concerned him.

Dr. Kendrick stepped away from the desk and took one of the chairs. Admiral Ra'aiah looked at 43 and 117, then began to describe what had happened.

"As you already know, the shuttle carrying your reinforcements from Earth was intercepted and captured by the Tandeeri. They did what I was planning to do. Somewhat."

Admiral Ra'aiah explained that the large Tandeeri capital ships had moved in to engage Captain Chastain and the rest of the fleet. At first, they didn't see any of the Tandeeri fighter squadrons, which was odd. When the fleet moved in to attack, they had made their first mistake.

Right as the S.C.E. shuttle, carrying their friends, started its journey toward the Firestar, a massive group of Tandeeri fighters emerged stealthily from Apogee station. Apparently, they'd cloaked themselves, outflanked the shuttle, and quickly surrounded it.

"When their fleet got close, they distracted us," Admiral Ra'aiah sighed. "We were out of position and there was no time to turn back. I sent squadrons to protect your friends. The Tandeeri fighters engaged them in a massive dogfight. There was no way to break their lines."

"We lost contact?" Serina asked fearfully.

"During the battle, we received a transmission from the shuttle. From amborgs... 8 and 9," Admiral Ra'aiah looked at the report and checked to make sure she had gotten it correct. "The Tandeeri used such a huge amount of energy that we barely saw their distress signal. I think the amborgs were attempting to bypass it and use their own power to call us."

Admiral Ra'aiah looked at Dr. Kendrick, then back at 43.

"We lost their signal when they were taken out past the moon," she said. "Blocked and pushed towards the enemy fleet. All attempts to escape? Futile."

Dr. Kendrick buried his face into his hands.

"They're gone?" he breathed.

"I don't think so."

43 glanced around the room. 117 noticed a spark in her eyes. She looked at 117 and thought carefully.

"They took prisoners," she said to him. "They kidnapped them."

"Uh," 117 nodded in confusion. "Yeah? Didn't we just establish that?"

"They didn't shoot down our shuttle," 43 turned to Admiral Ra'aiah. "They took them! Not kill them!"

"I see your point, 43, but where are you going with this?"

43 looked at Dr. Kendrick and moved to put a hand reassuringly on his shoulder.

"They could still be alive!" she said. "This is the first time we've ever seen the Tandeeri take prisoners!"

"That's right," 117 began to realize what she was saying. He also recalled all of the stories 43 had told and the missions she'd been on. "You told us that the Tandeeri never took prisoners. Everything was always left in ruins."

Dr. Kendrick's eyes fluttered open, and a glimmer of hope returned to his expression as he glanced at 43 and the Admiral.

"Then we can go get them!" he exclaimed.

"I can't do that," Admiral Ra'aiah replied.

"Why not?!" Serina asked. "You can't be serious!"

"I can't risk more lives," Admiral Ra'aiah explained. "Especially since we have no feasible methods that will ensure a safe return. Even if I was in touch with them and got permission from the council, they would never allow this mission. My orders are to hold our position and defend Earth at all costs."

She looked at Dr. Kendrick.

"In the long run, I need to prioritize your planet over... one shuttle crew and a small group of amborgs," she said softly.

Serina flashed a deep shade of red as she shook her head.

"Space cowards," she spat. "Typical."

"Serina!"

Admiral Ra'aiah remained silent, but Dr. Kendrick's sudden outburst directed at Serina caused her to lean back a bit. 117 couldn't help but admire her resilience. He'd almost wanted to raise his voice at Serina himself, but decided against it.

"You listen to me," Dr. Kendrick lowered his gaze as Serina obediently turned to face him. "We are still guests aboard a starship from another universe. Admiral Ra'aiah is our best chance at figuring this out. I'm with you, believe me, but we get nowhere by insulting someone who has sacrificed so much to help us."

"Not apologizing," Serina spoke defiantly. She turned to look at the Admiral. "No offense."

"None taken," Admiral Ra'aiah showed both her hands, conceding to them. "Normally, I don't like name-calling, but I think you earned a pass on that one."

"Look," Serina turned back to Dr. Kendrick. "There's a reason why sticking to rules and regulations doesn't always work! We just do it because we can and we must!"

"Still," 117 said cautiously as he stepped forward and interjected. "What you're suggesting is treason, Serina. Even if we aren't part of this ship's crew, we still need to respect their authority!"

"We're not officially part of the S.C.E.!" Serina countered. Despite her small size, 117 edged towards 43 warily. "And yet, we're living in Epsilon and the people taken were from Epsilon, too. So, we get jurisdiction and a say in what we do next! Right?"

"Serina," Dr. Kendrick tilted his head at Admiral Ra'aiah. "The shuttle that was taken was Alpha universe personnel. Also, the shuttle technically belongs to the S.C.E. in this case so both universes would be determining the jurisdiction."

"Admiral," 43 interrupted gently. "They both actually bring up a good point."

Admiral Ra'aiah glanced at the older amborg with interest. She clasped her hands and rested them on her desk.

"I'm listening."

43 pointed at Dr. Kendrick.

"We have no command authority over Dr. Kendrick and his amborgs whatsoever," she explained. "This is quite literally their territory. Perhaps, if they do come up with a rescue plan, it could be done off the books? Besides, jurisdiction applies to them."

"It is?" Captain Harrelson asked from the back. "It feels strange hearing that coming from an alternate universe amborg. Begging your pardon, ma'am."

Admiral Ra'aiah raised an eyebrow as she gazed questionably at 43. She turned to look at the others positively.

"We are floating in your universe's territory, your space, and your solar system," 43 suggested. "Even though it's our shuttle that has been taken by an enemy we are at war with, we can't just stray from our orders if it continues to violate the Epsilon universe's boundaries."

"This sounds way more politically complicated than what I was expecting," Harrelson mumbled.

"Coming to Epsilon without their official permission is by definition, a violation already," 43 told Admiral Ra'aiah. "It's like crossing the border without your passport!"

"Crossing universes *was* the biggest violation of this whole entire mission," Admiral Ra'aiah tilted her head. "Even so, the council determined that the needs outweighed the consequences so we have not committed any territorial violations. They would overrule this decision based on circumstantial evidence."

"Is this a courtroom or a starship?" 117 asked.

"My point is," 43 tried to finish her statement. "We are in their universe and their territory. We are cut off from our home universe and there's no way to receive or send any instructions until more reinforcements arrive. Without a higher branch of the S.C.E. here, Admiral Ra'aiah is the highest rank in our command. But even she would answer to the highest form of government on your Earth."

43 turned her gaze toward Dr. Kendrick as Admiral Ra'aiah looked down thoughtfully, her head slowly beginning to nod in agreement.

"She's right," she said. "If your leaders or the most powerful person on your home planet were to suggest we carry out a rescue mission, they would have to be aware of the situation."

"And he has!" Serina exclaimed giddily. She pointed at Dr. Kendrick. "He actually has!"

Dr. Kendrick blinked.

"Me?" he asked curiously. "I'm not the leader of Earth."

"Technically," 117 stated to the Admiral with a firm nod. "He is. The entire time that we've been in space, Dr. Kendrick maintained plenty of contact with the United Nations and the other world leaders. It's safe to say that he holds a lot of authority and respect from them. I think all we would have to do is ask the U.N. Secretary General for their personal endorsement. It would declare that Dr. John Kendrick, due to the fact that he is one of the smartest human beings on the planet, and also leading us in space, makes him one of the most qualified leaders of the human race. Oh, and he's our commander and the one in charge of us. Technically."

"I think that settles it."

Admiral Ra'aiah cast a supportive look to Dr. Kendrick, who was taking a moment to absorb everything.

"As your planet's advocate and leader of the amborgs of this universe," she declared. "I must issue a formal apology for not immediately assisting you, a trusted ally in this operation. You did recommend that we try to get our crew and your people back, but I failed to do so. I am open to suggestions on what you have in mind. I just hope that your ideas don't involve me taking my ship or fleet away from Earth. Otherwise, I will be disobeying my orders, and my superiors won't like that in my report."

All traces of sadness were gone from his face. Dr. Kendrick straightened his glasses and surveyed the room. The shift in atmosphere felt surreal, but uplifting. He noticed Serina looking up at him, giving an encouraging nod. She had switched back to a light blue color, which meant that she was feeling calmer.

"Huh," he managed to utter as he tried to think. He looked at 117. "So... did I accidentally promote myself to the leader of Earth?"

"I guess when I said, 'take me to your leader,'" 43 smirked, "I actually was taken to the right one."

Dr. Kendrick closed his mouth, bit his lip, and slowly nodded his head. Then he spoke again.

"Serina," he said. "If that's the case, then we need a plan. Or a suggested rescue mission."

"Sure," Serina grinned.

"Oh and Serina," Dr. Kendrick reminded her. "Think crazy."

Serina lit up brightly.

"Way ahead of you," she winked. "I need a few minutes."

"In the meantime, I think I remember 117 coming forward about something," Admiral Ra'aiah nodded. She turned to117. "You had something important to tell us? What was it about?"

"Yes. I..."

117 stopped when he suddenly felt his pocket shake violently. Puzzled, he looked down and reached inside. Argentum was buzzing like a cell phone. He pulled it out, ignoring the rest of them, and started reading the words that were appearing.

117, there is something unsafe about this room, it wrote across the silver surface. *I advise that a search of the room be conducted before discussing the visitor designated Oreo by your friend. Sharing sensitive information is unsafe in this vicinity. Proceed with caution.*

"Admiral," 117 said, forcing a smile, causing her to stare at him suspiciously. He looked around and said the first thing that came to mind to keep the conversation going. "Could you please tell us what that scratching post is for?"

117 held up Argentum for her to read the words on its surface. Admiral Ra'aiah was a bit stunned, but she quietly leaned forward to read the message. On the side, 117 transmitted to Serina.

"I know you're busy, Serina," he said on a private channel. "But please scan the room! Please do a deep and extensive one."

Serina cast an alarmed look at 117 and gave a quick nod. She vanished in a flash of light while 117 sent a transmission to 43. Dr. Kendrick remained seated, watching with keen interest as Admiral Ra'aiah signaled to 117 that she'd finished reading. 113 and 280 both glanced at each other, but stayed silent as they observed carefully.

"The cat scratcher..." she said as she cleared her throat. They noticed that she was beginning to blush. "It's mine. I use it."

"Didn't see that coming," Captain Harrelson raised an eyebrow.

"W-what?" 117 stammered.

All of them stared at the Admiral, who maintained her composure, but her cheeks now burned with embarrassment. Dr. Kendrick looked taken aback. How did she manage to say that with a straight face? As the conversation went on, Serina suddenly appeared in different parts of the room.

Out of the corner of his eye, 117 saw her zoom over to a painting. From there she jumped to one of the lights on the ceiling, then to one of the chairs, and then back to Dr. Kendrick. She flashed a deep shade of red, similar to the alarms that shined when they were in battle, every time she stopped.

"I don't use it for anything... intimate," Admiral Ra'aiah said quietly. "My mother is half-feline. So... when I was born, that technically means that I'm a quarter cat."

"Well that explains why your eyes looked slightly different at times," Dr. Kendrick stared at her, fascinated. "I knew there was something special about you."

"Thank you but not the point," Admiral Ra'aiah spoke softly, which prompted Dr. Kendrick to nod in understanding. "The cat post is for... when I want to scratch something or if I just want to take a nap next to it."

The thought of Admiral Ra'aiah, in uniform, taking a cat nap, popped into 117's head. He immediately deleted the image before it could fully form in his brain. They were all probably thinking the same thing. A grown woman in a military uniform being part kitty was not what they expected to hear at all.

Fortunately, the conversation came to an abrupt halt when Serina suddenly appeared on the desk.

"Discreetly, I found three bugs and hidden cameras," she said informatively. She pointed back at the three locations she had flown to. "They've been temporarily frozen and replaced with false images, so now we can speak freely. I've also filtered the audio with a fake conversation to throw off whoever is listening. Someone is definitely putting a collar on your neck. This might be a very precarious situation we just stumbled into."

"That's amazing Serina," 43 said, impressed. "You're planting a fake conversation?"

"It's a little hard," Serina said with a little bit of strain in her voice. "But while the images are false, I just took audio samples from everyone here and came up with a plausible and easy to believe script."

She then turned to Admiral Ra'aiah and looked up at her curiously. "So... you're part cat?"

"Can we get back on topic now?" Admiral Ra'aiah muttered miserably. "We can discuss my blood habits... later. First things first, lock!"

They heard a click. Everyone looked at the door and saw the light turn red. That must have meant that she had secured the room so no one would accidentally walk in.

"Yes. Indeed. We're getting off-track," Dr. Kendrick nodded. "What's going on 117? Why are we in a secure room?"

"Argentum just warned me..." 117 replied, holding the silver cube up to Dr. Kendrick. "It is... something I inherited."

"That something told me..." Admiral Ra'aiah shifted uncomfortably, "someone has been watching me."

"Admiral," 117 said. "Being watched does make someone feel uncomfortable. But I really need to..."

"My scratching post," she said, ignoring them. Her eyes widened when she came to a realization. "My privacy has been violated."

"Admiral," 43 coughed. "We can deal with that in a moment. 117, please. What's so important that... we have to make sure that we're talking in private?"

"Admiral," 117 nodded and placed Argentum on the desk. "I have to tell you something big. It's a game changer."

If it was going to speak, it could do so... however it wanted. Argentum didn't write anything else. Since there was no more movement, 117 decided to just say it directly.

"501 has, in his custody, right now, on your ship, a Tandeeri baby."

Dr. Kendrick shot up from his chair. He'd been staring at Argentum, but his attention instantly shifted at the mention of 501's name. Admiral Ra'aiah's expression transformed from embarrassment to utter shock. 43 walked over to stand at the Admiral's side, equally stunned.

"Shit," Serina said, turning a pale color.

"501 h-has a *what*?" Dr. Kendrick stuttered.

"Say that again?" 43 and the Admiral said simultaneously.

"Somehow," 117 stated as clearly as he could. He held up both his hands reassuringly. "501 has encountered a Tandeeri baby in a storage closet near the main mess hall. 917, 5, 6, and 3 were the ones who 501 asked to... spread the word because this is pretty much a problem."

"It is obviously a problem," Admiral Ra'aiah replied shakily.

"Can I see the video footage?" Dr. Kendrick asked, lifting a trembling hand. "You did record it right?"

"Oh yeah," 117 replied as he grabbed a data-pad from his pocket and played his memories on it. "Admiral, can you confirm... which we already did, that this alien is not known in any database of your universe?"

43, Admiral Ra'aiah, and Dr. Kendrick focused intently on the screen. It took a few minutes for them to watch the whole conversation between the amborgs involved. By the time the video finished and it showed him and 917 leaving the storage closet, 117 shut off the data-pad.

"Now that I've seen this," the Admiral spoke softly. "This is going to be one hell of a report."

"That's what we said," 117 replied as 43 gave the Admiral a sympathetic pat on the shoulder.

"You were right to come to me first 117," Admiral Ra'aiah said. "This information... if it got out, then I can't even begin to describe what sort of reactions we'd get. For now, we keep this a secret from my crew. Ulgo will find out, given my past experiences trying to hide important secrets from him. So I need to tell him. Unfortunately, I have no ideas at the moment to give... Oreo, back to the enemy fleet. We have standing orders to shoot on sight every time we encounter their fleet."

"But maybe we can try to offer some sort of peace offering?" Serina suggested as she turned a bright purple. "Oreo could be what we could use to... maybe open up talks?"

"A plausible idea," Admiral Ra'aiah sighed. "But my position is not going to be very helpful. I will leave this child to 501. He has taken the responsibility of watching and caring for it, so we need to protect them. We will learn all we can about the Tandeeri. In the meantime, I think 43 and I should focus on who is listening in on my conversations."

"Perhaps we could trace the bugs back to their origin?" Dr. Kendrick suggested.

"That'll work," Serina nodded. "It'd help if I had a physical represent-ation or an actual bug to take a look at. If I knew what it looked like, then I could cross-reference it in the database. Problem is, if we try to physically remove the bugs, they will lose the false imaging I programmed and the added fake conversations. We'd risk alerting whoever is listening in, and I'm already strained to maximum capacity keeping it all blocked out. This technology is way too sophisticated."

"You're broadcasting a fake conversation and false images with everyone in this room," 43 stared. "You can't get a physical copy of one of the bugs?"

"Nobody's perfect," Serina lifted an arm and wiped her holographic forehead.

Before they could continue their conversation, Argentum began to shake and vibrate on the desk, prompting everyone to lean forward to look at the writing it was scribbling.

Master, it read, *If you wouldn't mind, could you place me over one of the devices?*

117 stood up, grabbed Argentum, and went over to the chair where Serina had appeared earlier. Suddenly, more writing popped up.

I am close enough to the listening device, Argentum reported. *Place me back on the Admiral's desk and I will transform into the bug for a visual reference.*

117 placed the silver cube back onto the desk and Argentum began to morph its shape. They watched as it turned into a small cradle, and at its center was an exact copy of what they presumed to be the hidden device in the room. It looked really sophisticated and tiny.

"Well," Admiral Ra'aiah said angrily. "I haven't seen this type of bug in years. Very advanced and difficult to detect."

"I haven't seen those before," 43 said. "But at least we can now try and look for it in the database. If I tried to find information with you, Serina, could you trace it back to its origin?"

"Definitely," Serina nodded. "It'll take time though."

"Alright then," Admiral Ra'aiah stood from her desk. "43 and I will do everything we can to figure out who this interested third party is. We will also be planning an operation to attack the Tandeeri. Now, before you object, let me explain."

Dr. Kendrick also rose to his feet.

"Doctor," she said softly. "You and Serina can come up with a rescue plan. But we need to act like things are not out of place. Now, I'm officially, for my bridge crew to see, planning for an attack against the Tandeeri. It will look like a counterattack. Retaliation for our kidnapped shuttle. The crew will believe that and the fight continues on."

Admiral Ra'aiah walked up to Dr. Kendrick and 117.

"I am afraid that you will have to be the ones to figure out as much as possible about the Tandeeri," she said cautiously. "For your safety, you should tell the rest of the amborgs that it is not safe to wander alone. Gather what information you can and do what you think is necessary."

"Well," Dr. Kendrick sighed. He waved to the Fourth Group amborgs behind him. "117, would you mind if I went to see 501? 280 and 113 can escort me. I think it'd be safer if the space jumpers come, too. I'd like to see what we're dealing with. You do a check and get a handle on where everyone is. Understood?"

"You got it," 117 nodded.

"Serina," Dr. Kendrick said as they all prepared to leave the office. "You know what to do, right?"

"Yup," Serina winked. "The audio and images will return to normal the instant we leave."

As they left, Admiral Ra'aiah and 43 walked over to Commander Ulgo. Serina stayed with 43 while Dr. Kendrick and 117 went to the elevators. As the doors opened, 1 and 2 flew out.

"Dr. Kendrick!" 1 said desperately. "Is it true what happened?"

"Déjà vu," 117 sighed.

"Excellent timing," Dr. Kendrick said with a reassuring smile. "1 and 2, you're coming with us. We're going to find 501. We can explain everything. Come along."

"What?" 2 asked, raising an eyebrow.

"Get back in the elevator and we'll explain all that we can," Dr. Kendrick said.

He and 117 ushered them back in the elevator and, without a word, 113 and 280 joined in and mimicked the motion of pushing the First Group leaders inside. Captain Harrelson and his marines cheerfully followed them in.

"117," Dr. Kendrick said. "Your brothers wanted to ask you how you were feeling. Personally, I don't need to hear it again. Wasn't there something confidential you wanted to tell them about?"

117 nodded and then transferred his messages to 1 and 2 privately. While Dr. Kendrick continued to make small talk, he discreetly passed on to them what they had missed.

Out of nowhere, the amborgs received a call on the emergency channel. They quietly checked it and saw it was from 917.

"917 to all amborgs, can anyone read me?"

117 looked at 1 and 2, who both shrugged. He nodded and signaled to the two First Group amborgs that he would take the call. He was the leader of the Second Group, after all.

"117 responding to the emergency channel," he said as the others stood by silently. Dr. Kendrick kept making small talk to Captain Harrelson while the amborgs focused on the channel. "917, go ahead. What's wrong?"

"I've lost contact with Angel."

117 glanced at 280 and 113. The two of them blinked once, but didn't even crack a facial muscle. 1 and 2 looked worried, reminding 117 that there were still some human emotions circulating among them.

"What do you mean?"

"Well, if you try to call her," 917 replied, "you'll notice it going straight to voicemail."

"Well, if she doesn't want to talk, that's common. Right?"

"Really?" 917 asked.

117 picked up on 917's irritation loud and clear. In fact, he practically felt the word jab in his ears.

"The only reason I was calling her was because she tried to call me first," he explained. "Right as I was about to accept the call, it disconnected. All my calls to her after that have been unanswered."

117 looked at the others. They all stood there silently, tuning in to the channel. There were three main reasons why an amborg would go quiet after attempting to reach out to someone. First, 999 could have suddenly encountered something that required immediate attention. Second, she could have dialed the wrong number, which seemed unlikely. Or the third reason...

"She's under attack," 117 guessed.

"I agree and I really hope we're both wrong," 917 replied quickly.

"All amborgs," 117 declared into the channel. "999 has gone silent. 917 and I will be responding. Please standby. We will check in soon."

117 hurriedly asked the other amborgs to fill Dr. Kendrick in on what was happening. As soon as the elevator reached the deck with the archives, he rushed over. Once inside, he noticed 917 handing over his weapons to the receptionist.

"Hey," he acknowledged as he undid the gun holster around his waist. "What's up?"

117 noticed a sign that warned visitors to turn in their weapons before entering the archives. The receptionist had a tray where 917 was stashing his gear. As 117 put his gun in the same tray, he realized that 917's collapsible sword wasn't in there. He was probably keeping it on him discreetly as a precaution.

"The receptionist hasn't seen her leave," 917 nodded politely to the lady at the desk. "Then I heard the announcement that amborgs had been kidnapped, so I got worried."

"There's no way that could happen," 117 replied. "She's still onboard and her beacon is inside the archives."

"Even so," 917 said as the two of them entered the doors. They passed a security scanner that looked a lot like the ones found at airport terminals. "Come help me find her. I'm a little creeped out to be alone right now. That's why I used the emergency channel. Just in case I, you know, mysteriously vanish, too."

"Now you're giving me chills," 117 replied nervously.

They carefully stepped through to the other side, where a soft blue light illuminated the entire area in front of them. The aisleways and shelves glowed in a soothing spectrum of colors, providing a sense of visual comfort. As the door hissed shut behind them, they quickly power-walked down the halls. The archives were basically a futuristic, high-tech library, almost resembling a temple of light and wisdom.

117 and 917 looked behind them frequently as they checked the aisles. It was empty. Occasionally, they would walk past an officer sitting at a table or working on one of the computer terminals. They moved cautiously to avoid attracting unwanted attention and arousing suspicion. Even though there were a few others, the silence was slightly uncomfortable.

"What did the Admiral say?" 917 asked on a private channel.

"Probably what you would expect," 117 answered. "She knows about Oreo, but she doesn't have a plan. Tried hard to hide it by sounding confident but..."

"We're basically screwed, right?" 917 asked. "And now we have amborgs that have been captured."

"Yup."

"What are we going to do about that?"

117 turned to 917, and they both displayed the same level of concern. Of course, the awkward pause and hesitation meant that there was no plan. It was still in the works.

"Serina is thinking of something," 117 answered.

"Ah, that makes me feel a little better," 917 nodded.

They peered around a corner, but didn't find anything. Then, 917 asked 117 a question.

"Do you think it was because we have Oreo that the others were taken?"

"What do you mean?"

"Pretty common scenario," 917 explained. "Some people get angry when you cross the line and target their families. I mean... 18 has the perfect lecture about honor and structure in the Italian la famiglias. You go near a girlfriend or newborn infant of Alberto Biagino and see if you get away with that without consequences."

917 grabbed 117's shoulder and the two of them stopped. He looked around and made sure they weren't being watched. Even if they were mentally speaking to each other, they were still in a public setting.

"What if the Tandeeri think we kidnapped Oreo?" 917 whispered. "And then they kidnapped our people in response?"

"A symbolic move," 117 said, thinking about the shuttle struggling to make its way to the Firestar. "Either way, both sides must be angry. What if the next attack gets worse?"

"We need to get Oreo back before it's too late," 917 said. "As impossible as it sounds, we have to help 501 come up with something now. It's not safe for the kid if it stays here."

"The Admiral did say we aren't actually members of the S.C.E.," 117 pointed out, prompting a curious glance from 917. "So... we don't actually have to follow their orders."

"Hmm," 917 nodded as the two of them walked down another aisle. "That might be easier to work with than nothing."

"Did you hear that?"

Both of them stopped. 117 thought he had imagined it, but they trained their ears towards the end of the corridor. They were in a section of the archives that housed a set of private booths, designed for individuals to study, read, or browse in peace without interruptions from the outside world.

"501 told me that Angel took one of these booths when she first came in," 917 whispered. "Looks like we found them."

"Yeah," 117 said as they walked down past each one. "But I know I heard something. It's coming from the one at the end."

The two of them sprinted over to the last booth and found 999. She was indeed there, but the problem was, she wasn't alone.

"What the hell is that?!" 917's eyes widened in terror.

The first thing they saw was a robot holding 999 by the neck, pinning her against the wall. It was bipedal and humanoid in shape, similar to their security drones, but less blocky and more refined. It exuded a sleek and menacing aura, painted in deep, shadowy colors. Its eyes, two glowing red slits, remained locked on 999 the entire time.

Her face was covered in bruises and the entire inside of the booth showed signs of a deadly, close-quarters battle. The robot, its grip unyielding around her neck, abruptly extended one of its arms and unleashed a flurry of punches to her ribs.

"Angel!" 917 shouted as he tried to open the door. "Damn it! Our weapons are back at the entrance!"

They had nothing to shoot at the glass or the door with. Going back to the receptionist would be a waste of time. 917 placed his hands on the door's surface and tried to scan the materials for any weak points to strike at.

117 glanced through one of the windows and tried to figure out if there was a way to enter from the side. It didn't look like 999 was going to last long. Without hesitation, 117 raised his foot and aimed a powerful kick at the glass. There was a loud bong as he heard the glass vibrate slightly from the impact, but it didn't even crack. He let out a frustrated yell.

The situation took an unexpected turn. The commotion outside attracted the robot's attention. As it shifted its gaze toward 117 and 917, its red eyes locking onto them, it inadvertently loosened its grip on 999 just enough. She turned her eyes weakly to the both of them standing helplessly outside the booth. The sight sparked a glimmer of hope within her, and with the last ounce of strength she had, she refocused, reigniting her will to fight. 117 watched as she seized the opportunity and grabbed onto the arm holding her throat. With her bare hands, she strained and crushed the joints of the robot's arm in massive power grip. The broken joints released her, and she fell to the ground. However, the robot quickly pivoted to confront her and kneed her in the face.

She clutched her nose, but resumed struggling against the ensuing onslaught of her enemy.

17 dashed over to the door, lending a hand to 917 as they attempted to pry it open. 17 pressed buttons on the wall panel, but it only buzzed in response, glowing red with failure. It was locked from the inside.

"She's not going to last much longer!"

917 reached into his pocket and pulled out the sword that 43 had given him.

"Move 117!" he said as he pressed the button, extending the blade. "I'm going to break in!"

He lifted his arm and prepared to slice the door controls, but 117 stood in place, stopping him.

"No!" 117 said as he reached into his own pocket. "You do that, we could trap her in there!"

He wasn't sure what made him do it but for some reason, 117 felt that asking Argentum for help would be the right move. He looked down at Argentum as 917 changed his plan and began to batter the door. He kept trying to stab and swing his sword, but it only bounced and slid off.

"Argentum!" 117 shouted. "Uhh! Can you turn into a knife? Now?"

To what purpose do you require a stabbing article? Argentum asked as words flowed across the surface. *Remember, violence is never the best option.*

"We're trying to open the door to save 999, and brute force isn't working!" 117 explained quickly, watching as 999 was flung across the table as the robot advanced again. "I need to try and hack the door panel!"

Is that all? I have an alternative, Argentum replied. *Place me near the panel and I will open the door.*

117 immediately positioned the silver cube in front of the panel. Instantly, Argentum flew from his hand and adhered to the surface like a magnet. There was a sharp, electrical buzz as Argentum morphed and disappeared into the panel. The panel flashed in an array of different colors before Argentum shot back out, landing in 117's palm. The door panel turned green.

You are welcome, Argentum said as the door hissed open. *Enemy target is now exposed. You may kill it when ready.*

Ignoring the sadistic comment from the little silver cube, 117 and 917 ran inside and charged the robot. 117 tackled it in the midriff, forcing it into the wall. 917 yelled out as he slashed at the neckline with his sword. The head was sliced clean off the robot's body, but it was still trying to attack 999. As she struggled to escape, 117 kept the robot pinned, and then 917 went to work.

With a powerful swing of his sword, he severed the rest of the robot's limbs. Just as the robot's chest was about to hit the ground, he lunged forward and plunged his blade deep into its core. This final strike did the job; the robot whined before its lights dimmed and it collapsed lifelessly.

"Argentum?" 117 panted as he held the silver cube up to the dead robot. "Is this thing dead?"

I can confirm no readings, Argentum replied. *Good kill, 917. The danger has been averted.*

117 knelt down and scanned the robot, while 917 sheathed his sword and went to go help 999, who was coughing. He'd never seen anything like it aboard the ship before. It had to have a specific purpose.

"Alice," 917 said breathlessly as he knelt beside her. "What was that?"

"I don't know," 999 coughed and allowed him to wrap his arms around her waist. "Some kind of assassin drone? I took a bathroom and water break. That's when I called you. I felt... something strange before going back inside my booth."

999 looked around frantically as she struggled to catch her breath. 117 continued to listen while he inspected the broken enemy robot, its pieces strewn all over the place. She uneasily shuffled away from it, fearing that it would stand back up as 917 checked her injuries.

"I felt like something followed me and then I saw its red eyes appear," she continued. "Before I could shut the door, it came and locked us in. Didn't say a thing. I was trapped. It blocked my signal. Couldn't call for help. I remember hearing that the others were taken by the Tandeeri and then this. I felt... afraid."

999 buried her face in 917's shoulder.

"It was like... Before we were found... We...," 999 said, breathing heavily. "I couldn't fight it off. I couldn't run away. It cut me off. I needed to cry but... no one heard me. I thought I was dead."

"It's ok," 917 said, holding her in a soft embrace. "We're here now. Your nightmares will never come back. I promise."

999 kept her face hidden from the two of them, her breaths gradually becoming steadier as she found comfort in their presence. 117 turned away and kept examining the damage. Though she wasn't crying, she still cared about her appearance. Both of them understood why she couldn't bear to show

her face. It was a hard-won victory, but she had been through a terrifying and traumatic experience.

"What's with you and all these deadlock duels?" 917 sighed in relief as he held onto her.

"I had it handled," 999 replied.

"I know," he chuckled reassuringly.

"You called me Alice. Why?"

917 looked down at 999.

"Yeah I did," he nodded. "Because that's your name."

"But you always use Angel. You said you liked that one better."

"Yeah, but I thought I was losing you, right in front of me."

"Uh, I'm still here," 117 awkwardly cleared his throat.

999 withdrew from 917's shoulder and nodded. With him helping, she was able to get back up to her feet. They cautiously walked over to 117, who was examining the robot remains with Argentum.

"I've never seen this kind of robot before," 117 said. He had a flashback of the giant behemoth robots from the Dominoe Incident. He shuddered. "Did somebody build another army to kill us?"

"It doesn't look Tandeeri," 917 said. "But it was trying to kill her."

"Maybe it was what I found," 999 groaned as 917 helped her stand up.

917 pulled out a rag and wiped her forehead. She nodded her thanks and they all sat down at the table. 117 pushed the destroyed parts off the table but still, the three of them took seats as far away from it as they could. They had seen enough films that taught them that it could still come back to life.

999 showed them the data pad that she'd put together. Then she said something familiar that 917 had heard earlier.

"I know who started this war," she declared. "It has to end peacefully because it's all wrong. We've been dragged into something much bigger than we thought."

Chapter 23: Watch your back

"You figured out this entire war? In less than two days aboard this ship?"

"You'd be surprised at what people can do when they're properly motivated."

917 and 117 exchanged glances while 999 continued to load the files she had on her data pad. She also pulled out a thick stack of handwritten notes.

"I pulled files concerning every single past battle with the Tandeeri," she explained. "Ship engagements, colony attacks, sightings, and every encounter. When I started looking more into those files and reports, I found that most of them are sealed."

"That's kind of common in warfare, isn't it?" 117 asked. "Classified documents and any information that is disclosed without authorization could harm or damage national security back home. In this case, interstellar security?"

"I thought so too," 999 shrugged. "But why would something as simple as colony attacks and after-action reports threaten to lock me out? It doesn't make sense."

Before she explained what she had found, she gave a quick description of the S.C.E. procedure.

"After every fleet battle or engagement in space," 999 said, "the mission, details of the military operations, and after-action reports are always reviewed by a panel of admirals and by one designated individual called a 'Judge.' Now, since the Alpha fleet and starships here are cut off from their home universe, there's no panel. There's no way to establish a connection with them unless they keep a wormhole open for a short and sustained period of time."

She handed them papers that included dates and locations to look over. Half of them had red lines through them.

"Those red lines are all the missions that never had after-action reviews done by a board of admirals," 999 explained. "If the S.C.E. is this sophisticated and super futuristic organization, why are some of the reports redacted or simply not there? These reports are supposed to be public information so that the officers, captains, and commanders of the S.C.E. can be held accountable."

"So you were trying to pull up these reports?" 117 asked. "Or at least find them?"

"Yes," 999 nodded. "I wanted to read and listen to all of the survivors. Anyone that fought the Tandeeri or was there during those battles has to have some insight. Problem is, I don't think someone liked that I was investigating this. I think that when I got too close after my computer system threatened to terminate my clearance, I decided… to hack the system. It might have been what triggered the robot."

"Did you find what you were looking for?" 917 asked.

"You know how history is always written by whoever wins? The ones who are alive are the ones who determine the outcome," 999 stated. "Apparently, it was enough to get me marked for death."

"So, we're back to square one?" 117 asked calmly. "It sounds like you don't have an actual answer."

"I only have theories," 999 sighed. "The first one being that the S.C.E. are the ones who have been escalating this war. Not the Tandeeri."

"Even if that's a theory," 117 replied, looking impressed. "That's still a pretty serious one. Bold claim."

"I think that someone," 999 looked around and checked outside the windows of the booth. There was no one watching them, so she continued talking. "Or some group inside the S.C.E. are attempting to rewrite history or trying to shape this war in a direction that they want it to go."

"Yeah," 917 muttered as he picked up a data pad. "Intelligence that fears intelligence."

"And amborgs prefer to get to the bottom of secret plots," 999 said, eyeing the dead robot in between typing. "Even the crazy ones."

"So what was it that was restricted?" 117 asked.

"Ground battles and the destruction of colonies all across the Alpha universe. Ow, careful."

917 apologized as he gently dabbed some ointment over the bruises on her head.

"Something catch your eye?"

"Nothing," 999 shook her head. "That's what I'm telling you though. There's no footage or any video evidence of the Tandeeri appearing on a planet or at a colony that was eventually destroyed. Then I thought about us."

"Us?" 917 asked.

"117 got really upset when he found out his Alpha was dead," 999 stated.

"I wasn't that upset," 117 replied.

917 and 999 both looked at him. Her cold stare made him nod and admit the truth.

"Fine," he sighed. "I was really upset."

"Were you?" 999 turned to 917. "How did you feel?"

"I wasn't surprised," 917 shrugged. "Of course, I only found out for sure when 43 did that big speech filled with heartbreak and despair during your deadlock duel. But... how I felt? I felt a little sad about it."

"Would it help if I told you that you died very admirably?"

"I'm listening," 917 perked up.

"General James Weaver," 999 showed him a file. "That was your human name in the Alpha universe."

"I'm sorry," 917 looked slightly surprised. "James Weaver? That's the best that my Alpha could come up with?"

"Can we finish listening before another murder bot comes after us?" 117 said as he uneasily kept checking on the robot's corpse on the floor.

"Sorry," 917 sighed as he gazed at 999. "Continue."

"Your Alpha was one of the first amborg casualties just after the S.C.E. encountered the Tandeeri," she replied. "You and I both were."

"Whoa," 117 looked at the file. Their eyes widened in shock as they finished the report. "You were both killed in action."

"James and Alicia Weaver," 917 read out loud. "Decorated heroes of the S.C.E. were lost when the Tandeeri invaded and destroyed Centuria Rosa colony. No survivors when fleet reinforcements arrived. Hold on..."

"Exactly," 999 interrupted. "I haven't found any evidence that the Tandeeri were even there."

"But wait," 917 cleared his throat and leaned forward. "Our last names were Weaver."

He turned to 999, who awkwardly avoided his gaze. 117 looked at them inquisitively. The fact that their Alpha versions had the same last name meant one thing.

"We were married?" he asked, dumbfounded.

"Yes," 999 nodded. "43 told me that after my Alpha was injured during a mission, it made the two of us... them, think really seriously about the future."

"You knew this whole time?" 917 asked curiously.

"I did," 999 mumbled. "If you actually took the time to read about stuff like this..."

999 glanced at 117, who merely shrugged.

"What?" he asked softly.

"Aren't you going to ask me to get back on track?"

117 nodded in understanding.

"Right," he murmured as they went back to reading the files. "Can we talk about your... alternate relationship later?"

"Sorry," 917 nodded, dropping the matter.

"Every ship that responded to the Centuria Rosa attack had their files pulled and redacted," 999 stated. "But everything that I could find and pull up, everyone kept saying the same exact thing."

"The Tandeeri weren't at Centuria Rosa," 117 said.

117 and 917 both silently stared at 999.

"If the Tandeeri weren't there," 917 said quietly. "Who was? And who was responsible for our deaths?"

The three of them glanced at the broken robot on the floor. It just lay there, completely lifeless. They nervously waited for it to spring back to life, but nothing happened. Who did this robot belong to? Could they be the ones responsible?

"Any chance we could find anyone that could tell us about Centuria Rosa?" 117 asked.

"They're all dead," 999 stated. "Every ship that responded. Every person that reported that the Tandeeri weren't there... They're all gone. Missing or killed in action."

117 and 917 both fell silent. From what she was saying, it sounded like there were no witnesses. This was starting to feel extremely creepy.

"I felt the exact same way," 999 mumbled. "I think everything about this mission is a trap. If we stay aboard this ship, we will die."

"You don't know that for sure," 917 whispered.

"Oh really?" 999 asked, not taking her eyes off the dead robot. "Most of the video footage of the battles between the Tandeeri and the S.C.E. is all space combat. How is it that no one has seen or found any footage of a ground assault?"

999 showed them a compilation of video recordings and public images that the S.C.E released over the years. 117 and 917 looked at it carefully, then turned to scan the area around them, keeping an eye out for any other surprise attacks.

"Relax," she said. "Most of the files on this data pad are public record. I didn't use this one to look at anything classified. Just look."

The two of them reviewed the footage and everything reported by the media about the Tandeeri war. They read social media posts and sifted through many articles. 999 was right, there was no ground battle to be seen anywhere.

"Not one sighting of an actual live Tandeeri," she said.

117 and 917 snuck another glance at each other. Thanks to 501, her statement was about to be proven false. However, they decided it would be best to reveal that after her presentation.

"Look at all these deaths at the start of the whole war since the first contact," she activated a projector on the table and a map illuminated the center of the booth. "Outposts, colonies, spaceports... all destroyed. Alien embassies and cities attacked across several quadrants. All these planets and systems that came under attack are sporadic and out of the way..."

They saw several planets, systems, and territories appear on the map. Many regions were color-coded depending on what faction they belonged to. They saw blue, red, green, and orange, but it wasn't entirely clear to them.

"The Tandeeri are not the ones attacking," 999 stated.

It was a bold declaration, but 917 and 117 didn't completely buy it. It wasn't because they didn't trust her perspective. They had to wait patiently for her evidence to support her theory.

"Look at where we died."

999 began to highlight pulsing red dots that seemed to be close to the edge of planets that were marked in the blue region. 117 tilted his head.

"Everything in the blue region is S.C.E. territory," 999 pointed. "117. Your Alpha died here. Sent to maintain defense of the Kovark-S.C.E. joint colony. Killed in action when the Tandeeri eradicated the surface with orbital bombardments. After-action reports are all redacted and sealed, and there's no footage of the battle."

"When?" 117 asked as he looked at the pulsing red light on the map.

"Five years ago."

999 then brought up another dot. This one was also on the edge of the S.C.E. boundaries.

"Amborg 1 was part of a ship tasked with escorting refugees to safe space. All hands were lost when the Tandeeri intercepted them. No survivors. 501 and 466 are presumed missing here. 297's expedition was found decimated at Lunestris Seva. 777 shot down here."

More and more red pulsing dots appeared on the map. 117 began to feel sick as he watched them all start pulsing. Were these all battles that an Alpha amborg had been in? 999 had really done some serious investigating since they arrived aboard the Firestar. Now, it felt like they had stumbled upon something they really shouldn't have.

"If I can take a guess at where this is going," 917 looked at the map in horror. "Why does this entire war feel like a convenient means of getting rid of the amborgs?"

"I'm more or less going to agree with 917," 117 gulped. "I think it might be because someone was trying to avoid one of us figuring all of this out."

They both turned to 999, who looked down at them.

"Someone is trying to silence us," she said.

"But what about Alpha A.I. Industries?" 917 asked. "Alpha Dr. Kendrick? 43 said that he was alive, right?"

"There's no way to contact him or the other universe's A.I. Industries," 999 shook her head. "Not unless we go to the Alpha universe ourselves."

"There's also another pattern I see on this map," 117 said as he leaned forward. "Every battle with the Tandeeri are all avoiding the center of the S.C.E. systems."

"That's what I want to show next," 999 nodded eagerly.

999 tapped a button and the pulsing red lights stopped. Within the blue region on the map, she highlighted several big blue dots. They noticed that these were planets and different systems.

"Every blue dot here represents the major colonies and home planets for all species and members of the S.C.E. None of them intersect with a red dot," she said. "Most of these are military bases, spaceports, and capital worlds that the Tandeeri have never gone near. If they have such superior technology and the S.C.E. are losing the war, why does it look like they seem to be conveniently hanging around there?"

"A lot of battle tactics involve fighting on outlying outposts before you begin an invasion," 117 said. "But I assume you're about to tell me I'm wrong?"

"This isn't smart 117," 999 looked at him and pointed at the map. "You could lead videogame troops better than whatever all of this is. Why don't the Tandeeri just make a beeline for the S.C.E. Council? Why don't they try and take Earth? We have seen firsthand how powerful they are, and they don't even try to end this war? These red dots should be in the shape of a straight line right to the heart of the S.C.E. but instead, they're all over the place. Either they're really terrible at strategy or someone is using them as a scapegoat."

"117," 917 chuckled nervously. "I think I see her point clearly now."

117 looked past the map at the robot remains again. The bugs in Admiral Ra'aiah's ready room also hinted at something shady going on.

"So... a third party," he muttered. "There's someone that doesn't want us to figure this out. This would make sense, considering what Serina and Argentum discovered earlier."

"Serina and who? What do you mean?"

117 pulled Argentum out of his pocket and set it out on the table. 999 suddenly appeared annoyed, like she had just heard the punchline to a really bad joke. Without a word, she gestured to Argentum, wondering what it was doing on the table. 917 saw her expression and instantly tried to reassure her.

"It's a tool that Alpha 117 left for him," he explained. "It's handier than it looks."

"Your right-hand crawling into the bank to save hostages was handier," 999 replied. "What the hell is this? 117, are you taking advice from a rock?"

"Argentum is not a rock," 117 declared firmly. "But I'm sure it's very sensitive."

917 put a palm to his face as 117's confidence faded fast. They couldn't believe that he had said those words out loud.

"I admit," 999 shut her eyes and exhaled. "This little cube is pretty, but you've gone insane."

Argentum began to shake on the table. The three of them looked at the writing that appeared on one side.

Thank you for your compliment, it wrote, *sarcasm included. My master 117 has not lost his sanity. Everything he's saying is accurate.*

999 shook her head in disbelief. She didn't even feel like questioning all the weird things she'd been seeing lately.

"Your Alpha gave you a sentient pet rock?" she spoke in a trembling voice. "A pet rock?"

"Anyway," 117 explained. He picked up Argentum and pocketed it. "If it weren't for Argentum, we wouldn't have been able to get into the booth to save you. Also, we discovered hidden bugs inside Admiral Ra'aiah's ready room."

"This just got even scarier," 917's eyes widened.

117 explained what they had encountered earlier.

"The Admiral is working right now to figure out where they came from," he said. "Then Oreo and 501... That was just dumb luck or something. This robot and those bugs are connected in some way."

999 glanced at 917.

"Oreo?" she asked.

"There's no way to sugarcoat this. 117, why don't you tell her?"

117 rolled his eyes. Right as he was about to tell her, he suddenly had an idea. Though, he wasn't sure how well they would take it. It would follow the Admiral's recommendation to not follow S.C.E. protocol, but it would definitely involve the amborgs creating a significant amount of trouble. Failure meant putting their lives at risk. The fragile alliance between the S.C.E. and their planet Earth would be in jeopardy.

"117? You're drifting."

117 looked at 917 and 999 as his eyes widened.

"No," 917 stared inquisitively at him. "That's the face he makes when he's got a crazy idea."

"I think it is my turn to be stupid and crazy," 117 said, eyes wide as he took a deep breath. "917. 999. There's a way to end this war. It's a slim chance but we just need to figure out how to transport it."

"Yeah," 917 nodded. He had the same look as well. "And 501 is babysitting it. Oreo just might be the key to our survival."

"What is going on?" 999 shot them an angry and confused look, then stared at them suspiciously. "What are you talking about?"

"Well," 917 sighed. He and 117 exchanged glances. "501..."

"What?" she said warily. Now she was alert. "What did he do now?"

"It's not bad," 117 answered.

This answer was too vague for Angel.

"Now that's bull right there," 999 snapped, but fortunately, she wasn't hostile. Yet. She likely felt too exhausted. "How bad are we talking about? Is it like the time when you allowed him to drink gasoline when he thought it was lemonade?"

117 and 917 glanced at each other briefly. They remembered it like it was yesterday. On 501's birthday one year, 8, 9, 125, and 274 had devised such a clever scheme that many of the others hadn't been able to see it coming at all.

The four of them had spiked 501's glass with an extra ingredient on that special day, which happened to contain gasoline. They'd brewed it so well that nobody detected any trace of it. Even 501 couldn't taste or smell the difference. It was, without a doubt, a successful prank that harbored beautiful and glorious results when he blew out his birthday candles. Many people had been terrified because they thought that 501 had come up with a new and original party trick. Eventually, after they calmed down, everyone laughed because it was the dumbest thing that they had ever seen. Despite nearly burning down the house, 501 had said that it was one of the best birthdays he ever had.

Still, 117 and 917, after they finished reminiscing, shrugged as they faced 999 again. This was probably not as bad as the birthday candle fiasco. Probably.

"It's a little worse than that," 917 said, remembering the amborgs that had the misfortune of being in the line of fire of 501's candles, literally. "Like the time... 501 launched Dr. Kendrick's car into that office."

"That bad?" 999 looked shocked and her eye twitched with anger.

"501 found, discovered, and is currently watching over a Tandeeri baby," 117 stated immediately. "We were on our way to tell you, but you were occupied."

It took a second for her to take all that in. They had originally assumed that she would react in her own unique way. They were right. 999 looked annoyed and began to fume, but she didn't lash out.

"So..." she spoke softly. "It must have been after I yelled at him, and he ran off."

"501 did mention that he had upset you," 917 murmured.

"He has a Tandeeri child under his care?" she asked, clenching the data-pad in her hands as she began to tremble. "An actual one?"

"Yes," 117 nodded.

"So, this is extremely bad," 999 shook her head. "I almost got assassinated and now 501 has a child?"

"Don't you see 999?" 117 said as he leaned forward and placed his hands on the table. "We can bring Oreo back to the Tandeeri and get our friends back. If they accept this olive branch that we're offering, we can be diplomatic and then we can use this as an opportunity to get both sides to stop shooting. Maybe long enough to peacefully resolve this before we all get destroyed."

"Do I want to know why its name is Oreo?" 999 asked.

They both shook their heads.

"Did you stop and consider where in your simplified plan that we were supposed to just bring it back?" she continued bitterly. "How are we supposed to just bring an alien child to the Tandeeri fleet? This is assuming I believe you and that 501 adopted an alien baby. Oh god... he's a parent. Why would you allow that?!"

"What if we stole a ship?"

117 and 999 both turned to look at 917. They waited to see if he would take back his question, but the look on his face showed how much he'd meant what he said.

"What if during a battle or while undercover, we just fly to the Tandeeri?" he said. "117 already told me that we aren't part of the S.C.E. We can just do it without any sort of governing system to stop us."

"Easier said than done," 117 replied. "Even if we did everything correctly, then what? There's no guarantee the Tandeeri won't just shoot us down."

"If we don't go at them with guns blazing, then they probably won't."

"You see, that's the part where the military would say you're crazy," 117 said. "It's out of the question."

"We go by ourselves," 917 argued. "The less that are going, the less that are at risk. 117, what have we got to lose, for crying out loud? Everything that we have done these last few days has been totally improvised. Of course, it's easier to say it than do it. It's because we're choosing whether we want to be the first to act."

"Are you sure that's wise?" 117 replied. "You're acting impulsively based on the motive that you want to get there first. Think about what happened in... I mean... Just think."

"I'm saying that if we wait it out too long," 917 said, "the S.C.E. will do something before we get a solid plan in place, and then it will get worse. It doesn't help that we're being watched by some super-secret spy organization. We have to do this now."

117 turned to 999.

"What do you think?"

999 paused as she took a moment to consider everything they had discussed.

"I'm with him," she stated. "All of your ideas are crazy, but it's a start. You're the leader of the Second Group, so this is your decision."

"The only reason I hesitated slightly was because I wanted to come up with more options before we settled on a plan," 117 said.

"We can do it," 999 nodded. "We... chose to be amborgs because we wanted to do the things most people can't."

117 listened to 999 and immediately thought of how passionate 501 was about caring for Oreo. He wasn't sure whose quirks had rubbed off on who. Many of them had certainly come a long way in terms of their way of thinking.

"Yeah," 917 said with a smirk. "Because every person wants to cross the multiverse, fight on the front lines of an intergalactic war, and peacefully resolve it with murder-bots and unidentified alien races chasing after us. No pressure."

"I can't believe I'm saying this," 999 sighed and sniffed. "But I missed your sarcasm. Let me see your sword."

917, puzzled, grabbed his sword and handed it to her. 999 clicked the button and the blade opened. Suddenly she threw it at the parts of the robot. It went into the head. There was a loud crash, a brief burst of electricity, but there was no further movement. She had a really good aim.

"Sorry," she said looking at 117 and 917, who had both retreated a little. "I thought I saw it move."

"We should get out of here and go inform the Admiral," 917 replied as he went to retrieve his sword.

"Let's go," 117 replied. "We got to go warn the receptionist and security."

"Actually," 999 replied. "If it's all the same, let's keep this under wraps."

999 stood up and reached into her pocket. She pulled out a familiar tool that they had used on several occasions. She threw a red orb at the pile of robot parts. There was a bright flash and then suddenly, the parts disappeared, leaving only the orb behind.

"All clean," she reported as she went to pick it up. "I wouldn't want someone to make this evidence just mysteriously vanish. I'll keep it safe with me until we present it to the Admiral."

"So, we're keeping this confidential?" 117 asked as the three of them gathered all the data-pads. "We should head to the bridge and make sure that none of the amborgs are by themselves."

"Once we step out of this booth," 917 cautioned them, "we need to be careful."

The trio made their way out, treading carefully as they headed back to the archives' entrance. With every aisle way they passed, they kept a watchful eye out for any sudden movement. They remained laser-focused on the task at hand every step of the way. They ignored every crew member they walked past, doing their best to stay calm as they made their exit.

As they exited the archives, the receptionist gave them a polite farewell. 999 turned her face away since the ointment was still working on healing and hiding her bruises. 917 and 117 both smiled at the receptionist to cover for her.

They discreetly checked for any signs that she was aware of what had happened earlier, but didn't detect anything out of the ordinary. Still, they maintained 999's line of thinking. Trust no one.

Once they reached the elevator, they began to make their way to the bridge. 999 pressed the stop button unexpectedly.

"What are you doing?" 917 asked. "Elevators are never a good place to stop randomly."

"Just to be safe," 999 said as she massaged her shoulder. "117, perhaps it would be better to do the head count now? We should use the emergency channel."

"You're probably right."

117 activated his scanner. After having access to the schematics of the S.C.E. Firestar, he was able to project an image of the ship from his bracelet. Green dots appeared all over the ship, indicating where the amborgs were. The amborgs appeared to be grouped or clustered together in certain locations. 117 checked each dot to see which amborgs were together.

"It looks like 466 is with 501," 117 muttered. "1, 2, and 3 are there as well. They're meeting Oreo, I guess. 280 and 113 are escorting Dr. Kendrick, it looks like they're heading to the armory. The rest of the Fourth Group are there. Uhh, 5 and 6 have gone up to the bridge. 249, 593, and 49 are heading to us. Then there's... Wait. Where's 297 and 777?"

As 999 and 917 examined the map, they realized that 117 was right. 777 and 297's beacons weren't anywhere on the ship. They had disappeared.

"It's happening," 917 said fearfully. "Oh no."

"That is not good," 117 said as he quickly tried to call 297. Unfortunately, it went to voicemail. He tried to reach 777, but there was no response. "Just what we need right now. 999 almost gets killed and now two amborgs have gone missing."

"What if they were caught and ejected into space?" 917 asked.

"Not helping," 117 said, feeling shivers crawl up his spine. "Now let's think... When was the last time we saw him?"

"They were in the hangar," 917 replied immediately. "The three of us saw that crashed Tandeeri fighter, almost got killed from the explosion, but we helped the fire crew put it out. After that whole debacle, 501 called me and that's when I left them together to see Oreo."

"Great," 117 began to feel bad for ignoring 297 and 777. "Our best marksman and luckiest amborg haven't been seen since."

"But, their beacons were still on the Firestar," 917 said.

"I know how we can check. Serina?"

"Yo."

117 heard her voice clear as day.

"I need your help," he said. Then he heard some laughter in the background. "Is that 501 in the background?"

"It's so cute!" Serina exclaimed. "Oreo is having a blast! Captain Harrelson and 113 have been playing hide and seek with this little guy! Or girl. Or... gender-neutral Tandeeri! You know, even though the Fourth Group are so uptight, they're so good with kids!"

"Right, right," 117 nodded. "Listen, 917 and 999 are here with me. We need to check on something."

"Sure, sure!" Serina replied. "I have so many pictures and videos to share with you all when we get back!"

117 opened the channel so that 917 and 999 could listen in.

"Serina," 917 said, "the last time I saw 297 and 777 was when the Tandeeri fighter crashed. I left them in the hangar when 501 asked me to meet Oreo."

"Oh you mean when Oreo's ship crashed?"

917 perked up, suddenly looking pleased.

"You agree with me?" he asked.

"Oh yeah," Serina replied casually. "There's no other way that Oreo could have gotten aboard this ship. Unless you want to accuse the little cutie pie of being a stowaway for... who knows how long?"

"What are you talking about?" 999 raised an eyebrow.

"I'll explain later," 917 noticed 117 staring and dipped his head apologetically.

"297 and 777 are missing," 117 said. "We cannot see their beacons onboard the Firestar at all and we can't contact them. Can you find out when they disappeared?"

"That is really not good," Serina replied, concern bleeding into her tone. "Hang on, let me do a quick look at the security footage and cross reference it with all of our beacons when Dr. Kendrick enacted the buddy system."

"Be careful!" 999 blurted out.

917 and 117 turned to look at her, but they knew why she had that reaction, thanks to her wide-eyed expression.

"Hey, Angel!" Serina's voice sounded excited once again. "Be careful of what?"

"Murder bot almost killed her when she was looking at classified files," 117 replied.

999 fell silent as she bit her lip and rubbed her hands awkwardly.

"Just be very careful," she mumbled.

"I always am," Serina replied confidently. "Thanks for the heads up! But you owe me an explanation about the murder bot part."

"I think we owe everyone we trust that explanation..." 117 replied.

"Hey, just finished reviewing all the footage," Serina's response was fast. "You guys are not going to like what those two did..."

A video feed appeared in 117's field of vision. He enhanced the screen and watched. 297 and 777 were frantically talking to a pilot next to one of the S.C.E. shuttles. He sped up the footage and saw the pilot walk away after they finished talking. 297 and 777 then both ran inside the shuttle. He watched in shock as the shuttle actually began moving and then there was a camera change.

"Oh t-those crazy idiots," 917 stammered.

They watched the rest of the footage as the shuttle departed the hangar bay and flew out of the Firestar's airspace. Serina chuckled nervously.

"Yeah," she said, "their beacons flew very far away from the Firestar after the two of them got on that shuttle."

"When was this?" 999 fumed.

"It was right after they heard about the other amborgs being kidnapped by the Tandeeri."

297 and 777 had gone after the Tandeeri fleet.

"What were they thinking?" 117 groaned. "The two of them can't take on the big Tandeeri ships with a shuttle."

Suddenly, another call came in. Everyone paused and looked at each other when they saw who was contacting them.

"297!" they all said simultaneously. "777!"

"Wow, quadruple jinx," Serina snorted.

117 decided to take charge of the phone call as he added it to the channel.

"297!" he exclaimed. "Are you there? Where the hell are you?!"

117 got a lot of static in response. Then, he heard 297's voice come through.

"Yeah... kzzt... about that? Bzzt... 117, can you hear me?!"

"I need help clearing this up," 117 said to the others.

917 and 999 both nodded as they placed their hands on his shoulders. With the three of them combined, they attempted to filter out and lock on to 297's signal.

"I can hear you 297!" 117 replied. "What are you doing?"

"Saw the... krzzz... shuttle taken! I... bzzt... asked the hangar crew... krzztt... Flew out... bzzz... tried to locate...!! Krzztt... The Tandeeri flagship! 777 and I are ok!"

"You're what?!" 117 asked as 917 and 999 began to cringe in pain. Keeping the signal up was getting too hard to maintain. "297! What are you doing over there?!"

"Send...bzzt... help! We're going... bzzt... My communicator is... krzz... overloading! Attempting to board... krzzz... rescue our friends!"

The call suddenly cut off and disconnected from loss of signal. 917 and 999 retracted their hands, and they gasped in relief from the exertion of keeping the transmission intact. 117 tried to call 297 again, but it didn't work. The signal kept going out. It wasn't strong enough.

"Houston," Serina stated as they all looked at each other grimly. "We have another problem."

"Now what?" 917 asked.

"We're going after him," 117 answered softly.

He asked the elevator to take them to the bridge.

Chapter 24: The Rescue Mission Begins

S.C.E. Firestar
Ready Room

"Commander Ulgo?"

Tentatively, 117 stepped onto the bridge, spotting the commander standing at his post next to Admiral Ra'aiah's empty seat. He turned, a frown forming on his face.

"Yes sir?"

"Is Admiral Ra'aiah in her ready room? We need to talk to her."

Commander Ulgo shifted his gaze towards 917 and 999. His eyes lingered a moment longer on 999, but then he turned to 117 and nodded.

"The Admiral and 43 are still inside her ready room."

"Can we just...? You know?"

"Yes sir," Ulgo replied promptly.

117 gave a respectful nod and then turned away. He could feel the commander's piercing gaze burrowing into his back as 917 and 999 followed him to Admiral Ra'aiah's office. Could he be someone that they could trust? Or was he in league with whomever was operating in the shadows?

117 approached the door, which remained closed as he tried to remember how it worked. Glancing to the side, he noticed a panel and pressed the green button. A chime echoed from within, then they heard Admiral Ra'aiah's voice.

"Come in," she called out from inside.

The door slid open with a soft hiss, and the three of them stepped inside. As it closed behind them, they made their way to Admiral Ra'aiah, who was engaged in a discussion with 43 at her desk. 43's eyes widened when she saw 999.

"What happened to you?"

999 shook her head.

"Not until Dr. Kendrick gets here," she declared.

"I agree," Admiral Ra'aiah nodded. "43 and I were using my secure console here to do some digging."

117 privately messaged Serina. He told her where they were and that they needed help securing the room. In an instant, there was a flash of light as she appeared before them.

"You can talk freely now," she said, concentrating hard. "Just don't distract me while I'm fooling the bugs in here. Dr. Kendrick should be back in a few minutes."

"You're wearing a ton of ointment."

43 didn't waste any time at all. She rushed over and gently examined 999 from a respectful distance as 917 and 117 approached the Admiral.

"We have a lot to tell you," 117 stated.

"I understand," Admiral Ra'aiah nodded. "Do you want to go first? Or should we?"

She glanced at 999 with a worried expression.

"Are you alright?"

999 nodded to 43, then to the Admiral.

"Someone tried to kill me for looking at sensitive information. I think I might have gone too far."

"We're all in danger," 117 said. "Two more of my amborgs have jumped ship to go on a self-appointed rescue mission."

"297 and 777," 917 added.

"What?" 43 asked.

"Hold on a second!"

Admiral Ra'aiah held up her hands and waved them up and down like a signalman. The chatter immediately died down, and the room fell silent. Then, 999 stepped forward, sliding her hand into her pocket.

"I just have one question," she stated. "Do you recognize this?"

She pulled the red transport orb out and held it in her hand. Before Admiral Ra'aiah could even ask, 999 clicked the button to eject the contents. A piercing whine emanated from the orb as it sprang open. It released a blinding flash of light, causing everyone to avert their eyes, followed by a thunderous crash as something hit the floor. Shattered metal and scattered components skittered across the floor as if it had been tossed from the back of a car.

"What the hell?"

43 and Admiral Ra'aiah both stared at the robot. 999 watched their reactions closely. While 43 hesitantly backed away, the Admiral's gaze lingered, meticulously examining each part. She seemed quite fascinated, maybe even a bit too much.

"Huh," she gasped. "I never thought I'd ever see one again."

"You know what this is?"

117 and 917 shared a glance and stepped forward. 117 positioned himself on the right, while 917 took the left. In the middle, 999 stood firm, and they all took defensive stances. 43 regarded the three of them, then turned to the Admiral.

"I've heard of it," she held up her hands peacefully. "And before I was promoted to admiral, I saw one murder someone I cared about."

Admiral Ra'aiah stepped forward and pointed down at the remains.

"When I submitted a report, detailing what I had seen," she stated, "it was redacted. They said it was just a mistake. Wrong place at the wrong time. Everyone else decided to forget, but I remembered for years."

A chime sounded at the door. 917 and 117 drew their weapons, aiming them at the entrance. 999 merely turned her head as the room fell silent. Admiral Ra'aiah answered while they kept an eye on the door.

"Who is it?"

"Dr. Kendrick."

Admiral Ra'aiah unlocked the door, and it slid open, allowing him to enter. 117 and 917 quickly hid their arms behind their backs. Dr. Kendrick walked in with 113 and 280 at his side, Captain Harrelson and his squad of marines following closely behind. The entire gang was back in her ready room. Admiral Ra'aiah sighed, experiencing a familiar sense of déjà vu. The door hissed closed as everyone gathered around her furniture.

"Did you just point weapons at the door?" Dr. Kendrick stared at 917 and 117 questionably. "At us?"

The two amborgs slowly holstered their weapons. They nodded.

"It's been a rough day," 117 replied.

"Sorry," 999 stated. "They're just protecting me. I almost died."

As Dr. Kendrick tilted his head, he caught sight of 999's injuries. The second he noticed how much medical ointment they'd used, his expression suddenly shifted to one of pure outrage.

"Who put their hands on you?" his voice trembled angrily.

"Not who," 917 stated. He turned and pointed at the broken heap of parts on the floor. "That."

"What is that?" Captain Harrelson asked as the other space-jumpers whispered and murmured softly among themselves.

"Silent Eclipse."

Everyone looked up at Admiral Ra'aiah, who acknowledged them with a courteous nod. She looked down at the shattered remains of the lifeless robot.

"It's an assassin model."

"Hmm, this is very concerning," Dr. Kendrick kept his eyes glued on the parts and leaned forward. "What a dark design."

The amborgs quickly detailed the events that unfolded in the archives. The atmosphere grew bleak and cold as the entire group listened to 999's investigation.

"So anyway, the files that 999 was looking into triggered... this," 117 said. "It cut her off from us. It's creepier and much scarier when it's alive."

"Well done," Dr. Kendrick patted 117 and 917 on their shoulders. "You managed to protect Angel, and that was good."

"Your theories and statements concerning the Tandeeri are a startling revelation," Admiral Ra'aiah said. "We were all so caught up in fighting this war that we didn't realize that we were being played."

"So," Captain Harrelson muttered. "The entire war was faked? How does that even work?"

"What do you do when you face a bully that hits you?" Dr. Kendrick asked. "Captain?"

"You either do nothing or you hit back," he replied.

"From what Angel just described to us, the S.C.E. has been fighting the Tandeeri over the course of this war," Dr. Kendrick tried to simplify her story as best as he could. "This is what the public knows, correct?"

Admiral Ra'aiah nodded.

"Every battle and every encounter where they are reported," he continued, "the S.C.E. responds and sends their ships in. As the war progressed, military production kicked in. Enlistment rates increased. More ships built, more officers, more people to send into battle against the Tandeeri."

"Yes sir," Captain Harrelson nodded. "Every conflict requires a response."

"The war is a smokescreen," Dr. Kendrick looked at Admiral Ra'aiah like a teacher planning an exam. "If colonies along the borders of the S.C.E. are destroyed, they must be rebuilt. Outposts, military bases, and ports. All of this destruction so that the S.C.E. high command can swoop in and justify all of it by advancing and preparing for a stronger military expansion across their universe. Imagine all of that, but the Tandeeri are the ones being blamed."

"No," 43 shook her head.

"Yes 43," Dr. Kendrick nodded grimly. "The S.C.E. are the ones responsible for this war."

"That's not possible!"

"Think about it," 999 protested, confronting 43. "Your hunt for the Tandeeri has blinded you from who really killed Alpha 117 and your friends. This robot works for whoever killed all the Alpha amborgs. Only someone who craves power would eliminate friends and enemies to make sure that there is no competition to oppose them when they rise to the top. The S.C.E. aren't losing this war, someone is making it look like they are!"

"The military does this sort of thing all the time," 117 looked at Captain Harrelson. "During training, recruits are broken to be built back up so they are stronger. To reach their maximum potential."

"But, who is doing this? Why put the blame on the Tandeeri?" Captain Harrelson asked. "Didn't they attack us?"

"No!"

Everyone looked at 43. Her eyes were widening.

"I'm sorry if my theory destroys everything you vowed to uphold," 999 stated. "I know that you've been hunting the Tandeeri for years. Trying to..."

43 whirled around and interrupted her before she could finish her sentence.

"No, I mean," 43 shook her head. She held up a hand to silence 999. "I think you're right. Also, Captain Harrelson! They didn't attack us!"

43 looked at 117. It was in that brief pause she took to let him think that it dawned on him. The memory could've been pulled up and replayed, but he remembered...

"When they first appeared at Apogee station," she recounted the events they'd witnessed. "We shot them first!"

"They only fought in self-defense," 117 nodded in agreement.

"There's only one organization devious enough to knock down a few pegs in order to get ready to step in with their own agenda," Admiral Ra'aiah stated.

Everyone watched as the Admiral pointed a finger at the dead drone.

"The bugs in my ready room, possibly all over my ship," she muttered. "Allocating personnel, starships, fleets and resources all across our territories to be sacrificed for a war that they were never in control of to begin with. Sending me and my godfather into the Alpha universe... No, that's too much. Now this broken drone confirms it."

Admiral Ra'aiah looked at everyone in the room and spoke the name. "Silent Eclipse."

"That doesn't sound ominous at all…" Serina replied as she continued to concentrate.

"It was originally a covert-ops division within our organization," Admiral Ra'aiah explained to every Alpha-universe citizen in the room. "Infiltration, assassination, elite guerrilla strike tactics, everything you can think of, all in the name of preserving the S.C.E."

"I take it that their methods weren't good for your image?" Dr. Kendrick asked.

"My mother had stories about them when my grandparents fought in the first-contact war against the S.C.E.," she suddenly scanned the crowd and quickly continued. "Yes, my people were very skittish and prone to aggression, which started a brief conflict."

Several people lowered their heads, and there were a few scattered nods. Admiral Ra'aiah had already answered whatever questions were on their minds. Evidently, this wasn't the first time she had to address that subject.

"After a peace was brokered and they came to a settlement, my people joined the organization," Admiral Ra'aiah nodded. "Silent Eclipse had methods that were too extreme and as the S.C.E. continued to expand and induct more systems gradually, they were officially disbanded."

"Well, it looks like someone kept it running," Dr. Kendrick replied. "Do we have any ideas who could be behind this?"

"Anyone in the council," Admiral Ra'aiah answered, shaking her head. "Anyone with money. A commander at a desk job. Someone among the higher ranking admirals. It could be anyone as long as they know what corners to cut and how to hide in plain sight."

117 stepped forward and held his hand up.

"Ok, if we don't know who's running the creepy shadow organization that tried to kill my partner, then can we refocus our efforts?"

999 shared the security footage in the hangar of 297 and 777 boarding one of the shuttles during the last battle. The Admiral watched intently as 117 addressed everyone.

"What we need to deal with right now is the fact that 297 and 777 are over there with the enemy fleet trying to rescue our friends alone," he said. "We have to get out there and try to support them or get them back before they're lost."

"I agree with you David, but there's another problem," Dr. Kendrick said. They heard a faint tink as he kicked a piece of the robot with his foot. "This piece of scrap metal tried to murder your sister amborg under our noses. I have a nagging feeling in the back of my mind."

Dr. Kendrick looked at 43 and Admiral Ra'aiah nervously.

"What if there are more onboard this ship?"

"If there are, then my crew and the families aboard are in danger." Admiral Ra'aiah whispered with a tremble in her voice, her eyes widening in horror. "One of this ship's secondary objectives is to carry on a legacy if the S.C.E. should fall."

"Are you saying what I think you're saying?" 917 asked.

"If something destroys our home," Admiral Ra'aiah explained, "the Firestar is also designed to carry everyone onboard into deep space to locate a new place for us to live if we have nothing to return to. She was built with several other sister ships that had the same contingencies. One of them being to carry enough people to rebuild and repopulate should the worst ever happen."

"So if everything goes south, we would have to worry about another invasion?" Captain Harrelson crossed his arms. "From the S.C.E."

"That would have been a likely scenario if the Tandeeri had won the war against us," Admiral Ra'aiah dipped her head apologetically. "I am sorry for how that sounds, but everyone has emergency contingencies. Even you, right captain?"

"Well," Harrelson shifted slightly. "I have a bunker in my backyard in case of a zombie apocalypse. But nothing for invasion from outer space. Or maybe I could fortify my place to be shielded from nuclear blasts..."

"Anyway," Admiral Ra'aiah looked away, leaving Captain Harrelson to ponder his home improvement choices. "The Firestar would not have claimed Epsilon Earth if things went wrong. We would have left you alone."

"After we were destroyed? Or what about if we won the war?"

"The point is we're all hostages in space," she sighed, quickly getting everyone back on track. "If Silent Eclipse has any other drones hidden aboard, we're treading on glass. Let's also not forget that there may be crew aboard my ship that could be under Silent Eclipse's influence. We're all being monitored, even after being cut off from Alpha universe."

"We need to go and get 297 and 777 back," 43 stated. "Getting Oreo off the ship is also a priority. This little child is a dangerous target of opportunity, even if Silent Eclipse are the real culprits."

"You still think the Tandeeri are responsible for the war?" 917 asked.

"I'm slowly changing my mind," 43 replied. "But if Silent Eclipse is responsible, then I'm concerned about whether or not this dead bot has buddies. It'll probably be a matter of time before they realize this one is destroyed or that they lost contact with it."

"Meaning they could be triggered," 999 said. "At this rate, we probably won't have much time to get off the ship. The longer we talk about this, the more fighting we should prepare for."

"I have to secure the ship and put in my own safeguards before that happens," Admiral Ra'aiah thought carefully. "They won't stop. They'll perform every covert and terrorist act they can think of in their programming to get what they want. If the Firestar goes down, Earth will be next."

"That's why we're proposing we take this from two fronts," 917 explained as he looked at 999 for confirmation. She nodded, verifying that this idea was accurate. "We still want to help rather than sit around. Well, technically we have no choice at this point since C-3P0 went to the dark side."

"Not our first enemy robot uprising," 117 remarked with an amused look. "Although that was human-led, technically speaking."

917 smirked as 999 shook her head. He continued his proposal to the Admiral regarding the mission.

"Some of us will go after 297 and 777. We will try to return Oreo to the Tandeeri. Maybe it will offer us a chance to negotiate with them.," he declared. "The rest of us will stay behind to help the ship and make sure that it doesn't get captured or taken over. Those of us going out; we just need a shuttle and a crew willing to take us."

"We need to try to do this before more S.C.E. reinforcements arrive," Admiral Ra'aiah nodded. "Each ship that is out here right now needs to lockdown immediately and do a thorough search."

"The other captains and commanders in your fleet could open fire on your ship," Dr. Kendrick warned her.

"I will inform them that we'll be performing our first hit-and-run strikes against the Tandeeri fleet," Admiral Ra'aiah replied confidently. "They already know that I've been planning that for a while now. Any loyalist to Silent Eclipse might buy that as a cover story. Once I maneuver the Firestar close to the Tandeeri fleet, you get Oreo out of here while we try to put on a decent show."

"The more ships that arrive," 43 said, "the more we'll be outnumbered."

"It will work," 999 nodded reassuringly. "The Firestar moving out to carry out its original battle plan would be the perfect cover to distract the others so that we can leave. It would probably fool Silent Eclipse temporarily, but it would be the best way for us to make a break for it."

Another chime sounded at the door, suddenly sending everyone on high alert as Admiral Ra'aiah spoke up.

"Yes?"

"It's Commander Ulgo."

Dr. Kendrick faced the Admiral, looking concerned.

"Can he be trusted?" he asked.

"Normally, I would say yes," Admiral Ra'aiah shrugged. "This time, I say we find out."

She called out to the door.

"Come in!"

The door unlocked and hissed open. Commander Ulgo stepped through, hands resting at his sides. His eyes were downcast as he stepped over the threshold, and the door slid shut behind him. Once it was closed, he lifted his head and froze.

Captain Harrelson and the space jumpers stepped back from the commander as the rest of the group, positioned at a safe distance, drew their weapons. Commander Ulgo immediately raised his hands in a gesture of peace the second he heard the sound of guns charging up and noticed they were aimed directly at his chest and head.

"Pardon me Admiral," Ulgo said, his composure unwavering. He spoke deliberately and with a steady tone, ensuring his hands were clearly visible to everyone present. "But if this is a demotion, then it's a very poor method of getting the message across. Have I done something wrong?"

"Ulgo," Admiral Ra'aiah said, lowering her sidearm. "You are the one who selected my bridge officers and crew. Many of the department heads were handpicked, interviewed, checked, and approved of by you. Naturally, as my first officer, you hold influence. So let me warn you now, either you come forward with your true intentions or no one will ever discover your body."

Commander Ulgo's stiff expression seemed to soften slightly, giving way to a look of confusion rather than fear. He met his commanding officer's gaze with a skeptical stare, showing no signs of intimidation. This was probably the first time they'd seen him break away from his usual stone-cold persona since they boarded the Firestar.

"What in Horvo's name are you saying Admiral?" he replied stiffly. "I've spent all my years serving you and ensuring that your command was absolute. You sound like I just murdered your pet."

43 decided to add an additional test to their vetting process. She pointed at the robot on the floor and Ulgo looked down at the broken pieces.

"Recognize your friend here?" she asked.

"What is that? I've never seen that type of drone before."

"Silent Eclipse," 43 stated.

Ulgo glanced at 43 before shifting his gaze to the others. His eyes fell on the heap of broken robot components scattered across the floor, yet his expression remained a mix of shock and bewilderment.

"A what? What eclipse? I haven't heard anything about that," he said calmly.

"Serina?" Dr. Kendrick looked up at Serina.

"Well, technically the amborgs all have lie detectors," Serina said in a strained voice as she turned orange. "But he's telling the truth. I hear nothing but confusion in his voice. Commander Ulgo seems to be clean."

"Lower your weapons," Admiral Ra'aiah sighed with relief. "We were just checking if you were a traitor."

"Thanks?" Ulgo raised an eyebrow as he lowered his hands. "May I remind you, Admiral, that an actual traitor wouldn't actually admit to being one. That's the mark of an idiot. Pardon my language ma'am."

"Long story short," Ra'aiah chuckled nervously. "Commander, we have bigger problems. I need to make sure that I can trust you to death from this point on."

"Always Admiral."

"These parts are the remains of an assassination droid sent to kill our guest 999," Admiral Ra'aiah gestured to the pieces. "Turns out, we've been carrying more problems than we originally thought."

"Shall I inform security to sweep the ship?" Ulgo asked.

"No," 43 replied. "Not yet. We aren't ready with that particular part of the plan yet."

Admiral Ra'aiah stepped forward to address the commander.

"I want you to gather your most trusted people, Ulgo," she said firmly. "We need every officer that we can find. Those that will help us and who would not betray the S.C.E. Get as many people as you can under your influence and assist the amborgs."

"Oh?"

"Here's what we're going to do," 117 said. "We all will go to the armory, grab what we need, and then decide who goes and who stays."

"Then we need a shuttle and a crew," 999 said.

"We will pursue the Tandeeri fleet. It's time to begin our hit-and-run missions," Admiral Ra'aiah explained. "During that time, we will... ready our marine battalions to defend and secure all vital parts of the ship. Ulgo, if you would be so kind as to alert Wolf Squadron of an... escort mission, then that would help. It would seem that our rescue plans will be moved ahead of schedule. We will be underway to engage the Tandeeri within the hour. I don't suppose you'd also be interested in calling an impromptu lockdown drill for all personnel?"

Everyone turned and looked between the two officers. Admiral Ra'aiah had said quite a lot in such a short period of time. Did Ulgo even get all of that?

"As a matter of fact ma'am, a lockdown will be ideal for keeping the crew alert to all threats."

As it turned out, Commander Ulgo had understood the message loud and clear.

"I will inform the appropriate personnel," he said with a firm nod. "Perhaps the amborgs would care to accompany me to the armory?"

"Indeed," Admiral Ra'aiah winked with a smirk. "I can give you one hour. During that time, we advance towards the Tandeeri fleet and will... fire at them."

She turned to 117.

"If you aren't gone by the time the battle begins, you will be trapped here during the lockdown."

117 nodded subtly. Even though Serina was still masking bugs and the cameras in Admiral Ra'aiah's ready room, she was still implying certain details of the mission without directly saying so. This was actually her taking them back to when they had the whole jurisdiction debate earlier.

In other words, Admiral Ra'aiah was telling the amborgs that they had one hour to get Oreo off the ship. If they weren't gone by then, they would be stuck.

"Well," 117 said, glancing at the one person in the room who lacked much combat experience. "Dr. Kendrick won't be coming with us, naturally."

Dr. Kendrick's eyes widened as he scanned the room. "Uh, why not?" he replied, clearly taken aback.

"I don't advise it," Serina added warningly. "He's in no condition to go."

"6 gave me a clean bill of health!" Dr. Kendrick protested. "She used a cellular binding device and fixed my concussion!"

"We need some amborgs to stay behind to guard and protect him," 117 told Admiral Ra'aiah.

"Now, we can't just give me a personal escort the entire time," Dr. Kendrick said. "The amborgs that do stay will also need to protect the crew of this ship. That's my personal request. A lot of them came here because they wanted to save us. I know my safety is important, but there are innocent people aboard this ship. You will protect them as if they were family."

"That's going to be a really tough crowd to sort through," 999 said, eyeing the dead robot pieces again. "I'm glad I'm volunteering to get off this ship."

No one could blame her, especially considering what had happened earlier.

Commander Ulgo cleared his throat again, prompting a slight wince from Admira Ra'aiah. However, she met his gaze and gave a nod of approval. Once given permission to speak, he turned to 117.

"Begging your pardon but, how do we determine exactly who is going or staying?"

Admiral Ra'aiah smirked and placed a hand on 117's shoulder. He looked at her curiously.

"Oh," she smiled. Turning her eyes to Ulgo, she winked. "I don't believe that Epsilon matters are within my jurisdiction. Since they do what they want anyway, who am I to argue with residents of their planet Earth? Don't you agree, 43?"

"Indeed," 43 grinned at 117. "It would appear that the Epsilon amborgs have their own priorities."

"Then let's get to the armory," 117 said. "Dr. Kendrick, the amborgs who won't be going after 297 will report to you first before we leave."

"999, hide this robot," Admiral Ra'aiah said. "Let's leave this room exactly as we found it."

999 tossed the transport orb into the air. It activated with a high-pitched whine as it powered up. With a bright flash of light, the orb drew in the scattered fragments of the robot, leaving nothing behind.

"Impressive," Ulgo nodded without cracking a smile. "Most impressive."

"Very convenient," Admiral Ra'aiah noted.

Once they stepped out of the ready room, Serina appeared on 117's shoulder. Her small holographic form rested there, and she let out a sigh of relief.

"Wow," she panted. "Trying to fabricate a fake meeting for those bugs and cameras twice is taking a toll on me."

"What fake conversation did you substitute to hide our real one?" 117 asked.

"I played a bunch of scripts from sitcom shows and used audio filters to make the characters sound like us," Serina answered. "I used a lot of episodes of Hot Bot Suspect."

"You're obsessed with that show," 117 laughed.

"Well," Serina looked around cautiously. "Since there doesn't seem to be an uprising, I think Silent Eclipse bought the whole masquerade."

Admiral Ra'aiah made her way to her chair while 43 looked over the entire group.

"We're going to coordinate everything from the bridge," 43 stated to every amborg on a private channel. "I will protect the admiral and the bridge crew at all costs."

43 paused as she approached 117.

"If I don't see you again," she sighed. "Give them hell."

"You sure you don't want to come with us?" 917 asked.

"I don't think I'm mentally fit for that kind of mission," 43 replied. "I spent years trying to find the Tandeeri. Now, I have to stop thinking that they're the enemy. I think I can do better protecting the ship."

"But you're an expert," 999 mumbled. "You've been hunting the Tandeeri for that long, you must know things that could help us."

"I can send you all of the information I've gathered on my missions," 43 stated as she respectfully shook her head. "But I'm more of an expert in combat. If the ship is in danger, all of these people need protection."

"You know," 117 glanced at Serina, who smiled. "That is accurate. You are the best fighter, in this universe or the next."

"Ahem."

999 appeared slightly annoyed, causing 117 and 917 to sweat.

"Best fighter?" she grumbled. "I would have won."

"It was a tie," 917 spoke uneasily. "Can we move on?"

"With your permission," 43 chuckled as she turned back to 117. "I'll guard the admiral and I'll guide the amborgs staying behind. Are you sure I can't convince you to take Dr. Kendrick with you? Or we could try and... send him back to Earth."

"I don't think there'd be time for that once Admiral Ra'aiah orders the ship to leave," 117 replied.

"I think it's statistically better if he remains aboard," Serina said. "I have this weird feeling that if we tried to peel away and get him home, it'd be a waste of time."

"43!"

43 turned at the sound of her name and sighed.

"No time," she said. "Once you have your team ready, let me know who's going and who's staying. After you get off the ship, we're going to be securing every vital area. I'll need that information."

"Understood," 117 nodded.

"Sir."

117 turned to find Ulgo looking at him. The amborgs proceeded toward the elevator, and as the doors closed behind them, everyone began to ask Ulgo questions.

"So Commander?" Captain Harrelson said eagerly. "Does all of this mean that we get to borrow some of your guns?"

"Under the circumstances," Ulgo replied with a stiff nod. "I'd say that you have earned the right to defend yourselves. Fortunately, we have very advanced weaponry. I also have a question for 999."

999 perked up.

"Yes sir?" she asked.

"The drone that you fought," Ulgo whispered. "How fast was it? How strong?"

"It was dangerous," 999 replied. "You haven't seen it before?"

"No," Ulgo replied, shaking his head. "That organization that shall remain unnamed was always one of those stories that instructors at the academy mentioned to scare the underclassmen. With actual confirmation that they exist, then we have to assume that they are capable of terrifying things."

"Commander, you look older than Admiral Ra'aiah," 917 stated bluntly. "A story from the academy? How old are you?"

Ulgo glared at 917, and the two of them locked eyes. 117 nudged 917 in the shoulder.

"I promise," Ulgo looked at everyone in the elevator, "I don't have any connections to the unnamed organization. If what Admiral Ra'aiah has described back there is true, then I would never be part of that kind of group."

Everyone eyed him warily, but a sudden flash of light broke the tension, and Serina appeared near Ulgo's head.

"Guys," she said, waving her hands calmly. "I believe him."

Commander Ulgo looked slightly surprised that an A.I. was defending him. He graciously cracked a polite smile and dipped his head formally. Serina looked flattered.

"I am very fortunate to have you say that," he said. He looked at Serina closely and narrowed his eyes. "Pardon me but, I feel like I know you."

"I get that a lot."

"Let's get to the armory," Ulgo looked at the entire group cordially.

"He's smiling," 917 mumbled as he quivered fearfully.

"I see that," 999 stared.

"What's wrong?" Commander Ulgo asked.

"It's just... we haven't seen you smile at all this entire time we've been here," 117 laughed nervously.

"It's a day of firsts," Ulgo replied.

When they got to the armory, 117 sent out a signal to the amborgs aboard the Firestar. With that done, everyone quickly took their positions. Once the whole Epsilon team was inside, they started grabbing weapons, ammo, and armor in preparation for the possible battle ahead.

"Dr. Kendrick, I request permission to go on this mission."

Everyone stopped packing and they stared at Dr. Kendrick. Serina was standing in his hands and practically pleading with him.

"What on earth would you want to do by going on this mission?" Dr. Kendrick said in surprise.

He didn't seem angry, but her request was a bit of a shocker for him.

"If I can contribute in any way, then I don't think I can do that here," Serina said. "I want to learn about the Tandeeri and stay with 117. They need an A.I. backing them up."

The amborgs picked to embark on the rescue mission exchanged glances, their expressions a blend of uncertainty and apprehension. While 117 believed that having an artificial intelligence as powerful as Serina could come in handy, the others weren't so sure.

"If you go Serina," 1 warned. "It might be dangerous."

"Or they could have a computer system that I could access and help with decrypting any ways to communicate," Serina said. "Please Dr. Kendrick, I promise to come back. I just have a gut feeling the team needs me."

"I believe it is up to the leaders of the Second and Third Group to decide," Dr. Kendrick sighed. "I don't want you to go, but it would appear that your mind is made up."

"I say let her come," 466 said. "501 agrees, too."

"Yes," 501 said as he wrestled Oreo into a backpack with some other baby supplies that 466 had brought from the nursery. "Just like old times! Sort of."

Sneaking Oreo to the armory had been a piece of cake. Using a red transport orb, 466 had engulfed 501 and Oreo within it so that they wouldn't be seen carrying a Tandeeri in public. 501 was able to keep an eye on the baby while inside to make sure nothing bad happened to it/him. The little Tandeeri had apparently found the experience rather enjoyable.

"I agree," 999 said. "It would be good to have Serina with us."

Serina beamed and skipped a few times to show her appreciation. She then locked eyes with 117 and clasped her hands together in a pleading gesture. However, 117 flashed a grin, revealing that his decision was already made.

"That would be a great idea," he said, which made her do a backflip.

"Then that's settled," 6 smiled.

"Thank you!" Serina squealed as she flew over and zapped onto 117's shoulder.

"I can keep an eye on Dr. Kendrick since we're staying," 6 nodded as she slung a rifle around her shoulder. "I think we should make our way back to the medical bay. I can pick up more supplies that way."

The First Group and the Fourth Group had decided, after brief voting sessions, to remain aboard the S.C.E. to defend the ship and protect Dr. Kendrick as well as the vital sections of the ship.

6 originally wanted to go with 117's team, but she had reluctantly decided to remain behind. If the sole purpose of this mission was to find a peaceful solution, then she wouldn't have to worry too much about them. If Silent Eclipse had enemy forces hidden aboard the Firestar, the fighting would result in a lot of casualties, and she felt it would be better to help Admiral Ra'aiah's crew as best as she could. In the event of an emergency, each amborg already had sufficient medical training, but just to be safe, she had appointed 466 as the designated medic for 117's team.

280 and 113 both felt at home when given the chance to arm themselves. Given that their specialties were in close quarters combat along with the other Fourth Group amborgs, they were confident they could hold down the fort.

The First Group amborgs passed weapons to each other as Ulgo explained what each one did.

"You have a standard plasma repeater right here," Ulgo said, making sure that 3 was gripping it correctly. "Now on this model, you pull back on the catch, and the empty clip pops out. You do not need to insert anything. Just push the catch forward again, hear the click, and the gun is reloaded and ready to shoot again. It carries one bar which has four plasma cases. You can reload four times before a new bar has to be inserted."

"How many rounds does each case carry?" 3 asked curiously as she turned the repeater on.

"Two hundred shots of plasma per case," Ulgo answered as he helped 3 sling the weapon on her back. "You can carry three bars on the back of this pack. In the event of an enemy boarding, you may run out of ammo fast. Watch the indicators and be mindful of your hand on the trigger. I believe in your universe, this is the equivalent of a machine gun."

"Neat," 3 said with admiration in her eyes. She turned around and did a squat. "It's a little heavy but it'll work."

"Careful," 5 stared with an amused look. "She's out to hunt aliens."

3's pose and bladed stance looked very similar to a few characters from a classic sci-fi film franchise from a few hundred years ago. She stuck her tongue out at him and straightened up so Ulgo could teach her how to collapse the weapon and hang it on her back.

"Everyone has standard issue rifles and firearms," Ulgo said as he looked over 1 and 2's preparation of their weapons. "Amborg 6, I suggest you take this shield if you intend to heal injuries."

Ulgo passed a bracer, which had a thick rectangular-looking piece of metal on it. 6 took it and examined it curiously. She inserted her left arm into the bracer and then clicked the button. The metal on her arm immediately fell away, and a five-foot shield unfurled, reaching all the way to the ground.

"These are our standard issue melee defense," Ulgo explained as he opened more cases in the armory. "When one expends too much ammo, melee combat is another way to survive. These shields are designed to withstand plasma, electrical, kinetic bullets and more. They take a lot to break and are useful as portable pieces of cover on the battlefield."

"Much like the Romans in ancient history," 917 said, examining the bracer. "Are there other melee weapons?"

"Feel free to take a case of these in those transport orbs of yours," Ulgo nodded. "We have swords, extendable spears, and other gadgets we train our marines with. The shields also have multiple configurations so you can change the size."

"I can keep those with me when Oreo and I go inside the orb for transport," 501 smiled as Oreo nuzzled into the backpack.

"Now you won't have actual energy shields," Ulgo advised with caution. "But these paddings will still offer you good mobility and a suitable defense should anything go wrong. In the event of a water landing, increased gravity emergencies, or other dire circumstances, click the release button on the belt and all of your armor will disengage and eject."

The First and Fourth group listened attentively as they began to don the many pieces of armor in their own configurations. Several of them only wanted to wear light chest guards with a few pieces on their arms and legs. The numbers on their A.I. Industries uniforms were still glowing and visible underneath all the armor. 117's team only grabbed gear that was necessary for space travel.

"These pieces are good for light space travel," Ulgo said as he handed 117 a type of pack. "Your space suits in this universe are slow and bulky. Take these oxygen masks. We require these for EVA, space walks, and if you're ejected into space. This pack has a retractable helmet that reaches up from your shoulders and covers your head, providing you with enough oxygen for about an hour. There will be boosters on the shuttle craft which you can add on for flight mobility. And then the rest of your gear can be added."

"If we are trying to be peaceful," 117 said to the Second and Third Group, "then we will try to avoid using our weapons, except as a last resort. Our sole mission right now is to make our way to the fleet and figure out what 297 and 777 have done. Then we help support them."

"When the Firestar begins its diversion," Ulgo said, "Wolf Squadron will escort your shuttle around to the brunt of the fighting. Our best shuttle crew have volunteered to take you in. Be advised, once you close in on the Tandeeri fleet, Wolf Squadron's orders are to retreat in order to make it look less like an attack. We will focus on missing our shots, and defending the ship. Externally and internally."

"Hopefully," 1 said as he brought up video footage on his bracelet, "we can deal with any other stowaways who have a vendetta against truth seekers."

999 had shared the video of her struggle against the Silent Eclipse robot in the Archives. Both 117 and 917 grudgingly admitted that it had been quite difficult to defeat.Now, the rest of the team were working together to develop strategies and techniques to prevent someone else from falling victim to being attacked from behind, especially since no one possessed a sword like the one 917 used.

"Does anyone have any more questions?" Ulgo asked, looking at his watch.

"Can we trust Wolf Squadron? And the shuttle crew?" 117 asked as everyone checked their gear one last time. "They would be willing to do this for us? Just like that?"

"They should," Ulgo nodded and shifted his gaze to 917. "After all, it's your squadron, Lieutenant Commander."

917's eyes widened. He blinked, pointing at himself with a questioning look, which was answered by another smirk from Ulgo.

"My squadron?" he asked. "I don't follow."

"Commander," Ulgo stated, "your Alpha was deadly on the ground, and he also believed those that controlled the skies and outer space could turn the tide of battle. You were also an accomplished pilot."

"Well," 917 said with a bashful grin. "I'll be sure to thank them after we get through this."

"Ok," 117 took a deep breath. It was time to do a quick briefing. "Our objective is simple. We locate 297 and 777, return Oreo, and negotiate a cease-fire. The Second and Third Group's responsibilities are to contact the Tandeeri... or die trying."

117 looked at 1, who nodded. With that signal, he continued sharing the rest of the mission details.

"We stay behind," 1 declared. "The First and Fourth Group get the potentially more dangerous assignment of flushing out the rats aboard this ship. Even though we had a couple of days to explore the Firestar, she's still the size of a city. Alpha 43 will be our guide during the next phase of the mission. Our objective is to defend the ship and eliminate potential threats aboard."

"Oh," 466 said, raising her hand. "Please send someone to defend the nursery and the kids. I know we have to take care of the assassin bots but please, protect the people who are going to be in the most danger."

466 appeared worried as a few of them cast glances in her direction.

"There are kids here, a lot of them."

"We'll try 466," 1 said with a reassuring smile. "Our primary concerns will be, if more assassin droids appear, to defend the parts of the ship that are vital. The engineering section, weapons control, and the bridge are top priorities. Watch each person carefully as well. This... Silent Eclipse organization could be anyone, aside from the stand-out evil battle droids. Look for patterns, loners, exiles, people in places that they shouldn't be in. If you don't trust the troops that are with you, you restrain them or prevent them from trying to get ahold of you. If necessary, you kill them before they kill you."

"How do we tell the good guys from the bad?" 2 asked rhetorically, then immediately answered his own question. "If they shoot at you, they're bad."

1 and 2 were referring to potential hostage scenarios. They'd undergone extensive training to avoid hostage situations and to prevent any loss of life, but it was tough when criminals tried to play to their kind-hearted nature, exploiting their weaknesses in order to gain an advantage over them. Their countermeasures were shaped through experience.

"Even if we don't know these people," 1 said, "we will still protect them. They've been fighting for us. So that's what we do for them."

Everyone nodded and murmured their agreements. 1 turned to smile confidently at 117.

"Even in space... or an alternate universe," he chuckled nervously, "this is what we chose to do."

"Yeah!" 5 punched his fist in the air. "Crossing universal barriers and scaring the crap out of ourselves!"

6 playfully bumped 5 in the side with her fist, but laughter had already taken over the room. As 5 massaged the spot where she'd struck, he caught a glimpse of her cracking a smile, too.

"Hey guys," 5 continued as they all glanced at each other cheerfully. "Let's get a group photo."

It was an idea they could all agree with. They formed a line and had Ulgo snap the picture with 466's camera. Each of them were already capturing their own moments and compiling them into personal collections, but this was the big one that 466 wanted to save on her own camera.

"We'll get 297 and 777 in the next one once we get them back," 117 said as Ulgo figured out how to work the camera.

"Agreed," Serina nodded, turning a bright red to set the proper lighting.

"Hey guys," 5 said when Ulgo gave a thumbs-up, preparing to take the picture. "Let's save the world again as a family."

A bright flash illuminated the scene as the photo was snapped. In a heartbeat, they all forgot about the war, and smiles broke across their faces. That fleeting moment was captured, gone in an instant. As everyone checked their gear and prepared to move out, a sudden wave of reality washed over them, like a bucket of icy water splashing down over their heads. Their faces turned grave as they readied themselves for a fight.

"Doctor?" Captain Harrelson reached out. He grabbed a strap and tightened it on Dr. Kendrick's armor plating. "This looks loose."

"Thank you," Dr. Kendrick smiled. "It feels so light and comfortable now."

"You're a VIP," Captain Harrelson nodded. "We have to protect you at all costs."

117 shook hands with 1 and 2, then gave a brief salute to 113 and 280. The First Group's first stop was the medical bay so that 6 could grab supplies and then rejoin Dr. Kendrick. The Fourth Group and Captain Harrelson's squad of space-jumpers would escort Dr. Kendrick to the bridge. From there, the Fourth Group would deploy as needed under the direction of 43 and Admiral Ra'aiah.

501 and Oreo were carefully hidden in 466's transport orb as she followed close behind 117 and 917. 999 said a quick farewell to 6, and the two of them shook hands firmly. They wished each other luck as the amborgs split off. Commander Ulgo was going to take the three Second Group amborgs and the Third Group to the hangar bay where Wolf Squadron was waiting. 917 was quite eager to meet his Alpha's old squadron.

"This is the Admiral speaking," Admiral Ra'aiah's voice spoke over the ship P.A. "The ship has begun maneuvering towards the enemy fleet. All hands, prepare for combat."

After arriving at the hangar, Ulgo led them to a shuttle that was being prepped for launch. A small group of pilots loitered nearby, and as they drew closer, a few turned to look. Those that were sitting sprang to their feet.

"Wolves! Atten-hurr!!"

"Officer on deck!" someone responded.

The pilots reacted instantly to Commander Ulgo's shout, and in less than a minute, silence fell across the group. They immediately lined up and snapped to attention.

"Lieutenant Commander 917," Ulgo motioned for 917 to step forward. "Your escort stands ready. Salute the commander!"

"Uhh," 917 mumbled as they all saluted. Taken aback, he stuttered, "W-what's up?"

The pilots stared back, maintaining their composure. As 917 approached, they lifted their arms in a salute. However, he paused, unsure of what to do next.

"I suggest you give them a command," Ulgo whispered behind 917 so that the squadron couldn't hear him. "They'll listen to you if you take charge."

"You don't say 'what's up,'" 117 muttered uneasily as he forced a smile. "Not to them."

"I know. It was an attempt to open a friendly dialogue. I forgot that they think we have ranks," 917 whispered back. He quickly spoke to the pilots again as confidently as he could. "At ease."

The pilots all stood with their feet apart and relaxed their postures.

"Commander," one man stepped forward. "Glad to have you back. I've kept Wolf Squad up to speed since we last saw you."

"917," Ulgo introduced the man to the amborgs. "This is Wolf Squad's current leader, Lieutenant Chan. One of the best pilots in the inner quadrant and one of our finest and most decorated veterans."

"Wow," 917 said, shaking the pilot's hand. "You seem a little old to be a pilot."

Chan's eyes twitched at 917's remark. The other pilots instinctively recoiled, while the amborgs watched anxiously.

"What is with you and the old people comments?" Serina asked.

"Sorry!" 917 replied to them privately. "It slipped out!"

Lieutenant Chan continued to silently brood as Ulgo stepped forward.

"Calm yourself Lieutenant," he said warningly.

After a moment, Chan lifted his hand and 917 looked down. Despite his menacing gaze, 917 realized that he was waiting to shake his hand.

"Sorry," 917 said as they exchanged a firm handshake, feeling his hand getting crushed. "I didn't mean to be so blunt and offensive."

917 was surprised at how strong Chan's grip was. The military training the S.C.E. offered was definitely no joke.

"You were the only one that always told me the truth," Chan smiled. "Especially when it came to my age. It's good to have you back leading us."

"I think you're still the leader," 917 replied nervously. "I don't have a pilot's license for outer space."

"If you're not my commander on this mission," Lieutenant Chan said, "then don't apologize. You are a guest and the asset we've been assigned to escort. I look forward to the day that you get back in the cockpit and take up the wolf's mantle."

"I suppose I will have to earn that right again," 917 chuckled apprehensively. "Can I have my hand back?"

As 917 and Chan finally released their handshake, everyone around them visibly relaxed, letting out sighs of relief. The tension in the air lifted, and the group seemed to come together again.

"Chan will be the one leading his fighters to escort your shuttle," Ulgo explained. "That's all they need to know, and they will protect you."

"Very well then," 917 nodded. "Shall we get underway?"

Chan nodded. He quickly placed his helmet on his head. A visor slid from the top of the helmet down to the chin and clicked in place. The other pilots began to do the same.

"Wolf pack! Move out!"

As the pilots made their way toward their fighters, a couple of other crewmen led the amborgs to the shuttle. They clambered their way up the loading ramp as Ulgo waved them off.

"Good hunting!" he yelled as the hangar was flooded with noise.

Commander Ulgo disappeared as the amborgs filed into the shuttle. The crew joined shortly after, and everyone began searching for available seats.

"Hello."

117, 917 and 999 turned to see a female pilot standing before them. 917's eyes widened in dismay, while 117 and 999 merely stared.

"You," 917 said. "What are you doing here?"

"I told you we'd be in touch again," the ensign replied, tilting her head.

"Do you know this girl, 917?" 999 asked politely, but they could hear building animosity in her tone. "Wait, I saw you briefly."

It was the same girl that 917 had encountered in the supply closet. He was wondering how she'd ended up being assigned to their team as she offered them a friendly greeting.

She had wrapped her hair up in some kind of pilot cap, but 917 remembered her face. 117, however, didn't think she looked familiar at all.

"Girl?" the ensign replied with a raised eyebrow. "I'm no girl."

"Your voice. I remember you," 117 said as it suddenly dawned on him. "You bumped into 917 when we first came aboard."

"Then we met in the supply room," 917 said.

"You what?" 999 said angrily. "For what purpose?"

"Because she was one of the first crewmembers aboard that wanted me to start thinking that there was something wrong about the war," 917 said quickly as 999 glared daggers at the ensign. "After we… she left me alone, I wanted to go find you in the archives right away to discuss this but then stuff happened. 501 had a baby and then when 117 and I rescued you, I forgot to bring it up. Please quit staring at me like that. Nothing happened between us aside from the information hand-off. Anyway, what I want to know is, if it was so important for you to keep yourself a secret when we first met, why are you here?"

Braelynn glanced around at all the curious faces. Honestly, they might as well grab some popcorn for the drama potentially about to unfold.

"To make sure that my people's best hope of survival gets back alive," Braelynn answered his question calmly. "Just a quick note, I am a member of Wolf Squadron, temporarily, and will be taking you to the Tandeeri fleet."

"Got promoted huh?" 917 asked. "Or did your supervisor transfer you because you were so gloomy?"

"It helps when you work for Naval Intelligence," Braelynn nodded. "You got to blend in almost every department. For now, I'm your pilot."

"Well then get back to the cockpit where you belong," 999 ordered.

"Please don't start another fight," 117 groaned. "Is this going to be a problem?"

"Yes it will," 999 snapped. "Especially if she doesn't get us out of here now."

"Begging your pardon… ma'am," Braelynn snapped back, then indicated with her head to 917. "But my orders only come from the Lieutenant Commander."

The amborgs nearby gasped and nervously inched away. 999 looked like she'd been slapped… hard. Most people didn't survive the moment they dissed her. Even 917 was staring in shock, taken aback by how bold this mysterious ensign-lieutenant pilot was.

"Let's just get underway," 117 quickly interrupted before things could get out of hand. "Can we please go? We are on a deadline. Haha. Please, let's go!"

"Yes please," 917 said slowly, placing a hand on 999's shoulder.

Braelynn turned on her heel and strode to the front of the shuttle. Fuming, 999 was practically forced into her seat by 917, and the three of them settled in, pulling their harnesses down tight.

"You could've been a little nicer," 917 muttered.

"Absolutely not," 999 replied with a huff. "Don't trust her. Don't like her. It doesn't matter what she says 917, you can't believe that she won't hurt you in some way."

"Are you worried about my social welfare or my physical life?" 917 asked. "I don't think she's Silent Eclipse, but she's not that bad."

"Hey, don't come crawling to me for help if she turns into a Mata-Hari," 999 said as she turned her head away. "The instant she shows signs of sabotaging our efforts, she's dead."

"There must be some reason why you didn't kill her immediately when she stood up to you," 117 pointed out innocently.

"Hmph."

"Attention," they all heard Braelynn's voice over the shuttle's intercom. "We are now beginning take-off procedures. Departure in three minutes."

"We're probably going to crash into a meteor at this rate," 999 muttered as she continued to sulk. "Everyone fill out their wills?"

"Oh come on," 117 replied. "Earlier you couldn't wait to propose our plan to the Admiral. It is not the time to be negative."

"It'll be 917's fault if we don't live," 999 said accusingly. "All the amborgs in one singular shuttle, yeah that's not an ideal target at all for the bad guys. Good job."

"You cannot pin this entirely on me," 917 sighed.

"Actually I can. You forgot to tell me about her. Why, I wonder? Is she so attractive that your brain muscles sparked out? You compromised us the instant you recognized her aboard this shuttle and we didn't know about her until we were introduced. Highly suspicious. Over-explaining the details is a classic feint to avoid the truth. So this is all on you if we die."

There was no reasoning with her at this point. 917 sighed again and sank lower into his seat while 117 gave him some reassuring pats on the shoulder. It wasn't helping though, since 999 was still criticizing the whole thing. Now they were starting to miss when she preferred not to talk in general.

The roar of the shuttle's engines cut her off, sending vibrations through the hull plating. As the shuttle ascended, the sound of the engines sharpened, transforming into a piercing high-pitched whine. Everyone turned to the viewports, watching the hangar bay recede below them.

"Hangar bay cleared," they heard the pilots up front say. "Rendezvousing with Wolf Squadron. Escort position confirmed."

"Wow," 249 said excitedly. "Look at the fighters!"

"Amazing!" 49 agreed while 466 checked on her transport orb.

"Artificial gravity has been enabled," Braelynn announced over the intercom. "You are now free to move about the shuttle. Arrival at target in about fifteen."

The amborgs disengaged their harnesses like they were on a typical passenger airliner, but all of them kept to their seats. 117 was about to stand up and discuss their strategy to reach the ship that 297 was on when suddenly, someone from the front of the shuttle clambered back to them.

"You're welcome," Braelynn said as she tossed something at their feet. "Someone doesn't want your mission to succeed. You'll have to hope the Firestar doesn't get taken over."

117, 917 and 999 leaned over to examine the device. It took them a moment for them to realize they'd just eagerly attempted to understand an Alpha universe device that was completely unfamiliar to them.

"That there was strapped and hidden near the landing gear," Braelynn said pointing to it. "I disarmed it, but it was set to blow ten minutes from now—the perfect opportunity to get rid of our only shot at negotiation while making it look like we were killed in combat."

"So," 117 said, leaning forward in his seat. "Someone knows of our true intentions."

Without warning, 999 sprang to her feet and drew her firearm. It glowed with energy as it charged, and she took aim at Braelynn, who quickly raised her hands in defense.

"Whoa! Calm down 999!" 917 said as he stood and tried to put his hand on her arm. 999 merely shrugged him off and stepped away.

"How do we know you're not a traitor?" 999 said angrily. "You could have planted that bomb and pretended to disarm it so we would trust you."

"I am not a traitor," Braelynn said, rooted to the spot.

"Then prove it, or I shoot."

917 brought his hand back to his side. He turned to face Braelynn, but didn't pull his gun on her. 117 looked at the device with unease as Serina perched on his shoulder.

A couple more amborgs had also drawn their weapons, but they weren't sure who to aim at. 117 sent a signal for everyone to stand down. The last thing they needed was to accidentally kill each other in the shuttle.

"Take the bomb and put it in the hatch at the back of the shuttle," Braelynn instructed carefully. "That panel next to the hatch will close the inner airlock. There's an override which will open the outer door and eject the bomb from the shuttle. Then you can check me. I am entirely unarmed and I swear I will get you to where you are going."

"Get the bomb," 999 said to 917, who quickly rushed over to it.

917 lifted it gingerly and did exactly what Braelynn instructed. He moved to the shuttle hatch and placed the bomb inside. Then he hit the controls on the panel and the inner airlock closed. Once it hissed shut, 917 pressed another button. There was a brief whooshing noise as the airlock vented its payload. Then there was silence.

"There we go," 917 said as 466 walked over to Braelynn and began to body-scan her.

"I don't see anything else," 466 reported. 999 lowered her gun but continued to glance suspiciously up and down.

"Serina," 117 said. "Can you check the shuttle for anything else?"

"With pleasure," Serina said as she lifted off his shoulder like a butterfly.

Braelynn nodded and allowed Serina to float around.

"You can also check the cockpit," she said. "I've already taken care of my copilot."

917 and 117 looked at each other in alarm. 999 clenched the gun and kept her aim. 466 finished the body scan on Braelynn and stepped back nervously.

"What do you mean?" 117 asked as 917 ran to the front of the shuttle.

"Silent Eclipse does everything it can to make sure things go their way," Braelynn said insistently. "Once they're aware that you know of their existence, then they've already started."

"She's right," 917 called to them from the front. "I got a dead... robot up here. I thought it was... someone else earlier?"

"The shuttle crew assigned to you was killed," Braelynn explained. "They were replaced by two of those droids. I snuck my name onto the roster and prevented them from killing all of you."

"Who are you with?" 999 asked.

"Like I already said," Braelynn sighed, "S.C.E. Intelligence. I'm an agent! I'm with the people who want to see you live through this. While you've all taken your time coming up with a strategy, they've already got many contingencies in place to make sure your only plan fails. Please trust me."

"That doesn't answer the question," 117 said. "Angel, stand down."

"Is that an order?" 999 said coldly, her gaze piercing everyone with fear.

"You going to disobey a direct one?" 117 gulped, boldly saying it as clearly as possible. 917, carrying the dead robot, dropped it on the floor. 999 kept her gun raised while Braelynn continued to look back with a brave face. However, it became increasingly clear to those around them that under her brave façade, fear was starting to seep through. This seemed familiar to 917, who recalled a similar moment when he had once pointed a gun to her head.

"Alice," 917 said. "Listen to me if you don't trust her. Put. It. Down."

117 breathed. He let out a sigh of relief when 999's menacing look faded, replaced with wide-eyed astonishment. She slowly lowered her arms and holstered her weapon. Braelynn followed suit, relaxing her stance and exhaled.

"You used my real name," 999 said as she sat down. "Again."

"It's the only name that gets your attention," 917 said.

"Am I off the hit-list?" Braelynn asked with an uneasy hand-gesture. "Because you do need someone to fly this thing."

"Yes," 999 said, rolling her eyes.

"Ok," 117 said as the rest of the team relaxed. "Now that we're not killing anyone, what's the plan now?"

"My guess is, the assault on the Firestar has begun," Braelynn said. "When Silent Eclipse marks someone for death, all of them will know. When amborg 999 survived, that got their attention and they began to prepare for a takeover. We have to hope that the others can protect the Firestar from falling."

"Well we have to warn the First and Fourth Group," 466 exclaimed. "If there's an army of agents and assassins aboard, then... there will be so much fighting! So many people will..."

Everyone knew why 466 cared so much about the people aboard the ship. She was clearly thinking of the children in the nurseries and the peaceful matriarchs that had dedicated their lives to the younger generations.

"What do you think I did before we took off?" Braelynn said reassuringly to 466. "I already passed the word on to your friends. They know what to do."

"You've thought of everything haven't you?"

917 flashed Braelynn an impressed smile.

"Let's just say you should see me on a good day," Braelynn replied, returning a flattered smile. "As a strategist, I prefer to have control over the field of battle so that my allies have a fair advantage."

"Working against unfavorable odds is kind of our thing," 117 said. "So, the point being, we've got to finish this now. The only safe place now is the Tandeeri fleet."

"That's if you can get the Tandeeri to side with you," Braelynn reminded them as she climbed back into the cockpit. "Then you can make sure that Silent Eclipse never touches your planet."

"I trust 1 to keep things under control," 117 answered firmly. "Dr. Kendrick may be our most valuable hostage but if there's one thing I know, we won't go down without a fight."

"Oh crap," Serina said anxiously. "Now I feel bad about leaving him. Am I better off here or back there?"

"Don't worry," 117 replied. "They're all going to be fine. So what's happening now?"

"The Firestar has begun the attack," Braelynn informed them. "I could use a hand up here."

117 and 917 approached the cockpit together. 117 pushed 917 into the other pilot's seat. Despite not having a license for space travel, he was the only one among them from Earth who had flying experience. He told Braelynn that he was a fast learner.

"So," 917 said as he placed a hand on the console. "How did you know that your copilot was a robot?"

"I laced his helmet with a poison of my own design," Braelynn replied casually. "I mean, the robot's holo-disguise was helpful and would've fooled me but it was a dead give-away when it put on the helmet without feeling instant pain. So I shot it in the head."

"Right," 917 said nervously. "Anyway... You want to give me a crash course?"

"I can keep flying," Braelynn said as she tilted the control stick to the left. "Hit the blue buttons on your right-hand side. Second one on the left first and then the one next to it. It'll allow me more maneuverability on the thrusters."

"Is there any way we can track 297 or 777's homing beacon?" 117 asked as 917 hit the buttons he was told to press.

The shuttle made a brief whooshing noise. Suddenly, the shuttle seemed to move a lot faster as Braelynn gained more control. They saw the Firestar beginning its bombardment.

"Man," 917 said. "The shuttle feels like someone recalibrated the sensitivity on the controllers."

"This is the best way to fly," Braelynn nodded and licked her lips. "This is shuttle one to Wolf Squadron. You may break off escort."

"Roger that," Chan's voice came in through the comms. "Good luck shuttle one. We'll stay back far enough to cover you. Signal us if the mission doesn't look good. We'll be there."

117 and 917 stood by, watching the fighters take off and vanish from sight.

"Charge the weapons," Braelynn instructed.

"What?" 117 and 917 asked.

"How good of a shot are you two?" Braelynn pointed to a set of red buttons in front of 917. "Because if Silent Eclipse replaced any of Wolf Squad's pilots, then we're going to have a big problem."

917 quickly pressed the buttons she indicated. A small screen appeared in front of the two amborgs. They watched a targeting reticule appear and began to track the retreating squadron of fighters.

"The computer will automatically target and shoot at any incoming threats," Braelynn said. "Any target locks on us and we'll be able to fight. Now let's try and find your two missing amborgs."

She hit a set of buttons, and the controls lit up.

"I'm going to use the sensors to try and look for the signatures of the other two shuttles," Braelynn said as the Tandeeri fleet came into view. "If we find the signature, we can find 297 or 777 and hopefully identify which ship was the one they were taken to."

"Find the flagship," 917 said as the image became fuzzy. "Then we spacewalk over there?"

"If they see how small and really insignificant our shuttle is, then maybe they may let us approach," Braelynn sighed as the Tandeeri fleet grew closer with every passing moment.

117 quickly turned and called into the back of the shuttle.

"Hey 466!" he said. "I think now would be a good time to let 501 and Oreo out."

"Seriously? You named it Oreo? An Earth cookie?"

Braelynn stared at 917, who nodded.

"Yeah, that's not going away anytime soon," 117 groaned embarrassingly.

"It was 501," 917 explained.

"Well," Braelynn cleared her throat. "You guys did a good job of concealing that Tandeeri child. I've never seen that kind of technology before. But what are you thinking 117?"

"It's a long shot," 117 shrugged. "But maybe the Tandeeri would be more welcoming if they saw us carrying Oreo in? You know, I highly doubt they'd shoot their own kind, so maybe that's our way in."

"Well," Braelynn nodded. "Then let's hope that hunch pays off. The Firestar is pulling back. And we're still going in."

They watched as the missiles and lasers from the Firestar disappeared. The fighters were all withdrawing—none of them had actually attacked or fired any shots—and there had been no damage inflicted.

"How does the Admiral plan to report that the S.C.E. missed every shot?" 117 asked.

"If it was me," Braelynn said, "then I'd just say that our instruments and targeting sensors weren't operating at optimal capacity during the fight."

"You know," 917 interjected, "in the past, when workers were threatened by automation, they threw their wooden shoes called *sabots* into the machines to break them down. Hence, coining the word 'sabotage.'"

"Too bad," 117 said. "I mean, thanks to Silent Eclipse, the Firestar almost had their chance to beat the Tandeeri."

"Hey! 117! What did I miss?"

501 climbed up into the cockpit and 117 clapped him on the shoulders.

"Well," he said as 501 grinned. "We're close to bringing Oreo home."

"Oh wow," 501 said, gazing out at the Tandeeri fleet. "We are close."

There was a light pattering of feet behind them. They heard the amborgs in the back erupt into shouts as several objects were knocked over.

"Oh right," 501 said looking back. "We carried a lot of stuff in the transport orb. Guess Oreo knocked some things over."

117 looked down and saw Oreo climbing into the cockpit. The little Tandeeri cheerfully ran up to Braelynn's seat, then dashed to 917 with a ton of juvenile curiosity. It tried to look for a place to climb up until finally, 501 knelt down and motioned for it to come into his arms.

"Come here little one," 501 smiled. "You want to see?"

Oreo let out a grunt of delight and 501 scooped him up. As Oreo was put on 501's shoulders, they all looked at the fleet closing in. Braelynn glanced at

Oreo for a second and looked like she wanted to make a comment but instead decided to pay attention to flying the shuttle.

"Wow," 917 said. All of them peered out the viewport. "The ships are enormous."

"Are you running the scan?" Braelynn asked, her eyes glued to the closest Tandeeri ship.

"Getting a bad reading," 917 said as he and 117 both looked at the monitor. "I can't see anything and my own sensors are also going bad."

"Umm guys?" 501 said. "Do you hear that?"

A deep, ominous rumble echoed from outside. Braelynn brought them closer, and they all paused to listen. Suddenly, everything went quiet.

"Did that sound like a giant fart in outer space?" 117 asked.

"Oh good," 501 chuckled. "I'm glad I wasn't the only one thinking tha..."

A massive tremor hit, causing everyone to stumble. A red collision alert lit up on the screens and started blaring an alarm.

"What's happened?!" 466 yelled from the back.

"We've been stopped," Braelynn said as she checked the console. "All systems are running but... we've hit something. Our speed is dropping."

"I think we got tractor beamed," 917 said. "Look."

They all gazed out as a Tandeeri ship approached at an alarming speed. It was only then that 117 realized that 917 was right. Their ship was actually being pulled in. The shuttle was yanked forward and then lowered toward the ship's underside. Then, what appeared to be a hatch opened up.

"Do we ready weapons?" 501 asked meekly.

"No," 117 replied as he took a giant gulp. "Everyone! We are... boarding the Tandeeri ship!"

The only one that was enjoying the whole experience was Oreo, to no one's surprise. It seemed as if it was attempting to cheer, making noises that sounded like a tiny, compressed trumpet. Home sweet home?

"117?"

117 turned to look at 501, who was holding Oreo. The little Tandeeri looked excited as 501 trembled in fear.

"I love you," he said.

"I love you too buddy," 117 sighed. He turned to the back and shouted, "Everyone! Stay calm and get away from the exits! They're probably going to capture us and make us prisoners!"

917 and Braelynn watched as dark shadows crept over the cockpit, plunging the space around them into darkness. The shuttle was swallowed up, drawn into a mysterious void. Serina's glowing form became one of the brightest lights in the shuttle as she continued to scan and record everything.

"I've got a bad feeling about this," 917 declared.

"Finally," Serina said mockingly as she stared upwards into the darkness. "Someone said it."

Chapter 25: Later, buddy

The White House
Oval Office
Emergency Recall plus 10 days 2 hours

President Holland peered at the screen of a laptop one of his aides brought in. He looked into the camera, and the facial recognition signed him in. The following step required fingerprint authorization, so he positioned his right hand on the palm scanner. A prompt popped up, and two words appeared.

Lake Washington showed up on his screen. President Holland took a deep breath to speak the proper passphrase in order to complete the last security check.

"I took a fishing trip with my family," he said calmly and clearly into the microphone. "Something hooked my line and I was pulled into the water. It was deep, dark and cold. So cold that it pierces into your bones. I thought I was drowning as I tried to figure out which way was up. I thought it was all over until a strong and warm hand found me and I was pulled out. When my head broke the surface and I could draw breath again, I said to myself, "that was one of the most exhilarating moments that summer."

The prompt on the screen switched from red to green as the final security check was cleared.

"Identity confirmed," the voice on the computer reported. "Personal encrypted transmission from Dr. John Kendrick, CEO of A.I. Industries, to President Bill Holland."

The audio note from the sender captured President Holland's attention, causing him to lean forward with keen interest. He understood that this was a private message, not designed for the public eye. This meant that the recording he was about to view was intended solely for his eyes only. But what could be so important that Dr. Kendrick would resort to such extreme secrecy? This felt like overkill.

"Hello Bill."

Dr. Kendrick's face appeared on the screen. As the recording began, Bill listened intently to the familiar voice of his friend.

"I must be quick about this. In my last message to you and the rest of Earth's leaders, I told you how a fleet of starships from the other universe came over to help us. They are currently in a defensive formation protecting the Earth."

Dr. Kendrick's face on the screen was downcast, and he released a heavy sigh. As he raised his eyes, President Holland could see that something was bothering him.

"Please take care of yourself," he continued. "Up here, we figured out a way to possibly end the war. If we're successful, everything will be fine. If not, then prepare for the worst."

"Alien invasion," President Holland let out a shudder. "I hope it doesn't come to that."

"This message is to let you know that I value you as a friend and if something happens to me, I need you to make sure that A.I. Industries is protected and in the right hands."

"Shouldn't this message be for someone back there then?" President Holland raised an eyebrow.

"I already sent instructions to my employees back at my company," Dr. Kendrick said reassuringly.

It was as if the recorded message was reading his thoughts, anticipating the questions swirling around in his mind. The fact that their friendship put them on the same wavelength helped him momentarily forget about the global turmoil weighing heavily on his shoulders.

"I have a special document and set of files on my personal drive back home," Dr. Kendrick smiled, then bit his lip. "It's my uh... letter. *The* letter. The one we talked about before."

President Holland nodded slowly.

"Oh," he breathed. "Don't talk like that John."

"The files and messages on that drive are my last will and testament," Dr. Kendrick looked at the camera and smiled, but Holland could see his eyes glistening. Tears were welling up, slightly hidden by his glasses. It was clear that his friend was struggling to mask his fear. "I've been updating it for a few years now. It contains messages to be delivered, final requests, and last rites in the event I don't make it. My lawyers and the amborgs will know what to do when they open it."

President Holland thought about his own last will and testament. Everything he had planned to leave to his family and friends. While it might not have been as sophisticated as Dr. Kendrick's, he realized that if there were years' worth of requests or final wishes stored on that hard drive, it could take hours, if not days, to sift through it all. As he watched the recording of John, who was holding back tears, a pressing question lingered in his mind.

"What are you telling me this for?" President Holland asked. "John?"

"I know to a lot of people in your staff, I come off as an arrogant and self-righteous prick," Dr. Kendrick stated, which made President Holland chuckle. Dr. Kendrick paused, then grinned cheekily. "Oh wait, those were your words a few years ago on my birthday."

Both men laughed, like they were sitting face to face. President Holland felt a small spark of joy, sharing a virtual laugh with Dr. Kendrick.

"But you are my friend," he stated in the video, causing Holland to fall silent. "You've been one of the kindest supporters of my company, and you were the greatest and the most ambitious man I know. You still are. You're the President of the United States."

"And yet, your wife chose you instead of me," President Holland muttered wryly.

"In my will, I name who will be the successor. The one who will run A.I. Industries if I am dead, missing, or will never return," Dr. Kendrick stated casually. "There's a collection of messages, pre-recorded mail, and possessions of mine that need to be delivered. My fortune and business is in safe hands. I just... wanted to talk to you one last time in case things don't go well. Can I ask you for one last request?"

"I have no way to respond to your message, John," President Holland sighed as he waited for Dr. Kendrick to continue speaking. "So, since I have no choice, go for it."

"I want you to be the one to give my eulogy."

Bill looked at the screen. Dr. Kendrick smiled kindly at him.

"Yeah, you heard me correctly," he said smugly. "I want you to be the one to give the eulogy at my funeral, if I don't make it out of this one. I want it to be you, not as the President of the United States, but because you're the only one I know who can make it happy, be a symbol of hope for everyone who grieves, and... you just have a way with words that continuously inspire us."

"It's kind of in my job description," President Holland smiled, beginning to feel a little choked up.

"I know it's your job to always be proactive while inspiring the people," Dr. Kendrick said, "so I know everything will be ok if you make the people not feel alone. You gave my wife's eulogy and I know that you are the one I want to do the same for me if I die."

President Holland brought a hand up and wiped his eyes. He didn't want to tear up now.

"The reason I got my hopes up and wanted to go to space was because... I wanted to see if in another universe, I could see her again."

President Holland smiled.

"Of course," he nodded sympathetically. "You would have moved mountains if you had discovered a way to bring her back."

Under the circumstances, Dr. Kendrick had left the planet to go straight to the heavens. Initially, President Holland figured it was because being up there would bring him closer to her. But now, he understood that he meant it in a very literal sense. The thought of possibly seeing his wife, alternate universe or not, was probably what motivated his actions.

"And, if this is the last time I get to talk to you," Dr. Kendrick said softly. "Please go visit my wife. Tell her that it was worth it."

Dr. Kendrick was asking him to visit and possibly clean the leaves off Mrs. Kendrick's headstone.

"And when I'm buried," he smiled, "or when you build my gravestone, I want it to say... Father to the Nameless. Loving Husband. And genius extraordinaire."

"Really?" President Holland said sarcastically, raising an eyebrow.

"Kidding on that last one," Dr. Kendrick chuckled. "But I suppose if I'm dead, then I don't really get to overrule you. Since I'm the one asking one of the leaders of the free world to decorate my tombstone. You decide what it says, alright?"

"Oh I know exactly what to write on yours," President Holland grinned.

"Goodbye Bill," Dr. Kendrick said gently. "It's been fun. All my best to you. I'll see you on the other side. This is your friend, John Kendrick, signing off. Good luck to you."

The recording paused, and the screen went dark as it finished. President Holland stared at the display for several moments before he closed the laptop and set it aside. He reached over and grabbed the phone on his desk.

"I'm all done here."

The door to the Oval Office on his right swung open, and a handful of officers stepped inside. They offered a salute to the President before swiftly heading to the laptop computer. Once it was taken away, President Holland turned his gaze to the officer who stayed behind, standing before the Resolute desk.

"Was there anything else?" he asked politely.

"No, Mr. President," the officer replied firmly. "That was the only message that Dr. Kendrick asked us to deliver to you."

"Thank you," President Holland nodded. "Please send in the amborg escorts and the French President, please?"

"Yes sir."

President Holland rose from his desk and walked over to the window, looking out over the lawn briefly before hearing the door click. He turned to find a man in a similar suit and tie entering with a bright smile and cheerful demeanor. A pin of the French flag adorned his chest as he raised his hand in greeting. The two leaders exchanged a warm handshake, and President Holland invited him to take a seat.

"Bill! Thank you for seeing me before I left."

"Vincent," President Holland smiled. "I'm glad we had time to schedule this meeting."

President Vincent D'astier of France looked behind him and acknowledged the two amborgs that had escorted him.

"As you can see," he said in a rich, French accent while flashing a confident grin, "I'm in good hands."

While the two Presidents settled in for their discussion, 125 and 274 positioned themselves in the corner, vigilantly monitoring the room as their designated protectors.

"What was the last thing that Dr. Kendrick transmitted?" 274 leaned towards 125, lowering his voice.

"A rescue operation," 125 answered back softly.

"A rescue operation? That sounds awesome."

125 sighed.

"Still," he said. "We're here and they're up there. They're outnumbered and floating in the vastness of space. Not that I dislike our current jobs but..."

"It's still important," 274 replied. "We're also technically outnumbered down here too."

President D'astier had been visiting the U.S. when all the events in outer space went down. He had been traveling the world on a French goodwill tour of some kind, and visiting the White House was one of his last stops on the journey home. Some emergency joint cooperative bill or something like that had been proposed ever since the arrival of Serina 43.

With a surge of incidents unfolding in outer space, President D'astier's return to France was delayed. In light of the growing chaos and public panic, President Holland deemed it necessary for his Secret Service advisors to create a secure travel plan to ensure the French leader's safe and discreet passage home. The national guard and police forces were inundated with the fallout from the S.C.E. and Tandeeri war. When D'astier finally left, 247 would accompany him as an escort, while 125 would stay behind to protect the White House.

"Thank you *mon ami*," he said, sighing in relief. "I am very grateful we were able to negotiate an exchange. And all this trouble just to get home to my people, I can't even begin to thank you for going that far for me. I remember the days when we could just go out the front door and walk around in public without a care in the world. I shall never forget your kindness, even as the heavens light up above."

"Remember to go out with your umbrella," President Holland grinned. The two of them stood up and shook hands. "Safe journey. Your people won't be able to do without you. Especially your family. Please tell your wife congratulations on the additions to the French leadership."

"My third child," President D'astier nodded as they said their farewells. "I hope that we make it to see the future that they will be born into."

"We will," President Holland nodded.

The French president chuckled and shook a finger. As he turned to leave, he looked at 125 and 274 cheerfully.

"Jesse," he said, "I'm ready to return home."

"I will get you there safely and protect you until the end of this Emergency Recall," 274 replied with a firm nod.

Although 274 had already conveyed these sentiments to the French president, he felt it was necessary for President Holland to also hear his words. Their safety was, in fact, a high priority to A.I. Industries, and the amborgs were committed to ensuring that these leaders would continue to effectively guide their nations through this chain of events.

"See you back at home," 274 gazed at 125 as he began to follow President D'astier out of the Oval Office.

As they stepped through the door, 125 saw Secret Service and a handful of DGSE agents waiting. The French agents enclosed themselves in a small formation to protect their leader and 274. The outer group was composed of

President Holland's agents. The entire group would be escorted to President D'astier's transport.

"Marco," President Holland smiled. "Mind shutting the door please? I have a few minutes until my Chief of Staff comes in. Perhaps you could give me an update?"

"It doesn't sound good sir," 125 admitted as the door to the Oval Office closed again, barring the outside office from hearing them. "The last time we were in contact with Dr. Kendrick, they confirmed that our amborg reinforcements sent up into space were captured. Now there's some type of plan being concocted to go after them."

"Well, that explains the whole top-secret message he mailed me," President Holland stated. "Do you know what he sent?"

"No sir," 125 replied honestly. "If it was a heavily encrypted message, no one but you has seen it. If I may, we should consider the fact that there are rumors."

"Oh?"

President Holland stared at 125 suspiciously.

"What rumors?"

"I heard members of your cabinet trying to coerce your Chief of Staff," 125 lowered his voice. "They don't think that you have what it takes to lead us through this entire thing."

"Well, that's valid," President Holland shrugged. "I'm the 75th President of the United States and we have an interstellar multiverse war going on above our heads. I'm witnessing history unfold and there's nothing I can do about it except try to prevent my country from falling apart."

"All I'm trying to tell you is that some people are trying to get you out of office," 125 stated. "We already have too much going on down here. We're getting requests faster than we can process them."

"I understand," President Holland said. "You protect me from physical harm, so I'll concentrate on the politics. What are we dealing with right now?"

"Fortunately," 125 reported, "the national guard in all states have mobilized and have been dispatched all across the country to help the lower priority assignments. Members of all amborg groups are traveling the world and helping where they can."

"Could I ask you for information about one particular assignment?"

"Which one?"

President Holland lowered his voice and looked 125 in the eyes.

"The cargo ship in Los Angeles, where are we with that?"

125 nodded.

"We have dispatched amborg 723 to handle that one," he stated. "She will report in once we have a target to pursue."

"723," President Holland glanced away, trying to recall who that was. As the memory surfaced, he turned his attention back to 125. "Isn't she the former... amborg-killer?"

"Yes sir."

"And you thought she was the best option? Will she be alright on her own?"

"You forget, sir, that amborgs are more than capable of carrying out certain tasks on their own," 125 nodded confidently. "We are ready to back her up if she calls us."

"Well, the next time she contacts you, tell her that I support her 100%," President Holland dipped his head respectfully. "In the name of those that were killed in the Los Angeles harbor, we will find the ones responsible."

125 smiled as President Holland walked over to his desk.

"Marco," he said, settling into his chair. "We have a shuttle from Alpha universe with S.C.E. liaisons out on our front lawn. If some people in my staff want me removed as President, what will happen to them?"

"My mission is to protect you, Mr. President," 125 stated.

"What happens if I'm no longer President? What will you do?"

"I will continue to protect you," 125 repeated his instructions. "Being overthrown would only highlight the lack of faith your staff have for you. If they try to fight our friends from the Alpha universe or do anything harmful, my loyalty is to you."

"Thank you," President Holland smiled.

The door opened and they both turned to see one of his secretaries entering.

"Sir," he said, "Miss Seras is here to see you."

"Good," President Holland nodded. "Please send her in right away."

As the secretary stepped out, he looked at 125 and took a calming deep breath.

"Well," he exhaled, "if my Chief of Staff seems to be hearing about some dissent in the ranks, I think we should get to the bottom of this and nip it in the bud."

"Right away," 125 nodded. "Good plan, sir."

His Chief of Staff was someone named Emily Seras. She was a young blond-haired woman in a business suit who walked with haste. She greeted the President and 125 frantically.

"Mr. President," she said, "I have the latest reports from across the country."

"Let's hear it," President Holland nodded.

"Oil and gas lines have all been secured," she reported as she read a list on a sheet of paper. "Our power grids and refineries have increased security. We still have heavy amounts of mass transit that is slowly moving."

Immigration policies, economics, and the social infrastructure of the country was constantly changing. All the President could do was try to teach the American people that they had to continue adapting and improvising as best as they could.

"How are the banks doing?" President Holland asked.

"It was a good idea to keep the ATMs online sir," Emily smiled. "Letting the people have access to their money was a wise decision. With the banks slowly reopening across the country, the people are worrying less about financial issues."

After his announcement to the people, President Holland had asked the White House staff to close the banks straightaway. This would be a temporary solution since his economic and financial advisers predicted that the country and the rest of the world would be undergoing massive problems. Shutting down the banks for a few days would have been better than generating another Great Depression. If everyone had all decided to withdraw their money at the same time all across the country, the banks would have collapsed. He allowed the ATMs and credit lines to remain active, which proved to be a great decision.

President Holland then heard Emily share another issue that caught his attention.

"Say that again?" he turned sharply. "I'm so sorry, I lost focus for a moment. What did you just say?"

He'd looked away for a moment, lost in thought, and had only caught a snippet of something odd she just said.

"There's an anti-space movement that's taking place across a few states," Emily replied, "but it's being investigated right now."

"Anti-space? What does that mean?"

"Several online forums are posting about how we have to fight the alien invasion," she answered. "The visitors from the S.C.E. landing around the world are here to take over. A lot of citizens believe it's their right to defend themselves."

"Well that's ridiculous," President Holland stated. "The S.C.E. liaisons have been providing us with lots of enlightening information about their ways, their world, and their universe. They aren't the enemy. We even put a stop to launching nuclear weapons!"

"I understand your sentiment Mr. President," Emily nodded. "But the fact is, there are a lot of people that don't know the things you've discussed with the S.C.E. diplomats. A lot of radicalized militias and armed civilians are inciting trouble across the country."

"And why wasn't this at the top of our list?" President Holland asked.

"It's being contained," Emily replied quickly. "The military and police are handling these incidents as they crop up."

"Get the press corps together Emily," President Holland ordered firmly. "Let's set up a press conference so we can address this."

"Sir? Are you sure that's a good idea?"

"Yes! We need to try to put a stop to this before we accidentally cause the S.C.E. any problems," President Holland stated. "They're helping us defend our planet, for crying out loud. I want the American people to know that we should be fighting at their side and defending our planet together. We need to convince them that if they attack the S.C.E. diplomats around the world, it could lead to another war. Us against a futuristic military force that wouldn't even have to land on our planet to conquer us. Is that what you want?"

"No sir," Emily said as she hastily scribbled a note at the bottom of her paper. "I'll get them together."

"Is there anything else you want to tell me?"

Emily hesitated as she glanced at 125. President Holland gazed at her sternly. It wasn't wise to keep him waiting, so she cleared her throat.

"General Wingate has been requesting to take military action. There's an incident involving U.S. citizens overseas that he wants your approval for."

"Damn it, I told him that he shouldn't overstep his authority. Is he trying to make us look bad?"

President Holland glanced to the side and saw that 125 had lifted a finger and tapped his nose. Apparently, this was a signal. It looked like he was "on the nose" about this situation.

"Emily," Holland lowered his gaze at her. "Tell the General I want to meet him. Now. I took an oath as your leader to make sure that the country remains intact tomorrow and we will keep working to strengthen the nation. I will not have it undermined by someone who panics and pulls the trigger on other human beings!"

"Yes sir!"

Emily left the Oval Office hastily as President Holland glanced at 125.

"A very firm stance," he complimented him. "Very powerful."

"Let's hope it sticks," President Holland let out another sigh. "Come on, we still have a lot of work to do."

Epilogue:

Pentagon

"Major? You have a visitor."

Audrey looked up from her screen when she heard a knock on her door. It clicked and swung open and Janine, her secretary, poked her head in. Janine was always reliable and eager to assist, but Audrey could have sworn she'd directly left her orders that she wasn't to be disturbed.

"I can't see anyone at the moment," she answered nonchalantly. "I'm in the middle of all of these dispatches. You're going to have to tell them to come back."

Audrey gave Janine an apologetic look. The entire office floor was sorting through mountains of paperwork and files. She and many other officers were sifting through so much information that it felt like she hadn't left her desk for several days. Ever since her return from vacation, the overtime was a nightmare, but at least she could expect a nice payout after this. If she lived through this.

Since the appearance of the S.C.E., the military had been scrambling to get their troops back to a state of readiness. That was phase one, appropriately named by Audrey and her colleagues. It took about three days to successfully activate the National Guard in every state across the country. Even with the forces that were already prepared, the announcement of an incident in outer space was enough to throw everyone into disarray. Phase two involved deploying every police and military unit they had to try and handle problems from each state. The amborgs that were assigned to protect the U.S. would also be assisting wherever they could.

Audrey reflected on her time in school, remembering how it wasn't always safe to leave campus. Venturing into town or visiting nearby cities wasn't always pleasant, as chaos seemed to lurk around every corner. When the amborgs started cleaning up the streets, conditions improved greatly. When she lost her brother during the Dominoe Incident, the destruction and pandemonium of that brief conflict had ended so many lives and almost shattered the progress that society tried to cultivate. The events in outer space seemed to revert everyone back to a chaotic mass mentality of panic and fear. Things really felt like they did a decade ago—the same level of tension and anxiety hung in the air.

"Major."

Janine suddenly called out to her again, snapping her out of her daydream. Audrey straightened up and focused.

"Look," Audrey gestured to the stack of folders that hadn't been touched. "I'm really busy. For real."

"Well, he said that if you were available for a few minutes," Janine nervously stood her ground and looked to the side. "He knows you and your husband really well."

Audrey gazed skeptically at Janine.

"Amborg?"

"No."

"Ok then," Audrey struggled to form an idea of who it could be. "A.I. Industries?"

"No, he's from the White House."

"That still doesn't narrow it down, surprisingly," Audrey was still drawing a blank. "Fine, I'll see him. But in one minute, call me and tell me someone is on the phone for me."

It was a classic escape hatch. If there was something that Audrey didn't like about a conversation, she would have Janine call her from outside. First, she would use her own cell phone to dial the phone at her desk. Once she answered it, she would pretend to be chatting with a facsimile and then announce in Audrey's office that there was a caller on the line. This would give her the excuse to postpone or end the conversation.

Janine smiled and her head disappeared from sight. Audrey rose from her chair and straightened her uniform. She had to at least try and look presentable for whoever was visiting. Some footsteps came from around the corner, and she saw the silhouette of a man approaching. The door opened again and she lit up.

"So, I really hope it's not a bad time?"

"Brad!"

The first and last time that she'd seen Brad was at her and 117's wedding. He'd been a high school senior writing a paper about the amborgs a few years ago. He had befriended her husband and had the opportunity to speak to many people at A.I. Industries to get an exclusive, once-in-a-lifetime experience.

117 had invited him as a friend and that's how Audrey learned about how his senior thesis had been received well at his school. He managed to complete

an early-college program, moved to Pennsylvania, and got hired at a rather impressive job.

"How's it going for you, being one of the youngest press reporters to sit in the White House?" Audrey asked.

"It's kind of cool that whenever the President calls for a press conference, I sometimes get to throw a question at him," Brad smiled.

"Well, I don't mean to brag but I get to visit the Oval Office twice a month," Audrey smirked. "Three times, if I'm lucky."

"But have you actually gotten a chance to talk to him directly?"

"It's not a competition."

Audrey and Brad both hugged and laughed. This was a very nice and cathartic moment. It definitely felt much better than sifting through proverbial mountains of data and reading the stacks of paper folders on her desk.

"Well, clearly, it looks like you could use some help with these," Brad eyed her desk.

"Where's Carter when I need him, right?" Audrey sighed.

Audrey walked over, grabbed a file on the top, and read the title. She quickly picked up her pen, signed her signature on it, and strolled over to the wall.

"Another requisition that's going to go to another officer, and then another," she sighed again as she hit a button next to a small compartment. "Once a lot of people sign it, it's probably just going to get lost in the building somewhere."

"Why not just toss some of these?" Brad asked curiously.

The door to the compartment swung open. Audrey slid the form inside, and a green light swept over it, scanning the entire thing. Once it finished, a prompt appeared on the screen within. Audrey pressed a few buttons and then hit the "send" button. A green check mark popped up, confirming that it had been successfully sent to the intended recipient.

Audrey took the original file over to a small bin. Once she dropped it in, the lid closed tightly. She then pressed a red button on the side, activating it. Brad watched as a little bit of heat radiated from it, and a small amount of smoke lightly spilled out.

"You got the new document incinerator," he smiled, then the reality of what he'd just seen hit. "Wait, isn't that a fire hazard?"

"Yes," Audrey nodded as she sauntered over to her desk and picked up another file. "Only if it explodes."

"Does it tend to explode frequently?" Brad asked, taking a step back.

"Haven't had an incident since I got it," Audrey smirked.

"When did you get it?"

Audrey skimmed through the file before placing it on the middle stack reserved for her high-priority forms. Turning to Brad, she smiled and shook her head lightly.

"I know it's been a while since we've seen each other, but maybe we should just skip the nonsense. What are you doing here?"

"I needed your help to try and contact anyone at A.I. Industries for me," Brad said. "The number of emails, calls, and messages being sent there are overwhelming and it's difficult to get through. I was wondering if I could borrow your hotline?"

"I only have private lines set up for David, Mandy, and my A.I. Carter," Audrey replied. "What's wrong?"

"I needed to get in touch with 117's grandfather," Brad explained. "Some of my colleagues at work keep hearing a lot of troubling rumors. The main one I just heard recently is that the S.C.E. is not to be trusted?"

"What?" Audrey blinked. "Who told you that?"

"It's been circulating on the internet," he said in a soft tone. "Many people are arming themselves and itching for a fight. They all keep talking about defending the country or the planet from invasion. I don't exactly have much to offer, so I figured that you could get in touch with Mark's vigilantes."

"I can't just call him," Audrey replied nervously. "Not only would that be going outside the chain of command but with the whole war we have above the planet right now, everyone's really busy trying not to think about the fact that the planet could be gone at any moment."

"Tragedy makes people appreciate each other more or they become afraid of each other," Brad stated. "I'm just thinking about the people that are afraid of the S.C.E."

"I'll see what I can do," Audrey nodded.

"Also, do you think that the country won't tear itself apart if things go wrong?" Brad asked quickly.

"No," Audrey replied instantly. "There's so much tension in this building that one wrong move could send everyone over the edge. You know how quick to violence people can be when things spiral out of control."

"And what's your opinion about the S.C.E.? These visitors that have landed in D.C. and are enlightening the White House?"

"Are you doing an interview right now?" Audrey shot Brad an incredulous look. "Because if you visited me here just to sneak in these questions..."

"Oh no!" Brad exclaimed, immediately shaking his head. His eyes grew wide as he backed up a step. "Sorry, default work mode. I didn't mean to start it like that."

"Ok," Audrey exhaled as she sank into her chair. "Just be careful. I don't speak on behalf of the Pentagon. Any information regarding what's going on in outer space and here with the S.C.E. diplomats are not up to me to share. Can I trust you not to be that guy that adds more fuel to the rumor mill on the internet?"

"Absolutely," Brad nodded. "I just thought you should know that the anti-alien sentiment is mounting."

"I always knew that there were a lot of people that didn't believe in extra-terrestrial life, but I doubt it's going to escalate that much," Audrey replied.

"I'm just saying," Brad insisted. "You should start reading about what people are posting and get ready to start a lot of investigating. We need to get on top of the growing threats before these people do something extreme. Some are claiming that the S.C.E. diplomats are using mind control techniques, alien weapons invisible to us, and planning assimilation to make the people of Earth surrender their bodies to their new overlords."

"Where are all of these rumors coming from?" Audrey asked.

"I know that the Pentagon and the White House have some of the best cybersecurity specialists in the world," Brad shrugged, "but I really think that we should start taking some of these rumors seriously and not pretend they're not there."

"That's about a million things that we would have to check," Audrey mumbled.

"It is," Brad nodded. "I just think that as a friendly suggestion, we could contact more of our friends at A.I. Industries to expedite things."

Audrey sighed as she glanced at the mountain of files piled up on her desk. Sorting through them all was no small feat. People often said that being a military-style office worker was pretty significant, but she wasn't convinced she could be at her best staying cooped up in her office any longer.

"Alright then," she said. "Do you have anything from your sources that maybe we could consider looking into first?"

Brad pulled a thumb drive out of his pocket.

"Well, for starters, I'll leave this here with you," he said.

After Audrey accepted the drive, Brad left and promised to be in touch. She plugged it into her computer and started checking for anything suspicious or any hostile malware. The scan revealed nothing hazardous, so she opened the first document and started looking at some screenshots as she pulled out her cellphone.

She immediately dialed the hotline to Mandy and hoped that she was listening. After a few minutes, there was a click and her voice answered.

"Hello? Audrey?"

"Mandy," Audrey smiled in relief when she heard her. "Good to hear from you."

"Same," Mandy replied cheerfully. "You calling to check in? It's been a few days since your last text."

"Been busy," Audrey sighed. "I just got visited by Brad. He had some stuff he wanted me to send to you."

"Brad? Well, I'm glad to hear that he's ok," Mandy said. "What did he want to send?"

"Has A.I. Industries been investigating any leads regarding any anti-alien sentiments?"

"Don't get me started," Mandy groaned. "There's a small team of amborgs that 4 assembled that are dealing with those matters. They just finished arresting a bunch of bomb-makers in the middle of Wyoming. Their intentions were unclear. Many people are trying to claim that it's the end of the world in order to justify them committing a great deal of federal crimes."

"Ah," Audrey awkwardly looked at the rest of the files that Brad had left her. "So, all of the things that I'm reading here are useless then?"

"Not necessarily," Mandy replied. "Send me what you have and we'll see if Brad discovered anything that we haven't. More information doesn't hurt. We just need to sort through and prioritize what needs to be taken care of."

"Thanks Mandy," Audrey smiled. "I'll send you the files in a moment."

"Was there anything else?"

Audrey thought of 117. She glanced down at her wedding ring, then her eyes drifted to a small framed photo of her and her husband sitting on a shelf near her desk. 117 beamed with joy, his arms wrapped around her belly, highlighting a forming baby bump.

Audrey then spoke into the phone again.

"How's Sarah? Is... she doing ok?"

Mandy laughed.

"She's doing fine," she answered kindly. "She's waiting for both of you. She misses her mom and dad."

Audrey and 117's two year old daughter wasn't old enough to be aware of what was happening in the world right now. She had tried to justify to herself that her work was going to keep her family safe. After Brad had stopped by to ask that she contact A.I. Industries, something in her just seemed to snap. All of sudden, she felt scared and desperately needed to hear good news for a change.

"I should have been the one to get her," Audrey sighed in relief, but she couldn't shake off the heavy guilt that was weighing down on her. "We were on vacation and this all happened."

"You can't blame yourself for things beyond your control," Mandy replied. "All that matters is that you're helping out."

"I should be there with you and my daughter."

"Well, you can't go awol," Mandy said bluntly. "That's a court-martial offense. She's in good hands here. Don't worry."

"Thanks Mandy, but if you don't mind," Audrey clenched her lips. "Could I talk to her? Could someone put her on the phone? I need to hear her voice."

"I'll go get her. Hang on."

Audrey remained as calm as she could while the hold music played in the background. A nagging question in the back of her mind made her entire body burn with guilt as she anxiously waited to hear Sarah's voice. After a minute of waiting, she heard a click.

"Mommy?"

"Hi Sarah," Audrey breathed happily.

"Where are you?"

"I'm at work," Audrey sniffed, holding back a few tears. "How are you?"

"Ok, I guess."

"Ok?" she smiled. "Well, that's good! You should keep listening to all of your aunts and uncles!"

"When are you coming back?" Sarah asked in a gentle voice.

"Uh, soon, I hope," Audrey replied. "It's just been so busy."

"Is papa with you?"

"No," Audrey said. "He's working, too. He's off being a hero."

"Hero? Is he saving the world again?"

Audrey peered at the photo on her shelf again. She definitely hoped that 117 was ok and continued to do what he did best. There was no way she could tell her firstborn that she didn't know or that she hadn't been in contact due to her heavy workload. She had to be as reassuring as possible while she waited to hear from him.

"Yeah," Audrey nodded. "Papa is away being a hero."

To be continued: Files for T.H.I. Reditus have finished.

Thank you for utilizing the A.I. Industries public database.

Book Three coming next Fall 2025

The Human Inside:

Obstinatio

A.I. Industries Database Personnel Files
Special Notes and Data Entries Compiled by Dr. John Kendrick
Edition 3: **Note:** Some entries have been revised/omitted from previous files

Epsilon Universe

The Amborgs

First Group: 30 Active members. Initiated in 2115.

The first 30 humans to be cybernetically enhanced by A.I. Industries. Many refer to them as the originals. They have the highest experience in comparison to all amborgs that came after them. My wife always did care strongly about their mental health as much as their physical health. They are all wise and strong together and as individuals.

Second Group: <u>29</u> Active members. Initiated in 2127.

After the untimely loss of Melissa, I admit that I was temporarily unable to continue with my goals of expanding my cyborg family. Fortunately, after a personal hiatus, I found my way again and set to work looking for more volunteers. Another 30 amborgs joined the First Group as I continued perfecting the enhancement procedures. Tragically, the Second Group lost Serina 43, arguably the strongest amborg in all of A.I. Industries. Her number has since been retired and no replacement has taken her place. This was a decision made by the amborgs that I continue to respect to this day.

Third Group: <u>30</u> Active members. Initiated in 2128.

Under special circumstances, I had the Third Group amborgs training schedule accelerated when active members from the First and Second Groups encountered enemy combatants that had developed countermeasures against them. It was terrifying knowing that outsiders were finding new and creative ways to defeat the amborgs so I figured that a new group of them would tip the scales in a balanced manner. They joined the field, supporting their brothers and sisters with strong willpower and commitment. In 10 years, they lost one amborg (Amara 345) and a new member joined their roster in 2138; Lizzy 723.

Fourth Group: <u>30</u> Active members. Initiated in 2134.

After the Dominoe Incident in 2128, I devoted as many resources as possible to helping the US rebuild. My company is based in the Midwest and definitely wanted to help the country get back on its feet. Because of A.I. Industries' contribution, President Holland allowed me to initiate another group of

664

amborgs despite public opinion directing a lot of negative feedback. I managed to convince The White House and Congress that amborgs were still a necessity. I'm glad that everyone ended up agreeing.

■■■ ..

Leonard 1: First Group. Age 41.

I'll never forget the day I met Leonard on the streets. Or in this case, I'll never forget the time I caught him trying to steal my wallet. The very first human to successfully become an amborg. I witnessed his very first mission, his marriage to a lovely woman, and becoming the first hero of A.I. Industries. He is the leader of the First Group and the most experienced cybernetic being on the active roster. Many of the others look up to him and seek advice from him when needed. Discreetly, I know that he is currently single due to a quiet and personal divorce, which is all I will share.

Ziggy 2: First Group. Age 40.

Leonard 1's closest friend. Despite being the second person in history to successfully survive cybernetic augmentation, he allows amborg 1 to assume the leadership role since being in the spotlight isn't really his style. I'm not sure if it's out of habit that Ziggy tends to step aside whenever there are missions requiring a primary leader or if it's because he proudly wears the number two. Nevertheless, I've seen him set his limits on where he prefers to be in the chain of command. He's quite capable and comfortable with others taking the spotlight.

Missy 3 aka Melissa Carson: First Group. Age 38.

The iron chef of A.I. Industries. For recreational purposes, which has now become a key driving point in her life, she is one of the world's most renowned culinary experts. I am proud of her accomplishments. Food being her life is an understatement. When she isn't publicly wearing her amborg attire, she is the manager of Crystalline, a top-tier restaurant in New York. It's rumored that you need to book months in advance just to get a table. She has made quite a name for herself ever since she poisoned half the First Group when she started out. I can still feel the stomach pains from that incident... but let's not bring that up again.

Katrina "Kat" 4: First Group. Age 39.

When the First Group amborgs were initiated, they needed someone in their ranks to carry out logistics. The one woman that could handle that kind of responsibility is Kat. She is regarded as one of A.I. Industries' best coordinators for operations and is usually the one who drafts the mission briefs for all other amborgs. I have to admit, she is one terrifyingly smart amborg. She could probably run my company blindfolded with one hand and leg tied down to an anchor and she'd still accept any challenges thrown her way.

Johnny 5: First Group. Age 40.

Every group of friends has that one guy. Or perhaps in a unique and diverse family, there's always the one person who utilizes their sense of humor to pave the way for social interactions. It's hard to pinpoint which amborg from the First Group reconnected with their human emotions first. Melissa probably would be able to tell you but most would say that Johnny 5 was the one who did it successfully and more quickly than the others. Always keep them laughing is what he was taught and on many occasions, he always tries to lighten the mood with his quips and witty remarks. I never get tired of his jokes or his fun stories. He brings a large level of positivity all the time.

Vanessa 6: First Group. Age 39.

The doctor of the amborgs. Despite the fact that everyone has mandatory medical training, 6 has always demonstrated a passionate love for the medical field. Saving lives regularly is fulfilling, but caring for the health of the people she encounters is always a priority. There's a rumor that she's saved over a thousand people since her career as an amborg began. From what I learned, she only keeps track of one number; the number of people she's lost. The bigger that number gets, the more dedicated she is. I think she's quite remarkable in that regard.

Stuart 8: First Group. Age 38.

Although Johnny 5 is known for his humor, practical jokes are 8 and 9's specialty. If something catches on fire, he's usually one of the suspects. It's getting to be quite difficult to determine whether or not their antics are actually helpful in the field. I was concerned at first when I started reading their post-action reports from the missions they deployed on but now, I'm confident that the others can keep their antics under control. But... I keep an extra container of aspirin close by when I'm about to listen to their debriefings.

Christy 9: First Group. Age 38.

It was probably not a good idea to enhance someone with an almost unhealthy obsession with constantly breaking fire code and safety regulations. Despite her unusual and unorthodox tactics, she does manage to get the job done... even if it means the social media relations department has to step in and issue public apologies on her behalf to put out the, no pun intended, fires she ignites on the internet. I would be lying if I wrote in her personnel file that she didn't give me migraines every time I summoned her to my office for an explanation.

Clint 11: First Group. Age 40.

Clint 11 has always ventured out into the wilderness on plenty of occasions. Many of the amborgs learned how to survive thanks to his outdoorsy and adventurous background. Very few know this but he assisted amborg 1 in hiding A.I. Industries asset, codenamed: Nova in an undisclosed location for their protection. If you were to abandon him in a desert or frozen tundra alone, he would definitely show up at your doorstep the following day without a scratch.

Danielle 12: First Group. Age 41.

A quiet but skillful tactician, she always employs communication as her primary tactic for the most difficult situations. Don't let her kind demeanor fool you, she is just as deadly as the next amborg if negotiations fall short. Aggressive negotiations are substituted at that point to get the job done.

Kiden 18: First Group. Age 38.

If you wish to learn what it takes to go undercover, the expert is amborg 18. Onsite, she is the lead trainer and supervisor for all amborg physical exercises. She keeps every amborg at A.I. Industries trained and properly conditioned to carry out their activities at all times. In the field, she excels at maintaining secret identities for covert operations and being discreet. Over the last decade, she has secured a strong relationship with the head of the largest Italian crime family. I'm not exactly sure what led to this unlikely alliance but leaving that under her sole responsibility is giving A.I. Industries plenty of plausible deniability. I just hope that I don't have to participate in something extremely terrible because she got in trouble with the mafia.

Tiana 19: First Group. Age 39.

I discovered Tiana roaming on the streets of Boston. She has a huge personal connection to the East Coast. After the Dominoe Incident, she traveled across the states and primarily concentrated her efforts on reconstruction projects for anyone that had lost their homes. I was very grateful for all the help she provided during that time period. She remains adamant that no one else should lose the roofs over their heads and I love her passion for that.

Jennifer 24: First Group. Age 42.

Like several other candidates that went through A.I. Industries various programs, 24 doesn't have many memories about her family or past. She remains at A.I. Industries and chooses not to actively seek out more about her life prior to cybernetic enhancement. Many have commented that this decision seems questionable, but they respect it nonetheless. I absolutely respect her choice and appreciate that I can count on her at all times..

■ ■

David 117: Second Group. Age 27.

In my opinion, I would like to state for the record that David has made quite a name for himself since his initiation. The elected leader of the Second Group and one of the finest amborgs that I've ever seen. If anyone else had taken up the mantle or if he hadn't been there, the Dominoe Incident could have turned out quite differently. Despite being seen in public as shy or mild-mannered, he has a very open and friendly nature among friends. He's one of the few who still has a living familial relative. A paternal grandfather... mmm, Mark. After the loss of Serina 43, who was his girlfriend at the time, he continued his duties as an amborg and I worried that he was going to sink into a state of depression. I kept an eye on him, but saw that he was ok and managed to recover. Now he's become a husband and a father and I am absolutely proud of him.

Serina 43: Second Group. Epsilon Status: Deceased

Due to the fact that she is a legend at my company, I have to acknowledge and write this for the record. According to her peers, she is known as the best amborg to exist in the history of A.I. Industries and I will always agree with that statement. Serina and David had family members that worked with me. Even though I had sworn never to allow them into the amborg program, I promised them that if anything happened, I would protect them at all costs. Tragically, I failed her family's last wishes. She would become the first amborg to die and this would cast a dark shadow over the Second Group, her closest friends. Her life ended after the Assassin of the Dominoe Incident mortally wounded her. Despite using illegal technology to force her to defame A.I. Industries and my name, she devoted every moment of her life to serving the world. She passed away officially in 2130. Shortly after, we developed an A.I. at the company and named her Serina in her honor.

Jack 917: Second Group. Age 29.

An odd and peculiar case among the amborgs. He is probably the most controversial human being that the amborg program ever encountered. Everyone knows I enhanced 917 out of a coma to save his life. When he woke up, he had a severe case of amnesia and unfortunately had to live with the fact that he was different. He chose the name Jack because he had many talents and skills. It suits him. The enhancement was authorized by an unnamed savior, and I would like to respect their privacy as I continue sharing my thoughts. Jack is a very devoted amborg but at times, I feel that he's a loose cannon. However, I do think he is capable of great deeds. I often wonder... and I am afraid to ask him, does he resent me for saving his life? Should I have let him die? Was all of this what he wanted? Forgive me, I'm rambling. Let's move on. He has been rather distant since losing his former apprentice, Amara 345 of the Third Group.

Alice "Angel" 999: Second Group. Age 28

The lone wolf of the amborgs. She is known to be silent, deadly, and extremely lethal. Her personality contrasts with Jack 917 but they exhibit an indescribable bond as friends. She's his best friend, according to both of them. She is the former apprentice to Vanessa 6 and the former mentor to Amara 345. Oddly enough, she appears to be the current mentor of Lizzy 723, but I'm not entirely sure. From what she's told me, she visits a nice lady out in Portland whenever she asks for time off. It's actually quite relieving to hear that someone out there raised her with kindness before she came to A.I. Industries. She has been through quite an ordeal and despite how silent she is most of the time, I encourage everyone that tries to befriend her to be incredibly patient and respectful to her. Boundaries. She is really particular about her boundaries. May God help you if you so much as try to put a finger on her without her permission.

Carter 297 aka "Carter Richardson:" Second Group. Age 27.

I love my son Carter very much. Do not misunderstand this passage in his file. However, I was clear with him when he left A.I. Industries to serve as a soldier in the armed forces. When he sets foot off of company grounds, he will not have my support. I never wanted the amborgs to be military weapons—pawns for the government to throw headfirst into war. Yes, I know that it's a contradiction to send the amborgs out on missions where they have to fight. I will always stand by the fact that they do so as amborgs of A.I. Industries, not as conscripted soldiers. Carter has incredible accuracy and is very proficient in long-range combat. After the Dominoe Incident, he joined the US Special Forces and I acknowledge that he is one of the best soldiers in the world. He is always welcome to come home and we will be here to receive him with open arms, despite the horrific things he's seen and the inhumane acts that he's witnessed. Despite his trauma, I always look forward to the times when he comes home.

Katie 57 aka "Casey Owen:" Second Group. Age 28.

Katie has quite a career and legacy in the ranks of the Second Group. She moonlights as a police officer for the LAPD when not working as an amborg. She serves as a liaison to Commander Bradley at times. She recently discovered that she had a long-lost twin, which was a surprise to all of us. Both were separated from each other at birth. At a political function, we met U.S. Senator Leera Alden who bore a fantastic resemblance to her. I originally thought that it was an elaborate prank, and so did they. Since their meeting, A.I. Industries unexpectedly gained an influential ally. Twins seem to run naturally throughout the Second Group.

Luis 777: Second Group. Age 27.

The luckiest amborg, next to amborg 7 of the First Group that is. Whenever he is seen out on a mission, people have reported that seeing his number out in public brings them good luck. Many of the Second Group amborgs have the number 7 already in their designations but due to the fact that he is 777, he has brought the best amount of luck for many people. I certainly feel lucky whenever he escorts me around in public.

Ryan 35: Second Group. Age 28.

One of the few amborgs to remain behind at A.I. Industries after the end of the Dominoe Incident. He worked on several reconstruction projects and deployed on many missions as needed. Like David, Ryan has always been slightly quiet. He's not really a take-charge type of person and chooses to follow, rather than lead.

Marco 125: Second Group. Age 26.

Specializes in political relations. He is an outstanding liaison to The White House. During Emergency Recalls, I have complete and total faith in his ability to protect members of Congress and the office of POTUS. Although, I do admit there was one time during a previous Presidential Administration where he and the eldest daughter of the former President Layton almost caused quite the scandal. I'm glad that we mended that bridge after a long discussion.

Jesse 274: Second Group. Age 26.

Specializes in international relations. After the Dominoe Incident, he was appointed as a U.S. representative to the United Nations. Even with all of the world's languages available to the amborgs, I am still impressed with how many that Jesse has learned and become fluent in. Despite the antics and shenanigans caused by some of the others, he maintains a very professional and prosperous relationship with friends and allies abroad as well as at home. I am proud of him being one of the politicians helping to maintain world diplomacy. The UN certainly doesn't want me in charge no matter how many times I ask.

Keith 66: Second Group. Age 28.

I'm pretty sure that 'city-boy' is enough to describe him. Keith has never really enjoyed the missions that had him going anywhere near a forest, the mountains, or near the beach. What's wrong with the beach or anywhere tropical? Oh well, he spends so much time on his computers at home where he feels comfortable… Who am I to break him from his solitude?

Steve 92: Second Group. Age 30.

Remember what I said about twins earlier? I originally thought that Steve and his brother Jon were the only twin amborgs I would ever have at A.I. Industries. Like all biological siblings, they did eventually have to resolve some rather intense disagreements with a deadlock duel. Their differing perspectives on opposing sides was one of the few times I ever felt afraid of the fact that I could tell which one was which. Despite that one incident, the two have fought alongside each other. They are now inseparable.

Jon 93: Second Group. Age 30.

I'll just add some more of my observations on Jon's file to supplement his brother's. Wow, that was a little intense and went in a different direction than I thought. My apologies. Steve and Jon actually both care a lot about each other. On their own time, they enjoy participating in pranks that the others come up with. My personal favorite is when they switch uniforms or force us to try and distinguish the two of them. It's a game that the Third Group triplets certainly enjoy.

■ ■

Dominic "Donut" 501: Third Group. Age 25.

Like his mentor, David 117, he has gained a lot of influence and is also considered to be the leader of the Third Group. I will be honest, I am terrified whenever his name is mentioned or I see an incident report with him in the subject line. I would like to give him the benefit of the doubt but to be fair, he has a tendency to cause a lot of problems or is involved in situations that are way out of his comfort zone. If he ever gets stuck in a jam, he has family and friends that will protect him. I fear the day that none of us will be there for him when he's truly fighting on his own.

Carolina 466: Third Group. Age 24.

If anything happens to Dominic, I trust Carol will take care of him. Although sometimes, when she also participates in his shenanigans, I can expect a pretty interesting report from the two of them. Using the time that he was kidnapped as an example, I know that she'll stop at nothing to make sure that he's ok. She is a great partner and friend to him.

Amara 345: Third Group. Status: Deceased.

If I had days to talk about her, I will. But I'll keep this short. Her loss to the Third Group... no, all the amborgs, was demoralizing. Amara was incredible. Talented, optimistic, and... I don't know what it was about her but... she could make you feel... like you could do anything. She was the most amazing mathematician that I had met, even prior to becoming an amborg. When she injured her spine during our Third Emergency Recall, she was so strong and worked hard to recover. I wish that I had never sent her on that mission when she was cleared for active duty. Maybe, if we had done better, she would still be here. Unfortunately, she would tell me what many have already said to me; that there's nothing we can do about the past.

Lizzy 723: Third Group. Age 21.

Taking Lizzy into our ranks has always been a great subject of controversy. For the record, she has attempted to murder three of our amborgs. Unsuccessfully, if anyone was curious, and I am fortunate that not a single amborg was taken from us by her hand. In 2130, reports from overseas delivered troubling news. The UN security forces uncovered a secret installation owned by a foreign nation attempting to recreate my work at A.I. Industries. My company wasn't the only organization with cybernetically enhanced individuals. Lizzy was part of an illegal team of trained individuals brainwashed and designed for one purpose; to challenge the amborgs. Amborg-killers were what we called them. I dispatched a team to combat this situation and to my surprise, when they had the opportunity, the amborgs captured Lizzy alive and brought her home to A.I. Industries. At the request of Kat 4, we made her an amborg after we allowed Lizzy to make the choice. She is the only amborg replacement in the entire Third Group.

Roland 249: Third Group. Age 25.

Roland is a fine leader and quite capable. He maintains a positive relationship with the community and enjoys supervising company departments in his spare time. He is very eager to be a leader and wants to take on more responsibilities. I look forward to how well he helps me maintain and manage the company.

Sara 593: Third Group. Age 26.

When I think about Sara, she reminds me of Melissa at times. She's very bright, enthusiastic and is easy to talk to. Of course, with every amborg, I always try to maintain a strong connection with, but she definitely has a fiery spirit that reminds me of my wife. I know this is crazy to admit but I feel like she channels Melissa at times. Not really something that important to keep thinking about.

Chris 49: Third Group. Age 24.

Ever since I implemented the buddy system protocol, some amborgs in the Third Group really depend on it. Each amborg, individually, is quite capable but Chris acts like he can't be alone for more than five minutes. I don't mind the fact that he likes being part of a team, but he does need to step it up if separated from us.

August 95: Third Group. Age 25.

August has traveled the world frequently, which has given him a lot of insight into cultures that the rest of us aren't too familiar with. His stories are very entertaining and inspiring. His experiences are very unique and if he hadn't decided to become an amborg, he probably would have never traveled as much as he has.

Kayla 53: Third Group. Age 24.

The older amborgs certainly had a lot of things to teach her. Kayla is probably the only amborg in the Third Group that enjoys sneaking around. I guess that's what happens when she finds genealogical data that reveals her ancestors were possibly ninjas. This has helped her improve her skills and I am impressed. Maybe not so much about the part where I keep catching her trying to break into my office to read my personal files. I'm going to go check the lock on my office door after submitting this entry.

Anderson 331: Third Group. Age 23.

The eldest of the triplets of the Third Group. I've always seen him as the least strict of these siblings. I'm not exaggerating, he is in fact the troublemaker of the three triplets.

Allison 332: Third Group. Age 23.

The middle child of the triplets. With the Second Group twins as their mentors, she is the only girl out of the five of them. I always felt that being surrounded by brothers was isolating. I was wrong. Interestingly enough, this dynamic hasn't stopped her from being able to take care of herself and occasionally fight back. In fact, she actually takes charge whenever her brothers are about to do anything stupid.

Atkinson 333: Third Group. Age 23.

The youngest of the triplets. Definitely takes after his brother, Anderson. He is the most competitive of three. I wonder if he feels overshadowed by his brother and sister at times. I don't have a lot of information since he prefers action over words. Clearly, he has some growing up to do.

■ ■

Ally 113: Fourth Group. Age 21.

What worries me about Ally is the fact that she and the other Fourth Group amborgs seem to be adopting

a policy of no emotions. It's like some big event affected them to the point where I can't seem to get an emotional read on them. Even though she is quite capable, I hope that Ally reconnects with her emotions soon.

Alex 280: Fourth Group. Age 21.

Same notes for Ally apply to Alex. Both of them are the definitive leaders of the Fourth Group. Whatever they do or think, it seems to filter down to the other amborgs. I have to properly take some time to identify what seems to be on their minds.

Hugo 63: Fourth Group. Age 20.

Not enough information. I apologize. Ever since the technician program at A.I. Industries was disbanded, the Fourth Group amborgs do not have an official employee that supervises them like before. I maintain a personal connection with every amborg but until I know what has happened, the Fourth Group seem to alienate themselves from the others with their "behavior." You can see my finger quotes right? Ok, just checking.

Lisa 100: Fourth Group. Age 21.

Not enough information. I know that Lisa has attempted to work with the First Group at times but it has yet to yield any emotional results.

Terry 378: Fourth Group. Age 21.

Not enough information. Cold and efficient, just like the other Groups of amborgs before.

Riley 65: Fourth Group. Age 21.

Not enough information. If Melissa was still here, maybe she could properly psychoanalyze the Fourth Group.

Morgan 224: Fourth Group. Age 21.

Not enough information. I'm sorry. Nothing of significant note is coming to mind. The Fourth Group are

the youngest amborgs at A.I. Industries and I assumed that they'd be like the Third Group. However, their personalities have just disappeared. It's like someone locked up their feelings and threw away the key. Don't blame me now, I actually encourage them to search for their emotions.

■■

Amborg Industries aka A.I. Industries

Dr. John Kendrick: CEO

Oh, this is my data entry. Ok then, what should I say? I am... the only child of Dr. Ethan and Susan Kendrick. I am a third-generation scientist, the Creator of the Amborgs and C.E.O. of one the world's most powerful companies. Despite A.I. Industries being based in the U.S., I have the company registered as an independent organization. I created this company and my family in order to make the world a better place. I can only hope that my actions make our unwritten future a good one. If my parents or Melissa are watching over me and my amborgs, I hope I've made them proud.

George Ramirez: Media Relations

One of my oldest friends. Although he is not vice-president of the company, many have often mistaken him in that role. To be fair, he knows the company just as much as I do. Melissa and I met him many years prior to forming the company and made him the head of Public Relations for A.I. Industries. His family resides with him onsite as he maintains business with all outside sources that I cannot handle alone. Well, I need to update one tiny detail. His ex-wife Marina left him recently and with his daughter Thalia away for school, the poor man has been absorbed in work to distract himself. I do hope he's ok.

Dr. Robert Kolaski: Artificial Intelligence R&D Department Head

What? I'm not going to say too much about him. Last time, I put in the flashing alarms as a joke in his personnel file. It was funny then and still is today. But, I'm going to skip this entry.

Thalia Ramirez

George's teenage daughter. For a long time, she was a resident at A.I. Industries before leaving to attend college. Whenever she visits, we treat her well. I wonder what kind of career she'll choose when she graduates. You can see that she has both her mother and father's spirit. To a lot of the staff here, she is part of our great family.

■■■

The Technicians

Mandy Palmer

David 117's closest friend and former technician. At a young age, she was accepted into a program designed to care for and educate the amborgs. When the technician program was discontinued, I reassigned her to other logistical tasks at A.I. Industries. She is very talented and skilled, just like her husband Tom. They are great friends to this company. I remember when I offered to pay for their wedding, and they refused. They said that they wanted to work for that on their own. Mandy has always been headstrong and a valuable employee of A.I. Industries. Despite how young she is, she commands a lot of respect from everyone else. She is quite impressive.

Jacob Kelewski

Jacob has always told me that the only reason he remains one of my employees is because of how good the paychecks are. I have never been one to hold back what I believe they deserve to make annually. Deep down, I know the truth. He likes working for me because he gets to experience the most amazing things ever. I have no clue why he doesn't just admit it. Even after I offered him a position aboard Apogee station, I got nothing. No reaction. Serina tells me that he is excited, but he gets embarrassed whenever someone catches him acting childishly so he does everything in his power not to show it. I personally think that embracing his inner child is more true to who he really is.

Nova: Name redacted

Error. Files redacted. Information unavailable.

Artificial Intelligence Programs:

Serina:

Our best A.I. program. Very few know about her true identity. I would like to keep it that way. She has a much more eccentric personality than the other programs we've raised. She advocates for more rights for artificial intelligence and I trust her with my life. She is technically an upgraded version of a previous incarnation. With Robert and 6's help, she's the new and improved top-of-the-line program.

Carter:

Audrey Wright's former A.I. that has officially taken permanent residency at A.I. Industries. He is a rare older generation model that was discontinued. As a personal request, Audrey sent him to me and we upgraded him so that he wouldn't be declared obsolete and scheduled for deletion as a result. I wonder if upgrading his code and giving him a visual holographic body unexpectedly boosted his ego. He certainly seems to get into a lot of trouble in our systems. I swear to god Carter, if you are on my computer reading this and preparing to edit anything, I will confine you to your hard drive in your quarters.

■■

Apogee Station

When I started coordinating with NASA and began developing my space station, I knew that I needed a crew that could help provide protection and security. The following personnel are the bravest people I have ever had the privilege to work with.

Captain Lee Harrelson: 1ˢᵗ Platoon, B-Company, 205ᵗʰ Marines.

Lee Harrelson is one of the finest soldiers I've met. His parents were veterans of the Third World War, and he saw action with the amborgs in Texas, the Academy, and Washington D.C. Wherever the amborgs deployed, he was right there, ready to provide his support and back them up. During all Emergency Recalls in the history of my company, he went above and beyond and is a living legend. Naturally, I offered him a position aboard Apogee Station. He trained to become certified as an astronaut and took command of a company of marines. I know that under his watch; we are all safe because he and his troops are always ready to respond.

Captain Sheila Hicks: Echo 209, Foe Hammer

When NASA went to the Air Force to look for pilots, the selection process was very competitive. Sheila Hicks exceeded all of my expectations. Apparently, she had been disqualified from my selection process when I looked over the submitted applications. During the Dominoe Incident, she was told to ground her ship and not fly at night when the Academy was under attack. Disobeying orders, she continued to make trips into the war zone to evacuate all of the people that had been left behind. When I sat down and brought this to light, she simply told me that she kept flying because it wasn't right to leave people behind to die. That's when I made her one of the lead pilots of Echo Flight. I have never regretted this decision.

Captain Sam Planck: Echo 232, Night Song

Sam is also another equally skilled pilot as Captain Hicks. He tends to be a stickler for the rules. So much so, he reminds me of the amborgs at times. He once told me that the reason he loves to fly, across the skies or in space, is because it generates a feeling like no other. One time, he flew us in the path of a sudden storm front and instead of allowing fear to take control, he merely laughed. He laughed the entire time that his ship rattled and shook through that storm. For some reason, that made me feel better and reassured me that we would make it. He looks calm and professional, but I have some suspicions that he tends to go crazy. Is it weird that I consider that kind of person to be my kind of pilot?

Lieutenant Benji Frye: Copilot

You have to be a highly trained individual to be able to stomach the constant trips between outer space and Earth. Benji was in the astronaut training corps and became one of the qualifying candidates to join Echo Flight after he interned aboard my station.

Sergeant Dean Hammond: Crew Chief

I was warned before my first trip aboard the Foe Hammer shuttle about one very particular thing. Never refer to the Sergeant as a military flight attendant, otherwise he might just decide to kick you off the ship... while it's in flight. Apparently, there's a rumor that someone... disappeared and never made it to their intended destination. You would think that my position as CEO of A.I. Industries would give me a little leeway. I need to warn the rest of you that I was wrong and very wrong when I tried to make a joke. If Sergeant Hammond had actually decided to commit murder and hide my dead body, I have no doubts he would have gotten away with it. So please do not piss him off. He has no time for bullshit, but it makes him one very tough crew chief that knows how to maintain and keep the shuttles from falling apart after every trip.

■ ■

Acquaintances & Allies

Grandpa Mark

Almost all the amborgs don't have a living relative. Mark is the exception. He is David 117's paternal grandfather and the head of a strong group of vigilantes: freedom fighters for the people that assist A.I. Industries from the shadows or with extreme cases that the amborgs cannot handle alone. He's very energetic and sometimes acts crazy but he is a reliable friend. Not bad for an old man. All I really know is that he and David 117's father, my former employee, didn't see eye to eye. I assumed he was dead for a while and then I received word from the LAPD that he had stabbed David 117. It makes my blood boil that he decided to do that to get his point across, but it is what it is. It doesn't mean I have to like it. He is a tough old man and I'm glad we are allies with him.

LAPD Commander Marsha Bradley

Back in 2127, the streets of Los Angeles were in turmoil. Heavy casualties among the police elevated her to the position of Police Chief due to the lack of other suitable candidates. Her rank then was Captain. After the Dominoe Incident, the chain of command across the LAPD was restructured and heavily reformed, allowing her to step down as Chief, and she was promoted to Commander as thanks for her bravery and service. She has a mysterious relationship with Mark and she's one of the few humans that is aware of Katie 57's secret identity. I suggest not getting on her bad side.

Sergeant Paul Lewis

All I will say about Officer Lewis is... I have no idea how he's survived this long. Oh, that's not enough? According to my A.I. assistants, I need to say a few more words. He is probably the luckiest or the unluckiest officer in the LAPD.

Sergeant Joe Harrison

A legend among the LAPD. Personally, I remember meeting Officer Harrison around the time when Melissa and I were kidnapped. To see him serve the police and his community for decades is an extraordinary feat.

Officer Joe Johnson

In 2128, there was a huge shortage of police officers which resulted in Johnson suddenly becoming a sergeant. After things in Los Angeles had calmed down, he requested a demotion which was granted by his newly appointed superiors. He remains good friends with David 117 to this day and seems to be doing well.

Dr. Gene Wildman

The former doctor, mentor to Vanessa 6, and head of A.I. Industries' medical staff. After his family was kidnapped, he was forced to sabotage Serina 43 during the Dominoe Incident. Once the smoke cleared, he was arrested and imprisoned. He is currently waiting for a ruling to reduce his prison sentence. Through the amborgs, his daughter Tessa constantly communicates with him, hoping for the day that they can be reunited. I hope that we can accomplish this with the parole board. It's a constant battle with the lawyers.

Tessa Wildman

Tessa is one of the bravest individuals I know. Very few could go through what she was forced to experience and come out of it alive. From what I understand, she owns an adult entertainment business in New York. I have always wanted to visit it to see how she's doing. Get your minds out of the gutter, I am genuinely curious to see how she runs the place.

Major Audrey Wright

David 117 certainly kept their relationship under wraps. When things became serious and they got closer, I can still remember the look on his face when he told me that he wanted to marry her. It made my spirits soar when he happily asked me to meet her. Melissa and I never had a chance to have children of our own. But if I had a biological daughter, Audrey is definitely the right fit in our slightly larger-than-normal family.

President Bill Holland

It doesn't matter how high in the political field he goes, Bill is always going to be the idiot that once told me and I quote, "Bro, we should try flying with these paper wings I built!" It still makes me laugh whenever I think about the time that he fell off my roof. Who knew that he would become the most powerful man in the nation? Yes, I voted for him, even with his ridiculous spending bill. Now I'm not suggesting that our friendship has any impact on anything political that affects the nation, but I do appreciate the fact that there is at least one friend I know in Washington D.C. managing things. He was a groomsman the day I got married, and he's one of my oldest friends. I care about him a lot.

<u>Alpha Universe</u>

Ok, here's where it might get really weird.

Serina 43:

The alpha universe's amborg 43. She crossed the barriers of the multiverse to arrive on our planet. She behaves just like her Epsilon version. Uh... the version that we all know. Her skills are much more advanced and her strength is immeasurable. Hell hath no fury than an amborg scorned. I was heartbroken to hear that her choice to wear red neon stripes on her uniform was a mark of shame. She wears red to honor the friends and family she's lost.

Space Command Enterprise (S.C.E.)

Second Colonial... Defense Fleet

Was that right? I remember that was what Admiral Ra'aiah announced.

Admiral Ra'aiah:

Uh, she's a... Third Admiral... which is apparently a low ranking admiral. A little confusing but we'll gather more information about that. She doesn't have gold stripes, like the higher ranking officers. But, they also aren't the silver color either that I see the lower ranks wear. They're almost... shiny, from what I see. It's like if starlight was sewn into her sleeves and the stars on her collar.

For someone from a parallel universe... alternate universe...? From next door... she is quite... captivating. It's probably rude of me to say this but she is incredible for her age. I always thought that admirals were those old and wrinkly senior citizens that were battle hardened and weary from their careers serving aboard starships. When you look at a woman like Ra'aiah... wow. It amazes me that she's very close to my age and she looks so much like a recent college grad. I'm not sure if that's something I'm allowed to say since she is in command of a massive starship and is here to protect us all. I hope my comments do not offend her if she sees this file.

Commander Ulgo:

Uh, he wears gold stripes and he's the First Officer of the Firestar. If I had to describe this man in one word, I would choose the word: Intense. His seriousness and stoic attitude kind of intimidates me. Sure, he treats me like a guest but if looks could kill, this man probably could do it. Not too chatty but he is quite cooperative whenever I have questions.

The Fourth Expeditionary... Reconnaissance Fleet.

I really hope I got that right. The S.C.E.'s organization is really... organized in a unique way.

Captain Chastain:

The commander of the Alexandria. From what I was told, he refuses to be promoted and that this man is Admiral Ra'aiah's godfather. Is serving in the fleet a family trade? He sent Alpha Serina 43 to us. I admire the fact that he risked his ship, his fleet, and thousands of lives just to send us a proper warning of what was coming. He has an amazing sense of humor to complement his professionalism. His calming attitude almost makes you forget about the fact that we're at war.

Lieutenant Commander Riley:

First Officer of the Alexandria. I have only had a few interactions with her. She seems a little inexperienced but under the guidance of Chastain, I have to trust that she'll become a strong leader. I'm not the best judge of character for people from alternate universes.

"Everything I've done... and everything I will do, thanks for being an anchor point in my life."

For Felicity, Jay and Karina

The Breaking Point

By

Yee-Ron Ted Cheng

A.I. Industries
Psychological Post Mission Debriefing
2116 April

"I wonder what's on their minds."

"Oh please, you're just worried about whether or not I'm going to clear them for the next mission."

John Kendrick turned sharply, giving his wife a hard stare. She glared back defiantly as they stood face to face.

"They can handle what goes on out there!" he said.

"When you take the time to talk to them," Melissa replied, "you'll notice that each time they leave and come back here, a small part of them gets etched away. You created them to be the strongest human beings on Earth."

"And they are," John snapped.

"So let them be human! The reason we hold these psychological meetings is to determine whether or not they still have an understanding or their own mental health!"

"They are fine!"

"Damn it, John!"

They both paused before the fight could escalate. They broke eye contact and turned away from each other.

"You can't keep doing this to them!" she protested.

"Doing what exactly?" John replied. "You want me to stop saving the world? You want me to tell those government pricks that we're just going to stop protecting the people out there? Undo everything we've built?!"

"I'm talking about their lives!" Melissa shook her clipboard in his face. "I never liked it when you inhibited the amborgs' emotions! They have to live with their actions for the rest of their lives. Who knows how many hundreds of years that's going to be! They are not playthings! They are our family!"

"I know that!" John replied.

"Clearly, you don't," Melissa shook her head. "Leonard was kidnapped by a self-entitled asshat and pushed dangerously close into something he would have regretted for a very long time."

"They are all strong and capable of handling these situations."

"Physically? Yes. But how long until they mentally break from this cybernetic lifestyle?"

John pointed at the room on the other side of the observation glass. It was empty at the moment, yet he acted as though someone was already sitting inside.

"The only way to know how strong you can be is by testing your limits," John stated.

"And I'm telling you that Leonard's limits were almost broken," Melissa countered his argument coldly. "He just doesn't know how to show it anymore because of you."

John Kendrick clenched his jaw, glaring at her in irritation. She held her ground, releasing a frustrated breath.

"They look up to you like a father," she said, "and I'm married to you, so that makes me their mother. It's my job to nurture them and help them feel. They're not machines."

"Alright," John sighed. "So, what do you recommend?"

"You let me talk to him while you observe from outside."

They glanced at the clock and noticed it was four in the afternoon, the exact time they had scheduled this debriefing.

A door swung open at the far end of the room. Leonard 1 stepped through, right on time. Outside, amborgs 2, 3, and 4 peered in. All of them displayed neutral expressions as the door closed, leaving 1 alone. He settled into a chair and waited in silence.

Without saying anything else, Melissa left John at the window and walked out into the hallway. She rounded the corner and entered the debriefing room.

"Leonard," she smiled pleasantly as she stepped through the threshold. "It's good to see you!"

"Dr. Kendrick," 1 replied.

"Now now," Melissa said kindly as she approached the table and gazed into his eyes. "Use my first name."

"Is Dr. John Kendrick watching?"

1 glanced at the tinted protective glass. They couldn't see who was on the other side, but Melissa politely nodded.

"Yes," she said. "John is watching, too. But let's take a second and talk, ok? Remember to use my name too."

"Yes. Dr. Melissa."

Every time they did one of these debriefings, Melissa always tried to encourage the amborgs to use their names. It would make conversations more personal if they could just find a way to relax and not talk to each other like coworkers. The whole point of why they called the amborgs their family was so that they could be the greatest human beings on the planet.

"Leonard," Melissa said, looking at her data pad. "I wanted to talk about your last mission. How do you feel?"

"I don't understand."

"How do you feel?" Melissa repeated the question gently.

1 remained silent. Melissa sighed and turned her gaze to the window. She sensed her husband's quiet presence on the other side. When she faced 1 again, she peered deeply into his eyes.

"Have you been crying? Leonard?"

"Amborgs do not cry," 1 replied flatly.

"Were you upset? When they rescued you?"

"No," 1 stated.

"You know I can tell that you're lying, right?"

Melissa looked at 1 with a soft expression, tilting her head slightly. She pulled a notepad from her pocket and put it on the table. She flipped it open, took out a pen, and began to write.

1 didn't respond. He didn't deny her last statement, which either meant that she was on the nose, or needed to do a little more digging. John had made the amborgs quite resilient when it came to emotional inhibition.

"Ziggy and Katrina reported that you were angry, violent, and had to be subdued," Melissa stated. "Missy has also been telling me that you haven't eaten anything in a week. They're all telling me the same thing. They're concerned for you."

"Yes ma'am," 1 said softly. "I am alright."

"Are you sure?" Melissa asked. "I can get them in here to join us for this debriefing."

"I was already debriefed," 1 stated. "Perhaps you are not referring to this meeting correctly? Is this a psychological evaluation?"

"Yes, it is, Leonard," Melissa nodded. "You're very sharp."

"There is nothing on my physical body that is... sharp," 1 glanced down at himself. "You must be referring to an alternate means of praising my intelligence."

"You are incredibly smart and intelligent," Melissa agreed. "But you aren't taking care of yourself."

"I am functioning within acceptable parameters."

"But are you ok?"

Melissa kept jotting down notes while keeping an eye on 1's body language. She observed the way his hands shifted and any changes in his breathing. The smallest movements told her all that she needed to know.

He stayed very quiet, deliberately trying to avoid talking to her. The pressure of it all felt increasingly heavy. Melissa began to count the number of times 1 blinked, realizing he was struggling to maintain eye contact.

"You were hurt." Melissa reported as she looked at the data pad. "It's in the debriefing. Leonard, what happened?"

"I have already written my mission report."

"If you feel like it," Melissa said, "I'd like to hear about what happened to you. Is that alright?"

1 looked down at Melissa's pen, then his eyes wandered onto the data pad. After a few seconds of thinking, he looked up and nodded.

"Very well," he said. "I would like to finish this session and retire to my quarters. Sharing the events will expedite this evaluation."

"I don't want you to rush into it," Melissa stated. "Take it slow and describe to me what you saw and how you felt."

"4 and I were on a transport assignment. We were escorting a large steel shipment across the country. There were reports that convoys were being attacked by criminals and gang members. The two of us oversaw supervising and monitoring the shipments. Sometimes, we would even join the escorts and ensure that the steel reached their destinations."

"Why weren't the two of you together?"

"There were over 53 shipments that were traveling to various parts of the country," 1 stated. "Sometimes, it was easier if we both split up and managed individual convoys on our own."

"And you were separated from your partner?"

"4 and I were talking about... a psychic that we had met," 1 reported. "Two months ago. A woman reached out to me, grabbed my arm, and said the phrase, 'tread carefully or else fire would consume me.' In an effort to interpret this with 4, she told me that it was impossible."

"Why? What does this have to do with your mission?"

"4 stated that fire doesn't affect us," 1 said, shaking his head. "She also described that psychics do not have special abilities. Predicting the future was a gimmick and a special way to con normal people."

"Alright Leonard," Melissa took note of what he'd said so far. "So you're telling me that you and Kat had a disagreement?"

"I simply stated that some people are allowed to believe in certain practices," 1 nodded. "But 4 told me that it was only a tool for con artists. She doesn't believe in psychics."

This was a little surprising to hear. Melissa gazed inquisitively at 1.

"Does that mean that you do?" she asked politely.

"I don't know," 1 answered. "There is no scientific evidence to support what that lady told me. But when she said those words, I felt... a little bit of fear."

"Like you knew something would happen?" Melissa suggested.

"4 told me to stop being distracted," 1 replied. "She told me that the reason I was afraid was because that psychic had implanted the idea, and the power of suggestion did the rest. When we couldn't resolve the discussion, we had to go back to work."

"So, is it safe to say that when you got back to doing your tasks, the two of you had a disagreement?"

"I shouldn't have gotten upset at 4."

Melissa blinked. She briefly glanced at the tinted window. That comment caught her attention right away. Did 1 just admit to being upset?

"What do you remember?" Melissa asked. "What made you upset?"

"I didn't let it bother me," 1 replied. "Actually, I chose not to let her see that her words had upset me. I was distracted and then it happened."

Melissa glanced down at the data pad, confirming the events that followed.

"You were then kidnapped," she said. "Who was it that managed to knock you out?"

"There was a female supervisor when I managed to finish escorting the shipment," 1 described. "When I got out of the transport to begin observing the unloading, she handed me a signature pad. Then I felt a massive surge of energy. Everything went dark."

"Can you remember what happened after?"

1 took a moment to think. He closed his eyes and dug into his memories. It was a very handy technique for recalling the details of everything he had seen.

"I woke up and I wasn't where I originally was."

Leonard 1's eyes fluttered open, and a sudden sharp pain surged through his body all the way up to his brain. He shot upright, his gaze darting around as his left hand instinctively clutched his right wrist. The source of the pain drew his attention, and he pulled back his right sleeve just enough to reveal the traces of an electrical burn. Then he remembered.

The supervisor. She had handed him a little electronic scanner to get his thumbprint. They needed his signature to confirm delivery of the shipment. He hadn't questioned it at all since he had done it several times over the last week. This one, he recalled, had discharged a very strong electrical pulse. Before he even had time to register what happened, everything had gone dark.

1 realized he was on some luxurious couch. The cushions were comfortable, but he stood up and got to his feet. There were all sorts of special items on display: trinkets, decorations and other fancy pieces of art and furniture. It looked like a museum, but all of the chairs looked too expensive for public use.

"What am I doing here?" he asked, puzzled when he didn't recognize anything.

Before he could try to access his transmitter and call for help, the door at the end of the room opened.

A man and woman stepped through the door. The woman, he recognized immediately. It was the "supervisor" that had handed him the scanner. Before he could ask his questions, he took a closer look at the man, and his facial recognition software activated. It was the man who'd contracted him for this job.

"Oh," the man gasped. "How... wondrous! Look at him!"

1 walked cautiously towards the two of them as the man continued to smile gleefully. He walked forward with his hands raised.

"So vibrant and full of life!" he exclaimed. "So strong too! The detail! The balance!"

This man was Lestor Sullivan. He was the owner of The Sullivan Steelworks corporation. He had asked for help from A.I. Industries to escort his shipments to major construction sites on numerous occasions. John and Melissa Kendrick had dispatched a couple of amborgs every now and then.

Lestor was an older and more refined gentleman. He wore a semi-formal tunic of some kind. A button-down sweater seemed to keep him warm, and 1 noticed silk pajamas underneath. The pants that he had on were slacks. In comparison to John Kendrick, Lestor looked like an old man about to take a smoke break or was heading to the kitchen to make a cup of cocoa or warm milk. He certainly had a rich grandpa-like aura about him.

"Didn't I tell you Vera? Didn't I tell you?" he turned and looked at the woman with a grin. "Magnificent. What a remarkable piece of work."

1 decided that it was time to speak. He activated the silver bracelet on his left wrist. It glowed and flashed with a bright green light with every word he said. 1's mouth remained shut as he transmitted what he wanted to say.

"Why have I been brought here?" he asked calmly.

The reaction he got was unexpected. Lestor gave a shudder as he let out an excited laugh. 1 was perplexed as he watched the man hunch forward like he'd just been tickled. He waved his hands in front of him and slowly began to walk around 1.

"Oh!" he beamed positively, while 1 turned his head to keep an eye on him. "The voice projection! It's amazing! Ha! The voice coming out of the bracelet! No vocal chords! Amazing!"

Lestor continued to circle around 1.

"The inflection, the timing..."

Suddenly, Lestor snapped his fingers to the left, the right, and then down across towards the ground. 1's eyes tracked each movement intently. He laughed again, clearly pleased.

1 was about to ask the question again when suddenly, Lestor snapped to attention and cleared his throat. 1 leaned back when he abruptly raised his voice.

"It took...! Great effort, effort...!" he shouted.

1's eyes grew wide in surprise as he paid close attention. Why was this man shouting? Lestor seemed to realize he was overreacting and then lowered his voice.

"Great effort," he repeated in a plain tone. He smiled mischievously. "To bring you...!"

Lestor pointed at 1, then at the ground.

"...here!"

He turned to Vera.

"I was sure it'd be worth it," he said normally. "I was right."

1 raised his hand.

"I've been delivered here against my wishes. I would like to know the reason."

"Certainly."

Lestor walked up to 1 and raised his right hand. 1 realized that he wanted a handshake, so he gently took the man's hand. They shook a few times and then let go.

"You have been brought here," Lestor smiled, taking a step back. "For my enjoyment... and my appreciation."

"Am I to infer that you intend to hold me captive?" 1 asked.

"Captive? *Captive*?" Lestor looked taken aback, his smile fading. He looked up thoughtfully, then waved his hand and rolled his wrist. "Oh, that's such an inappropriate description. My dear amborg..."

Lestor paused, and his eyes widened. He looked at 1 in concern.

"Excuse me, where are my manners," he said. "May I call you... Leonard? I'm told that's the name the Kendricks call you?"

"That is my given name," 1 nodded.

"Leonard," Lestor nodded and broke it down. "You will be... catered to, fawned over, cared for. Like you've never been before. Your every wish will be... fulfilled."

1 realized what the old man was saying. He had been captured so that he could become a servant. A plaything. This was definitely not the ideal living situation that he wanted to be in. Therefore, after listening to what Lestor had just described, he quickly transmitted a firm response.

"I wish to leave," 1 stated.

Lestor spluttered as he let out a laugh.

"*Almost* every wish," he smiled, shaking his head.

"This is unacceptable, sir," 1 replied. "I have no desire to remain here, and even if I did, my duties as an amborg to A.I. Industries would not allow it."

Lestor turned to Vera.

"He's so... simple-minded, isn't he?" he asked. "Just like the other ones."

"Very persistent," Vera responded.

It was the first time that he had heard her speak since he'd last seen her. 1 examined Vera's features closely. She had brown wavy hair that didn't fully cover her face, striking blue eyes, and a pointed nose. She wore a rather comfortable-looking suit, which contrasted to Lester's casual attire. She looked like a secretary of some sort, or perhaps a personal assistant. Vera reminded

1 of his wife, Daphne. That was another problem. Wouldn't his wife and A.I. Industries be looking for him? He needed to determine precisely how long he had been unconscious.

"But," Lestor held up a finger, "he's very polite, which is an awfully nice touch."

He pivoted to 1.

"I decline to allow you to go," he formally stated.

"Then I am forced to attempt escape," 1 replied. "Excuse me."

1 walked towards the door that they'd come through. He noticed that Lestor and Vera followed, but didn't try to stop him. They watched curiously as 1 approached the door and realized there were no handles. He lifted his hands and put them on the surface. He attempted to push the door open, but it didn't budge. Even as he increased his strength, analyzed the door frame, and attempted to force it, it remained stuck tight. It was built solely for the purpose to keep him, or something big, from breaking out.

"Uh, ten amborgs."

1 glanced over his shoulder to see that Lestor was smiling confidently.

"Maybe ten amborgs could open the door," he said. "They just might be able to force it open. I'm afraid there's nothing you can do."

Lestor raised his hands playfully.

"It's keyed to galvanic skin responses and DNA patterns. Sorry."

1 turned on his heel and stalked towards Lestor.

"Then I must have you open the door for me," he said.

Lestor nodded, smiling pleasantly as 1 attempted to open his arms to try to grab him. However, the instant that 1 put a hand on the old man, a sharp burst of electricity hit him in his fingers. 1 quickly retracted his hands and stepped back.

Lestor turned his back on 1.

"Are you feeling well, son?"

1 rushed in for another attempt to grab Lestor. The result was the same when his hands touched his clothes. An even bigger jolt of electricity zapped him and 1 felt crippling pain lance through his entire body. He fell backwards, falling to the floor in a heap.

He looked up, wincing from the pain as Lestor faced him again.

"Oh," he feigned surprise. "I wouldn't do that again if I were you. I have defense mechanisms that prevent any bodily harm."

1 allowed the pain to subside. He slowly sat up.

"I fail to understand the value you place on my presence," he said.

Lestor waved and gestured to the rest of the room.

"Oh, well, have a look around! Everything in here? This collection is from all over the world."

1 rose to his feet, and Lestor gestured for him to join him at a nearby shelf where a vase rested. It was an exquisite Etruscan vase.

"This one was recovered from a dig site in Rome," he said excitedly as 1 leaned forward for a closer look. "Amazing, isn't it? An old vault buried underground was discovered when workers were trying to expand the underground subway system. How spectacular that we're still finding buried treasure! This one is from the Ming dynasty! Very rare."

He showed 1 a strikingly tall vase crafted from red clay, reminiscent of a colossal Tetris block. The vase featured ornate gold handles at its peak, yet it was the vivid red hue of the body that really caught his eye.

"A 2035 rare vase," Lestor described. "Created by Luke Bennington. He just had a way with these sculptures."

1 was led away and shown a dali wooden statue, a few artistic portraits, some small miscellaneous items, and several other expensive-looking items. Lestor then brought 1 over to what appeared to be a display case. Inside was a trading card.

"Look at this! This is the only known Roger Maris card from 1962!"

1 examined the photograph. It featured Roger Maris, the renowned baseball player from the New York Yankees. Attached to it was a small metal plaque that provided a written description.

Born: September 10th, 1934, Hibbing, MN

Died: December 14th, 1985, Houston, TX

Number 9: Outfielder for the New York Yankees.

Played 12 seasons of MLB and set a single-season home run record of 61 home runs in 1961. Highest recorded until it was broken in 1998.

Lestor gently opened the display case. The glass door swung open smoothly, and 1 realized there was a smell emanating from the trading card. Taking a deep breath, he recognized the familiar and delightful scent of bubble gum.

"The smell?" Lestor grinned. "If you smelled bubble gum, then you'd be right! I preserved it in the case!"

Lestor gingerly closed the case, and the bubble gum smell dissipated. He then put his hands up to his chin and thought for a moment.

"Let's see..." he mumbled. "What else? Oh yes! How about the chinchillas?"

Lestor gestured toward a nearby enclosure. Curious, 1 stepped closer and peered into a beautifully designed case. A family of chinchillas nestled inside, their cute, fluffy forms bustling about.

"Short-tailed chinchillas," 1 tilted his head. "They are an endangered species."

"Oh yes," Lestor nodded. "Very few locations have them. The surviving ones don't live in the wild anymore."

Lestor activated a button on the side of the enclosure. There was a faint rattling sound as some food dispensed into a little dish inside. The chinchillas eagerly scurried over to the bowl and began to indulge themselves.

"Everything you see in here is priceless!" Lestor raised his arms and turned on the spot. "Just like you, my dear boy. You are one of a kind, if you'll forgive the pun."

He showed a luxurious and fancy chair sitting on a pedestal. A plaque attached to its base with his name on it snagged his attention.

"This is where you belong, too! Sit, sit."

1 glanced at Lestor solemnly. The old man's smile faded.

"Sit!" he repeated the command.

1 refused. He remained where he was. He kept his feet planted and rooted to the spot in defiance. Lestor appeared confused.

"You think, perhaps, it might be uncomfortable?" he asked. Then he leaned his head back and grinned again. "Oh, but you don't give a thought to comfort, do you?"

Lestor turned to look at Vera again.

"When Dean gets a good look..."

He waved at 1.

"...at that! He's going to be so jealous! I can't wait to see his face!"

1 was beginning to feel afraid. Most situations, he could handle. This, however, was too much. The kidnapping of an amborg was a serious offense. If his friends couldn't locate him, or if he couldn't call for help, this was going to escalate too far. He was alone and cut off from help.

Lestor looked at 1 again and clapped his hands.

"You, Leonard 1, the first cyborg in all of human history!" he chuckled gleefully. "You are, um, you are the crown jewel... of my collection! You're a treasure beyond comparison!"

A faint beeping noise snagged their attention, prompting them to glance over. Vera walked over to the wall console and pressed a green button.

"Yes, go ahead," she stated.

1 couldn't hear who was on the other end. Lestor cleared his throat, and 1 turned to listen to what the man was saying.

"I think you should be flattered."

"I am not, sir," 1 declared. "Most living beings would find involuntary confinement offensive and inequitable. Moreover, you have violated the law."

Lestor raised his hand and shrugged it off. He didn't seem to care.

"I know, I know," he said in a boorish tone. Then he gave a rather disturbing and pleasant smile. "What I've done? Super immoral, evil, selfish, unprincipled, illegal. Well, I've learned to live with it."

"Excuse me sir."

Vera was calling out to Lestor.

"Fujikawa is calling you," she explained. "Says he wants to buy a shipment of spices from you."

"He had four days to decide!" Lestor yelled.

The clear change in his demeanor and emotions was frightening. A lot of red flags and alarms were going off in 1's mind. Was he going senile or something?

"Why do they have to decide right...!"

Lestor dropped his hands and approached Vera with a laid-back stride. 1 observed silently, noting how he lowered his voice.

"Right," he said, preparing to depart. "All right then."

1 kept a close eye on Mr. Sullivan's movements as the door swung open. It appeared to identify both him and his assistant from a distance. Maybe he had a remote control hidden on his body. The galvanized skin response or DNA security recognition were likely designed to be external in order to gain access to the room.

"Mr. Sullivan?"

Lestor and Vera paused in their tracks, turning their attention to 1.

"I must emphasize," 1 stayed rooted in his spot, making sure that his voice reached their ears clearly. "Mr. Sullivan. I consider this captivity a hostile act on your part."

"Oh, well," Lestor shrugged as he turned to walk out. Vera followed him. "You get used to it."

The door shut and 1 found himself alone in the room of collectibles. The artifacts of Lestor's collection were quite impressive, but he definitely wasn't going to be part of it. He had to figure something out, and fast. 1 double checked the time.

It had been 8:78 PM when Vera shocked him unconscious. When he came to, his clock showed it was 6:12 AM the next day. Somehow, he had been moved discreetly to Lestor's home or... this place was probably just a safe room that housed these prized possessions. The question was, where was he?

He was supposed to check in at 10AM every day and 10PM every night. It was a standard routine for the amborgs whenever they were out on a mission. Hopefully, the others would have begun checking his last known location when they realized he had missed last night's attendance. He knew that both Dr. Kendricks would be immediately searching all over the world for him.

"I hope I'm not on the moon," 1 said softly as he walked over to the wall panel and tried to press some buttons. "That would be problematic."

Even with all the money in the world, 1 doubted that a rich man like Lestor Sullivan could secretly transport him into orbit. It was ludicrously expensive to have a personal spacecraft that was not registered or licensed with a space agency. Anything in outer space was under NASA's jurisdiction, so there was no way anyone could have launched him to the moon.

"Well, since I'm not in space or on the moon," 1 crossed his fingers. "I have managed to narrow my location down to the planet Earth."

It was the most obvious conclusion, and he realized the others would have probably laughed at him for thinking so stupidly.

Tinkering with the wall panel wasn't helping. 1 already knew that he'd need to have the correct DNA or fingerprints to access it. Vera had pressed the green button to answer a call, but when he tried it, a red light flashed and a buzzer went off. He didn't have access. 1 knew it wouldn't be that simple.

About two hours later, 1 had surveyed the interior of the room multiple times. He'd considered smashing up everything in the room as an option to force Lestor to set him free, but John and Melissa Kendrick had taught the amborgs to preserve history, to keep it out of harm's way. If he willingly destroyed humanity's legacy, what kind of monster would that make him?

The door was built like a tank. Lestor had to use his connections as a rich steel tycoon to get it constructed. He must have scouted out a really secluded spot in the world for this level of tech and his priceless collection. If 1 hadn't been whisked away to another country, he was likely holed up somewhere inland or remote. Maybe he ended up in the mountains, a desert, or tucked away in a city. Depending on the kind of transportation they used, where could they have taken him in just five to six hours?

"Lestor Sullivan wouldn't have put me on a plane, civilian or private," he contemplated the travel time to fill in the gap. "Trains would be fast but there would be limited spots to go to. Perhaps a truck or heavy vehicle. But even if I identified where I was, I still need to contact home."

Suddenly, the door opened. 1 made a dash for it, but then Vera walked in. As soon as she crossed the threshold, it slammed shut behind her. If he had lunged for the opening, they both would've been crushed. Perhaps the next time the door opened, he would wait at the entrance? Thinking back to what happened to him earlier, when he tried grabbing Lestor, 1 decided that was probably not the wisest option. There had to be a way to neutralize that defensive ability.

"Lestor wants you to sit in your chair," Vera lifted her arms, and 1 noticed she was holding some clothes. "Please put this on."

1 shook his head.

"I have no reason to accede to Mr. Sullivan's wishes."

"He will give you reasons if you force him to," Vera said cautiously. Her harsh tone became fierce as she stepped closer.

"Mr. Sullivan is deluding himself if he believes he can keep me here," 1 stated. "The other amborgs of A.I. Industries will find me. This, I am certain of."

"They'll never find you," Vera scoffed, shaking her head. She sternly held out the clothes again. "We've put out the word that you've taken on another mission. Personally."

"They will come searching for me," 1 replied firmly. "Whatever you have done will easily unravel. Mr. Sullivan will be charged with kidnapping and holding me captive."

"We've come up with some very convincing stories before to throw people off track."

"Clearly," 1 shook his head, "Mr. Sullivan has no moral difficulty with my imprisonment."

"He has no moral difficulties at all," Vera explained. She looked away grimly.

This got 1's attention. She seemed to resent what she was saying. Maybe she could be persuaded. It was possible that working for Lestor Sullivan was challenging considering the behavior he had witnessed earlier.

"Do you?" 1 asked quickly.

Vera gazed at 1. A glint in her eyes caused her to sneer.

"Clever, amborg," she said, displeased. "Is it in your programming to seek out vulnerabilities in your enemies?"

"Yes," 1 replied honestly as he scanned her and kept an eye on her movements. "Are you my enemy?"

"I obey Mr. Sullivan and so does everyone here in this facility," Vera stated.

"Why?" 1 asked curiously.

This seemed to trigger something. Vera shook her head at him, her demeanor suddenly becoming defensive.

"You are a curious thing, aren't you?" she groaned.

"Do you object to the question?" 1 shrugged.

"He will do anything," Vera snapped. "He will always find ways to get what he wants from people. His rewards for loyalty are lavish. His punishments for disloyalty are equally..."

1 noticed Vera start to tremble a bit. She raised a hand to her cheek, her gaze dropping for a moment, then she met his eyes again. She finished what she was saying while trying to regain her composure.

"...lavish," she whispered, almost menacingly. She shook her head again. "You won't find anyone here that will help you escape."

She headed for the door, dropping the bundle of clothes on the couch he'd woken up on. As she walked away, she lifted a hand and gave him a soft wave.

"Face it, amborg. He has you."

1 called out to Vera as the door opened and she stepped out.

"It appears...!" he spoke up, watching her turn back to face him. "...He has us both."

Vera said nothing as the door shut. 1 looked at the clothes she had left him and let them sit there on the couch. He hoped that what he said to her would slowly tear away at her conscience. For the time being, he decided to continue being defiant.

After about an hour, 1 curiously stepped over to the Chinchilla cage. Vera had given him a couple of clues in her responses. If this was a facility of some kind, he had to assume that it was possibly at one of Lestor's industrial locations, or maybe a corporate office. Perhaps it was the main one.

"Lestor has a family of Chinchillas living in a room with so much art and memorabilia," 1 checked on their food and water dishes. "He must live close by or maybe there are a few assistants like Vera that come in here to take care of his pets."

As 1 gazed into the cage, he heard the door open again. This time, he saw Lestor rushing in. He took one look at 1 and let out an exasperated sigh.

"What are you doing? Why aren't you dressed in the new clothes yet?" he said, putting his hands on his hips.

"I am an amborg of A.I. Industries," 1 stated.

"You are not *in* A.I. Industries anymore," Lestor lifted his hands, clenched his fists, and walked slowly towards him. "It's time you adjusted your programming and accepted reality."

"Even if I chose to do so," 1 replied, "it is doubtful that my programming would be altered to accede to your wishes."

"Oh?"

John Kendrick's design for the amborg implants were quite sophisticated. He had spent a lot of time developing 1's advanced neural net. The CPU built into him wouldn't comply. Lestor didn't seem to be comprehending what he was saying.

"When I was designed and unveiled to the world," 1 continued, "the Kendricks taught me to have a fundamental respect for life in all its forms. I admit that I have caused harm to certain people in the interests of safeguarding and protecting the world, but the amborgs are a symbol of peace in uncertain times."

"What a marvelous contradiction," Lestor leaned back and seemed to wobble over to the couch. He was physically mocking 1's explanation. "A military pacifist. Tell me, whose dreadful idea was it that got you to sign up to join A.I. Industries?"

"My skills and everything I ever wanted was to..."

"Leonard, Leonard... no," Lestor interrupted him. "Big mistake. Grievous error. No. You belong at A.I. Industries about as much as I belong in a verbal contract. Tell me, have you killed someone yet?"

"In 25 missions," 1 stated, "no. But I am trained and programmed to use deadly force in the cause of defense."

"Shame on you."

1 fell silent as he watched Lestor sit down on the couch next to the clothes. The old man wagged a finger at him and shook his head.

"Shame on you," he repeated. "How neatly you rationalize your capabilities. How can you just casually accept your role in murder?"

"I would not participate in a murder," 1 replied.

"Really?" Lestor let out a yawn. "When word on the grapevine is that a few other amborgs have done some serious business?"

"You are wrong," 1 spoke confidently. "The others wouldn't do such things. Perhaps you misunderstand."

"Can't you see how much better it'd be for you here?" Lestor waved to the rest of the room. "The intellectual rewards alone. A lifetime of comfortable living. I am at war with no one. That's the beauty of it. I am your liberator. Young John Kendrick just doesn't fully recognize what you inspire. A.I. Industries just wants you to be a hero. A war object to shape the future in his image."

"You are a fine debater, sir," 1 acknowledged the old man with a polite nod. "It is a pity you have used your verbal skills for mere hucksterism and the advancement of your own greed."

"Perhaps," Lestor stood and walked over to 1. "Perhaps you would not judge me so harshly if you knew of my desperate youth wasted... wasted on the streets."

1 saw Lestor's face. A few tears streamed down his cheeks. The gas lighting and the emotional manipulation was strongly detected. 1 stood his ground and didn't change his stance.

"Your past doesn't excuse your actions," he declared. "You are unethical and immoral, sir."

"Well, that doesn't matter, it isn't true," Lestor immediately stopped crying and shrugged. He tilted his head and smiled. "My father was actually quite wealthy. He was a thief."

Lestor turned to the couch and grabbed the clothes that Vera had left.

"Leonard," he held them up, allowing the outfit to drop down and hang from his arms so that he could show it. "Why don't you put on these lovely clothes and go sit in your chair?"

"I must decline," 1 replied.

Lestor angrily rolled up the outfit. 1 carefully observed his behavior, remaining in place.

"You are going to be much more of a challenge than I first thought," his voice trembled slightly.

Lestor stalked over to a cabinet, and 1 heard the sound of a lock click as it opened. He couldn't see what was going on, but he could hear water trickling into a glass. 1 couldn't help but wonder why Lestor had a hidden bar like that. It seemed rather suspicious.

"Here is something that I want your logic to understand," he said as he lifted the glass, then dumped what was in it over 1's uniform.

1 heard sizzling and he peered down to find his jacket literally melting away. A quick scan confirmed that he'd been splashed by some form of sulfuric acid.

"I'm not exactly sure if your skin will be damaged," Lestor shrugged as he sat down casually. "I guess we have plenty of time to learn about you. But I believe that your uniform will dissolve thanks to my specially designed compound."

1 sensed a fire igniting within him. It wasn't just the physical sensation of his jacket burning away; it was something deeper. Lestor Sullivan had desecrated the uniform of A.I. Industries. He had treasured this outfit because it was a special gift that made him feel part of something special. Now it was ruined.

"Personally, I don't mind you running around naked," Lestor scoffed. "I assume you have no modesty. But then... I guess that decency is a rule of your training."

1 watched silently as Lestor strolled to the entrance.

"In any case, Leonard," he said cheerfully. "Why don't you make a decision about which alternative you dislike the least. Make your choice by dinnertime tonight. I've invited a guest to meet you."

He tilted his head down and glared at 1 menacingly.

"And I *expect* you to be as entertaining with him as you have been with me."

After the door shut, 1 immediately took off the remnants of his A.I. Industries jacket and let it drop on the floor. He hadn't been hurt underneath, so he tried to come up with a way to wash off the acid. He quickly ran to the Chinchilla enclosure and borrowed their water pan to try to wash the acid off. Unfortunately, it didn't have any effect. The acid continued to dissolve his jacket completely.

"You wish to see entertainment?" he growled quietly. Rage bubbled under his skin. "Fine, I shall gladly demonstrate."

Although Mr. Sullivan had deliberately ruined his amborg jacket, he wasn't completely exposed. He grabbed the jacket Vera left behind and slipped it on. Underneath, he still had a short-sleeved undershirt. He wasn't about to fully give in to his demands.

1 continued to examine the rest of the contents in the room. Maybe something in here could help him.

"I could destroy the baseball card..."

1 looked at the display case and took a few steps towards it.

"No," he stopped himself. "If I do that, who knows what Lestor would do. If I tried using his collection as leverage, I might have to contend with other obstacles he could throw my way. I must wait."

A few hours later, 1 continued to wait. Then he saw the door open. Instead of taking his seat, as instructed, 1 stood upright and froze on the spot.

Without turning to look directly at the door, he watched everything out of his peripheral vision while impersonating a statue.

Lestor and Vera entered, and between them was another man that 1 didn't recognize. They had their arms wrapped around each other, as if they were trying to carry a drunk friend home.

"...With the pearls intact?"

Lestor let out a laugh as the man in the middle shook free and cackled.

"Please," Lestor sputtered.

"The pearls were intact?!"

"The pearls were actually added to increase value," Lestor replied.

"Oh, I see. Hey. What's that??"

1 kept his gaze fixed ahead, emotionless and unresponsive. Lestor and Vera exchanged glances as they watched their guest look at 1 with curiosity.

"Something new, and you didn't tell me?"

Their guest turned and shook his finger like a parent about to scold their child. Lestor and Vera merely laughed.

"Ah yes," he exclaimed. "Leonard! My boy! I am delighted to see that you dressed for the occasion. This is my friend Ronald and..."

The chatter died down as everyone looked at 1 closely. He noticed their smiles fading, replaced with silent stares. Lestor chuckled awkwardly and urged Ronald to approach the amborg.

"Say hello to my friend, Ronald Winstrom," Lestor smiled graciously.

1 remained perfectly still. No blinking, no changes to his expression, and no movements whatsoever. He wasn't even breathing.

"Uh," Lestor stepped forward as Ronald continued to watch curiously. "Leonard, say hello. No need to be shy."

Even though he wasn't reacting at all to the conversation, 1 began to feel a little bit of satisfaction from watching Lestor's demeanor go from happiness to sheer embarrassment.

"I see," Ronald stepped forward, examining 1 closely. "It's a mannequin of sorts… right?"

"This is not a mannequin," Lestor replied. 1 could hear a faint trace of annoyance in his voice. "This is Leonard! This is formerly Leonard 1, the very first amborg in human history from A.I. Industries!"

Ronald leaned in closer, and 1 caught a whiff of his cologne. It had a fresh scent that he found nice, but he kept that to himself. Sticking to his act, he stayed perfectly still, pretending to be frozen.

"He doesn't seem to be very active," Ronald shrugged.

"It's because he's playing a stupid little game," Lestor insisted.

"Well, someone has certainly played a trick on you," Ronald chuckled, shaking his head. "Did you acquire this from Japan? I'm told that they design the most amazing mannequins. They can replicate almost anyone."

This seemed to antagonize Lestor more as he looked to his friend and 1. Each time 1 saw the old man look his way, he could see the rage building.

"I don't find this amusing," Lestor glared at 1. His lip curled as he stepped into his face. "I demand that you behave normally."

"You are not my parents," was what he wished he could say.

Lestor moved to 1's left side. He could see him out of the corner of his eye. Was the old man going to hit him?

"Behave… normally!" he snapped his fingers loudly near 1's ear.

If only you knew, good sir, 1 thought privately, *this is actually normal behavior back at A.I. Industries.*

"I know you can hear me!" Lestor shouted.

Then 1 felt something smack his shoulder. Lestor was still equipped with the electric-shock defense mechanism on his person. 1 felt a sharp zap as the surge of power sent him falling forward. Instead of reacting, 1 decided to allow himself to tumble over like a felled tree. He fell face first into the couch, bounced off the cushions, and rolled onto the floor. Continuing to stare straight ahead, 1 stared up at the ceiling.

"He falls well," Ronald said.

"I apologize for this," Lestor mumbled.

"Don't be sorry," Ronald laughed. "This is actually quite entertaining. Now, come along Vera! Let's go find that other girl Sandra! I'd like to play around with her now. Let's leave Lestor to his broken toy."

If I was not putting on this act, 1 remained prone on the ground, *I would take action against you.*

As he looked straight up at the ceiling, Lestor's face loomed mere inches from his own. He looked absolutely livid, his lips curling up into a snarl.

"You'll regret this," he whispered.

Then he stood up and left. 1 could hear his footsteps stomping towards the door. When he heard the door hiss and close, he sat up.

"In the words of my wife," 1 smiled, turning to look at the door. "Screw you."

When the coast was clear, 1 stood up and straightened his clothes, feeling quite pleased with himself. He'd recorded every bit of footage of Lestor Sullivan's awkward moments and stored them in his CPU. The more that he had, the more evidence the jury could use to nail him down.

He went back to examining and admiring the pieces in the collection.

Another hour passed, then 1 heard the door open.

Lestor walked in alone and was wiping sweat off his forehead. He cleared his throat.

"I would... like to. I mean, I would very much like our relationship to change."

1 delivered a casual response.

"You may expect me to use every means at my disposal to resist your wishes," he declared.

"Why couldn't you just comply?" Lestor let out a small whine. "Why do you have to argue all the time?"

He glanced at the chair with the plaque engraved with 1's name. He gestured toward it and attempted a soft smile.

"Couldn't you just sit in the chair?"

1 remained rooted to the spot.

"Come on," Lestor began to sway to the side as his smile disappeared. "Go... sit on the chair."

1 wanted him to feel anger and frustration. His lack of cooperation had to have lasting effects. He wanted Lestor to make a mistake.

"I do not want to sit in the chair," he spoke defiantly.

"You will," Lestor sighed. "You may not believe it right now. But, you will."

1's eyes followed Lestor as he made his way to a glass case affixed to the wall. Inside, a beautiful necklace caught the light. Lestor waved his hand close to the glass, and a beep echoed as the case extended outward. 1 noticed that it was built on top of some sort of hidden wall safe. When it stopped moving, Lestor began to enter a combination.

Suddenly, he paused. He turned around to find 1 watching closely. He laughed mischievously and stepped in front of the panel, intentionally blocking his view so he could enter the rest of the code. Once the last number was keyed in, there was a click and Lestor opened the safe. He reached inside and pulled out some type of baton.

"Do you know what this is, Leonard?" Lestor held it up for 1 to look at.

"That is an electric disruptor," 1 replied, scanning the device instantly.

"Correct!" Lestor smiled as he closed the safe. "It is one of five prototypes of the class C disruptor. I own three of them."

"The class C disruptor was banned," 1 stated. "It was supposed to be a non-lethal tool for law enforcement until it was recalled from the field. Too many casualties during many police arrests."

"I sleep with one next to my pillow and I sleep very well knowing it's there. Do you know why?"

"It is a lethal weapon," 1 replied.

"Not just lethal," Lestor replied. "It's vicious. It shocks and slowly melts your insides. Excellent for torture. I've always wanted to try it."

"Fine," 1 replied calmly. "I do not want to sit in your chair. Not now, not ever."

"You will," Lestor brandished the disruptor threateningly.

"I doubt you will destroy me," 1 said with complete certainty. "You assigned so much value to me, I infer that you will not go through with it."

"That goes without saying," Lestor shrugged.

1 watched as Lestor approached the panel on the wall, the same one where Vera had answered a phone call. He pressed the button, and a chime sounded.

"Please come in!" he said clearly into the microphone.

The door opened again and Vera stepped through. Lestor graciously walked up to her and smiled as he gave her a hug.

"Vera! Now tell me, my dear, how many years have you been working for me?"

"14 years," Vera replied.

"14 years," Lestor repeated cheerfully as he caressed her hands. "How wonderful! She was barely an adult when I found her."

It was quite disturbing, 1 thought as he examined the two of them closely. If it hadn't been for the fact that he couldn't touch either of them, he would punch this man and leave. The way he talked to her and put his hands on her was disgusting.

"She was idealistic, naïve, and full of dreams," Lestor led Vera to the couch and she took a seat. "I made those dreams come true. Didn't I?"

Vera nodded, giving Lestor a big smile. Her smile faded when she saw him pull out the disruptor and activated it.

"I'm going to miss you," he smiled sinisterly as he raised his hand and prepared to strike.

Horrified, Vera gasped as Lestor towered over her.

1 had to do something fast. Without hesitation, he decided to comply. He couldn't allow someone to be hurt as a result of this. Lestor was completely unhinged. This crazy old man was the most infuriating person he had ever encountered.

"Lestor Sullivan!" 1 shouted as he scrambled to the chair and sat down in it.

Lestor looked up at 1 and a big smile of satisfaction spread across his face. Vera's terrified expression also turned in his direction.

1 clenched his fists on his knees as he watched Lestor from the chair.

"Was that so difficult?" Lestor asked pleasantly, deactivating the disrupter and hung it on his belt.

1's expression began to contort with rage. He'd decided to do one thing before he escaped from this prison. He was going to kill this man.

Lestor turned triumphantly towards the door. He suddenly stopped and headed back to the wall safe. He entered the code again, purposefully hiding it from 1's watchful gaze, and stored the disruptor inside. The safe receded and hid itself back in the wall.

Then he walked towards the exit.

"Let's go Vera! Time's a wastin'!"

Vera, trembling, stood up and quickly followed. Before she exited the room, she turned and looked at 1 for a heartbeat, then left. He noticed the pain in her eyes and how defeated she looked. That might be the key to winning her over. The door clicked shut behind her, and 1 jumped to his feet.

He walked over to the display case with the necklace and mimicked Lestor's actions. To his surprise, the wall safe slid back out. Lestor must have been incredibly confident that 1 wouldn't be able to figure out the combination. The controls for the wall safe were likely not coded to anyone specific. Curious, 1 leaned in to examine the keypad.

It was a nine digit pad, and had only managed to catch a glimpse of the first three numbers before Lestor obscured them. Despite knowing the initial digits, there were still millions of combinations left to consider. Using an infrared scanner, 1 could identify which numbers Lestor had pressed. He noticed more pronounced fingerprints on certain digits, recalling the series of beeps that followed Lestor unlocking the safe.

There had been eight beeps. There were eight numbers in the passcode.

1 slowly went to work. He made a mental note of all the number combinations. He needed to try and figure out what he knew about Lestor. Maybe an important number in his life was the combination. It was always easy to set a passcode as something special. Perhaps eight digits was a specific date. Month, day, and then the year.

1 began to brainstorm what dates might be important to Lestor and he went to work trying as many of them as possible. He remembered Lestor's birthday from some public records, so he tried that one first. He also tried the date when his company was founded and even the day Lestor graduated from college, among other possibilities.

This went on for a few more hours as he continuously tried to guess what date might unlock the safe. He was thankful that it wasn't locking him out despite his repeated failed attempts at entering the passcode.

Just then, 1 heard the door open, expecting Lestor. Instead, it was Vera who burst in, her expression wild and frantic. 1 watched her intently, sensing something was off.

"If I help you escape," Vera pleaded, "will you take me with you?"

"The consequences if we are caught..." 1 started, but Vera rushed up to him.

"I know," she exclaimed. "I know! He's asleep right now, and I'm aware of the consequences! Now might be our best chance!"

Vera placed her hand on the panel. She deftly punched in the numbers on the keypad, and a moment later, a click signaled that the safe had been unlocked.

"14 years," she muttered angrily. "You learn a few things."

She pulled the door open and stepped aside. 1 reached inside and grabbed the disruptor.

"I'll lead you out of here."

Even though he considered that this might be a trap, 1 nodded quietly. This was the best news he had heard so far.

Vera and 1 positioned themselves near the door, and it hissed open. As they stepped outside, 1 took a moment to survey his surroundings. The corridors gleamed with a polished finish, but what struck him as odd was the biting cold that surrounded them.

"Where are we?" 1 asked.

"An underground city that was built to withstand and sustain a population of survivors from the fallout of World War Three," Vera explained. "Lestor had it converted for his own personal use. I'll take you to a vehicle you can use."

"I need to establish contact with A.I. Industries," 1 stated.

"No," Vera replied as they turned down another hall. "Lestor keeps all communications in this facility centered from his personal office. If we steal one of his cars and get away safely, you can send out a transmission."

1 followed Vera to a flight of stairs and they ascended to the next floor. Then she led him to an elevator. Once they were inside, she used her access key to send the elevator up to the highest floor.

Every moment inside made 1 nervous. They couldn't linger in here too long. If they were discovered, the elevator was the perfect place to trap them.

Fortunately, they made it and the doors opened. After a quick jog, Vera took 1 inside the garage.

"We can use one of his cars," Vera pointed at the row of vehicles.

1 glanced around.

"I think you should use one of his cars first, without me," he said. "Get in the driver's seat and tell me where the door controls are located. Once the garage opens, you can escape. I'll be right behind you."

"What?"

"I am a very fast runner," 1 explained.

A deafening bang echoed throughout the entire garage. 1 turned his head sharply and whirled around. Vera had frozen in place, as if an invisible force had stopped her. Then he saw a stream of crimson oozing from her heart.

"Did you really think that I wouldn't have noticed my own personal amborg had left the room? The security system flagged me the instant that Leonard was outside of his room!"

1 rushed forward and caught Vera as her eyes bulged in shock and tears began to well up. Blood trickled from her lips as she struggled to breath. She trembled as 1 held her in his arms. Turning, he spotted Lestor lurking at the garage entrance, smoke curling from the gun he'd just fired. 1 glanced down at Vera, who choked and looked terrified. He realized he had nothing in his medical kit to ease her suffering. The gunshot wound was fatal. She was slipping away right in front of him.

"Your fault," he heard Lestor call out to him.

This triggered 1. Furiously, he spun around to face the old man. A few security guards had shown up and were observing the scene closely.

"I-it's your fault," Lestor stammered, waving the gun. "You knew the price for disobedience. So did she."

Seriously? He was that far gone?

"Well, there's always more people I can pluck off the streets to replace her."

1's breathing became ragged as he clenched his jaw and glared daggers at Lestor and his security team. Before he set Vera down, he looked at her.

"Vera?" He spoke gently.

Vera didn't say anything. Her breathing became shallow and soft. Her gaze drifted upward, and her body went limp. 1 watched her pupils dilate and become lifeless, and he mournfully dipped his head. He gently lowered her to the ground before rising in a surge of fury.

Lowering his gaze, he marched towards Lestor.

"Stop!" he yelled. "Stop, I say!"

1 began quickening his pace.

"Shoot him!"

Guns fired as 1 faced them head on. He stood his ground without taking any damage, but he realized that the clothes that Lestor had given him weren't bulletproof. He could feel the bullets tearing through the fabric as he defiantly marched forward through the storm of bullets.

When the guards ran out of ammo, they closed in and tried to subdue him. It didn't work. The only thing that 1 was aware of was the fact that any time someone got in close, he pummeled them.

He threw one guard over his shoulder. He punched another one so hard it fractured the man's spine and he crumpled onto the floor like jelly. Even after the other guards watched their colleagues get decimated by the one single amborg, they kept trying. 1 felt satisfied at the fact that they all chose the stupid option. He tore their limbs, broke bones, and inflicted maximum pain, all so he could reach the one target he needed to take care of.

1 reached Lestor, stopped a few feet from him, and pulled out the electronic disruptor. He switched it on menacingly.

Lestor gulped in fear as he remained rooted in place.

"You won't hurt me," he trembled. "Amborgs have a fundamental respect for life in all its forms. That's what you said. I'm a living being. Therefore, you can't harm me."

"Yes I can," 1 glared at the old man. His limbs burned with anger.

"Empty threats," Lestor replied. "I'll just shoot more people dead until you comply. I can always find more. Their blood will be on your hands, just like Vera. So, in order to finish this, you must shoot me."

"You are crazy," 1 said.

"So do it," Lestor said smugly. Sweat continued to pour down his face. "Break your rules. Stop resisting and give in to your feelings."

"I am not a monster," 1 brandished the disruptor and held it up towards Lestor's face. "You are."

"Oh, if that isn't the pot calling the kettle black," Lestor spat. "You defy me with your logic and moral principles. You can't even act out the desire for revenge when I killed Vera. When you became an amborg, you became a monster and the Kendricks forced you under their control. Don't let them use you. Just stay here with me."

"No," 1 snarled. "I cannot allow... this, to continue."

Lestor inhaled sharply and tried to step back. 1 lifted his hand, ready to plunge the disruptor into him. Suddenly, a hand grabbed his wrist, forcing him to stop.

"Stop."

1 blinked and looked to his right. Amborg 2 stood beside him, eyes fixed on him. Behind them, 3 and 4 had also arrived, their attention focused on the unfolding drama. 3 looked horrified, whereas 4 examined the scene intensely.

"Found you," 4 stated.

"1," 2 spoke gently. "Are you alright?"

1 bit his lip as he felt 2's grip tighten. He dropped the disruptor, and it fell to the ground. He looked at his friends and the rage dissipated, only to be replaced with grief and pain.

"I'm... fine," he forced out.

He glanced at Lestor, then turned away.

"Please take Lestor Sullivan into custody," 1 stated. "I am charging him with kidnapping, theft..."

1 cast a grief-stricken look at Vera's body.

"...and murder."

"And what happened after that?"

1 blinked and looked up at Melissa in the debriefing room.

"You're crying," she said softly. "Are you ok, Leonard?"

"If... if the others hadn't found me in time..." he spoke softly.

"You were held captive for almost a full day," Melissa said. "What happened after the others got to you?"

"4 was the one who took Lestor Sullivan into custody," 1 reported. The memories became clearer to him as he recounted the story. "3 got me out of there and contacted 6 to check on my condition. 2 coordinated the police effort and confiscated everything. I think I scared everyone."

Melissa stopped taking notes and listened intently.

"Vera was killed," 1 shuddered. "She spent 14 years of her life working for an egotistical delusional asshole... He had no ounce of responsibility. He said it was my fault."

"He gaslit you," Melissa sighed. "And it made you angry?"

"I killed his security team," 1 shut his eyes and leaned forward. "I couldn't touch Lestor the whole time, but I could hurt his security guards. I took it out on them."

"Does it make you feel better that a few of them are still alive?" Melissa asked. "They'll never walk or stand properly anymore but... you didn't kill all of them."

"I wanted to torture and inflict as much damage to Lestor, but I couldn't touch him," 1 said. "If I had just a few more seconds..."

1 looked up at Melissa and continued to cry.

"...I would have killed him, right then and there."

"I believe you," Melissa said, nodding her head sympathetically. "I totally understand that feeling. I'm also glad that you didn't. When the other amborgs found you and stopped you...I'm grateful they were able to stop you long enough for you to calm down."

"I almost wanted to fight the others off," 1 responded, his voice shaking. "Am I a terrible person for almost wanting to hurt my friends, just to kill Lestor?"

"No it doesn't," Melissa replied. "It makes you as human as the rest of us."

"Can I go back to my room?"

Melissa's mouth fell open. 1's bracelet hadn't flashed or transmitted this question to her. She had witnessed 1 open his own mouth and his voice came out in a rather hoarse and raspy tone.

"Yes, uh... yes!" she replied, her eyes widening. "Leonard... For the record, I just want to let you know that we are putting you on temporary leave. It is my recommendation that due to your mental condition, I am restricting you from active duty until I deem it necessary."

1 rose from the table. He lifted a hand and wiped his cheeks. Then he opened his mouth again and she heard his broken and shaky voice.

"Under---stood," he said, before turning to walk towards the door. "I would... like... see my wife."

Melissa stood and watched as 1 turned his head to look at her again.

"Please?" he rasped and coughed.

"Sure."

The doors opened and 1 stepped out of the room. She remained where she was, listening to his footsteps receding down the hall. Then, she heard a set of soft footsteps enter the room a moment later.

"He's clearly not fit for duty," Melissa sighed. "He needs some time off."

"Yes," John's voice answered her. "I have to admit, I wasn't expecting to see such strong emotional responses."

"You programmed them to inhibit their feelings," Melissa shook her head. "Then when he got pushed, he almost destroyed everything in his path."

Melissa grabbed everything on the table and turned to look at her husband.

"How long until this happens to the next amborg?" she asked. "What about all of the future amborgs? Are you going to brush aside all of their emotions?"

"Let's... discuss this with the rest of your department," John nodded. "We'll look into some programs or alternative methods that the amborgs can participate in to help their recovery after each mission."

"Thank you," Melissa gave him a small smile.

The two of them walked out of the room, and 1 wasn't anywhere in sight. He'd already gone back to his own quarters. Something then popped up into Melissa's mind.

"By the way," she said, "did you ever meet Lestor Sullivan?"

"No," John shook his head. "He was always seclusive and was never really friendly to me. I always thought he was rather... eccentric."

"Well, he kidnapped our firstborn cyborg," Melissa muttered grimly. "That's a given. What happened to his collection?"

"It's all confiscated evidence now until his trial," John replied. "Most possessions will probably be returned to the rightful owners or their descendents. 2 actually recovered some items that didn't get taken into police custody."

"Oh?" Melissa gazed at him curiously. "What didn't the police want?"

"How do you feel about raising chinchillas??"

"You didn't?!" she exclaimed, a smile forming on her face. "You brought them here?"

"Well, they are endangered," John shrugged. "I also saw the footage from 1's memory drive. Maybe they'll help him feel better. Emotional support."

"Dr. John Kendrick," Melissa let out a sigh. "You just keep trying to find ways to make our superpowered family bigger."

The couple continued walking down the halls of A.I. Industries to their next task. The day wasn't over yet.